THE GAMESTER WARS:

The Alexandrian Ring
The Assassin Gambit
The Napoleon Wager

By William R. Forstchen:

The Ice Prophet Trilogy:
  ICE PROPHET*
  THE FLAME UPON THE ICE*
  A DARKNESS UPON THE ICE*

INTO THE SEA OF STARS*

The Gamester Wars:
  THE ALEXANDRIAN RING*
  THE ASSASSIN GAMBIT*
  THE NAPOLEON WAGER*

With Newt Gingrich:
1945

*Published by Ballantine Books

THE GAMESTER WARS

The Alexandrian Ring
The Assassin Gambit
The Napoleon Wager

William R. Forstchen

A Del Rey® Book
BALLANTINE BOOKS • NEW YORK

A Del Rey® Book
Published by Ballantine Books

Copyright © 1987, 1988, 1993 by William R. Forstchen

ISBN 0-345-40049-6

Manufactured in the United States of America

First Edition: August 1995

10   9   8   7   6   5   4   3   2   1

Contents

THE ALEXANDRIAN RING

Bring me a map and let me see how much
is left to conquer all the world.

—MARLOWE

chapter one

Corbin Gablona leaned over the dinner table, sweeping the precious dinnerware onto the floor. "Here was the Carthaginian position."

He picked up half a dozen diamond-studded spice shakers with his large, beefy hands and laid them out in a line. Knowing that he was the center of attention, Corbin smiled happily at the ten Humans and half-dozen Gavarnians who sat around the dinner table.

"These are the feared Numidian horsemen." Several of the Family heads nodded in appreciation. Corbin then picked up a decanter of Malady Ambrosia and waved it in the air.

"This, why, this here is Hannibal." He laughed softly, so that his one hundred and sixty kilos shook like a wave-tossed jellyfish. With a dramatic flourish he placed the decanter in the center of the line, facing the upturned wine glasses that represented the Roman infantry.

"Now, what can we use for that Roman general—what was his name?"

"Scipio Africanus, you mean."

Gablona looked up at the speaker. "Ah, my dear Bukha Taug. I'm impressed that a Gavarnian would have known such an obscure fact."

Bukha smiled from the other side of the table, even though a Gavarnian smile usually signaled that someone was being considered for dinner. "Why, Corbin, even a Gavnar, and particularly a Gavnar of Koh status, is expected to know something of alien history. But, my good friend, your Hannibal was second rate, truly second rate."

Two Gavarnians came up to Bukha's side as if in support of their friend. All three of them smiled. Their forward canines glistened in the candlelight. The nap of their pelts stood on end.

"So you think Hannibal was second rate?" Zola Faldon interjected in his high rasping whine, ready, as always, when facing a "Gaf," to defend any Human, right or wrong.

"So you think Hannibal was second rate?" Bukha replied in a fair imitation of Faldon's whine, which was the more comical coming from a heavily furred creature two and a half meters tall. His fearful appearance was offset by his being the worst dresser of a species noted for being among the least stylish in creation. Bukha was wearing one of his more conservative outfits—a polyester jumpsuit of electric blue, accented by hot yellow stripes.

"You might not like my voice," Zola snapped back, "but by all of space, I wish you Gavarnians could do something about your damn musk. This place stinks like a kennel."

"You Humans don't smell any better. No wonder your ancestors and mine hated each other on sight."

"Ah, now those must have been the days . . ." one of the Humans replied, and there was a general murmur of agreement around the table.

"We could settle our own differences then." Another Human sighed wistfully.

"No damned Overseers," a Gavarnian growled from the other end of the table, while he poured a drink for the Human sitting next to him.

"Yeah, those damned holier-than-thou Overseers," shouted the sole Xsarn, who was stretched out on a couch in the far corner, six tentacles wrapped around a covered feeding trough that none of the others dared look into. The Xsarn pulled its feeding tube from the trough and waved it in anger. However, as such displays usually resulted in a Xsarn's regurgitating its most recent meal, the diners shouted for it to stop.

"Come now, gentlemen, my fellow Kohs," Corbin interjected as he produced a bottle of brandy and a box of cigars from the sideboard and passed them around the table. "Let's be realistic. By the greatest of coincidences all three of our species discovered the transspace jump point into the Large Magellanic region at nearly the same time. Why, it was the greatest planet-grab in history, and the devil take the hindmost. It was fabulous—but somewhat bloody, I daresay."

"Ah, those truly were the days," the Xsarn replied.

"Easy for us to say today," said Sigma Azermatti, the oldest and richest of the Humans present. "It was also one of the biggest bloodlettings ever. We scrambled for the few places the

First Travelers hadn't already mined and stripped. Why, we slaughtered each other by the tens of millions, and you're *nostalgic* about it? You Xsarns are crazy."

"The death of the one is meaningless," the Xsarn replied, attempting to sound superior.

"If we tried to kill you now," one of the Gavarnians interjected, "you'd drop that meaningless line, and damn fast."

"Gentlemen, no violence please!" the Xsarn shouted. "After all, we in the Magellanic Cloud are civilized now."

"Precisely my point," Sigma responded. "We're civilized beings now. The fighting in this region of space shattered trade and isolated hundreds of millions on planets that could support agrarian economies but lacked the significant natural resources for higher tech levels. It was rare to find a planet in this Cloud that the First Travelers had not completely exploited hundreds of thousands of years ago; with the collapse of trade support due to the war, this entire region reverted. I thank the heavens the Overseers came through here when they did and forced our forefathers to come to peace. Otherwise all of us would be living like our barbarian cousins on the majority of planets in the Clouds, rather than sitting here aboard Corbin's yacht."

"Does this mean," Corbin interjected quietly, "that you've converted to the Overseers' nauseating preachiness and will no longer join us in an occasional wager or game?"

"No, of course not," Sigma replied quickly. "But I am saying that 'the good old days' weren't so good. The Overseers were quite simple and direct—they abhorred violence so they put a stop to all technological forms of mass destruction."

"Holier-than-thou pious bastards," the Xsarn interjected.

"Bastardy is impossible for you Xsarns—you're asexual," Bukha replied with a smile.

"Come now, gentlemen," Sigma continued, "their high ideals have kept the peace in space for nearly two millennia. They're even gaining control over some of our interspecies fighting on the primitive worlds. By keeping such fights local and forbidding our involvement in any way, they keep us from escalating local conflicts into interplanetary wars like the last one, which nearly destroyed us all. Gentlemen, if it wasn't for the peace imposed by the Overseers, we wouldn't be sitting here drinking brandy together, I can assure you.

"If they pulled out of this corner of space tomorrow, we'd be back at each other's throats before a standard year passed."

No one responded, and Sigma looked around the table triumphantly.

"You know that nineteenth-century earthside is my specialty," one of the Gavarnians responded, "and I daresay Sigma does have a point. We're like the nobility of Europe during that time. We speak each other's languages, we drop by for visits with each other and share the refined things that civilization has to offer. If those poor fools had had the Overseers to keep the peace, they might've been able to save their civilization from the twentieth-century wars. We, at least, do have them, no matter how much we dislike their paternalism."

"Thank heavens at least for the games," Bukha interjected. "They've yet to catch us doing that, at least, or else we'd all go crazy for a little action."

"Xsarnfood, those damned Overseers are Xsarnfood," a Gavarnian muttered, then nodded in the direction of the insectoid in the corner. "Apologies, my old friend, but you know what I mean."

"No bother, no bother at all," the Xsarn replied. "But, gentlemen, I don't see why you view this excellent dinner of mine with such loathing. Why, the stuff you Humans produce is like a rare vintage to us—especially when you've been eating spicy food. And as for Gavarnian—"

"Shut up!" the others roared together. The Xsarn dropped its head, realizing that a discussion of Xsarnian cuisine was not appreciated by the present company, even though they were its producers.

"I must say," a short, red-pelted Gavarnian next to Corbin replied, "I much prefer sharing brandy and cigars like gentlemen to ripping each other's guts out."

"Good chap, good for you!" Zola interjected. They all nodded their heads and congratulated one another on being so gentlemanly about such things.

"All right, Corbin," Gragth said at last. "I've enjoyed the socializing, but you didn't drag me fifty light-years just to look at my hairy face and hear me toast my siblings and curse the Overseers. What is it then? Are you organizing a game, because if so, by the memory of my brothers departed, we need one! It's been a little too peaceable of late."

"A game—did I hear someone say a game?" Zola called in reply. An expectant hush fell over the room as all eyes turned on Corbin. The Xsarn stopped its meal, grabbed a scented towel, and wiped off its feeding tube to join its companions around the table.

Corbin sat back and gestured. Those around him fell silent. With a dramatic flourish he lit his cigar, took a long pull, and then exhaled the smoke in a shimmering blue ring.

He pointed up to the ring and smiled at his own wit for starting his proposal in such a novel way. "Remind you of anything, gentlemen?"

"You mean the smoke?" Zola asked.

"No, not the smoke, I mean the shape of the smoke."

Silence reigned for a moment.

"You refer then to the Kolbard, the ring-world of the First Travelers?"

"Very good, Azermatti Koh," Corbin replied, and he placed a slightly sarcastic emphasis on the word "Koh," an honorific used only by Family heads controlling more than a hundred worlds or planetary consortiums. "You, of course, have seen before the others. Yes, I am referring to the Kolbard."

"And what in hell is the Kolbard?" Yeshna Veder, who was second only to Bukha in the Gavarnian hierarchy, asked in his soft silken voice.

"I can understand your not knowing," Bukha interjected to spare his friend a sarcastic reply from Corbin. "It's on the other side of the Cloud from you. In fact, it's nearly three thousand light-years in, toward the home galaxy and several degrees off the plane of approach. No resources worth exploiting."

"Thank you, Bukha. I couldn't have said it better myself," Corbin replied as Bukha came around the table to sit next to him. Bukha nodded to Corbin as if prompting him to say something.

"Ah, yes, maybe I should point out that . . . well, you see, Bukha and I got together on this little idea a couple of years ago, or was it longer than that, my good friend?"

"No, quite right. Make it about two years standard. But rather than hear it from me, perhaps there is somebody waiting here who can explain all this better than I."

With a dramatic flourish Corbin pushed at the paging disc on his wrist. The doorway at the far end of the room opened to reveal a short, rotund Human and a tall, slender Gavarnian. The Human's hair was gray and thinning, combed forward in a vain attempt at covering the balding top. He might have been slender once, but that was long past. His stomach bulged and he had the

ruddy complexion of someone accustomed to taking his entertainment in liquid form. But intelligence gleamed in his eyes.

The Gavarnian next to him was obviously of an advanced
age, since his pelt was going to white. But his dark, almond-
shaped eyes mirrored a sharp, eager mind. His suit was a sub-
dued combination of orange and gray stripes; for his race, a
being of impeccable taste.

"Aldin Larice and Zergh Tumar," Zola shouted with glee.
"Then it's going to be a game after all!"

Aldin smiled and nodded in Zola's direction. "I thought that
after losing three hundred–odd worlds to Corbin in your last
bet you'd curse the day you saw me again."

The others laughed good-naturedly at Aldin's comment—the
way beings have laughed throughout the ages when an expert in
their favorite sport makes a joke, even when the joke is on
them. Aldin was a vasba, a professional battle and simulation
arranger, and considered by many to be the best in the entire
Cloud.

Aldin smiled in his tight-lipped way, reached over, and,
without asking permission, poured himself a half snifter of
brandy, knocking most of it back in one gulp.

There, *that's* better, he thought, trying to calm himself. Good
stuff, that Ralindin Brandy, far better than the stuff he could afford. He wanted to let the tension build a bit more, but didn't
dare push it too far. The men admired him for his grasp of
Terran military history stretching all the way back to its legendary origins on Earth, but they were still the most powerful men,
Gavarnians, and Xsarn in the Magellanic Cloud, and as such
were not beings to be trifled with. Accidents for enemies, real
or imagined, were not unknown—even in the days of the Overseers.

Aldin placed the snifter to one side and smiled. "Most honored Koh Gragth, in your estimate, who in the history of the
origin planet of my species was perhaps the greatest general?"

Gragth of the Esag Consortium flashed a wide, frightful grimace. Snifter in hand, he rose from his chair and looked across
at Aldin.

"My personal favorite was Saladin," he replied smoothly.
"Now *there* was a Human who understood how a Gavarnian
makes war. I could also mention Ali al-Gadah, but his little
campaign wound up destroying half of your planet; and besides, his own country was radioactive and heavily cratered by

the time it was over. But of all my favorites of Earth history, the greatest general would have to be Alexander. We Gavarnians admire him not only for the way he made war but for his own reckless courage, as well. He was the stuff of legends, as if touched by the gods. And know that even today many of us, including myself, believe that the Unseen Light does single out some beings for great things, for so it was once said by Kubar Taug. I think you humans call it the Great Man Theory of History, where it is postulated that occasionally a truly great man of exceptional worth is born, his destiny—to rule."

Aldin looked around at the table and quickly took over the conversation, for he could see where half a dozen others were about to advance their own favorite theories regarding who was best, along with the various pros and cons of the Great Man Theory. "Thank you, Koh Gragth, for such a well-phrased analysis. I am gratified that you mention Alexander, for he is the subject that I wish to discuss."

"Then you plan to make a simulator of Alexander for our gaming pleasure—is that it?" Zola interjected enthusiastically.

"Not exactly."

"Then why are you here?" the Xsarn asked. "You are the best procurer of primitive battles in this region of space, otherwise Corbin wouldn't have locked you up with that lifelong exclusive contract. Now Corbin mentioned the Kolbard—have you found something there? Come on and explain yourself, Aldin—I care not for riddles."

Aldin smiled; he had their undivided attention. "Gentlemen, would you be at all interested in betting on Alexander the Great?"

"A computer simulation of Alexander?" Azermatti inquired.

"No, most noble Koh, I mean Alexander the Great for real."

"Just what in the name of my most beloved food are you talking about?" the Xsarn asked excitedly.

"For half of my lifetime we've known the location of old Earth," Aldin replied. "And the location of Lhaza, the Gavarnian home planet, has been known for several generations. Therefore, at the request of Corbin and Bukha, my colleague Zergh and I have been out exploring time."

Sigma was already nodding eagerly. The old fox has guessed what's coming, Aldin thought. He gave a nod of recognition to the eldest Koh.

"But what good is that?" Zola asked. "We've found half a

dozen nexuses of time distortion, to be sure, but none is near enough any place of interest. They're just like space-portal jump points, ninety-nine percent of them are off in some half-ass corner that isn't any good. Lucky for all of us that we found the dimensional jump from our galaxy to the Cloud, otherwise we'd all still be back there."

"Damn it, Zola," Bukha replied heatedly, "it was we Gavarnians who found that jump point first, and you Humans just sneaked in behind us."

The Humans all started to roar back at Bukha; the issue of who arrived in the Cloud first was still a source of contention. Only when the Xsarn threatened to add its shockingly fetid breath to the shouting did they finally calm down and return their attention to Aldin, who, wearing a patient look of disinterest, sat through the storm with his friend Zergh.

"If we could continue, gentlemen, I would like to state that Zola was right about time jump points. The vast majority of them are useless. You can only go through for a brief period and the effect is local. The hardest trick has simply been to learn how to control the points so that you can get a fix on the exact moment you wish to enter. After all, what the hell good is there in jumping through time if you can't decide where you want to go?"

"You've found a time nexus in near-Earth space, and you've learned how to control it!" Azermatti said.

Aldin nodded in acknowledgment.

The Family heads broke into a wild flurry of excited conversation, and Aldin caught Corbin's eye. The rotund Koh was beaming with satisfaction. Corbin had spent nearly a billion katars and Bukha another billion on the research, and they were about to cosponsor the greatest gambling event in the history of gaming.

Corbin stood up and extended his hands. "Gentlemen, gentlemen, *please*! Bukha and I have a little announcement: we wish to propose a game, a betting arrangement unlike any in history. Gentlemen, would you please lend your attention to my master vasba, and he'll explain the gaming scenario. And remember, gentlemen, we aren't talking about a simulation, we are talking about a game unlike any in the history of games."

Aldin bowed in acknowledgement to Corbin and the rest fell silent again, eager to hear the new wrinkle to their oldest, longest-lived passion—military history combined with gambling. A century past, Corbin's father had doubled his holdings in one day by wiping out the Demano Family in a bet centered on a simulation of Crécy that they had managed to arrange between two tribes on a primitive world. Thus had started the rise of the mighty Gablona fortune.

The legendary battles of Earth held the Humans' particular fancy. Earth was no more, having been destroyed in the war between the Humans and Gavarnians—and thus their nostalgia for it was even greater. With the outlawing of warfare by the Overseers, nostalgia over the pageantry of ancient times held sway among the Cloud's ruling classes. On many of the primitive planets, as well, memories of humanity's distant heritage were still kept alive across millennia and light-years beyond imagining. The same was true for the Gavarnians and Xsarns, who had lost their home planets in the war, as well. The ruling classes in the Magellanic Cloud came to know their worlds of origin's battles and strategies the way other ruling classes once demonstrated refinement by their knowledge of horses and operatic arias. And in such a society a master vasba, though technically still of the lower classes, was a man who could sit and share a drink with aficionados who held the most exalted positions.

"Gentlemen, the wager will be on the real Alexander the Great, brought across five millennia to fight again."

"But my dear vasba," Sigma interrupted, "if memory serves, the legendary Alexander died in 323 B.C. from malaria or poison, and our records show that he did not have any long, unexplained absence. Now, to the best of my knowledge, the theory of the indestructibility of the past has been fairly well proven. How do you expect to retrieve him, since you cannot alter the past?"

"A most excellent question, Azermatti Koh. However, you should look again at your Arrian. For it was written that Alexander retained his lifelike appearance for many days after his death. And—here is the interesting point—his body was left alone in a sealed room for some time while his generals argued about the succession.

"Now, gentlemen, I propose that he was, for several days, in a deep coma after the doctors of his time had already pronounced him dead. Therefore I shall take my vessel through the time nexus then transport down to the chamber where his body lies in state. It will be a simple matter to take his body measurements and then leave a replication in his place. The people of his time will never know the difference, and the theory of the indestructibility of the past will not be challenged in any way. History records that his body was taken to Egypt. I believe that the body was indeed someone other than Alexander."

"This is absolutely remarkable!" Zola cried. "You mean to bring back the real Alexander for a game?"

Aldin nodded.

"But for what game, and where?" Gragth responded. "Now I do confess that such an event would interest me, but at the risk of sounding ethnocentric, I must state that, as a Gavarnian, I do feel a little left out."

"Ah, the best question of all," Corbin said, as if waiting for the Gavarnian protest.

"How so?" Gragth replied.

"I think I could ask any Human here who was the best of the Gavarnians, and the response would be the same."

Corbin looked at his fellow Humans and, as usual, it was Zola who responded first.

"Now, there might be some room for debate here," he said with a professorial tone, "but I think we'd agree it would have to be the Great Uniter of all the Gavarnian races, Kubar Taug, who disappeared after the battle of Oaertam. He went up to the mountain of prayer with his standard-bearer and never returned. I daresay that he just might have taken a trip longer than any the ancient Gavarnians could ever have imagined."

It was Gragth who grasped it first. "You mean to say that you've not only found a time nexus near Earth, but one near our home, as well?"

"It is true," Zergh said, finally breaking his silence. "I was there. It is possible that soon we shall all see the Great Unifier, Kubar Taug. Neither Corbin nor I could visit the time frame of our proposed generals, since it appears that crossing a nexus once sets up a pattern of disturbance that does not settle for years. But we are confident that both Kubar and Alexander can be taken and, in fact, we plan to do so within the month."

"I had mentioned the Kolbard somewhat earlier," Corbin continued, in spite of the excited conversations going on around him, "and through a little research we've discovered several interesting facts. The ring, as you most likely know, is several million kilometers in diameter and nearly five thousand in width. Much to my surprise, it is a fertile location for our little wagers, for it appears the Overseers are not even aware of it. Certainly none of their patrols has ever ventured by for a visit."

"To know what the unknowables do, that is a new form of power, and mysterious to us all," Yeshna interjected.

"Let's just say I prefer my sources stay anonymous for right now," Corbin replied. "Nearly two and a half standard millennia ago Humans, Gavarnians, and Xsarns settled that unique world created by the First Travelers. But since it was artificial, there were no raw materials. The naturally formed worlds all have something by way of ores and minerals, but this realm has nothing to help a tech-level rise. Currently half a hundred conflicts go on around the ring's periphery. The fools have no real skill in such things, and as a result, the best of the fights are nasty but inconclusive. Metal is scarce and therefore highly valued.

"On one of the smaller continents an ugly little war is going on between Gavarnians and Humans. It's been waged inconclusively ever since the Great War, which nearly shattered all interspace commerce and cut off thousands upon thousands of settled worlds. It really isn't even a war, just an endless series of raids, usually by the Gafs—excuse me, Gavarnians—against a completely degenerate Human population in desperate need of a leader. The cultures are unique, as well; the Gavarnians are a fair approximation of the twelfth dynasty, the time of Kubar himself, while the Human side is similar to Novgorodian Rus. Alexander is known to them, a part of their legends of the Old-World Gods. That conflict will provide fertile ground for the two beings to forge new empires.

"I might also add that, as a test of the Great Man Theory of History, it would be interesting to observe two individuals who must start with nothing and rise up again to positions of power."

"Fascinating!" Sigma exclaimed. "A true test of the theory at last."

"And, of course," Zola interjected, "we'd be doing the poor sods down there a service by ending the war for one or the other, rather than let it drag on forever."

Most of them were not sure if Zola's comment was sarcasm or not, but they all nodded dutifully and muttered polite platitudes about helping out the less fortunate creatures in their universe. Having thus reassured themselves about the moral implications of the game, they turned back to Aldin.

"Therefore, gentlemen," Aldin continued, realizing that Corbin had finished his little monologue, "I propose that we send Alexander and Kubar there. The people of the region are aware of their historical past; both species view their heros as beings from the legendary golden age of the past."

As he finished, the would-be bettors were so excited that they immediately shouted agreement and demanded to be included. Corbin and Bukha smiled at each other; as organizers of the event, they were entitled to five percent of all winnings. From the enthusiasm visible, before the betting was done they would likely collect five percent of everything the other families owned.

"Of course, there has to be a game controller to insure honesty and fair play," Sigma interjected.

"Ah, yes, but of course," Corbin replied, reminded of an inconvenience he wished had been overlooked. "Since its national pride, shall we say, is not involved, might I suggest our good friend the Xsarn?"

The Xsarn rose up as if to give a speech, but remembering its manners among non-Xsarns, it simply nodded an affirmative rather than subject its companions to an extended sampling of its breath.

"It should receive the standard one percent, as well," Sigma stated.

"Outside our five, of course," Bukha replied.

"That's not the standard way," Sigma interjected.

"But our expenses in organizing the game and doing the time research were beyond imagining."

"Oh, I can just imagine," Sigma replied sarcastically. "But to show we understand and do appreciate what you and Bukha are doing for us, shall we say a quarter-percent each from the two of you, the other half-percent to be assessed against the bettors."

A mumbled chorus of agreements rose on that point, as well.

"May all Overseers kiss our hairy behinds, for a game is on!" Gragth shouted and raised his glass in a toast.

"Actually, sounds rather appealing to me," the Xsarn replied as it slipped its feeding tube into a half-empty brandy bottle.

Corbin gazed around the room as his fellow Kohs drained their drinks and cried out with delight at the prospect of the most exciting game that had ever been offered.

The royalty fees alone would make him rich, and his stature in the history of gaming would be forever untouchable. Of course, he'd make a killing in the game, as well. The betting would follow chauvinistic lines, Gavarnian and Human betting according to race, but Corbin had another angle, and before the game was over, he'd have the bettors cleaned out, especially Sigma. He nodded toward his hated rival while finishing his brandy.

"So, they bought it all," Aldin said to his companion as they walked back through the corridors of Corbin's yacht in a frustrating attempt to find their suite. Corbin loved mazes; some of the corridors in his new gaming yacht had been designed to amuse him.

"Left here," Zergh muttered.

"No, it's right."

Zergh, shrugging his massive shoulders, decided not to argue, and followed his old friend until Aldin finally gave up.

"There is one thing though," Zergh whispered cautiously despite his jammer. A good vasba always wore a jammer; a gaming bettor would go to any length for inside data. Bugging the food was not unknown.

"What's got you worried now?"

"All of them, every last one of those rich bastards. This will be the biggest game in history. I know you Humans are habitual liars and cheats, and I suspect the Koh will do anything, including murder, to win the fortunes that will be wagered on this one. Aldin, I said in the beginning this project was a little too big, it will bring out the worst in you Humans."

"Oh, thanks for the compliment," Aldin replied evenly as he stopped in confusion at a ten-way three-dimensional corridor intersection. He finally decided to take a hard right.

"There's one question you've yet to answer for me," Zergh said softly, looking around suspiciously. "That fat slob Corbin cheated you blind on your commission for the last game. That's nothing but Xsarnfood when he claimed the winnings you invested were lost in a freighter accident. His royalty statements are the longest lies in history. As his exclusive vasba, you're supposed to receive ten percent of all *his* game earnings after expenses. You've made him billions but what have you got to show for it? Thirty years of service to that bastard, and when payment time comes something has always gone wrong, or those lying thieves called accountants have doctored the books. And then like a damn fool you still take the contract for this Alexander venture that he offered you."

"It looked interesting," Aldin replied quietly.

"Interesting. Listen, my friend, maybe it's because I'm a Gaf, and we have this thing about pride and honor. But by my three brothers, if on top of all of that someone had seduced my only niece and heir, and then turned her into a brazen court mistress, well, I'd—"

"I would prefer you don't talk about it. I'm a vasba, a game procurer, and the Alexander contract will be the biggest event in the history of gaming. So please don't trouble me with prudish Gaf honor. Tia's nineteen years old, it's her life. The money, well, I was foolish to trust him, and that's that."

Aldin stopped at the next intersection and looked around. "I think I've been here before," he whispered.

"Only the third time. Now follow me for a change. Do you actually think you can trust him, this time, to deliver your ten-percent cut of his fees for arranging the game? I know my Bukha is good for it, but you know about the honor of Gafs."

"Considering my current credit rating and how my creditors rearrange one's appearance when not paid, I can only hope that Corbin's good for it," Aldin said wearily.

It was always the same, Aldin thought, with Kohs such as Corbin, who were the new breed of wealth coming up. In his own father's time, a gentleman was a gentleman. But Corbin was one of the new rich, like Yeshna of the Pi to Infinity Consortium. They were the damned new breed of money before everything, without sense of honor, family breeding, or scruples. To them a vasba was amusing to be around, but was still a servant in the family court.

"Anyhow," Aldin said wearily, "I made the mistake of marrying one of the Gablona cousins; you can imagine what my alimony payments are like."

Now that had been the craziest move of his life. He had been young, trying to rise above his station. She had married him because, for a while, it had been fashionable for women to marry "tradesmen." The fashion passed and the divorce had followed and Corbin took insane delight in reminding him of "dearest Edwiena" at every opportunity, pointing out to him her latest indiscretion.

"So, my good friend," Aldin said, trying to force a smile, "love the Gablona dynasty or not, I need a job."

Turning the next corner, the two came up to a blank wall.

"I can't stand that man's idea of fun!" Zergh shouted in exasperation.

"If Corbin plays this game as I think he will, that will be an understatement," Aldin replied coldly.

chapter two

"Really, Aldin, I can't see why you must snap your commands at me. After all, do remember my station!"

Exasperated, Aldin turned and looked at his niece. "Listen, Tia, just because you are Corbin's mistress doesn't mean that I've got to speak to you in a tone of reverence. You were my apprentice long before Corbin laid hands on you. I know he wanted you on this trip just to make sure his investment in Alexander was not tampered with, but I am still running the show."

Tired of the eight-hour running argument, Tia figured the last statement simply wasn't worth responding to. She made a third check on the deep-range scanning system, reconfirming the adjustments to their nexus jump. They were still blaming each other for the "little miscalculation," as Tia put it, that had caused them to appear a thousand years off in time and thus lay the groundwork for a radical departure in a nomadic tribe's religious philosophy. Thinking about that caused her anger to boil up again.

"And another thing, Uncle," Tia snapped, "remember you yourself said that the past cannot be altered. Therefore it must have been preordained that you appeared on top of the mountain in front of that old guy. Don't blame me for it—just count yourself lucky I snapped you back up here."

"Just shut up. It's lucky for me I remembered the story so I didn't foul things up." Aldin was feeling guilty about that one. He had debated whether to land a couple of days later to try to clear everything up, but that just might make matters worse. He regretted, as well, that he hadn't tried to omit a line from the stone tablets, perhaps the one on adultery . . .

"Are you sure that the date is right this time and that we're orbiting at the proper position?"

"Care to check my instruments?" Tia asked in a hurt tone, as if she had just been accused of lying or wishing to cause yet another little mix-up.

Aldin got up and leaned over Tia's chair to double-check the data. All instruments indicated that they were in geosynch above Babylon on the morning the histories claimed Alexander died. The calculations were relatively easy since the records indicated Alexander's passing as eight days before the summer solstice of 323 B.C. and twelve years after a major lunar eclipse in Anatolia. With that information punched in, the ship's navigational system simply had to calculate the date in relation to the relative positions of the Earth, the Moon, and their angle to the sun.

He hoped that Zergh would have the same success. Lhaza had no moons and the astronomical records for the twelfth Gavarnian dynasty were far from complete. There was no way of communicating with him since they were in different time periods a thousand light-years apart.

Satisfied with the nav reports, Aldin left Tia to her job and went back to check on their passenger.

Opening the doors to the medical bay, Aldin took one last look at Wiyger Luciana, a former plastacement contractor for the Gablona Family. Aldin had met him on several occasions to discuss minor bets, and lost on all of them. A rumor was floating among the Family retainers that Wiyger had built a substandard foundation for Corbin's palace on the ice world called Vol. Of course, Corbin and Luciana, Inc., had publicly agreed that the collapse of the palace was due to a freak summer storm, an unfortunate occurrence for the three hundred Family retainers who froze to death.

Aldin looked closely at the corpse. He hoped that the build and height were relatively close to those of Alexander. Once he and Tia had obtained the data, it would be fed into the medicomp, which would alter the body and deliver a full replication within twelve hours. Then the retrieval would simply be a matter of switching the bodies.

To pull it off, Aldin thought, and here came the difficult part. Arranging primitive combats and computing odds was his business, but he was about to enter Alexander's palace to steal the body while the successors were already coming to blows in the same building.

He was terrified. He had been tempted for weeks just to bolt on the whole arrangement, but Wiyger was an instructive object lesson for anyone who wished to cross a Koh. He had tried to talk Corbin out of it, but that had been useless.

"After all," Corbin had replied smoothly, "you did sign the contract."

"But I thought that you'd hire someone else to actually snatch Alexander."

"What, and run up even greater expenses? Your contract stated that you were to design and implement the project, so start implementing and stop whining."

"But I'm a vasba!" Aldin ventured bravely. "I simply arrange the game and calculate the bets."

"Go back to your contract and read the fine print," Corbin said. "If memory serves, section Y, paragraph three."

"Couldn't we renegotiate?"

Aldin turned away from the corpse and returned to the forward cabin. "Better get on your traveling robes."

"Couldn't you make them of something other than wool? It chafes my skin."

"I'll chafe your skin—the skin on your butt with the bottom of my boot."

"If my Corbin heard you address me like that . . ."

"I know, I know. But Corbin isn't here, and since he asked me to train you as a gaming consultant, train you I will. Now, is your speech implant working?"

"Agricola puerum amat."

"That's the farmer loves the boy, and you're speaking Latin. Remember, just think that you want Greek and it will automatically slip into your neural processes and have you thinking and speaking in the appropriate language. Within a couple of minutes the synapse link will merge into the language and you won't even notice the difference from your normal speech. The damn thing's worth a hundred thousand katars, so for heaven's sake, don't get clunked on the head and smash it up. Otherwise it comes out of my expenses. All right, try it again."

"I bear greetings and gifts from the philosophos Aristotle to the king. Trained in the mysteries of the Delphi, I have been sent to my lord Alexander in his hour of need—"

"Fairly good. Let's just hope the accent is correct, that's one thing I'm afraid we can't know till we land. Remember, if their Greek sounds strange, just explain to them that we're originally from a trade post near the Pillars of Hercules. The implant will quickly register the difference and automatically alter your speech process."

"It will all still be Greek to me," Tia replied. She jumped beyond the range of Aldin's kick.

"Are you set, Tia?" Aldin could see that even the usually unflappable Tia was nervous at the prospect of transjumping down to ancient Earth. The youngster had a touch of the hypochondriac about her, and in spite of the vaccinations Tia was absolutely terrified of bubonic plague and the common cold.

"Just remember, if you get a runny nose, use your sleeve."

"I jolted up on a megavac, just in case."

"Let's hope your megavac is proof against a Macedonian sword." And before Tia could cry an objection, Aldin punched the stone on his belt buckle, activating the relay to the ship's transporter system. He experienced a momentary blackout as his molecular structure disintegrated.

It was the hour before sunrise and already the eastern sky was washed by the early light of a purple-blue dawn. Beneath the walls of Babylon his consciousness returned in a moment of disorienting blindness and pain that was typical of a beam jump.

Instinctively he felt his body, making sure that everything was still present. The beam jump had been perfected a millennium earlier, but like many another traveler he still had his doubts, fearing that one day he'd come through with a body part missing or attached to the incorrect region.

Raising his head, he made a quick recon of the area. As near as he could estimate, the ship's computer had dumped them precisely on location, in a small ravine near a minor gate, where an infrared scan had indicated that no one was about.

"Tia?"

"Over here."

In the early-morning shadow, Aldin could barely make out

his niece. He should have darkened the jumproom to aid his
night vision, but it was too late to worry about that.

A faint cool breeze stirred the reeds along the canal bank,
the canes rustling and sighing with a gentle hypnotic swirl.
Good, Aldin thought. There *should* be a special feel to the time
when a legend is breathing his last. The moment should have
a magic, a gentle stirring within that awakens an awareness of
some deeper link with destiny. Aldin tried to reach out and feel
that moment even as the morning breeze wafted across the
open fields, carrying with it the first stirrings of a city about to
awake. Enthralled, Aldin climbed to the edge of the ravine, his
eyes adjusted to the light, and looked out to the walls that girdled Babylon for a score of miles.

"The Xsarns would love it here," Tia whispered. "Take a
whiff of that breeze."

"Ah, shut up! You sure know how to kill a moment."

"I mean, *smell* it! Damn, I never thought a place could stink
this bad."

"Come on, let's walk to the gate," he said, the romance of
the moment having evaporated. "It should be opening soon."
Even as they stepped out onto the road, the world around them
seemed to stir with life. The greatest king in history might be
dying, but for the multitude it was a day that still had to be
lived. Dung- and reed-fired meals were being prepared along
the roadside as hundreds of travelers, who had arrived beneath
the walls after the closing of the gates, prepared to enter the
greatest city of the once-mighty Persian empire.

In preparation for a day of trading beyond the gates, merchants were soon setting up their stalls along the side of the
road, and their shrill cries filled the air.

"What a cacophony. You'd think these people would at least
have the dignity to wait for dawn before getting started," Tia
complained.

"Think of speaking in *Greek*," Aldin whispered in reply.
"Remember, the language implant will work properly only if
you think *Greek*. Start doing it now and it should be an unconscious act within minutes. These Greeks and Macedonians are
rather snobbish about their language—speak anything else and
you lose face with them. Remember that."

"I'll try," Tia replied, her response, in Greek, shaky but
passable.

Aldin felt for a moment that bringing her along might have

been a mistake, but if worse came to worst it would be good to have someone to cover his back. Hoodwinking the Macedonian successors to Alexander might look easy on paper, but it would be quite another thing to pull off. Even as they practiced their Greek in whispers, the gate of the city was before them, and the guard, a Macedonian by his uniform, did not seem in the best of moods as he shouted curses at the waiting line of people.

Aldin quickly surveyed the scene and as he did so a single horn sounded in the distance. In an instant it was picked up by another and yet another. Stepping back from the brooding height of the city walls, Aldin could see columns of smoke rising from the top of the ziggurats within. The ascending swirling clouds were tinged with fiery red, a reflection of the first light of dawn, which now broke across the open plains and marshes to the east.

The crowd around the gate grew silent for a moment, some of them going to their knees and bowing to the east, while others extended their hands to the heavens and cried out their greetings to the dawn. And the gates that stood twelve meters tall swung back, as if guided by the hands of giants unseen.

"Let's go," Aldin whispered, and he started forward, joining in with the pushing, jostling mob.

"Do you know where we're going?" Tia asked.

"No."

And without another word Aldin walked up to the Macedonian guard, a soldier well past his prime. The guard duty was likely a bone thrown to the old soldier who could no longer keep up. As Aldin drew closer he saw that the man was missing part of his nose. An ugly scar had been gouged upward from the missing part to an empty right-eye socket. Whatever the man had tangled with, it had taken a good part of him away with it.

Aldin's heart was pounding. For his entire life ancient soldiery had been a question of academic speculation and a source of data for gaming. He was about to speak to a man who might have served with Alexander from the beginning, who might have stood in the phalanx at Guagamela, or charged with his leader across the Granicus. This was a man who had truly *been* there.

"Excuse me. Ah, I'm bearing a—a greeting from . . ."

"Step aside there, you're blocking the road," the guard shouted in a barely recognizable dialect.

Tia hurried to Aldin's side. "Let me take care of it," she whispered.

Tia minced up to the guard, whose bulk made it appear as if a Bathsheba were approaching a Goliath. "Who is your hegemon?" she barked.

The guard stared coldly at Tia.

"*You*, yes, I'm speaking to *you*. *Who* is your hegemon?"

"Aristophane. Why?"

"Then I would suggest, soldier, that you get him. My companion Cleitius and I are envoys from the famed Aristotle, sent with a gift for the king."

The guard looked closely at Tia and his military bearing started to slip. "But my lord Alexander, he's dying. With the others I marched past him but yesterday, and I saw. He is dying."

"Do you know of Aristotle?"

"He whocedon. He was the teacher of my lord."

"Then you know he had many special powers. We might be able to help our king if you do not delay us. But if you do cause delay, I would not want to be you when the truth is learned."

The guard looked to his companion who was listening to the conversation, and there was a quick nod of agreement.

"Follow me," the guard said eagerly, and he pushed a way for them through the shouting dust-covered crowds shoving through the city gate.

Tia gave Aldin a quick wink and a self-satisfied nod, but when she glimpsed Aldin's expression of extreme distress, she quickly imitated him.

Once they had passed through the massive bronze gates, the guard turned into a squat, mud-brick barracks hall. Following his lead, Aldin stepped in after him, where he was assailed by the smell of unwashed bodies, dung fires, cooking food, and leather. It was a rich heady smell that made him slightly dizzy.

The guard stopped before a bunk where a short barrellike soldier lay stretched out on a rope-weave bed.

"All right, just what the hell is it now, Parmenion? You're the most shiftless son of a mutilated dog that has ever cursed my presence. Besides, you stink like an Egyptian sewer." The man groaned as he opened his eyes and looked at the guard.

In a nervous and excited voice Parmenion started to explain. Aldin tried to follow the conversation but it was held at such a rapid clip that it was difficult to run with. He hoped that his implant would analyze the data and learn to function in the proper dialect and faster.

As Parmenion spoke, the noise in the room died down and Aldin noticed that the other men were staring at him.

In short order the three were back out on the street with Parmenion leading the way down the main avenue, which approached an area of the city devoted to the myriad of cults and religions that prevailed in the Persian Empire at that time.

A feeling of anxiety seemed almost palpable, and the shrines were crowded. For the Persians were old hands at that sort of thing. The death of a king and civil war were synonymous, and most expected that the streets would run with blood as soon as the bronzed warrior from the west breathed his last.

Aldin noticed, as well, that more than one cast a hostile gaze upon him. For a moment he feared that his origins must somehow show. Parmenion somehow sensed his anxiety.

" 'Tis nothing personal, you see. They expect that we'll be at each other's throats, and some of their throats might get in the way, if you get my meaning, if the worst should happen and the great king goes to his fathers."

Aldin noticed a genuine note of pain in Parmenion's voice. So the legends are not legends, Aldin thought, the men must truly love him. The Greek or Macedonian soldiers that he passed *did* have a dazed and distant look to them.

They crossed a great square that was strangely empty, and Aldin sensed that they must be approaching the palace. A low wall in front of them was pierced by a single gate and, approaching, he could hear wild shouts of confusion from the other side.

A heavy guard was posted at the gate, but one of the men, recognizing Parmenion, waved them through.

In the courtyard beyond, men ran to and fro shouting wildly, some walked in shock with unseeing eyes. Others, weeping in anguish, were shaking their fists at the heavens. Some stood in groups and gazed suspiciously at any who drew close.

"I fear it might be too late." Parmenion groaned. "Too late." And as a heavily armed soldier raced past him, he called out a sad greeting. "Ho, Antonilius, how goes it within?" He gestured toward the Persian palace that occupied the far end of the courtyard.

"He speaks not. He slips away," the man cried and ran on.

"Quickly," Aldin cried. "Perhaps we can still help."

He pulled Tia closer. "As soon as they think he's dead, the arguing will start, there'll be mass confusion. We'll never get in if they think there's no need for a physician. I'll divert their attention. You hold the scanner in your palm like a medallion and point it at him. The computer will gather the data and do the rest."

"What's that?" Parmenion asked, his voice edged with suspicion.

"Nothing of importance to one such as you," Tia snapped.

"Now, now," Aldin replied, playing the opposite role, "don't berate the guard—caution is his job. I was merely reminding my friend to pray with her sacred medallion, presented to her by the oracle of Siwah. For our king is beloved of the oracle, and perhaps the medallion will help."

The conversation was cut short as they arrived at the main entrance to the palace. Parmenion stood in confusion a moment, dismayed that no guard was posted. "This cannot be allowed. Something is terribly wrong, terribly wrong." He shrugged then led the way in.

Grabbing hold of the first man who looked like he held some authority, Parmenion pointed out the two travelers and gave a hurried account.

"I don't give a good damn," the officer cried. "He's gone, he's gone so it doesn't matter."

Aldin stepped forward and grabbed the officer, who was edging into hysteria. "You know of my master." And as if to lend authority, Aldin pulled out a sheaf of "letters of introduction." "We are physicians, and even when others despair, we may still be of help. Lead us to his apartments, and you may yet save your king."

The officer hesitated, but even as he debated what to do, loud arguing and the clashing of weapons echoed in the next room. "Follow me," he said at last, and pushed his way past a knot of shouting, bawling men.

"In here." He pointed to an open doorway that seemed to lead into an audience chamber. It was packed with men.

Surely this can't be the room, Aldin thought, it's chaos in there. But he pushed his way into the crowd.

Parmenion hurried to Aldin's side and helped him to shoulder his way through the crush. All order and discipline have simply disintegrated, Aldin thought. The most powerful man in the ancient world dies and within minutes his empire and the order he has created are sucked into the darkness with him.

Suddenly the way was blocked, and Parmenion started to explain their story again.

"They don't look like physicians to me," someone cried, and the crowd, which seemed on the point of becoming a mob, turned its attention to the confrontation between the fat guard and a bantam-size officer.

"In fact, they seem more like troublemakers than messengers. I can't believe you'd be so stupid as to let them in here," the officer shouted.

The crowd that surrounded them stepped back a couple of paces. The officer's hand already rested on the hilt of a sword. "I think they should be thoroughly searched before being allowed to approach the presence."

Damn it, Aldin thought, this could take hours, and we're so close! Over the head of the officer he saw the thin veil that must mark the separation between the bedchamber and anteroom.

"Who are you?" The voice was low and gruff.

Aldin turned and faced another soldier, one who had the look of the desert and a lifetime's hard campaigning etched into his features.

"Messengers of goodwill from Aristotle," Aldin quickly replied.

"My lord has not had converse with Aristotle since the betrayal by the philosophos' nephew. Why should that old conjurer wish to send messengers now?"

"We were to bring this gift as a renewed offering of friendship." And Aldin reached into his pouch and produced a gem-studded pendant. It was a cheap trinket back home, but gold and emeralds still impressed Macedonians. At least, that had been Aldin's reasoning.

The man said nothing, but took the pendant and held it absently in his hand while continuing to scrutinize Aldin and Tia. So much for theory.

"We hastened here," Aldin continued, "abandoning our retinue when we heard that the great king was sick. The good soldier by our side escorted us from the great gate to the palace." And he pointed to Parmenion, who was standing stiffly by their side.

"That fat wreckage a *soldier*?" A smile almost crossed his face.

"I was at Granicus, and Guagamela, my lord Ptolemy." Parmenion's voice revealed the insult that he felt.

Ptolemy nodded in reply and turned away.

"We have studied medicine under Aristotle; perhaps there is still some way we can help."

"He is gone," Ptolemy said sadly, and as if in response to his words the lamentations in the room increased in volume.

"If he is truly gone, then we cannot hurt him. There have been times when men have been thought to be gone and yet are not. At least let us look and try. Surely we cannot harm."

Ptolemy hesitated for a moment, and then turned to a young aide standing beside him. He leaned over, whispered something to him, and then strode from the room.

Ptolemy, Aldin thought, and he looked in wonder as the man disappeared into the press. He wanted to shout to the man that he would found a three-hundred-year dynasty in Egypt, but Tia was already pushing him forward. The crowd parted before them and the light curtain was pulled back.

"And what of his half brother?" someone in the background shouted. "He should be the rightful heir."

"He's a half-wit," came the heated reply.

"You're the half-wit, by Zeus, and I still pledge myself to the brother."

"And what of the unborn child? Heh, what do you say of that?" screamed another.

Aldin suddenly heard the unmistakable sound of swords being drawn.

The military historian in him was fascinated, the man terrified, but another task remained, so Aldin turned away even as the men poured out of the room and the sound of fighting erupted in a corridor beyond.

He approached the silken curtain and hesitated. To Aldin's time, the man beyond it was dust for five thousand years, but if the scam worked, soon he would be a living, walking presence in a realm beyond imagining.

Aldin pulled back the curtain.

He was more beautiful, in a rugged masculine way, than Aldin had imagined. It was as if a Hellenic Greek statue had been given the texture and coloration of life. The form of Alexander had influenced a century of sculpture. Many had thought those sculptures to be idealized. Aldin saw that in fact they had never done justice.

A muffled sob distracted Aldin. He looked behind him. Parmenion's face was bathed in tears.

What sort of man was he, Aldin wondered, that could bring an aged veteran to display such emotion?

Aldin drew closer. He had imagined Alexander to be bigger; only a giant could bestride fifty centuries. This man was small, even for his own age, but his body was perfect in its proportions. His reddish blond hair was damp with fevered sweat and hung in loose, tangled knots.

His features were drawn—his eyes sunken.

Aldin looked around the chamber. A slender young man sat on the floor in the corner. "Bagoas?" Aldin asked.

The young man nodded in reply.

It was Alexander's eunuch lover, and Aldin stared at him for a moment, fascinated at such a strange love that had survived in the history of a man who most believed had conquered only through bloodshed.

"He is gone to his father," Bagoas whispered.

"But still I must check," Aldin replied. He walked up to the side of Alexander's bed and nodded to Tia.

She unshielded the medallion and pointed it at Alexander. "I know a girl whose name is Jewel," Tia said in common speech.

Aldin looked at her and rolled his eyes. The phrases would be gibberish to Parmenion and Bagoas, and as such would seem like an appropriate incantation. But still, the girl should have some respect!

"And this here girl did love to screw!"

"Tia!"

But she was away, full tilt now, reciting a stream of obscene limericks.

Aldin tried to ignore her as he unraveled the bioscan system from his traveler's pouch. There were no external signs of respiration and the body was extremely pale, but there was no cyanosis and in the stultifying heat decomposition should have started within several hours of death. Aldin produced a small mirror and held it before Alexander's mouth and nostrils. And then in a quick single motion he let his other hand slip behind

Alexander's neck, where he pushed a flesh-colored scan/med dose unit between Alexander's shoulder blades.

The skin was disturbingly cool to the touch. If Alexander hadn't languished in a deep coma after his apparent death, the whole trip would be a waste. Facing Corbin with the news would be no great pleasure.

The pickup unit in his ear clicked on as the scan/med dose unit activated and broadcast data to Aldin and the ship's computer.

"Heart rate, thirteen per minute," a small voice whispered. "Pressure sixty over thirty-five."

Aldin struggled not to show his exultation. He was right!

Tia looked at Aldin. He gave a subtle nod, then forced himself to show a look of anguished pain.

"Brain scan nominal on all counts, projected damage threshold within seventeen hours. Pleurisy, pneumonia, and major aberration in pancreatic function—initial diagnosis. Termination line within seventy-two hours."

Parmenion had drawn closer, trying to contain his grief. But there was a curious look in his eyes, as well, as he looked at Aldin and then back to Tia.

"Did I hear you say something?" Parmenion asked.

"Ah . . . no."

Parmenion looked at him with a curious expression. Aldin returned his gaze and forced himself to look distraught. "It is as I feared, he is gone."

"Unless otherwise overridden," the computerized voice whispered, "will administer stabilization medication as programmed."

Aldin ran his finger across the medallion signaling his assent to the ship's computer. The comalike state would be maintained while medication prevented further deterioration. As he did so, his other hand brushed against the adobe wall, and he applied a pinhead monitor unit that could observe the room, so they could check out the area before jumping back in with the replacement body.

Tia gave him a quick nod. The scan was finished. All they had to do was step into a side room, get pulled out by the ship, then reinsert later with the reformed body.

"There's nothing more we can do here," Aldin whispered sadly, trying to force a tear to his eye. "My friend and I will leave now."

"Just a moment." Ptolemy's aide stood in the corner of the audience chamber. "Did you say you were from Aristotle?"

"Yes."

"Strange, ever since our late lamented Alexander executed his nephew, we haven't heard a word from him. And suddenly on the day he dies, you show up on our doorstep. Some of the men in that hallway believe there is a plot afoot, that *poison* might have been at play here. I understand that Master Aristotle is quite knowledgeable in such areas."

Aldin shrugged his shoulders. "I would not know of such things. I am merely a messenger from him to our late king, nothing more. I have his letter in my pouch if you wish to see it."

"Yes, but of course. My lord Ptolemy will inspect that later. For now, he insists that you remain here at the palace so that he can talk with you when time permits." As the aide spoke, the sounds of fighting erupted again.

He gave them a cold, sinister smile. "You, guard!" The aide pointed at Parmenion. "You know where to show them, and you are responsible."

The aide turned and strode out of the room.

Aldin suddenly felt a heavy hand resting on his shoulder and, turning, looked up into the scarred face of the Macedonian guard. "Now, sir, there's nothing to worry about."

"Of course not," Aldin replied gamely.

He knew all about the famed Macedonian hospitality. It was just the standard practice of torture that preceded questioning that had him worried.

chapter three

"What do you think they'll do?" Tia whispered, forgetting to use Greek.

"Just shut up," Aldin hissed, and then nodded a smile

toward the far corner of the room where Parmenion sat by the doorway, drawn sword resting on his knee.

All their belongings had been taken, including their medallions. Fortunately his belt with its concealed electronics had not been touched; the only other way to communicate with the ship was through the small transmit unit he had swallowed just before departure. He had no desire to wait until that key component rematerialized.

He had made the mistake of asking Parmenion the time, and that had aroused further suspicions, since the measurement of time in this era was a haphazard thing at best. However, from the gradual darkening in their room he guessed that it must be drawing toward evening, and he estimated that replication should soon be completed.

Even as he smiled at Parmenion there was a short burst from his audio pickup.

"Replacement ready to be transported. Awaiting your signal."

"So tell me, Parmenion," Aldin asked, rising to his feet, "I heard you say that you fought at Gaugamela."

Parmenion shifted and looked up at him with pride. "I was in the front rank, opposite the first chariot assault. Ah, now that was a sight."

Aldin only half listened, and he gave a subtle hand gesture to Tia, indicating that things were ready back aboard the ship. If the situation turned ugly, they could have themselves pulled back to the ship. To return, however, would be impossible, for the hue and the cry would be up for the two "sorcerers."

". . . I saw this ugly black-bearded dog," Parmenion roared, still talking about Gaugamela, "he was coming straight at me with spear lowered. And then you know what I did?"

"I couldn't possibly guess," Aldin replied, and Parmenion continued on with his tale.

Aldin stretched and stepped closer to Parmenion as if engrossed in his tale. The arguing and occasional clashing of weapons outside had been going on with increasing frequency as the day progressed. All they had to do was to somehow put Parmenion out of action for a couple of minutes and then make a dash back to the room where Alexander lay in a coma. But how to do it?

"Guard, just what the hell are you prattling about?"

Parmenion shot up and stood rigid at attention. It was the bantam-size officer standing in the doorway.

He looked over at the two prisoners and advanced toward Aldin with an air of superior contempt. "I think you have a little problem, friend."

Aldin, sensing the man's mood, didn't reply.

"You see, a number of envoys have arrived today. Even now my lord Ptolemy has taken the time to meet with them. And you'd never imagine where they are from."

Aldin could only shake his head, not wishing to say anything that might enrage the captain.

"They're from Pella, where your so-called employer is supposed to reside. They traveled the same road you should have, and they claim no knowledge of an embassy from Aristotle, who, I might add, is just one step removed from arrested now that Alexander is gone."

Aldin simply smiled and shrugged his shoulders.

"And besides," the captain continued in a gloating manner, "those travelers carry a letter from Aristotle, as well, bearing his official signature and seal. Which does not, for some strange reason, match the signature on your letter at all."

Aldin shot a quick sidelong glance at Tia, who had visibly paled and was already looking quite guilty.

"So we have here an interesting situation." The officer advanced closer. "Perhaps you are part of a plot to kill our king and were sent to make sure that he was indeed dead and, if not, to administer another dose.

"Then again," he said with a smile, "you just might be two innocent fools who didn't know the game you were playing."

His left hand was resting on his sword hilt, and Aldin watched it carefully. But it was his right hand that shot out like lightning, caught Aldin in the solar plexus, and sent him crumpling to the floor, gasping for breath. Tia backed up against the wall, her eyes wide with terror.

"But I think you're guilty," the captain hissed. "And I'll take personal delight in helping to smash your body to a shapeless pulp until you finally talk. After that I'll pull your eyes out of their sockets.

"You, guard, my men will be here shortly to take these two to their questioning." With an ugly laugh he strode out of the room.

Aldin lay on the floor trying to regain his breath, and Tia came over to his side.

"Could you help me get him over to the cot?" Tia asked, looking imploringly at Parmenion.

"Get him there yourself," the guard growled.

"Please, he's an old man," Tia begged. "I tell you we're innocent. Do you think we would have rushed to Alexander's side after we had heard the news that he was dead if we intended harm? We would have stayed clear and been safe. I tell you we're innocent, and my friend here is hurt. Please help me."

Parmenion hesitated for a moment, and then with a mumbled curse he came over to Tia's side and started to bend over to pick Aldin up. In one swift movement her foot came up and caught Parmenion in such a way that he would be walking with difficulty for some time to come. His breath escaped in an agonized *woosh*, his one eye bulging out as he doubled over.

"Good going, girl," Aldin groaned, staggering to his feet.

Parmenion was still bent over, gasping, as Tia snatched up a small stool and raised it up high.

"Not too hard," Aldin said, actually feeling a touch of sympathy for their guard.

The stool caught Parmenion across the back of the head and he fell forward, his arms outstretched and grabbing for Aldin. He caught him on the belt.

"Xsarnfood!"

In horror, Aldin fumbled to release Parmenion's grip on his belt buckle, but the damage had already been done. The signal for the body transfer had been activated.

A dull shimmer suddenly appeared at Aldin's feet, right next to Parmenion's twitching body. Before Aldin had time to react, the shimmer turned into an even pulsing glow as the energy field formed. There was a faint outrushing of air, and then, with a faint *pop*, the field distorted and disappeared.

An exact replica of Alexander's body lay on the floor. Parmenion, who was still semiconscious, gave a gasping moan of horror and then his one eye rolled up as he passed out, either from fright or the blow to the head.

"Well, that throws the crap in the fire," Tia whispered.

"Damn good job that computer did," Aldin replied. "Damn good job. Can't tell the difference at all." He found the thought so amusing that he had to chuckle as he realized that if they pulled it off, a shady plastacement dealer would be the center of a shrine for centuries to come.

"Now what are we going to do?" Tia asked.

Without even trying to formulate a plan, Aldin grabbed hold of the cloak around Parmenion's shoulders, yanked it off, and wrapped it around the body.

"Parmenion's helmet, get it off," Aldin hissed. "And his belt, too!"

A minute later the door to the main corridor opened and a very frightened Tia peeked out, fearful that she'd get a spear in her face.

She looked back at Aldin.

"Why don't we just transport over to the room with Alexander?" Tia asked hopefully.

"Can't. The transport only locks on to living tissue and what we are wearing, nothing else. It can send a corpse down, but not back up. We'll have to haul it there ourselves."

"Please, Aldin, I beg you. Corbin will understand, I can work on him. Let's just get the hell out of here. If we get caught hauling this body around . . ."

"If you don't shut up, they'll catch us anyhow and we'll get crucified. Is it clear?"

"There's a group arguing down the end of the hall," she whispered.

"Fine, let's go."

Aldin kicked the door wide open and staggered out, the arm of the corpse slung over his shoulder.

"Help me, damn you, or by God's blood I'll yank that transceiver off you and leave you here."

Tia came to the other side of the body and grabbed it, helping Aldin to drag it out into the corridor.

"You're crazy!" Tia hissed.

"Stay calm, this place is in an uproar. They'll never notice us. I read that for most of the night Alexander's room wasn't even guarded, so it'll be simple, now let's go."

Still trembling from the blow to his stomach, he soon broke out into a sweat as they dragged the corpse down the hallway and past the first group of arguing soldiers.

The Macedonian guards barely spared them a glance; men being dragged out from the brawling was a common sight. Aldin only hoped that no one insisted on pulling back the helmet and taking a look.

They turned the corridor and started up the stairs to the main audience chamber where Alexander lay unattended.

"Ho there, is that Certius?"

Aldin kept on moving, ignoring the shouted command.

"I say, there, is that Certius?" A heavyset officer stepped in front of them.

"No, sir," Aldin replied in a differing whine, keeping his head low as if in subservience, "this be Aristophane. Too much to drink in grief, that's all. And him still sick with the fever and all. I heard it's catching good, sir."

With a mumbled curse the officer stepped back and let them pass.

A file of soldiers marched past them, brief snatches of their conversation echoing in the dimly lit corridor.

"Machus claims he'll personally yank out the fat one's teeth, one by one."

"I don't care, just as long as I can have some fun with the girl first."

"Ah, we know what kind of fun you want, Tremenichas." The others laughed crudely as they shouldered their way past Aldin. Tia, in a near panic, tried to pick up the pace, but Aldin held her back, partially out of not wanting to draw attention, but also because he was out of breath.

In another minute they would know if the approach to the main room was clear, but in another minute the guards sent to pick them up would be raising the cry. It would be a close thing.

They came out on the last landing of the staircase and turned toward the audience chamber.

All was quiet as the three drew closer. In the shadows he could see a sentry and Aldin felt his heart sink.

"Stop and identify."

Aldin knew he didn't have the strength to overcome this man; he would have to rely on simple salesmanship.

"Ah, soldier, it breaks my heart to bring my brother here." He tried to raise the corpse up a little bit as if he wanted to show it to the sentry. "It breaks my heart indeed. We followed the king from the beginning. I can still remember the clear bright day when Philip brought him out into the courtyard, and we raised the shout for the newborn lad. And now he is dead."

Aldin felt himself getting so into the part that there was even a faint shudder in his voice.

"I couldn't serve him, I was short of wind, you see." He coughed slightly to add emphasis. "But my brother here"—again he nudged the corpse—"was in Hephaestion's brigade and fought from Issus to the Indus. So overcome was he that he near drank himself to death tonight. So I beg you, good sir, please let us in for just one moment so that we might gaze one last time and bid our farewell."

"I've got orders, the room is closed. I can imagine it's not too pleasant in there right now, what with all this damned heat."

Even as he spoke they could hear shouted cries in the distance. The alarm was being raised.

"Look here, it's all my brother has." Aldin dug his hand into Parmenion's pouch, hoping that there'd be something. He felt some cool metal and pulled out a handful of copper and a couple of silver coins. To a collector back in the Cloud they'd be worth a thousand katars, enough to buy him a month in the finest pleasure palaces of Quitar, but he couldn't quibble now.

"A gift from my brother, please take it."

The guard hesitated and looked to his companion in the shadows.

The man nodded his approval and the guard took the bribe.

"Go on in and make it quick. And see that your brother there doesn't make a mess."

Even as he spoke he and his companion walked past them to the head of the staircase to see what the commotion was all about.

The door pushed open, and the two dragged the body inside.

It was cooler in there, dark and eerie. The great chamber was empty and echoed to the padding of their sandals as they dragged the body across the room.

Aldin approached the dais and again he was taken by the beauty of the man whose body was illuminated by a single torch, which flickered fitfully at the head of the bed.

There was no time for formality now.

Aldin dropped the corpse by the side of the bed.

"Come on, let's go," he hissed, and motioned for Tia to grab hold of Alexander's feet.

"So help me, Aldin, if we get out of this, I'll never—" She hesitated for a second. "What the hell is that?"

"Someone's coming, now move it!"

Forgetting all ceremony and respect, Aldin pushed Alexander off the dais.

Rushing around to the plastacement contractor, Aldin yanked off the helmet, belt and cape, tossing the equipment onto Alexander. Then with a strength that surprised him, he lifted the replacement up and dropped it where Alexander had lain only seconds before.

"Drag him over by the window," Aldin commanded, even as he struggled with the sheet that had covered Alexander and tried to arrange the corpse to look as if it had not been disturbed.

"Alarm. Body thieves. Alarm!"

A form suddenly leaped through the doorway, knocking Aldin off his feet. Aldin swung with desperate blows, pummeling his assailant on the shoulders and head.

"Help! Alarm!"

He could see Tia dragging Alexander away from him, moving toward the window.

"Not away from me, you idiot," Aldin screamed. "The beam, the beam, get next to me—*Yowlll*!" he cried out in anguish as his attacker's teeth sank into his leg.

Tia, at last comprehending, turned around and dragged Alexander back toward the struggling pair.

In the distance Aldin could hear more shouts, and the sound of running feet. The guard was closing in.

The hell with this guy on me, he thought, and when he saw that Tia was within range he hit the activation button on his buckle. There was a panic-filled moment when nothing happened and he thought all this punching, kicking, and other nonsense had broken something vital—then the distortion hit.

A faint popping *hiss* brought him to consciousness as the distortion shut down. Instinctively he checked his body to make sure that nothing important had been left behind.

"By the teeth of Zeus!"

"Damn it, Aldin, you brought that guard with us!"

Aldin could feel the grip around the lower half of his body relax and then go limp.

He kicked his way clear and stood up.

Parmenion was sprawled out, unconscious, and for a second Aldin wasn't sure whether he had simply passed out or the shock of transjumping had killed him.

"Now what the hell are you going to do?" Tia asked.

"Never mind him, it's Alexander I'm concerned about."

Aldin crouched over the unconscious form and touched him lightly on the throat, even as he realized that a pulse would not be noticeable. The body was cool to the touch and he felt a quick tug of fear.

"Help me," Aldin cried, and together they picked Alexander up and took him into the med-support room that had been previously occupied by the substitute body.

Aldin placed him on the now-empty table and hooked a direct monitor line to the patch he had attached earlier to Alexander's back.

He scanned the instrument's readout and breathed a sigh of relief.

"Initiate revival?" the computer queried.

"Affirmative, but keep the subject lightly sedated."

"By all the gods, I am ready," came a weak cry from the next room.

Fearful that the momentarily interrupted scuffle would resume, Aldin slid up to the open door leading into the transport chamber and peeked out.

Parmenion was on his hands and knees, his body shaking like a jellyfish.

"So you've decided to accompany your king to the next world?"

Aldin gave Tia a look of reproach but didn't stop her.

"Happily and without hesitation." Parmenion moaned.

"Then why did you assault the messengers of the gods?"

"Really, Tia, give him a break."

Parmenion snuck a quick peek at the two standing in the doorway, and with a loud moan he quickly averted his eyes.

"I—I was serving my king. I knew not that you were sent by the gods to take him to the next realm. And remember, noble ones, that it was I who led you to him, and I who helped when the bigger of you was hurt."

Aldin drew Tia back from the doorway.

"We should send him back," Tia whispered. "We pulled the switch and he was the only witness, but now he thinks we're gods. Let's give the poor man a drink and then send him back down to the spot that we jumped down to last night."

"He let two prisoners escape," Aldin replied. "They'll give him the punishment we would have received."

"Well, I guess it's your problem," Tia replied. "He was hanging on to you when you came through, so—"

Her comment was cut short by the high-pitched shriek of the ship's alarm, which was counterpointed by Parmenion's agonized wail of fear in response.

"Ship approaching," the intercom boomed, "ship approaching. Signal from unidentified vessel that we are to prepare for boarding."

"Who the hell?" And together they ran for the forward control room, nearly tripping over Parmenion, who was still prostrated on the floor.

"Ship design and probable origin," Aldin shouted as he leaped for the command chair.

"Unable to determine," the computer responded.

"Punch us out of here!" Aldin cried. "Take evasive action and run for the time nexus."

"Receiving message from approaching vessel, it is in galactic standard."

"Hook it in." Aldin groaned. "I think I know who it is."

"Unidentified vessel, bound out of Magellanic Cloud, currently Earth orbit. We have reason to believe you are involved in illegal process, procuring participants for gaming situation. This is an Overseer vessel; you are to cease any attempt at flight."

"Get us the hell out of here!" Aldin shouted.

They were slammed back into their seats as the ship's pulse system engaged a fraction ahead of the inertia damping unit.

"Cease all movement." The voice was Doppler-shifted as they accelerated up and away.

"Damn all self-righteous Overseers," Aldin raged. "Bastards never mind their own business."

"Ship attempting to flee. Such action is a violation of Overseer Law. Cease action at once."

"Aldin, they might shoot to disable!" Tia cried.

The Overseers were dedicated to pacifism, but it was pacifism at the point of a gun, and Aldin knew she was right.

"Ship command, evasive maneuver radical."

"Acknowledge, evasive maneuver about to engage."

Even as they shifted, the first beam of blinding light arched across their path. The simple act of evasion could possibly throw them into a beam and kill them, and he knew that the Overseers hoped such a thought would prevent him from his course of action. And he hoped, as well, that they'd stop shooting rather than risk a kill on the "destiny of their souls," as they called it.

"You are undoubtedly engaged in an illegal action. If you cease your evasion and allow boarding, we will merely provide counseling."

Oh, heavens, Aldin thought, the last thing he needed was several hundred hours of moral lecturing about the folly of his ways by one of their damned missionaries, and six months in one of their damned peace reorientation centers.

"Eat Xsarnfood!" Aldin cried, and Tia cackled with delight at his reply.

"Approaching first distortion field to nexus," the ship advised after transmitting Aldin's gastronomical advice, which prompted another shot across their bow.

"Do you think we'll get away?" Tia asked. "I've heard about their counseling; I'll be damned if I'll take any of that crap."

In fact he half suspected that the Overseers would not appreciate six months with her, either. The thought of surrendering just for the fun of it crossed his mind, but he pushed it aside; the commissions for the game far outweighed the pleasure of possibly discomfiting an Overseer.

"Go back and strap in Alexander, and make sure Parmenion is strapped in, as well. The turbulence will be rough at this speed."

"You're not gods!"

Turning, they saw Parmenion standing unsteadily in the doorway.

"Maybe not," Aldin shouted, remembering to switch back into Greek, "but by all the heavens, there's somebody chasing us who thinks he is. And if you give us any trouble we'll push you off this sky-wagon and let you fall into their hands. Now go help the girl with your king."

Parmenion hesitated for a second, and then with a shrug of his massive shoulders he followed Tia out of the room as she shoved her way past him with a mumbled curse.

"First nexus approach in ten seconds."

"Ship full stop," Aldin cried impulsively.

"Say what?" Tia cried, rushing back into the room.

"Just shut up. Maybe I've decided that life with them is better than life with you," Aldin yelled.

"Oh, yeah, well, Corbin will give you the same that Luciana got if you pull this on me."

"Shut up and see to Alexander!"

"Overseer ship decelerating," the computer chimed in.

Aldin noticed Parmenion's confusion over the computer voice, but an explanation would have to wait.

"Transmit, but provide usual voice distortion to avoid identification."

"Proceed."

"To Overseer ship, we surrender. Our primary drive unit is overheating. We accept your offer of counseling, but please get us off this ship, I think it's going to blow."

"We are glad that you have seen the folly of your ways," the Overseer pilot replied. "Switch on coordinate beacon and prepare to be placed aboard our ship."

"Ship nav, prepare for full acceleration," Aldin whispered.

"It will not be so bad, friends. You'll soon be enlightened to our higher ways."

"Oh, yeah, well, kiss my butt!" Aldin yelled. "Ship computer, hit it out of here."

In a blinding flash, they leaped away, leaving the Overseer vessel in their wake. Parmenion and Tia were knocked off their feet, and Aldin's vision blurred as they hit the edge of the field. Even as the pursuit ship started to accelerate, they crossed the first time nexus and disappeared.

"So long, suckers!" Aldin cried.

"So long, suckers?" Tia asked.

"Oh, yeah, I forgot you kids don't study your history of linguistics any more. It's an Earth term that means that you've taken someone for a fool.

"Well, let's get back to our passenger," Aldin said happily. "I hope that jump through didn't knock him off the table."

"The king!" It was Parmenion shouting from the next room.

Together Aldin and Tia rushed into the medical chamber. She stopped in the doorway with a gasp and Aldin nearly knocked her over.

"Am I in the realm of my fathers?"

He lay on the table, his eyes open, staring at them as if from some great distance beyond measure. Parmenion knelt by his side, tears of joy streaming down his face.

"I guess I better start explaining," Aldin whispered, his voice edged with awe and fear.

chapter four

"So I'm not dead?"

Aldin smiled softly and shook his head.

"Then if not dead, where am I? Have I been taken prisoner?"

Again Aldin smiled, trying to project his best bedside manner, which he knew couldn't be very reassuring.

"Majesty, they've snatched you for ransom," Parmenion blurted out. "They are in league with some evil god."

"If I'm in league with an evil god," Tia hissed, "rest assured I'll cut off a very important part of your body if you say another word."

Parmenion looked at her defiantly, started to open his mouth, and then, mumbling to himself, he turned away.

"Leave me alone with him, and I'll explain," Aldin said softly, still looking straight into those strange, mysterious eyes that seemed to hold an almost hypnotic power.

"Majesty!" Parmenion turned, ready to defend his king in spite of Tia's threat.

"It's all right," Alexander said weakly. "If they mean my death, they can have it. But I think not, otherwise I would not have been brought back from the doorway. Go, soldier, I command it."

Parmenion bowed low and walked out of the room, but the tone of his mumbling was obvious to everyone, even Alexander.

"A good soldier," Alexander said softly, and a faint smile crossed his lips. "Now tell me, how?"

"Might I ask what you remember?" Aldin replied. "And then perhaps I can better explain."

Alexander stopped for a moment and his brow creased as if he were searching for some half-forgotten thought.

"It was as if I were falling." He sighed. "A slipping away

46

into the darkness, to be embraced by the cool of a summer night.

"I could hear them all the time, like voices from beyond the pale. They cried that I was dead, and I tried to tell them not to lament. I heard them arguing, and then fighting."

He hesitated and looked at Aldin.

"They will die without me. The dream of unity will be lost. You must heal me so that I can return and lead them again."

"I can't."

"Then I am to die. Or am I already dead?"

"No, you'll live, Alexander. But return you, I cannot."

He could see the flicker of anger surface. He had said no to the most powerful man on Earth. The most powerful man on Earth, and Aldin realized that already that time was five millennia past, and all those to whom he had talked only hours before had returned to dust.

Alexander tried to sit up.

"I command . . ." he began, but fell back trembling with pain and exhaustion.

"You must believe me, O King." The words felt funny, but somehow Aldin felt no discomfort using the phrase with such a man. "If I could fulfill any wish of yours, I would. But to return is not possible. But do not lament, for destiny has given you the chance for a higher calling."

Alexander looked at him searchingly, suspicious of what he was hearing.

"And what worlds are there still for me to conquer?" Aldin whispered.

"What was that?" Alexander asked.

"Oh, just a quote attributed to you. Now you're still weak and should rest."

"But I must know why and how."

Aldin could only smile. He would have to ask him about Aristotle and the training he had received at the tutor's hands so that even now his mind was questing for answers.

"Computer med unit," Aldin said softly, "mild sedative, continue with standard medication and nutritional program."

"Acknowledged."

Alexander looked around, startled by the soft feminine voice of the computer. "Who was that?"

"Soon enough, soon enough. Now sleep."

Aldin could see the sedative taking effect, yet Alexander

fought to hold consciousness, as if he feared to ever close his eyes again.

"But I must know," he whispered.

"You will." Even as Aldin spoke, his patient drifted away. Aldin sat by him watching the gentle rise and fall of his chest, his breath still rasping from the congestion of pneumonia. The medic servobot unit nudged Aldin aside and hooked an oxygen tube to Alexander and deftly inserted an IV.

Aldin felt a sense of awe at what he had just accomplished. He had reached across the millennia and saved one of the greatest generals in history. He had expected to feel a slight condescending attitude to this man—after all, there was five thousand years of civilization separating them—but he was indeed a leader of legend. Aldin wondered suddenly if the Gavarnian leader Alexander was to meet would ever be able to match him. His thoughts turned to his fellow vasba Zergh, and he could not help but wonder if Zergh was feeling the same way he was at this moment.

"I am not sure I understand, Zergh."

Zergh stood up and stretched, his reddish-gray pelt expanding out and swaying gently as he rocked his body back and forth. "Nearly a day must have passed, exalted one. You should rest, there is still time to talk."

"No, I wish to know all."

"You're still weak from the poison. Why not sleep and I'll return later."

"No." It was no longer a statement, it was a command.

With a sigh Zergh sat down and signaled for his assistant to bring another drink.

"I'll have one of those, as well."

"But, exalted, think of your health."

"I am thinking of my health." He barked a short gruff laugh, and Zergh had to shake his head in amazement. Either he had the endurance of ten or he was delirious and would soon pass out.

"You're thinking about how I can stay up like this for so long, aren't you?"

Again he displayed an ability to somehow read another's thoughts.

"I think I should be watchful of my thoughts around you,

Kubar Taug, for you seem to be able to pull them out of the air."

Kubar laughed again. "If I could not feel such things, I would never have lived as long as I have, nor would I have conquered a world. A conqueror must know his enemies, but even more so, he must know the thoughts of his friends and how far he can trust them.

"Now you're starting to wonder about the poison and why I drank from the cup offered by my spouse before I went to the mountain to meditate."

Zergh could only shake his head.

Kubar smiled. "Funny, that was only three days past. Three days and what you call four thousand years ago. And now I ride to another world, not as a dead man but as one still alive for yet another adventure."

He shook his head and his mane gently rustled behind him. "I should be grateful. Indeed I am honored by the place that history has given me. But did you ever think that I was simply tired of war and conquest?"

"But you conquered an entire world and united us," Zergh replied. "What greater thing can one aspire to?"

Kubar looked at him and smiled. "Returning to what I was just talking about, I will say that I did suspect that cup, but I drank anyhow."

"Why?"

"Tired, perhaps."

Zergh looked at him and didn't believe.

"Perhaps, as well, it was a test of loyalty. I guess you know I loved to do such things as a proof of my trust, and, well, that time I was wrong. But no, that is in a way a lie to myself. You see, I had just won my greatest triumph; the unification was complete, and I knew, as well, that the Council could hold it together after I was gone. So I thought on the words of Lagata, our greatest warrior-poet, when he said that it is good when one makes his mark upon his world, but it is better to know when to leave, so that the mark will shine the brighter."

Kubar fell silent for a moment as if lost in thought. Zergh wanted to say that somehow he had been right; that by "disappearing" when he did, he became the martyr to the unification and thus made it complete. For half a thousand lifetimes the legend had been told and retold how Kubar Taug had come to unify and when his task was completed he had returned to the

Unseen Light. But he felt that such words, such praise, would be mere platitudes to one as great as Kubar.

Kubar looked up at Zergh again and smiled. "So tell me, what is it you call them?"

"Humans."

"Yes, Humans. But most of all tell me of this one they named Alexander."

"You've told me how, but you haven't told me the reasons why."

Startled, Aldin sat up from his bunk to find Alexander sitting by the foot of the bed, smiling at him with a distant, enigmatic smile.

"You should be resting, you're still not completely recovered."

"I suspect that my name has somehow survived across five millennia not because I was one given to rest. There is not enough time, Aldin. The gods gave us sleep to cheat us of our glory. To sleep is to be dead."

Aldin shook his head and, turning to the serving unit, he punched up a coffee and made a gesture of offering to Alexander.

It had amazed him how quickly this man had adapted himself to the technological shift, accepting the various shipboard computers and servobots with an eager curiosity. He had rebelled slightly at the language implant, expressing the Hellenic disdain for any other language but his own. But the practicality of it finally won him over. He accepted even the question of translight space travel with barely a shrug, thus laying to rest the concern of several Kohs that the shock of his surroundings would render him useless.

Perhaps the greatest source of interest for Aldin was teaching Alexander how to access the history library and then to watch as Alexander read the accounts of his own life. His rage at Plutarch's ridiculous fables about his drunkenness and debauchery had echoed through the ship for hours. And Aldin could little blame him, wondering how he himself would feel if his life's history had been so badly distorted, and then believed across hundreds of generations.

"So now your questions turn to the future."

"There is nothing else but the future, Aldin. Though I know you and these demigods of your time find me interesting, I doubt if you went through the trouble of this little transfer simply for your own amusement. And my guard has pointed out to me that we seem to have been chased by something that you were evidently rather fearful of."

Aldin felt as if the eyes were boring straight into him. It was a searching look for truth, and there was no getting around it, for this man would know when someone was lying.

"I've been sent to take you to another world where there is a war."

"I am flattered by the interest in me, but again why me, why not someone from your own time?"

"Because it is you, Alexander. If you could conjure Hector from the dust to fight by your side, would you not do it?"

Alexander smiled at the mention of his hero, and in spite of his attempt to appear aloof, it was obvious that he was honored by such a comparison.

"So you wish a Hector for your war, is that it?"

Aldin nodded slowly, and said, "I'm taking you to a realm like few others in the hundred thousand inhabited worlds of the cosmos. It is a place made by a most ancient race known only to us as the First Travelers. It is believed by some that they trod upon our Earth ten million years ago and played a part in the birth of man, and of the Gavarnians, as well."

"The Garvarnians?"

"In a moment, but let me explain the First Travelers. They had such power that they even built worlds for their own amusement, the way you would build a city. One such world they built in the shape of a ring—a ring so large that the land area of a hundred Earths would fill but a small part of it . . ."

Alexander was silent, intent, and listened to Aldin's every word.

"Twenty-five hundred years ago this world was found by men, and it was empty of intelligent life. The First Travelers seemed to have built it only to abandon their work and move on."

"Why?"

"We don't know. We have never seen them, even the Overseers . . ."

Aldin cut himself short, not wishing to get into that angle.

"Something you'd prefer I didn't know about?"

"Well, of all the things you need to know about, that is one of the least useful, shall we say."

"I shan't force you. Continue then."

"They simply built such things as the ring and then disappeared. As I was saying, those who settled this place lost contact with the other worlds while a great war was fought. Only recently have we found these people again, but their knowledge had slipped back to the most basic of things. How shall I say it, they were somewhat . . ."

"I think you mean primitive, as in my time."

"No insult intended," Aldin replied.

"Nor taken. I would be indeed vain if I thought that man's knowledge of the world stopped when I died. Of course there would be progress."

"So what we found," Aldin continued, "was a loosely knit civilization locked in a war with a race of aliens."

"Aliens?"

"Oh, I see, I think we forgot something in our earlier conversation. You remember that I mentioned the Gavarnians?"

"Yes."

"They have the intelligence of men, but they are not men."

"You mean they are another race of creatures?" Alexander paused for a moment, a look of wonder coming to him. "I had always hoped that beyond Bactria I would find such a thing, and now, at last."

Aldin shook his head and smiled. "On the level of combat that we are speaking of they are nearly impossible to defeat. They walk like men, and talk like men, but their appearance is more that of a wolf."

Alexander gave him a quizzical look, as if Aldin were stretching the truth. "On the level of combat? What do you mean?"

"Simply that war on this ring-world is no different than in your time. It is sword, spear, and bow."

"So none of your new machines or discoveries apply there? How is that, for men will always seek better ways to make war? My father and Dionysius of Syracuse learned this and used men of knowledge to build machines that could destroy. Why aren't your machines used in this fight?"

"Neither we nor the Gavarnians knew of this war until recently. And I might as well tell you that there is a third race, the Overseers, who have forbidden all war and thus prevent new machines from being brought into this conflict, even if we wanted to."

"Even if you wanted to?"

"Why should we? Our machines would only serve to provoke mass destruction. Far better to let them settle their differences in the manner of your time."

Alexander smiled as if he could sense the hidden meanings in Aldin's words. "A little more interesting, as well, isn't it?"

Aldin was silent.

"So that is why you reached out for me across the eons. You want me to take over this war and to fight it to a successful end."

"Precisely."

"But I am a stranger to them. Why should they accept me?"

"These people are not all that warlike, and they are disorganized. A man such as you will be able to find his way and soon prove himself."

"An interesting challenge. So, without title, name, or army I am to forge my own way."

Aldin shrugged his shoulders. "They do know of you, and in fact admire their ancient history. If you can convince them of who you are, so much the better."

"This sounds like the dream of a madman," Alexander said coldly.

"But what a challenge."

"Will you be with me?"

"Once I leave you upon the ring, the demigods whom we call Kohs forbid all contact with either you or the Gavarnians. That will be your challenge."

"The challenge is always safer, Aldin Larice, when it is not you who must face it."

"Then you refuse?"

"I didn't say that, but it is a difficult problem. I assume that little machine you put in me will help with the language, but what of the customs of these people?"

"We shall place you near a mountain tribe much like your own Macedons. They are in fact descendants of people north and east of Macedon. But the legends of your deeds are known to them."

"I still think you are crazy. I mean, why should I do this?"

"Well, there are the Gavarnians to consider, and Human honor to uphold. You see, even now a Gavarnian leader, as famed and honored as yourself, will be placed upon the other side. He will attempt to organize and lead his people against the men of this world. The men have the potential advantage of generalship such as yours; the Gavarnians, however, have the advantage of simple brute strength. It takes two, even three men to match one Gavarnian for strength."

Aldin was hoping that this point alone would lure him in, and he didn't have long to wait for a response.

"Tell me of this Gavarnian leader that I must face."

"Orbital matchup with Kolbard is complete, current position as indicated."

Aldin swiveled away from the command console and looked at the three standing behind him.

Tia attempted to look uninterested, but even someone as jaded as she was awed by what was before them.

Their orbital path ran along the periphery of the Kolbard. Two barrier walls several hundred kilometers high ran parallel on either edge of the ring, enclosing the region's atmosphere. As they edged close into the barrier, Aldin commanded the ship to pull in toward the mid-region of the arc. They skimmed the wall then slipped over it, and there below them was a world of shimmering blues and greens, as if they floated above a lush planet girded by a ribbon of light that arched up into infinity in either direction.

"Upon the back of a tortoise," Alexander muttered, "which rests upon the back of an elephant, which rides atop the back of a lion."

"What's that?" Tia asked.

"Oh, just how one of our teachers attempted to explain what the world rests upon . . ." His words trailed off as he shook his head in amazed bemusement.

With a low moan and a curse about evil wizardry, Parmenion turned away from the view.

"Soldier, I saw you stand at Guagamela against the Persian chariots, so why should something like this disturb you?"

"That I could understand, that I could fight. But this smacks of evil magic." He squinted at Aldin, as if he were about to sprout wings or breathe fire.

"There'll be a lot more for you to see," Aldin replied, then turned his attention back to Alexander.

"Are you ready to go down there?"

Alexander shrugged his shoulders and smiled. "Somehow I must view all of this as a bonus given to me by the gods. It is a chance to prove what I am, without my father to lay the groundwork. To build an empire from scratch, as he did, now *that* is a worthy challenge. I'm ready."

Aldin couldn't help but smile at the response. But Parmenion didn't seem to be happy at all.

"But what about me?"

"Why, you're staying here with us," Aldin replied.

"I can't leave him go down there by himself. I mean, it just isn't right. I'm his sworn guard."

Aldin had been afraid there would be a problem over this and he tried to reason.

"The Gavarnian is landing by himself. It wouldn't be fair to give Alexander an assistant."

"And you hid my sword, you dirty scum; why, if I had it in my hands right now I'd—"

"Enough." Alexander stepped forward, putting a restraining hand on Parmenion's shoulder. "It would be nice to have at least one countryman with me. Couldn't it be arranged?"

Aldin shrugged his shoulders and shooed them out of the room. He knew that Zergh's ship was already in place on the opposite barrier wall of the ring. Now that they were both positioned, a signal from Corbin would start the game.

He punched into the Gavarnian channel. "Aldin to Zergh, are you ready for drop-off?"

"This will be an easy bet to clean up on, Aldin," Zergh replied in his clear gruff voice. "Kubar is even better than I had imagined. Care to make a little side bet?"

"Ten thousand katars?" Aldin offered.

There was a moment of hesitation. "Done. Now, what do you want?"

"Just a minor wrinkle," Aldin said. "I inadvertently picked up a guard. I'll present my full records to the Xsarn as verification. I was wondering if you had run into a similar problem and if so, perhaps we could arrange a companion for each."

"Thank the stars. I have a half-crazy spear carrier in the next room. I had to lock him up to keep him from killing me whenever I didn't show Kubar the proper respect."

"Agreed, then?"

"Agreed. Drop-off within the hour then. I'll notify Corbin that everything is ready."

Parmenion's initial enthusiasm was somewhat dampened as Tia explained in the simplest of terms how the beam system would work. He looked sideways at Alexander, trying to mask his fears.

Aldin came up to Alexander and extended his hand, which Alexander took in a firm, confident grip.

"May your gods watch over you and bring you glory."

"Ah, yes, glory." He smiled again. "An entire world. Let's just hope they agree with my methods."

Tia came in from the com center and nodded. The signal had just been given.

With a wave of his hand, Aldin turned aside and activated the beam. There was a shimmer and a *pop*, and the two were gone.

Aldin stood silent for a minute, feeling a tug of guilt that he had not been more honest with Alexander and explained the real motivation for bringing him to Kolbard. But that was no longer his concern. It was time for him to get to Corbin's new gaming yacht, which was berthed atop one of the hundred-kilometer-high weather control towers. This action might take a year or more to manage and already the bets were pouring in.

chapter five

"Sire, I'm afraid."

Alexander looked back at Parmenion and smiled. Aldin's ship was long since gone, and for hours they had been climbing up toward the high ridge of a line of hills. Parmenion was panting for breath as sweat dripped from his body, staining his tunic and leather armor.

Alexander stopped for a moment and took a deep breath, exhaling it with a sense of wonder. Ever since the arrow had torn his lung in a battle years before, breathing had been difficult. Aldin's miraculous machines had somehow made him whole again, and for that, at least, he was grateful.

"What do you fear, Parmenion?"

"Look to the sun, Alexander, it moves not. Therefore time moves not, and we are trapped here for eternity."

"Interesting logic; you sound like a Euclidian. But remember we are not walking upon our world but another, so fear not."

"Walking upon another world," Parmenion mumbled, "and he tells me to fear not."

Alexander looked up at the sun again. So strange—it was a sun, but different. The light was sharper, somehow more white, he thought. And he wrestled again with his own fear.

He was the companion of fear. They never knew, none of them ever knew nor would he ever tell them of the fear he had so often felt in his own heart. But of course, he could never tell, for that must be part of his legend: that Alexander was without fear, even here, on what that man had called the Kolbard—an eternity away from home.

And what of home? What of Roxana, or the unborn one that would be his heir? His mind raced over what he had overheard in the death chamber of the Babylonian palace, even as he felt his life slipping away.

He almost had to smile at the memory. They had been his wolves, his ravenous ones, to unleash upon any who stood in the path of his glory and his dream. And he had heard them turn upon each other. Out of the dim recess of coma he had listened as they fell one upon the other, even as wolves do when their leader should falter or die. Turn they would, and turn again, until the new leader was anointed.

But they were dust now, dust, their names linked only into the shadows of his glory, or so the fat one, the one whom he had first thought was a god-messenger, had told him.

Five thousand years ago. He shook his head, feeling overwhelmed by the thought. *Five thousand years.* He looked again to the sky as if somehow out there he would see his world and, by seeing it, regain balance and understanding of the whys and wherefores of what had happened to him.

Five thousand years and what the fat one, Aldin, said was 150,000 light-years away. Aldin tried to explain that, as well, but the number was meaningless to Alexander. He pushed the thought aside as was his custom. Whenever there was something that he could not understand, he would worry over the question, but if no answer came, he would push it away until such time or place as he could again devote himself to learning about the unknown.

But now, there was a far more immediate concern. A new adventure was beginning for him, and he thought about the unusual circumstances of it for a brief moment. What was the real reason for this Aldin to do what he did? Granted, curiosity about himself must have been a factor, but there was something else, and he felt it was not only to unite these people and lead them against an invader. For if Aldin and the demigods called Kohs had wished that, they would have landed him with great fanfare and pomp to awe the barbarians into doing his will. But instead they had landed him there as a thief in the night, almost as if Aldin had wished no one to see what was being done. But that was not his immediate concern, either.

He slowed his pace for a moment and surveyed the hills around him. The land was not unlike that of Bactria: high hills lightly forested and capped with snowclad peaks. The air was fresh, bracing, and clean as it had been in Bactria when compared to the hot, humid stench of Babylon. Directly before him was a mountain beyond all imagining, a towering behemoth that rose straight into the heavens until it seemed as if it would reach to the very sun. Aldin had explained that it was used as a port for the massive ships that sailed the heavens, and also as a tower to cool the air and thus balance the temperature, and that such mountains bulged like spikes on the outside of the ring, as well.

Such a thing was beyond Alexander's grasp, and he could only believe that these First Travelers whom Aldin said had made this place were in fact gods, or children of gods. Even as he gazed upon the tower in the shape of a mountain, he called it Olympus in his own mind. Aldin had told him that it was viewed as a holy place, and that a dozen or more villages surrounded it. What looked to be almost next to the mountain—but was in fact more than fifty leagues away—was a replica of the first mountain, and then four more beyond that. Aldin said that several hundred thousand people lived in the region of the first three towers, but beyond, to the far north rim of the ring, was desolation except for occasional hermits and brigands. The other three towers were in the region held by the creatures known as the Gavarnians. He looked in their direction for a moment, hoping to see the signs of their capital city on the ocean's coast, off to what in his own mind he called the west.

But from such a distance all he could see was the shimmer of the ocean shadowed by a high floating bank of clouds that trailed from the three distant towers.

Hundreds of leagues away toward what Alexander decided was the east, the direction he was heading in, there appeared to be a purple wall that seemed to reach to the heavens. Aldin explained that such barriers were set at regular intervals, otherwise the winds generated across the vast expanse of open space could create weather far worse than anything encountered in the great plains of central Asia.

Again the realization of what had happened to him started to well up inside, but his disciplined mind forced the emotion away. If fear of the unknown or the dangerous had ever taken hold of him, he never would have taken an empire, nor could he build a new one on this world. Looking back over his shoulder to the west, he could see the same type of wall, but this one, running north and south, appeared to be far closer.

Since the world he was on curved up, rather than down, the horizon did not disappear. Parmenion was still terrified by that sight alone, but already he was growing used to it. He'd have to, he realized, otherwise he'd go mad.

Not good country for a phalanx, Alexander realized. It was rough and hilly, cut by narrow ravines and brooding heights of bare windswept rock. Aldin told him that the terrain of this region varied greatly, since the First Travelers had apparently taken delight in forming the land without logic, guided by a whimsy to place one thing next to another in wild confusion. A single day's march to the south would bring them into open plains of unbelievable richness, but that was held by whomever he was to lead his new people against.

And then another thought struck him with awe: he had merely conquered a world; these First Travelers had actually built a world.

"Sire, listen!" Parmenion was at his shoulder, whispering even as he pulled him toward a rocky outcropping that offered concealment.

Alexander cocked his head, turning it from side to side, listening, and then he heard it, dancing at the edge of recognition like a distant wave one was not sure was heard or imagined.

He looked at Parmenion for confirmation.

"Sounds like a scream," Parmenion whispered, "a Human scream."

Alexander shrugged his shoulders and started to uncase the bow that Aldin had given him. After a brief struggle he strung it and tested the pull. It was as good as a Scythian weapon, perhaps even better since it was made of a metal, most likely a highly tempered steel, he thought. And again he shook his head in wonder.

He pulled one of the arrows from the quiver and held it, testing the balance. It was light, so very light; the four-barbed head glinting wickedly in the multihued manner of a razor-sharp weapon. Such precision, Alexander thought, and such cost to make one of these in Macedon.

"Shall we?" Alexander inquired of his companion with a smile.

"Ah, sire, it's really none of our business."

"But it is, Parmenion. We have to meet these people sooner or later, so why not now? Eh, unsheath that sword, if it is not rusted in place, and come along."

He said it with a smile as if joking, and shamed, Parmenion fell in behind his king.

I never thought I would someday lead an army of one, Alexander thought, but there must be a start and why not here? And he realized, as well, that the more humble the origin, the greater the glory if he should survive.

Survive—already he was a legend as he had wished, so this adventure was merely an extra reward, as if the gods had decided to give him an even greater challenge. Perhaps that was it, the gods were challenging him further. He smiled at the thought.

If that were the case, he would not disappoint them.

The cries grew louder as Alexander approached the crest of the hill. Crouching low, he approached the ridge-line with caution, moving from boulder to boulder.

There was another cry. This one high-pitched and filled with panic. He suddenly realized that to come to battle like a thief was unbefitting one who was king. Standing erect, he strode forward, as if by his mere presence the disturbance on the other side of the hill would somehow cease.

"By the gods!" Parmenion gasped.

Alexander felt his old companion again, the tremor of fear—but this was a fear unlike anything he had ever faced before. He had feared his father, at least in the beginning, and there had been the fear of failure, but unlike those around him, there had never been the fear in battle. Now he felt it.

The screams were Human, to be sure, and they were screams of panic. And the cause of those screams was to his eyes a moving nightmare.

The creature was wolflike, but yet not. Human, but not. It was as if the two had been blended together into one unholy mating. It rode astride a beast that was twice the size of his Bucephalas. It was like a horse, but somehow fiercer and wilder.

There were a half dozen of the creatures mounted on their nightmare steeds, and he could hear their voices as if they were laughing in triumph. Each of them wielded a lance, and they rode forward in attack formation, spears lowered. One of them carried a Human under its arm, and it was from her that the screams came. He realized now that the screams were ones not of pain but of rage, as she shouted imprecations at the men who were running away. That made him realize for a second that he could indeed understand what she was saying, even though it was not Greek, Persian, or any dialect he was used to. The implant of Aldin's worked even here and he could understand, as well, the fear in the voices of the men she was swearing at.

Before her captors nearly half a hundred men were running in panic, casting aside their flimsy spears to allow for a more speedy retreat. All this he saw in a glance, and he knew what he must do.

Alexander flexed his bow once more to test its balance and pull. He reached to the quiver strapped to his back and pulled out a shaft of gleaming metal. In an easy, fluid motion he nocked the arrow and pulled back, sighting on the beast who was bringing up the rear of the charge.

He knew this was the moment of the testing, and he knew, as well, that the moment he shot they would turn their wrath upon him.

The arrow snapped out—a sliver of lightning streaking on a fatal path. It caught the creature high in the back, punching straight through what appeared to be a corset of mail. With a loud piercing shriek he pitched forward, lifted from his seat by the impact. The horse sheared to one side, bearing its master out of the attack.

Already the second arrow was nocked, aimed, and away.

This one hit a second creature lower in the back but had the same effect. And then the others were aware of him slowing their attack and turning to see where their unseen tormentor was located.

"I think, Parmenion, you'd better ready your pike and prepare to receive cavalry."

But his command was unnecessary as Parmenion had already sheathed his sword. He took the top section of his pike, inserted the socket into the second section of ash, and locked it in place. He stepped to Alexander's side, knelt down on one knee, and snapped the weapon to the present position, so that a charging horse, if foolish enough to press the attack, would impale itself on the long barb.

Parmenion was trembling with fear. He had withstood many a charge, but never one from a horse that stood twenty-five hands tall.

The third arrow winged out and missed its mark as the creature pulled his mount up short just as Alexander fired. The arrow disappeared into the rising cloud of dust.

"Sire, one of them has a bow," Parmenion shouted, and Alexander suddenly noticed the creature that had pulled up short. He was unslinging his bow even as he goaded his horse into the attack.

Another arrow snapped out. This one nearly lifted the creature out of his saddle, the bow falling from his hand.

The remaining three hesitated for a second, then the one carrying the Human female dropped his prisoner to the ground and, with a thundering roar, goaded his horse forward into a lumbering charge.

"Look, look how slow," Alexander shouted. "Impressive, but too slow. The elephants of Pontus were far worse."

The creature lowered his lance, pulled his shield up high for protection, and came forward, all the time howling with a high, piercing keen that set the hair on edge.

Alexander nocked an arrow and stepped forward several paces, stopping just short of the iron head on the end of Parmenion's pike.

"Sire, shoot," Parmenion shouted. "You can get off two or three before he hits!"

"I want to watch," Alexander said. "It's almost beautiful."

"The sight of our blood won't be beautiful, not in the slightest."

But Alexander ignored him, caught up in the remarkable display of the moment. Onward the creature came, now standing high in what Alexander took to be ropes that extended down from either side of the saddle. The horse was indeed impressive, but slow, not able to go much faster than a trot. The armor looked fairly good, but appeared to be nothing more than a leatherlike jerkin.

"Sire! Please shoot him!"

"Another moment."

The creature was closing, so that above the howling he could hear the puffing of the horse, the rattle of the accoutrements. And the creature, as if sensing what he faced, did not blanch, but rather stood higher in the saddle, displaying his defiance.

Alexander shook his head and then drew the bow. His opponent raised his shield up, protecting his side and face.

The bow snapped, and the howling stopped. A riderless horse trotted past Alexander. The beast came to a stop to one side as if it would now watch the outcome of the struggle.

Alexander looked to the other two, who were silent, watching. He strode forward for a dozen paces and cast his cloak aside so that his bronzed and silvered armor shone for the first time in the light of another world.

"I am Alexander, known as the Great, son of Philip, once ruler of half the known world."

He dropped his bow and unsheathed the sword that Aldin had given him. It felt light, well balanced, finer than any steel of the Aramaic sword makers. He was touched by the fact that Aldin had engraved the blade with his titles and the names of his greatest victories. Even across five thousand years they had remembered that. He looked at how the blade shone in the sunlight, and again his gaze turned heavenward.

He looked back again to the remaining two. One of them stood in his stirrups and held his lance aloft. His shouts drifted on the wind and Alexander realized that this creature was speaking to him, but the words held no meaning and he was disappointed that Aldin had not taken care of that, as well.

He assumed it was a challenge, and in response he started to walk down the hill, but even as he started to advance, the two turned their horses about and trotted away.

Reaching the crest of the opposite hill, they looked back again for a moment and then disappeared from view.

"Sire, a good shot that one, but what a devil it is."

Parmenion had advanced over to the body of the one that had charged. Alexander came over to join him. The arrow had driven clear through the shield, catching the creature in the throat. He still could not understand what it was that he had just fought, but he knew that bravery at least was one of its virtues. The creature must have known that he was going to die but still he came forward, rising up in his saddle to meet what Alexander was forced to deliver.

"If this is what we must face, then we have a formidable foe."

"And if those running cowards are what you must lead," Parmenion muttered, gesturing in the direction the men had fled, "then you really have your work cut out."

Alexander knelt down by the side of the creature. It was half again as tall as he was, covered from head to foot in a light matting of soft black hair. Again he had the feeling that he was looking at a Human, but it was a Human that was nearly half wolf. Picking up the still-warm hand, he examined the fingers, which were almost manlike except for the remarkably long thumb that sprang from the wrong side of the wrist.

He looked to the creature's face. The eyes were still open, oriental in appearance with a double folding. The ears were nearly on top of the creature's head, protruding from either side of a studded leather helmet. The armor was well made, but there was hardly any metal; it all appeared to be of leather. Alexander touched the creature's eyelids and closed them. Standing, he picked up its cape and laid it across the body.

"A worthy foe," Alexander said softly, and then looked back to his companion.

"Parmenion, I think it time that we go and meet our subjects."

Parmenion could only shake his head in wonder. This man, this one from the gods, had no doubt, no question; he knew that they were indeed already his subjects.

The horse stood to one side, eyeing the two of them with suspicion. Alexander slowly extended his hand to either side and, speaking softly, he started to approach the beast. The creature shied and stepped back.

"Parmenion, give me a cloak."

Alexander took the cloak that Parmenion snatched up from the body of his fallen foe and draped it around his body. He sifted around the horse in a wide circle so that the wind was at his back, and then started to advance.

The horse was still.

He approached the creature head on, reached up and stroked it lightly on the nose, all the while talking softly. After several minutes he started to work his way to the horse's flank, still stroking it lightly.

It was bigger than any horse he had ever seen, almost the size of a yearling elephant. The pommel of the saddle was well above eye level, and he could just barely grasp it with his hands. The horse shied slightly and nickered, but Alexander hung on, all the while speaking softly.

He took a deep breath and, with a quick graceful movement, pulled himself up then swung his leg up over the horse's back.

The creature started to buck and Alexander fought to stay on. He could barely straddle the animal with his legs, so wide was the back, and he struggled for balance as he reached for the reins.

"Sire, try putting your feet into those leather loops," Parmenion shouted.

Alexander looked down one side of the horse and saw the loop Parmenion was shouting about. But they were too low, and then he saw the strap that adjusted them.

The horse was still bucking even as Alexander reached over and struggled with the strap, pulling the loop up higher. He somehow knew that he was being watched, and to fall off now would be a loss of whatever mystique he had gained in the fight. The loop was high enough, at last, and he slipped his left foot in. He reached over to the other side and quickly hiked the second strap into place and seated his foot in the loop.

He placed his weight down on the ropes and felt a sense of control. They were remarkable, and the utter simplicity of the idea stunned him. Why hadn't he, or one of his cavalry officers, thought of them? Grabbing hold of the reins, he stood up in the stirrups, and with a sure gentle hand he quickly brought the beast under control.

Then with a kick of the heels he urged the creature into a run. After the horses of the Scythians and the finest of Persian stock, the creature was disappointingly slow, but he knew that a massed charge of a thousand such beasts would strike terror even into the best of his armies—the way the Elephants of Porus had once done. He realized that this creature combined the best of both. The terrifying mass of an elephant, but also the greater agility and control of a horse, and could forage on its own and not require a mountain of fodder every day.

He galloped up alongside of Parmenion and reined the horse in.

"Come on, Parmenion, better to ride on Bucephalas than to walk." There was the trace of a distant smile on Alexander's lips.

"You still miss him, don't you?" Parmenion asked, more like an elder brother than a lowly soldier. For like many of his now-distant army, Parmenion could remember his king as a young boy, and could remember, as well, the boy's lifelong companion who had carried him on a hundred fields of strife, to finally die on the plains of the Indus. He could still remember, as well, their leader who by then was nearer to being a god than a man, resting the head of his companion on his lap and crying like a boy who had lost his first dog. His memory must have showed in his eyes, for Alexander nodded and turned away for a moment.

"His soul came back to serve me here in my hour of need," Alexander said softly. "Again I ride Bucephalas. Now climb up, you sentimental old fool. Let's follow those cowards and see where they hide."

Parmenion accepted his king's hand and scrambled up behind Alexander. He was frightened beyond words by the beast, but he refused to show his fear.

"Speaking of those cowards, did you see where the girl went to? At least she had the courage to curse them."

"No, sire, she disappeared in the confusion."

"Somehow I have a feeling she's still in the area, so keep a watch."

Together they trotted off, riding into the high hills in search of those who had run away.

"Do you smell that, Parmenion?"

"Not as bad as Babylon, sire, but still, what a stink."

They had been climbing into the high hills toward the massive mountain for what Alexander thought must have been several hours; it was impossible now to tell, for the shadows never changed, and always the same crystalline white orb hung motionless, directly overhead. To either horizon he could see the blue-green band extending upward like opposing horns, until they disappeared in the glaring light. To either side ran white barrier lines that Aldin said prevented the air from rushing away. He understood, but still he could not believe.

Even these high hills had been constructed and contoured by godlike hands. That, he realized, was the context he'd have to place this madness into. Otherwise he would indeed lose all perspective. This was the realm made by yet other gods, just as his gods, his sires, had shaped the world of Macedon and the vastness of Persia.

The path they were on narrowed down to a defile barely wide enough for two horses to pass through.

"If any unpleasantness is planned, it will be here," Alexander said softly.

Parmenion lowered his pike, while Alexander nocked an arrow. Even as he pulled the arrow out of the quiver, there was a faint rustle from the defile and then the blowing of a horn.

"Well, let's not come in skulking like thieves," he said, and spurred the horse forward.

There was no one at the defile, but there was evidence of a hasty retreat. Several lances and a number of shields lay scattered about.

"Ah, the dogs, they run again," Parmenion shouted.

"Could be a trick; always remember the Scythians."

They pushed forward, making yet another turn on the trail, and he pulled Bucephalas up short.

The trail ended a short distance ahead in a rude stone palisade that enclosed a small stockade. Looking around, Alexander realized he had wandered into a small valley of green fields and blooming orchards. The fields looked well tended; if anything, these people appeared to be good farmers. There was the faint scent of flowers, but the predominant smell was one of death. Upon the walls of the palisades hung several corpses in various states of decomposition.

"Just like home," Parmenion said with a chuckle.

There was a grunt of a reply from Alexander, and Parmenion could sense his displeasure at the sight. The man before him had ordered such ends for countless thousands and he couldn't understand this sudden disdain. As if sensing the emotion, Alexander turned in the saddle.

"There's another enemy. What fools to kill each other like—"

His words were cut short by a wild cacophony of horns that

caused Bucephalas to shy away and snort with fear. As if in answer, a volley of arrows snapped out.

"Well, at least they have archery," Alexander shouted as he and Parmenion together raised their shields. The bolts scattered around them, none striking the two soldiers or their horse.

Alexander stood up in his stirrups and drew back on his bow. Aiming high, he released and the arrow sang upward, soaring far above the wall then disappearing from view.

There was a loud shout of amazement from the defenders, who still remained hidden, but their volleys stopped.

Alexander stood in his stirrups.

"I am Alexander," he cried, hoping that the implant was doing its work. The words formed in his mind and he spoke them knowing what they were, but still he couldn't be sure.

"I have been told of your suffering at the hands of these creatures called Gavarnians. I, Alexander, known as the Great, King of Macedon, Hegemon of all the Greeks, King of Kings of all the Persians and such lands to that of the Indus and the Eastern Sea, have been sent to you from the world you once called Earth."

"Ah, go on," came a derisive cry.

"I tell you I saw it," shouted another from the fortress. "He killed four of them, he did. You saw him shoot."

"The man's a crazy," replied the first. "Look at him out there."

"If you think he's a crazy," came a high voice from behind Alexander, "then come out here and say it to him face to face."

Alexander turned and looked to where the voice had come from. It was the girl.

She strode forward, barely sparing him a second glance. She was clothed simply in a tunic that nearly reached her feet and was tied around the waist by a knotted cord. Her blond hair hung in two thick braids that fell across her high arching breasts. Her features were light—an oval face and high cheekbones, and a sharp look that expected a response of deference.

"At least he saved me," she shouted. "More than you fools could do."

"But, Neva, what can you expect? There were six of them."

"Open that gate, you damn fool."

"But, Neva. What about him?"

She looked back at Alexander as if noticing him for the first time.

"Most of them are idiots," she muttered, and then she looked back.

"He killed four of the Gafs," she shouted toward the fortress, "what do you think we should do? Let him in and honor him as he deserves."

"If we do that," came another voice that held a note of sarcasm as if speaking to a despised child, "and the Gafs find out, they'll really be after him and us. There's a price on him already, I daresay."

"Enough of this, damn it, now let us in!"

She turned back to Alexander and she smiled.

"If there's a price on you," Parmenion interjected, whispering to Alexander, "then how can we trust these cowards? They might kill us in our sleep."

"Because the leader of the town will swear your protection," Neva responded as if offended by Parmenion's suggestion, "and the word of a Ris will be honored."

"If there is a price on me," Alexander interjected, "know then that I bring conflict with me."

"But of course." Neva smiled. "You can train these people to fight against our neighbors, the Kievants."

"I thought your foes were the Gavarnians."

Neva pointed to the bodies hanging on the walls. "Those are Kievants. The Gafs pay us for each one brought in."

"I think you have your work cut out for you," Parmenion muttered.

"Bring me to your leader," Alexander said wearily. "I want to talk to him about Kievants, and Gafs."

"But you are talking to her right now; just don't tell my uncle—the fool still thinks he runs the place!" Neva replied with a smile, then she turned away.

"Now open those damned gates, you pinheads, or I'll personally come in there and cut off somebody's balls and feed what's left to the Gafs."

"Amazons," Parmenion mumbled. "Damn that Aldin Larice."

chapter six

"Gentlemen," Aldin said, "the payoff for first encounter betting is five point five to two in favor of Alexander."

Turning from the screen, Aldin stepped over to the room-length window that provided a panoramic view of the Kolbard beneath them. The view was stunning as he looked straight down to the floor of the ring a hundred kilometers below. The fertile lands held by the Gafs were to his left. It was a well-managed patchwork of green fields and woodlots, intersected by half a dozen rivers that flowed down to the vast inland sea. Reaching almost to the sea, and providing a natural boundary between the western end of the Gavarnian lands and the hills occupied by the Humans, was a shimmering open region. A million years of wind erosion had peeled off the topsoil to reveal the substructure of the Kolbard, creating a vast open desert of bare, polished metal.

To the right were the steep rolling hills and deep ravines occupied by the Humans. Almost straight down he could see the place where he had dropped Alexander off only hours before. A quick punch up on the keypad by his side brought to the screen a high magnification view from one of the hovering drones positioned to monitor the action. He watched Alexander for a moment, still amazed at what he had just managed to accomplish. Turning away from the screen, Aldin looked back at the Kohs in the control room.

Corbin's yacht, *Gamemaster*, was docked to the support bay constructed atop one of the cooling towers of the Kolbard. Except for the monitor and control equipment set into one wall, the rest of the room presented an image of an old, well-endowed hunting lodge, or gentleman's gaming club. The furniture was overstuffed leather, the walls were highly polished teak imported from one of the tropical plantation worlds. Even though the ship was less than a year old, it already had that old familiar masculine smell of expensive cigars, quality brandy, and leather. Of course, the entire vessel was the envy of the other Kohs, and Corbin gloried in this ability to upstage his business rivals.

The servobots quietly made their rounds serving drinks to the Kohs.

"Excellent, my good Aldin," Corbin said, his tone reflecting his pleasure at the auspicious start of the activities, "most excellent indeed. Alexander is everything I had imagined him to be."

"Imagined him to be, and even more," Zola interrupted as he appeared at Aldin's side. "It was foolish of me to bet against his initial contact. I shan't do that again."

"Human-to-Human contact is one thing," Bukha responded, still facing the tote board. "But let me assure you, the first organized encounter between Gavarnian and Human will be a straightforward and foregone conclusion. Alexander or no Alexander."

"But you saw it from the remote scan," Corbin replied evenly. "He lifted four of your much-vaunted Gavarnians out of their saddles without taking a scratch."

"You know," Zola said silkily, coming up to Bukha's side, "maybe your warriors are simply not up to snuff."

Bukha turned toward Zola and gave him a full toothy grin, with his fangs slightly bared.

Zola stepped back. "Well, no need to get barbaric about it."

"Not at all, not at all, just yawning. No hostility intended."

"Gentlemen, the first segment of betting has ended," Aldin interrupted. "You may settle your accounts through the main filing system. As is custom, our hosting Kohs Corbin Gablona and Bukha Taug shall provide feasting in celebration."

"Any word on Zergh and the delivery of Kubar Taug?" Sigma asked.

"Drop-off will occur shortly," Aldin replied. And there was a muffled round of excited conversations as the Kohs went over to the table that floated into the room, laden with the finest delicacies to be found anywhere in the Magellanic Cloud. Even the Xsarn was joining them, putting aside his regular diet for once, to eat what he considered to be uncooked food.

Looking over his shoulder, Kubar Taug saw that his squire was with him, bearing the Vota, the silver rod of office that he had designed for himself back across the millennia. But that was the past, lost to dust, across two thousand estas, what Zergh told him was measured now by the Human term of four thousand years. Dust, they were all dust. All his friends, the tens of thousands of his host, the grand and massive players in the drama of uniting a world—all gone to dust.

And his siblings, his three brothers who had died before him. Cliarn was dead just days past, or was it four thousand years? He turned away from his squire and closed his eyes. His three brothers, he thought, and the aching filled his soul as it did for all Gafs. For like all Gavarnians, he had come into the world at the same time with his three other brothers and a single sister. But the brothers had left before him, to wait in Binda, the Hall of Quiet Repose and Longing, waiting until the four were again united and thus could journey together to the Unseen Light.

Oh, my brothers, he thought sadly, how long have you waited for me. Have you sat in silence across the millennia watching as all others were united but still I would not come? Have you feared that I would never stand in the Portal of Light? Or did your spirits come with me through time, as well? Were they granted that reprieve, at least? Did Cliarn, whose dying eyes had looked into his but days ago, did he bring the two who had died so young?

"Cliarn, forgive me," he whispered, as he had said to himself ten thousand times while journeying across the heavens to this new world. This new world. Opening his eyes, he looked again upon the alien sun, which was blinding white, rather than the soft ruby glow of home. He averted his gaze and looked at the upward sweep as the horizon curved up and away to either side—twin horns of blue green with occasional streaks of brown.

Looking to what Zergh said was the equal of north, he could see three soaring mountains that seemed to loom nearly overhead, even though they were at least dozens of leagues away. Behind him there were three more, one coming straight out of the great sea. The city he was walking toward rested at the base of the mountain which already he called Valdinca, the Mountain of Spirits. When this thing, this quest was over, he would climb up Valdinca, if such a thing were possible, and see where the great sailing ships of the stars had once docked. Back home he had sailed the sky, and the memory filled him with joy, for it was during his reign that balloons first rose above his world, floating from the heat of fires and also from the breaking of water. He had won his greatest victory at Heda with that tactical surprise. Perhaps that would be the way to reach up to the mountaintops when this was over.

When this was over. He smiled to himself at that thought. How often, how very often he had thought that phrase "when this is over" during the darkest days of the fifth coalition, or in the exile of a hundred nights. How often he had dreamed of the beginning, when it had only been himself and his three glorious brothers of blood birth, united together.

But his brothers were ashes. And she was ashes, too, as were the children. All that, the price to conquer a world. He looked again at Paga, and Paga as always had the expression of worried concern for his lord.

He was a squire. Kubar had begged Paga to take the ranks that he truly deserved, but always his old childhood friend had refused, wishing only to serve him. It was Paga who had saved his life more than once when there had been only a score of them, hunted and despised—the hunting more a blood sport than war for the nobles he faced. It was more than half a lifetime ago when he had organized the first company of a hundred from his village to rebel against the established order of serfdom and overlord. Yes, Paga was the last of that glorious company.

There again the word glorious. When the campaign of twenty estas was ending at last, how often they had used that word. Glorious, that was the lie to give the bereaved. Somehow that one word made the burden more bearable for some as they united not only a people but a world into one class of free beings—a union that had to be paid for with a generation's worth of blood.

He looked again at the upward sweep of a world that his senses told him was somehow made backward, or out of a mirror where the horizons did not behave as they should. So for the passing of five hundred generations his name had been enshrined—how he had gone to the mountain Valdinca after the last battle and the death of Cliarn, and there disappeared, to join his ancestors.

He chuckled to himself. The disappearing had been the final act, the final cement that had united them under his semidivine legend—and here he was now, an age later, asked to do the same thing all over again by his most distant descendants who had swept out to the stars, as he had dreamed they would.

He smiled at Paga and motioned that they should kneel and wait. It would not be long, of that he could be sure, for Zergh had told him that they would be placed next to a much-frequented path that the patrols often rode upon. Patrols of an overlord—the mere thought of it made him shake his head in sadness. For though they glorified his name they had forgotten once again. In his name the dream had held until new worlds were gained, but there the old corruption had taken hold, and once again there were overlords and serfs, warrior class and downtrodden.

They revered him yet they forgot what he had stood for. The prophet Jesdha was right when he said that it was the curse of prophets to always look beyond what normal beings could see, and thus break their own hearts in the process. So he would have to start again, here on this new world that a fellow Gavarnian had taken him to aboard a floating ship of miracles. He pondered on that for a moment, and had the feeling that he had not been told everything, but he would let that matter pass until his task was over.

He sighed with the realization of what had to be done. Zergh had told him that the old conventions before the unifying had again taken hold. It was as if these descendants, fearing the future, had returned to the distant past. Therefore he would proclaim himself as in the old legends and then the proofs would have to be given—and for that he had to prepare.

With a ruffling of his silken robes, Kubar Taug knelt in the dust of the roadside and assumed the position of the first contemplation, and Paga, standard-bearer and weapons carrier, knelt with him. They did not have long to wait.

He heard a rhythmic noise in the distance. It sounded like the canter of a dispa, but he knew already that their two-legged beast of burden was not used on this world, but was replaced instead by a beast taken from the hairless ones, and bred to a larger size.

He closed his eyes, his breathing controlled, looking inward to the source, wherein he had first come to realize his calling to a higher destiny. The approaching riders drew nearer and clattered to a stop.

"You, gray one, you block the way of the feday, the messenger of the Taug."

Kubar was silent. So his own name had come to be the name given to a ruler, but he could not now react to the insult. He extended his hand in the subtlest of gestures for Paga to restrain himself.

"I say, you, gray one." The voice was impetuous, having been slighted by his lack of response. "I spare you for you are elder to me, but move aside or my breeding and station shall be forgotten, even though you wear the garb of an ancient."

Kubar remained motionless, his eyes closed.

He heard his challenger dismount, his armor creaking, his boots crunching on the hard gravel of the road.

"If you seek your end, gray one, if you wish to join your brothers, then I shall be forced to oblige."

He could hear the sword being drawn and with it the intaking of breath from Paga.

"I shall command you but once," Kubar said evenly, "for I am Kubar Taug, across the generations come yet again to unite you all as one." And as he spoke he rose up and faced the warrior who approached him with sword already drawn and poised to the third chord, the position known as the Macna, used for the killing of someone whose social class you were not sure of. So that old useless relic of etiquette had survived, as well, Kubar thought.

The warrior changed to the sixth chord of contempt and smiled. "You are a mad one and as such must lie and thus hold no class. Prepare to die."

As soon as the warrior had said the word lie, Paga started forward bellowing with rage, but he was already too late.

In one fluid motion, Kubar's sword snapped from its scabbard. Before the warrior's expression could even change from a smile to one of pain, his head rolled from his body. With a flick of his wrist Kubar snapped the blood from his blade and returned to the kneeling position, in the spreading pool of blood.

Paga faced the stunned companion of the dead messenger. "How far to the one you call your taug?"

"Half a dozen dimmings away, but his brother is less than a dimming ride from here."

A dimming? That was something the one called Zergh had neglected to explain. He only hoped that this dimming was not too long off.

"Go and announce to him," Paga shouted, "that Kubar Taug has crossed time to lead yet again!"

The messenger looked at Paga in disbelief.

"Go then, or you must face my sword as well."

"I've already seen enough from the hairless ones that is strange, so that one more strangeness to report is nothing," the messenger said, and he held up a bandaged arm as if this were a proof. "I shall bear that message."

Spurring his mount, he rode around the body of his companion and pressed on.

Paga felt a light touch on his shoulder, and he stirred from his meditation.

"I think I understand the term of the dimming," Kubar said thoughtfully.

Paga could see that his master's curiosity was aroused and came to his feet to stand by Kubar's side.

"Notice that it is darker, yet no cloud covers the sky. I felt it some time ago, a slight cooling of the air. Do you notice?"

"It is darker," Paga said excitedly, and he looked again to the strange white sun, which still hovered directly overhead in the same position.

"Is it dying?" he cried suddenly, looking around and trying to control his fear.

Kubar chuckled softly. "Astronomy was not your interest, my warrior blood kin. I remember my observers of the night said that some stars did glow brighter and then dimmer. This world, this Kolbard, as Zergh put it, does not turn its face away from the sun above, but a form of night occurs nevertheless when the light of the sun dims."

Kubar looked back up the road toward where the messenger had disappeared.

"They said less than a dimming, therefore I must assume they shall return shortly. I hope we don't have to go through another such wasteful folly." As he spoke, he looked at the now-rigid body at his feet.

"I hope not, as well. I think that those for whom we wait are coming," Paga replied evenly, pointing down the road the messenger had taken. Secretly he feared that the warriors of this world would think the two of them mad and blood challenge would follow blood challenge until they were both dead.

It was still confusing that the horizon did not act as a horizon should, but Kubar could see where Paga was pointing to a serpentine line advancing toward them.

"I must contemplate before I act," Kubar said softly, and returned to the kneeling position.

"There are now two dead," Paga said evenly as he gazed at the second headless corpse, which had fallen on top of the first one, the fresh blood pooling into the gravel to mingle with the dried black stain from the earlier killing.

A murmur arose from the circle of warriors that surrounded them.

Kubar again sheathed his sword and looked straight at the leader of the party.

"I am Kubar Taug, and I lower myself to speak in answer but speak I must to explain. I am not mad. Only a madman would lie to those whom he wishes to serve with, at least it was so in my day. Or have the Gavarnians grown degenerate?"

He already knew the answer to that question, for Zergh had told him that the age-old injunction to tell the truth within the clan, which had come up from the distant, preliterate past, still held true on the Kolbard. Even through the mindset of the translation implant, he could sense, as well, that certain words could still be traced back to their root, and the references to truth saying and lying were remarkably the same. There was a significant smattering of words whose roots were unknown to him—the translator implant handled them, and he could only imagine that they were of alien origin.

The fifty warriors that surrounded him were silent, all dressed in the same lacquered armor, the only color to them a single red ribbon used to tie their queues. He knew that one of them had to be the kin leader but the gambit was to find out which one. Motionless, he started to hold each in turn with his gaze. Most quickly turned away, some tried to fight his will, and some avoided his glance altogether. From the corner of his eye he noticed the warriors looking to one in particular.

This one did not look like the kin leader, at least not from physical appearance. He must rule by his intelligence and wit rather than strength, Kubar thought, and he will have the strong arm of a sworn champion to defend him.

"I turn to the leader who has seen," Kubar said softly, staring over the leader's head to avoid a challenge, "and in your wisdom you must decide if yet another is to die to prove my claim."

The leader snorted and spurred his mount to draw closer. "I have seen, and will not call you an untruthspeaker, but such a claim . . ." His words drifted off to silence.

Kubar was motionless with Paga at his side holding the silver staff of office. "I can understand your questioning and blame you not, for you must be possessed of wisdom and judgment to lead."

He could sense the inner sigh of relief from the leader. Kubar had avoided a confrontation of proof and a direct blood challenge, at least for the moment.

"Let us eat and talk as the dimming moves, and then perhaps we will see the path to light."

With the third round of the *musa* the mood between the two had started to relax as the soothing effects of the mild narcotic drink coursed through them.

The leader sat on an intricately woven rug, the group surrounded by a windscreen of pale-green cloth that bore the repeated pattern of a single blue flower.

Not a word had been passed between them, for the first to speak would lose face, and each continued to stare at the ground in front of him to avoid direct eye contact, which could be taken as a challenge.

Kubar found this to be of some interest since the ritual was almost the same as from his time—right down to the simple fact that both he and the kin leader had subtly let the hair on their body extend outward, just enough to show calmed assurance—not so much as to be interpreted as a sign of hostility, nor so little, to be taken as a sign of subservience in the presence of a superior.

Finally it was a standard-bearer standing to the side of the leader who spoke first, breaking the silence.

"And you who are Kubar, you have no lesser blood kin to speak first?"

"As you should already know, if my name has survived, my first blood kin died at Mutacha, my second at Vollen, my third—" he hesitated for a moment—"you should know of Cliarn, as well. Therefore your question to me is obviously a trap, but this time I shall not take offense. Is your leader present here the last blood kin?"

He looked up at the one across from him, who gave a slight nod of acknowledgment.

"I speak for Hina co Kalin," the standard-bearer replied, "second to his eldest brother Kalin called taug, who are brothers to Swanika, killed by a fall from his mount, and Uta, killed but a dimming ago by a hairless one."

Kubar detected shame in the speaker's voice, and the statement was greeted by a low murmur. Kubar realized that to die at the hands of a Human was considered dishonorable.

Kubar nodded in the direction of Hina, who was the second of four brothers and thus standard-bearer to the taug. With formal introductions completed by both sides, there could no longer be a killing out of hand, for names had been given and the death stories of brothers exchanged. Zergh had told him that this ritual had survived, as well, so he knew he had achieved the first step.

Hina now unbuckled his sword and placed it on the ground to his left side, and Kubar followed his example, not confident of the symbolism, but feeling that it must be a sign of trust.

"I shall not call you untruthspeaker," Hina began, "but by the souls of my brothers and father, you must see what you are asking me to believe is almost beyond belief."

Kubar could only smile. Until a score of days past, if someone had walked into his council room and announced that he was the legendary Gretha, slayer of the beast Vis who had once entwined the world in its coils, he would have been hard-pressed not to take insult for being lied to.

Kubar chuckled and look up at the dim star overhead.

"Hear me, Hina co Kalin, brother of the taug. If someone had told me that I would be sitting on this world called a Kolbard, five hundred lifetimes into my future, and discussing such impossibilities as casually as this, why, I would not have hesitated to treat him as he deserved. Have you ever heard of Zergh?"

"No."

"Too bad, he is a most remarkable Gavarnian—part thief, part spirit god."

Hina was silent.

"I know that fifteen hundred estas ago your ancestors were travelers from other worlds."

Hina nodded.

"That your ancestors came to this world, and then a great

war, a cataclysm, cut them off from their brethren who have never returned."

"That is known by all," Hina replied.

"But did you know that there are Gavarnians who live almost like the gods of our ancient legends, that still journey among the stars?"

Hina was silent for a moment; a look of confusion crossed his face and then understanding.

"Yes, that word is in our Coda. It is a light in the sky that cannot be seen. Stars hovered in the sky when the world of our ancestors turned as dark as a cave. Stars . . ." He fell silent for a moment as if looking off into some great distance.

"All of us remember the stories of our childhood, when our brothers still walked by our side and we knew not which of us would be the first one called by fate. To all of us there are legends of our sires and our heroes long gone. And first among them—first warrior, first strategist, first conqueror, and then uniter—was Kubar do Ladg, first-named taug. He is our idol, he who united together the various clans of the Gavarn, he who first rose up and set all Gavarnians free, so that together we could leap outward to the stars. He was my dream, and thus your words are either the cruelest of jests or a dream that has come to walk among us."

Hina was silent again, daring to lock gazes with Kubar.

"And somehow, I always thought Kubar Taug to be bigger than life, his voice bolder, and gaze purer, his strength stronger, a radiance emanating from his soul. And instead I meet someone dust covered, someone with an infinite weariness in his eyes, his pelt already thinning, and who stands barely to the shoulder of most of my guards. And that someone claims the name of Kubar Taug."

"And yet Kubar Taug does sit across from you, or I would not be a truthsayer, and then would my strength diminish and I would die."

Hina's gaze would not break from that of Kubar.

"This is Das," Hina said, drawing his blade and placing it before Kubar.

The admiration of the blades, Kubar realized—yet another ritual that had been revived—and he suddenly knew just how important this act would be. It was a ritual, but it could now be a proof, as well.

"And this is Tagak, of purest steel, unknown to your own world."

There was a gasp of amazement as the sword slipped from its sheath, reflecting the light of the dimming sun. Extending the hilt, he leaned over and presented the blade to Hina. Etiquette was forgotten as the warriors gathered around to gaze admiringly at the shimmering blade. Taking the hilt in one hand and the tip of the blade in the other, Hina looked over at Kubar, who nodded his approval.

Hina's muscles coiled as he pulled the blade back until it bent nearly double. The audience was silent. Their own metal would have snapped from the tension. When he released the tip of the sword, the blade snapped back to its original position.

"It is truly a blade of the ancestors," Hina said softly, as he admired the watery lines and luster locked into cold steel, perfect except for a single notch near the hilt.

"Tagak," Paga replied. "And I now carry its sister sword, the blade of Cliarn—Tusta." And he withdrew the sword from its scabbard and laid it before the assembly. The two blades were identical down to the single notch cut into each near the hilt. Hina reached out and touched the single imperfection on the one blade and then the other.

Hina looked up at Kubar, and closing his eyes, he started to recite.

> Coming together, equal to equal,
> Steel flashing fire,
> Coming together, blood to blood,
> Life spilled by brother,
> Thus the joining complete, and the sacrifice made,
> Sacrifice made,
> Death of a brother, a race joined as one.

Kubar fought for composure. The night Cliarn died, he had heard Shesta, the laymaker, first sing those words. And they had survived, along with the dark memory.

Hina reverently picked up the sister swords, one after the other, and presented them back to their owners. By such an act he acknowledged acceptance into the circle of the clan. However, Hina had only displayed his blade to Kubar and had not offered it. Therefore he was not pledged to protect in return.

Kubar made a subtle gesture to Paga not to react to the implied snub. He realized that full and immediate acceptance was of course something impossible to expect so soon. That could only come with time. Even if Hina fully believed what he had said, Hina was not taug. His first brother held that position and thus Hina could not make an acknowledgment that his brother might not accept. He was wise, this one, and cautious, as any of a ruling family should be. Already Kubar liked him, even though he was of this ancient noble system that had returned to life on the Kolbard.

Kubar noticed that it was still getting darker. The light was as dark as if a monsoon-laden cloud had passed before the sun, yet still the sky was clear. He could not help but turn his gaze away from Hina and look to the dark-blue heavens.

"Will the light return again to its former strength?"

Hina laughed. "But of course you would not know that, would you?"

Kubar could detect no testing in that question and knew that the first step toward ultimate acceptance had been passed. He would simply have to prove to them that their greatest legend had indeed come. He looked from the sky back to his arms and legs.

Yes, the legend had come. Even if his fur was thinning out, he thought, and he scratched the bald spot at the back of his neck.

chapter seven

"You there. Yes, you with the sloping forehead. You'll never have the makings of a pikeman of the first rank." Parmenion's voice was cracking with rage. "Yes, stupid, I mean you, step forward!

"And you think you'll be a soldier?" Parmenion stepped closer and leaned forward standing on his tiptoes in a vain attempt to come to the soldier's eye level. "Well, come on, man, speak. Or are you struck dumb, as well?"

The object of his wrath could only look at him goggle-eyed with fright. His mouth was open as if he were trying to speak, but only inarticulate sounds came out.

Parmenion threw up his hands in exasperation, and the pikeman in training jumped back.

"That's it, jump back. I'll see you jump back when you stand your first charge. By all the gods, I'll see you with my sword sticking up your butt if you waver one god-cursed inch. I swear that." His voice was near to breaking. "I swear it by the shadows of my father. I swear it by Alexander himself."

"Try not to drag my name into this."

Parmenion turned on his heels and with a quick flourish presented his pike as Alexander drew closer.

"General Parmenion, if you would be so good as to inspect the latest workings of the smithy, I'd like a word with these men."

"Smithy? There isn't enough metal in this entire stinkhole to make fifty pike heads. And even less intelligence to fashion them."

Parmenion passed through the gate back into the town, the roar of his cursing causing the villagers to bar their doors yet again and to hide their children from view.

"You may rest," Alexander said evenly, and a grateful sigh went up from the three hundred men and handful of women who stood in the ranks.

He tried to imagine them as something different, to see again the serried ranks of his Companions, the five thousand men of the finest phalanx in the world, marching across the plain of Guagamela to dispute the kingship of empires. But there was only the harsh reality.

His "army" was a ragtag, scurvied, thoroughly unmilitary rabble of cowards and thieves. Their city was a hideout for petty robbers who would snatch up an occasional unarmed traveler. They were good for the bludgeon blow to the back, or the even more despicable hunting of their neighbors to collect the Gavarnian reward for heads, but as he had seen not a score of dimmings ago, they routed when a handful of Gafs on horseback decided to chase them for some sport.

This was his army. Starting with this band of scum, he

would have to unite all the tribes in a region larger than Anatolia and then turn that force against the Gafs who, to make matters worse, were ruled under a common king of kings, known as the Taugech, or some such thing. Alexander knew as well that if this Taugech sensed but for a moment that a uniter had come to bind the men together, he would not cease until that man had been hunted down. It was of course what he would do if the roles were reversed. Therefore a task that should take years would have to be accomplished in months, otherwise the common enemy would destroy him.

He looked back to the unit.

"General Parmenion is right." He almost stumbled over the words. There had been another Parmenion, most trusted general of his father and right hand to his own early conquests, until he had been accused of treason and then executed. Alexander had never quite forgotten what he had believed at the time was a betrayal, and still his dreams were haunted by that old weather-creased face. So now there was a new Parmenion, a bulging, one-eyed, illiterate guard who was his only link to a different past. A new general Parmenion for a new world.

The men were silent, sullen, and most of all resentful that this stranger, with claims to a legendary grandeur, had so thoroughly mucked up their lives. Alexander knew they'd most likely stab him in the back at the first chance if not for the fact that Neva—who had the strength, both physical and mental, to cower the thieving lot—would kill the first man who tried. He half suspected that when the Gafs had snatched her, the men had run away not in panic, but in relief. Even her uncle, Ivarn Black Teeth, who was the nominal ruler of this filth patch, seemed overawed by her at times. There was something about her that did not fit this place. But now was not the time to ponder that point.

"So far you've fought only as individuals," Alexander said in a voice that he used when he was speaking in a comradely fashion. "For what is to be done you must learn to fight as one. You must move as one, level spears as one, and if need be, die as one. Damn you all, you must realize that if but one of you fails, if but one runs, then the rest of us could die.

"Have no pity for the weak in your ranks, for he could cause your death. Now, I have told you that a hundred times already, but now I tell you something different. Tomorrow we advance against the Kievants. Tomorrow with your newfound skill and courage you will vanquish your foes. All of you have told me how you hate the Kievants, how they piss in your drinking stream and steal your women and young boys for their perverted lusts. With my leadership you will punish them and show them that the men of Ris are to be feared!"

He finished that statement with a rhetorical flourish, expecting a resounding cheer. But they were silent, dumb. After an embarrassed moment, he turned away.

"Now lower those spears, damn you, and advance at the walk pace."

Ivarn, as usual, was already into the latter stages of drunkenness, roaring how tomorrow he would personally cut off the ears of the fallen bandits of Kievant. Alexander sat on the stool across from him, with Parmenion at his back. The room was illuminated by a smokey dung fire that filled the chamber with a choking stench, until finally some of the cloud, after having watered the eyes and fouled the air, curled out of a hole in the roof.

The dimming was nearly half over, but Ivarn was in rare form and already raving.

"And that damned Borst, him will I personally castrate and then hang out on the walls of his miserable dung heap."

Alexander nodded absently and spared another glance toward Neva.

As usual, she was trying her best to give a seductive look toward "her savior," as she called him. He quickly turned his gaze away. The problem with sex was here, as well. Even in his youth he had somehow felt removed from the lusty talk of his comrades. He simply did not feel the same desire, either for the love of another man, so praised by the Thebans, or for the desire of a woman. It seemed to him that he played half-heartedly in a game, more to humor his friends than to take pleasure in the game itself.

And then there was the simple fact that she was the only female relative of the chieftain of this miserable village. The fact that he had rescued her from the "Gafs," as these villagers called them, had raised his prestige, and then his promise to Ivarn to help him destroy the Kievants had, for the moment at least, secured his position. He didn't want to take any risks.

"So tell me again, O legendary one," Ivarn roared, and his

half-dozen bodyguards snickered at the witty sarcasm, "how do we do it?"

Alexander looked over at Parmenion in order to stifle any protest or sarcastic comments.

"It's quite simple, O king of kings." Alexander almost choked on the words, but he had to play the part. "I am simply showing you a secret way of defeating your enemies and expanding your glory. By fighting together as one team, you can overcome ten times your number."

"And then I can drive my enemies before me?" Ivarn asked, almost childlike in his tone.

"That is correct."

"And if you fail us tomorrow?" one of the guards grumbled.

Alexander gave him an even smile. "There will be no failure."

"You should hope so," Ivarn said evenly. Alexander knew that he was on a fine balance here. The bow he carried was worth more than all the possessions of this entire village, and it was only the promise of victory against the rivals in the next valley that kept his head on his shoulders.

"Here, another drink," Ivarn suddenly called as he staggered to his feet, offering a sack of fermented goat milk to Alexander.

"Don't you think some rest should be taken?" Alexander asked. "The dimming is more than half passed. It's best to be the first ones moving, for we can expect that the Kievants already know that something is afoot."

Ivarn waved the advice aside and collapsed back onto the stool that he called a throne.

"I think I shall see to the guards," Alexander replied coldly, and rising up, he gave a curt nod to the chieftain and strode out of the hut. His instincts were still expecting that nighttime would be dark, whereas during a dimming the intensity of light dropped only to that of a cloudy day, or the light of a full moon on the snow-covered steppes beyond Bactria. He looked in the direction that in his mind had come to mean northwest, and in the far distance, clinging to the side of Olympus, there floated a flickering smudge of light and a thin plume of smoke. In a few short hours he would march up to them and take the first step toward his new empire.

Again he was flooded by a sense of wonder. He looked to the west, and curving farther up and away he could see rivers of blue, what appeared to be a distant ocean, dark mountain valleys, green forests, and high pillars of white until the colors merged into a dark blue-green arching up overhead—to be lost in the glare of the dimming sun.

"You know he plans to kill you once you've defeated the Kievants for him."

He turned and Neva was standing by his side. He had smelled her approach, since like all the rest of these robbers she viewed bathing as an insult and complete waste of time.

Alexander realized this girl could be quite attractive if cleaned up and dressed in the way that he was more accustomed to. She drew closer to him and lightly touched his shoulder, pressing her body to his side.

"I could be available to you for the rest of this darkness, if you wished."

"I thank you for the honor," Alexander whispered in reply, hoping that Parmenion at least had the sense to keep an eye on the girl's other hand, which he knew was resting on the pommel of her dagger, "but it is nearly time to rouse the men. And before I go to battle I must have my strength, or the gods will not help me."

"A man such as you surely has the strength to know three women in a night before going out to cut the throats of his foes."

"Ah, yes, of course. But I wish to serve your uncle to the fullest of my strength."

"That old goat, didn't you hear me say he is in there right now planning to kill you?"

"Why are you telling me this?"

"Isn't it obvious?" She started to move her body against his in what anyone but a blind man could see was a reasonable imitation of what she had hopes would occur in very short order.

Alexander suddenly grabbed hold of her and, choking down a gag, he kissed her on the neck. She gave a shudder and groaned with delight. Parmenion, keeping an eye on her dagger hand, could only grin with lewd delight.

"My dear, I want to as much as you," he whispered, "but if I don't win this fight, your uncle will have my head no matter what. I need all my strength and more to win, and then you'll see my reward." He kissed her once more then quickly released her and stepped back.

She looked at him hungrily, her eyes glazed with lust.

"Just look out for Lothar. He's the big dumb-looking one. He'll do anything Ivarn says; the others are too cowardly to try for you in the open."

"Thank you. And know that your desire will soon be fulfilled." He gave a curt glance to Parmenion and muttered, "Let's get the hell out of here." Backing away, he left Neva still panting with desire.

Parmenion started to whisper a ribald comment, but before the first word was out Alexander's gaze let it be known that he would be crossing into very deep waters if he continued.

She watched him disappear around the corner. She was still trembling with desire and now he was gone. Her thoughts centered in on Lothar, who had already staggered back to his hut to sleep off the party. Well, arrangements could be made, she thought, and though Lothar was dumb, he certainly did have a couple of advantages. She smiled with anticipation.

"Remember, at a walk," Parmenion roared. "And be sure your shield covers the man to your left!"

In the distance the horns of the enemy sounded louder. The town looked like an anthill that someone had stirred with a stick, setting the nest into a boiling swirl of activity. The Kievant warriors were pouring out of the gate, shouting and cursing. Alexander could only shake his head in absolute amazement. These people had to be even cruder than the men following him.

It was exactly as Neva had predicted. Combat between the various towns was half blood-vengeance and half blood-sport. When rival sides went to the field, they would meet before one gate or another and spend most of the day shouting insults at each other. To them, that was the civilized way of having a good fight.

Occasionally, she said, someone would work up the nerve and sally toward the other side with much shouting and gesturing. A rival from the opposing tribe, shouting curses in return, would venture out from his camp and then amid elaborate shouts, gestures, and an occasional toss of spears, they would close in. The fight would be joined until either a lucky blow killed someone or one of the combatants was wounded. The wounded man would flee back to the support of his comrades who had been shouting encouragements and, of course, placing an occasional bet on the side. The injured warrior's fellow tribesmen would ward off the spears and random arrow shots of the victor's companions, and the match would be over.

On rare occasions it would boil up into a more general action with a couple of dozen men and an occasional woman trading blows, but that was the extent of organization to their brawls.

After several days of this, one side or another would acknowledge defeat and either pull back inside its walls or march back to its own village leaving their dead, as custom demanded, to be taken as trophies. Of course, the heads would be cashed in to the Gafs for a bounty. If enough fresh heads were presented, the Gafs would take that as a tribute and leave the village alone.

It seemed remarkable to Alexander that men could sink so low that they didn't even understand how to wage a good war, but his own experience with trying to train these men was evidence enough. He thought for a moment of Homer and the heroes of legend who fought one-on-one beneath the walls of Troy—but those men were heroes, these characters were nothing more than brawling thieves.

Alexander surveyed his rag-tag army, marching in a column, four abreast, from his elevated position on Bucephalas. He could well understand how the Gafs had triumphed over them centuries ago and driven them from the fertile valley into the high hills where they were hunted for sport, the way he would hunt for a wild boar.

"Sire, we're drawing closer. I think it's nearly time."

Alexander nodded to Parmenion and gestured for him to order the men from the closed, marching rank into attack formation. He had to keep his own men moving and not let them have any time to consider what was about to happen. Neva's estimates were off when she said the numbers were even. There were at least five or six hundred men pouring out of the fortified village. But the odds could be ten times as great and still it would not have worried him. Discipline against numbers would even the score, as it had on nearly every battlefield he had ever fought upon.

Parmenion struggled, kicked, and shouted to get the unwilling warriors out of their column and into an attack phalanx sixty wide and five deep. Alexander had agreed with his recommendation that with so few men the phalanx would have to be shallower than was customary in order to make it wide enough to wedge the flanks on either side of the ravine through which they were advancing.

Alexander nocked an arrow to his bow and guided Bucephalas to the rear of the advancing column. It galled him to have to lead his troops from behind, but he realized that his presence in the rear, mounted on a Gaf horse with a nocked arrow ready for the first deserter, would go far toward winning the battle. It was far better to guide from the back of the phalanx than to lead from the front and discover that his "army" had decided to go home.

The chanted insults of the Kievants could now be plainly heard.

"We piss on your heads, you scum."

"You are downhill from us, we are above you."

That one he couldn't figure out. Why the relative location of one to other had any relevance was beyond him. It was an absurdity that even Parmenion could grasp as craziness. But the Ris believed it significant and now cried out in rage.

Parmenion, holding the standard, which was nothing more than a ragged piece of cloth upon which was a crudely drawn representation of Mount Olympus, turned to look back at his men and held the flag aloft.

Alexander looked over his shoulder to where Ivarn, surrounded by his half-dozen guards, sat beneath the shadow of a low-hanging cliff, watching the fight from a safe distance. He knew the dirty old coward would hang there in the back until things were decided, one way or the other.

"All right, Parmenion, let's get this over with," Alexander said, half disgusted at just how ridiculous this motley host looked. A boy standing next to Alexander started to beat out a rhythm on a drum, while Parmenion, holding the standard high, advanced toward the Kievants who were shouting gleefully at the strange display.

More than one man looked over his shoulder toward Alexander. And a simple gesture with the point of the arrow was enough to convince him to stay with the task at hand.

They advanced up the ravine toward the milling crowd of warriors who stood several hundred paces beyond the wall of their village. The range closed, and individuals could now be easily discerned.

* * *

Aldin had the telecams up to full magnification, and was even able to artfully fade between different views as he shifted the scenes back and forth. There wasn't any real serious betting going on over this match; it was more of a professional interest than anything else, but he needed to observe this thing, as well. This was the first time anyone of this age had a chance to witness Alexander in an organized battle. Perhaps there would be some clues that could be applied to later bets.

He knew Corbin would be watching with special interest, and some of the other Kohs would want copies of the action. But with no major fight between the Gavarnians and Humans anticipated for some time, all except a couple of the Kohs had departed the yacht to return home for business or other sport. Once the action started to heat up, they would be back—and a tape of the early fights would be of interest to them.

Somehow it almost seemed a little pathetic to see this once-mighty king reduced to leading such a despicable band. The presence of the man still haunted him. He had, if anything, expected a certain haughtiness, like the attitudes of the Kohs whom he served. There was a certain regal bearing, to be sure, but in spite of that, Aldin could not help but like and finally admire the man. This was not because of the place he held in history, which was cause enough for admiration. It was on a more personal level. Alexander had remarkable gifts, and rather than arouse a sense of envy or distrust, they created instead a desire to like him. At times he seemed like an eager boy confronted with a whole new universe to explore, and yet just below the surface was an infinite sadness. Aldin tried to shake the thought away but he felt as if he, too, supposedly a hard-bitten professional, was somehow under his sway. He could only hope that events of which Alexander was not even aware would not destroy him completely, without a shred of self-respect to soothe his passing.

"To the half left, turn!"

The advancing phalanx, as was typical of such a formation, had started to drift to the right, since each man instinctively moved toward the protection of the shield held by his neighbor.

They were now within a hundred paces of the Kievants, whose shouted taunts had died down to an uneasy silence. Almost all the men turned as commanded, except for a handful who weren't sure of their lefts and rights. The ranks tangled up for a moment, but the men were pushed along with the crowd and quickly faced in the right direction.

"Half right, turn!"

They were now bearing down more or less toward the middle of the Kievants, who jumped about halfheartedly, not at all sure of what was going on. After all, normal men would, at this point, start calling out their individual taunts, start strutting, and generally parade up and down for a couple of hours before working up the nerve to go in. But these men were strangely quiet and came on like a wave.

"Spears down!"

The sight of the spears dropping, more or less, as if guided by a single hand, sent a chill down Alexander's back. It was almost like the old times.

"Don't bunch up, don't bunch up!" Parmenion's voice was cracking with excitement. It was his first command and he was obviously enjoying it.

The Kievants were absolutely dumbfounded. Some of them cast their spears—most dropping short—but a couple hit into the ranks and a man went down screaming in pain. The advancing formation started to waver.

The timing was all important, that is what won a battle. He knew the time was now, or the men would break apart and revert to their cherished but completely absurd methods of combat.

"Now, my Macedons," Alexander shouted, caught up in a strange fantasy, "charge them at the double."

He spurred Bucephalas into a canter, angling his mount to the right flank, and with his shouted cry the men surged forward—the tension breaking in the release of the charge.

As Alexander knew was all too common in these affairs, the battle was decided before the first weapon was crossed. As the three hundred men shouted out their curses, the Kievants, seeing what was coming, cast aside their shields and departed for a safer neighborhood. Within seconds the battle, if it could be called that, had disintegrated into a footrace as the Kievants, looking over their shoulders and crying in fear, surged toward the protection of their gate, the phalanx hot on their heels.

Alexander surged through the crowd, Bucephalas now up to full speed, which was just about as fast as a man could run.

Slinging his bow, he unsheathed his sword and applied it lib-
erally to anyone who came near, using the flat of the blade
since he already had plans for these men. As he charged forward, the Kievants parted before him, not daring to face such
a man riding atop a Gaf beast.

He arrived at the gate ahead of his own men. The Kievant
chieftain who stood by the portal made threatening gestures, as
if challenging Alexander to a fight. But when Alexander lowered his sword and acknowledged that he would be more than
happy to comply, the chieftain cast aside his shield and fled
into the town, disappearing into the screaming mob of women
and children who had lined the mud brick walls of the town
only moments before.

Alexander turned in the gateway, suddenly aware of the fact
that he had surged so far ahead in his cavalry charge of one
that the entire Kievant army was now between him and his
own men. And since he held the portal of escape, he would
have to hold it alone until his men came up.

He turned expecting to face a cornered mob that would fight
with desperation to get past him, but what greeted him was
something totally unexpected.

The Kievants were falling prostrate, crying out in anguish,
raising their hands in supplication, looking back over their
shoulders toward the still-advancing phalanx and then back to
him. The battle was won before it had even started.

Amazed, he sheathed his unbloodied sword and signaled
Parmenion to stop the advance.

It took a couple of minutes to calm the men down, and
Parmenion had to knock a couple of Ris flat to keep the excited men from falling on an old rival and slaying him. There
was a strange uneasiness as captors and captives looked at
each other, neither side having much experience in these affairs
and now totally lost as to how to conduct themselves.

Alexander shouted that the chieftain of the Kievants should
come out before he could count to one hundred or that he
would start to execute all the prisoners, and with that command there was a loud wailing from within the town. He could
only hope that they knew how much a hundred was, but before
Alexander got past forty the women of the town dragged the
chieftain forward, bruised and bleeding, and threw him at Alexander's feet.

Suddenly from the back of the press Ivarn pushed forward,

brandishing a massive two-handed club. And with loud shouts and curses he advanced toward the kneeling chief.

"Old scum, thief, one who sleeps with his own sisters, now I've got you!"

The chieftain looked at Alexander and then back to Ivarn, then threw his hands up to Alexander. "Spare me, one who must be a god. And I, Borst, will serve you faithfully."

Alexander looked over at Ivarn. And after weeks of play acting it was a pleasure to let his real feelings out.

"Enough, Ivarn, this man is mine now. In fact, all these men are mine, and not one of them is to be harmed. The Kievants are now the second company of phalanx."

"What? After I won this fight!" Ivarn screamed, and he gave a sly look to Lothar, who had walked up with his commander and stood by the side of Alexander's horse.

"After I finish this scum, I'll deal with you, you damned foreign upstart."

Ivarn advanced on Borst, club held high, and Borst fell to the ground wailing in terror. Alexander started to turn Bucephalas and bring his sword up, preparing first to take out Lothar and then Ivarn. His only hope was that this wouldn't trigger the phalanx into a revolt when they saw their chieftain killed. But he knew now for certain that Ivarn would have him dead, now that he had learned all he felt that he needed to know.

Lothar moved far faster than he could have ever imagined.

With a leaping stride, the wrestler came up alongside of Ivarn, and with a quick sure movement he snatched the chieftain off the ground and twisted his body into an impossible contortion. There was a loud, audible snap—and Ivarn hit the ground, his head lolling obscenely to one side.

The men were silent, stunned by what they had seen. Lothar looked to the gathering and then turned back to face Alexander.

"Hail Alexander!" Lothar screamed, raising a clenched fist into the air.

"Hail Alexander!" And the two tribes joined their voices into one shouting his praise.

Already Borst was at his side shouting out that he knew a perfect enemy that lived above them and he pointed "up," toward a ridgeline that shimmered above them in the blue, cloudless sky.

He could see Neva standing off to one side and noticed that

Lothar was already standing next to her, whispering something into her ear. So that was the arrangement, he thought, and he gave her a nod of acknowledgment. She was a dangerous one, to be sure, arranging the murder of her own uncle, even though he was a beast. He realized that he'd have to keep a little promise of reward once dimming came, and he shuddered at the thought.

"Tell me, Borst," Alexander asked, trying to be heard above the roaring shouts of the men. "I come from a distant place, and it is my custom to wash with hot water once a fight has been finished."

Borst shuddered and tried to hide a grimace of disgust. "But of course, O Alexander. I can arrange it."

He looked back again at Neva and tried to smile. "And see that there's one available whenever I want it. Even if it's in the middle of a dimming."

Borst shrugged his shoulders at such a strange request, but he was so happy to still have his head attached to his shoulders that he didn't argue.

chapter eight

"You realize, that sounds really disgusting," Neva said, as if he had just suggested that they engage in some of the practices usually associated with Egyptian royalty.

"But it really is quite pleasant," Alexander replied. "I can assure you that you'll feel like a new person."

"What! And lose the accumulation of dirt and smell that I've built up through several hundred dimmings! Are you trying to say that I'm not attractive to you?"

There was a dangerous look in her eyes and he could only smile at her, hoping that what he was really thinking wasn't too obvious.

"Now that you've had your third bath you should be ready

again," she said, reaching out from under the covers, ready to grab hold of him, preferably in one area more than another.

"Ah, yes, indeed if I had the time I would love to, but there are other duties calling. The dimming is almost past, and I should be up and about."

Before she could voice a stronger protest, he quickly called for Parmenion and exited from what was called "the palace."

Sleepily Parmenion came out of a side room and kicked at the sentries posted to guard the doorway, and who at the first opportunity had slumped down and gone to sleep.

"Damn fools. I'm sorry, sire."

Alexander ignored his apologies and simply looked at the sheepish guards with barely concealed anger that made the men look nervously at their feet.

He strode down toward the gate, his guards stumbling after him.

"Where are we going?" Parmenion inquired.

"To get a better look at that." And he pointed at Olympus, which dominated half the sky above the village. Parmenion fell silent and Alexander knew that he had listened perhaps a little too much to the superstitious sayings about the mountain that Aldin had called a heat exchanger.

Clearing the gate, they walked through the encampment of the Ris army. Some of the men were already rising, and at the sight of their commander they gave a ragged cheer, chanting his name with their curious lisping accent. Alexander motioned for them to be quiet, but their shouts were still echoing as he disappeared up the trail leading to Mount Olympus. The guards accompanying him started to mumble to themselves that this place was known to be the realm of gods, and with a wave of the hand Alexander bade them to go back down the mountain and wait. They didn't need to be told twice, and with a clatter of spears, they took off down the mountain trail.

"You know, one of the Ris told me that there are places up there"—Parmenion pointed up to the brooding heights—"that they say can't be scratched, and shine like the sun."

"You're telling me this to try to persuade me that maybe we should leave well enough alone."

Parmenion was silent, and Alexander looked at his one-eyed companion and smiled. "I've been told that several hundred dimmings past, an oracle came to live up here. These villagers hold the man in awe, saying he serves the gods. If we bring him into my service, it will increase our prestige among all the people of this region. Anyhow, Parmenion, I have to go and see this place and this man; otherwise I wouldn't be Alexander."

Parmenion could only shrug and mumble something about the difficulties of living with legends. Wheezing like an asthmatic in a dustbin, he struggled to keep pace as they followed the narrow path up the immense, white-capped mountain.

As they climbed ever higher, the rushing wind swirled louder and louder around them. It was Parmenion who first realized that there was a faint vibration to the ground, as if an earthquake was starting.

Alexander struggled with his fear, for having witnessed the destructive power of the gods when they shook the earth, he viewed such an event with trepidation. The two of them stood for some minutes, bracing for the shock, but none came, just the steady vibration and the gentle howling of the wind.

He looked up again at the towering height that appeared to go straight up, ten times or more beyond the highest soaring reaches of Asia.

He could not help but wonder why the Ris had not placed their fortress up there where they would be forever "higher" than anyone else, and would thus not have to view their neighbors as having insulted them. But then again they seemed so fearful of the mountain that he could well understand their reluctance to tread its slopes. He understood, as well, that many peasant fears often times had some foundation in fact, and he could only wonder what the mystery was.

A loud roar soon filled the air with deafening thunder, and, after turning at a branch of the trail, they beheld a mighty river shooting out of an underground passage so wide that a hundred men could march abreast into the cavern. Alexander realized that this tremendous flow of water originated from within the mountain, and the phenomenon filled him with awe. Where did the water come from? he wondered. He had seen underground springs before, but never a cataract of such immense proportions, with a flow almost as great as the mighty Tigris.

The light of the sun was already at its peak, flooding the far horizon with its crystalline light. Turning away from the river, they pushed on up the trail, until, pausing at last on a windswept ledge, the two men stopped to rest. The village of the Kievants was far below them, an insignificant speck on the landscape. In the distance they could see the village of the Avars perched on its miserable hillside. Gazing out in every direction, they saw dozens of signs of habitation throughout the hill country. The gentle curve of the Kolbard swept up and away to either side, and now that they were above the low clutter of hills they had a clear, unobstructed view as the twin horns of either horizon cut upward, narrowing into blue-green ribbons of light arching up to the never-moving sun. The two other towers now seemed so close that he felt as if he could almost reach out and touch them, while farther away rose three more towers whose foundations rested in the realm of the Gafs, a hundred leagues away.

With the unobstructed view he now had, Alexander could see the clear checkered pattern of well-tended fields cut by the undulating swirls of half a dozen rivers. The land looked gentle, rich, and full of life. Whoever had created this land must have lived in those distant gardens, Alexander thought wistfully. There was land enough there for all who lived in this region, but as was always the way, he realized, richness was held by a few, while the rest starved.

He remembered yet again the sharp hills and the narrow valleys of his own homeland, and the awe in his heart when first he beheld the great rich plains of Persia, with their well-ordered fields and vast endless spaces—the realm he had taken from Darius. Darius, he thought, shaking his head at the memory. How he dreamed of meeting him one on one, before the eyes of half a million, to struggle for control of the world; the emperor of the Persians who was his enemy yet somehow the only one in the world whom he could test himself against. But it had ended instead with a squalid murder by the roadside, a dying emperor abandoned by his own men, to lie in the dust, cursed and despised.

"Darius," he whispered, as if the sounding of the name could again conjure his foe out of the dust.

Parmenion looked over at his companion and then leaned back and looked up toward the squared-off peak above them. "Maybe we've already gone too far, and the oracle lives somewhere down there." Parmenion gestured vaguely back down to the lower level.

"If that were the case," Alexander replied, his thoughts returning to the present, "then why does this trail continue on upward? I think you're just looking for an excuse to stop."

"Who, me?"

Alexander didn't bother with a response and, rising, continued on with the climb. The wind swirled around them, plucking at their cloaks, an occasional gust threatening to knock them off balance, so that the two travelers were soon forced to lean on each other for support.

Turning a bend in the upward spiraling trail, they dipped down into a small valley a quarter of a league across, and both of them cried aloud with wonder when they first beheld the sight before them.

It gleamed with brilliant intensity, reflecting the white light of the sun as if it was made of burnished bronze. The wind pushed at their back, trying to push them toward what appeared to be a huge, gaping cavern at the lower end of the valley.

"Well, shall we go take a look?" Alexander ventured. Parmenion was silent, but his expression was more than sufficient to give an answer.

"If I were you," came a voice from behind, "I'd think twice before going on."

Parmenion whipped around, drawing his sword, but Alexander remained motionless, his back turned to the speaker. "If he meant us harm, Parmenion, he wouldn't have given us a warning."

"I just don't like people sneaking up on me," Parmenion replied gruffly.

"Perhaps I could argue that you were sneaking up on me," the speaker replied, stepping out of the shadows to reveal himself.

He stood tall and proud, though obviously an ancient. His hair was gone, his features wrinkled like old parchment, and he leaned on a wooden staff for support, as if the removal of it would cause him to tumble down. He drew closer to Alexander and squinted at him, betraying the dimming of his vision, as well.

"Are you the oracle that we seek?" Parmenion asked.

"What? Oh, no, not another damn youngster coming to seek truth from the oracle." The old man cackled softly. "You searchers are always such a pain in the butt end, coming up here, expecting to hit me with some smart-ass questions and then go back claiming that you found enlightenment. Well, if that's what you came for, then just get the hell out of here and leave me alone."

"Do you know who you're talking to?" Parmenion demanded.

"No. Now let me guess, could it be the new chieftain of the Kievants? Well, if it is, just remember, young man, that I'm higher up than all of you and piss always rolls downhill."

Parmenion started to raise his sword, but Alexander, laughing, beckoned for him to hold his anger in check. "By the heavens, Parmenion, it's good to hear a man speak frankly and without fear. Not since Pindar of Thebes have I been spoken to like this."

"Pindar of Thebes?" The old man looked at Alexander, then turned to his companion. "Parmenion?" he said questioningly as he gazed at the one-eyed guard.

"Sound familiar?" Alexander asked tentatively.

"Why, yes, of course it's familiar. I've read my Arrian and my Renault, which is more than can be said for the rest of the muckers down there." He waved toward the lowlands with a vague gesture of disgust. "And might I ask why you're running around on this climate control and docking tower, speaking in the first person, as if you were an ancient Macedonian king from Earth?"

Alexander looked at him with openmouthed astonishment, not sure at all where to start on this one.

"Well, go on. Stop goggling at me like a fish out of water, tell me what all this is about."

"I am Alexander, son of Philip, known to you as the Great."

The old man looked at him appraisingly for some seconds. Alexander could sense that Parmenion would most likely pounce if this man gave what should be a typical reaction.

"Go on now," the oracle replied, and Parmenion held back, not sure if the man's tone was mocking or incredulous.

"It is the truth, old man," Alexander replied in Greek, forcing himself to remember that once-familiar tongue.

"Now you've added a new angle to your argument," the oracle responded, with just a trace of a broad highlander accent.

And now it was Parmenion's turn to be amazed. "How in the name of the gods do you know our tongue? Why, I was getting sick of talking the gibberish spoken by these barbarians. It's good to speak again with a civilized man."

The oracle shrugged, obviously feeling flattered. "Let's just say I've studied the old works. But come, let's get out of this howling gale and talk where we need not shout our words into the wind."

He beckoned for the two to follow him on a narrow side path that led into a cleft in the hills.

"Where does that lead?" Alexander asked, pointing toward the gaping entrance to the mountainside that they had originally been heading toward.

"Watch."

The oracle wandered off the trail and poked at the ground with his staff. After a brief search he scraped up a loose stone and walked to the edge of the valley. With a gentle underhanded toss he lobbed the stone onto the sloping metallike surface. The stone started to slip away, like a river-smoothed rock skipped out onto a frozen lake. It accelerated as it fell toward the cavern opening, driven by the howling wind in its downward slide. Falling through the mouth of the cave, it disappeared from view.

"Care to follow it?"

Parmenion gulped and shook his head.

"If we had stepped onto that surface, that would have been our fate," Alexander said more as a statement than a question.

"Don't go fooling around intake vents, especially where the substructures have been revealed through wind erosion. You wind up in a cooling fin and it's all over. Oh, yes, you finally get pumped back out as liquid fertilizer, but that's a small consolation. No glory, no funeral pyres . . . just fertilizer.

"Quite the system, this," the oracle said, pointing to the mountain around them. "Remote sensors monitor the climate below, feed in the data, and then these mountains act as the regulators. The mountain is honeycombed with heat exchangers that cool the air when needed, and return the moisture either as rain or as a river. If it wasn't for that, this place would have fried out eons ago. Creating a variable star only solved part of the climate control problem. Smart fellows, those First Travelers. I've spent a lifetime figuring out how they did it. Now, you definitely don't want to go near the moisture dump system farther up, that place is a real killer."

The two Macedons looked at the oracle as if he were speaking some sort of alien tongue that their translator implants simply could not pick up on. The oracle, realizing that he had lost his two visitors, stopped short with a shrug of his shoulders.

"Oh, anyhow, hold your thanks for my saving your lives. You'll pay me back later, I'm sure. Now let's get out of this damn gale. Come on, you want enlightenment, I'll give enlightenment. If you don't want enlightenment, then get the hell out of here and go mumble your Greek someplace else. It's all the same to me."

"You still don't believe that I'm Alexander?"

"Well, let me put it to you this way. If I came wandering into your court, and said that I, Yaroslav, the most brilliant oracle and wise man of my realm, had traveled across space and time from a ring-planet, made by a race known as the First Travelers, and they built this place for the hell of it, what would you think?

"And then to top it off, I told you that I'd been transported by some man named Aldin who gave me this mission to unite all mankind." He stopped for a moment, leaned back in his chair, and took another swig from a wineskin. "Now, where was I? Ah, yes, if I showed up with a story like that, what in the name of Zeus would you do?"

Alexander could only shake his head.

"Now, those simpleminded fools down there might buy it, but me?" He shook his head and chuckled.

"Let's leave this old dodderer," Parmenion said gruffly. "We don't have to prove anything to him."

"Nor do I intend to," Alexander replied evenly. "So sit back down, Parmenion, I've still got some questions."

"Listen to him, Parmenion," Yaroslav said, again speaking in Greek. "After all, he is the great Alexander, so show the proper respect."

"You know, your Greek is really quite good," Alexander replied good-naturedly.

Yaroslav waved away the compliment as if he did not need such things. "Here and there some small centers of learning still survive. I spent a lot of time studying what you claim was your time."

"Where?" Alexander inquired.

"Never mind that, but anyhow, do you have any idea just how big this structure is?"

"I think I have a grasp of it."

"Even I, who've spent a long time studying this place, still have a hard time getting a grasp of it."

Yaroslav stood up and walked to the far corner of the room that he called his private study.

The room was richly appointed, and did not give any feeling whatsoever that it was in fact a cave. The walls were paneled with what appeared to be oak, the leather chairs that they sat upon were heavily padded and, to Alexander, seemed out of place somehow for a hermit living atop a mountain. If Yaroslav was an oracle, he certainly was a comfortable one. Alexander could only wonder as to how this old man had managed to haul so much material up the mountain to this distant cave.

Yaroslav pulled open a cabinet door and, mumbling a series of curses, he rummaged around inside the walk-in closet for some minutes before reappearing, dragging a massive scroll as thick around as a man's waist. Grabbing hold of one end, he gave it a toss and the scroll unraveled across the floor—only a small fraction of it was revealed before coming to a rest on the far side of the room.

"Now, where are we?" he mumbled meditatively. "Damn thing's always so big, it's such a pain working with this damn parchment. Damn primitives."

"Is that a map?" Parmenion asked, standing up and peering over Yaroslav's shoulder.

"Of course it's a map, you idiot. Can't you see that?"

Parmenion made a significant and age-old gesture at Yaroslav's back, then got down on the floor beside him to look at the details.

"No, no, not here." Yaroslav pulled the parchment across the floor so that it continued to unravel from the far corner.

"Could it be there, where it's marked in red?" Alexander ventured, pointing to a section that had just unraveled from the scroll.

"Ah, yes, that's how I marked our particular region in question.

"Now, to give you an idea of what we are dealing with," Yaroslav said in a pedantic tone. "Remember first of all that this world was built by a race we refer to as the First Travelers."

"Who were they?" Alexander asked. "Were they gods?"

"You could call them that, at least in your classic Olympian sense, as beings who still had the foibles and desires of men. You see, I believe they built this ring simply as an exercise, an amusement. The way a child might build a huge sand castle simply to prove to himself that he can do it."

"Do they still live here, then?"

Yaroslav hesitated for a moment, as if judging his response.

"I don't think so," he replied slowly, "though there are legends among the current inhabitants that the 'Ancient Ones' still live beneath, in the subterranean passageways."

"The what?" Alexander asked.

"Remember this Kolbard is of artificial construction, like a massive building. There are literally millions of tunnels, access ways, cooling fins exposed to open vacuum, and repair ports honeycombing this entire structure."

"Are we near an entryway now?"

"If you ever get curious, just go through that opposite door. Though after a couple of leagues I can't remember which way to go," Yaroslav said quickly, his voice full of warning. "So you might not get back."

Alexander eyed him with curiosity.

"Is it locked?" Parmenion asked suspiciously, as if the opposite doorway was an entry to the dark underworld—which in a sense, it was.

Yaroslav only smiled in response.

"Where are we on this map?" Alexander asked, pointing to the section outlined in red.

"Ah, yes, now let's see." Yaroslav leaned forward and after a brief search he pointed out the high range of hills that ran along what he called the "northern" section of the continent.

"You notice a scale line down there." He pointed to a series of graph lines. "Distance is measured in versts, and comes out to about three versts to one of your leagues. Now, there are several hundred continent areas on the Kolbard; some are smaller than Europe, while others are ten times that of Asia."

"How are they divided apart?"

"There are oceans, to be sure. From up here you have no problem seeing the Iras Sea to our west. That is nearly a million square versts in area, with a number of islands on it. So, like Earth, the various continents can be divided by oceans, but they are also divided by barrier walls that soar up beyond the upper levels of atmosphere."

"Why the walls?" Parmenion asked.

"To break up wind-flow patterns. Otherwise, due to the co-riolis effect, there would be hurricane-force winds building up, if the terrain didn't interrupt it. In some places the wind has gradually stripped away the topsoil. The locals around here refer to it as the Anvil."

Alexander couldn't understand some of the terms, but grasped what the old man was saying.

"And what is this 'Anvil'?"

"You noticed the open shimmering area down toward the Iras Sea? It's the bare metal of the support structure. Strong stuff, that metal, damn near impossible to scratch, and definitely impossible to pull up and use. That Anvil down there is a small one, only a hundred versts long by a hundred wide. Now picture an area like that a hundred times larger. In some regions it acts as a barrier from one area to another. Nothing grows, it's damn difficult even to move on it. Nothing gets across except for an occasional nomadic merchant. It's as good as an ocean to divide things off."

"Nomadic merchant?" Alexander asked. "Does that mean that all the wheel is occupied?"

Yaroslav smiled.

"I think so, but it is so massive it is hard to tell. Nearly three thousand years ago, more than halfway back, in fact, to your time, mankind first made landfall here. Colonists settled it at a number of locations. Those muckers down below came from north of your original empire. They've pretty well reverted back to precivilized standards, thanks to the Great War, which cut off thousands of worlds and left them isolated. What made it even worse was the fact that the First Travelers had stripped most of the planets of their resources a million years ago, and thus there was next to nothing as far as basic materials to rebuild through the various technological levels.

"Here, as on innumerable other places in the Magellanic Cloud, we found ourselves competing with the Gafs, along with another race, for control of all the inhabitable worlds. I can only speak for this area, but there are rumors that there are dozens of different races living on the various continents, for the First Travelers seemed to take delight in dropping off interesting specimens to populate this little project of theirs, long before we ever arrived on the scene.

"Damn it, I've heard of plantlike creatures in the next continent over, and insectlike beings that breed humans for food and as slaves. Why, there're almost limitless probabilities to this place."

"What I'm interested in now," Alexander interrupted, "are the Gavarnians."

"Ah, yes, we call them the Gafs. So why the interest?"

Alexander stood up and smiled at Yaroslav. "I'm Alexander, should not that be answer enough?"

Yaroslav chuckled, more to himself than to his guests. "So another war of conquest. And those scum down below are to be your army, is that it?"

Alexander nodded in reply.

"It's a far cry from your Macedons. And your foes will have no Darius to hamper them."

"Yes, Darius," Alexander said softly. "Do you know then of their leader, this Kubar Taug?"

"Ah, no, can't say that I do." And he fell silent.

Alexander noticed that Parmenion was watching their host intently, but he voiced no opinion.

"So you plan to unite the tribes into a host and to train them to your task?"

"That's the general idea."

"Ah, well, I best be packing then."

Without another word Yaroslav walked into the next chamber and the two wanderers heard the sound of drawers opening and slamming shut, with occasional mumbled curses and groans. After some minutes Yaroslav reappeared with a pack slung over his shoulder and a fairly good imitation of an archaic Greek helmet on his head and a rounded shield at his side.

"Best be off, then. I shan't miss the fun of this, so I guess I'll tag along."

"Old man," Parmenion mumbled, "in your condition, one day's hard march will leave you dead. Stay here and live off the offerings of the fools that come to hear you."

"Old man, is it?" And Yaroslav advanced on his taunter. "Look at that belly," he roared, poking the overweight guard in the stomach. "It's a wonder it hasn't sagged to your feet so that you trip over it when running from your foes! I'll outmarch you, outwench you, outfight you, and outdrink you. All this clean living of a hermit has worn a little thin. I've been waiting for an adventure like this, now let's be off."

Alexander was silent, looking closely at this newest recruit.

"Look, Alexander son of Philip—and yes, I do believe your tale, no matter how improbable it sounds—like Augustine once said about his religion, 'It's so damn improbable, I have to believe it.' I can read, I know this world, and I'm passably good as a healer, as well. Besides, you need a chronicler for this tale, and that I shall be, because you're not going to find anyone down there that can hold a quill correctly, let alone have the intelligence to know how to use it. And believe me, I'll write a far better history than some of the damn fools who've scribbled out a pack of lies about you. So let's take the map, you'll need that, and be off."

"We can't carry the whole thing," Alexander said, looking at the impossibly long parchment roll. With a quick flash of his sword he cut out the area marked in red.

"Just like with Gordius," Yaroslav replied philosophically as he gazed on his mutilated trophy. "I'll come back with some bearers later to bring the rest, along with my library and easy chair." And then he turned away and strode out the door without a backward look.

"So, this is the army of the great Alexander." Yaroslav groaned sarcastically.

"My father's grandsire had not much better than these when he started," Alexander replied, and Parmenion could sense the touch of despair in his master's voice.

The Kievants, after a dozen dimmings of intense training, had been judged ready to serve as the second phalanx and were now drawn up in battle formation beside their former enemy. The cavalry force had been doubled, as well. A Ris hero—that at least is how Alexander had named him—had come in with a report of a lone Gaf scout who was mounted and searching the area where Alexander had made his first encounter. The sighting of the Gaf could only mean that his opponents were out looking for him. Parmenion had taken a contingent out and returned three dimmings later, mounted uneasily atop a towering horse. His stature now was second only to Alexander's, for all soon were told how he bested the feared warrior alone, one pikeman bringing down a mounted swordsman.

Several of the Ris were bloodied from the foray. Not by the Gaf, but by the sound thrashing Parmenion had given them for breaking and running when the warrior charged. And as was sometimes the case with such men, they now held him in high esteem as a man to be reckoned with and one that had near-mystical powers. And they were quick to pummel any man who spoke out against the fat chieftain of the "golden one," as they now called Alexander.

Alexander nodded to Parmenion, and his second in command nudged his mount to a canter. Parmenion trotted down to stop in front of the regiment of Ris and a spontaneous shout went up from that command.

Good, Alexander thought, already we are accepted, and some of them must sense, as well, the start of what comes here today. He looked out at eight hundred men assembled before the gates of the city. They were still filthy and ragged; there was no semblance of uniforms except for brown headbands on the Ris and dirty white for the Kievants. Their armor, if they were fortunate to have any, was a boiled leather tunic backed with felt or wool. Only one in three carried a metal-tipped spear.

But he could remember the stories the old soldiers had told him in his youth, and somehow he could see here the resurrection of those legends from his past when the Macedons were nothing more than barbaric shepherds and thieves. Yes, these men could be a start after all.

He stood up in his stirrups. "Soldiers! I call you soldiers, for now, for the first time, you are soldiers and worthy of that honored title."

Yaroslav gave a sarcastic sniff, but Alexander ignored the oracle.

"Once you called yourselves Ris and Kievants. Once you fell upon each other and squabbled like ignorant children in the dirt. But no more. Look now to each other. When divided against yourselves you were nothing. But now, united, you are powerful. Can you not sense the strength here? Can you not sense the power that can be yours as long as you are united?"

He stopped for a moment, and there was a gentle murmur in the ranks as the men turned and looked at each other.

"Behold!" Turning to Yaroslav, he took the single stick that the oracle offered to him.

Alexander grabbed hold of the stick at both ends. His muscles knotted, and the stick snapped in half. Again he held out his hand, and this time Yaroslav gave him two sticks. Holding them together, he tried to snap them also, his muscles knotting in a great show of force—which was indeed show, for he did not want his lesson to suddenly break. The two sticks held.

"Thus in the two sticks is your lesson. Alone you are like a twig to be snapped, united under me you cannot be broken. And stronger yet you shall be before we are done, as stick after stick is added to the bundle."

A mighty shout went up from the assembly.

"You, the Kievants, have told me that the people of Novgor piss downhill on you. Today we march on Novgor."

A wild cry greeted his words, for both villages had managed to maintain a longstanding feud with their other neighbor, as well.

"We go not to destroy them, but to take them, so that in another dozen dimmings there will be a third regiment in our command, adding to our strength."

There was some quiet muttering at this, but Parmenion merely had to urge his horse forward a couple of paces and the complaints died away.

"Listen to me, soldiers. For I, Alexander, shall tell you all. Once the Novgor are at our sides, we shall split our army, half marching to Avar, the other half to Boroda. Then in a dozen more dimmings there will be yet two more regiments, and they in turn shall conquer and recruit yet two more, so that soon there shall be a hundred regiments. And when we gather together at one place, our shouts shall drown out even the roaring of the cascade coming from the mountain I call Olympus."

The men were silent, enrapt at the realization of what he was proposing. Some of the wiser men started to cry out about whom they should attack next, once the conquest of the Humans was complete.

"Already some of you can see where I shall lead," Alexander shouted in response. "For when we are strong enough, we shall march down to the sea. The oracle Yaroslav has told me that where the Anvil meets the sea there is a great hill of iron that fell from the sky eons ago. This is where the Gafs get their metal, and there we shall meet the Gafs. We shall face the Gafs and take from them the mountain of iron and the flowing sea, and the rich lands, to call our own. I, Alexander, son of Philip, called the Great, promise this."

They stamped their spears upon the ground, roaring their approval.

"Listen to me now, Ris and Kievants. From today onward

you are no longer two people. When you joined me in this cause, your old names of the past were left behind. From my realm there was one people above all others, and henceforth all that join me shall be known by that name.

"From now on you are Macedons!"

The men looked one to another, saying this new word tentatively at first but soon chanting it proudly, as if it were some spell or talisman.

Drawing his sword, Alexander pointed to the goat path that led off toward the village of the Novgor, and the ranks fell in behind him. As he rode past the wall, which was barely higher than his head, Neva leaned over, revealing her ample charms to him. He had convinced her to stay behind as his regent. That way she would be out of sight, and smelling, for several dimmings, at least. With a well-acted look of pained parting, he gazed at her for a moment and then cantered past.

Yaroslav was trotting by his side, and reaching down, Alexander hoisted the old philosopher up behind him. For several seconds the old man gazed closely at Neva with an intent curiosity, as if he had suddenly seen a woman for the first time.

"Really, that rabble back there, Macedons indeed," Yaroslav said, turning away from the woman. "Scratch that thin layer of bravado off them and they're still a pack of thieves. Macedons indeed."

"They will be," Alexander replied, his voice distant, "they will be."

And no one noticed at that moment the look that so many had seen on another world, when his followers would say that he was gazing toward a glory that only he could somehow see.

"And what do you make of this report, Kubar Taug?"

Long he had waited for this question. For the passage of four-score dimmings he had waited, as if in Binda, for a question regarding the current situation. Here at last they had finally recognized him at a clan gathering. The game of waiting that he had been forced to play was now entering its next phase.

Upon his arrival at the court of Kalin, Hina's brother the Taug, Kubar had withdrawn into solitude and waited. He knew that if he was to lead these people it would not be as someone who came bearing warnings and calling to lead. Rather it must be that they should come to him in the end and ask. And now they were asking for the first time. It was only a simple question, delivered in a slightly mocking tone, but it was the start nevertheless.

"First, Kalin," he said slowly, as if stirred from deep sleep, "first tell me what you yourself think, and then I shall speak in turn."

Kubar stopped speaking and looked around at the assembled Gavarnians. Nearly sixty warriors were present, each of them representing one of the noble families that inhabited this region of the Kolbard they called Kia Valinstan, "the realm of blossoming flowers."

They were all dressed almost identically wearing the traditional lacquered-armor tunic that flared into a long hanging skirt of shining leather that reached nearly to the ground. Upon the right breast of each was painted the family standard—for some, flowers; for others, geometric designs; and for yet others, symbolic representations of honored ancestors who had been the legendary first settlers in the murky, distant past.

Having come from all points of the realm, they now were gathered at last in the central courtyard of Kalin's castle, the main bastion of Sirt, the single large city of their realm. Cities were anathema to those who ruled the land from their own private fiefdoms; Sirt's status had grown merely because it was the personal domain of the taugs, the acknowledged elder family of their world.

To some from the distant marches, this was the first visit to Sirt in their lifetimes. The pagodalike central keep that rose high into the air and the sloping battlements of stone that covered nearly a square verst in area filled them with as much awe as the fact that they were in the presence of Kalin Taug. Some, as well, though they kept the fact hidden, were in awe of this stranger who claimed to be legend come to life.

Kubar returned their curious stares with a polite nod and then faced back toward Kalin.

Kalin turned and looked back at his personal court, who were members of his immediate family and the family retainers. He knew what they already thought of this meeting, for few of them believed, himself included, that the one who sat before them was the Taug of the legends of the past to them. But word of this stranger's presence had spread through the city, and at last, bowing to pressure, Kalin had allowed him to attend the clan meeting.

Kubar noticed the two females who were allowed to sit in the council. One was Kaveta, the wife of Kalin. Kalin, as the eldest, was the only one of his four brothers allowed to marry. But he already noticed that her eyes rested more often upon Hina than her spouse. Judging, so far, between the two, he could well understand why. But he knew that as a Gavarnian of noble rank it would stop merely at looks, for to do otherwise would be the worst possible disgrace for her, and one of the ultimate betrayals possible for a brother.

He noticed, as well, the looks the other one gave. Her name was Liala, the one sister of Hina and Kalin. She was attractive beyond measure, her almond-shaped eyes unusually large and full of vibrant life. He had found himself looking forward to their brief conversations as they passed each other in the corridors of the castle. He could not help but see the look in her eyes when she gazed upon him. But he could only think that he was already old and graying, and that her looks were one of simple admiration, and he thought no more of it.

Kalin rose up, his red-lacquered armor creaking, his gaze straight at Kubar, as if waiting for a challenge.

"It is simple enough," he said gruffly. "The hairless ones, the scum beneath our contempt, have found some leader. He has united together a score of their filth-covered clans, and even now moves to bring the entire hill region under his control. If we moved against them today, we would face an organized foe of perhaps ten thousand. It is reported that he is doubling the size of his force every thirty dimmings. They call this one Iskander, the name you first mentioned upon your arrival here. It is obvious you knew of him before us, and that mystery in and of itself is troubling."

Kalin fell silent, as if he had spoken too much already by acknowledging Kubar's foreknowledge of the threat. Kubar realized this was not the time to press his case so he quietly changed the direction.

"How many can he draw upon in the end?" Kubar asked evenly, not staring straight at Kalin, to avoid an unnecessary challenge.

"We keep no count of the scum. They are there for our sport when we wish it, or when we need to punish their thieving. After all, they are only hairless ones, not even worthy of this formal attention they now receive."

"Be that as it may," Hina interjected, "they are in need of

our attention now. My border watchers report that maybe forty, perhaps as many as sixty thousand, can be brought together. That is more than all the nobles and landless servants in our entire realm."

"To bring together that many in one place up in the hills would be impossible," came a voice from the back of the room.

Kubar smiled and looked to the shadows behind Kalin, where the speaker stood. It was Wirgth, the court advisor to the taug clan. Such a position was an old and honored one in Gavarnian tradition. The advisor, or Kaadu, was traditionally the closest friend of the sire who ruled before the current taug. Upon the death of his friend the Kaadu became the most cherished advisor to the son who ruled. Thus a ruler chose his closest friend carefully, looking for one who was loyal, intelligent, and with the moral strength to speak forcefully and with truth at all times.

Kubar recognized those qualities at once when he met Wirgth. The graying, ascetic-looking Gaf had spent many a long dimming with him, questioning carefully, endlessly probing Kubar and his story. Kubar knew that his presence at the meeting was Wirgth's doing. The Kaadu had accepted him as the true Taug.

"Explain, honored Kaadu," Kalin said coldly.

"It is simple enough," Wirgth said, advancing to the center of the room. "The hairless ones need at least a wreth weight of food per day in order to keep their strength. Thus if their army came together in one place, they would require sixty thousand wreths of food a day. In one day they would devour everything in even their largest village. We've denied them horses, taking the breed for ourselves with that consideration in mind. Without horses and wagons it's physically impossible for them to supply a large number of people in one place.

"Thus they must do one of two things. They must either disperse, or they must move down out of the hills and into our richer lands, where they can gather enough forage to stay alive."

"They'd be fools to dare us," Kalin roared. "I don't give a good damn if they organize in their hills, they can stay there and rot, for all I care. But they would never dare to face the shock of one of our mounted regiments."

"But I think they just might," Wirgth interjected. "For this unifier, whoever he is, must be unifying for a reason. If he allows his men to spread out once again, he shall lose control in short order. Therefore I believe that his only logical move is to come forward with the intent of driving us."

"Hairless ones driving us," another underlord shouted, coming to his feet. "That is beyond all reason. Your reading has addled you, Wirgth. Whoever heard of a hairless one driving one such as us? They are there for our sport, not as a challenge."

"Arn, they might have been sport for you in the past," Wirgth replied, "but the days of sport with the hairless ones are over."

Wirgth fell silent, and before Arn, the lord of the northern marches, could reply, thus starting an argument he was obviously looking for, Hina interrupted.

"Kubar, I am curious as to your response regarding Wirgth's comments."

"Iskander, as you call him," Kubar interjected cautiously, "has come to this world for but one purpose—to organize the hairless ones and then turn them against us in a war of conquest. That is why I am here at this time. There is no coincidence in this. It is a simple logical fact. Iskander will invade. He must invade and do so shortly, and when he comes there will be sixty thousand men behind him. Do not underestimate this man, for he is the best in the entire history of the Humans—conjured from their past to destroy us."

There was a low rumbling of growls from most of the underlords. Kubar gave a quick hand gesture to Paga, who was sitting behind him, as he sensed his standard-bearer's anger.

"Let them come then," Kalin roared. "We shall carpet the ground with their dead!"

The vassals in the courtyard came to their feet, shouting their approval.

"It shall be a hunt like no other," Kalin screamed. "We shall drive our enemies before us until the hills run with blood. Let them dare to come down, and then they shall see the wrath of the Gavarnians. I have said all along that this is a race beneath our contempt. Let us exterminate them and have an end to their filth!"

Knowing better than to try, Kubar still felt compelled to give warning. Standing, he turned to face the family heads behind him. Their wild demonstration lasted for some minutes, but

one by one they saw his visage, and as if sensing his power
they fell quiet in his presence.

"They'll send out a decoy on the extreme right flank," he
began softly. "The flank farthest removed from our center of
concentration. Thus as we advance out to meet them our own
flank will be exposed to their position in the hills. Then their
main force will cut in from behind, forcing us to give battle.

"I must warn you now, do not underestimate them." His
voice now rose up and those around him could sense the cold
calculation and determination in it. He was speaking as if he
had already read a history of what was to come.

"They know nothing of your honor, the way you fight, or
the way you expect your opponents to fight. They will laugh
at your conventions, the calling out of family names, the seeking of a worthy foe. Do not underestimate them."

"Are you the taug of my people?" Kalin replied harshly.

Kubar turned and looked back at Kalin.

"No," he said evenly, trying not to betray the despair in his
heart, for it was obvious to him where the arrogance of Kalin
might lead. It was the same arrogance the nobles of his own
time had shown when first he had stood up to face them.

"Then are you the general that shall command our army?"

"No, I am not the taug of your people, or their general. For
I have not been asked."

His phrasing was well calculated and revealed to all present
what he would finally expect. They would have to come and
ask him to be the taug.

"You are nothing but an impostor," Arn shouted, coming up
to Kalin's side. "An impostor, a charlatan, and I would rot before serving you instead of the true taug."

"Paga, hold," Kubar shouted. Arn had offered a direct challenge, which in moments could descend into a bloodbath. The
moment was dangerous. And it was Wirgth who finally retrieved it.

"For your service to our taug, in offering him advice, I
thank you, Kubar," Wirgth said evenly, stepping forward to
place himself between Kubar and Arn.

"You have the courage of a Kaadu to speak as you now did,
offering fair and honest advice. It is the same advice I now
give Kalin Taug. Do not underestimate this one called Iskander."

The words of a Kaadu were considered sacred, and the tension in the courtyard started to ease off. Hina, who was standing by his brother's side, looked to Kubar as if offering a warning not to speak further. Kubar could see the anxiety in the younger brother's eyes and nodded in response.

"I know you believe him," Kalin snarled, watching the interplay between his brother and Kubar.

"I can believe him and his words yet still be loyal to he who is the same blood and flesh as I," Hina replied. "I will ride by your side and serve, as I am sure Kubar and Paga shall do as well."

"But of course," Kubar responded diplomatically. "And of course I wish the honored Kalin luck and the blessing of my brothers departed when he goes to meet them. Know that I shall be there when Kalin goes to meet Iskander."

"Goes to drive them," Kalin snarled.

"But of course," Kubar replied evenly, without a trace of emotion.

chapter nine

From: Aldin Larice
To: All participating Kohs
Subject: First stage completion report for the Alexandrian/
           Taug Encounter

The primary campaign of Alexander has been completed as of game day 127, standard. His accomplishments are as follows:

As of the date of this report the last active resistance to his consolidation has been eliminated. For all practical purposes resistance to his unification drive collapsed by the start of his fifth campaign when he was capable of fielding ten regiments. From thenceforth, except for one or two minor cases, the Human inhabitants flocked to his banner, throwing open their gates. Most all of them already accept the fact that he is in-

deed the Alexander sent from their historic past to redeem them.

The northern hill region measuring nearly a million square kilometers in area is under his sway (see enclosed maps).

At this date he can marshal nearly fifty regiments of heavy pike, twenty of skirmishers, one of ballista artillery, but less than half a regiment of cavalry. Full tote records evaluating performance of each regiment is enclosed, along with evaluation of command structure and control.

Several skirmishes have developed, but the Human forces have yet to venture into the lower plains where the Gavarnian cavalry is most effective.

Intelligence reports indicate however that the Gavarnian advance into the northeastern hill region is in fact a full-scale penetration. As you can observe from evaluation printouts, Alexander's forces are reacting in an appropriate manner, which indicates that they are fully aware and deploying for a counterstrike. Therefore this memo should be considered a full-scale battle alert. Primary odds have been computed along all lines. As is standard operation, all considerations have been fed into the game standard evaluation program. Any and all bets can be processed through access code 23–alpha–alpha–873. Portfolios of all corporate assets wagered will be evaluated by a blind system-three program for total worth. Security clearance to data is through coded access only by party or parties responding to bet offer.

Duplicate reports of Kubar Taug's progress, as submitted by Zergh, are enclosed with cross-comparison evaluation of results.

As of this date, standard, daily tote odds will be printed. Today's odds are as follows:

Survival of Alexander—day, standard 87:1
Survival of Kubar Taug—same 1,221:1
Battle to occur within seven days, standard 3.7:1
First victory to Alexander 2:7
Submitted—Larice

"A little short on the odds, there, my dear Aldin, aren't we?"

Aldin looked up from the navigation board and, standing, offered his chair to Corbin Gablona, who could barely manage to squeeze his massive bulk through the doorway.

The pleasure yacht had cost him an even fifty million, a value greater than some planets, but for some foolish reason the master designer had never considered the bulk of its owner when it came to the command and control area of the vessel.

The designer was currently dealing with a most unpleasant job retrofitting organic fertilizer ships.

"Do remember, my lord, that conflict analysis through statistical measurement is a complex process. Take for instance the question of Alexander's death."

Aldin looked closely at Corbin as he spoke, but there was no response.

"Yes, Alexander's death."

The two men turned as Bukha Taug came into the room with Zergh at his side. Zergh nodded politely toward Corbin and then came up to Aldin's side, extending his huge paw to his fellow game master.

"I was just discussing such an event with my Koh Bukha," Zergh said evenly. "My analysis of course matches yours as to the odds of his death, which shows the ability of our programs, along with our own skills at data gathering and profiling, but one does not always agree with analysis, even when it is your own. Do you not concur, my friend?"

"There is the possibility," Aldin replied smoothly, "that our mathematical models of Alexander are not precise. Remember that I merely provide data input with some judgments of possibilities, but the computer is the one that analyzes this data and produces the final outputs. A Game Master of the First Degree, of which there are only two"—Aldin nodded to the Gavarnian who was his only equal—"can only provide probabilities. We cannot calculate a particular arrow or its flight and how that will intersect at a given moment with the line of Alexander's life."

Corbin was silent.

"In my analysis," Zergh interjected, "which was interplayed with that of Aldin's, I gave a slightly higher probability of death or serious injury to Alexander. But the computer rated Aldin's projections higher due to his specialization with this particular warrior. But I daresay, either way, it could make an interesting side bet."

Corbin nodded toward Bukha. "Rather than the private bets through the computer, shall we say a little public wager?"

"I do hate betting on the death of a Human I could almost admire, but the loyalties of race are thick."

Bukha looked straight at Corbin as he spoke, but there was no response.

"Shall we say control of your Cersta System?" Corbin said. "If I'm not mistaken, the automatic mines on the three worlds there are showing a significant return on your initial investment. For my part, I shall wager my pleasure world of Marrakesh; the Human females there might even meet with your approval."

Bukha, as was befitting a properly repressed Gavarnian, hid his revulsion at the mention of interracial sex, which was in fact practiced but viewed by the moral of both races as bestiality.

Bukha nodded to Zergh, who pulled out a pocket unit and ran a quick financial check.

"Relative worth comes out more like one point eight to seven," Zergh reported.

"Throw in the Dias Consortium, as well, then."

"But you are merely co-owner along with Zola."

"If I lose, I daresay that effeminate lout will be more than happy to sign me out and you in."

Zergh ran another quick check and nodded his approval.

"Two point three to seven."

"I'll draw the documents," Aldin said matter-of-factly.

"Come, come," Corbin replied smoothly, "we are all gentlemen here, are we not?"

Bukha smiled evenly, even though to his own race a smile was an act of hostility.

"My lord Alexander, they are responding as you said they would."

Alexander looked up at the sweat-covered courier who sat astride a small Gavarnian mount.

"Where did you get the horse, boy?"

"I took it in the ambush." The boy beamed with obvious pride.

"Parmenion and his troops?"

"They're not a verst behind me. Staying just ahead of the pursuing force."

"Good, very good. Go to supply, draw yourself some wine, you've earned it."

"I should return my lord Alexander."

"Follow my orders, rest yourself. They'll be here soon enough."

The boy saluted and kicked his mount to a canter. Alexander looked up from his map table and smiled at Yaroslav. "Did you hear that, he took it from a Gavarnian."

"Only someone as young as he would be crazy enough to mount such a beast."

"I've got fifty horses now. Already the men are learning that taking a horse means an end to walking—they've lost their fear."

"They'll soon get it back," Yaroslav said pensively, looking at the rolling cloud of dust approaching from the east. "Best you start the final briefing." And Yaroslav stepped out of the tent to beckon for the regiment commanders to come in.

"Do you all know your positions?" Alexander asked, looking to the regiment commanders once they had gathered around the raised sandbox that was used to illustrate their position since most of them still were not used to the idea of symbols on parchment representing hills, rivers, and men.

The men were silent. He could sense their fear. It was one thing when they had come to his banner, one after another to march against other Humans, but this was their first go against the Gafs. They were petrified, and at this moment it was only their greater fear of him that kept them to their task.

"Remember, it will be simple enough, we just let them come to us. They'll deploy in the way that Yaroslav here said they would, for war to them is as much ritual as it is a matter of death or victory. Just let them come. They have only eight thousand mounted and five thousand retainers on foot compared to our forty thousand deployed here. But if one of you breaks, the rest of you will break, and we'll all be slaughtered, for you can't outrun them. And besides, you have no place to run."

There was a faint rumble from the back of the crowd, but his look of challenge silenced them.

They were indeed in a trap. Nearly a fortnight ago the Gaf army had marched from their capital and advanced northeast, into the hill country. Alexander had led his force out into the plains after the Gaf army had passed, severing their lines of communication, thus forcing them to turn back and attack his prepared position. A lesson he had learned from Darius at

Issus. But he had positioned himself in the fork between the Volsta and Benazi rivers, thus eliminating any hope for retreat. If they broke and ran, the rivers would block any chance of escape, and everyone in his army now knew this.

There was no way out, and some now looked at their leader with hatred and suspicion.

"Go to your posts, and those on the left, remember. If you show yourself before I come to lead, I'll personally take your heads. If any of us are left alive. Now go."

The men turned and left.

"If the battle goes against us," Yaroslav mumbled, "they'll seek you out first and cut you to ribbons before they themselves die."

"I'm not worried," Alexander replied almost cheerily. "You see, my friend, if I don't plan to lose, I won't."

"Oh, just grand, next thing I know you'll be telling me that your father Zeus assured you of this victory."

Alexander merely looked at him and smiled.

"My lord Kalin, they've stopped their retreat. See, just before the crest of the next hill."

Kalin, commander of the first host, reined in his horse and looked to where his aide was pointing.

"Still only fifty or so, and they've backed into the fork of the river rather than make for the last ford. The stupid fools are trapped."

"We've yet to sight the rest of their forces," Wirgth cautioned.

"Oh, they're in there, behind those hills and waiting. He's not sure of his men, this Alexander. He knows he has cowards, so he has trapped them into a position where they must fight or die. This makes it far easier to finish them even before the dimming."

"So why attack?" Hina replied. "If they're trapped, let's bottle them up. Within several passings we can starve them out."

"What! Even against the hairless ones I would not do such a thing. Have you no honor at all? Let's slaughter this rabble and go home."

Kalin turned in his saddle and looked at Kubar, who sat silently behind him. "Or does the most ancient and honored Kubar have another opinion?"

" 'Tis your host, not mine, therefore I merely observe and speak not."

"With such a lofty claim as yours, do you wish to announce first?" Kalin sneered.

"It is your army, your fight, and pray, your victory. Therefore I shall not partake from your honor but shall merely observe."

"Wise enough," Kalin said coldly, as his staff snickered at the apparent cowardice of an obvious liar. "Hina and Wirgth may stay with you, by the way."

The two turned and started to voice their protest.

"It is only as tradition demands," Kubar replied softly. "Hina as the last surviving youngest brother should not ride into the same conflict as the eldest lest the family line itself be threatened, and the Kaadu must not risk his life, either, less his advice be put to peril."

"For once we agree," Kalin said coldly, but there was a strange look in his eyes as he spoke, as if he had himself been pushed into a trap that he was only now becoming aware of. Kubar held Kalin's gaze for a moment and then bowed in a show of respect. The warrior turned his horse and galloped away, leaving the three to the rear as the army of nobles jostled for position in the advancing line.

"Classic formation," Yaroslav said, as if observing an academic problem on a sheet of parchment, rather than the maneuvering of thirteen thousand warriors.

"No logic to it, though."

"Ah, my Alexander, by your standard, not theirs. Remember, the nobility rides, as is their birthright, the non-noble marches. Titles and rank must be given and exchanged, that is the proper way. Thus the mounted unit deploys in forward line ahead of the infantry, highest rank closest to the west, lowest to the opposite side, and then the swordsmen behind."

"Foolishness. The same waste of cavalry that Darius used against me at Issus."

"Perhaps. But they can still fight. Look, that must be Kalin." He pointed to the far left of the enemy line where a single horseman had detached himself from the line and advanced across the open field that separated his serried ranks from Alexander and his troop of fifty horsemen that lined the low crested hill that stretched like a barrier in front of the river fork.

Like a rippling wave the line started to advance from the Gavarnian left, each horseman waiting until the one to his own left had started forward, thus not riding ahead of someone decreed to be higher in rank.

When he was less than half a bowshot away, Kalin reined in his mount and then stood in the stirrups.

"Human, I give you honor by addressing you. I am Kalin, eldest of Kalin's sons, called taug. I am the eldest of the eldest for eight generations, and the sword arm of my people. Thirty-eight of your kind have I hung inverted from my saddle. You are not worthy of my blade, but today I shall give you the taste of it. You without honor or love of brother, you whom they call Iskander, come forward and give unto me your history before you die."

Even before he had finished speaking, the next Gaf in line drew up by Kalin's side and started the same litany and then the next one and the next one so that soon the wild growling of hundreds of voices echoed against the hill as the noble Gafs advanced, shouting their family names with pride.

The sound gradually thundered away down the line while Alexander remained silent and motionless in the saddle.

An expectant hush settled across the field, for the Gafs now believed that histories would be given in turn, even if they were only hairless ones, and once given the Humans would advance in single line to meet them.

Alexander rode forward for a dozen paces and, reining in, he stood in his stirrups. He looked back to Yaroslav, wondering for a second if this were not some elaborate ruse to humiliate him, but the aged scholar simply beckoned for Alexander to go ahead, even as he started to back up in anticipation of the Gaf response.

Reaching down, he prepared himself, and when his gesture started to be obvious, an angry growling came up from the Gafs.

"I now piss," Alexander shouted, his voice echoing even above the angry roar. "Kalin, hear me, for I piss on the honor of your brothers, and may their bones be rubbed in it!"

He never had a chance to complete what he had started and Bucephalas snickered with surprise at the sudden soaking as Alexander hurriedly tried to finish, for an earsplitting roar came up from the Gafs. As if guided by a single hand, they drew scimitars and charged.

Reining his horse about, Alexander urged it into a semblance of a gallop and headed back for the crest of the hill. Already his cavalry troop streamed before him; panic-stricken, they looked over their shoulders. Parmenion hung to the back and came up by his side.

"Lucky we are in a trap," Alexander roared, "otherwise those bastards would keep on running."

Parmenion looked over his shoulder at the advancing host, for now their infantry, enraged at the ultimate insult, was surging forward, as well. From the look of blood lust in the advancing host of wolflike giants, Parmenion found himself half wishing there was an escape route after all.

The troop of cavalry crested the hill and surged between two fluttering pennants, with Alexander and Parmenion bringing up the rear. Pulling up the pennants, Alexander followed his horseman carefully in order to stay between the chalked lines that marked the safe path.

Coming over the top of the slope, he could see the raw slash of entrenchments that ran more than half a league to the north and ended in the far riverbank. Nearly every foot of the entrenched line was faced by sharpened sticks that would hit a Gaf at chest height. At regular intervals the barricade had small openings, like the one he was now making for, which were flanked by three-meter-high ramparts of earth. The roar behind him grew louder and suddenly burst over them as a wave of horsemen crested the hill.

A thundering shout came up from his own line, but he could sense that it was a cry of fear more than of rage.

Clearing the gate, Alexander turned and watched as a dozen men dragged an entanglement of sharpened logs out and quickly threw them across the open barrier.

He stood in the saddle then leaped up to the platform where Yaroslav and several regiment commanders stood, awestruck by the rampaging advance.

"Told you it would make them angry," Yaroslav shouted, his voice barely heard above the outraged roar that was sweeping down upon them.

Alexander was silent, intent on watching the opening stage of the battle. Parmenion was already galloping down to take

command of the center, prepared to rally the line if it should
start to give.

Alexander looked to the broad, open trench behind the
stockade and moat where his men stood three ranks deep and
then back over his shoulder where the reserve attack phalanxes
were drawn up, each in a column of eight. At least they were
still holding, even though most all of them were white with
fright.

"Here it comes," one of the commanders shouted.

The wave of horsemen, having crested the hill, were now
picking up speed as they advanced down the slope, with Kalin
at the head.

"There goes one!" And a shout of triumph went up. It was
as if the earth had opened up to swallow both Gaf and horse.
Suddenly another, and then another went down, falling into the
concealed traps. Yet still they came on, chanting their family
names. Kalin continued to push forward as if guided by fate,
heading straight for the battlement where Alexander now
stood.

He was oblivious to the disaster around him, as singly, and
then by the tens and the hundreds, the advancing wave of cavalry fell to the checkerboard pattern of traps, pitfalls, and hidden entanglements of rope.

Alexander watched as the enemy captain somehow found
his way onto the safe path through the line.

"I must meet him," Alexander shouted, pulling out his
sword as he prepared to leap off the battlement wall.

"Wait," Yaroslav shouted, even as he pointed at the enemy
captain whose horse had veered from the safe path.

Caught by a trip line, the horse spun over, hurling its burden
forward. Kalin hit the ground hard, right at the base of the
tower. From the way his head lolled to one side Alexander
knew there was no need to face him now.

"So brave, yet so foolish," he whispered sadly.

"Shall we go forward to see?" Hina asked quietly.

"There is no need," Kubar said sadly. "For we can sit here
and yet still know all, even when we see it not. It is far too obvious. And the words of that Human were but a confirmation
of their plan. How I wish I could have warned your brother
and have him believe me, for there is nothing worse, Hina,
than to see disaster coming yet be powerless to stop it."

Hina tried to suppress his desire to go forward in order to blot out the insult that had been given. It was obvious by now that a disaster of undreamed-of proportions was taking place on the other side of the hill.

It had been some time since the last of the infantry had swarmed up over the slope into the thundering roar of battle. Now there seemed to be a continual stream of riderless horses and wounded warriors staggering back down the slope. Something was obviously going wrong. There had yet to be a paean, the unified shout of victory at the striking down of a rival chieftain. Instead, there was just a wild and constant roaring that somehow held in its turmoil a note of growing fear.

"Clear the barrier," Alexander roared as he finished his gallop down the line to the position on the far left.

Turning in the saddle, he looked back at the serried ranks of the Ris, who held the position as the farthest most regiment on the left.

"Remember not to break ranks!" he shouted to them, his strong full voice carrying above the thundering roar of battle. "And follow me."

The last of the logs having been drawn back, he pushed his way forward, keeping pace with the skirmishers who poured out in front. They were on the extreme right of the enemy line, faced only by an open deployment of infantry.

For what must have been an hour or more, the Gafs had thundered against the entrenched position. Those who survived the deadfalls and entanglements had pushed against the fortified lines, all semblance of control forgotten. It had been a maddening assault that was terrifying in its intensity, but useless for any practical purpose.

As the casualties piled up, the enemy formations had contracted to the center. Alexander had been up and down the line, helping to plug the few breakthroughs that were made, and had finally worked down to the extreme left where his final punch was concealed.

As he cleared the gate he looked farther up the line and signaled for Parmenion to start his regiment out, as well. The plan was simple enough: punch through the crippled right, pivot, and roll up the enemy line. Clearing the last of the entanglements, his men shook out their line to form a phalanx a hundred men wide by ten deep. In a minute they were ready, and pivoting forty-five degrees to the right, they set out at a double pace.

The few weary Gafs that were before them broke at the sight of the inexorable wall bearing down from the north, and the sight of their enemies' backs heightened the spirit of the men. In staggered formation Parmenion's regiments fell in on the right flank of the expanding line, and half a dozen more regiments swung in as reserves.

Looking down the enemy line, Alexander could see that they were well extended beyond the Gafs' position. Holding his sword up high, he pointed for them to pivot another forty-five degrees. They were now a wave, rolling down the length of the enemy line, curling it up like rotten wood collapsing beneath a razor-sharp blade.

The roaring anger of the Gafs now gave way to fear. Here and there a lone warrior, beyond caring, held his ground and was washed over, taking a Human or two with him, but the once-proud host was pushed beyond all their ability to comprehend. Gafs were supposed to fight as by the law. Humans had always run like animals of prey, for that was what they were. But now the beast had insulted them, then fought in ways beyond all comprehension.

The men behind him knew, as well, that somehow this strange warrior who claimed to come out of the past from the legendary Earth had created a new thing. It was a moment beyond their wildest imaginings. And in it they took courage, and found themselves, after all, to be men.

The chant started from the back. A single voice calling out the name to the beat of their advance, their accent changing the word, but still recognizable.

"Iskander, Iskander."

It swept like thunder down the line, so that thousands of voices cried as one.

"Iskander, Iskander."

And counterpointed to it came the dismal shouts of the Gafs as they broke and ran in a stampeding herd toward the river, which was their only hope of escape, now that their flank was completely turned.

As they ran their weapons fell, wounded were abandoned, horses left to capture, and the Human wave bore down upon them.

"Iskander, Iskander."

Reining in his horse, Alexander let the ranks pass by. His practiced eye noticed that already the formations were breaking up, but that was beyond control. He had to remind himself that these were men under arms for less than a score of weeks, and not the thirty-year veterans he had led out of Bactria and the Indus.

"Iskander!"

The cry came from his left, and turning, he saw a Gaf driving a spear through the body of a man who stood by his side. Alexander instantly knew that the man had leaped in front of a spear that had been meant for him.

Spurring his horse around, he came up on the Gaf and with a single blow finished off the enemy who had let the Humans march over him in order to get at their commander.

After leaping from the horse, he came up to the dying man and knelt by his side.

"Iskander," the man whispered, "it is a good day to die, for I have seen them run." And then he was gone.

"A glorious day," Parmenion shouted, coming to his captain's side. "By Zeus, it's as glorious as Guagamela!"

Alexander came to his feet, that curious, distant look in his eyes.

"Yes," he whispered, "even I will say it was glorious." And unfastening his cloak, he laid it across the body of a beardless youth.

chapter ten

"Brother Kalin, go now to our brother Swanika. Brother Kalin, go now to our brother Uta. Oh, my three glorious brothers, wait for me in the hall of Binda beyond the shadows. Oh, my three brothers, wait for me, until at last I cross over the shadow, as well, where again we shall be joined as one. Together we shall be joined and face then the mystery of the Unseen Light, for together from the light we came, and at last, together, we shall return unto it."

Choked with grief, Hina turned away from the cracking, blazing pyre. The four keepers of the flame, dressed in red robes, bowed to the heir and took from his hand the flaming torch that had ignited the blaze.

Kalin's body alone had been given the honors that were proper. It had come the dimming before, under Human guard with a message from Alexander saying that he wished to return the body of an honorable warrior to his people. The courier had then inquired as to the proper custom of disposing with the other ten thousand corpses of the host.

Hina's guardsmen wanted to tear the Humans apart on the spot but he had prevented it, for to do so would be a loss of face. And he had allowed the envoys to depart.

He looked at the few survivors of the once-proud nobility. Nine out of ten had fallen on the field. As custom demanded, a place was still kept in the line for the slain during the mourning period; but where sixty family heads had once stood, only five were left. Half a dozen younger heirs stood in the place of older brothers or sires, but for the other families every male heir of the direct line had been lost, for the convention that applied to the heir of a taug was not practiced for lesser titles. Besides, they had only been hunting Humans, and as such, none had wished to miss the sport. If there was no heir to stand for a fallen nobleman, the vacant place was occupied instead by a sheathed sword set upon the ground.

Hina composed himself. First he nodded to Kubar, who stood silent by the flaming pyre, then he bowed to the assembly.

"Honored nobility, the mourning time for all of us shall continue as is our ancient custom, but still we must prepare."

"Prepare for what?" came a shouted taunt from the back. Hina recognized the graying speaker as Arn, the Wu-taug, or family leader of the Paka clan, whose family estates encompassed the region now occupied by the Humans.

Arn stepped from his assigned place in the assembly and walked to the foot of the dais that Hina occupied. That action alone, which implied a challenge, drew a murmured response from the nobles.

"There was no honor for those who fell at the forks," Arn roared. "There was no name giving with the Humans, and no blood debt paid by the victors so that families would be satisfied. What honor was there, answer me that?"

Hina was silent while a murmur of assent greeted Arn's words.

"They were slaughtered by Humans, by cattle that we hunted for sport and for meat at the time of holy days. The Humans did not fight, they denied all honor. And then to add insult, you suffered this envoy, the voice of this Iskander, to live even when he was in our camp, sword about his waist."

"Is it not said," Hina quickly replied, "that the head of an envoy, the voice of a family, is sacred when he comes to your fire? Even if he is a man, I will follow our law."

Arn ignored the quote from sacred tradition. "They have done something new, something strange beyond our understanding. They have taken the honor of war and torn it asunder like the peeling of the bark from a tree. There is no honor left. It is time for us to chant our names, and return back to that cursed hill of death—and there to end it, once and for all."

The survivors of Arn's clan gathered around him, shouting their approval at his suicide plan.

Hina extended his right arm, and even though the sun was dim, still the object in his hand glinted in the shadowy light.

"This is the circlet of the taug," Hina cried, and the warriors fell silent at the sight of the sacred object. Kalin had worn it into battle and it had been returned with his body.

"This crown," Hina shouted, "is the symbol of the taug. On your naming day you swore an oath of loyalty to it. Remember the oath is to the symbol of the taug, not simply to he who wears it. Two score lifetimes ago we came to this ring in the great migration, and then our brothers who crossed the stars disappeared in the Great War with the hairless ones. For two score lifetimes we of the hundred first families grew in numbers about the Iras Sea, and always did we honor the rule of the taug.

"It was the rule of the taug that set the rules of war, thus preventing us from destroying ourselves, and taught us that war is an honor of nobles who serve the one taug. The symbol of the taug is sacred and must be obeyed, else we shall disappear into the night of legend, where there is no light and none may see."

Arn knew that age-old tradition would win out over the

discontent of his followers. He bowed his head in acknowledgment.

"Of the hundred first families there were but sixty left before the Humans changed. Now there are but eleven. If we follow the desire of Arn and march back to fight yet again as we did, there shall be none.

"War was once for honor and the reputation that a Gavarnian took to his pyre. Now it shall be different, it shall be for the survival of us all."

"War and honor are one," Arn replied coldly.

"That must change." As Hina spoke he held the crown up so that all were silent. "And I am not capable of the task," he said evenly.

Arn looked into his rival's eyes, looking for the weakness, but there was none.

"How can that be?" another cried. "The clan Brug has been above all rivalries since the migration. Your clan alone is bred to be the final judge."

"I know nothing of the new warfare that has to be fought," Hina replied. "And we must learn this and acknowledge who shall teach us, if we are to survive."

There was an expectant feeling in the air. Hina stared at Arn and could see a sudden look of hope in the old warrior's eyes.

He turned away from Arn and walked over to Kubar's side. "At this moment I hold the power that you are all sworn to obey. I am the last heir of the Brugs, thus whatever I do shall be the law. Watch now what I do, and obey this decision."

Before anyone could voice a protest, he turned and placed the circlet of steel on Kubar's head.

"I acknowledge the truth of this one's words. Once before in legends past there came the first Taug, whose very name became the title for all since who have ruled. He was the first Taug, and from out of legend he has been sent again to save us as he did our ancestors. Kubar Taug is the one Taug of the Kolbard."

A scattering of cheers arose from the assembly, but most were silent. As oath-bound, they were sworn to serve, but they were not sworn to love what most of them believed was an impostor. And believe him as taug, or not, all knew how the first great Taug had ended the rule of the landholders and thus united his people ages ago. Such things were fine when they were legends—but legends were difficult to live with when come to life.

Kubar looked over to where Liala was standing in the corner of the courtyard. Their eyes locked for but a moment, and he could see that her look was simply not one of admiration. His wife, who had been a wife in name only, was dead now for four thousand years, but she was still a memory alive but a brief time ago. Liala's interest created a momentary confusion on his part and he turned away to look back at Hina. He could imagine that his friend was suffering from the same confusion, since by tradition, if the older brother was married, the wife of the brother remarried the younger one. But Hina had other things to concern him at the moment; they would talk of it later.

Hina was looking to Arn, awaiting a response. The clenched fist was finally raised, but the eyes glowed a defiance that was evident to all. Kubar noticed, as well. It was a look he had faced a thousand times, and it was a look that more than once had nearly led to his death.

"Close one for Kubar," Zergh said quietly, staring into the brandy that Aldin had poured for him.

"You had it plotted out well in your initial prognosis. And it followed remarkably close to what you had said," Aldin replied to his old friend.

"You are a Human; the inner weavings I can expect you to know here"—Zergh pointed to his head—"but in the heart, that is something only a Gavarnian can truly understand. They want to believe that he is Kubar, sent to redeem them. But have you ever admired someone who was too perfect? You want to be by their side, yet at the same time they are a living proof of your own limited abilities, and thus create pain."

Aldin, as usual, looked like he had taken one drink too many, and Zergh wrinkled his snout when Aldin pulled out a less-than-pleasant-smelling cigar and lit it up.

"You sure the room aboard this ship has been debugged?"

Aldin nodded in response and pointed to his own counter-snoop, which rested on the sideboard alongside the half-empty bottle of brandy. The stasis field, which blocked out all sound and was impervious, as well, to laser sensing, was already locked on, but it was possible nevertheless to have a microplant floating in the air and inserted into the room before the stasis had been turned on. Corbin was noted for such little forms of trust and hospitality.

"There's been an interesting ripple in the betting flow," Zergh began cautiously. "Why, just on that last fight alone, nearly eight percent of all the real estate in the Cloud changed hands. If that much went up on the first battle, I can imagine how it will run when we get down to the last encounter."

"Now's when the real action starts," Aldin replied, pulling on the cigar and watching the pattern of smoke as it hit the edge of the stasis and flattened out.

"After that last battle the free-float odds chart shifted three point seven three to one in favor of Alexander."

"I know that, Zergh. It's my business to compute it."

"But there's been no sign of Corbin's money coming into the game. Sure, he's placed the usual handful of bets, a world here, a multisystem business there, but no reports of anything major."

"What about Bukha?" Aldin replied.

"He's a Gavarnian of the old school. He'll bet some on Kubar out of loyalty but so far he's been slow to enter, as well. But come now, Aldin, what about Corbin? You know what kind of man he is. What's happening with him?"

Aldin turned his gaze to Zergh and fixed him with an even gaze.

"I'm in the employ of Corbin as his master vasba. I trust he'll abide by most of the rules. But beyond that . . ." He shrugged his shoulders.

"Aldin, I've watched you grow in your profession for thirty years, or have you forgotten you apprenticed under me? You're a damn good historian and gaming analyzer, but a piss-poor judge of Human qualities. Corbin must be up to something. This game's turning into the biggest gambling operation in history, and I've suspected from the day Corbin first mentioned this project that he had something up his sleeve."

"A Gavarnian trying to tell me about Human qualities?"

"I've tried to tell you more than once about Corbin, but oh, no, you wouldn't listen. So the son of a bitch robs you blind, and that cousin of his soaks every last ounce of alimony payments out of you. Then yesterday you told me that his royalty payment to you will be partnership in the Zswer Mining Consortium. Come on, Aldin, that's a sucker's deal if I ever heard one. He'll skin you clean out of that in six months' time and then where will you be—broke and on the beach with nothing to show for three years' worth of work."

Aldin was silent, ignoring his friend's words as if to listen would cause him to betray the trust of yet another friend.

As Aldin finished up his cigar, Zergh finally arose complaining that he needed a breath of fresh air. Aldin did not even acknowledge his departure as he prepared for yet another shot of brandy.

"The nobility is dead," Kubar said quietly, and looked across the table to his friend on the other side. "I'm not saying that because I relish the idea. Always remember, Hina, that I was of noble birth, as well—the same as you."

Hina leaned back in his chair and grimaced.

"You can say that around me," Hina replied, "because I know that. Remember, I saw them go down to their defeat. The nobility died in the field facing this Iskander. But don't ever say that around Arn, no matter what his oath of allegiance to the circle of steel." He pointed to the thin crown of metal on Kubar's brow.

Kubar barked softly and grimaced. "Remember, I had an entire world of nobility to deal with and to unite. And, oh, how they wanted me to end the slaughter—and to still keep their titles once the slaughter had ended. I think I know how to tread softly around Arn."

"Realize, though, that if Arn ever comes to truly believe that you are the Taug, then he'll have the lesson of our distant history, as well, to show what remained of the old orders once you had finished. Your contemporaries did not have such an advantage. Don't count on your legendary status too much with Arn. Remember, close exposure to a legend tends to lower him a notch or two into the realm of mere mortals."

Kubar chuckled at the thought. So he was a legend, placed even higher than Narg of the Shining Blade and this other Gavarnian of over three thousand years past who, according to Zergh, had discovered the means to jump from star to star.

"So why do you accept me?"

"Because I guess you could say I'm a romantic. It was assumed even when my brothers were still alive that Kalin would be always the one to rule. He was first from the womb of my mother, and thus is was his right to start with. It was I of the four who was the one allowed to read and to dream of distant glories."

Kubar thought it a curious throwback, that reading should one day be viewed with disdain, a compromise with the strength of a warrior's word.

"I dreamed that we were not the only Gavarnians to survive the Great Wars with the Humans and the other races. And your presence here, and your story of this Zergh who flies through space and time like a servant of the Unseen Light, have proven that, at least. I dreamed of greater things and knew in my heart when I met you that your coming was the sign I had hoped for."

Kubar could only smile at the romance in his friend's mind. Hina reminded him of those first comrades who had rallied to his banner when his revolution was young. They had all been so young, so full of dreams for tomorrow. And all of them, except for old Paga, who sat sleepily in the corner of the room, were now dead. He muttered a silent prayer for his friend that the dreamer of fate would not dream of darkness for this companion.

"Tomorrow we shall start," Kubar said evenly, drawing the conversation back to the practical concerns that faced them.

"If this Iskander is any type of commander, he will not let the initiative for this campaign pass into our hands. The stone walls of this city and the fact that we face the sea and can thus gain supplies from ships most likely will prevent him from launching a direct attack and siege."

"Then where do you think it shall come?" Wirgth finally interjected, entering the conversation that until now he had been observing silently.

"An army that big devours supplies like the bottomless stomach of the giant *Gress*. His men must spread out and forage the countryside."

"Why not come straight on to the city and finish it?"

"Ah, I must assume that this Iskander is good. Never underestimate your foe, even if he is a hairless one. Always believe that he knows everything you think and is smarter than you in all things."

"Unlike my brother," Hina said darkly.

"Your brother fought in the way he thought all wars should be fought," Wirgth replied diplomatically.

"As I was saying," Kubar continued, "Iskander must assume

that we shall not make the same mistake again. If we pull back to the city, the walls of stone will require a long siege. With the harbor behind us supplies are no problem, for as yet the hairless ones have no ships. No, I think he is too shrewd to attack us in that way. Besides, a siege requires engines and supplies of metal for equipment and weapons. Most of those men we faced were still carrying wooden-tipped spears. You can't take a stone-walled city with that. Even with the supplies they looted from our army, they still do not have enough to mount a proper siege. And, besides, it will take several score of dimmings to rework the weapons they've taken to fit Human hands."

"Then he must gain three things," Hina ventured, "before he can make his killing blow. While we need but one to win."

"Go on."

"Supplies for his men, ships to close off our harbor, and metal to equip both men and ships."

Kubar barked a muffled tone of satisfaction. With the tip of his finger he pointed to a black oval on the map before them, two hundred versts north of the city.

"The wrecked ore carrier that rests thirty versts to the northeast of Mount Lequa, that is where he shall drive for. That destroyed vessel of ancient spacefaring Humans has enough iron ore to supply an army a hundred times the size of Iskander's. Your own people have been mining it since you first settled here. Where it rests on a bay of the Iras Sea, it is just south of the hill country that the Humans can withdraw back into if they are attacked and defeated. Yes, that is where I think he will come. But do not neglect the southward approaches, either, for there are some of our richest farmland. Now that they have horses, they are sure to raid in that direction to take supplies, as well."

"You mentioned the three things for the Humans," Wirgth interrupted, "but what is it that we need?"

"We need to relearn the art of war," Hina replied coldly.

"Never call it an art," Kubar responded as if he were suddenly too tired to continue. "Rather it is learning how to butcher on a massive scale.

"Your ancestors on this ring were wiser than all but a few realized. They knew that if ever massed warfare was allowed to take hold with their descendants who were marooned here, the slaughter would be catastrophic. So they changed the equation, made combat a highly ritualized thing that would kill but a handful before it got out of control. Now you all will have to relearn the older, far more efficient way, and that is why I am here."

Kubar sat back for a moment, the thought suddenly taking form, a thought that he had been far too busy to consider in a serious way. It was this Iskander who had united the Humans and taught them the new way, which in fact was as old as their history. And he had been brought across time to do yet the same service, if service it could be called, to his people, as well. Why? For what reason was this bloodshed escalated? Granted, in the end it would settle the difference between Human and Gavarnian on the Kolbard once and for all, and across ten thousand dimmings, more lives might be saved than lost. But still there was the nagging question of why. Such endless rounds of slaughter, and for a moment his memory drifted back to Cliarn and the fields of his last battle—that last battle that finally united Lhaza. Cliarn.

"So how shall we do it, then?" Hina asked, interrupting Kubar's line of thought.

"We shall raise up the landless laborers and those of the city."

"They'll not fight as a noble would," Hina replied evenly. "They serve as border warrens, but you saw how useless they were in that fight. Most of them broke once Iskander's Humans came out of their fortress and charged."

"Because, in the end, they had no real reason to fight. They are landless peasants, without title or respect. Really, Hina, there is an entire continent we can give them out there as reward for fighting."

Hina was silent, understanding the implication, knowing it was needed, but still frightened by the revolutionary impact of what Kubar was leading to.

"As of tomorrow there shall be no more landless class. Each shall be given his estate to work by the sweat of his own labor. They will fight for such tangible reward."

"But what about the nobles?" Hina replied coldly, and in his words even Kubar could sense a tone of identification with his own class.

"If they do not agree, then they doom themselves anyhow, for without an army to face the hairless ones, Iskander shall win and there will be no estates, period. Besides, there will be rewards for the nobility, new titles to have, decorations for valor to wear, and pageantry to lull them. The first draft of levies will come from those family estates that were wiped out in the battle of the forks, or from lands already overrun by the Humans. We'll leave the others working, for now, to bring in what harvest they can before the Humans arrive.

"With the passing of this dimming, we shall start. The training will be essential, for the troops must learn to fight as a unit—their bodies subject to the will of but one mind."

Again there was the old paradox. Here he wished to create a society where each was equal to another, yet in order to achieve that he would first free the landless and then immediately set out to bring them under his unshakable will, so that they would finally be willing to die at his command.

"Arn will try to block you," Wirgth said. "He's too shrewd to fall for a mere bauble or decoration to ease him while you dismantle an entire social order."

"I assume he will. But you shall be surprised how quickly some of the other nobility will be willing to rush to their death in order to earn a hunk of metal hung on a useless ribbon. As for Arn, I shall let him assume that once the war is won he'll be able to eliminate me and reestablish the status quo. I need him and his nobility too much right now, to train and lead the new levies of troops."

With a yawn Kubar stood up from the table and stretched. "This world without a night is too confusing to me. How I miss the twilight that filled the sky with a lavender glow."

To Hina, who had never seen such a thing as night or the stars, Kubar's words sounded as if they came from the world of myth. And then he reminded himself yet again that he had just given his crown to a myth. A myth who while saving them would most likely destroy them, as well.

With a polite nod to Hina and Wirgth, Kubar started to the door, and Paga, roused from his nap, came in behind his master.

Tomorrow they would start in earnest. There were a few other things that he planned to start, as well, but best not to overwhelm Hina with those little experiments that he had in mind. He had already placed a request for the lightest sheets of fabric to be found, along with enough copper to nearly strip the kingdom of every pot and pan. But that would be his little secret, for now.

It would be an interesting diversion from his other tasks.

Long before, he had found that working with such things cleared his mind so that he could better deal with the far more important problems. And problems there would be. Iskander, of course, came above all else. He would have to fathom how this Human made war and then find a way to counter it. There would be the training of the levies, the preparations to defend the ore carrier, and of course Arn. But for the moment his thoughts were centered on Zergh. He knew that to waste time contemplating the one who brought him here was foolish. But the question of "why" would not leave him, even as he tried to settle into a restless sleep.

"Not a bad arrangement, so far," Corbin said lazily, as he examined the contents in his goblet. Leaning back, he drained off the rest of the brandy and smiled at his companion.

"Sure you wouldn't care for a drink?" Corbin asked.

"No, I'd rather keep my head clear."

"Ah, Tia, my shrewd little mistress, you never did care for drinking."

"Just because, from no choice of mine, Aldin is my uncle does not mean that I inherited his cruder vices. Besides, he's my uncle from my mother's side of the family, which makes you my third cousin. If I've inherited any vices, my dear, it comes from our mutual blood, not his."

Corbin threw back his head and laughed. "You inherited your mother's sharp tongue, at least. But let's not quarrel about such trivial things. How goes your work with Aldin?"

"He's fat, he never washes, he's of the lower classes and acts it. Why you respect him as a vasba is beyond me."

"I never said I respected him. I use him because he is useful, that is all."

"So why have you forced me to serve this man you use?"

"Because you had no choice. With your mother gone, you are family obligated to obey my wishes. It's that simple. Anyhow, I did have a significant investment with the Alexander game and I wanted someone close to me to observe him, with my interests in mind. Your report was quite concise and informative."

Tia was silent, waiting for the real reason for this required visit to come out.

Corbin smiled in what was a caricature of loving indulgence. "Knowing the arts of the vasba can't hurt you. In fact, it can help make you wealthy as you get older."

"Since I'll never inherit the family control, I'll need that knowledge, won't I, my dear, or have you finally decided to declare which of the mistresses you'll make your legitimate wife?" As she spoke she drew closer, running her hands up and down his bloated body.

"Now, I never said that you were not the one in my will," he said laughingly, while returning her caresses in a more direct manner.

"Don't patronize me," Tia responded, suddenly pulling back.

"Ah, Tia, my darling, you'll be well taken care of, just trust me. Anyhow, I think there is a little something you might be interested in. You have shown a decent knowledge of how the games work, as well as a certain desire to give me any pleasure I desire."

She leaned forward again, ready to hear what he was going to offer. From the beginning she had suspected there was something more going on behind the scenes with Corbin, otherwise his placement of her with the recovery team for Alexander would have made little sense.

"Ah, now my greedy young child is all ears for what Uncle Corby has to say."

"Just get to the point, and don't call yourself Uncle Corby. It makes my being your mistress sound a little too perverted."

Corbin extended his hands in an innocent gesture, as if he had been wrongly accused. "Well, let's get down to business then, shall we? First off, I needed somebody in the family to learn a little more about this vasba business. I see a big future in it now that we've discovered a way to harvest old Earth for interesting arrangements. Yes indeed, there are endless possibilities for gaming in our future."

"But you have Aldin to run that angle."

"Your uncle or not, he is getting old."

"What you really mean to say is you want to cut him out of his ten-percent commission and keep it in the family."

"Did I say that?"

Tia could only smile knowingly. It could be a lucrative agreement. She knew Corbin had been cheating Aldin on his royalty statements for some time. With the commissions from the Alexandrian game, Aldin could find himself to be a very rich man. So that was Corbin's offer, for a start, at least.

"So I've learned something about being a vasba. It's a dirty lower-class job; what else do you have in mind?" Tia said, smiling. "Come on, I know you well enough to realize there's something else."

"All right then, girl. I need you to make a special arrangement."

"Go on."

"First off, I want you to report on anything suspicious about Aldin."

"I assumed I was to do that from the start. And I daresay that he assumes that I am to do that, as well."

"Things are going to get a little tense very shortly," Corbin said, leaning over to fix Tia with his gaze. "I need your help, and the reward will match the help."

"Such as naming me your legitimate spouse?"

"Don't push your luck," Corbin replied coldly. Then leaning back, he smiled again. "But anything is possible, once this is over with.

"You see, betting is running strongly on xenophobic lines. Now, the Gafs have some interesting worlds, to be sure, but it's the possessions of old Sigma Azermatti that really interest me. His systems sit astride the jump point back to the home galaxy. I think this little time device can have some interesting implications for going back to trade markets not yet exploited—and Sigma would get the duties. Also, the worlds he now owns are rich in and of themselves."

"And besides," Tia interrupted, "he vexes you simply because of the respect all the other Kohs have for him. Along with the fact that he's the wealthiest Human Koh in the Cloud."

Corbin grunted angrily. She was right, he had always hated Sigma for the air of disdain that he had shown for the "Gablona upstarts," as he termed them when Corbin was not within hearing distance.

"I plan to wipe him out in this game."

"His estates are four times the size of yours," Tia responded, "you can't match him on bets. Secondly, he's betting on Alexander, the same way you should be. After all, the trends indicate a continued win on his part."

"Oh, really," Corbin said knowingly.

"All right, what's the scam, dearest?"

"Your overall analysis report was perhaps far better than you thought, and, if anything, confirmed what I believed would happen all along."

"And that is?"

"We're betting on two societies in conflict, but we are betting on two personalities, as well. But there is a significant ingredient to victory for either side that's being overlooked."

Corbin leaned back, beckoned for Tia to fill his brandy snifter, and then continued.

"You see, for Alexander to succeed it will be through the strength of his own character that will mold a shapeless society together, giving it order. For Kubar, however, victory comes from merely transforming a complex social system already in place. Up until the first battle, I had my suspicions as to the overall outcome, since Kubar had to deal with an entrenched system of nobility. Oh, they might admire him as a legend, but they damn sure weren't enthused about having that legend bearing witness against them. But conveniently for me, that social system died in the first battle. Kubar has an open ticket now to transform the Gafs into the only type of army that could beat Alexander—an army modified to defeat phalanx tactics. Once he's trained them, it doesn't matter if he lives or dies."

"But if Kubar should die," Tia replied, "Alexander's superior generalship would win the day."

"Oh, of course, if Kubar should die first."

She looked at him suspiciously. "What are you driving at, Corbin?"

"Come now, Tia, do I need to spell it out?"

"I suspect that there's a deal in this for me. There damn well better be. But before I get dragged in, I want to hear it straight from you."

Corbin leaned forward and suddenly his voice was full of menace. "There'll only be two other people besides myself who know about this. Let me tell you the negative first, if you should decide not to cooperate."

"I'm dead, just like the plastacement contractor."

"His little accident, at least, was quick and relatively painless. There could be far worse things."

Tia reached over and picked up Corbin's hand and rested it lightly upon her breast. "You were the first to touch this, Corbin. When I met you that's all I had to offer. That's more than can be said for that cheap slut Regina, whom you seem to be favoring more than me."

"She's got bigger teats than yours, Tia, but not the brains. That's why I'm talking to you and not her."

She certainly did, Tia realized, and the dirty old lecher in front of her, like most men, considered an extra ten pounds of swollen glands to be far more significant than a woman's brain. Damn, she knew he'd wind up cutting her out in the end for that swollen, shrill-voiced, vacuum-headed cow. But maybe this scam was the way out she had been looking for ever since she allowed herself to be dragged into Corbin's net. Corbin was a path to prominence in her family. In fact, he was the only path since he did have a propensity to squash any of his relatives who had pretensions of grandeur, especially if the relative was a woman.

"I know what you'd do to me if I failed you," Tia replied, putting on her best seductive smile. "So go ahead and tell me, dearest."

"Cut the 'dearest' crap. This is business, plain and simple, and you fit the bill. You're Aldin's niece, even if it is only through marriage. The old dodderer has a liking for you and always has. At the same time, you're part of my family, so there's a self-interest there. And finally, I sleep with you."

Corbin leaned back and smiled his cold, sinister grin. "I plan to murder Alexander and thus throw the game."

Her expression did not change or flicker, and she returned the smile that he gave her.

Good, he thought quietly. No moral outcry, no whining, because if she had, her next drink might have been her last.

"How long have you been planning this?" Tia replied evenly.

"For over two years, right after my research people started to show some promising results with the time travel studies and I realized the game might be feasible.

"I came across an obscure paper, printed by some fool academician back at one of the universities that I endowed for public relations purposes. It was a study of the Kolbard and an examination of some of the cultures. The old fool who wrote it made some good points, and he created a scenario outlining how the Humans we finally chose for the fight could win or lose. The model fit Alexander and Kubar, since he pointed out that both societies needed some sort of charismatic leader to transform them.

"It was the classic Great Man Theory all over again. But once transformed, the Gafs would most likely win, since they would still have a better organizational structure. In fact, the historian actually cited Alexander, comparing his empire built around one man to that of the Romans, which was more of a societal team effort. I must say, that paper helped to center my attention on Alexander. That paper was the inspiration, Alexander and Kubar are merely interesting window dressing to draw the suckers into the biggest scam ever played. The author was quite the intellectual; I could have used him, but the stupid alky disappeared right after the paper was published."

"So in spite of the current Gaf setbacks," Tia said hurriedly, "you still plan to kill Alexander?"

"The setbacks make it all the better, and again, it's just part of the scam. As I said, I plan to kill Alexander after secretly wagering a fair portion of my fortune in favor of the Gafs. I've held off till now since the odds were fairly even, as I anticipated they'd be. But I also anticipated that Alexander would have little difficulty organizing, while Kubar would take some time. Thus Alexander would win the opening rounds. Those opening victories would drive the odds up maybe as high as five or six to one in his favor. Now that that is happening, I plan to start to funnel my money secretly into the Gaf side. Once the market has been driven as high as it can go in Alexander's favor, I'll trigger his death. The Human side collapses, since as was pointed out in that paper, the Human society will be built around just one man."

"The same as in the Wars of the Succession," Tia replied. "Once Alexander died, his empire disintegrated into civil war. The dream of unification was lost."

"Ah, Tia, you have been studying then, as well."

She smiled quickly and shrugged her shoulders.

"With Alexander dead, the Humans lose and I clean up."

"Against whom," Tia replied, "and how are you planning to filter this money in without anyone knowing? After all, if word got out that you were betting against Alexander, it would blow everything wide open. All the Kohs would be hot on your trail to find out why. When Alexander gets it, even if they couldn't prove it, the bloody finger would still be pointed in your direction."

"Ah, Tia, Tia, so now we come to the point, and that's why I'm bringing you in. For the last two years I've been quietly creating a large number of corporate fronts, creating holding companies that hold other companies in turn. Hell, that plastacement contractor still holds controlling interest in nearly a hundred worlds through a dozen companies held by one of my dead bodyguards. It's all been cleverly arranged, my dear, all of it. But I cannot act in this little drama directly. The risk is too great. My every move is being monitored by the other Kohs. As of yesterday, nearly ten and a half percent of the total wealth of the Clouds was tied into the game. With that much money floating around you can be sure that large amounts are being spent just trying to figure out who is doing what, looking for the inside angle on the game.

"Therefore I have to remain above all suspicion, and assume that everything I do is monitored. I want you to handle the portfolio and to filter the money in. It will merely mean that you'll act as the middleman, so to speak, dumping the corporations into the betting when I give you the signal. No one will ever meet you, it will all be handled through your contact to the controllers of a particular firm. Code systems have been set up, and it will appear as if a consortium of minor Kohs have learned of the game and are stacking their life savings on the action.

"The bets will be placed anonymously through you, and they all must be specifically targeted against the holdings of Sigma Azermatti."

"When you win, though, it will finally come out that the Gablona Family is holding the Sigma fortune," Tia replied.

"Oh, eventually, but by then any attempt at tracing the death of Alexander will be impossible. In fact, I want Sigma to know, two or three years down the road, that I, Corbin Gablona, finally cleaned him out."

"Of course, my dear," Tia said smoothly, "I'll do it. I'll do anything for you. But this will take a lot of effort on my part, and there is some small risk involved."

"Ah, yes, the payoff," Corbin replied smoothly. "How does one percent of all winnings sound to you? One percent can make you a minor Koh in your own right."

One percent! The cheap bastard. That simple offer in and of itself showed what he felt for her. So, Regina or that twosome of Mpnoa and Bithila, who would work on Corbin together at the same time, would be the ones that wound up with the bigger bucks. She fought to control her anger. She could see, as well, that making her his mistress had nothing to do with desire or love. She had often wondered about that, since she had always felt so insecure about her own appearance. The other women around Corbin were simply voluptuous while she was all skinny angles with a bobbed, upturned nose and hair that could never get past shoulder length without looking like a home for various vermin. So that was it all along—he had picked her for her superior intellect, the knowledge taught to her by Aldin, and her innate ability to help pull off such a scam.

He was certainly a cheap bastard, but then she had known it from the very start.

"It's agreed then," she replied smoothly.

"Ah, I knew you would see the potential in this for you," Corbin replied, smiling.

"But one question. How do you plan to kill Alexander? That playing field down there is crammed with surveillance equipment. The Xsarn's done a masterful job at insuring that everything is legal and that all contact is impossible. Even our own trip to Earth and every contact with Alexander were scanned to make sure no slowacting agents might be introduced by either side. So how do you plan to do it?"

"As I said earlier," Corbin replied, "only two people will know about the plan. But neither of them will know more than they need to. Don't ever ask about Alexander again."

She backed off, sensing the threat in his words.

Smiling again, Corbin turned and pulled a bottle of champagne from the sideboard, leaving the alternate bottle, the one he would have used had Tia balked, in its place.

After the bottle was uncorked, the two smiled at each other as the drinks were poured. So now she knew and apparently had taken the bait. This woman was a good choice, as he had sensed years before when she was still but a young girl first flowering into adolescence.

She'll do well, and he almost regretted what he'd have to arrange once this was over. Give women too much power, he thought, and they start to run amok. That's why in the end he preferred the dumb ones who knew their place. It'd be a shame to use the other bottle of liquor on her the way he already planned for the other participant. He smiled again at Tia, wondering what she was thinking.

Looking over her glass, Tia returned his loving gaze.

chapter eleven

"By all the gods," Parmenion roared, "Stand on that flank or I'll kill you myself!"

The wavering men looked in his direction and then nervously back to the approaching line of Gaf infantry.

"You've got to hold!"

They were really outnumbered this time, and the enemy was pouring around the flanks, ready to threaten the small fortified camp that guarded their toehold on the edge of the Anvil.

At Alexander's orders, Parmenion had led two thousand men ahead of the advancing column with orders to capture the strange mountain of iron by surprise before the Gafs could reinforce it. Half of them were all of Alexander's mounted strength, the other thousand being the elite Ris and Kievant phalanx that had ridden across the Anvil double-mounted with the horsemen. But even as he reached the edge of the Anvil, he knew the hope of surprise was lost. Gafs by the thousands poured out of the fortress to meet them. Somehow the enemy must have second-guessed their intentions and reinforced the position that had been reported near empty only half a dozen dimmings before.

Looking back behind him, the Anvil glimmered even in the dimming. He could see the dozen columns that marked Alexander's approach. Distances were hard to measure though, and he guessed that at best they were more than a half day off, but one column on the left did appear to be closer. He could always break off and withdraw back across the Anvil, but to do so would mean the loss of the one prize he had managed to take.

The Anvil—to the men in his command it was nothing out

of the ordinary. Merely a desert of bare windswept metal that stretched for thirty leagues. But in his mind it was still a fear-shrouded dream. He had heard often enough that this was a world created by the godlike First Travelers. But gods made worlds from dirt and stone, not metal that could barely be scratched and was flat as a griddle for as far as the eye could see.

They had crossed it in two dimmings, riding hard, their march guided by the lump of darkness that as they approached took shape into a collapsed structure that was larger than many a town he had seen back on Earth.

Parmenion was still amazed over the fact that he was looking at a ship that once flew through the air like a winged chariot, bearing more iron ore than all the mines of Anatolia could have produced if worked for a hundred years. Yaroslav said that it was an ore ship, sent to bring desperately needed raw material for the first crew of Humans who had landed on the Kolbard. Yaroslav said that such vessels had been ships that sailed without men aboard. The vessel would land on a world, carve out the side of an ore-bearing mountain, then fly away to bring the ore to a world that needed it. But the ship had somehow crashed, perhaps destroyed by one of the sky-chariots of the Gaf demigods. Such knowledge made Parmenion feel as if he were living in a drunken nightmare where all truth had been turned upside down. Alexander could smile his curious smile when confronted with the new and strange, but not he. It damn near was driving him mad.

The iron city was less than a league away from the position they now occupied with their backs to the Anvil. Parmenion had been amazed to see that a town was built into the ruins of the ship, complete with watchtowers shaped from ore rock, and ringed with walls of that same metal. Why, there was enough metal there—

"They're charging!"

The Gafs had learned quickly! The heavy line of infantry was advancing on the run. His infantrymen, who had ridden across the Anvil clutching the backs of their mounted comrades, lowered their spears.

"Right flank horse hold. And don't let them get around you!" Parmenion roared to a messenger who wore the headband of the Avar horsemen.

The rider saluted and galloped to his young commander

Sashi, a youth barely able to shave, but who had demonstrated such skill with the Gavarnian horses that he quickly earned the respect of all who aspired to Alexander's mounted arm.

Knowing that the only way to win in this form of combat was to attack, Parmenion drew his sword and cantered up to the left side of the Ris and Kievant phalanxes.

"Front spears down, and watch your spacing," he roared.

As if guided by a single hand the weapons dropped, the spears in the second, third, and fourth ranks coming forward past the first line, so that the approaching enemy would have to face a wall of sharpened death.

Gaps were opened at regular intervals so that the slingers could pull out from the front and reach the protection of the rear, where they would continue to hurl their missiles of death over the heads of the line.

The Gafs were surging forward, and in imitation of Parmenion's own formation, the Gavarnian cavalry was posted to either flank, rather than follow their older concept of lining up in front of the infantry.

"Macedons! Forward!"

The two phalanxes, a hundred and twenty men wide by eight deep, stepped forward while the cavalry extended its screen to either side.

Parmenion let the men advance while dropping to the rear, where he could better survey the action as it unfolded.

This endless probing and skirmishing had been going on since yesterday's dimming without any chance for rest. A dozen times the Gafs had swarmed out from the fortress to threaten them. The first eight times they had broken and retreated before contact could be established.

The last three times, however, they had ventured closer, and along a number of points had actually come into contact. The vast majority of them were still nothing more than a formationless mob of five or six thousand warriors. But Parmenion feared that they were about to introduce something new.

An hour ago, a new unit of Gafs had come up from the southward road, which led back to their capital. And this formation marched and had deployed in near-perfect imitation of a phalanx. The only thing different was they were armed with swords.

The marching cadence of the Gaf formation started to falter as the Ris and Kievants raised their battle chant.

"Iskander, Iskander."

Damn them, Parmenion cursed, they were supposed to stay silent so that the signal horn could be clearly heard.

"Parmenion!"

He turned to see a squadron of mounted men galloping in from the edge of the Anvil. Several of them were pointing off to the south, and rising up in his stirrups, he saw a shimmering dark column coming out of the heat. It had to be Alexander, leading a flanking march, but they were still a fair distance away. The couriers drew closer.

"Alexander commands that you fall back, if need be."

"And abandon that?" Parmenion roared, and he pointed down toward the edge of a small lagoon at his back.

"What in the name of the world-makers is that?" the courier cried, goggle-eyed at the strange device.

"It's a Gaf ship," Parmenion shouted, "beached here for repairs. We took it before they could burn it."

"A ship? What is that?"

Parmenion ignored the boy and turned his attention back to the fight.

The discipline of his regiment was holding, they were continuing down the slope toward the Gafs, who had almost come to a stop. Good, maybe they'd pull back again without a fight and then he could detach his cavalry to cut up the flanking forces.

"Damn them, here they come!"

With a wild roar the Gaf line suddenly surged forward, losing all cohesion and semblance of formation.

Urging his horse forward, Parmenion came up to the rear of his line, which was starting to waver. "Hold them, hold them, my men!"

With a deafening shout the Gafs rushed forward, waving their scimitars, and the impact came as several thousand Humans and Gavarnians smashed together in a wild cacophony of roars, curses, and dying screams.

The weight of the impact shuddered the Human line, pushing it back half a dozen meters as the alien warriors pushed against the men, who seemed almost childlike when fighting against their roaring opponents.

"Rear rank spears," Parmenion cried to his signaler.

The horn sounded high and clear, three piercing notes, and the last four ranks of spearmen lowered their weapons, leaning

into them as if advancing into a storm. More than one Ris or
Kievant was speared in the back by his own men, but most of
the men were able to guide their ungainly weapons through
gaps in the line where their sharpened steel points, fashioned
from trophies from the Battle of the Forks, pierced through the
leather armor of their opponents.

The line of impact shifted and pushed as some Gafs gave
ground against the impenetrable wall, while others, caught up
in the old way of battle, leaped into the fray regardless of orders.

To either flank of the main fight the Gafs held back, kept at
bay by the cavalry forces that stood like anchors to either side
of the fight. But this anchor was weakening, as well, as squadron after squadron was detailed off to screen the enemy flanking forces that spread out wide to either side.

Parmenion could only hope that Alexander was pushing his
forces forward as rapidly as possible. The Gafs were learning
far too fast the art of engaging a phalanx.

"Call them off."

"But my lord Taug," Hina ventured, "their line is starting to
buckle! We just might destroy them."

"That's not what we're fighting for today," Kubar said quietly. "Remember, never let the scent of victory blind you to the
possible stench of defeat.

"Look over there." He pointed toward the advancing block
of men coming in off the Anvil.

"The Humans are still several versts away. By the time they
come up . . ."

Kubar looked at Hina and the half-dozen staff members by
his side. "This battle is a lesson to us, we watch and learn.
Twelve times we've attacked them, each time to watch how
they deploy, to see how they use their weapons and combine
their men on foot with those on horse. It is a lesson to understand the mind of their commander."

He stopped for a moment and looked again at the distant
man on horseback who commanded from the back of the Human wall formation. Was that the one called Iskander?

"That is why we have fought today. And be sure you remember what you've seen."

"But the ship on the beach?" Wirgth said. "I'm not at all
comfortable with their possession of that."

"It is an unfortunate loss," Kubar replied. "In battle one must weigh the gain against the price. We could retake it, but in doing so, that column,"—he pointed toward the advancing Humans—"could close our retreat back to the city. We have but one group of warriors trained to fight as a unit, that group down there, which is earning its first blood. Those warriors are to return to our capital to train the others.

"The recapture of the ship is not worth the loss of their experience. Now pull them out before it is too late."

Seconds later, half a dozen kettle drums started a rolling beat, to be picked up by the signal drums of the unit commander.

Still not disciplined, Kubar thought, watching as a significant portion of his warriors still surged forward, even as the rest of their unit started to pull away.

"Senseless," he mumbled, "what senseless waste." The Humans gradually swarmed over those who continued to fight, while the rest of the formation backed away and then, turning, started to run back up the hill.

"This is the hard part," Kubar said, as if lecturing a group of students in the classroom. "Going into a fight is always easy. It is the backing away that requires real discipline, elsewise your warriors might break and just keep on running."

"A true Gavarnian never runs from a Human," Arn said coldly from the rear of the assembled staff officers.

Kubar was tempted to retort with an inquiry as to how he had survived the debacle at the Forks, but let it pass.

"A true warrior," Paga said softly, looking straight at Arn, "learns to defeat his opponent in the end. All that happens before is without meaning."

Arn was silent, knowing that those around him were completely under the influence of this newfound leader who fought without honor.

The flanking units started to pull back, as well. As planned, the cavalry that Kubar had held in reserve swung out from their concealed positions behind the hill to screen the retreat of the infantry. That had been a hard lesson for Kubar to explain—the need to keep cavalry in reserve, in order to exploit a victory or cover a retreat. To the Gavarnian warriors, there was no logic in not throwing all your strength in at once. But he could see those around him nodding and speaking to themselves as the cavalry did its job of stopping the Human advance. Good, this little affair was having precisely the effect he wanted. Without committing to a major battle, his future officers were learning in the field the truth of his lessons. Now it was time to follow up.

"Good, we've learned much today," Kubar said quietly. "Now what have we seen?"

"They never fight as individuals but always as a group," Wirgth replied. "It makes good sense. One to one we could kill them out of hand, but a wall of spears, that is hard to argue with."

"Very good," Kubar replied. Realizing that there was little time left before the relief column arrived, he decided to convey what he had seen himself, rather than let his pupils say it for him, and thus feel that they had discovered it on their own.

"Note the following and remember it. The cavalry stays on the wings, covering the flanks of their formation. They wait until their opponent wavers and then send it in for the killing blow. Your cavalry *reserve* behind the center can be shifted to either wing, attack up the middle, or can cover your retreat as you've just seen. They would have done that now to us, if their commander had not been so anxious to protect the prize they've captured.

"I can see now that swords against lowered spears are useless. The weight of our attack almost took them, but the length of their spears prevented that."

"Therefore we should use the same weapons?" Hina ventured.

"I don't think so. It takes time and training to get a large group of warriors to fight in formations like that. One or two warriors losing their head in the heat of battle could cause a line to crack wide open. They only barely hold themselves, we could see that. The blood of our warriors is not cool enough yet to fight so coldly. We must figure out how to break those formations before we hit them."

"Archers?" Hina asked.

"That was a sport of nobles; it takes a long time to train one archer and even longer to make the right bows. We have not the time nor the skilled warriors in numbers. But those we do have shall be used accordingly. At least that will be a sport our noble warriors will enjoy."

Arn was silent.

"Hina, it's best that you rejoin those men now. I need to

think on how to break the Humans' formations; I'll send my ideas to you by the messenger birds that I brought with me."

The staff looked at Kubar incredulously.

"But you're coming back with us to the city, are you not?" Wirgth cried.

Kubar barked softly, as if they were joking. "This mountain of ore behind us must be held. If the Humans take it, then they have another ingredient toward their victory. It will take time yet to train our army back at the capital. If this citadel falls, then they can form a living chain to haul all the ore they need back up into the hills where it can be forged into stronger weapons. No, I shall stay here."

"No, Kubar," Hina replied anxiously, "I'll stay here and you go back."

"Listen to me. This is where the battle will be fought for at least the next thirty dimmings. Here I can observe how they fight and plan for the time when our forces march out to meet them. Besides, you here might accept me as taug, but it is you, Hina, who in the eyes of many are still the true taug, no matter who wears the crown. You alone have the force to counteract those who would oppose our plans. Now go."

As he spoke the last words, Kubar looked significantly at Arn, who returned his gaze with defiance.

The others hesitated for a moment, then bowing, they turned to leave.

"Oh, by the way," Kubar said as an afterthought, "I could use one or two of noble birth to aid me. Would you be interested, Arn?"

The warrior turned and grimaced at him. He knew he was trapped, for to refuse would be a mark of cowardice. Silently he turned away and, mounting his horse, he started back alone to the citadel.

"And, Wirgth, I could use your help, as well, if you would wish to be of assistance."

The Kaadu, for once allowing his emotions to show, nodded with delight. Bowing low to Hina, who signaled his approval, Wirgth stepped over to Kubar Taug's side.

"Now move before those men cut off our retreat."

"Kubar, I still don't like this," Hina said. "If they should block the harbor, you'll be cut off."

"Then train your army quickly. I'll look for you in thirty dimmings."

Mounting their horses, Hina and his retinue cantered back down the slope where the battle-tested regiment was drawing up.

Thirty dimmings, Kubar thought, as he looked at the iron fortress. If Hina failed, or the nobles revolted, or Iskander tried some new trick, then all would be for naught, and he would die at last. Would he then return to the time he had been snatched from, to rejoin his brothers at last?

Feeling the bittersweet ache for his departed kin that only a Gavarnian could understand, Kubar Taug mounted his horse and rode back to the iron fortress that he knew would soon be drenched in blood.

"They're learning how to fight," Alexander mused, between gulps of warm beer that one of Parmenion's aides offered him.

Guiding his horse around the clumps of dead, he worked his way across the open field that had been a scene of nightmarish chaos less than an hour before. "How did our men stand?"

"Not bad for raw recruits. Ah, but if only I had but one regiment of our old troops," Parmenion replied gruffly, "I could have had that fortress for you as a present."

"You're turning into quite the general. Almost as good as my old Parmenion back on Earth."

Parmenion was silent. He was already forgetting his old station as a lowly drunken guard back home.

Across the valley, almost within hailing distance, Alexander could see several mounted Gafs looking in their direction. Was one of them the Taug?

"From what you've said of their fighting, I daresay they were observing us, seeing how we react and then forming their plans in response. So far they're responding to us. I wonder when they'll finally be forcing *us* to respond?"

"The fact that they brought that regiment up, fought it but for an hour, then sent it back to their capital almost confirms that suspicion. It leads me to believe, as well, that they knew we would strike here first."

Again he looked across the open field at the Gavarnian horsemen.

One of them moved his horse forward by several paces and then raised an arm into the air. It almost looked like a salute.

"Well, that must be him, damn it," Alexander said, smiling, and raising up in his own stirrups, he returned the salute.

The Gavarnian turned and galloped back toward the city.

"Is the encirclement complete?" Alexander asked, looking up from the rough charts that he had drawn himself.

"We've completely surrounded the fortress," Yaroslav replied. "The men are starting to dig the defensive positions facing the enemy capital."

"Position that blocking force on the southern road correctly. Make sure they have a clear field of vision, so they have several hours' warning of an approach."

"I've already seen to it," Sashi replied. "As you advised, I'm moving patrols up to within sight of the city. We should have at least one dimming to warn of any approach from that direction."

"But there is still the sea," Alexander said quietly. "As long as that line is open to them, they'll have supplies. We must cut off the sea."

"We can post artillery at the narrows," Parmenion interjected. "I already have men working to construct ballistae. When posted on both sides, it can sweep the main channel."

"Still not enough, damn it. We need more metal for the ballista fittings. Oh, we'll smash some of them, but even two or three ships a day getting past our blockade will make a difference. I'm racing time here," Alexander replied wearily. "Every day we wait gives them another day to train for our method of war. I would not want to see what would happen if they fielded an equal number of phalanxes trained like ours. We must take that mountain, and quickly. Then we must convert its metal into weapons and siege equipment for our entire army if we wish to take their capital. Damn it, if we give them six months, they'll drive us back into the hills, and then the war could drag on for years. I want to end this thing now!"

"Sire, the unit we faced yesterday was hardly trained," Parmenion replied, "if that's what you're worrying about. They came on in formation, but once we closed, all cohesion broke down and they fought like Gafs."

"Even then," Yaroslav interjected, "our casualties were almost equal, and our line damn near cracked. Even you've admitted that."

Parmenion was silent.

"Even so, there is still the question of cutting off their capital from the sea. If only I had some Cretan shipwrights with me."

"What are Cretan shipwrights?" Sashi asked.

"Oh, nothing we have here, boy," Alexander said sadly. "When I heard they had a regiment at least partially trained and then pulled it out, I knew then that we were in trouble. Those Gafs are starting to learn how to fight like Macedons. That regiment will be used to train the others. Therefore we haven't got much time. We need to seal up this ore city tight, take it, and then use it. What might very well tip the scales is that the Gaf have metal and we don't."

"So why not march straight on the Gaf city?" Sashi replied.

"I've thought of that, boy. But the fortifications there are immense. We would need heavy siege equipment to breech it; they could hole up there by the thousands while we're spread out in a circle twenty versts in length. Besides, if we leave this place in our rear, it could cut us off from the hills. Finally, we need to cut them off from the sea if we're to take that city.

"I need ships, Parmenion, otherwise this will be another Tyre, a year-long siege we can't afford. I had hoped, my friend, that your lightning strike could take the mountain in one quick march, but the gods did not will it so."

"Ah, yes, Tyre," Yaroslav interjected. "Bit of a rough time taking them before you got a navy together."

Alexander had to remind himself again that this man had read the history. And that thought alone chilled him. He was *history*—five thousand years old.

"Do you have any suggestions, Yaroslav?" Sashi asked hopefully.

"Too bad we don't have any sulfur," he said quietly, as if musing to himself, "but then again . . ."

The others were silently looking at the aged philosopher, who merely smiled and then changed the subject.

"Now, the Romans in the first Punic War faced the same problem."

"Romans. Too bad things didn't work out the way I planned," Alexander replied. "A pesky little people, them. Arrogant as anything. I had hoped to pay them a visit."

"Now, that would have been interesting, too bad it couldn't have been arranged." Yaroslav fell silent again for a moment.

"But as I was saying, the Romans faced a similar problem

and introduced a little something called the assembly line, since they, like you, didn't have a skilled shipwright in the lot."

"What's this assembly line?" Alexander asked.

"Simple enough. The Romans were fighting with—" He hesitated for a moment. "Well, never mind that, just say that they discovered a wrecked ship of their enemies. They took it apart plank by plank, right down to the last peg, then trained several hundred men to make one part and one part only.

"Now, each man could turn out a number of parts a day, which then were numbered. The numbered parts were put together by other unskilled laborers, and behold, within days they had a replica of the first ship. Within a month they had half a hundred ships, within six months they had a fleet of half a thousand. Granted the vessels were made of unseasoned wood, but they did sail. Meanwhile, the Roman general set up rows of benches and trained the men how to row and keep the pace."

Alexander's eyes were gleaming. "We only need half the men here to develop the siege lines and launch probing attacks. We could turn our least trained regiments to the task."

"But, sire," Parmenion interjected, "the Gafs don't seem to have any warships. That vessel we captured is simply a miserable sailing craft."

"So we'll just remove the mast, punch in holes for oars, and mount a ram up front. Yaroslav, you'll be responsible to start on it at once. I'll sketch out the changes we'll need."

"Maybe I should have kept my mouth shut," Yaroslav muttered.

"Come now, I hereby appoint you admiral of my new fleet."

"Oh, thank you, sire," Yaroslav replied evenly. "It's just the title I've always wanted."

There was a solution as he always knew there would have to be. With a nod to his staff, Alexander left them to their planning for supplies and stepped out of the tent. For a brief moment he felt disoriented. The fact that he was exhausted made him think that it should be night, but the sun as always was motionless, forever hovering in the same spot.

It was the middle of a dimming, and the heavy overcast that had set in caused the light to have an early-twilight cast to it. In fact, it was the darkest he had seen the countryside since his arrival.

The clouds stretched out from Olympus and its companions, which still dominated the entire northeastern horizon even though they were now well over a hundred leagues away.

For weeks there had been little if any rain, only an occasional thundershower, and the temperature had slowly climbed to near summer heat. Now, with the cloud cover spreading out, he could already notice a slight cooling. He wondered for a moment if the mountains to the northeast and their twins to the south had something to do with the change.

Walking to the crest of the hill, he saw that his army was resting, except for the occasional patrol that rode far afield in a giant protective arc. The center of all his attention was the ugly cylinder of what had once been a ship that sailed between the stars. It seemed a honeycomb of caves and scaffoldings, while around it rose a wall that stood three times the height of a man.

He was tempted to storm it once enough engines and towers had been built to sweep the battlements. Was that Kubar he had seen earlier? Two hands suddenly wrapped around him from behind, nearly locking his arms to his side.

With a cry he whirled around, breaking free from his assailant's grasp.

She greeted him with a laugh, and then he recognized his attacker.

"Neva, I thought you were back running the villages!"

"I grew lonely, and besides, those stupid oafs can run themselves now that you've managed to drag away all the quarreling men. In fact, it was so peaceful it started to get boring. You remember Divina, the girl who had an interest in Parmenion. Well, we kept talking about the two of you and finally decided there was only one way to solve our problem and get the treatment we've been needing for some time."

"I'm sure Parmenion will be happy to hear this," Alexander replied, imagining how useless his second in command would be once Divina had finished a night with him.

"Just do me one favor, tell Divina not to wear him down too much. I need him."

"Maybe you should worry about my wearing you down," she said softly, moving her arms up around his shoulders.

At least she's bathed for the occasion. Alexander, smiling, looked into her eyes.

For a moment he thought of Roxana and the devotion she

had for him, then his thoughts turned even to Bagoas, the Persian eunuch boy who had been his lover, as well. Again he wondered why the pleasures of the flesh had not held him slave the way they did the other men he had known. Perhaps because he had truly loved but one thing—the pursuit of glory, the conquest of a world.

Neva gradually let her hands slip off Alexander's shoulders and drift the length of his body. For the moment, at least, the obsession with glory disappeared, and he led his eager companion to his tent.

chapter twelve

"My lord Taug, what in the name of the Unseen Light is that?" There was a note of awe—edged with fear—in Wirgth's voice as he pointed to the drawings spread out on Kubar's desk.

"Perhaps we should not discuss that just now." Kubar returned to his desk and hastily rolled up the sheaf of drawings.

"It looked like some giant bubble. Is it a new weapon?"

"One could call it that. Now, why don't you tell me what it is that has brought you here unannounced?"

"Oh, yes. Arn reports that a dozen ships approach, running close-hauled to the wind. It must be the supplies and reinforcements."

"Fine, fine."

"He also says that there is some unusual activity going on across the bay."

Kubar looked up from the drawings that he was concealing. "What sort of activity?"

"We can hear horns and such—that, and a column of men was seen running off the hill and disappearing back into the bay that the hairless ones have been protecting so carefully."

That didn't sound good. Something had been going on over there. He had attempted to run some scout ships up, but the Humans had mounted half a dozen huge rafts at the bend of the bay, each carrying one of their giant bows, thus making approach almost impossible.

"I'm coming," Kubar replied, tossing the drawings into a cabinet.

Leaving his study in the center of the ore carrier, he stepped out into a small open area surrounded on all sides by shear walls nearly fifteen meters high. It had at one time been the central core of the ship, and the Gafs, when they had started to mine the wreck, discovered that the central section of ore was a remarkably high grade of iron nickel. Thus they had left the other sections nearly intact while clearing out the best of the metal.

Down in the lower courtyard nearly a hundred women, the only ones in the fortress and most of them wives and daughters of smiths who lived there, were still busy at their work, stitching the layers of silk that Kubar had taken with him from the capital before the siege had started.

A light rain fell upon them as they sat beneath makeshift shelters, the object of their work spread out, filling nearly the entire floor area of the chamber.

"This damnable rain," Kubar cursed softly. It had been falling nearly constantly since the siege had started thirty dimmings ago.

"My lord Taug," Wirgth said softly, "Arn is up there." And he pointed to the high watchtower built into what had once been the stern of the ship.

Following Wirgth's lead, Kubar ascended what appeared to be an endless series of ladders. Coming out onto a high platform, he stopped for a moment to examine the new heavy crossbow that had been installed within the last dimming. Its proud crew bowed toward him as he nodded in their direction.

The workmanship was not bad at all. "Any luck?" Kubar asked.

"Nothing today, my lord Taug. We've tried a couple of shots on that group over there." The warrior pointed toward the ten-meter-high siege towers positioned four hundred paces back, near the lowest part of the wall. "They're moving men up, it might mean something."

Kubar looked to where the soldier had pointed. Half a dozen wooden towers covered with leather were positioned just out of bolt range. There did seem to be an unusual level of activity. Turning his gaze across the bay, he saw a flurry of activity in the Human's secretive position over there, as well.

Damn it all, if only his secret was ready. But he knew wishes were useless in the face of war. Yet he did not need any secret weapon to surmise what might very well be happening. Turning to the west, he could see the convoy of a dozen ships rounding the outer point and then he looked back at his opponent's preparations.

"Sound the alarm," Kubar said softly, looking over at Wirgth. "I think the Humans are preparing some sort of surprise."

"By all the gods, I get the sickness of the sea." Parmenion groaned.

"Shut up and lead them out," Yaroslav shouted, jumping up and down excitedly from the shoreline.

"I never should have tackled that damned Aldin, *never.*"

A horn sounded from atop the watchtower guarding the passage into the narrow channel.

"Remember, steersmen, just keep them at a steady pull," Yaroslav cried.

"Yaroslav, we can still trade places."

"Are you crazy? I'm the philosopher, you're the warrior, now get going."

"All right, you bastards," Parmenion roared, "let's get this over with."

A feeble shout went up from the twenty galleys drawn up in line along the shore.

"Come on, you scum," Parmenion cried, looking to his own crew. "Start the count." And he nodded to the drummer boy who stood by his side.

The boy brought a mallet down against the leather head of the drum. Most of the rowers managed to pull together on the first stroke, but several of the men tangled up as their oars bit the water for the first time.

They had been practicing on land for thirty dimmings, sitting on wooden benches and pulling their shafts against thin air. And while they had practiced, the assembly line had developed around them, turning out the first score of rams based upon the clumsy design on the Gaf sailing cog. The shipyard had been constructed in a narrow channel with no room to practice, and the assigned crews dared not go out into the bay where the Gafs would have observed the birth of Alexander's new navy. The launching of the attack would be the first attempt for all the men who had come down from the mountains to now fight upon the sea.

The drummer kept a slow but steady pace, and even though some of the oars tangled up, Parmenion managed to keep them guided toward the channel opening while Yaroslav ran along the bank shouting encouragement.

"That's it, that's it. Remember to back up once you ram!"

"If I don't get back from this," Parmenion cried, "my ghost will haunt you forever!"

"Nonsense," Yaroslav shouted. "Pure superstition."

But Parmenion had no time for a retort as they approached the sharp bend in the channel that led out into the open bay.

"Left side stop," Parmenion cried, forgetting the nautical terms that Yaroslav had tried to teach the new sailors. Fortunately most of the men knew what he was referring to, and as the other side continued to row, the galley pivoted through the channel.

"All oars and increase speed!"

The bay opened up before them. Half a league away the Gaf fortress rose up from the waterline and he could hear the distant horns blowing. They must have guessed something was up.

Off to his right he could see the convoy running the narrows. One of the ships was on fire, having been hit by the artillery posted on the bluffs, but the other twelve ships were already clear and running for the protection of the enemy harbor.

He spared a quick glance back over his shoulder. Damn it all, one of the rams had simply continued on straight and run clean ashore, but so far most of the others seemed to be keeping pace. Already half a dozen of them were out of the channel, advancing in a more or less ragged line.

He had seen such a sight before during the siege of Tyre when hundreds of ships had maneuvered as if guided by a single hand, and Parmenion knew that this was a ridiculously poor imitation of that. They had all known that any attempt to organize the maneuvering of their raw fleet would be absurd, so each ship's commander had simply been told to head for the nearest enemy ship and to ram it and then back away.

He could only hope that they all wouldn't turn coward and

run, or worse yet, completely forget how to maneuver their vessels.

"Bring up the speed," Parmenion commanded, and the drummer increased the beat.

Most of the rowers were keeping together, but there were several who were hopelessly out of rhythm and tangling their comrades ahead and behind them.

"You there, Gris, pull your bleeding oar in and stop rowing," Parmenion cried. The uncoordinated rower did as he was commanded and looked up at Parmenion with a foolish grin on his face.

"All right lads, I'm steering for the lead ship now."

Several of the men slacked their pace to look over their shoulders.

"Don't look, damn you." The ship skewed to starboard due to a sudden tangle of a half dozen rowers.

"Don't look. I promise to give you plenty of warning before we hit 'em."

Within minutes they had closed to the point that he could see individual Gafs running about the deck of their lead ship.

Looking back over his shoulder again, he could see that over half his fleet had made it out of the channel. The remainder, however, were either tangled up with the beached vessel, a knot of them completely blocking the channel, or they were spinning about in circles like a fly with one wing broken off. Two of them had managed to roll over, and their terrified crews were clinging to the wallowing wrecks. Not a single man in his command knew how to swim properly, and he cursed aloud at the graphic reminder. He couldn't swim, either.

There was a loud shout of triumph off to his left and he saw that the ram crewed by the villagers from Kievant had pulled ahead of his own men from Ris. These two villages, being the first of Alexander's army, had expressed their insult when first passed over for the new navy. Realizing that such esprit was essential, Alexander had agreed that they should be represented in the fleet. Parmenion cursed them silently, believing that their loudmouthed insistence had resulted in his own assignment as the attack admiral, allowing Yaroslav to sit back on the shore. "All right, lads, *ramming speed!*"

The range was down to a long bowshot, and the Gaf fleet was in a panic; several of the ships to the rear were attempting to turn about and run back through the narrows, while the others ran as close into shore as they dared. Since they had yet to come abreast of the Gaf fortress, the catapults that Alexander had positioned in anticipation of such a move were already firing, sending their flaming bolts out across the water.

But Parmenion turned his thoughts away from all other concerns as he aimed his vessel on an intersecting path with the first Gaf ship.

It was obvious they had no experience with rams, otherwise the captain of the other vessel would have turned his vessel to meet them, Parmenion thought. They must assume we'll just come in alongside and then try to board.

He gripped the tiller tightly; it was less than half an arrow-flight to go.

Half a dozen bolts arced out from the ship; one of them skimming in low caught a rower square in the back. With a scream the man stood up, the bolt sticking out of his chest, and as he tumbled forward, his oar tangled up with several others.

The ram skewed to port and Parmenion fought to bring it around.

"Ramming speed!" Parmenion cried. "Keep at it, men, ramming speed."

A hundred paces, now fifty. He was looking up at the deck now. A Gaf archer stood up and fired, the bolt slammed into the deck by Parmenion's feet.

Twenty-five paces.

"Ramming speed!"

Seeing at last what was about to happen, the Gaf commander pulled the tiller hard over. It was too late.

With a thundering impact the ram drove into the Gaf vessel close to the stern. Rigging lines snapped, splintered planking rose into the air, and every rower was knocked from his bench into a tumbled, squirming mass of men.

Screams of panic and rage echoed from the Gaf ship.

"Up, damn you, up," Parmenion roared. "Back to the oars."

He jumped from his perch astern and charged down the narrow deck kicking the men back to their positions.

A Gaf archer appeared above him. Parmenion dodged to one side as a bolt skimmed past him. After picking up one of the spears stacked on the deck, he hefted the shaft and hurled it upward. The Gaf warrior disappeared in a shower of blood.

"Now pull, damn you," Parmenion cried, "pull us out or we go down with it."

Less than half the men were back in their positions, and working feverishly, they foamed the water with their oars. Parmenion could feel the stern of their ship rising slowly out of the water, as the Gaf vessel quickly filled from the hole torn in its side.

"Pull!"

With a shuddering groan they snapped free. As they backed away, they exposed a gaping hole in the enemy's side, and the vessel slowly started to roll over.

Gaf warriors and sailors spilled off the deck, screaming with panic.

"*Back!* Get us the hell out of here!"

The ram swung backward, but due to the imbalance of rowers, the vessel swung to port cutting an arc around the ship.

"Now forward," Parmenion cried. "All together, pull!"

The rowers reversed the direction of their oars, and the water foamed around them as they stopped their backward drive and then started to move forward.

"Harder!"

With slowly increasing speed, they pulled away from the sinking ship.

"Parmenion!" The cry came from forward, and looking up, he could see Gris, the clumsiest of the rowers, struggling with his oar.

A Gaf was clinging to it. The creature was fighting desperately to hang on, a look of wild panic in its eyes. And in that gaze Parmenion saw a mirror of his own panic if he were to be suddenly cast into the ocean.

"Hold the tiller steady, boy," Parmenion commanded. Giving the helm to the drummer and running forward, he came up alongside Gris, who hung on to his oar, looking like a fisherman who had suddenly hooked a whale.

The Gaf had worked its way up the wooden shaft, so that it was nearly alongside the boat. Before reason or logic could show him the possible danger of reaching out, Parmenion extended his hand and the Gaf grabbed hold.

For a second he thought the creature was trying to drag him in, and he pulled back with a fierce desperation, but the Gaf hung on, coming right up over the side.

A look into its eyes, though, showed that it was filled with panic and terrified beyond all reason.

He pulled it up and over, and the Gaf, dressed in a long red flowing robe, collapsed onto the deck.

"Tie it up," Parmenion commanded to the rower next to him, and turning, he rushed back to the stern.

Taking the tiller back from the drummer, he suddenly had enough time to look beyond the range of his own personal struggle.

At least half a dozen other ships had been rammed. The Kievant ship had already disengaged from its target and was rowing desperately after another ship, which was drawing nigh the protection of the enemy harbor. He could see where one ram had buried itself so completely into an enemy ship that both of them were going down together, their crews struggling against both each other and the deathlike embrace of the sea.

The three Gaf ships that had turned about were already running back through the narrows. Another one was aflame from the batteries on the hill, while several enthusiastic ram crews pursued them.

There wasn't much left to do, other than to help pick up survivors and shepherd the fleet back to their base. The second phase of the assault was up to Alexander, and Parmenion looked off toward the position where the half-dozen siege towers had been constructed.

"Parmenion, I tied her up."

It was the rower from up forward.

"What?"

"The Gaf, I tied her up."

"What do you mean?"

"I think, sir . . . at least it seemed like it, sir. You know, I think she's a woman."

"Most ingenious on their part," Kubar said softly, looking out at the wreckage of the supply convoy.

Even as he spoke he could still hear the distant sounds of the fighting. Two ships had managed to break through, one of them with its port side railing below the water. The pursuing rams were already turning about and heading back to their base on the other side of the bay, while off in the distance the two ships that had managed to break free of the trap had cleared the narrows, leaving two flaming companions in their wake.

"Is that all you can say?" Arn shouted. "We've lost several

hundred reinforcements and the precious supplies, and all you can say is 'most ingenious.' "

"What else can I say?" Kubar said, turning to face the raging noble. "One must remember, more than anything else, that a commander must never let rage rule his emotions. Kalin learned that lesson, but too late."

Arn looked for a moment as if he would strike the Taug, and the hair on his neck bristled. A soft growl of challenge came from Paga, who stood by Kubar's side. Arn looked to the others for support, but they averted their eyes—a sign that he had shamed himself by the outburst.

"Come now, Arn. I feel your pain at our loss." Kubar walked to Arn's side as if to put a hand on his shoulder, but Arn shrugged the gesture off and stalked to the other side of the watchtower.

"So they know how to fight now upon the water. I should have forseen these ram ships, but our history had no warfare upon the open sea . . ." He turned his eyes landward.

"I must assume that this Iskander has let but one-half of his plan fall." He looked at the siege towers. "They'll hit us there. Now let's see if it's our turn to spring a little surprise."

Even as he spoke the signal horns from the enemy camp sounded and a mighty shout went up from the Human army.

"Forward, my Macedons!"

Dismounted, Alexander marched to the left of the advancing siege towers, each of them pushed by a full regiment of five hundred men.

He knew the attack was still premature, but he hoped that the Gafs would be demoralized by the victory of the fleet which, combined with the sudden assault, would result in the Gafs' capitulating. He had but one fear for a capitulation, that the army, still only half disciplined, would turn a surrender into a massacre, thus hardening the future defense of the capital city. He needed a surrender with honor to use as a lever to weaken the resolve of the last redoubt.

All around the perimeter, the Humans raised their battle cries, as the ten regiments of heavy troops advanced at a slow walk toward the metallic ramparts that surrounded the ore carrier. Having the advantage of a slight downhill slope, the six siege towers advanced without incident.

As he stepped in front of the ranks, Alexander turned and

looked back at the advancing line. Swinging up his shield, he raised it high as a signal, and all across the front the wooden shields of the heavy infantry were raised up in response.

The towers were slowly gaining momentum as they rolled down the slope, so that the men were now braking the ungainly mountains of wood.

The attack was within arrow-shot range now but still no response, and not a Gaf was to be seen on the battlements. Alexander knew that no Gaf resistance at all was too good to hope for; there must be some preparation. He could sense the nervousness in his men. The silence from the other side was unnerving, and here and there along the line some of the men started to falter. But most kept moving forward as if drawn into the conflict by the six mobile platforms. Suddenly from all along the line, pillars of hot sparks showered upward.

The men hesitated, many of them crying out in fear. But no weapon was seen. There was another outburst of sparks, and then another, in a slow rhythmic pattern. Yet no weapon was seen.

Alexander leaped to the fore of his line. "Forward, my Macedons! Forward! They're setting fire to their own city." He knew it was a lie, but this was the moment to set his men into motion. Drawing his sword he started forward, his blond hair streaming out from under his helmet. For a moment he was alone, a sole warrior rushing toward the enemy, plainly visible to all the thousands on either side. It was a fitting stage for the glory that had always been his dream.

As if caught up in the power of their commander's vision, the host surged forward shouting his name, so that it echoed from the walls and the hills beyond. "Iskander, Iskander!"

The siege towers rolled forward, gaining speed, their crews not wishing to be left behind. More than one man stumbled before the advancing juggernauts of wood and was crushed, yet the engines of war pushed relentlessly forward.

The line swept onward, commander to the fore, and the base of the wall was gained. The race was over and he had grasped the fleeting vision yet again for an all-too-brief moment.

As if dazed, he looked about him as his host crowded beneath the battlements. Ladders were raised up and down the line. The towers were nearly to the wall, and the men struggled back to avoid being crushed, while their crews struggled des-

perately to stop the vehicles before they crashed into the wall.
And then the reaction came.

Up and down the line, hundreds of Gafs suddenly appeared,
their deeper growls cutting through the shouts of the Humans.
A shower of rocks cascaded down, while a volley of spears
arced out, smashing into the upturned shields of the defenders.

"The towers!" Alexander roared. "Drop their draw-
bridges!" But his words were lost in the wild crescendo of
screams, curses, and shouts of pain.

The first tower reached the wall and the Gafs revealed their
response.

The showers of sparks became continuous along the wall.
Alexander, as if sensing that something was wrong, started to
look straight up.

A blinding sheet of fire and smoke arced out over his head,
hissing like a red-hot sword thrust into ice. The sheet of fire
came down behind him, and turning, he watched as dozens of
men fell to the ground, thrashing and screaming. A garish light
exploded to his right, and looking over his shoulder, he saw a
river of flame cascade down from the nearest tower.

For a moment he thought the untanned hides from slaughtered Gaf cattle, hung on the sides of the towers, would repulse
the fire. But so intense was the heat that it ate right through the
green leather, and the wood beneath it burst into flames.

The shouts of triumph from the Humans changed in an instant to that of panic, as the army stood beneath the battlements, unable to respond.

The river of fire over his head stopped for a moment, and
after sprinting out from the relative protection of the wall, he
pushed his way over the burning thrashing men on the ground.

A shadow passed over him and he ducked down, holding up
his shield, but nothing struck him. Looking up, he saw a log
swinging out over his head, suspended by a series of cables. At
the end of the log dangled a series of grappling hooks.

The log smashed into the tower, the hooks snagging into the
structure. To his amazement the log started to move straight
up, and stepping back, he saw a heavy cable was tied to the
front of the log. The cable stretched back up to a high battlement up on the ore carrier, where half a hundred Gafs were
turning a windlass. With a creaking groan the tower lifted up
onto one side and tottered, leaning over in his direction.

All at once the Gafs released the windlass, and turning, Alexander started to run. The tower crashed down not two meters behind him, sending a thundering shudder through the earth.

Another river of flame hit the ground in front of him, and looking up, he saw a fire-wreathed nozzle sticking out from the battlement, while a shower of sparks rose up behind it. A jet of flame arced out again, and he dodged backward, realizing that the Gafs aiming the nozzle were trying to hit him. A searing pain whipped across his legs and he stumbled backward, holding his shield up to protect himself from the scalding heat.

Even as he struggled to survive, he knew the assault was lost. All around him the men streamed to the rear, most of them throwing away their shields and spears. Half a dozen pyres of flame leaped into the air—all the towers were lost. Unlike his old Macedons, these men would not rally by a personal display of bravery on his part. None of them would even bother to look back over his shoulder until they had reached the encampment atop the hill.

Turning, he started back up the hill.

The roar of the Gafs thundered behind him and then died away, to be replaced with a deep guttural growl that sounded like a chant that he could almost distinguish.

"Taug, Taug, Taug."

Alexander turned again and looked back at the battlements a hundred meters away. Another river of fire shot from the wall to reignite a smoldering tower. Lowering his shield, he looked at the bossing. It was covered with beads of still-warm metal, and he looked again at the rhythmic showers of sparks, as if they were coming from a forge.

They must have used a massive series of bellows to shoot molten metal out onto the troops, while using some sort of combination of logs and ropes to lift the towers and toss them onto their sides.

He noticed that the Gafs were looking toward one individual who stood upon a battlement, next to one of the crews that had lifted a siege tower from the ground.

Alexander felt that this one was looking straight at him, and on an impulse he raised his sword up in the air.

There was a flash of metal from the other side as a scimitar was raised in response.

So that is the Taug, Alexander thought, and turning, he followed his demoralized men back to the encampment. He knew that it would be a long night of bracing up the morale of his defeated army. But his having had a sea victory first, before the defeat, would help to balance that out.

But there were any number of other problems, as well. And he knew that the Gafs were only just beginning to show that the war was not over yet.

"My brother Kohs," Sigma Azermatti said, looking around the monitor room at the assembled gamblers, "there's a problem with the game."

"How can there be a problem?" Zola shouted. "A sea battle—imagine, an actual sea battle!—too bad it wasn't worth betting on, though. But still it was interesting nevertheless."

There was a general murmur of postgame comments from the other Kohs gathered around the room. Zola, in a ridiculous attempt at merriment, had appeared wearing a flowing robe in the Grecian style with an olive wreath perched jauntily on his brow. The Humans thought it was rather immature and shocking, but several Gavarnian Kohs had quietly asked him who his tailor was. Sigma turned away from the panoramic window that provided a magnificent display of the world below Mount Olympus and stared angrily at the Kohs.

"Come now, Sigma," Corbin began lazily, "we have the Xsarn's oversight of the action, and it has reported nothing amiss." He turned. "Have you, my friend?"

The Xsarn looked up from its feeding trough and wagged its head in what it felt was a good interpretation of the negative, which coincidentally was used by both Humans and Gafs.

"See, Sigma, if there is a problem it would be the first to report it."

Sigma settled back into his chair. "My concern is that the betting is getting, how shall we say, somewhat out of hand. The latest public tote sheets report that nearly eighteen percent of the total capital investments and corporate wealth of the entire Cloud is committed to this game. Eighteen percent! This damned thing is tying up an outrageous part of all our operating capital. Capital investments in general are now on hold, for no one is sinking anything into their projects once the assessments are made for betting purposes. Gentlemen, this is getting way out of hand."

"Come, come, Sigma, it's merely a game," Zola remarked.

"Merely a game, you say!" Sigma replied heatedly. "In

some areas the economy is at a standstill, for without capital investments entire heavy industries are on hold, with resulting financial disruptions and unemployment. Gentlemen, the Overseers are bound to notice this, and seeing that it is out of the usual pattern, it can result in their getting curious."

"Let the bastards get curious, we've covered ourselves," Corbin replied. "We've got good security on the Kolbard, they'll never find us out."

"But that's just part of what I'm concerned about," Sigma replied coldly. "With eighteen percent of the total wealth of the Cloud now resting on the lives of one Human and one Gaf down there, the situation is ripe for someone to try to take advantage."

"Oh, come now," Yeshna interjected, "we are honorable gentlemen."

There was a chorus of "well saids" and "here, heres."

Sigma realized he was not being heard, and taking his brandy in hand, he rose and started for the door.

"Go ahead then, gentlemen. I've fallen prey to this game lust, as well, far too much so, I daresay. And I'm not happy about getting sucked into it. If it all comes crashing down, don't say you haven't been warned."

He stopped at the doorway and then looked back coldly at Corbin. "And might I add that if Alexander dies, I shall suspect the worst. And if ever I can prove it, then Overseers be damed, I'll have my revenge." He slammed the door behind him.

"How dare he," cried Zola.

"I *never*! And to think, he is a gentleman, no less," shouted Gragth.

But Corbin was silent, smiling as if to himself as he poured another drink. So Sigma was starting to feel the pressure. Tia had been doing her work, all right. Odds just before the day's action had stood 4.1 to 1 in Alexander's favor. Granted the battle was a draw, in a tactical sense, but strategically they could all see the implications when Alexander had started to build his fleet. Overall, the odds would continue to climb in favor of the Macedonian. Sigma's little tantrum was, most likely, a clever ploy to scare off some of the pro-Alexander money so he could suck up a bigger share for himself.

Clever son of a bitch, Corbin thought. Tia was doing her job properly—and Corbin's other player was all primed and ready.

* * *

"Did you send a message that you wanted to see me?"

Aldin looked up at the open doorway as Zergh bent low to enter the room.

The old Gaf stopped speaking as he noticed who was sitting across from Aldin. "I didn't know you already had company."

"Come now, Zergh, I can remember a time when you'd sit me on your knee and delight in telling me old Gavarnian legends."

"That's before you grew up, Tia." She could not help but notice the sarcasm in his voice.

"Come, come, Zergh," Aldin said softly, "I don't like it, either, but our little Tia had to reach maturity some time."

"Stop being so protective of me, Uncle. I can take care of myself."

"It's just that I've worked for Corbin for thirty years, that's ten years longer than you've been around. The fact that you've allowed yourself to become his mistress—"

"Look, Uncle, girls have sexual desires, too."

The old Gavarnian, embarrassed as all Gavarnians were by the predilection of Humans to openly discuss sexual activities, rose up again as if making to leave. Among male Gavarnians sexual longings were suppressed, for only the oldest brother, or the last surviving brother, had the right to mate, since the male-to-female ratio at birth was four to one. Some males did engage in homosexual activities, but that was something no Gaf would ever dream of openly discussing with another Gaf, let alone a Human.

"Don't leave, Zergh, there're some things I want to discuss."

Zergh looked back over at Tia, who returned his gaze with an even smile.

"I know," she replied to the look of distrust in his eyes, "now that I sleep with Corbin you'd rather not talk about certain things in my presence. I can take a hint."

Without another word she rose and left the room.

Shaking his head, Aldin pulled out the bug scanner and gave a quick pass of the room, as if Tia might have left a listening device behind. Satisfied that all was secure, he motioned for Zergh to close the door.

"Listen, Aldin," Zergh said, settling down in the chair next to his friend, "I've been running some discreet checks on that mining consortium Corbin promised you as part of your royalty payment. It happens I've a friend in an accounting firm that reports to the Overseers. Now, those guys doctor the books like mad for the do-gooders, but they know the inside news, as well. The damn thing's a dummy. Its assets were stripped six months ago then transferred over to an Eldarnian World bank account, and Eldarnian World accounts are handled strictly by code words, no names involved."

"So you're saying that Corbin is cheating me once again," Aldin replied dejectedly.

"What I've been telling you from the beginning. Once this game is up, you'll get taken and then dumped."

Aldin could only shrug his shoulders and pour another drink for himself.

"Enough of that damn drinking," Zergh replied. "That stuff's killing you, man."

"At least that's one thing Corbin keeps me well supplied with."

"Yeah, 'cause he knows what it does to you. You'll fall into another binge, he'll come along after the game is over, help you to dry out like the last time, and then take you for another ride.

"There's more you should know about, as well," Zergh continued. "My friend in accounting says that he thinks *billions* of Katars are being laundered through the Eldarnian banks. *Billions*, all of it impossible to trace. I can't help but think that Corbin is up to something."

Aldin shrugged his shoulders.

"And you let your niece, the girl you practically raised, hang around with that bum."

Again Aldin's shoulders shrugged.

"By the way, was there any reason for that visit of hers? I haven't seen her since the two of you got back from picking up Alexander."

Aldin looked over at him and smiled. "Just family business."

"You mean she was just checking up on you?"

"You could say that. It was just family business, as usual, that's all."

chapter thirteen

Alexander looked at the Gavarnian female and smiled. He had learned in recent days that such a gesture in Gaf society did not hold the same meaning, but she had already explained that in her thirty days of captivity she was learning the nuances of Human gestures, as well.

This was so like Darius again, he thought. After Issus he had captured Darius' mother, wives, and concubines, and from them learned the subtleties required of a Persian emperor. The female before him was the only sister of Hina, the Gaf who would have been the taug ruler if not for Kubar.

The language implant had quickly allowed him to converse with her, and she in turn was learning Human speech. She was shrewd, to be sure, revealing nothing of military value. Nevertheless she was showing him the way of the Gafs, and thus providing information that would be needed in the days ahead.

"So, I am honored again by your presence," Liala said, beckoning for Alexander to sit by her side.

"You are comfortable?"

"Captivity is never comfortable for a Gavarnian. But I had assumed all along that I would be tortured and killed if I fell into the hands of the hairless ones. So in comparison I must confess that you have made me comfortable. But tell me, why have you come to me in the middle of the dimming?"

"It's just that I've had a suspicion, and now I wish to confirm it."

"And that is?"

"Ever since your capture you've never told me why you were aboard that ship. I would never have known you were the only sister of Hina if you had not made the mistake of speaking to yourself while I was standing outside your tent."

"Iskander, that was a violation and most rude. When a Gavarnian speaks to the Unseen Light, they do so with open voice. To listen while I called for the protection of my brother was shocking."

He could see that she was gently chiding him, and there was nearly a sense of playfulness in her voice. He could not help but like her. She was intelligent, straightforward, and dignified. In their conversations, she had spent hours reciting the Balda Hista, the great ballad of Kubar Taug, which had been passed down across four thousand years of Human time. He realized that if anything this woman was putting a face on the Gafs, revealing them as cultured, with a history and tradition as rich as his own. They were no longer beasts in his eyes. They were opponents truly worthy of respect.

"But you were saying that you wish to venture another guess as to why I was aboard that ship, so do entertain me with your assumptions."

"It took me some time to learn to read the emotions of a Gavarnian: I had to learn the inflections in the voice, the interplay of words with facial expressions, and the look in your eyes while you spoke. I think now that I'm beginning to see."

It was the same, he realized. Until Issus, Darius was nothing but an image to him—a distant warrior sighted across a field of battle. But then he saw him at last through the eyes of someone who loved him, and through Darius' mother he learned to see Darius as someone's son.

"Go on, Iskander, tell me what it is that you've surmised."

"Without your brother's knowledge you hid yourself aboard that ship. For no brother would allow his sister to go into the peril you chose to face."

She started to grow uneasy.

"I realized it last night when you were reciting the part of the Balda Hista that spoke of the last meeting between Kubar Taug and his wife, just before his final battle and the betrayal. I knew then that you loved him, and that is why you tried to reach the city we now lay siege to."

Liala was silent and turned away.

"Thank you for sharing Kubar Taug with me," Alexander said softly. "You know it is my fate to face him and to cast him down, but know that you shall always have my protection. I have sent a courier to your brother telling him that you are safe but that I cannot release you until this thing is over. For you have seen too much of our armies, and far too much of me, as well. If you wish, I shall inform Kubar Taug of your safety."

Liala turned back and looked into the eyes of the Human who would try to kill the one she loved, and saw far more of him than he would ever reveal to any of his comrades.

"I thank you for your truthspeaking, but I ask that you not send a message to Kubar since he thinks I am still safely back in the city," she said softly. "Now leave me. For now that you know, I wish to pray for the safety of Kubar Taug."

"I tell you, it leaves a trap wide open."

"It sounds like cowardice to me."

Kubar was glad that Paga was not in the room, otherwise a blood challenge would have been offered. He desperately fought to control his own exasperation. Just once, if only for one time in his life, he truly wished that he could give way to his temper and let his true feelings surge to the surface. All his life he had met illogic with calm reasoning, never had he raised his voice in anger to those who followed him. He turned back to face Arn and the other half-dozen nobles.

"Let me try to explain this simply. What is the purpose of our defending this fortress?"

"To deny it to the hairless ones," a section commander growled.

"And you've all done that most admirably. But there were some other reasons, as well. First of which was to act as a bait, to draw Iskander's army out into the open while preventing it from ravaging our croplands to the south, or from threatening our capital. That purpose has been served."

"And we need but hold for another half-dozen dimmings and then we can catch him in the vise between our army and Hina's. We know that Hina's ready to march."

"So we wish," Kubar rejoined. "And if it were that easy, we could end this campaign in a dozen dimmings. But never underestimate what Iskander is."

"He's hairless scum," Arn's sword-bearer snarled.

"And brilliant—otherwise could he have come as far as he has against the best we can offer?" Kubar replied slowly.

There was no response.

"Now listen to me. We did not want him to take this sky-ship, since he could mine it to make more weapons. We've held it for nearly sixty dimmings, and from our last messenger

hawk we know that Hina marches in but three more dimmings."

"To our relief and then to victory."

"Our relief, yes; victory, I doubt. Look at the map, just look
at it." He unrolled the soiled parchment across the table.

"The Anvil is an open plain to the east. The Horth estuary
a barrier to the north, our capital to the south, and the sea to
the west. If Hina advances, Alexander will not meet him, he
will in fact withdraw back across the Anvil and there will be
no final confrontation."

"Then he is a coward."

Kubar, struggling with his emotions, let the comment pass.
"Why would he run?" Wirgth inquired.

Kubar almost breathed a sigh of relief for the timely question. "Because it is what I would do," he replied, knowing that
such a statement would draw a scoffing response. But there
was only silence in the conference chamber.

"He will not advance to meet Hina because to do so would
leave a fortified position at his back, threatening his line of retreat and supply. On the other hand, he could throw everything
he has against us, but the victory might be so costly that again
he would be forced to retire in the face of Hina's fresh units.
Either way he turns, there'll be an enemy at his back. Therefore, if this fortress holds, there is only one alternative for
him—withdraw back across the Anvil and promise his men the
booty that can be looted from our farmlands to the south."

"Then we'll meet him there."

"On our own farmlands?" Kubar asked quietly. "You don't
know what that means, I do. Far too many times I've seen it.
We'll be forced to scorch the land, then they will burn it, in
kind. It will be raided and counterraided as each side grapples
for position. It will take an endless cycle of dimmings before
the issue is brought to grips. And when finally one side has triumphed over the other, there will be little if anything left for
the victor.

"Believe me," he said coldly, "I've seen war, real war—
without honor or glory in it, and I know what it produces. I've
seen the farmlands burning from horizon to horizon. I've
seen the numbed looks on the faces of defeated armies retreating at
night. And I've seen the families, the thousands of families—
waiting, forever waiting for a return, when all hope is already

dead. Yes, my friends, I've seen that. I spent a lifetime helping to produce it—and I don't want it again."

He fell silent and looked away from them for a moment, as if wrestling with the memory. So strong was the conviction in his voice that none dared to respond. Even those few who still doubted his authenticity as the true Taug paused for a moment.

"I want this war ended here and now!" Kubar roared, smashing his fist down on the table with such force that the wood beneath his iron hand cracked.

"Honored nobles, it is no coincidence that this Iskander and I arrived on this world at the same time. I, from our legendary past; I must assume that the demigods of the Humans have done the same in the choosing of Iskander. Therefore I also must assume that he is their best. I say this without false pride or that even more dangerous trait, false humility. It is merely a point of logic, nothing more.

"Therefore I want all of you to realize, I want every warrior in a position of command to know, that Iskander in his Human form, no matter how distasteful, is equal to me in all abilities. If Hina marches and this fortress still stands, he will withdraw."

"But why abandon this fortress?" Arn said slowly, as if he had conceded the logic of Kubar's argument.

"As the hook in the bait. There'll be too little time for Iskander to mine this place, but once he's taken it, he will be loath to leave it. With the threat gone from his back, he will feel confident to use this as a base as he turns to meet Hina. From the beginning I assumed that his plan was to take the fortress, mine it, then turn southward to meet Hina before the walls of the capital. One ingredient is missing—the ability to mine it. For when we leave, we shall smash our forges and drag the tools with us. There will be little time to use this resource, and then he will be forced out to meet Hina.

"He will not retreat once this place is his, since he will not be willing to come take it once again. And, besides that, there is the question of the morale of his men, for a retreat after a string of victories will be beyond understanding to his troops, and he knows that, as well. No, we cannot let him deny us this battle. We must give him the fortress."

"But couldn't he hole up in here?" Wirgth asked.

"Not likely. Too many men under his command, first of all, to fit in here. He most likely understands that his control of the sea is tentative, at best, and that we will respond. No commander will allow himself to be pinned into a siege deep inside enemy lines. When we do defeat him in the field, he might even fall back here, hoping that he can lure us into another attack on a fortified position. Then we can finish him off."

"If he doesn't march into our capital first," Arn replied.

"Then it will not matter for any of us, including myself."

Kubar looked around the room and sensed that the logic of his argument was taking effect. He must act now before there was chance for any opposition to regroup.

"When the next dimming comes, we move."

"That is one point you haven't clarified," Arn said smoothly. "Or have you forgotten that we are surrounded and our sea route is cut, at least for the moment? Must I assume then that you simply plan to cut your way out of here?"

"Wirgth has told me there is a chamber into the underworld that leads down to the coastal tower."

There was a loud murmur of dissent.

"No one has gone in the catacombs and survived," Arn shouted angrily. "No one!"

"But Wirgth has the maps."

Wirgth nodded, and with a quick snap of his wrist, he unrolled the parchment atop the plans to the fortress and the surrounding countryside.

"The diagrams have been in my family line for generations and clearly plot a course directly beneath this fortress. The entryway is connected into the catacomb we have been using."

The others mumbled quietly, not wishing to show their fear.

"It could be a trap, or some such foul machination, of the gods who made this place," one of the warriors mumbled while making a sign to ward off evil.

"I doubt that," Wirgth said quietly.

"Do you doubt the word of one of our most valiant captains?" Arn replied.

"But of course not, sire," Wirgth replied. Only Kubar noticed that the pronunciation Wirgth used for the word sire was in fact an archaic form not used since his own time, when such a term, for a while at least, was only use derisively.

He looked at Wirgth closely, but the old Gavarnian only smiled at him, his rheumy eyes twinkling as if they were sharing a private joke. But how could he have known such a thing? Kubar wondered.

"Then if we can march out," Arn inquired, "why not move Hina's army in here in force and catch Iskander by surprise?"

"The tunnel path comes out to the north side of the great mountain," Wirgth replied, "a good five leagues from our own line. I've not mentioned it before simply because it would be useless to bring supplies or a large army up through it. But a thousand of us appearing out of it will cause quite a stir. If Hina has already passed, then we'll simply follow up behind him."

"It still sounds like witchery to me," one of the other warriors said.

"I've already been there," Wirgth said offhandedly, "and I certainly wasn't afraid of any godspirits or ghosts. Now, my good sires, surely if they didn't frighten me . . ."

The others could not respond without sounding as if they were afraid of something that the old Kaadu viewed with disdain.

"There are nearly a thousand of us," Arn interjected. "How do we propose to pull out without their overwhelming us?"

"But that is the final point," Kubar replied. "You see, in fact, I *want* them to overwhelm us."

"What?"

Control your temper, Kubar thought desperately, control it, and he attempted to force a smile.

"Iskander!"

He was already buckling on his armor, even before Parmenion had torn the flap aside and burst into the tent.

"They're sallying?"

"They've already hit the line in front of the main gate."

"There shouldn't be that many," Alexander stated, trying to give an outward appearance of calm, even as all around him the camp was in an uproar.

"It's not the men," Parmenion cried. "They have another of their machines."

So this Kubar had invented yet another device to confound them. His interest aroused, Alexander grasped his sword and strode out into the chaos that surrounded him.

"By all the gods," he whispered softly.

The first siege line was already breached, but there were no

Gafs in sight. Instead the Humans were confronted by what appeared to be a tortoise shell the size of a small shed. And already a second one was emerging from the gate.

"It's merely a type of siege tower," Alexander said out loud in an attempt to calm those around him.

"But look!" one of the men cried, and even as he spoke a tongue of molten metal arced out from a nozzle mounted on the side of the tortoise, sweeping the trenchline with fire. Panic-stricken men burst out from the escarpment and ran for the rear, while from the fortress walls a volley of arrows and catapult bolts rained down, catching half a dozen fleeing Humans in midstride and pinning them to the ground.

Alexander looked for the commander of the Ris and Kievant phalanx, whose men served as his elite bodyguard. Catching the man's attention, he gave the signal for the phalanx to be formed.

As he waited, the second tortoise cleared the gate, and a third one appeared behind it. Having the advantage of moving downhill from the elevated gatehouse, the machines moved along at a fair speed while playing out a heavy cable behind them. Alexander's artillery opened fire with a shower of bolts and rocks, making a number of strikes, but without effect. A number of Gaf skirmishers sallied out, as well, and Alexander could see where a heavy unit of horse was forming up just within the fortress wall.

"Do you think they're trying a breakout?" Parmenion cried, trying to be heard above the ever-increasing roar of battle.

But Alexander was silent. They had managed to pierce his first siege line but there were two more beyond that, and then two leagues farther out was another series of protective ditches facing southward toward the enemy capital. If they were trying a breakout, it was certainly a desperate move. But this was a time of desperation, both for him and the Gafs. He assumed that their preparations in the capital would soon be complete. He was planning to assault the ore carrier before the Gafs marched, but now they seemed to be coming out, thus possibly eliminating for him the need for a desperate assault, since the earthen ramp that he was building toward the east wall was still six meters from completion.

"Sire, we're formed," the Ris commander shouted, and the Kievant nodded his assertion.

"We charge straight at them, open formation," Alexander

shouted. "When we've closed be sure to stand clear of the noz-
zles then drive your spears in through the slits or try to jam
them up underneath the wheels. There, do you see it, it's being
pushed by Gafs walking inside. Pass that back to the men."

Damn it, if these men were his real Macedons there would
be no need to explain, they'd simply do it, the same as when
they faced the elephants of Porus. The men had opened ranks
and let the beasts pass, and then attacked them from the flanks
and rear. He could still remember the cries of the wounded
creatures—he blocked out the thought.

"Forward!"

The phalanx swung into a four-rank formation behind him
and advanced down the field at a walk. The skirmishers deployed to the right flank in an attempt to deliver harassing fire
against the wall and thus keep the enemy archers down.

The third tortoise stopped in the gate, having skewed to one
side and then crunched down, as if its forward axle had broken. Suddenly he could see his chance.

He looked back up to where Parmenion was watching the
action, but there was no need to point out the enemy's plight.

Parmenion was already shouting to his signalers, and within
seconds the horns sounded five steady notes and then a sixth
note an octave higher, to be repeated again and again as the
camp stirred into action. Up and down the line the men saw
what had happened and a wild shout rose to the heavens.

"To the right flank in column," Alexander screamed. "Follow me to the gate!"

Half a hundred Gafs were gathered around the tortoise, trying desperately to push it out of the gate. But the harder they
pushed, the more the front edge dug into the ground.

The damned fools, Alexander thought, they should push it
back, not forward.

"Faster," he cried, "before they close the gate, faster!"

The other two tortoises stopped and the back ends split
open—a score of Gafs poured out of each and dashed up the
slope even as the phalanx came down from the flank.

It would be a near thing, and some of them, falling behind,
turned in desperation to trade their lives as dearly as possible.

One warrior, singling out Alexander at the head of the column, drew a scimitar and charged. As he bore down, Alexander braced for the impact, driving his shield in low in an
attempt to knock the towering creature off balance.

He felt as if he had run into a stone wall. A crashing blow numbed his arm and sent him staggering backward, but the host pushing down behind him charged over the Gaf and bore him under a tide of shouting men. Alexander was pushed to one side, but nothing could stop him at this moment. Casting aside his shield, he pushed to the front of the charging column.

The Gafs, seeing the tide of men bearing down upon them, backed up, forming under the portcullis.

"Forward, my Macedons!"

And the line at the head of the charge smashed into the wall of screaming Gavarnian warriors.

Panting for breath, Kubar looked over his shoulder. The reserve line was gone, the last of the warriors were off the wall and had retreated into the inner citadel.

"Go on, Wirgth. Paga and I will stay here only a moment longer."

"Not until you leave," Wirgth replied, his eyes locked on Kubar.

Kubar quickly turned and looked back at the fighting that was raging in the gateway a score of paces away.

"Those are all first or second brothers," Wirgth said coldly. "They pledged to hold the gate and put on the fight to deceive this Iskander. They want to die here and you cannot stop them, nor should you blame yourself. Now leave."

But Kubar did not move, and his hand rested on the half-drawn sword in his scabbard. It was one thing to order warriors to battle, it was far different to ask men to go to certain death. But a hundred would have to stay to die, and he had been forced to ask. Those who had older brothers still alive had cried for, had almost begged at times, for the honor. Again their damned glory and honor.

"You are the soul of our fight," Wirgth said softly. "If you die then we all die at the swords of the hairless ones."

He looked back at the gate again. A lone man was battering his way through the gate, ducking beneath the blows of the Gaf warriors and coming in low with an up-driven blade. But the man was lost from view as Paga, Wirgth, and half a dozen guards forced their commander away from the fight.

Suddenly they were out of the courtyard and into a rough stone passage that cut downward into the heart of the ore ship. Every twenty paces they passed a torch stuck into a socket, and the last guard in the detachment knocked the torch down after they had passed.

The downward descent leveled out as they came into a low vaulted chamber. It was quiet, cool, and damp—a startling change after the heat and roar of battle aboveground.

They stopped for a brief moment before a jet-black stone that stood alone in the middle of the chamber. Its surface was scorched, the entire rock illuminated by a circle of light from overhead. Kubar leaned over the stone and looked straight up into the dim light of the sun, which seemed to float at the top of the chimney directly above. The stone had been pushed aside, revealing a circular hole that seemed to drop like a well.

There was a smell of death in the room. The half a hundred dead who occupied this place, unable to be cremated because of the shortage of wood, had been dragged back out and laid in the streets and in various apartments throughout the fortress. They had been denied the right of final rest upon the cremation stone and the rising of their ashes to the Unseen Light above.

They could still serve in death, Kubar had explained. Their bodies would serve to deceive the enemy as to the numbers who had survived to the end.

Each of them bowed to the altar, then following Wirgth's lead, they started down.

Two of the guards stayed behind and Kubar suddenly realized that Wirgth had not told him about one final detail regarding their retreat.

"Wait!"

But it was too late. Even as he cried out the guards leaned into the stone, and with a shuddering grind it slid over the hole, closing off those who were looking up. With a *boom* the altar dropped back into place.

He had to brace himself, to give the example, but his mind could not tear away from the thought of those two warriors who would soon die, trading their lives so that his deception and stratagems could be played out.

He had to set the example, and cursing silently, he followed Wirgth down the ladder. Far below he could hear a rising murmur of voices. The rest of the garrison was waiting for their arrival. He set his face, and reaching the last rung, Kubar let go and landed on his feet in the middle of a broad corridor.

* * *

For a moment he was stunned, and he knew that his amazement and fear showed.

The corridor was so wide that half a dozen mounted Gavarnians could have ridden abreast. From overhead a soft yellow light radiated from translucent panels, flooding the corridor with a comfortable warm glow. It was dry and held a comfortable cool scent. When Wirgth had said that he knew of a tunnel that stretched for nearly three days' march, Kubar had imagined groping in a dank, fetid darkness.

He was disoriented and looked over to Wirgth, who motioned for him to follow.

After several minutes Kubar gained the head of the column. The warriors were quiet, fearful of the strange spotless surroundings.

Ahead of them the corridor was in darkness. Kubar was about to call for a torch when Wirgth, as if sensing his command, stepped forward a dozen paces and suddenly a battery of overhead panels lit up.

Those who had yet to see this phenomenon jumped back with startled shouts and several of them drew their blades, but Wirgth simply motioned for the warriors to be silent.

"Shall we start, Kubar? After all, it is a long march. There was once a hairless one who said something about the first steps of journeys . . . but I can't remember it now."

Again there was that strangeness, as if this old advisor somehow knew too much, but Kubar realized that now was not the time to pursue the mystery.

Following Wirgth's lead, he fell in alongside the bent-over Gavarnian, and behind him there was a stirring rustle as the survivors fell into line.

"Everybody else got out?" Kubar asked, looking over to Paga.

"Yes, everyone but the hundred volunteers who stayed behind. The tools for the forges have been hidden down here, and the material for that project of yours is being pulled along in one of the carts."

"And my clothing and armor, they were used as I requested?"

Wirgth merely nodded. And Kubar did not wish to inquire as to which body was selected to be his substitute.

They walked in silence for a time, until Kubar quietly remarked on the large number of side tunnels.

"The entire Kolbard is honeycombed with these access chambers and service tunnels. They reach right through the shielding of the ring to the other side, out into open space."

"Open space . . ." Kubar muttered, his words trailing off. It was still hard for him to realize that he was living on the inside of a world, not the outside, and that down was in fact up, and up—the thought was overwhelming.

But if Wirgth's comment was true, then it would be possible to go downward and see the stars. He wondered about that; would they seem the same as they had at home?

"This tunnel, I believe, was once a transportation link for great vehicles that girdled the Kolbard at speeds beyond our imagining."

"And if we followed this tunnel?"

"It would go on forever. We could walk it for a lifetime, and after a hundred generations our ancestors would one day come back here at the starting point. I've heard rumor that there are indeed races that live down here and do just that, moving forever in a great circle."

Kubar involuntarily shuddered at the thought of subterranean beings forever walking beyond sight of light or stars.

"How do you know of these things?"

"Oh, shall we say, it's just bits of old legends passed down through the generations of my family. No one else was ever interested in exploring this part of our world, and there are perhaps reasons why that is best. When that ore carrier crashed during the Great War of the demigods, it revealed a section of the tunnel which my ancestors covered over with the altar, so that as time passed it was all but forgotten."

Kubar was silent. Why was it that such a thing was covered over? Why hadn't they used these tunnels to move quickly from one place to another in comfort? Or was it some sort of primal fear that kept both his race and the Humans out of the subterranean world beneath their feet?

Hours later the column started to straggle, but Kubar wished to push on as long as endurance would hold. It was essential that he return to the fight as quickly as possible. There was a gentle stirring of wind to his right, and turning, he looked into a downward-sloping side tunnel. It was the first such opening that they had encountered, and Kubar hesitated for a moment, his curiosity aroused.

"I wouldn't turn in there if I were you," Wirgth said quietly.

"And why not?"

"You might get lost."

But he could sense something else in Wirgth's tone.

"Call a rest halt," Kubar said quietly. "I'll be back shortly."

The command filtered down the line and the column sank wearily to the floor, mumbling and groaning as soldiers have always done, when a long-anticipated rest is finally called.

Without another word, Kubar turned and started down the side tunnel. Knowing that argument was senseless Wirgth and Paga followed. The panels overhead lit up at their approach, but the coloring was softer and gradually shifted toward red as they moved along.

"My lord Taug, perhaps we . . ."

"Why are you trying to stop me?" Kubar asked, turning to look at Wirgth.

"Perhaps it's just that you're not ready for this."

"Let me be the judge of that, please."

Wirgth mumbled something to himself and fell silent.

For nearly a verst they made their way down the sloping corridor until finally the only lighting was a dull, shimmering red. Up ahead Kubar saw that the tunnel was coming to an end.

A room spread out before him, lost in darkness, and he sensed that he was in a chamber of immense length. No panels lit up to illuminate the way.

"By the names of my brothers!" Paga cried, leaping backward even as he grabbed Kubar and tried to pull him along.

Suddenly he felt as if he were falling into endless darkness, and his mind struggled against the panic. But no, he was standing on something after all.

He closed his eyes for a moment and fought for control, while removing Paga's grip. He took another step forward, then opened his eyes again.

Beneath his feet, the heavens were spread out before him. The swirling cloud of the galaxy arched beneath his feet.

"Our home, our long-lost home," Wirgth said softly, "is somewhere in that cloud of stars. For you it was a home you left but yesterday, for me it is a world lost long ago. You are at the bottom of the Kolbard, Kubar Taug. And here, again, you can see the everlasting sea of eternity."

Orientation returned and he could not help but laugh, and

his voice echoed in the darkened chamber. How strange to look down and see the stars between your feet.

"Wondrous," he whispered softly, "simply wondrous. Why then the fear in your voice and in your heart when you came to this place?"

Paga's grip returned to his shoulder, and Kubar could feel it tighten in panic. There was something else to this place, and turning, he looked back at Paga and then in the direction his comrade was staring.

The hair on the back of his neck stood straight up.

"Because," Wirgth said softly, "this is the Mausoleum of the First Travelers, the builders of this world. This has been their resting place for a hundred thousand of our lifetimes, and still their attendants who have no flesh see to them, and through those attendants I have learned why you are here."

From out of the darkness a corpse floated into view, and for the first time since his childhood Kubar screamed in fear.

chapter fourteen

"It's up to eight point eight to one," Corbin said, shaking his head with amazement. "Not even in my wildest dreams did I ever think it'd get this high. Have you pushed the rest of my assets into the game?"

"Right after the capture of the ore carrier and Kubar's disappearance, the odds peaked. I put the remainder of your twenty percent into the game matched straight against Sigma. Nearly sixty percent of his total wealth is tagged into the operation."

"Fabulous," Corbin gloated, "simply fabulous!"

"But all monitoring of Kubar ceased eighteen hours ago," Tia replied. "Corbin, if he's dead, Alexander might pull it off."

"Not to worry, my dear, not to worry. First off, we picked up a wavering in Kubar's signal for several minutes before it shut down; secondly, the body they dragged out into the square, though dressed as Kubar, doesn't match up to the computer analysis. I'm not worried yet; besides, Alexander will be taken care of shortly. The individual to do the job is already in place."

"How, Corbin?"

"Let's just say that if I see any possible threat or shift he'll be taken care of immediately. If I can swing even *higher* action, I'll let him last a bit longer."

Tia leaned forward. "How?"

"There's no need for you to know," Corbin replied guardedly.

"So where the hell is Kubar?" she asked suddenly, realizing that it was safer to change the subject rather than push it.

"Remember, the Kolbard is honeycombed with millions of kilometers of passages. It is possible, after all, that the Gafs know of these. For that matter, why shouldn't they?"

"There is one concern though," Tia replied.

"And what's that?"

"As far as I know, the Xsarn has no monitoring through the bottom of the Kolbard."

Corbin was suddenly silent. Good for her, this girl was certainly on top of the angles. "Any of the Kohs off ship right now?"

"Bukha and Yeshna are on their home worlds. I understand Sigad of Monta is in transit back here. Otherwise all the other Kohs are accounted for."

"All right then, just run a discreet check. If any of them leave, make sure a bug is placed on their personal vessels. What about Aldin and Zergh?"

"They're out deploying a new set of monitor drones."

"All right then, girl." He waved his hand as if to dismiss her, and taking the hint, Tia rose and left the room.

She was doing a good job of looking out for her interests but she was just a little too inquisitive about his contact with Alexander. Getting the contact in place next to Alexander had been the real headache. The problem had been an interesting one, a problem the solution of which he had arranged privately a couple of years earlier, with a number of discreet forays down to the Kolbard long before the project had started. The direct-wire contact from the top of Olympus was secured, as well. There'd be no over-the-air message, therefore no possible way for the Xsarn to find out. Now all he had to do was wait.

Turning, he opened the door into his private recreation chamber. It was about time for a little interesting diversion.

As the door closed behind her, Tia heard the door into Corbin's private chamber slip open and a female giggle echoed in the room. Damn that Regina, she thought quietly, and then, smiling, she continued on down the hall.

The endless monsoon of the last two months had finally broken, and with it came a fresh-scented breeze from out of the east. The sun, as always, hung motionless in a perpetual noonday sky, and for a moment Alexander ached for but one clear sunset to reflect its fiery light off the snowcapped pinnacles of the Hindu Kush.

The reports had been filtering up from the south all day. The enemy was giving every indication that they were about to march.

And what had happened to Kubar? That was the disturbing thought. Again he remembered his hunt for Darius. For years he had pursued him across the Persian Empire, across a thousand leagues and two major battlefields, in the end only to discover him murdered by two traitorous Persians. How he had dreamed that in the heat of battle he would step forward from the line, his armor gleaming in the morning sun, and there meet Darius one to one in a fight that would decide the fate of an entire world.

They had shown him the body of the one called the Taug. Though it bothered him to do so, he finally brought Liala to view the body as it lay in state in his own command tent. She had gazed silently upon it, then without a word turned away. She had not spoken since and refused to acknowledge if it was indeed the remains of Kubar.

"Still thinking about the number of casualties?" Yaroslav asked from behind him.

"Just a hundred dead and another fifty scattered around the fortress. Somehow it just doesn't add up."

"Did he take wing then?" Parmenion asked, looking over to Alexander from the brim of his cup.

"I would not be surprised," Alexander said softly. "And yet another thing, the tools for the forges—nothing, it's all gone, even the bellows used for the flame spouters have disappeared. There must have been another way out of here."

"But we have a perimeter several leagues deep completely encircling this place."

"There are other ways," Yaroslav said softly, and Alexander looked at him knowingly, remembering the place of their first meeting.

"Yaroslav, take five hundred men," Alexander commanded. "Start at one end of this ore ship and tear it apart to the other. There must have been another way, and I plan to find it."

Kubar was like him, Alexander knew that. And if all had been lost, his army destroyed, and he surrounded, he would not have met his death huddled in some alleyway. No, he would have donned his finest armor and stood atop the highest place, so that all might see how a king should die.

How a king should die. And his thoughts turned back to the bed of pain he had been taken from in Babylon. What was it from the holy book of the Jews, who called him a liberator? "By the waters of Babylon . . ." He could not remember the rest. On an impulse he almost turned to Yaroslav to ask if he knew. But no, he wondered too much about that man already. If Yaroslav knew an obscure book from a people most likely forgotten, that knowledge would just compound Alexander's concerns. He pushed the thought aside.

By the waters of Babylon . . . and he thought of the strange unseen god that the Jews had worshipped. Were the gods or god truly so remote? Faceless judges who ruled without passion? But even their god had shown anger, and had rained down death upon those who displeased him.

Or were people merely the playthings of the gods after all? Why had he been brought here? Who was this demigod named Aldin, who had a belly like Parmenion and had spoken fearfully of yet higher gods called Overseers?

"Did you ever hear of a god named Aldin?" Alexander suddenly asked, looking over his shoulder at Yaroslav. Parmenion stopped what he was doing and looked over at the aged philosopher, as well.

Yaroslav was motionless. Almost too perfectly so, Alexander thought.

"What god was that, my lord?"

Alexander smiled his knowing smile and looked away. Was this all some elaborate plaything of the gods? He had often wondered that when he lay alone at night, as they crossed the vastness of Persia. Did the gods of Olympus watch his actions, did they care? In his heart of hearts he had dreamed of being their equal, of one day holding all the world in his sway so that even the gods would look upon this one of mortal flesh with envy and admiration. For a god could be worshipped only from afar, and his voice was never heard, while he, Alexander, could arrange the world to his vision. Arrange the world.

He looked to the southward plains. From what appeared to be but a short march away rose another tower, then beyond that, across the shimmer of the sea, rose yet another and then another. Mountains made by gods, an entire world made by gods, and he was merely an actor upon their stage. Were they watching now? And almost by instinct he looked back to the tower that he had called Olympus. If you are watching, he thought, then watch carefully. For beyond all else, I am still Alexander.

"Prepare the rest of the army to march once the dimming has come," Alexander said, turning to face his staff. "We'll have to go into battle with the weapons we have."

"Why not stay here and let them come to us?" Parmenion ventured.

"We can't let them gain our left flank and cut the approaches to the Anvil. If so, we'll be pinned against the bay, and in spite of our ships, I'll not risk a supply and retreat line across water. I wish to face the enemy as close to his city as possible, so when we beat him he'll have no time to reorganize before we have already gained the gates. Get the men organized. We march within the hour."

The men saluted even as he turned away and strode out of his command tent.

The real reasons for his advance he would not share. In their first battle he had allowed himself, in fact had sought, a position from which there was no retreat. Knowing how the enemy fought, he was confident of success as long as his men were forced to stand.

But this time he was uneasy about it all, and he had no desire to be pushed back into a fortress from which there was no retreat. The ore citadel had fallen far too easily. It was as if the enemy had read his own mind, for he had already resolved that if the ore carrier did not fall before the reinforcements marched from the Gaf capital, he would pull back across the Anvil. Otherwise he'd be forced to fight an army of unknown quality, with yet another enemy force entrenched to his rear.

Not only did this one know what I was thinking, Alexander thought, but he had also studied how I fought, as well. Desperation could breed desperate actions, or at times it can create a whole new way of thinking. If Kubar was alive, Alexander knew that there would be no desperation in the coming battle.

Bowing low to the single urn that contained the ashes of his three brothers, Hina touched the talisman around his neck. Within its leather casing was a miniature of the urn upon the family altar, and like its larger counterpart, this miniature urn carried the ashes of his three brothers, as well. The tradition of the last surviving brother carrying the ashes of his three male siblings was old even in the time of Kubar. It served as an everpresent reminder of the bond that united four souls who came into creation together and who would one day face the judgment before the Light together, where the brothers would be judged as one for all their deeds. It was the last survivor who could continue the line, but it was the last survivor, as well, who carried the heaviest burden. For it was his actions more than any other that weighed the heaviest in the final judgment.

His three brothers lingered in Binda, the Hall of Waiting Rest, and their ashes about his neck were a reminder. For they could see his every action and know his every thought, and if he failed, they would know even before he rejoined them that his actions had condemned them all.

"It is time." He felt a light touch upon his shoulder.

Turning, he saw Kaveta standing in the doorway to the family temple. She was part of the inheritance from Kalin, as well, for if the oldest had married before his death, the last surviving brother took his wife. But for Hina that was no burden; he had loved Kaveta from afar even as Kalin claimed her, and in his heart he knew that she had preferred him, in spite of her clan obligations to Kalin. She drew closer and brushed her hands over his shoulders, and his hands gently touched her on the abdomen.

The day before she had told him that she was pregnant, and that the children would be his. To him that had been more a proof of her love than anything else, for no children had been born between her and Kalin. It was believed by many that a Gavarnian female could control her breeding cycle. If that were so, she had allowed the cycle to begin the first night they had been together, after the twenty-dimming mourning for Kalin had ended.

So there would be five lives soon—the four sons and a single daughter that came to all of the Gavarnian race. Three of the sons would be named after his brothers, and the fourth would be named after their father, for so it had always been. And the daughter would be named after Kaveta's mother, honoring her line, as well.

She looked so like Liala. The damnable fool, sneaking aboard a supply ship to reach Kubar. At least this Iskander had again shown that he understood chivalry when he informed him that his sister was safe in his care. The damn fool, and he could not help but wonder what could have so strongly motivated her to go to Kubar, who had not even noticed her during the brief time he had stayed at the court. As long as she was safe, though, then his thoughts turned back to his brothers.

Would he already be with his brothers when Kaveta came due, when the next quarter had passed and the rains came again?

"I love you more than my own life," he whispered. "If I should fall, tell my sons and daughter that I love them as I love the memory of my own brothers."

She smiled gently, and taking his hand, they left the temple and stepped into the glaring light of the palace courtyard.

It was empty except for a single horse, and beyond the sight of all others he hugged her close one last time then swung into the saddle.

Beyond the city wall the ranks were drawn up in thirty-five columns of a thousand, each of the thousand broken into ten separate groups of a hundred. And at the sight of their commander a wild roar rose up, terrible and proud. These warriors who had been landless and titleless could sense a new change and power in their lives.

Hina galloped down the road, and his staff of signalbearers and officers fell in behind him. His first regiment, the veterans of the first battle at the ore carrier, lined the road on either side. Each man held a short spear in his right hand. The wooden shaft, as long as a Human was tall, measured as thick around as a warrior's fist. The top of the spear was capped by an iron shaft, to which was affixed a barbed iron point. Each warrior carried two more of these ugly-looking weapons mounted to a harness on his back, and by his side he carried the long, curved sword.

Getting the swords for his new army had nearly caused an open rebellion at one point. Since it had been impossible to make the number that were needed in the short time available, he had been forced to requisition them from the noble families. But swords had histories and lineages the same as any Gavarnian, and the nobles had come near to rebellion when the supply staffs had shown up at their individual estates to take the weapons the army so desperately needed.

Still there were only enough for half the warriors to be thusly armed, and as a result a fair percentage of warriors were merely armed with the three short pikes and somewhat shorter imitations of the Human phalanx spears.

All of this was desperation; the plans that arrived nightly by messenger hawk from Kubar's position had laid it out step by step, but there had been no message for three dimmings. Hina was on his own.

Without looking back, Hina continued down the road. As the cheering died, the thirty-five thousand warriors of his army fell into marching formation, then spread out across a broad arc to either side of the road. The army moved north to the final confrontation.

"So you think it will come within the next three days?"

Aldin looked up from the data board and nodded to Zergh, who fell into the cushioned chair alongside him. The Gavarnian vasba held up an uncorked bottle of brandy; in his other hand were two goblets. Aldin nodded in agreement, both to the question and the offer, and Zergh poured half a snifter out and handed it to Aldin, who took a long gulp without any of the usual effete rituals practiced by the Kohs.

"I'll be glad when this damned game is over with," Zergh said wearily. "I haven't had a decent night's rest for the last bloody month. The betting from my half is pouring in faster than can be handled by the computers. Damn my eyes, Aldin, it was for a total worth over a *trillion* katars. One bet came in right after the taking of the ore carrier for over twenty billion. Just one bet, specified against some of Sigma's holdings."

"That bet must be some sort of record," Aldin muttered absently.

"It is. I already checked."

"Who placed it?"

"It came out of some code-named accounts from the Eldarnian banking system, no identification; somebody is trying to keep his placings quiet. I don't like that, the game's supposed to be limited to those with Koh status.

"Yeah, well Xsarnfood on that. Half the damn Cloud must know about this thing by now. Hell, I'm changing my private contact number twice a day now to keep away from the damned calls for tips, bribes, and long-lost relatives looking for a deal.

"Twenty billion . . . By the way," Aldin continued, "did Sigma make any inquiries as to who was betting against him?"

"Not a word. I contacted him personally to confirm it, and he just smiled and agreed. That's not like him, he's usually more cautious than that."

"Then why have you bothered to tell me?"

"Oh, no reason, no reason at all," Zergh responded, looking meditatively into his drink. "By the way, do you have one of those awful cigars of yours?"

"Need you ask?" Aldin fished around in his jacket pocket and pulled out two slightly bent brown cylinders, one of them already half smoked. After putting both in his mouth at the same time, he picked up a lighter from the desk and quickly had both of them pumping out twin plumes of curling smoke. He offered the longer of the two to Zergh and watched as his old mentor leaned back, took a pull, and then doubled over with a coughing spasm.

"At your age, you should take better care," Aldin ventured.

"I doubt if *these* things will take me, it's what's in my food that I tend to watch more of late. I tell you, Aldin, this profession isn't what it used to be. When I first brought you into it, it was still a sport of gentlemen. That's when nobles knew how to be nobles. There was a breeding to them then, and I admired their dignity. But these games have become like a drug, each one having to be just a little bit bigger than the last. Each one having to be more elaborate, with more variations and side bets to satiate their appetite for amusement. I don't see a gentleman in the lot, except maybe for Bukha and of course old Sigma. But I daresay he's the last of a dying breed. Why do we serve these thieves, Aldin?"

"It's what we're in business for."

"This is my last one," Zergh said softly as he pulled on the cigar again, and this time managed to inhale the smoke without choking.

"Retiring then?" Aldin asked quietly.

"Call it what you will. But this game has taken something out of me. Before this we merely watched a fight on a primitive world. We'd sneak in, set up the monitoring unit, evaluate the odds, then manage the bets. There was no way we could have stopped the fighting anyhow, since the Overseers control and forbid all contact with the primitive worlds. But now we've become involved, we've taken those two geniuses of destruction from their own worlds and placed them in a situation ripe for mayhem."

"You didn't voice these scruples when we started this venture."

"There was no reason to. My people and yours had been spilling blood down on the Kolbard since they first settled there nearly three millennia ago. I thought, as you did, that Kubar and Alexander would settle the issue once and for all. Besides, it was a question of more than passing interest—the thought of taking two legendary characters and pitting them against each other. I felt, as well, that in the end the victor would set about to raise his people from barbarism."

"Zergh, Zergh, you are starting to sound as if you have succumbed to the philosophy of the Overseers."

Zergh was silent and showed no anger over the gentle insult from Aldin.

"What is it that you really wish to discuss, Zergh? I've not known you to dwell overlong on philosophy and ethics, I've always thought that was more my department."

Zergh looked meditatively at the end of his cigar, and putting it in an ashtray, he tilted his head back and knocked down the rest of the brandy in his snifter.

"An individual becomes a Koh only because his family has consistently bred generation after generation of cunning and sharpness. There was a time when they also bred at least gentlemen with a rough code of ethics, but alas that's gone by the board."

"And that's not your main point, either."

"I'm breaking my ethics, as well, in discussing it."

"Go on," Aldin said softly, "this room was swept not an hour ago for bugs. If there had been any on you, my counter-system would have detected it. This chamber, at least, is clean."

"Just being on a Corbin gaming yacht makes me feel . . ."

"Damn it all! Say it!"

"All right then. Why would someone field in a twenty-billion katar bet? A sucker bet, at that, especially with Kubar still missing and presumed by more than one to be dead."

"Come now, you know more about Kubar than you'll ever say. And I can tell from your actions he's not dead, and gaming ethics be damned."

Zergh did not respond to the implications in Aldin's words. "Look, Aldin, I think that twenty-billion bet came from Corbin. It had to."

"Why do you say that?"

"I haven't been in this business for a lifetime without learning to smell out a good bet, or also learning how to smell out a game within a game."

"So why are you telling me about it?"

"Because, damn it, man, if he's secretly fielded a twenty-billion katar bet, something is up. Besides that, he's screwing you out of your royalties if that bet pays off; a vasba, as a consultant, is supposed to get a cut of all winnings. Damn it, Aldin, your advice has made that man billions, and you get shit from it.

"Bukha at least has been somewhat honest. Oh, his accountants are creative, but the money finally does trickle down to me nevertheless."

"If only you wouldn't blow it on bad women on some of those pleasure planets, and even worse card games," Aldin replied.

"But at least I have it."

"At least you *had* it."

"Listen, if Corbin is up to something, you should be tracking it down. But what do I find you doing here instead? Playing with old gaming programs on your computer and fiddling around with useless holotapes and replays of Alexander and Kubar. Damn it, man, stop looking at those old tapes and start getting involved with your own survival."

"But I am," Aldin said evenly, "I am."

He looked over at Zergh with a smile, and then, picking up the bugging sensor, he did another quick check of the room before settling back in his chair and offering his companion another drink.

chapter fifteen

"By the gods," Parmenion whispered, "look at them. When will they stop coming?"

For hours the Gaf army had been deploying on the opposite ridgeline a verst away. Unit after unit had swung out of column and filed out to either flank. What was occurring in the valley beyond the opposite ridgeline, they could only imagine, since the last of the Human scouts had been driven in hours ago.

Alexander could only assume at this point that what was being revealed on the opposite ridgeline was only a minor portion of the total enemy forces. Since it was an obvious goal of the Gafs to cut the Humans off from the Anvil, Alexander assumed that most of the hidden forces were shifting to threaten that end of his line. Out on the edge of the Anvil a majority of the cavalry from both armies was positioned and already engaged in a swift series of raids and counterraids, but neither side was willing yet to commit to a full-scale engagement.

Alexander studied each move carefully from the command post in the center of the line. He had chosen his position carefully. It was a third of the way up toward the enemy capital, with a defensive line that followed a ridge just slightly higher than the one opposite them. The far left was anchored on a rounded hill that dominated the rest of the line and looked out over the flatness of the Anvil, which came up to the very base of the hill. The right curved back gently and was anchored in a low outcropping of bared subsurface, surrounded lower down by a thick tangle of woods.

To match his position, the Gafs would be forced to deploy on the outer side of the curving line, thus occupying a longer front, which meant their positions would be more lightly held if both sides were equal. It also meant that he had the advantage of being able to shift reserves across the inside of the curving position, rather than the outside, as the Gafs would be forced to do.

He had weighed the advantage of the position against the possibility of advancing forward rapidly and trying to catch the Gaf army while it was still in column. But their numerical edge in cavalry prevented such a bold stroke and might have forced a confrontation on a field that did not offer superior advantages. The other problem with a swift attack was the simple fact that the closer he came to the capital, the farther he would have had to extend his flank to the left in order to prevent the enemy from turning his line. It was not in his nature to assume a defensive stance, but in his heart there had been a warning to not press his luck any further. In spite of his victories, most of his troops had yet to face the Gafs in an open encounter, and for that he wanted the advantage of position to place the odds in his favor.

The last column of a thousand had swung to the left, and after some minutes no more troops had appeared.

"Have you noticed," Alexander said, looking at the regiment commanders around him, "that their units seem to march and maneuver in groups of a thousand? While we operate in units of five hundred. I think they plan to mass them in depth and use their superior size and weight to crash through our lines."

The commanders were silent and looked nervously one to the other.

"When we go at them, it will be in the formations we drilled with—fronts of a hundred by ten deep. The first wave will have ten regiments across, a front of a thousand paces. Field catapults will deploy behind the advance and move in with it. But remember, we want the Gafs to come to us, and you'll withdraw before contact is made. They'll be expecting the main blow to come on the left, but, gentlemen, there'll be twenty regiments in a column five regiments deep on the right, concealed there." He pointed down to where the men were already deployed behind the clump of trees.

"Once we gain their flank, we'll be between them and their line of supply and retreat."

"But what if they anticipate that?" the Avar commander asked.

"I doubt that, since they know that if they can turn our left the battle is theirs. These Gafs seem to think only in terms of the offensive. But I plan to be with you on the right, and there is where the battle shall be decided."

The men were silent and Alexander smiled in an attempt to encourage them. "Don't worry, that's where I'll be. And wherever I am, that is where the battle is decided."

Alexander looked at Parmenion, who would be responsible for the left, and smiled. But his second in command had a look of worry in his eyes.

"What is it, Parmenion?"

"Just remembering what you've always said, my lord."

"And that is?"

"That this Kubar was their version of you. Even though he is missing and there are no indications that he rides with that army, still I worry that his spirit might be guiding those warriors over there. Otherwise they would not have come to us with such confidence."

Is Kubar dead? For a moment the thought chilled him. He had wanted to meet the legendary Gaf, to replay his hunt of Darius, only this time to a conclusion worthy of a king. Until this day he had never lost a major battle, and the words of Parmenion lingered with him.

But he was Alexander, and with a smile of confidence he turned away to look out across the field that would soon decide the fate of an entire realm. To either side the Kolbard arched up into a distant cloud-studded blue, and he dreamed the dreams that only he could understand.

"Let's just say I wish to make sure my bet is perfect," Corbin said smoothly.

"You know something, I can't help but think that you want him dead simply because over the months he has come to symbolize something superior to you and your damned Kohs. He's a man with integrity and honor."

"Come now, my dear Tia," Corbin replied smoothly, "integrity and honor are for fools. Too much of my wealth has been pulled into this game already. Remember, the technical wording of all bets centers on the final victory of the armies, not on the actual presence of the commanders. The life or death of Alexander and Kubar were secondary bets that only fools would play. There are too many random factors involved when betting on individual lives; it's the overall scope, which is more predictable, that interests me."

"Which you can control better, as well."

"Precisely. Just remember that one percent you're taking, and let the death of Alexander to insure that percent be my concern. The Gaf armies still have Hina, and after all, they're fighting now for the survival of their kingdom and this new social order that Kubar has brought about. Really distasteful, that, allowing the rabble to gain political control. But the Humans have only Alexander: with him gone the army will collapse, be driven into the hills, and the Xsarn will declare the game finished. Anyhow, the arrangements have already been made, as you well know, and shall be carried out shortly."

"As I well know," Tia said softly.

"Prepare to advance, Hina roared. Checking the strap on his helmet one last time, he nodded to the signal drummers. The deep, rolling thunder of a half a hundred kettle drums started, to be picked up by the regimental signalers up and down the line.

"Remember," Hina cried, "the center only, unless I give personal orders otherwise. We don't know where their real strength is! Remember, on my order only."

He knew his proper place was to stay on the hill, that's what Kubar would have done. But he could not order his warriors in and not go with them. He had to set the example. It was foolish Gaf honor, he knew, but regardless of what was foolish or not, he could not live any other way, in spite of Kubar's admonishings. And where was Kubar now? Was he dead in the fall of the ore carrier as a Human prisoner had claimed?

"Sire, there's no need for you—"

"Forward!"

The pipers started up and down the line and the five vustas, the elite regiments personally trained by Hina, stood up in position.

"They're starting to deploy," Parmenion cried. "See? There, in the center."

Alexander merely nodded. "They're meeting our center with their center. Now the trick is to get them to deploy the rest of the formation once the center is engaged."

With a steady measured pace the ten regiments of his own line started forward at a slow walk. Alexander kicked Bucephalas into a gallop and swung down toward the extreme right flank of the advancing line. They'd meet right in the middle of the valley, but so far the enemy had given no indication that it would commit either flank to the assault. The Gaf leader was holding the rest in concealment, the same way he would, and he was not happy with the thought.

All up and down the line the pipers were now in full play, blowing a shrill, dissonant cry that literally set the hair on edge. This made Gaf warriors look even more ominous. The range was down to only several hundred paces, and the slope of the hill was shallowing out into slightly marshy ground. Ahead, skirmishers from both sides were engaged at long distance, and showers of rocks and arrows arched up, passing each other in midflight to rain on the opposite lines.

The Human line started to pick up its pace, and the quiet thunder of wood striking wood rolled along the ranks as thousands of spears were lowered into attack position. The majority of weapons were still wooden tipped, but here and there along the line the cold burnish of tempered steel shone in the light of the never-moving sun.

"Spears up!" Hina cried, but the command had already been given for most of the regiments, which had suddenly come to a stop.

The Humans picked up their pace, drawing closer. Hina looked over his shoulder and saw that the regiments were reacting as planned, the formations suddenly breaking open into a checkerboard pattern of a hundred warrior units, three ranks deep and thirty-three wide.

Less than a hundred paces away, the Humans were out onto the flat, open space. A wild thundering cheer broke from their lines, drowning out all other sounds.

"Now!" Hina screamed, "Now!"

His command went unheard, but the training had not been forgotten. Thousands of spears arched skyward, and such was their mass that a visible shadow raced across the ground beneath them. But it was too soon. Most of the spears fell short, sticking in the ground in front of the Human ranks like a forest that had suddenly sprouted unlooked-for in the middle of the plain. However, this new form of attack had its effect nevertheless. Stunned by the awe-inspiring sight, the Human line slowed to a walk; the back lines, unable to see what had happened, still pressed forward. Hina saw that it was the moment.

Directly before him rode a single warrior, his armor shining in the sunlight.

It was he, it had to be he. And suddenly all that he had been taught by Kubar was forgotten. It was as if the old days had returned, if only for a moment. The honored warrior of the most westward position riding to face the most honored of the other side. The memory of his brothers could not be denied, not now.

Calling the name of his father, and his father's father before him, Hina unsheathed his sword and started forward. The warrior saw him, and unsheathing his own sword, he stood in his stirrups, his arms outstretched as if to gain his attention. But the fates that guided Hina's clan had decreed otherwise, and he never saw the arrow from the Human footman. He never saw the face or heard the family name of the man that drove a meter-long shaft into his body.

"I think this is it," Bukha said sadly. "Our army is breaking up and retreating to the rear."

The other Kohs had turned away from the monitor units. The high-resolution cameras could pick out individuals and had followed Alexander and Hina as they had rushed toward each other, and several hurried bets had been placed. But there had been a universal groan of disappointment when the arrow had slammed into Hina's body, lifting him out of the saddle.

The Gaf assault had broken the moment their commander fell. All along the front, the Gafs had pulled back, abandoning their positions to stream to the rear. It was only the age-old character of them that had saved the army as here and there units had suddenly swung around without order and plunged into the Human line, slamming it to a standstill, until finally the action had broken off as the Human host fell behind and the Gaf retreat was covered by their own cavalry pulled in from the right flank. Nearly an hour had passed and the dimming had set in, cutting down on the clarity of the images. Several of the cameras had shifted over to infra to provide a clearer view of the two armies, which were still deployed on the reverse of the two hills.

Betting for Alexander had climbed to nearly eleven to one, and Corbin had sat to one side, smiling quietly to himself. He

had placed, over his secret wire down to the surface, the order
to eliminate Alexander. But he saw no indications that Alexander was anywhere near his operative. He had assumed that his
target would pay his usual visit the night before the battle, but
that had not been the case. And suddenly it looked as if Corbin's fortune might be in the balance. There was a chance that
Alexander would rout the enemy forces after all. Corbin had
felt a moment of fear when Hina fell and it looked as if the
Gafs would break, but Alexander had held his assault.

All the monitors but one had been reporting clearly. It had
taken a good bit of manipulation to scramble that particular line,
but then again, after all, this ship had been of his design, just for
use in this game. A discreet check in his private quarters had
confirmed what the others didn't know. Kubar Taug was only
minutes away from the front, bringing up a small reserve and
his leadership skills which would help to tip the scale. The betting was at an all-time peak, he realized, and he almost regretted
not having held back some capital through Tia as a reserve.

Corbin was surprised when Bukha, who had been watching
him from one side, suddenly stood up and motioned for him to
follow him back to Corbin's own chambers. Leaving the other
Kohs, he followed the Gaf down a narrow corridor into his private wing of the ship.

Corbin felt the static field click on, and a quick check
showed that Bukha was clean.

"I'll get straight to the point," Bukha said evenly.

For a moment Corbin felt a sense of panic. Had Bukha
somehow detected the jammed transmission, or was it worse
than that?

"How about a drink first? That last action was a little unnerving. I think your army's had it and will be beaten without
much more of a fight. Do you mind?" Corbin pointed over to
the liquor cabinet, and without waiting for Bukha's reply, he
went over to the sideboard and pulled out a bottle of brandy,
uncorked it, and poured out half a snifter.

"Little early in the day for that?" Bukha ventured, but Corbin ignored the tone of insult in his voice.

"What is it that you want then?" Corbin asked coldly, looking straight at the head Gavarnian.

"Just that I was wondering if you would care to make a
personal bet on all of this."

Was this merely a scam? Corbin wondered, or had the runaway gambling bitten Bukha, as well?

"Whatever for?" Corbin replied. "Don't tell me you still think your side can win."

"I don't," Bukha said evenly. "In fact, I think it's all up for my side."

"Surely you're not suggesting that I bet for the Gavarnians to win in all of this?" Corbin asked. "I mean, somehow that would strike me as being, how should I say, disloyal, to bet against Alexander."

"Come now, Corbin, I've called you many things, but I never thought of attaching the word loyal to your name. No insult intended, of course."

Corbin was silent.

"It's just with odds of eleven to one, I thought you might be interested."

"But why would you be willing to bet against your own people?"

"Just call it a hedge against the other side, since I've already sunk a tidy sum into this. I wouldn't mind picking up some money on Alexander's win to cover my losses should the followers of Kubar lose."

"This is absurd." Corbin finished his drink and made as if to leave. There had to be a trap in this somehow. "I think we should return to the others. After all, as host of this ship I do have certain duties."

"All right then, let me get straight to the point. Let's just say I represent a little consortium of financial interests. We know your assets, and we were wondering if you would be at all interested in placing 100 billion katars against 931 billion? I realize that's slightly below the current printouts, but that's all we've agreed to front."

By the gods! Was this Gaf crazy?

"What is it that you know that I don't?" Corbin asked suspiciously.

"Let's just say a gut feeling that Alexander has a sure thing and we want to recoup. If I bet with anyone else, word would spread, and I would lose honor for having gone against my own kind. This secret would be between us, since both of us would lose face if the others knew. Call it greed if you want, but I wish to win back at least some of my losses. Now, I realize that a hundred billion is damn near sixty percent of your total assets, and why should you bet on a sucker bet like this? Let's just say I think you're a gaming man, and in one swoop this could make you the richest being—Human, Gaf, or Xsarn—in the entire Cloud."

"But why should I bet against my own?" Corbin asked, only half listening now. Bukha's comments had hit the mark. Bukha was only doing precisely the same thing that he would do under the circumstances.

"I think you'd be interested in taking it because you, too, wish to hedge your bets against any unforeseen events. If you've bet anything at all on Alexander, especially early on before the first fight, then you got favorable odds. So this little bet could be a match up, balancing one side against the other."

"Ah, yes, of course, of course," Corbin said absently. "Quite a bit, as a matter of fact."

"Then look at it this way. Alexander wins, you'll most likely still come out about even, but if not . . ." The Gaf shrugged his shoulders.

Richer than I ever dreamed, Corbin thought. I'll be the richest single being in the entire Cloud.

"I have the papers here," Bukha continued, "already bonded by Zergh in private and cross-registered through memory systems. Just remember that this is private, and if I win, the transfers will take place through an intricate series of holding companies as outlined in the contracts."

Corbin snatched up the papers and examined them briefly. They were straightforward and clearly bonded and registered. After removing a pen from his pocket, Corbin signed the papers then pressed his thumbprint down next to Bukha's and Zergh's. Taking the document, Corbin inserted it into the banking register of the computer, where it would be officially logged and become indisputable fact.

"Very good," Bukha said smoothly, "now I can sleep better." And without another word he strode from the room.

Corbin could feel a cold sweat breaking out. He had just laid well over half his total holdings on the line. But still, the thought of what he was about to win . . . With a wild laugh of delight he poured another drink.

In the distance he suddenly heard a number of Gafs break into cheers, but he already knew what had happened. The odds would shift downward again, the peak had been passed. So now the others knew, and he was already chuckling to himself since Bukha had taken the bet at higher odds, which even now were dropping.

Then the battle alarm sounded. So Alexander was moving again. By this time tomorrow, Corbin gloated, he'd be the richest Human in history.

"The Taug!" Kubar struggled to make his way through the swirling host of cheering Gavarnians and up to the command post situated atop the crest.

He had met the lead elements of the army a half hour before. They were already withdrawing in good order down the road. There had been no sign of disorder or rout, it was simply that the warriors had started to disengage and withdraw. Why Alexander had not taken advantage was beyond him, and then he had heard the word that Hina was dying. Ordering that his strange baggage be unpacked and a fire to be built on the left flank, he pushed forward, rallying the troops as he went.

The guards by the command tent parted at his passage through their ranks, and the worried staff gathered around the bedside moved aside quietly as he approached the bed.

He could see that it was almost over, but at the sight of him Hina struggled to rise up on his elbows. As the blanket fell off him Kubar saw the scarlet bandage wrapped around Hina's chest.

"I knew you were not dead," Hina whispered. "I knew you'd come back to save us all. I'm sorry, sorry that I failed."

Why, why did they always look at him that way, even as they died because of him? And Kubar fought with his emotions. How many countless times had he come like this to the tent of a dying warrior, only to have an old comrade apologize for dying and leaving the task undone?

Kubar took Hina's hand.

"You did not fail," he said softly, looking into Hina's eyes. "I've seen what you've done. You've made them equals and you've made them proud. They'll win with your name on their lips."

"You are my Taug," Hina said, his voice starting to slur. "Honor me by lighting the pyre. Tell me, O Taug, did I do my duty?"

"Yes," Kubar said, his voice breaking, "you did your duty well. Now go to sleep."

Suddenly Hina forced himself upright, as if struggling against an unseen force.

"He is the Taug, the one true Taug!" Hina cried. Desperately he fumbled for the small satchel about his neck, and a gentle smile crossed his face. His eyes shifted away as if gazing unto the face, or three faces, of those who had gone before him. He slumped forward into Kubar's arms and died.

Sobbing, Kubar held the body close, until finally unseen hands gently took the burden from him. For long moments he sat in silence until he finally became aware that there were others in the tent with him.

He stood and saw in their eyes the acknowledgment. They were united now—perhaps it had been his miraculous return, or that final cry of Hina's, but now they believed that he was who he had claimed all along. And he knew the word would spread; it was said that the last cry of one who was dying were always words of truth, for at such a moment the knowledge of the Unseen Light was so often revealed. It was not the placing of a steel circlet that had anointed him, it was instead the cry of a dying friend that united the people under his command. He looked at Arn who stood outside the tent, and even he bowed his head.

"Paga!" And his second came up to him.

"You know how to prepare what it is that I made."

"But of course, remember I was with you when the great Ulseva made one."

"You'll use it then. I shall stay here in the center. The rest of you prepare for the assault. Our right flank shall open, then the center, and finally we commit our reserves after we see how the enemy is deployed."

He walked from the tent out into the dim light of the middle dimming; from down in the valley came a continual roar of conflict as thousands of skirmishers from both sides maneuvered for position.

He looked back over his shoulder at the mountain he had just come from. So now he understood why this war was happening, and his rage knew no bounds. And there was the darker memory just below the surface; the metallic image of the thing Wirgth had called a First Traveler. He had seen the servant machines on Zergh's ship, but they were small, innocuous. What he had seen in the passage beneath the Kolbard was no servant—it was a machine that was a master.

It had towered over him to twice his height, a thing of a hundred arms that snaked out in every direction, appearing and disappearing from hidden recesses within its body. Its form was covered with curving metal armor that shimmered in the starlight, having the vague outline of humanoid or Gavarnian form. The multitude of arms made him think of some mythical god that could strike at will in any and all directions.

It floated past, as if drifting upon unseen legs, smelling of oil and the sharp pungent odor after lightning has struck from the sky, and Wirgth had bowed at its passage. The First Traveler had taken no notice of them, as if they were beyond its realm or its caring. So those were the creators—things not of flesh. They had created the world for their amusement, but the war being fought upon it was not of their doing or concern.

Then Wirgth had told him what he knew of the gods who were of flesh, who at this very moment were watching them from above, for Wirgth knew the language of the First Travelers and they told him of all that they saw.

Kubar looked toward the east, to the mount the Humans had come to call Olympus, and he cursed silently.

chapter sixteen

"Macedons, forward!"

At last they were turning again to face him. Just the simple fact that the Gafs had a longer stride had been telling in the retreat, that and the organized cavalry that was pulled in to cover the withdrawing army. In order to cover what at first appeared to be a rout, the Gafs had pulled in their right flank, breaking off all contact with the Anvil and forcing Alexander to pull in, as well, to strengthen the center. But now they had turned, and after a brief flurry of orders he shifted his men out of columns and back into attack formation. Fortunately his massive reserve on his right flank was intact and not yet detected, concealed just on the other side of the slope. When the moment came, they would charge at the double and smash right through to the capital road, thus cutting all retreat.

All along the line the spears were leveled once again, and he pushed forward into the assault. The cloud of javelins had given him pause. It was a new tactic of the enemy, and if they had held for but another twenty paces before throwing, his ranks would have been overwhelmed by the sheer volume of heavy bolts. That more than anything else had caused him to pause for several hours as he reconsidered how to approach the Gafs and then communicate that information out to the phalanxes.

He had faced javelins against the army of Porus, but those were light things of bamboo, dangerous only to an unarmored man. But these Gafs were strong, and the spears had hit like an avalanche, punching right through the leather armor and wooden shields of his men. There was only one way around it, and that was to send a lighter line forward to lure the enemy into throwing early and quickly charge in with the main van before another volley could stop them.

And what of their commander who had been struck down? For a fleeting instant Alexander thought that he faced Kubar, but when the Gaf went down he could clearly hear the warriors crying the name of Hina. He could not help but think of Hina's sister, and he resolved that once the action was decided he would go to her personally and tell her what had happened.

But the most important question was where was Kubar? That thought was predominant in his mind.

All these doubts were wearing at him. However, there was no time now for such distractions—the battle was about to be joined, and he could not let other things cloud his judgment.

The Gaf army poured down the slope and again they broke into the strange formations he had noticed last time, a checkered pattern in units of a hundred. Curious, he thought, they would have no weight against a phalanx.

"Just hold the left, Parmenion. Simply hold the left and don't let them turn you."

Parmenion nodded and, with his staff falling in behind him, the overweight general galloped off. Damn him, that old one-eyed Macedon was as good as any of the original Companions.

The Gafs continued down the slope. He could see no hesitation, and the shrieking of their pipers was maddening as the enemy drew closer. They were not silent this time, their howls of rage and anger thundered over the field like a cataract.

Something had happened to them to renew their spirits. Troops who had been retreating only hours before did not come in to an assault like this.

The pace of his own advance slowed, as up and down the line the men suddenly realized that this time they were facing Gafs who would stop at nothing, unless it was the razor point of a lowered spear.

The skirmishers started to pull back, but the Gafs held their javelins. All up and down the line the front ranks of the attacking host drew blades that shimmered in the pale light of the dimming.

Alexander positioned himself in the center of the line, directly behind the company of Ris, his own guard regiment.

"Brace your spears," Alexander roared. The men directly to his front heard the command, and kneeling down on one knee, they braced the butts of their spears into the ground and leaned back on the weapons in preparation for the shock of impact.

There could be no fancy tactics now, Alexander realized, he could only hope the line would hold. The Gafs up forward came on and broke into a full run while the checkered pattern of units behind suddenly slowed.

Even as the front ranks of the enemy line hit the picket wall of spears, a shadow arched up over the line. With a thundering impact, thousands of twenty-pound spears rained down on the line along a front of nearly half a kilometer. Seconds later a second shadow rose up, and then a third. It seemed as if thousands of Gafs and Humans disappeared in an exploding sea of blood. The enemy hacked through the openings carved by the javelins.

Now he could see why the Gafs used the small formations of a hundred. Wherever an opening had been cut the Gaf unit would break out of the checkered formation from the rear and rush to exploit the opening.

From behind his own line the hundred-odd field catapults slammed out a steady fire of two-meter-long spears that slammed into the opposite slope, sometimes pinning two or three warriors with a single bolt.

The Human line started to surge back a meter at a time as the superior weight of the Gafs pushed doggedly up the slope.

Alexander nodded to the signaler next to him, and above the roar of battle half a dozen horns cut through the cacophonous thunder while other signalers waved the red flags atop the signal pennants carried by Alexander's side.

From the far side of the ridge, the second wave of five thousand men appeared charging down the slope at the double. The slowly retreating line was suddenly pushed from the rear by the onset of ten more heavy regiments, and the flow of battle started to reverse. The Gaf line slowly started to fall back as thousands of men pushed up over the mounds of dead and wounded who covered the field.

The Gafs, as always, had the advantage of size and weight, but the Humans still were better able to hold formation and had the advantage of agility against their larger foes.

The fighting raged across the bottom of the valley and then slowly started to push up the Gaf slope. Another wave of reinforcements came down from the Gaf center, and as they hit the rear of the battle line, three more clouds of spears arched up and into the Human line, slamming the assault to a halt.

In the front, it was as if the pent-up hatred both sides held for the other across three thousand years was finally unleashed. Men whose spears had been smashed leaped barehanded against their enemies, viciously stabbing with the small daggers that most of them carried. Gafs down on the ground and dying would still slash out, cutting at anything in their way. In places the casualties piled up two and three deep. The fighting would pause for a moment while the warriors from both sides struggled to push the bodies aside so that they could get at their foes.

Nowhere was quarter asked or expected. It was a fight unparalleled in the history of the Kolbard. The slow minutes dragged by inexorably as the two sides remained locked in a bloody duel. Here and there the line would start to shift, suddenly stabilize, and then shift back yet again. All up and down the front Alexander rode at the rear of his men, watching in amazement as both sides drove at each other with a fury beyond his wildest nightmares. His Macedons had fought coldly, with a dark, fierce professionalism, but these men . . . They had suddenly learned what they could be if united, and they fought with a savagery he did not imagine was in them. But still the Gafs held.

He had to push this assault, and he nodded to his signalers and barked a command.

After several minutes a column of troops came over the slope from the left flank and deployed down the line. He had committed his reserve to the left, but his main knockout punch was still intact on the right. But that he would not commit until they had gained the top of the slope, to see the deployment of the rest of the Gaf army.

With the additional weight thrown in, the Gaf line started to buckle dangerously in the center, while the left and right flanks still held. The center of the line surged forward. The crest was only half an arrow's flight away, and suddenly the assault stopped up and down the line as a wild cry of panic filled the air.

"Release the hold-downs."

The Gavarnian warriors were awestruck, but since their Taug showed no fear, but rather a look of delight, they fought with their own emotions and said nothing.

"Just write it down and drop the messages," Kubar roared as Paga slowly lifted up beside him.

He stepped back from the crackling heat of the fire, and Paga quickly scurried up the rope ladder and alighted on the dangling makeshift basket.

The hot-air balloon lifted slowly into the sky. Fearful that panic might seize his own army, Kubar made it a point to climb up onto the makeshift command platform next to the moorings so that all up and down the line his warriors could see that he stood beneath the fearful object without hesitation.

The balloon continued its rapid ascent, while the ground crew played out the lengths of guide rope that prevented the silken bubble from floating away with the wind.

Paga felt as if his stomach were dropping away, to be left on the ground. For a moment he thought the contents of his last meal was begging for release, but such a thing would be a disgrace, so he fought the urge until it passed.

The battle was raging just on the other side of the ridge, and already a light stream of catapult bolts came skimming over the top of the hill to hit into the concealed formations waiting to be sent forward. Looking down the length of his own line, he could see the massive column of reserves deployed to the center.

The ridgeline dropped away and suddenly the entire panorama of the battle was beneath him. But even as he looked down upon them, the sound of strife changed in its tone. The Human formations looked like a long coiling snake that undulated slowly down its verst-long length. The balloon was starting to slow in its ascent. Kubar had explained to Paga how it would ride up on the column of smoke from the fire but as the smoke cooled the balloon's ascent would slowly be checked, and then it would start to come down again.

He strained for a view over the opposite ridge. In the far distance he could clearly see the ore carrier atop its high hill. But closer up, the next valley over was still blocked from view.

There, he could see something! Even above the cries down below he could hear them from the opposite slope. The balloon shifted and jolted with the wind but he barely noticed it as he grabbed hold of the rope ladder that curved up the balloon's side. He tried to scurry up it, but the giant bag of silk started to roll with the shifting of his weight.

The opposite ridge dropped away. They were all on the right! Alexander had stripped his reserves from his own left in order to reinforce the center! Their right was extremely powerful, but the left—there was next to nothing there!

Picking up a piece of charcoal, Paga quickly sketched a map showing the deployment of Alexander's line. After tying it to a rock, he looked down to the ground over thirty meters below him.

Even as he had worked, the balloon had reached its maximum height and was already starting to descend. But there was no time to wait. He spotted where Kubar was standing and tossed the rock in his direction. His task completed, he turned his attention back to the fight.

It had all changed! The Humans were starting to break! For a moment he was confused, since there was no visible reason why such a thing should happen. Not when they had only moments before been pushing the Gaf line back.

And then he understood. The eyes of nearly a hundred thousand beings had been turned to him. For half, it was a symbol of the strange power of their Taug, and they had taken hope and courage from that. But for the other half, it must appear to have been a new weapon of terror, and their fear had cut the courage from their bodies.

There was a wild shout to his right, and pouring downward like a freshet burst from its dam, twenty thousand Gafs started their charge—driving straight toward the enemy right—and Kubar rode at their head.

* * *

"Hold them, you've got to hold them!" Alexander screamed, but even as he shouted a wave of fugitives swept past him, taking half the command staff along with them in a wild panic-stricken run.

Reining Bucephalas around, he galloped up the hill, riding just ahead of the panic-stricken army. From his left flank he could see a knot of horsemen approaching—it was Parmenion and his staff.

Reaching the crest of the hill, he turned quickly to survey the field of strife. Half his army was on the run, casting aside their cumbersome spears, crying in panic as the Gaf host bore down relentlessly. There was no chance to rally the shattered line; men ran past him blindly, as if he did not exist. He had harbored a hope that by standing alone, exposed on the ridge-line, his shattered regiments would see his example and rally. But these were not veterans of a dozen campaigns, and they ran past with unseeing eyes.

Parmenion came galloping up, and Alexander could see the fear in his eyes, as well.

"What in the name of the gods was that?" Parmenion cried, pointing back to the opposite ridgeline where the balloon was slowly sinking from view.

"There was a Gaf riding it," Alexander shouted. "It was some device to see where our own troops were hidden. If only Aristotle were here."

But he was not, Alexander realized. Even the location of his dust had already been forgotten for five thousand years.

"Commit the reserves," Parmenion screamed, "you've got to commit the reserves!"

Alexander looked to his right. The twenty thousand men were still in formation. He knew that he was breaking an age-old rule of war, that one should never reinforce a failure. But he realized, as well, that if the men behind the ridge in reserve were ever turned around in retreat, they would not stop running. Already the Gaf assault was gaining the crest of the hill a league away. Within minutes they'd cut the road back to the ore carrier and the Anvil beyond. He'd have to meet it here and now.

"Parmenion, go to the right. Lead them in, try to strike that assault on the flank and smash it. Do you understand? Smash it!"

"Where are you going?" Parmenion cried.

"We still have the reserve cavalry regiment back at the com-

mand tent on the next ridge. The Ris and Kievant regiments
might be rallied back there. Those men are tough, they'll know
they need to stand! I'll try to hold the center till you come up.
Now move!"

Parmenion looked into his commander's eyes and saw
something there that drove a cold tingle of fear into his heart.
Reaching over, he grabbed Alexander by the shoulders and
hugged him close, then turning, he galloped back down the
slope.

"We're driving them!" Arn roared. "Look at them run."

At the head of the advancing column Kubar and his staff
crested the ridge. Before them they could see thousands of Humans running off in every direction. The entire enemy to the
right had disintegrated, but that was only half the army. Looking down the length of the enemy line, he saw the dark masses
of Alexander's reserves. There was a leakage of men from the
rear of the line, but the sheer mass prevented those to the forward and in the middle from breaking. A column of horsemen
were galloping down the length of the line, and as they passed,
the men behind them started to ripple forward. The assault
would be joined in a matter of minutes.

Kubar realized that if he could keep driving the broken enemy wing, they could cut right through to the outer edge of the
Human fortifications. If they could reach the lines and punch
through before the Humans had a chance to rally, the war
would be won. He was torn. Should he turn and meet the Humans on his left or push on? There was the chance of a partial
victory in smashing the reserves, or pushing straight in, expo-
sing his flank by taking the ore carrier back and thus cutting
off all hope of retreat. Directly ahead, not a verst away, a thin
line of infantry backed by all the Human cavalry was forming
up as a blocking force to phalanx formations that were advancing forward. A line of cavalry was deploying next to what he
assumed was the command tent. Alexander had to be there,
he had to reach Alexander!

"Forward!"

"But, Kubar, that flanking force!"

"We've got to hold them here," Alexander cried, "until the
flanking force can close in."

The single regiment of cavalry swung into attack formation, flanking either side of the two exhausted phalanxes.

"They're still in column," Alexander roared. "Hit them at the head of the column and slow them up. We can still win this if Parmenion hits them hard enough in the flank!"

Looking over his shoulder, he saw the second regiment of cavalry swinging into position on the left flank.

His staff crowded around the command tent, snatching up the rolls of paperwork that followed behind any army and working frantically to load them into a cart, so that the information could be taken to safety.

He saw Yaroslav pushing his way though the disorganized troops still streaming to the rear, holding Neva by his side. Through the swirling crowd of men, Alexander pushed up to their side.

Neva was looking up at him silently, while Yaroslav held her arms by her side, as if to restrain her from doing something foolish.

"Everything's all right now," Yaroslav yelled.

It was a strange way of putting it, but there was no time now. With a nod of farewell Alexander turned and started back to the front.

The enemy column was spreading out, deploying from column into line of attack. It was the moment when an army is at its weakest, when it is changing a formation, knocked off balance, and there could be hope, some precious minutes till Parmenion came up.

"Faster!" Alexander screamed. The foot regiments were left behind as the cavalry slowly picked up speed. But were they really moving faster? He felt as if it were all going far too slow, as if time were winding down, with each heartbeat passing twice again as slow as the last.

There was the Taug—yes, it was he, riding to the forward of the column. At last, as last the dream of a lifetime would be played out against desperate odds. He was somewhat to the right, and Alexander started to shift himself in the direction of the Taug even as he charged forward.

They were going to catch the column in midturn. Some of the Gafs, in their eagerness to engage, broke from the ranks and came charging individually down the hill, shouting their family chants. The first javelins arched up, then more, and finally a virtual blizzard of iron and wood lifted into the sky. Alexander held his shield up high. A shaft slammed into it, hanging fast, and he cast it aside. He dropped his spear low and braced for the impact.

The line of horsemen crashed into the enemy line.

Screaming with terror and pain, hundreds of horses went down, caught by the javelins or the Gaf swords. But their sheer size alone devastated the front of the enemy line. Alexander suddenly felt Bucephalas give way, rolling over onto his side. Leaping from the saddle, Alexander crashed into the side of a Gaf, knocking him off balance. Coming in low, he drove his spear clear through the enemy's body, dropping the warrior to the ground.

All around him was a nightmare confusion of screaming Humans, terrified horses, and enraged Gafs pushing forward into the line of death. Men and Gafs fell over each other in the confusion. None could pick his target as the battle line heaved back and forth, as if the thousands engaged had suddenly become a single living serpent, twisting and coiling upon the ground.

Alexander could see him. The Taug was not a dozen paces away.

"Kubar!" Alexander roared, and he struggled to meet the one who he knew was an alien mirror of himself. He felt as if he were pushing forward against a flood. Everything seemed to be locked in slow motion; each thundering beat of his heart seemed to shake his body. But the crush of bodies pushed him back and away, no matter how desperately he struggled to reach the Gavarnian commander, whom he knew did not see him.

He was fighting for his life now as he never imagined possible. All around him, by the dozens, the Ris and Kievant warriors were swept away. The defensive line stumbled back, driven like a wood chip on the foaming crest of a blood-red wave. But still they held.

Alexander stumbled, tripping on a body. An armor-clad Gaf loomed above him, his sword raised high for the killing blow. A spear suddenly drove through his chest, sending the Gaf over backward, while eager hands grasped at Alexander and pulled him back into the momentary safety of the phalanx line.

It was nearly impossible to think. The roar of battle had become so loud and constant that it caused a sense of deafness, as if there were no sound at all. A warrior turned to him, trying to scream something, but he could not hear the words. Then, as if in silence, the warrior collapsed—his head smashed in by an enemy spear.

He noticed that they were at the crest of the hill, the command tent was suddenly alongside him, the Human warriors pulling in to surround this, the highest point of land for their desperate stand.

A wave of javelins arced up, darkening the sun, and then came thundering down. There was no pain, only a ringing, stunning blow to his head, and he was down again.

Though he would not have believed it possible, the roar of battle increased yet again, so that he feared the very earth beneath him would split asunder from the sound.

A wave of Gafs surged over him, and then seconds later was pushed back. Desperately Alexander tried to regain his footing.

Several warriors gathered around, screaming hysterically, but he could not hear their words. And he feared that either he was going mad or that the blow to his head had destroyed his ability to hear.

He looked at them uncomprehendingly. The warriors dragged him to his feet and pointed, yet still he did not understand. They dragged him back toward the tent, where, to his amazement, he saw Bucephalas streaming blood from half a dozen wounds, yet still alive. How he had managed to get through the action and, as if by instinct, return to the command tent was beyond Alexander's understanding. He was so overcome that for the moment he broke and started to weep.

The warriors pushed him over and grabbed hold of his body, helping him back into the saddle. He looked down into their faces, and as if for the first time realized that most of them were still just boys, terrified, yet caught up in the wild delirium of battle. One of them handed him his sword, and then another shower of spears rained down, and most of them were swept away.

The knot of men around him had shrunk to just a small remnant of the once-proud phalanxes that had first marched with him so long ago. He saw a tall gangly youth, whom Parmenion had taken special delight in berating because the boy could not tell his left from his right, standing to the fore holding the dirty strip of cloth that was the standard of the Ris. In his right hand he held one of the massive scimitars of the Gafs and fought with the fury of despair, while clustered around him were a mere score of men—the last survivors of the regiment.

And now, at last, he saw why his men had been shouting to him and pointing off to the right. The sacrifice of the cavalry and the Ris and Kievant regiments had not been in vain. Parmenion's attack had come at last.

Along a front of nearly half a verst, they came at the double, their spears held low. The Gafs swung out to meet them. Their dark volley of javelins filled the air, and it seemed as if the entire front rank of men went down, but the army surged forward, climbing over the bodies of the fallen. And then the shock of battle hit as thousands came crashing together.

With that impact, the pressure on his own front suddenly stopped, as the Gaf army turned to face the new threat. He noticed now that the men around him were looking back over their shoulders, and turning, he saw to his amazement that the regiments which had broken earlier were starting to stream back into the fight. The majority of their men were missing, the weaker hearts having lost all stomach for the fight. But at least a dozen units, some with only fifty men, others with two or three hundred, were straggling back into the fight. His desperate stand had given them time to reform on the next ridgeline, and seeing that the battle was still not lost, they had come back in.

His gaze returned to the ground around him. It was carpeted with the dead and dying.

"My Macedons," Alexander whispered. He felt a warm trickle running down his face and absently he tried to brush it away. His hands were sticky and he looked at the blood, not sure if it was his or from someone that he had fought, for Gaf blood looked just the same.

Gavarnians. Where was Kubar? He must meet Kubar and decide this thing once and for all. As if in a dream, he tried to urge Bucephalas forward. He suddenly felt as if he were riding up the side of a mountain toward a scorching sun of hot white fire that spun and spun before him . . . and then darkness came.

chapter seventeen

There was somber consternation in the monitoring room. Entire empires were on the point of changing hands at this, the climax of the game. The scene displayed was one of absolute carnage. Estimates were that close to one-third of both armies were casualties. It was exhaustion, not victory, that finally ended the struggle; both sides collapsing on the ground that they held, not willing to withdraw from their hard-fought gains. In the end, neither side possessed the advantage; they had fought each other to a standstill there on the plains between the ore carrier and the Gaf capital.

There had been cold tension and silence in the gaming room as the desperate struggle finally wound down, if only for a brief rest, before the carnage began again. Both Gavarnian and Human Kohs had never expected this. No one had ever thought that this game would come to such a bloody final encounter, where neither side would finally admit defeat and graciously withdraw, thus ending the war.

For that matter, they had all expected that Alexander or Kubar would be proven the superior general. But in the terms of Zola, who was an old racing fan, the battle was "a dead heat." Both armies, though fighting in different ways, were equally matched, and both generals were matched, as well.

It was now or never, Corbin realized. He had been in a near panic when he realized that the nerve agent most likely had not yet been introduced. It would be a simple thing, merely a drink, and within minutes a mild hallucinogenic agent would take effect, slowly reacting, distorting judgment and vision.

Merely a drink, that's all she had to do. Both armies had fought to a standstill, but all that was needed now was for Alexander to be struck down, and it would be over with. For, knowing Alexander, Corbin expected that the moment had come for the grand gesture.

* * *

The dimming had passed and the exhausted armies rose from their numbed sleep. Across the open fields fifty thousand Humans and Gafs slowly formed into ranks. From behind the lines came a steady nightmarish sound as thousands upon thousands of wounded cried in anguish while waiting for the attention of the healers. The dead were silent. Their only form of witness to what had happened was the sickly sweet smell that now rose with the heat of the sun.

Silently Alexander walked the length of his line, stopping to speak to the battle-shocked men; kneeling occasionally to hold the hand of a dying warrior or to comfort a hoplite pushed to the edge of reason by what he had seen and done only hours before.

"They're veterans now," Parmenion whispered, as they walked away from the four score of men who were all that were left of the once-proud Ris and Kievant regiments.

"But at what a price," Alexander replied. "They've been pushed to the edge—in fact, beyond it. These men aren't Macedons born to warfare, imbued with the glory of dying for me."

He spoke the last sentence with a tone of infinite sadness, and Parmenion was shocked to see tears in his commander's eyes. He had seen Alexander cry at the death of a friend, or horse, but this was somehow different.

Alexander turned toward his second and smiled. "Did you ever wonder why the gods have allowed all of this to happen?" And as he spoke his arms swept out, pointing across the field of battle.

"Which gods? Our gods, or the gods of this world?"

"Any of the gods, all of them. I'm sick of them all and curse them." He thought again of Darius and for the first time Alexander felt that at last he knew how that tragic king of the Persians must have felt—when abandoned, he turned his face to the sky and died.

"But I shall play my part for them all," Alexander said softly, looking at Parmenion.

"What do you mean, sire?"

But Alexander had turned away even as Parmenion spoke, and looked back at the exhausted assembled ranks.

"Do you think they see any glory in all of this?"

Parmenion turned and surveyed the warriors drawing up behind him.

He could remember so clearly the fields of another world.
But the memory was not one clouded by drink in a tavern hall,
while spinning tales that would bring another free mug or the
attention of a wide-eyed girl. No, he could suddenly remember
it as it had actually been. The crossing of the Issus, against the
leveled spears of the Persian host. Or the taking of Tyre, and
the boy, his nephew with an arm hacked off, bleeding to death
while he fumbled blindly to somehow stop the torrent of
blood. Or the smashing blow of a Bactrian arrow plunging half
his world into night.

He could remember it all as he looked into the faces of the
men behind him, and the terror, the gut-tearing fear that would
scream through his worst nightmares, returned.

Parmenion looked at his king, a man whose father he had
first served and who he now had followed across two thousand
leagues of Earth and then across the heavens themselves.

"They see the same glory in it that I now see," Parmenion
replied. "It'll be the glory in a history book or in the tales of
aging men before a warm fire. But you are Alexander the
Great, and for you the world is different."

Alexander looked toward Yaroslav, who was now standing
behind them. But the old philosopher could only smile and
shake his head.

Alexander nodded and looked back at his soldiers smil-
ingly.

"They've had enough," he said evenly. "This is my fight
now. It's time that I became the actor upon the stage.
Parmenion, send a herald over to the Gafs. Inform Kubar Taug
that I shall meet him alone, upon foot in the valley between
our two lines. There let the fight be decided once and for all."

"Sire, are you mad," Parmenion cried. "You're wounded already, it knocked you clean out. And that's a Gaf you'll be facing alone. We've managed to hold them, and you've said it
time and again: we beat them by fighting together, but one to
one we're doomed."

"Just do as I command," Alexander said with a strange and
distant smile upon his features. "It shall be the plains of Ilium." He looked back toward Olympus and smiled.

* * *

"My lord Taug, don't accept. Not now!" Arn shouted. "We've backed them into a corner. One more assault and we have them."

"Have them for what?" Kubar responded. "A third of our army is down, do you want to spend another third to finish this? Think of the price, just think of it. Those Humans over there have done nothing less than prove their worth. For a hundred lifetimes you and your nobles have hunted them with contempt, and finally they've stood up and shown us all that they have the courage of a Gavarnian in their blood. In my mind, it is already settled."

"What do you mean?"

But Kubar turned away from Arn and gazed at the single Human warrior before him.

"Tell your lord Alexander that I shall meet him."

"It'll soon be time," Yaroslav said softly.

"I know, but there is something I have to do first." And turning, he walked back up the slope to the command tent, which had been the scene of such bitter fighting only hours before.

After entering the tent, he went into the back chamber. He knew he should have sent her back to the ore carrier, but there was something in his heart that had told him not to.

Liala rose to her feet when he entered.

"I think you know what I am about to do," he said softly.

"I know, Iskander. You are like him and he is like you, therefore I know."

"I just wanted to say . . ." And he fell silent.

She drew closer to him. "It is your fate, O Taug of the Humans. You know my wish, of course, that Kubar should live. But still my heart breaks for you, as well. For if you win, you shall understand all that he now is. And yet if he wins, he will yet again feel what he never wanted to face, ever again.

"There is an old Gavarnian custom," she said softly, and turning, she reached for a goblet of wine resting on a table.

"I knew you would come to see me before this thing you must do. For a woman of my race to offer a drink to a male is an act that she may do only for her spouse, for the one she loves, or for her brothers. In some strange way I sense that even across our races you are like my brother and also in a way, like the one I love. So drink, Iskander."

He took the cup from her hand and raised it to his lips.

She smiled knowingly at him as he drained the goblet.

"Now, Iskander," she whispered, "no matter who wins, I shall mourn. For I have in a sense betrayed the honor of being a Gavarnian, by being the first to thus pledge myself to a Human."

"I've already made Parmenion and Yaroslav pledge that if this thing should go against us, you are to be released at once. Tell Kubar . . ."

And again he could not find the words.

"I think I know what I should tell him," she said quietly. "Now leave me, Iskander." Turning away, she covered her face and sobbed.

Alexander stepped back out into the glaring light of day.

"If I should die," Alexander said calmly to the men drawn up in front of him, "that is to be an end to it all. Hold the men in check, Parmenion, and under signal of truce meet with Kubar. Try for the best terms you can and then evacuate. Even if we lose here today, the shape of this world shall never be the same. The Humans will have the hills and, I daresay, no Gaf shall ever trespass there again. There'll be more wars, to be sure, in the future, but never again shall they treat us with contempt. Do you understand me?"

Alexander looked over at Yaroslav and smiled.

"I don't care what you say or think in this, but it will be to the death. The things you told me earlier this morning . . ." He fell silent.

"If only I had realized earlier what I had truly been facing. But that is past now, and I must face Kubar."

"It doesn't have to be," Yaroslav said evenly.

"But it must be, if only for my own honor and his. That's what it has been about since the beginning. Thus it shall be ended here, once and for all."

"My lord."

Alexander turned and noticed Neva standing to one side. Guards on either side of her, as Yaroslav had ordered. Now was not the time, he did not want that type of scene before the assembled troops. Without another word he turned away from her, and her wild sobs filled the air until Yaroslav finally ordered her to be taken away.

For the first time since the game had started, Corbin felt a cold rush of fear. Suppose something should go wrong even now? But no, that was impossible. Only minutes before his personal paging implant had given three short beeps. She had finished her task for him at last; the agent had been administered and even now should be taking effect.

"They're doing it. They're actually doing it!" Zola screamed excitedly, pounding the armrests of his chair.

"Look, it's going to be a one on one."

Corbin's fears were forgotten as all eyes turned back to the battery of screens. The room grew quiet, as if any sound that they made might affect what was happening on the surface of the Kolbard a hundred leagues below. At maximum magnification the cameras planted on Olympus and on hovering drones zoomed in, while the remote and shield drones hovered directly above the field.

"If only Aldin and Zergh could see this," Yeshna said softly.

"They're being paid to monitor the equipment, not to watch a fight," Corbin replied coldly. "They're out there hovering above the playing area. Now shut up, they're closing in."

Kubar was already in the middle of the valley and he slowed his pace; in his right hand was one of the throwing spears, and a similar weapon, taken from a dead Gavarnian, was in the hands of Alexander.

The two of them stopped, not a dozen paces separating them.

"At last we meet each other, Kubar Taug," Alexander said, the speech of the Gafs coming with difficulty.

All the Humans were small to Kubar, but even in the stature of Humans, this one was smaller still. But that was merely in physical size. Here at last was his Human equivalent, the one who if he had lived long enough back on Earth would have united all their western world two thousand years before it actually did unite.

"I can somehow sense that you understand what is happening now, as well."

Alexander nodded sadly in reply.

"Can you see no other way then?" Kubar asked.

"No, there is no other way—it must be to the death. For your people and mine have suffered too long against each other, and we are the blood debt, in spite of what others think or do concerning this. Yesterday ten thousand died at our command, and now one of us will die at their command."

"My people have a belief," Kubar replied, "that in war one

must seek out an opponent who will make one's death worthy. We have found that with each other, Iskander.

"Then to the death?"

Alexander nodded. He hefted the spear in his hand and Kubar responded in kind.

Not a sound was heard; the last snatches of idle chatter died away. The two toylike images circled on the screen.

The Human feigned a rush, Kubar swung back bringing his shield in low while holding his spear high. Alexander backed up.

Again Alexander came in low, and Kubar jumped to one side, slashing out with the point of his spear. They backed off again.

Suddenly the Xsarn turned in its chair and started to punch up a stream of data on one of the side boards. The Kohs ignored it. To turn away for a second might mean the missing of the kill.

"Ah, gentlemen," the Xsarn shouted, "there's a problem."

The others roared for it to be quiet.

"Gentlemen, it's Aldin calling in, there's a problem!"

The monitor screens started to flicker, and like sports watchers throughout history who were interrupted during the climax of the game, the Kohs reacted with near hysteria.

But their shouts were drowned out by a warning alarm, and the screens suddenly flicked off, to be replaced with Aldin's image.

"This is a warning, this is a warning," Aldin was shouting, "an Overseer patrol is closing in on approach three seven oh two. I think—"

His words were cut off as the Overseer vessel started to jam.

"The battle!" Corbin screamed. "We've still got time. The battle, damn it!"

The monitors showed only static. The room was a scene of wild pandemonium as some of the Kohs were already rushing to the exits for their personal vessels, while others screamed at the Xsarn to pull the signal from the drone monitors back in.

All six appendages of the Xsarn were working furiously punching up different control boards and bypass channels.

"I can't get it, the Overseers are jamming it. Just a minute, just a minute, it's opening up."

A picture suddenly snapped into soft focus. Alexander was

down on one knee, and all in the room froze. Kubar was standing back, his spear raised on high for the killing blow.

The spear snapped from his hand and Alexander fell to the
ground, his shield upraised. The spear drove right through the
metal.

A wild cheer went up from the Gafs in spite of their other
concern. But no, the Human was still alive, as he cast his shattered shield aside.

Drawing his scimitar, Kubar rushed in for the kill. Alexander rolled to one side and came up, his own spear braced low.

The two came together and for a moment it seemed as if the
image had frozen, the Gaf and Human commanders locked together in a deadly embrace.

Kubar rose up to his full height and stepped backward. A
cry went up from the assembled Kohs.

Ever so slowly the Gavarnian chieftain crumpled to his
knees, clutching the spear that was driven into his chest. He
rolled to one side and then was still.

The camera swung up and panned across the field—the Gaf
army was breaking, running. The camera quickly swung to the
other side, and as if moved by a single hand, the entire Human
army came sweeping down the hill waving their weapons on
high. Alexander had won.

The image suddenly distorted. For several seconds Aldin's
picture filled the screen, but there was no sound and then it
snapped to another image.

Overseer!

The only thing visible was his head, and most of that was
cloaked by a veil. But the disquieting array of eyes and breathing apertures was still enough to fill the Humans and Gafs
with terror.

"This is an Overseer patrol," the voice said quietly, as if admonishing a wayward child. "We've suspected for some time
that there was an illegal interaction with primitives in progress.
Your foolish efforts to conceal the economic disruptions caused
by this game were soon traced by our agents. All of you will
stay exactly where you are. Boarding shall occur shortly. All
assets involved will be confiscated and organizers shall be sent
to reeducation sessions.

"This is an Overseer patrol . . ."

The Xsarn snapped the screen off.

"I declare the game as finished," the Xsarn roared, spraying everyone with the contents of its last three meals. "Decision to Alexander. All bets are logged in my personal computer. Let's get the hell out of here!"

"What!" Corbin screamed hysterically. "This is impossible. It's damned impossible, Alexander was losing!"

The others ignored him in their wild panic to get away. Chairs were upset, bottles of brandy spilled, and burning cigars dumped on the pile carpeting as the high nobles of the Cloud rushed for the single exit. All of them were screaming into their communicators calling for the servobots aboard their personal vessels to power up for an evasive jump out.

"If you don't get out of here now," Sigma yelled, "they'll have you for reeducation!"

His sense of survival finally took hold, and Corbin followed his rival out the door. There was no way that he could possibly get the massive pleasure yacht undocked from the tower in time, but he could still punch out through his personal life vessel and abandon the yacht to the Overseers. Of course, they'd know it was his and eventually they'd catch up, but in the meantime he could get his legal people working on it and come up with the necessary alibis.

Turning the corner to his escape craft, he saw Tia standing by the entryway.

"Not enough room, girl. It only takes two, and Regina's one of them," Corbin roared.

"That's why I smashed the control panel," she said coldly. "I knew, dear uncle, that you'd leave me behind, so I figured I could use some company."

"You damned bitch!" he roared, and pushing up the access hatch, he saw that she wasn't lying—the control panel was in ruins.

"I'll kill you for this!" he screamed.

"Cheating on the games is one thing," she shouted back, "but killing your mistress and third cousin, now how would you explain that to the Overseers? It'd be life in a reeducation camp."

With a wild roar he rushed past her into his private chamber. Seconds later he reemerged dragging a half-naked Regina behind him, her hair still in the permaformer, and the two of them disappeared up the next corridor.

Tia stood alone and listened as a series of vibrations rumbled through the ship as one after another the Kohs punched out to make good their escapes.

Several minutes later the vessel was quiet, the only sound the occasional whirring as a servobot rolled by picking up the refuse left by the fleeing Kohs.

The sound of footsteps approached from a side corridor and Sigma stepped into view.

"So he took your ship."

"At knifepoint, no less."

They looked at each other and smiled, as if this betrayal by Corbin was some sort of secret bond.

"Shall we go forward and see what's happened?" Sigma asked.

"Nothing else to do," Tia replied evenly, and together they returned back to the forward deck.

Returning to the empty room, Sigma walked over to the sideboard and pulled out a fresh bottle of brandy.

"No, not brandy, let's have some Mium Champagne for a change."

"Ah, but that's Corbin's private stock. He doesn't even share it with his brother Kohs."

"The hell with him, we deserve it after this."

Together they settled into the extra-large seat formerly occupied by the Xsarn, but not before a servobot had scrubbed the area down.

"Shall we take a look?"

Sigma leaned back and broke into near-hysterical laughter. "It was precious, absolutely precious. Why, you and Aldin had that planned right down to his hijacking my ship!"

Tia smiled.

"Everything, just everything, you two set up was remarkable. That fake holotape of Alexander killing Kubar, the warning signals Aldin patched into the Xsarn's board, why, even that phony Overseer. By the way, where the hell did you get that?"

"I'll explain that twist later, it is an interesting story. That will teach that son of a bitch Corbin to offer me one percent and to cheat my uncle besides. With our split of the take from Corbin, I'll make forty times that amount."

Sigma looked over at his coconspirator and smiled.

"But anyhow," he said quickly, changing the subject, "it was simply marvelous. To think that Corbin felt he was cheating us and arranging the game right from the beginning, when in fact you and Aldin had him outfoxed at every turn. Did you see the panic in his eyes? By the heavens, I don't know if he was

more distressed about losing his shirt or his fear of the Overseers. You stung that old bastard good and proper. It's a shame
no one but you and I will ever know."

"Well, there are Aldin and Zergh, but they'll keep quiet."

"And there're two others, as well, who now know what the
gods have been doing."

"Alexander and Kubar," Tia said, and Sigma could not help
but notice a strange touch of emotion in the girl's voice. Something he had not expected from someone who was now one of
the ten richest Kohs in the Cloud.

"They're still fighting down there," Sigma said quietly, as he
leaned over and called up the genuine signal from the battle.
The fake holotape had kicked in the moment the first one raised
a weapon. "To those two, this is all on an entirely different
level. It's not money for them, it's their lives, God help them."

Tia could not help but notice the sadness and guilt in his
voice.

Exhaustion had drained both of them. The spears had been
smashed long ago and now the two circled each other wearily,
swords in hand.

Kubar fought to keep Alexander at a distance, hoping to
bring him down with a wide sweeping blow, while Alexander
fought to duck in under Kubar's guard for a finishing cut.

Not a word had been spoken between the two and each was
locked in his own thoughts. For Kubar it was the memory of
the Plains of Oler, where alone and with one blow of the
sword the Unification Wars, and Cliarn's life, were ended.

Cliarn had been his own brother, so that even as he drove
his blade home, he cut out of his own heart forever any hope
for joy and happiness. Where was Cliarn now? The brother
who in the end had fought against him for what he in his own
wisdom believed was right—the preservation of the old order
of nobility. Where was the shadow of the very brother he had
slain in order to unite a world? Why had the Unseen Light ex-
acted such a price from him? And in his weariness he looked
at Alexander who wondered that same thought, even as Kubar
raised his sword up high.

There was Darius, at last. The hunt across the high plateau,
the hunt across the Issus and the plains of Guagamela come
now to its end. There was Darius, the man whose own mother
had turned away from her natural-born son to proclaim Alexan-

der as the son she should have borne. There was Darius, whose own wife had come to Alexander's bed, willingly asking that he father a son that would be more worthy to be a king.

But no, they were dust. Five thousand years of dust behind him, and this was the Taug, and they were on the plains of Ilium. Was Hector watching? And what would Achilles now say as they battled before the gaze of the gods?

The gods . . .

Kubar's sword came down—he ducked to one side, coming in low.

The opening, Kubar was open and Alexander looked into the eyes of Darius even as he cut in. His eyes . . .

Kubar staggered back, the sword dropping from his hand, numbed by the slashing blow that laid his side open.

The sword came back poised for the drive to the throat that would end it all. He could hear tens of thousands of voices rise up—some in triumph, some in pained fear—as the fate of all hung on the edge of a razor-sharp blade.

Where was Cliarn, was he laughing now? No, not Cliarn, not his beloved brother, he was weeping for the pain of his beloved brother about to die.

The eyes of Darius.

The sword pulled back further, as if coiling like a serpent ready to drive into flesh. And there it hung, suspended in time.

"Darius!"

The blade flashed but there was no cold searing, no flash of light that beckoned into the night.

Alexander drove his sword into the ground with such terrible force that the handle snapped from the blade.

He bent low for a moment as if gasping for breath, then Kubar realized that he was sobbing. The cries of all those around them died away to silence.

"It's finished," Alexander said, looking up. "I once said that only a king may kill a king. But I now say, as well, that only a king may spare a king."

Kubar looked at the Human before him. This one had reached at last the understanding of the Gavarnians, and at that moment Kubar suddenly understood the Humans, as well.

"The war then?" Kubar asked.

"Over."

"The terms?"

"The lands we occupy are ours. That which you have is yours."

Kubar looked over Alexander's shoulder back to the ore carrier in the distance and Alexander turned to follow his gaze.

"That's the only supply of metal on this whole continent," Kubar said softly. "Do you plan to hold that, as well?"

"Your people did for two thousand years. But there's something called trade."

He could see the justice in it. "Tell me, Alexander, did you know about these gods who had created all of this?"

Alexander nodded. "No better than the gods of my own time. Those gods I had worshipped, wishing to be like them. But these . . ." He looked back toward Olympus. "Their messenger Aldin and his accomplice on this planet are in my camp right now. He told me all, just before I came to meet you. It seems my own mistress was set to poison me just before this fight, but Aldin stopped it, and then tricked the gods into believing that the poison had been administered.

"Somehow I don't think the gods involved in this will be all that amused."

"You Humans have a phrase: 'They can go screw themselves.' I like that."

Alexander smiled, looking at a king who he knew understood. Finally there was another who was his equal.

"We'll talk again," Alexander said quietly. "There are legends across five thousand years to be shared. Come to me tonight, there is someone there whom I hope you will find pleasure in meeting."

Turning away, they started back up from the valley to tell their people the war was over.

chapter eighteen

"So you were in on it, as well?" Alexander asked.

Yaroslav shook his head, smiling. "Well, let's put it this way.

I just so happened to have written a little paper on this ring-structure years ago when I was a teacher. Aldin and I go way back, back to when I even thought he'd wind up being a professor himself, before he got into this damnable vasba business. Aldin here's been planning this thing for years, and he made sure a copy of my paper got into Corbin's hands. Corbin took the hook, and Aldin snuck me out and dropped me off down here. Oh, it was good fun suddenly being an oracle and all that."

"But why didn't you say anything?"

"We knew that Corbin had managed to plant someone here with the intent of killing you, we simply couldn't risk it."

"Why not?" Kubar asked, leaning across the table. "Just bring it out in the open or, for that matter, settle it once and for all." As he spoke he looked accusingly at Zergh and Aldin who sat in the far corner of the room.

"Let's put it this way," Aldin responded. "Your two races were both locked in stagnation. The Humans were nothing more than lawless brigands degenerated to the lowest form, while the Gavarnians were atrophied by a feudal system that showed no possibility of ever ending. The synthesis of this war was the radical transformation of both societies. Granted, there was a price, but view it as payment on the future. Already, in just the last thirty days, trade has started between your two societies. And each of your races has learned respect for the other.

"Yaroslav was nothing more than a little insurance to make sure that, how shall I say, the Olympian gods did not interfere beyond setting this situation."

"But didn't you interfere?" Liala asked softly from the back of the room.

Aldin could only spread his hands and smile. "Would you have rather had our interference, or the nerve agent that Neva would have provided?"

Kubar could only shake his head. Granted, more than one Gaf would rather have had a total victory, the same as the Humans. Arn was still proving to be a problem. He would give Arn time.

"This Neva, whatever happened?"

"Did you kill her?" Paga asked. "After all, that would be only justice."

Alexander shrugged his shoulders. "Aldin dropped her off on the next continent beyond the wall."

"Humans are there?" Paga asked.

"Ah, yes, and you should see what they're fighting against," Aldin replied. "Lizard things that practice Human sacrifice! Now, if ever creatures needed stopping . . ."

Already Alexander and Kubar were looking toward each other.

"Marlowe," Yaroslav whispered.

Alexander turned to Yaroslav and smiled.

And even Kubar nodded in agreement as Yaroslav called for his parchment roll to be fetched from the command tent.

Then Aldin and Zergh rose to leave, and the two kings looked up at them.

"We'll never know all the reasons why," Alexander said softly, a trace of a smile on his lips. "Yaroslav told me enough the evening of the great battle. I do not hold a grudge toward the two of you or toward your gods, for if anything, you've given me life and an entire world to unite, and thus begin the dream again."

Kubar came up to Alexander's side and nodded silently as the two vasbas left the room. Aldin turned to look one last time—the two were already back at the table, gazing at the map spread before them. Liala had shifted around the table to stand behind the two, and Aldin noticed that her hand was in Kubar's.

Leaving the two kings behind, Aldin and Zergh started through the ore carrier toward the underground corridors that would lead to the docking bay on the outside of the Kolbard.

As they turned into the main corridor they ran into Parmenion, who was calling for someone to follow.

Even though he had been used to seeing the godmessengers, he still stepped back for a moment.

With a grumbled curse the old one-eyed warrior pushed on, and from around the corner behind him a slender female appeared.

"Who's that?" Aldin asked as the girl hurriedly slipped past him.

Parmenion stopped for a moment and a smile crossed his face. "I found her this morning over at the Avar camp. She's the daughter of their commander. Her name's Roxana. Can you imagine that? So I couldn't help but think a little introduction . . . Well, you know." Cursing softly, the overweight general pushed on.

"May your gods watch over you, Parmenion," Zergh called.

"Some gods." Parmenion snorted. "I'll put my trust in Alexander." And then he was gone.

Several hours later Aldin and Zergh finally reached the docking bay that Kubar had discovered in his long underground march. After punching in the security code, the ship's entry lock opened and the two clambered aboard. There were no signs of the First Travelers that Wirgth had reported. That in itself fascinated Aldin. It was something definitely worth looking into. After all, there were always interesting possibilities.

That was one point of the puzzle he still couldn't figure out. How did Wirgth know about them? Let alone be able to communicate with them and thus find out about the Kohs' locations and what they were up to.

He had asked Zergh, but his old friend was stumped, as well. In the end he could only suspect that though he had been playing an elaborate game within a game, perhaps Bukha Taug had been doing the same, even before he was pulled in at the last stage of the scam.

At least Corbin had been wiped out. They still had no idea where he was hiding—in fact, most of the Kohs had taken off to parts unknown. So now it was simply a question of getting control of his assets and then enjoying the comfortable retirement he had been planning for years. And this time there would be no worry about royalties.

Zergh finished with the access code and together they stepped into the main salon of the ship that had been their secret command post for the last stage of the game.

"Damn it, Aldin, will you please stash that dummy Overseer?" Zergh cried, stepping back from the three-meter-long android lying deactivated in the far corner of the ship.

"I kind of like it. You never know when we might need it again."

"Damn thing gives me the creeps."

"All right, all right." He called a series of commands, and the droid came to life and crawled through a hatchway into the aft storage area, whining all the time about not being treated with respect.

"So, you pulled it off," Zergh said, uncorking a bottle of Mium Champagne.

"Yeah, not bad. No one's caught on yet, they're still shaking in their boots, hiding from one end of the Cloud to the other.

It will be a couple of years, at least, before anyone realizes that Tia has controlling interest in any of the corporations that changed hands. And I get control of half a hundred worlds in payoff. Finally I can retire."

"And you finally got even with that bastard Corbin."

"Yeah." Aldin leaned back in his chair inhaling deeply on one of Corbin's prized cigars.

Zergh started to punch in the exit commands to the ship's nav comp. "You serious about retiring?"

Aldin looked over at his old friend and smiled. "Just about the same as you are."

"You know, Sigma was talking about a little private arrangement."

"I'm all ears."

"Later, later." He typed in the activation command, and the ship dropped away from the bottom of the Kolbard, cutting a straight line out, as the dark underside of the structure filled the heavens above them.

Accelerating, they cleared the edge of the structure and the sun above them flooded the cabin with light. Several million kilometers in diameter, the Kolbard floated above them—a gleaming circle of blue green studded with white, floating in the vastness of black and endless night.

"What was that thing about Marlowe?" Zergh asked, as he leaned back to admire the most spectacular view in the Cloud.

"Earth author—Marlowe." Aldin could not help but smile as Alexander and Kubar's ring floated above him.

"Bring me a map and let me see how much is left to conquer all the world."

THE ASSASSIN GAMBIT

Friendship and honor are two of the rarest gifts to be found, and thus this book is dedicated to four who have shown me the value of such treasures.

For John Mina, Tom Seay, and Donn Wright. When special friends were needed you three were there. A lifetime of dedications could not repay all that you have done for me.

And for Kevin Malady, who has always exemplified for me the spirit of bushido and the honor of samurai. When a question of honor arises, it is your example I strive to follow.

acknowledgments

While researching for this book I came across the history of the Japanese Emperor Tsunayoshi and his dog decrees. Tsunayoshi was one of the first animal rights activists and placed special protection on dogs, believing them to be, and rightfully so, the most loyal and noble of creatures. I wish such laws, with the appropriate punishments for harming dogs, could be passed today to protect our canine friends, who ask only to serve and be loved.

Thus a little acknowledgment here to Tsunayoshi and to an old loyal friend, who's sat by my feet for many a book, sharing the ups and downs, always eager to see me smile, always ready to understand when I don't. A special thanks therefore to Ilya Murometz. I paid ten dollars for him a dozen years ago, the finest investment I ever made.

I hope my human friends don't mind sharing an acknowledgment with a canine and a dead emperor, but I'd also like to extend a special thanks to Tom Easton and Karsten Henckell for their help with probability theory, to Susan Schwartz and Joel Rosenberg for the right advice at the right time, and to Stephen Sterns, my always patient and understanding editor. Of course there should be a comment about Mer, but it goes without saying that without her loving support none of my books would have ever been created.

prologue

Yedo, Japan, 1702

"Come out, coward. Come out and face Oishi Kuranosuke of the Asano clan!"

"Murderer, you have no right," a voice shrieked to him from out of the darkness of the shed. "You are nothing but dishonored ronin; your master deserved the death he received!"

"Right? What do you know of right?" Oishi cried. "And of honor? You soil the very word by letting it pass your lips. Come out, Kira, you are still a lord to the emperor. Bear yourself with dignity."

"Go away," Kira screamed. "You break the emperor's law by attacking me!"

Oishi drew his long sword and, with a flourish, presented the hilt to the cornered nobleman.

"Take my sword, you are weaponless. I will face you alone then with but my short blade."

"The others," Kira shrieked. "You are the loyal league, the forty-seven ronin. They are out there with you."

"But I am the leader," Oishi said softly. "Come face me one to one. If you defeat me, you are free."

"I will not soil my hands. I am a noble courtier," Kira cried, backing away from the proffered blade.

With a sigh of exasperation Oishi shifted the blade to his left hand and then drew out his second sword.

"Then if you will not fight me, take my short sword. The moment you cut yourself, before the first drop of blood has touched the ground, I will serve as your second and end your pain."

Kira's eyes grew wide with terror.

"I did not mean to cause the death of your lord!" Kira screamed.

Oishi struggled to control his rage, to allow this noble, even though a hated foe, the final dignity his class deserved.

"You taunted my lord Asano without mercy. Rather than help him learn the etiquette of court, you goaded him and humiliated him, until he broke the law of the emperor against the drawing of weapons at court, and raised his blade against you. You fled rather than fight him, and my lord was put to death, while you hid away and continued to hide these last two years from the family of Asano."

Oishi stepped into the shed, sheathing his short blade while holding his long sword up high. He was so close to Kira that he could smell the fear of his foe.

"It is time, Kira," he whispered.

Screaming with terror, Kira leaped at him.

Deftly Oishi stepped back and to one side. So quick and sure was the strike that Kira's body continued forward for several more steps before it finally collapsed to the ground, showering the darkened room with a river of scarlet.

Oishi bent down, picked up Kira's head, and strode out of the charcoal shed.

"It is finished," he said evenly. There was no cheer, no shouts of joy from his forty-six companions. For all had known, from the moment they had sworn to take Kira's life in payment for the death of their lord, where the path they had chosen would lead. In fulfilling the code of honor of the samurai, they had responded to a law that transcended even the decrees of the emperor—not to walk beneath the same sun with one who had caused the death of their lord. But they would now have to honor the law of the land, of their emperor, and all of them knew that there was but one response he would give to the killing of his favorite courtier—death by seppuku.

"We have played the game the fates have decreed and have faced it with honor," Oishi said. "Let us now prepare to meet our fathers."

Kirdhuk, Armenia, 1256

"My master, it is hopeless. They have gained the last gate to the inner citadel. Already they are bringing up the ram."

"Then it is time at last to face our fate," Hassan said, his dark face contorted with anger. "Tell the remaining men to retreat to the library. There we shall light our pyre."

Without a word the Refik withdrew from the audience chamber.

Hassan stirred himself from his throne and gazed about the empty room. Once hundreds had stood there to serve him, the Refiks and Dais, the higher echelons of the order, and beneath them the instrument of their policies, the sword arm of the Ishmaelites—the Hashshāshīn.

Through the power of the assassins, they had ruled a shadowy kingdom within the heart of Islam for two hundred years, a kingdom that was slipping away.

In the distance Hassan could hear the echoing boom of the battering ram that would soon force the final gate.

So here is the end of all things, Hassan thought wistfully. They had dared to defy the Mongol horde that had come out of the east. And defy them they could, their holy order entrenched atop a hundred mountain fortresses from the hills of Lebanon to the mountains that looked down upon the Caspian. But the ruler of the order, the Old Man in the Mountain, had forgotten all that their founders had taught, and in his madness had tried to negotiate with the Mongol khan Mangu.

After revealing the secrets of the order, he had surrendered their capital fortress of Alamut, and with it the lists that showed where the thousands of initiates, the hidden assassins, might be found, concealed among the vast humanity of a thousand hamlets and cities. Their greatest weapon, the fear of assassination, was thus removed, and the Mongols had then swept forward, killing the hidden agents and daring the attack no prince of Islam had ever dreamed of.

And now the last fortress was falling, and he, Hassan, the last master now that the Old Man was dead, was about to die, as well.

The Refik appeared again in the doorway, as if to hurry him along.

"There are only forty-five of us left," the Refik whispered.

"Are they ready?" Hassan asked.

"Ready to die with honor in your name and that of the Prophet."

Hassan chuckled softly. "With honor, you say?"

The Refik looked at him with confusion.

But of course, Hassan thought, this one is imbued with the dream of honor, of dying a martyr for the honor of the Ishmaelites' cause. But that was nothing but a lie, for a Refik was one who still believed, who would never have the final inner mystery revealed.

The dream of martyrdom, of sacred honor, was a narcotic for fools. Only the masters, and grand masters, had the final truth revealed, like a corpse laid open upon the table.

Honor was meaningless, the promise of paradise a tool used by the masters to entice the young, dreaming of martyrdom in the name of the Shiite Ishmaelites and the martyr Hussein, to come to them. In hidden gardens they would be drugged with hashish and live for a time immersed in the pleasures of Alamut. And then they would be whisked away, brought back from their drug-fevered dreams, and told that they had glimpsed paradise. To return forever was simple, they were told, as the knife was pressed into their hands and the victim pointed out. And so they would rush forth to die and, in dying, fulfill their true purpose—to maintain the power of those who ruled.

The inner circle of masters and grand masters knew the real truth—all that mattered was power and the terror it instilled; those who believed anything else were fools.

"Come, let us die with honor," Hassan said coldly. "Soon we shall recline amid the pleasures of paradise."

The light of belief shone in the eyes of the Refik as he gazed upon the face of his master, not knowing the rage that lurked in Hassan's heart.

Planet Livola, Large Magellanic Cloud, 3-15-3145 C.A.

Message From: Xsarn Prime
To: Bukha Taug
Subject: Potential for Game

Received your message dated 3-14. Approve your suggestion for possible "diversion while accountants try to straighten out the mess from the Alexandrian game."

Any suggestions as to possible historical periods that could be included? Since you mention that "a question of honor to the order of Koh's was violated," I might be able to make one or two suggestions for combatants that could prove meaningful.

Join me for lunch today, we'll talk about preliminaries.

chapter one

"Aldin, look out!"

Oh, Gods, not again!

Aldin instinctively dived for the nearest cover, which in this case was behind a stack of wine barrels.

The first shot exploded the barrel right next to his head. Shattered wood and a shower of sparkling burgundy washed over him.

"Aldin, he's on your left!"

Aldin was blinded by the still-fizzing foam as he scrambled around the stack of crates.

Two more explosions echoed through the storage chamber, one blowing another barrel to splinters as the high-velocity round vaporized a rare selection of Halparinian muscatels, a favorite with Gaf connoisseurs.

"Yaroslav!"

There was no answer. Damn it, did they finally get him?

Another flurry of shots answered his call, touching off a chain reaction of bursting champagne bottles.

Aldin scurried across the floor, groping at last for his pistol, the plastic stock filling his hand. Somehow the weapon was supposed to make him feel more confident, but if anything, it gave him the shakes.

He backed up against a stack of crates, sank down to a crouching position, and snapped the safety off.

Five times, Aldin thought, five damn times in the last six months. Wouldn't Gablona ever give up?

But he realized that any hope for an end to this was ridiculous. To have thought that the sting pulled off in the Alexandrian game could have held up forever was absurd. Corbin Gablona had finally found out how he had been scammed out of his empire, and Aldin suddenly found himself hunted by his former employer from one end of the Cloud to the other. No,

Gablona would never give up. The only satisfaction was the thought that Corbin Gablona languished in an Overseer reeducation camp, but that still wouldn't stop the contract from being fulfilled by the Gablona family retainers.

Aldin stiffened. A hand appeared from behind a stack of crates. In the hand was an Erik 10, a potent piece of artillery that punched out a 10-millimeter exploding shell that could blow through the latest set of ultramesh body armor, even the double set he was wearing beneath his clothes. Aldin brought up his own piece and waited.

The hand extended to reveal an arm, and finally a terrified eye peeked around the corner just as Aldin started to squeeze the trigger.

He let out a trembling sigh of relief. Yaroslav, his old companion and fellow conspirator in the last game, crept out to join him.

"How many?" Aldin whispered.

"Only one, I think."

"How the hell . . ." Aldin began but knew that his companion was as much in the dark as he. They had taken passage aboard this third-class tramp freighter bound for the Rafta-ne system where his old vasba companion Zergh had found a safe house for him. The ship had several hundred passengers on board, each of them a potential killer, but that was the chance he'd had to take. His days of private flying were over; the third assassination attempt had totaled his ship, and there was no way in hell he'd be able to buy another. To buy a ship meant credits, and the moment a credit check for purchase was run into the banks Gablona's boys would find out. Then again they weren't always boys—the fourth attempt had been rather enjoyable, that is, until she tried to nail him in the eye with a poison flick dart.

For two weeks he had endured the passage, hidden away in his cabin, and only minutes from docking above Rafta-ne he was jumped in the baggage hold, all for trying to lift a couple of lousy bottles of wine that a Xsarn steward had told him were being smuggled in and just waiting to be taken.

Yaroslav's eyes widened with fear. Aldin swung around, holding down the trigger, his pistol recoiling half a dozen times, wiping out more cases of wine.

The assassin popped up from behind the shattered crates. Terrified, Aldin snapped off the rest of the clip, churning a couple of hundred gallons of the finest juice into a foaming spray. With a wild scream Yaroslav leaped up and in a two-handed stance emptied his weapon as well, the thundering shots echoing throughout the narrow cargo hull. The assassin flipped over, sprawled on the deck, kicked for a moment, and then was still.

A stream of red ooze bubbled out of the massive holes where his chest had been. Yaroslav drew up to the body while reloading. Just as he was about to kick the gun out of the assassin's hand, the man sat upright, raising his weapon. Yaroslav put his gun to the assassin's head and emptied another dozen rounds into it.

The head was gone, but still the body flopped and kicked for several seconds, until finally it was still.

Cautiously Aldin came up alongside his friend and gazed at the corpse.

"Our first shots should have killed him," Aldin whispered.

"It's a humanbot," Yaroslav replied nervously, kicking the gun out of the android's hand.

The two looked at each other wide-eyed with fear. It was bad enough that Gablona was trying to kill them, but to use humanbots . . . Replications of intelligent species were highly illegal—servobots by law were limited in abilities and, more important, had to look like bots. As killers they were even more dangerous than mere living beings, for bots knew no fear of pain, of punishment, or of dying, and as such were damn near unstoppable once programmed to kill.

Turning, the two ran for the door, trying desperately to make it out of the cargo hold and back to the main deck.

They came to the last row of cargo pallets, cautiously looking in all directions in case the bot had a friend around.

"Clear," Aldin whispered, then sprinted for the one doorway out. After grabbing hold, he yanked the barrier open and was shocked to find on the other side the Xsarn steward who had tipped him off to the wine.

Smiling, the steward was looking straight at him. Aldin gazed into the creature's eyes and knew.

"It's a trap!" Aldin cried, trying to back up but tripping over Yaroslav. The two fell to the deck as the steward pushed through the doorway, towering over them.

The Xsarn pulled from his tunic a heavy Erik 15, a weapon

that could damn near blow a hole right through the side of the ship.

"A little present from some of your old friends," the steward whispered, an evil smile lighting his face. "Their only regret is that they aren't here to see this.

"Time to sleep." And pointing the gun at Aldin's chest, his finger tugged the trigger.

"Brother Corbin, time to rise."

"First of all, I'm not your damned brother, and secondly, I don't feel like rising."

The Overseer's pale bloodless lips curled into a benevolently superior smile. Floating in the air, his long robes trailing to the ground, Losa drifted into the room and hovered over Corbin's sleeping pallet.

"Ah, Brother Corbin, we are all brothers in spirit here. It's the hour before dawn and time to start your day."

"Listen, Losa, or Loysa, or however you wanna call yourself, you're talking to Corbin Gablona, see. I've had it with this reeducation shit and I'm going on strike right now."

"As you wish," Losa whispered, his features just barely flickering from the Overseers' usual holier-than-thou smile.

A faint tingling snap cut through Corbin's body. "You bastards. Why, if I didn't have this juice suit on, I'd wring your scrawny neck!"

He cursed inwardly even as he barked out his defiance. Losa raised an admonishing finger, as if scolding a defiant child.

The tingling wasn't quite painful—the Overseers could never be accused of torture with pain—but it was nearly as bad, with a sensation like ten thousand mosquitoes settling in for a feeding frenzy.

Thrashing and cursing, Corbin tore at the juice suit that fit him like a second layer of skin. It even looked like flesh, molded to fit every bulging curve and contour of his three-hundred-pound body.

He tried to hold out, but both he and Losa knew that it was only a matter of time. Some mornings he'd last for two, even three minutes. But what's the use? he thought, even as he also realized that each giving in was yet another tiny victory for them.

"All right, all right!" Corbin screamed, and instantly the maddening sensation stopped.

"Why, I'd like to—" Losa's upraised finger stopped him in midthreat.

"Come, come, my dear brother. Someday you'll thank me for showing you the path to brotherhood. We Overseers only want those beneath us to live in peace. We abhor violence and so should you. You know that our liberal, enlightened approach is far superior to your primitive warmongering, reactionary ways. Isn't that right, brother?"

Corbin glowered at him. "Yeah, sure."

"Brother," Losa said sweetly, his smile still rigid.

"Brother," Corbin mumbled as he climbed out of bed, to face the eighty-seventh day of his "reeducation." Eighty-seven days, and only two thousand nine hundred and thirteen to go— that is, if he got a sentence reduction for good behavior.

Minutes later the two went down the main corridor, Corbin walking with hunched-over shoulders behind the floating Overseer.

At least they hadn't tapped into his thoughts yet. But he knew that would only be a matter of time. They'd loosen him up for a year or so and once that conditioning was complete, they'd go for the neuro-links and get him on the inside, too. He hated to think that no one ever beat these bastards at their game. In the end, anyone coming out of a Class One reeducation was nothing more than a simpering fool who'd debate for days on end the moral implications of eating a salad for fear that the plants might have feelings and not appreciate someone taking a bite out of them.

Damn. He had walked straight into their trap. Overseers were sticklers for the letter of the law, and Corbin figured his legal boys could so tie them up in the courts that it'd take years before he'd even come to a hearing. All he had to do was lay low so they couldn't nab him with a claim of protective custody.

But someone had squealed, and while hiding out on a pleasure barge all the way over in the Lesser Cloud, half a dozen Overseer ships had cut off all retreat and had him in a juice suit within the hour.

"What are you thinking about, brother?" Losa inquired, looking over his shoulder and fixing Corbin with his full four-eyed stare.

"Ah, you'd only juice me again," Corbin growled.

"Brother . . ."

"All right, all right, but I know you'd only juice me again, brother," Corbin snarled, placing a threatening emphasis on the last word.

"No, brother, we Overseers always want truth. In fact, I'd be far more distressed if you spoke an untruth merely out of fear. You see, brother, it is truth and total peaceful coexistence that we seek to give to you, our less-enlightened heathen natives. So do not fear, speak your heart, my friend."

"I was just wondering who squealed on me . . . brother."

"Since the truth can bring no harm, I'm pleased to tell you that it was your old rival Sigma Azermatti. His people found out where you were hiding and contacted us."

"Why, that rotten scum eater. He broke the code. He broke the damned code against squealing to you bastards."

"Brother," Losa said coldly, a flicker of disapproval crossing his features.

"Brother," Corbin quickly replied. He knew the Overseers were very squeamish about their mating rituals and the legitimacy of their offspring, and smiled inwardly at the Overseer's discomfort.

"That's better. And anyhow, I must say that he did the proper thing. There's hope yet that he might find the Path to Peace. After all, Brother Gablona, you were the organizer of another one of those disgusting games, and then to our dismay you went so far as to try to cheat."

"Yeah, you come down on me for a little fun, but you guys once wasted half a dozen of our worlds in a single day. Now explain that to me, brother!"

"Come, come, Corbin, I've already been through that. We did not 'waste,' as you say, your worlds, you did. We merely put the devices in place. And we did allow the worlds to evacuate first. The explosions were set to go off only if your ancestors continued to fight. They fought, and the worlds were destroyed, thus it can be argued that you yourselves caused the destruction.

"Tragic," Losa said sadly, "but it did work—the wars stopped. We then disabled all systems for running and making devices for interplanetary conflict and have prevented you from using them ever again. Sad that there are so few of us, so that we cannot be all places. At least we've stopped your major conflicts. But it pains us when some such as you still encourage fighting among the primitives and then cheat on the event."

"Cheat, is it? I just was smarter than those guys, and anyhow, they cheated, too, and wrecked the game up good. Hell, I was only doing unto them before they did unto me."

"You are quite incorrigible, Corbin Gablona. But give us enough time, and you'll see the folly of your ways. Now, here we are for today's lesson."

The Overseer stopped and pointed toward a door, which swung open before them. In the outdoor courtyard were half a dozen servobots that looked vaguely like Overseers, who along with Losa and Overseer Vush were the entire staff of this particular reeducation center, all of them ready to work on him and him alone.

"Oh, no, not the Meeting for Peaceful Support." Corbin groaned.

"Come now, we have a full series of lectures about the Path to Peace prepared for you. It is the seventh in a series of two hundred lectures; the bots have been eagerly looking forward to enlightening you."

"Just let me out of here," Corbin suddenly whined. "I'll do anything, sign anything, but let me out of this joint, I can't take another day of this crap!"

"Now, now," Losa said, "your distress is a good sign, for it shows that you are becoming more pliable to the truth. Now go on in, it'll be good for you."

"I never trusted anyone who told me something was good for me," Corbin shouted.

Exasperated, Losa started to raise his hand, indicating that Corbin was about to get another tickle of juice. Suddenly a high piercing whistle sounded in the distance.

"Stay right where you are and don't move," Losa commanded, turning away from Corbin and beckoning to the servobots in the room.

"What's going on?" Corbin shouted as the piercing whistle increased in volume with each passing second.

"Nothing that should concern you for now."

A faint shimmer suddenly popped into focus in the main courtyard, followed seconds later by half a dozen more.

"Zergh!" Corbin roared as the first form took shape, coalescing into flesh as the jump-down beam completed its transfer.

Losa swung around to face the Gavarnian vasba who had helped to organize the Alexandrian game.

The other forms snapped into focus around the aging Gaf. Half a dozen more came in behind them . . . and all of them Xsarns, weapons pointed at the Overseer and his servobots.

"This is highly out of form," Losa said, still maintaining his composure, the faintly superior smile not even flickering.

"It took long enough to find out where you hid him," Zergh said evenly, "and a lot of time to knock out your sensing system so we could approach, but we're here for Koh Gablona."

"That's it," Corbin shouted gleefully. "Give it to him and let's blow out of here."

"I'm afraid I can't let you do that," Losa said quietly. "He's still required to spend nearly three thousand days in protective custody."

"Screw the protective custody." Gablona laughed, walking up to Zergh's side. "Blast the bastard and let's get out of here."

"You know that killing an Overseer can produce the most unpleasant aftereffects," Losa cautioned. "I'm not saying that for myself, of course, just out of concern for you, my brothers."

Corbin laughed harshly and started to reach for Zergh's weapon.

"Don't worry," Zergh replied, "we're just here for Gablona."

Without saying another word he swung his weapon around and pointed it straight at Corbin's chest.

"It's sleep time," Zergh said coldly, and he squeezed the trigger.

"Gentlemen, gentlemen, please, let us have some order. Gentlemen, please!"

The Xsarn's excitement had finally become too much, and with his last words he had the typical Xsarnian reaction to too much stress: the contents of his last meal sprayed out across the room.

The shock of the fetid spray stopped Bukha Taug from driving his balled fist into Zola Faldon's solar plexus. As one, all the Kohs stopped in midargument and, turning, started to scream imprecations at the Xsarn who was attempting to preside over the meeting.

A couple of the Xsarn's companions came up to either side of him and rose up on their hind legs.

"Either shut up," one of the Xsarns roared, "or you'll get the same treatment from us!"

That finally settled the uproar, and the assembly of Kohs backed off, most of them still mumbling threats at each other, but more softly now so that the presiding Xsarn could at last be heard.

"Gentlemen, please, may we all return to our seats. Do remember the old adage that time is money. At last count there're at least two thousand lawyers and twice that many accountants waiting in the halls downstairs, and all of them have their meters running."

Silence at last settled over the room, the only sound coming from the servobots that were mopping up after the Xsarn and cleaning the table where one of the minor Gaf Kohs had spilled a little blood during a disagreement with his neighbor.

"Good. Remember that we are Kohs, and as such should show some dignity."

The others tried to nod in agreement even as they glared at each other.

"Now, back to the bottom line of the proposal, which is in plain words that all corporate assets transferred in any way whatsoever because of what is now commonly called the Alexandrian game shall be frozen as of noon today, standard time. Each company must present its full financial records to the specially convened auditing board. This board will then work in turn with the accountants and lawyers for the previous owners to discover which assets had been stripped once it was discovered that the game was a fraud. Finally, the board shall work to retrieve those assets before company titles are returned to the original owners.

"Is that agreed?"

One of the Gaf Kohs started to stand up to speak. There was a brief flurry of curses as two or three other Gafs, led by Bukha Taug, stood up and surrounded their compatriot. The discussion was short; the group broke apart.

The Gaf who had started to rise stood with a pained expression on his face, and with a lame shrug of his shoulders he sat back down.

"Good. Then that at least is agreed upon," the Xsarn intoned. "All of you please affix your marks to the memo boards."

As one each of the group extended hand, paw, or feeler to

their electronic pads and by touching the device noted their agreement.

A gentle sigh went through the room.

"That at least is the first step," Bukha said quietly. "But there is another problem."

"Another problem?" Zola interjected. "Damn it all, it will take a hundred years to sort out the first problem. First off, nearly half the Cloud's total assets were bet on that cursed Alexandrian game. Then the rumors start to fly that maybe something was amiss and the results weren't what we thought."

"And that's when all you fools," the Xsarn said coldly, forcing himself to remain under control, "rather than coming to me as director of the game, started looting the assets of any corporation that traded hands.

"This problem would have been a lot easier to solve if the freeze on all assets had been put out at once. We could have traded the companies back to their original owners and all would have been solved. But oh, no, all of you got greedy, thinking you could strip the corporations before being forced to give them back."

"A minor problem," Yarvin, one of the minor Kohs, intoned pompously.

"A minor problem, is it?" Vol, a Human who had lost heavily in the games, roared back. "My accountants report that I'll be lucky to get back half the true wealth of what I lost under false pretenses, and it was you Gafs who took the big profit."

"That's a lie," Bukha shouted, coming back to his feet again.

"Listen, if you want to make this into something more," Zola replied ominously, "then we Humans would be more than happy to comply."

An uneasy hush settled over the room. The implied threat that had been hanging over the meeting for days was at last out in the open. All suddenly realized that they stood on the edge of the abyss. Overseers or no Overseers, there was blood in the air.

"Gentlemen, please remember our stations in life, our reputations," the Xsarn said softly, extending his primary and secondary arms in a calming gesture. We've already made the first step by agreeing to freeze all assets as of today. Accountants and lawyers from each of your houses will now have total access to the books of your previously owned companies that are held by my arbitrating firm. In short order they'll be able to report what assets have been siphoned off after ownership was transferred and return them, minus the fees, of course, to my firm."

There was almost a universal growl from the Humans and Gafs over that point, but both sides realized that without the Xsarns as arbitrators the legal tangle would be impossible to unravel.

"But the legal and accounting fees to your auditing firm, who's going to cover that?" Zola replied. "Those bloodsuckers and calculator pushers will suck us dry. Damn it, just the retainer for Leecher's House of Barristers came to an even hundred million."

"Ought to have killed all the damn lawyers back in the final war," one of the Gafs growled. "Oh, I know we need them, and I agree there should be schools for lawyers, it's just that the moment they get their diplomas they should be shot as an example and protection for the rest of society."

"Here, here, I'll drink to that," several of the Kohs cried at once, and together they raised their glasses, finding the first grounds of agreement in many a day.

"Gentlemen," one of the Gafs interjected, "I propose a game. Let's find a planet, fill it with lawyers, bureaucrats, and politicians, and whoever strangles the other with reports and paperwork first wins!"

The others roared their approval, and for the moment a bit of calm settled over the group. The first major hurdle had been passed, and at least they had agreed in principle to rectify the damage created by their last betting spree. The Xsarn settled back on his lounger and waited for the next step.

"Before we get too self-satisfied," Zola suddenly interrupted, "my fellow Koh Bukha stated earlier that there was another problem. So go ahead, Bukha, please enlighten us."

"A simple enough question and one that I now feel is appropriate to bring up."

The other Kohs leaned forward to hear, sensing that Bukha, as usual, had held back his inner thoughts throughout the first days of the meeting, waiting for the right moment to spring.

"Go on, out with it," several of the Human Kohs shouted, smelling that something was afoot.

"What about the two Kohs not present?" Bukha asked softly.

"Gablona and Sigma, yeah, what about those bastards?" Vol seconded. "If Gablona hadn't tried to rig the game, and Sigma, finding out, hadn't then played along, all of this confusion would never have happened."

"And don't forget Aldin Larice," Yarvin added ominously. "A traitor to the code of the vasbas, that one."

Bukha settled back. He noticed the hard stare that Zola was giving him and he returned the look of inquiry with an open, innocent gaze. After all, he'd been able to prove on the first day of the meeting that it had merely been rare good luck that had guided him through the last game, and not insider informa- tion leaked from Aldin.

"Tell me," Zola asked softly, "do you perhaps know of something that the rest of us here do not?"

Bukha extended his hands and shrugged.

"Well, perhaps now would be the best time to tell you about the little solution my compatriot Bukha Taug and I have worked out," the Xsarn said quietly.

"And that is?" half the Kohs intoned together.

"It was you who tried your brother Kohs *in absentia* and found them guilty of fraud."

The group nodded with satisfaction over that point; it was the first item of business and had taken them less than two minutes to vote upon.

"However, we must all realize that we have only three choices for punishment. We can strip them of their assets, but, gentlemen, I don't think anyone here would like to set a prec- edent that could be used against the rest of us later."

The economic consortiums of the Cloud, covering hundreds of planets, were the closest thing to governments. All realized that economic backstabbing and the other assorted games of fair business was one thing, but confiscation by collective force was quite another.

"For a second choice, would any of you wish to publicly turn your old comrades over to the Overseers?"

A shout of rage went up from the assembly. Any of them might tip off the hated Overseers privately, perhaps, but in public, never.

"Anyhow," Zola interjected, "there's a rumor afloat that Gablona isn't really in hiding and that the Overseers already have him."

The others muttered their outrage over that fact and thus showed their solidarity against intrusion from the outsiders.

"The third choice then is simply to kill them," the Xsarn continued.

A hushed silence fell over the room. All of them were survivors of the rough-and-tumble world of Cloud economics. After all, they were Kohs and, as such, family heads of economic syndicates. But one of the supreme rules was never to make a hit on a Koh or the members of his immediate family. Once started, they knew it could never be stopped.

"I suspect then that you've arrived at another alternative, since the first three are unacceptable," Bukha said quietly.

"Precisely," the Xsarn replied, his mandibles pulling back to reveal what he thought was a smile.

chapter two

Groaning, Aldin Larice opened his eyes. The servobot by his side stared back with lifeless eyes of glass and metal, the dripping hypo still in its extended tentacle.

"Where the hell am I?" Aldin asked, sitting up and tentatively swinging his legs off the sleeping pallet.

The servobot made no reply.

Wherever he was, Aldin suspected that the situation was not to his advantage. The memories started to return. He felt for his chest; no hole, so obviously rather than an exploding slug the Xsarn had nailed him with a sleep jolt.

He had faint, dreamlike memories of semiconsciousness and then darkness again. The Xsarns must have taken him and put him on a doze unit until now, whenever now was.

The doorway swung open and two Xsarns entered the room.

"Aldin Larice, we have some friends who would like to see you."

"Oh, yeah? Well, maybe I'm in no mood to see them. First off, why the hell did you guys doze me out?"

"Would you have preferred a ten-millimeter round from one of Gablona's killers?" one of the insectoid Xsarns, wearing the red crest of a Xsarn of the Koh's house, asked in their usual polite, almost self-deprecating manner.

They did have a point, Aldin realized.

"Our agents have been trying to track you down for some time," the other Xsarn continued. "We were trying to lure you into that ship's storage area so we could take you quietly, but one of Gablona's bots got there ahead of us. We had a security net around your cabin, even took out a bot that tried to get through. We didn't know another one had been smuggled aboard and hidden with the wine. It went as we planned, however; the bot failed and we took you into protective custody."

"Yaroslav, is he all right?"

"In good health. We released him since he is no concern of ours."

"Well, thanks for the help," Aldin said, standing up, "but I think I'd rather be going now."

"Impossible. There are some friends who want to see you first."

"And suppose I don't want to go?"

"There is no sense in arguing. You will go with us."

The two Xsarns drew closer. At the very least they'd have no problem dragging him out, Aldin realized, but even worse, they might get excited in the process, with the usual unpleasant aftereffects.

"I'm coming, I'm coming."

"We're so glad you're cooperating. We have a special surprise in store for you."

Aldin didn't like the sound of that one.

"Gentlemen, I think we can all therefore agree that confiscation, murder, or turning the offending Kohs over to the Overseers is simply out of the question," the Xsarn stated, looking around the assembly for a dissenting opinion.

"Then what is the fourth possibility?" Zola asked, growing impatient.

With a nod the Xsarn turned to one of his assistants, who walked across the room to the far doorway and pulled it open.

"Aldin Larice!" Zola shouted excitedly. "You thieving, cheating scoundrel!"

Trying to maintain his bravado, Aldin looked to his two escorts and gave them a nod as if in dismissal and then stepped into the room.

If he showed fear before the Kohs, he was ruined, but suddenly his knees felt like jelly. For thirty years he had arranged games for them and thus gained access to the most powerful men in the Cloud. But after helping to arrange the sting in the last game, his one goal had been to find a quiet corner somewhere in the Smaller Cloud and simply count his profits.

With a flourish he gave a bow of acknowledgment and strode into the room. Not all the faces that turned to stare at him were angry ones; some in fact showed actual delight at his presence, and finally it was one of the Gafs who caught on.

"If the first three punishments were unacceptable choices, then the fourth must be a game!" Yarvin said with excitement.

"A game?" Zola cried, his anger suddenly diverted. "Upon my soul, I thought I'd never see one again. Damn it all, Xsarn, speak up!"

"What other solution could there be, gentlemen?" Aldin said smoothly, stepping up to the table and pouring himself a goblet of wine from one of the decanters by the Gaf end of the table. It was some of their damn muscatel but he gave them a knowing wink after downing the glass, as if he had partaken of the finest nectar in all the Cloud.

"We haven't quite discussed the details, Aldin and I," the Xsarn said staring with a jaundiced eye at Aldin, "but let me introduce the other components."

The portal on the other side of the room swung open to reveal two portly men busily shouting insults at each other.

"You thieving bastards," Vol roared, springing from his chair and starting for the door, followed a second later by half the Kohs in the room, while the more levelheaded ones sprang up to try to hold their enraged comrades back.

The two men in the doorway, suddenly aware of their enraged audience, dropped their own argument for the moment and tried to step back from the angry rush. Pandemonium reigned until finally the Xsarn called in half a dozen of his comrades, who by cajoling and various threats managed to get everyone back to their seats.

In the explosion of anger, Aldin, seeing who was in the doorway, had tried to quietly slip out of the room but was stopped and escorted back in. He had been attempting to hide from the wrath of Corbin Gablona, and now at last he was to meet him face-to-face, along with Sigma Azermatti, who Aldin realized still owed him a sizable commission and kickback.

"So I see you've got that lying thief who started this whole problem," Gablona shouted, storming into the room and pointing a finger straight at Aldin.

Another eruption was kicked off by that comment, and it was some minutes before the Xsarn finally shifted the focus of the meeting back to his original intent.

"Fellow Kohs, the first purpose of this meeting was to set the groundwork for repairing the damage that these three created with their manipulation of the game."

All three of the accused tried to respond.

"Shut up!" the Xsarn roared, and the three blanched and fell silent.

"That's better," he said quietly. He wiped his mouth clean, and continued.

"Now, of course, we all trust each other here, some company excluded—" and he nodded toward the three offending parties, "—but I think we all realize that it will be several months at least until the last arbitration is worked out between our various lawyers and accountants. Now, since this issue deals with most of your wealth, I think we've all become resigned to the fact that we're stuck here for the duration of the accounting."

A groan went up from the audience, for all of them knew that to be true. There'd be no pleasure-planet visits for some time to come, and that thought alone made them feel ugly. The banking world of Ator was the logical place for this conference, but it was famed as one of the most boring worlds in the Cloud, since, after all, it was inhabited almost solely by bankers, accountants, stockbrokers, and those who served them. The bankers of Ator were not noted for creative imaginations when it came to having fun.

"So I realized," the Xsarn continued, "that given the dreary place we're stuck in, we can handle several problems all in one nice little package and have some entertainment on the side."

"What sort of game did you have in mind?" Zola asked.

"We've agreed that the alternatives mentioned for punishing these three are out of the question," the Xsarn replied, "so let us make the fourth consideration a game to resolve the crisis."

"I object," Sigma sputtered. "I've not been consulted about

this. Your henchmen interrupted me while I was on a private meditative retreat, kidnapped me, drugged me, and dragged me halfway across the Cloud against my will . . ."

"Better that than what would have happened if we had not found you," the Xsarn cut in. "We can show you the documentation later, but Gablona had a shipload of his humanbot assassins above your planet ready to pounce."

Stunned, Sigma looked at his old business rival.

Gablona could merely give him a weak smile in response.

"Let's hear your proposal," Sigma replied, looking back to the Xsarn.

"The game arrangement will be simple enough. I propose that our two friends Gablona and Sigma be set down on a planet for the duration of the legal proceedings up here. They will be allowed up to fifty guards of their choosing who must be living beings, that is the only stipulation. Once the last audit and transfer is finished up here, the game will be declared over. When final preparations for the game are made, we should know the estimated closing date for the Alexandrian paperwork, and thus set the time limit.

"Whatever you do to each other on the planet is fine with us. Live in peace if you want, or kill each other, it's all the same. Of course, a wager here and there on the outcome will help us to pass the time while waiting for our accountants to finish."

The room was silent for a moment and then the import of what the Xsarn proposed suddenly sank in.

"It's a gladiator match," Zola said gleefully. "They can do anything they want to each other while they're down there."

"Precisely!"

Savagely Gablona and Sigma looked at each other, their mutual hatred blocking out all else. Turning to the Xsarn, they nodded their agreement.

"But there's more," the Xsarn continued. "We've all been concerned about the cost of the audits—surely it will run into the billions. Therefore it is proposed that if either Gablona or Sigma dies then his estate will be attached for the purpose of paying off our expenses."

"Fabulous idea," Zola shouted, and a universal cry of delight went up.

The two Kohs suddenly looked a little less enthused about

the proposal, but both were already calculating and assuming that it would be the other who would pay.

"Then it is agreed?" the Xsarn asked.

A roar of approval went up.

"And one final point," the Xsarn said. "Aldin Larice will play in this one, as well."

There was a moment of silence. For after all, Aldin was not of the Koh class, and several of them now wondered if it would be proper to allow a mere servant to perhaps be involved in the killing of a Koh.

"It's fine with me," Gablona said, stepping up to Aldin and poking a finger into his stomach. "He'll be dead inside of ten days."

"Would you care to put a wager on that?" Bukha interjected calmly.

"Ten million katars," Gablona shouted back.

"Done!"

The side bets started to fly and for some minutes the other problems were completely forgotten. Some of the Kohs who only hours before had sworn to kill Gablona were already at his side discussing bets and sharing brandies with him.

The Xsarn looked over at Bukha and the two quietly nodded to each other. The problem of numerous possible schisms among the Kohs had, for the moment at least, been sidestepped. The diversion would unite them and keep their imaginations occupied with gaming rather than possible mayhem against their fellow Kohs.

"There are a couple of questions," Aldin said, his voice cutting through the general conversation, and the room fell silent again.

"Go on," the Xsarn prompted, figuring that it would be Aldin who would want the details first.

"You said that we can select any fifty living beings that we want."

"Precisely. Only living beings will be allowed. Our good friend Gablona broke an important law when he manufactured those humanbots for killing you and Sigma. They're strictly out of the game, and we shall find a way of disposing of them."

Gablona looked over at the Xsarn and gave a weak smile, realizing it was best not to debate the point.

"That's fine," Aldin said quietly. "And next, where is the game to take place?"

"Ah, now that's the interesting point," the Xsarn said. "You see, we'll want something close to Ator. So I felt it best to actually stage the game right in this solar system. We also need a place where security can be kept at a maximum. A place where there is limited access, so there can be no interference like last time."

The room grew quiet.

"Therefore, gentlemen," the Xsarn said quietly, "the game of the Kohs shall take place in what the locals around here call 'The Hole.' "

"You can't do that," Aldin cried, "it isn't fair!"

"But, gentlemen, the rest of us already heard the three of you agree," the Xsarn said slyly. "And anyhow, it will make the action far more lively."

A chorus of chuckles echoed around the room.

"Ten million that all of them are dead within the week," Zola said.

"I'd make it three days," Vol replied evenly.

"Well, this is certainly a fine mess. Just remember I tried to warn you fools long before you started to cook up that Alexander scheme," Zergh announced, coming through the door.

Aldin and Yaroslav looked up and motioned for their friend to poor himself a drink before coming over to join the conversation.

"Any word on what Gablona or Sigma is doing, or how arrangements are going to be made?" Aldin asked.

"The Xsarn has declared that the three of you are under house arrest and will be forbidden to pick up the guards you elect, though you may designate a proxy to do it for you. Also, you can't meet with your people until the game begins and you start down for the Hole. I guess he fears all three of you might incite a riot if you and your designated guards have too much time together."

"Don't blame him," Aldin mumbled. "And the other two?"

"Word is that Sigma's thinking of Gavarnians as guards."

"Interesting choice," Yaroslav commented, "but slow in close combat."

"Basak berserkers," Zergh continued, stirring his sparkling

burgundy and throwing in a dash of anisette before coming over to join the others.

Yaroslav and Aldin looked at each other and nodded. Aldin had arranged a wager on the Basak some fifteen years back. They were noted for their fanatical bravery in battle, considering death by any means other than combat to be a disgrace that could bar them from joining their brothers in the afterlife.

"Good choice on several counts. In a straightforward attack they're damn near impossible to stop, once they get going," Aldin said slowly. "But down in the Hole, against the Al'Shiga, I'm not so sure."

"You two have been keeping me in the dark a bit too long," Zergh said slowly, and as he spoke he brought out his personal antibugger and waved it around to make sure there wasn't a tap on the room. "Isn't it time you filled me in on this? Somehow I can't believe that you're innocent victims letting the Kohs run the show. When the Xsarn gave me the orders to pick up Gablona I couldn't help but feel that there was something more to this—a game within the game, so to speak."

The two looked at him and merely smiled.

"Don't complain," Aldin said softly. "I was fingered with the last game, but my keeping quiet covered your hide and Bukha's from getting pulled in, as well. I hope you've reminded your good friends of that, and don't ask any more questions."

"At least then tell me about the Hole. It's more a concern of you Humans rather than Gafs. I've never studied it, nor had any desire to do so."

"But one of the six clans is made up of Gafs," Yaroslav said.

"Gafs we of my race would rather forget about," Zergh replied coldly. "Totally without honor. They're more like you Humans, in spite of their claim that the cult was first founded by them."

"But a most interesting cult, the Al'Shiga of the Hole," Yaroslav rejoined "founded during the first colonization wave into the Cloud. The Humans of course claim they founded it, and the Gavarnians take credit, as well, though most likely it was simply a fascinating cultural coincidence that led these two groups to share a similar historical legend. There are several other cases that some think are tied into the First Travelers, but that is pure conjecture. Anyhow, from the Human side they're believed to be linked to a radical religious tradition that nearly destroyed Human civilization in the twenty-first century."

"The Shiite Twelvers of the Middle East," Aldin interjected. "The survivors were exiled into space after the Second Atomic War."

"Yes, that was it," Yaroslav replied. "And the Hidden Taug cult among the Gafs had a similar history of causing mayhem.

"Both taught that their particular form of religious worship was the only true one. It's a cult of persecution, in which they believe their rightful place was denied them. Assassination is their path to salvation and power. They practiced it with glee, feeling it was a religious act. For a while, immediately after the Overseers imposed an end to interplanetary warfare, they were quite a force. But their numbers were small, and finally all three races banned them.

"Our ancestors were for eradicating the lot, but the Overseers stopped them, and the Al'Shiga were exiled down to the Hole, where they've stayed ever since, the technology to get off-planet having been denied them. Since the Hole is the sole source of green amber, there is some trade, but any modern devices are strictly prohibited. I must say that Hole traders in my mind are insane—most don't live a year before a Shiga takes them out. It's practice, you see, killing traders and, of course, each other."

"Practice?" Zergh asked.

"They've broken into six rival clans," Yaroslav stated. "Assassination is a game between them, their main form of recreation, if you will. Anyhow, they believe that there will come a day when one of the clans, the purest in the cult, will rise above the others and its leader will be revealed to be the hidden Ema, the great leader who will return them to the stars."

"Ema?"

"It means 'great teacher,' the one whose coming each generation claims is just around the corner, and who will lead them back to the stars when the proper sacrifice is made."

"What sacrifice?" Zergh asked, showing his confusion over what he was hearing.

"If they knew, they would have made it by now and gotten out of the Hole," Yaroslav said, chuckling grimly.

"A force like that could cause chaos out here," Zergh said slowly.

"Exactly," Aldin replied. "And that's why the choice of the Hole for this little game hasn't struck me as all that amusing. The Al'Shiga are a bunch of murderous madmen; we have a lot more to fear from them than from each other. I still can't understand why the Hole was chosen. I figured it'd just be some primitive world, maybe even back on the Kolbard."

"It was the Xsarn's idea," Zergh replied, looking closely at Aldin after his last comment.

"Where did you hear that?"

"Through Zola."

Aldin and Yaroslav looked at each other and nodded, as if a certain event had been confirmed.

"So that can explain Gablona's choice," Zergh continued.

"Ah, yes, my dear friend Gablona," Aldin said grimly. "What's he been up to?"

"Tried to bribe the Xsarn, for starters; rumor has it he offered a hundred million to get out of the game."

"If the Xsarn leaked that one out, I wonder what the real offer was?"

"My thinking exactly," Zergh continued. "But going down to the Hole can explain Gablona's choice."

"What then?" Yaroslav asked.

"Ishmaelites from medieval Earth. I've heard you mention them before; they sound difficult to counter."

"It figures," Aldin said coldly.

"So back then to what we were talking about before you came in," Yaroslav interrupted. "Looking at what we're facing, Aldin, and Gablona's choice confirms it, you've got to find a group as treacherous as what we're facing with the Shiga, and now Gablona. Sigma's choice is also an offensive move, one aimed straight at you, I daresay. If I had my choice, I'd go with the Eytor. They're not the best in stand-up combat, but they're deadly with poison and would kill their own mothers as a joke."

"Why not the Ashantor of Gree?" Zergh interjected. "Some claim those bastards can walk through walls—some of the best infiltrators and murderers throughout the Cloud."

Aldin looked at the two as if he didn't quite hear what they were saying. "What? And be like Gablona or those damned Shiga?"

"Fight fire with fire, I say," Yaroslav replied coldly.

"You don't seem to understand," Aldin said sadly. "What was my motivation in the last game?"

"To get rich," Yaroslav replied.

Aldin could only shake his head. "Sure, that was part of it, I won't deny that. But get rich with the money that Gablona had owed me all along. To me it was a question of honor as well. My personal honor versus Gablona's greed. A hope that I could somehow retrieve the honor of my niece Tia, and also to preserve the honor of Alexander and Kubar."

"Honor." Yaroslav laughed sadly. "Honor's nothing but legend to inflame the imagination of youth to do the bidding of those who would use them."

"But I think honor can be a weapon as powerful as anything the Shiga or Gablona could offer."

"Try using honor when the Shiga come for your head." Yaroslav sniffed.

"Nevertheless it's how I see life and what makes it worth living," Aldin said grimly.

"And it's why you've been screwed by life," Yaroslav replied.

Throughout their argument Zergh sat quiet. For Gafs honor was an intrinsic part of their nature, but three thousand years of contact with Humans had tempered that somewhat with a cold realism that allowed them to live inwardly by a personal code but could justify subtle deceit against those whom they came into contact with.

"Go with the Ashantor," Zergh said grimly. "Remember you're facing Gablona."

"No, damn it," Aldin said.

"Then who will be your guards?"

"The forty-seven ronin of ancient Japan," Aldin said softly, an almost dreamy look in his eyes.

"Why them?" Zergh asked, shaking his head.

"Because," Aldin replied, "in this age in which I feel so out of place, I've looked to them as an example. I discovered their story years before while still a student; a certain old friend had pointed them out to me in an ancient text," and he looked over at Yaroslav, who smiled at the memory.

"They knew there would be no reward for their loyalty. They believed there would be no praise of them, no memory of their action, only death. But honor to them was more important than life or any reward. Such men could perhaps show this age a thing or two about honor and a forgotten path to victory."

"You'll all be dead in a week, Aldin," Zergh said ruefully. "Honor can't stop a blade in the night. This isn't some damn philosophy exam, it's life and death, and I say you've got to fight in the manner your opponents will or you will die."

Aldin only smiled and shook his head as if Zergh was a child who couldn't understand.

"If his mind is made up, it's his life," Yaroslav interjected. "But let's look at the practical question in this. If you want honor and loyalty, they're fine. But if my history serves me correctly, after they finished their deed they all committed suicide in front of witnesses. Since history can't be altered, how the hell do you suggest to pull that one off?"

"The Xsarn confiscated the humanbots. Alter them to look like the men in question, and pull a switch. The Xsarn said any fifty that I want. I want them. To me loyalty is going to win this, and nothing less. I want the most loyal men in history."

"But how are you going to get such men to serve you?" Zergh asked.

Aldin looked at his old wolflike friend and smiled.

"I think I know a way," he said softly.

"If you insist," Yaroslav said, "but I think you're insane. Those men will be eaten alive down on the Hole. But I've got other things to worry about. This Hole thing I never expected. I'll have to think about it if you're going to get through this in one piece."

Aldin sat back in his chair and poured another drink for himself and his two companions.

"You know, I wonder what Zola's dreaming up at the moment," Aldin said softly. And Yaroslav chuckled at the thought.

Zergh looked from one to the other.

"I can't help but think I'm being kept in the dark," he said. "But what the hell do you mean about knowing a way to convince these samurai?"

"Trust me," Aldin said. "You'll enjoy yourself."

"All right, show him in, Zola said, and after releasing the paging button, he settled back into his chair and pushed the lift command.

The dais upon which his desk and table were set rose nearly a meter into the air, creating the illusion of a judge, or a person of great power looking down from a great height. His insecurity about his slight one-and-a-half-meter stature showed in most everything he did: the oversized pleasure ships and the gargantuan size of whatever he built; his taste in ample, towering women; and his need whenever possible to be looking down on someone.

The doorway opened and in walked a tall slender man with a narrow, ascetic face. He was pale, as if exposure to the sun happened only on the rare occasion that he emerged from some hidden room. He had the look of books and an academic life about him. In his midthirties, Kurst was no stranger to Zola. He'd employed the academic as a consultant in the past whenever questions of gaming probabilities came up, but to see him on Ator was a bit of a surprise. Kurst worked at some obscure university that Zola couldn't even remember, back on the other side of the Cloud. Something must really be bothering this man for him to come this far and then to camp on his doorstep for the last twelve hours, refusing to divulge to anyone the reason for this unannounced visit.

"So, what brings you to Ator?" Zola said, not at all unhappy to see the man who'd won him some good bets in the past. "Coming to check up on some numbers just for the fun of it?"

Kurst looked up at Zola and, squinting, pushed up his glasses, which as usual were riding too far down on the bridge of his nose. Glasses had been quite a fad with the intellectual crowd a dozen years back, the popular feeling being that they provided an air of classical scholarliness.

"I've had this idea," Kurst said excitedly.

"Oh, really, an idea so important that you couldn't simply put it into a memo the way most of my employees and consultants do?" Zola asked half tauntingly.

"Oh, no, I couldn't do that," Kurst replied, shifting his feet back and forth nervously.

"All right then, out with it, but it better be worth my time."

"Zola Koh, when I have an idea, I really have an idea," Kurst said smoothly. "As soon as it came to me, I booked the first express here at great expense."

"Which you expect me to reimburse you for?"

"Well, you do know that the salary of a professor of probability theory is not all that great."

"I see," Zola said coldly. "Well, out with it, and then I'll decide."

Kurst stopped for a moment, as if he were about to burst either from nervousness or simply from excitement that he could finally talk about the idea.

"There's rumor that you and the other Kohs are going to have a game."

"Oh, really!" Zola said crossly. "From where?"

"It's been floating around for nearly a month."

"Your sources?"

"It's just that all the Kohs are assembled in one place, and there were reports of three special ships arriving here under high security. Nearly every lawyer and accountant in the Cloud is already aware of the last game and the consequences, so the gaming of Kohs is no longer a secret. Two and two always equal four, and among some of my friends the deduction started to spread that three men are to be pitted against each other on a barbaric planet. It's been on the com links now for quite some time."

"Good Gods!" Zola roared.

He turned away from Kurst. If the lawyers knew and were chatting about it through the hookups, then the Overseers most likely knew, as well. What the hell was going on? How come the Overseers hadn't already moved in?

How come? Could it be then that the rumored encounter between the Xsarn and a representative of the Overseers wasn't a rumor after all?

He looked back at Kurst.

"Go on then," he said.

"The rumor of this game is spreading across the Cloud, and I had a tremendous idea that could turn it to your advantage."

"And that is . . . ?" Zola asked, relaxing ever so slightly.

"A lottery!" Kurst shouted, expelling the words as if they'd been pent up inside him for weeks. It really wasn't his idea, at least not initially. It had come up in a barroom conversation with a friend who'd been interested in discussing the game, knowing of Kurst's contact with Zola. The friend had commented that it could be a hell of a diversion for the masses, and after buying one more round of drinks, Kurst rushed out of the bar and booked the next flight to Ator. So, while it wasn't his idea initially, in short order he'd thought out the more fascinating permutations it could offer and thus by the time he landed on Ator he felt the idea was his, and his alone.

"What do you mean, a lottery?" Zola asked.

"A game for everyone in the Cloud!" Kurst announced triumphantly.

Zola sat silent for some seconds and then gradually the dais started to lower. Zola stood up and, stepping off, came up to confront Kurst.

"Are you mad?" he said, slowly enunciating each word savagely. "The games belong to us, the Kohs. They are not for the ill-bred rabble such as yourself!"

Kurst backed up a step, his fear obvious.

"I meant no offense to one of your illustrious class," Kurst squealed.

"Besides, it would mean that everyone in the Cloud would know," Zola said coldly. He left out mention of the Overseers, since such beings were creatures of legend to the people of the Cloud, and the Kohs never acknowledged their existence, or power that they held, to the lower classes.

"But let me explain," Kurst pleaded.

"Explain then. And when you're done taking my valuable time, I hope you've booked your own return passage."

"As I was saying earlier," Kurst ventured, "I had a wonderful idea for a lottery around your game. Now, from what I've heard, two Kohs and a vasba are going to be marooned on a barbaric planet for a certain number of days."

He stopped as if looking for confirmation, but Zola said nothing.

"Well, knowing the refined nature of those of your class, I can well see where all sorts of interesting wagers will be set on the finer points of combat between the three, but I had something else in mind."

"Go on," Zola said.

"Let's look at it in a logical progression. You have three players. Let's call them X, Y, and Z. Now, there is actually a fourth element, the natives, we'll call them N. Starting with player X, there are five possible outcomes. He could be killed by the natives, he could be killed by either of his opponents, or he could be killed even by his own people. The fifth alternative is that he lives."

"I think I understand," Zola said, the faintest look of interest crossing his features.

"Fine then," Kurst replied, warming to his subject. "Now, if only one person is involved, there are five possible bets. With two people, every combination comes out to twenty-five possible results, from both of them living to both of them being killed by natives."

"And with three players, like we have?" Zola asked, growing excited.

"One hundred and twenty-five possible outcomes for the first day!"

"The first day?" Zola replied.

"That's the beauty of it. Let's go back to one example. How long, might I ask, is the game intended to run?"

Zola looked closely at Kurst. No one was sure on that yet.

"Say sixty days," Zola said softly, already starting to anticipate what Kurst was driving at.

"Good, very good," Kurst replied, rubbing his hands. "There are four probable events a day then for sixty days."

"I thought you said five."

"Living all the way to the end is simply added on, it's a nonevent otherwise. So in the end there are two hundred and forty possible outcomes plus one. Now, with three players we therefore have as a total number of probable outcomes a sum equal to two hundred and forty-one to the third power."

Zola looked at Kurst dumbfounded.

"To be exact," Kurst replied sharply, "the figure comes out to thirteen million, nine hundred and ninety-seven thousand, five hundred and twenty-one different betting potentials. You sell them like lottery tickets, with people buying bets that could read, for example, X dead on day three by Y, Z dead on day forty-nine by the natives, Y lives."

"By heavens, I should have thought of this," Zola whispered.

"Not to worry about that," Kurst replied triumphantly. "I am your consultant and that's my job."

Zola looked at Kurst, a smile lighting his features. Why, he could sell billions of such tickets. Granted, some bets were better than others, and the mob would latch onto them, but all he had to do was make the payoff low, say 25 percent, and he'd still come out on top. There were problems, to be sure. First and foremost was the Overseers, but with the profit this could offer, he'd figure out a way to deal with them.

"Sorry if I was a bit cross earlier, you know how it is with the weighty concerns of business," Zola said good-naturedly, putting his arm up over Kurst's shoulder.

"How about a good cigar and a drink?" Zola continued, leading Kurst over to a chair by his desk.

"Don't mind if I do!" Kurst replied, amazed when the Koh even went so far as to light the cigar for him.

"Where are you staying, my friend?" Zola asked.

"Oh, I've got an old girlfriend working here with the stock market," Kurst replied, slightly embarrassed.

"Ah, but of course," Zola responded, chuckling and nudging his companion in the ribs.

"I'll see you first thing tomorrow. I want to make some calls on this. See my secretary on the way out and have her call accounting. Have them draw you a retainer for, let's see, would twenty thousand be enough?"

Kurst looked at Zola goggle-eyed.

"Only the beginning, my good man," Zola replied expansively. "Why, it's only the beginning."

As the door closed behind Kurst, Zola could not suppress a smile. Through some maneuvering and a couple of very expensive bribes, he'd already managed to get to one of Sigma's primitive guards. The usual promises had been made of untold riches and the bait had been taken.

Zola already knew where his money would be riding.

chapter three

Yedo, Japan, 1702

Oishi Kuranosuke looked down at the silken pouch resting in his lap, and was pleased. He gently pulled back the drawstrings, reached in, and drew forth the prize. He held up the head of Kira Yoshinaka by its topknot, and a sigh of fulfillment came from the forty-six samurai who knelt in a circle around him.

So here at last was the end of their quest, Oishi thought sadly. All that they had lived for, had dreamed of for the last year and a half was completed. Was it really such a short time ago? he thought wistfully. It had seemed an eternity, an endless succession of days, tortured with dishonor and shame, since their lord Asano Nagamori had gone to his shameful death.

With tear-streaked eyes Oishi looked into the grave of Asano in the center of their circle.

Only two years before Asano, brave, impetuous Asano, who still embodied the samurai spirit of old, had answered the call to serve in the court of the emperor and upon arrival was made answerable to Kira Yoshinaka, a craven courtier of the new school, who looked with disdain upon those not born and raised in the refined atmosphere of the court. At the mere thought of that cursed name, Oishi looked to the severed head in his hands, the head of Kira, as if to reassure himself that the hated enemy was indeed dead.

Oishi had been with Asano, and saw the daily insults and taunts to which the cowardly Kira had subjected his lord. In the days when men with swords had ruled, such taunts would have been answered at once. But such days were gone, and Kira knew himself safe, protected by the edict of the Imperial Court, where the drawing of a sword, even to avenge an insult, was punishable by death.

So the insults came, day after day, the effete courtier taunting the old warrior Asano, calling him bumpkin and uncultured barbarian, goading him like a boy teasing an eagle locked in a cage, and laughing behind his hand as Asano struggled to learn the elaborate rituals of Yedo. Of course Asano could have ended the taunting by paying the necessary bribes to Kira that all others finally paid him. Then Kira would deem it within his dignity to teach Asano all the finer nuances of court procedures, but Asano's pride prevented him from paying such a bribe, and so the taunts and laughter continued.

But the laughter finally died when the eagle broke its cage. If only he had been there, Oishi thought, if only he had been there that day, he could have restrained his lord, or drawn sword for him, but the fates had desired the drama to be played out without him.

While preparing for a reception with the Emperor Tsunayoshi, Kira had insulted Asano for not knowing a minor point of court etiquette and then held him up for public ridicule. With a shout of rage Asano drew his sword and went for

Kira, who fled shrieking. The first blow cut into Kira's fore-head.

Before he could swing again a dozen courtiers swarmed over Asano, bearing him to the ground, while others carried Kira away.

The justice of the Emperor Tsunayoshi, the emperor known for his edicts protecting all canines as the Dog Emperor, was swift. Before the sun had touched the western horizon, Asano was dead, believing that he had at least killed Kira, even while he drove the dagger into his own body in payment for his crime.

But Kira lived, the blow having stunned him and nothing more. The emperor decreed that the affair was finished; there was to be no blood vendetta from the house of Asano against Kira. If sword was drawn by any member of Asano's clan, death would be the punishment.

The emperor had spoken, but the law of the samurai, the samurai of old, was plain, for was it not written that a man could not walk under the same heavens with the slayer of his father, but even more so the slayer of his lord?

It was plain to all, at least those who believed yet in honor, that Kira with his taunting words had driven the blade into Asano's stomach, as surely as if he had held it with his own hand.

And so the "Loyal League" of forty-seven samurai was formed—to avenge the dishonor to their lord. And all who joined Oishi in this quest knew that there could be but one possible fate for them, for in answering one law, they surely would violate that of the emperor.

Now at last it was finished. Kira knew of them and had guarded himself well, hiding within his fortresses. But tonight he had let his guard down, thinking Oishi and his companions were far away.

And so they had struck, gaining entry to Kira's stronghold and finding him at last, cowering in the charcoal shed, without even a sword in hand.

Oishi stirred from his contemplation, raising his eyes to gaze at the other members of the Loyal League.

He had led them to this moment—it was the dream that had driven them forward, had filled every waking moment. And now they would die. Each had already made his farewells to family and friends. Each had already drawn in, preparing, already walking down the unknown path. For all knew that the moment Kira's head was struck from its body, the moment they had fulfilled the vengeance of their dead lord, they stood condemned.

Oishi smiled wistfully as he gazed upon his young nephew Seiji, who sat proudly by Takashi, his father, Oishi's older brother. Takashi caught his eyes for a moment. Both knew the other's pride in the youngster who had behaved well in their first and final fight, and both could sense the pain at what they had condemned him to.

"My lord Asano," Oishi said, bowing low before the grave, his comrades doing likewise. "I humbly beg you to accept this the fulfillment of our pledge to you."

After rising, he stepped forward and then knelt again by the foot of Asano's grave. He didn't want to release the offering, for once he had let go, it was finished, the purpose of the league completed.

His grasp lingered for a moment, and then bowing lower, he placed the freshly washed head of Kira Yoshinaka upon the grave of his master.

A sigh of contentment stirred through the empty graveyard, and for a moment Oishi was not sure if it came from his comrades or from the spirit of old Asano, satisfied that his honor was restored at last.

Oishi brought his hands together in prayer—prayer to Asano and to the ancestors of the clan that now they could rest peacefully, and prayer, as well, for himself, and for the league, so that all would face death unflinchingly. There was but one step left: to go to the head abbot of the local temple and there stay till the emperor's men arrived with the decision that all knew could only be a command to commit seppuku.

He knew he was lingering too long; it was time to act.

"Sogio, Fumio!"

"Hai!"

"The two of you are to go at once to the Censorate. Report to him what has transpired, and tell him that we shall present ourselves for arrest at the abbey."

The two rose up from the circle and hurried off.

"Terazaka!"

"Hai!"

"Leave at once, go to our lady, and inform her that the honor of her husband has been avenged."

Terazaka followed his two comrades into the darkness.

So now there were only forty-four of them, a good number that, Oishi thought wistfully.

He looked around the circle and, giving a slight nod of command, rose to his feet again, the others following.

"Are we all ready for what must be?" Oishi asked softly.

As one, his comrades nodded in reply.

He found himself struggling to hold back the tears of pride. Each knew that all he had to do was to melt into the darkness, and a populace that by and large sympathized with their cause would give them shelter and hidden passage into the countryside. But not one turned away; they had crossed the line together and would now die together. They would force the emperor himself to pass direct judgment and set an example of loyalty and courage in this decadent age.

"Then you all understand what is to come," Oishi announced.

They looked at him in silence and nodded.

"Then let us face our destiny."

"Oishi!"

Turning, Oishi saw the look of terror on Seiji's face, a terror that cut into his own heart as well.

For a moment he stood frozen and then fell to his knees, his forehead touching the ground. A stunning glow of crystalline brilliance washed over him, and he struggled with his fear.

"Oishi Kuranosuke!" a voice out of the light intoned.

Oishi dared a glance at his companions surrounding him; they were prostrate on the ground, none daring to raise his eyes. For who would dare to do so in the presence of their lord Asano Nagamori!

Surely there could be no answer other than that the pulsing light over the tomb was their lord, come from beyond to tell them of his pleasure with their deed.

"Oishi Kuranosuke, rise and come forward."

Despite his years of training, Oishi was ashamed to realize that his knees were trembling. What would his lord think at such a sight? He could only pray that Asano would understand, that visitors from the other world could cause even a samurai to tremble.

Struggling to master his fear, Oishi gained his feet and, with head still bowed, approached the light that now fully encompassed his lord's grave.

"You may look up, Oishi."

"Yes, my lord Asano."

Oishi raised his gaze. With a startled shout he drew back. It was not the spirit of Asano, but rather some god or, worse, a demon!

The others, roused by his cry, looked up as well, and with a shout came to their feet, some with swords already out and poised for defense.

"Silence!" the apparition roared.

The group fell quiet. The wolflike creature towered above them, his sharpened teeth glistening in the strange aura that surrounded him.

"I am not your lord Asano," the creature intoned, and then his voice fell to a whisper. "Just call me Zergh."

Zergh looked out at the assembled samurai. Damn it all, he thought, they should have sent a Human to handle this, but, oh, no, he had listened to Aldin and in the end could not refuse. He only hoped that the Xsarn crew could pull him out of here if these men decided to take offense at his presence. Aldin had assured him that the samurai of this period would hold a creature that looked similar to Earthly canines in high esteem and that they wouldn't lynch him with xenophobic delight, but he still found most primitive Humans decidedly unhealthy to be around.

"Your Emperor Tsunayoshi," Zergh said, trying to find the right godlike voice by using a small reverb mike attached to his collar, "is known even in worlds beyond for his edicts protecting all creatures that you call dogs, making it a capital crime to harm such beings. Even you, Oishi, have gained recognition for your kind treatment to such creatures. Would you and your comrades now raise blades against one who might consider such creatures to be kin?"

Startled by this statement, the samurai looked one to another. The creature was right. Some thought the emperor mad, but over a decade ago he had passed "the dog laws," which commanded all in his realm to treat dogs with compassion and forbade the harming of such creatures under the pain of death. Some thought him mad, but others, Oishi among them, saw the nobility in caring for the most loyal of all beings.

Oishi looked to his companions.

"Sheath your blades," Oishi commanded. His fear, at least for the moment, was under control, and he strived to set the example for the rest by calmly stepping forward, right to the very edge of the cone of light.

"I am Oishi Kuranosuke," he said, bowing low, giving the proper respect due a superior.

"Good, very good," Zergh replied with relief. "I wasn't sure if I was in the right place. The directions here weren't the best."

Oishi looked up at the being that stood atop Asano's grave and gave him a quizzical stare.

"You come from my lord Asano, to accept our offering?" Oishi asked, nodding first to the grave that the being stood upon and then to the head of Kira that lay before it.

The creature looked at the head and gave a slight grimace. He then gazed down at his feet, and as if realizing that he stood upon a grave, he quickly hopped off. As he did so the light that surrounded him faded and then disappeared.

"From Asano, you ask," Zergh said. "Well, not exactly, let's just say from a friend of your lord. You come highly recommended, you see."

"What friend of my lord Asano?"

"Let's just say that where I come from, beyond the heavens, you men known as the Loyal League of Forty-Seven Ronin are famous. One of the lords beyond the heavens is in desperate need of loyal men. He has asked permission of Asano for your service and Asano agreed, now that your pledge to him is completed."

"What lord?" Oishi asked, suddenly cautious, feeling that this creature was somehow hiding the full truth.

"The lord is a man of power in other heavens. He is besieged by enemies who wish his death. He needs loyal retainers, not more than fifty, and throughout the heavens it is known that the most loyal of men are the Loyal League. Your lord Asano has released you, your pledge to him is complete." And so saying, Zergh nodded to Kira's head. "Now there is another lord who needs your service."

"And his name?"

"The great lord Aldin Larice," Zergh replied, trying to keep from smirking at the thought of announcing his old potbellied friend in such a manner.

"Aldin Larice?" Oishi asked, stumbling over the strange-sounding name.

"I never heard of such a lord," Takashi announced, brazenly coming up to stand beside his comrade.

"A most worthy lord," Zergh replied lamely, hoping that the translator implant wouldn't convey the uneasiness he was feeling in the inflection of his words.

Takashi and Oishi looked at each other.

"I'm here with a request from the lord Aldin that you will find most interesting," Zergh quickly continued.

"And that is?" Oishi asked.

Zergh looked at Oishi and then at the other samurai who ringed him. He couldn't simply tell them that they would die if they didn't come with him. They had already decided to face such an event before his arrival. He'd have to sell them on coming, remembering Aldin's comment that the appeal of an honorable quest would be the best approach. If all else failed, he could call up to the Xsarn ship and have them snatched, but he could see that wouldn't go over too well with men whom Aldin would be entrusting with his life.

"My lord Aldin commanded me to bring him some honorable men," Zergh replied quickly.

"But we must face the emperor before we do anything else," Oishi replied grimly.

This is going to be a long night, Zergh thought to himself. How the hell was he going to explain humanbots, time travel, and a place called the Hole?

"Trust me," Zergh said, trying to smile. "I'll have you back here by morning."

Kirdhuk, Armenia, 1256

Incredulous, Hassan stood before the apparition.

"You claim then to be a jinn?" he asked.

The creature looked Human, to be sure, but was cloaked in a fiery light that blinded any who dared to look straight into it.

The men about him were on their knees, some crying ecstatically that Allah had sent this ally in their hour of need. In the distance the sound of the Mongol ram boomed louder and then suddenly stopped. They'd taken the last gate, now there was only the door to the library to stop them from the final onslaught.

"I am that what you think. I serve a prince of another land who seeks men such as you, and he has sent me to fetch you."

"Then if you are a jinn, smite our foes here," Hassan snarled.

Too long he had been a master of the inner secrets of his order. Secrets that taught that ultimately there was no Allah, no angels, demons, or jinns—merely the raw hand of power that men of reason could wield, using such legends to get others to do their commands.

"Such things are not the reason for my presence," the apparition replied coldly.

Hassan looked appraisingly about him. In another few minutes he would be dead with the last of his followers, the last Ishmaelite stronghold in the world falling before the Mongol storm. In the first moment that the apparition had appeared he had almost believed that perhaps the teachings of the inner masters were wrong. But cold logic ruled against it.

"Then if you will not fight against our foes, what shall you do?"

"My master bids you to come away with me from this place and to serve him faithfully beyond the heavens."

A look of disbelief was on Hassan's face.

"You mean you can take us beyond this?" he asked, waving his hand back toward the door through which the Mongols would burst at any moment.

"I can."

"And the price?"

"Obedience unto death for one who believes in your cause and seeks men such as you to serve him."

Hassan looked about at his surviving men, several of whom now looked up at him with hope in their eyes.

Hassan turned back to the apparition and smiled.

"I've just received word from our time-jump ship," the Xsarn announced with a dramatic flourish, strolling upright into the conference room. "It's safely made the jump-down back from Earth and will be arriving here in three days. Both sets of guards requested have been obtained. Gentlemen, I think we are going to have a most interesting game."

The Kohs stopped in their conversation and broke into polite applause.

"Sigma's guards will be docking with my gamemaster ship within the hour. According to my crews, in seventy-two hours standard the game will commence. Our legal people have given us an estimate that the paperwork from the Alexandrian fiasco will be cleared up in forty-three days. Therefore I am declaring that the exile down on the Hole will last for forty standard days. Once the other ship arrives, carrying the guards from Earth, all three teams will be awakened and they'll be transported down.

"As I explained earlier, all three contestants and their guards have had microtrackers implanted so we'll know where they are. Each tracker gives off a minute forcefield that interacts with any tracker from any opposing player. Any object touched by them picks up a slight tracer, as well, so even a poison or missile weapon can be linked back to whoever used it. Remote scanners have already been placed in the Hole, and they will register all microtrack contacts and feed the information back to the main gaming computers for cross-referencing if there is a question about a kill. Thus we'll be clearly able to register who kills whom throughout the game."

"The permutations of betting are most interesting," Vol said, standing up to address his comrades. "We can of course go for what I'd call the Trifecta bet, to use an ancient word of great tradition, that all three will die down there."

"And don't forget betting that the natives will do the job," one of the Gaf Kohs replied. "Hell, that's where I'm placing all my money."

"Of course, we can consider various weapon types, as well," Aster, another Gaf Koh, replied while pouring a brandy for his Human neighbor. "Quite a number of interesting side bets here, to be sure, such as on individual combats between, say, the samurai and the Basak berserkers."

"That's all child's play." Zola sniffed, giving the Kohs a glance of disdain. "Gentlemen, you're all being fools. There's profit to be had here, big profit."

"How is that?" the Xsarn asked.

"I have a question for you," Zola said, looking at the Xsarn.

"Ask then."

"You see, my good friend, in our previous games, there's been two sides: you either bet for or against. The bets are personal and direct between two gamers, with a gaming sponsor acting as the arbitrator and taking his cut. The same as in the last game."

"Yeah, Xsarn, just like the last one, when you were the

game administrator," Vol interjected, and this time Zola looked at his rival and nodded approval.

"Your point?" the Xsarn asked, growing cautious.

"It's just that the betting potentials are so complex and so interesting that they shouldn't go to waste. Usually for betting potentials this rich there's a house bank set up against which gamers can gamble. Therefore we were wondering what your plans were."

"Simple enough," the Xsarn replied. "I was gong to venture my rather significant holdings as the bank. I've retained a young vasba who's already worked out the programs and delivered the potential rates and odds on all permutations."

The other Kohs looked at each other as if the answer were what they expected.

"I think Zola has a point," Vol responded. "You seem to be making far too much profit of late. First, the retainer for the Alexandrian game, next the retainer for arbitrating this conference, next the retainer for overseeing this new game, and now we find out your bank is the house. It smells like shit to me, my friend."

Several of the Kohs laughed at Vol's choice of words, since what was a derogatory comment to them was in fact a high compliment to Xsarns, but the Xsarn nevertheless understood his meaning.

"Are you questioning my integrity?" the Xsarn asked, rising up on his hind legs.

The Kohs quickly backed up, shouting their apologies.

"Not at all," Vol cried, "not at all."

"So we'll have our little side amusements then," Zola continued. "Gentlemen, our good friend the Xsarn seems to have arranged this little affair not just for our amusement, but also for his profit."

"And to keep the league of Kohs from shattering apart," Bukha said softly.

"Oh, to be sure, most noble of him," Zola replied smoothly. "However, I think that our good friend, in his altruistic concern, has ignored the far wider potential for profit, which as Kohs should be our first and foremost concern."

"And that is?" Bukha asked.

"A lottery for the masses," Zola said.

"Are you mad?" Bukha roared. "The games are the entertainment for Kohs, not for the people. It has always been for individuals of refinement who can appreciate the subtleties of the military arts. Why, the people would turn it into . . . into . . ." And Bukha fell silent, as if grasping for the right phrase.

"It'd turn betting on warfare into a crude blood sport." The Xsarn sniffed.

"Exactly," Bukha shouted. "Lottery indeed! Now, on to the next item of business."

Zola remained silent, a thin, self-satisfied smile crossing his features as the other Kohs looked uneasily from one to the other.

"Just wait a minute," Vol said. "This is an open forum. I must say that I'm curious as to what Zola means by a lottery for the masses."

The room fell silent and as one the Kohs looked down the table at Bukha and the Xsarn.

"That's right," Aster chimed in. "We're all equals here, and I say let's hear what Zola has to say."

"Thank you, gentlemen," Zola said, not waiting for a response from the other two. "I've done a little research, you see, and have come up with the idea that we open the game up for everyone in the Cloud to bet upon."

"Madness," Bukha shouted. "First off, what about the Overseers?"

"You know how they feel about our gaming arrangements," the Xsarn replied coldly. "Noninterference or else."

"I took it upon myself to meet with an Overseer representative and told him all about it—my idea and the game that's about to be played."

"You did *what*!" the Kohs roared as one.

"This is unheard of!" Vol shouted.

For one of them to go voluntarily to the Overseers reminded many of them of Mad Duba, who nearly a century earlier had renounced his Koh status and went voluntarily to a reeducation camp. It'd caused a shake-up, for he spilled everything he knew and more than one illegal interference with a protected planet was shut down as a result.

"Perhaps we put the wrong Humans down on the Hole, but then again there's always room for a fourth," one of the Gaf Kohs growled.

"Gentlemen, gentlemen, please," Zola nervously interjected. "I merely went to tell them that I was setting up a lottery and that it was all perfectly legal. I pointed out that we were not interfering in any way with the Al'Shiga of the Hole."

"And they accepted that?" the Xsarn asked.

"Signed right here," Zola announced, and reached into his attaché case to pull out a heavy scroll, which he tossed on the table. Everyone knew what sticklers the Overseers were for legalistics, and the sight of a contract signed by them, and granting such rights, was unprecedented in the history of Overseer Koh relations.

Bukha and the Xsarn looked nervously to each other but said nothing.

"They've promised no arrests in relation to the game and noninterference in the collection of bets and payment of winnings. They've also agreed to drop their investigation and prosecutions resulting from any situation arising from the last game."

A loud murmur arose from the Kohs. They'd all been sweating out the last six months since the end of the game. Gablona had already been nabbed, and then to top it off the Xsarn had been crazy enough to arrange his being sprung. They'd all feared arrest, and now Zola, the one usually held in contempt by all the others, had gone and gotten them amnesty.

"Is this genuine?" Vol asked incredulously.

"Take it," Zola said, tossing the document down the length of the table. "The seals are all correct. Check into your system for the com line used by the Overseers, and you'll find a copy of this document there as well. The access code's in the attached paperwork."

Zola leaned back smiling. All his life they'd been looking down on him, doing cheap imitations of his falsetto voice, laughing at him behind his back. But now they owed him, and he basked in their shouts of astonishment and praise.

"Well done. Always knew you were the smartest of all of us," the Kohs cried, coming around his chair and patting him on the back.

Bukha and the Xsarn, however, did not join the rush, and Zola eyed them coldly.

"I think I speak for all of us," Bukha said, trying to gain everyone's attention, "when I thank Zola for managing to negotiate an amnesty. After all, we're forced to be here together for the next forty-odd days while our accountants and lawyers straighten out the mess. Security was our biggest concern and now we need not worry—" he paused for a moment, "—if this document is true."

"That can be checked," one of the Gaf Kohs standing behind Zola said defensively, "but I'm not worried. Otherwise Zola Koh would not have brought the agreement before us."

"Be that as it may," Bukha replied, "we've yet to hear of this lottery that Zola wants."

"Come, come, Bukha," Zola said, "we're all beings of business here, first and foremost. And like any good businessman I need to find ways to build my business. After all, the last game you helped launch has wound up costing all of us a lot of expense and time."

He let his words sink in, and more than one Koh, even some of the Gafs, looked toward Bukha with a cold stare.

"The lottery is a way to help us recoup those investments and expand our capital bases."

Zola looked out at the group and smiled. He'd assigned a special team to explore the marketing of the game and to set up the organization, and kept them all under the strictest of security arrangements. If the other Kohs had found out and had enough lead time, they could have set up their own operations, but now it was too late: the Xsarn had announced the game and no one other than he could launch the operation in time.

Softly at first, and then with growing excitement, he launched into a detailed analysis of his plan, repeating what Kurst had told him more than a week before, starting with an explanation of how lottery tickets could be sold with players betting on who would kill whom, and on which day. As he talked, a look of growing astonishment appeared on the faces of the Kohs, each of them inwardly frustrated that he had not thought of it himself.

"Now, the Xsarn has just announced that the game will last forty days," Zola stated, finishing up his presentation. "By a quick calculation I see that there are over four million possible outcomes. Now for the fun part. The game will run for forty days, but through a nice piece of celestial mechanics, a day down on the Hole is almost exactly one-half of a day standard, just a shade over twelve hours. Therefore, if bets are based upon days down on the Hole, we have eighty game turns. The result is an increase in possible bets by a factor of eight to over thirty-three million possible outcomes."

The Kohs were silent, looking at each other dumbfounded.

"Several other points," Zola continued. "The bet on death by one's own side might seem a weak one, but suicides, death by natural causes, and of course murder by one's own guards would all fall into that category."

"How much of a payoff?" Vol asked.

"Ah, the interesting point. Twenty-five percent. For us that would be a fool's bet, but for the mob who buy tickets on the first day it'll still be eight million katars. There'll only be one modifier. An analysis of odds would show a high probability of death by the natives, so we'll call any bets involving natives black tickets. Black tickets will pay off at half the normal rate; that'll protect us and shift bets into other areas.

"Finally, the lottery will be open till all three are dead or until there are only five days left. As each game day progresses, the mob can still buy tickets, but at a reduced payoff, of course."

"This is astonishing!" Aster exclaimed. "You're talking an average profit base of seventy-five percent, with only operating costs to deduct. There's no major capital investments other than tickets, advertising, and record keeping!"

"Why, one of my people even thought up a slogan for the ad campaign," Zola announced. " 'Spend a katar and win the Cloud!' "

The Kohs looked at each other and excitedly voiced their approval.

"My psych people, in talking with my probability people, have pointed out that once this starts it will mushroom. We've been fooling ourselves if we think our games have been secret. The masses have known all along, and being allowed to play will stroke their egos."

"Play the game of the Kohs and win the stars," Vol shouted excitedly, and his friends congratulated him on his talent for thinking up a possible ad slogan.

"Very good," Zola replied good-naturedly. "That is part of the appeal of the bet as well, and of course this is far more dramatic, a game involving Kohs in combat."

"A blood sport to them, and a loss to our dignity if we allow them to bet upon us," Bukha interjected calmly.

"Yes, indeed," Zola replied, "and the mob will love it and want part of the action. Gentlemen, the business of Kohs is business. Think of the profits we can squeeze."

Zola looked about the room in a conspiratorial manner.

"One projection model," he whispered, "worked up by my psych people runs out that every citizen of an Alpha-class world will spend a minimum of a hundred katars if the game runs a full eighty days. Now, census figures are rough as far as the ten thousand spacefaring worlds go, but I think it comes out to somewhere near two trillion katars total, with a projected profit line of one point five trillion in profits."

There was stunned silence.

"That's nearly all our personal wealth combined." The Xsarn gasped.

"It certainly is," Zola replied coolly with a smile. "Now, I'm sharing this knowledge with you because for this to go big, we must act big. We control the communication lines, the computers needed to handle the bookkeeping, the terminals to print out the tickets, and most important, the security system to record each bet so that no one can print a false ticket.

"We've got our organization structure sitting right beneath us." And as he spoke he pointed to the panoramic window that looked out over the enclosed stadium field far below. Spread out below them were acres of temporary work areas, where thousands of their accountants and lawyers had set up an office city.

"Our computer lines are all tapped in from here and out to our transjump radio hookups for instant access to the entire Cloud. From here we can run the entire game and have it up and ready to go thirty-six hours before the three contestants go down to the Hole. I've already lined up my ad people so the videos are ready to be beamed and flood every airway.

"Now, gentlemen, I've got the potential to start this game on the five hundred–odd worlds that I control, and with you or without you I plan to announce it to them within the hour. What I propose to you is simple. I can hook you into my system so that every world that we either control or have economic contact with can be part of this as well."

"What's the price?" the Xsarn asked.

"Call it an investment. You invest into it, open up your worlds for markets, and together we rake the profits. I'm selling shares in the business; each thousand-share block will cost twenty million, and that entitles you to market the game on one world. Of course, that entitles you to profits from the company as well. My friends, we'll all make hundreds of billions."

"How many shares will you hold?" the Xsarn asked coldly.

"Fifty-one percent," Zola replied evenly, "beyond the ones that I'm now offering to you."

"That means you'd get two hundred billion out of us, if you sold every share," Bukha said coldly.

"Ah, yes," Zola replied evenly. "Of course, you can refuse, but the profit sharing for all holders could run as high as seven hundred and fifty billion."

"You're selling shares?" one of the Gafs asked cautiously. "Why should we buy into yours, now that we know we could just go and run our own lotteries on our own worlds?"

"Ah, the knowledge is free, my friend, that's why I'm sharing it, but I should caution you that it'll take several weeks for you to get your game organization set up. Each day that passes means you'll lose billions in potential profits—this is a volatile market. And what's more, suppose our three friends below are so discourteous as to get themselves killed before you've started."

"This is obscene," Bukha interjected. "True, we're betting on our friends, but it was professional, weighing the skills of each, looking at the finer nuances of tactics and military strategy. You're turning it into a cheap thrill for the masses."

"You don't have to join us if you don't want to," Zola replied sanctimoniously. "But as I was saying, my system is in place, I've got the guarantee from the Overseers, and like it or not, I plan to run it. Now, the rest of you can join in the profits or not, as you see fit."

"And out of the goodness of your heart you're sharing it with us?" Bukha snarled.

"Let's just say I'm a prudent businessman. I'm spreading the risk a little. You can all buy shares, a day later the game ends and I've made a profit. If the game lasts eighty days, I wind up sharing out more than I made off of you, but still I'll make a profit. I'm covering both ends, that's all. Besides, without the rest of you, the game can't reach to all corners of the Cloud."

"I suspect," one of the Human Kohs said, "that you had this thought out weeks before and held the knowledge back from your friends so you could turn your own profit out of it first."

"Would you have shared it, if you'd thought of it first?" Vol replied evenly, coming to Zola's defense.

"But of course," the Human said, and his response was greeted with hoots of derision. To Zola's pleasure, most of the

Kohs quickly voiced the opinion that old Zola only did what they would have done and he was to be respected for it.

"So that's the bet," Zola replied. "Of course, among ourselves we'll still play it out the old way, just betting on who will win based upon our knowledge as connoisseurs of military gaming."

"But of course," they all replied.

"Good then. I'll call in my people with the prospectus and we'll sign now. My technical crews are waiting below. Once you've signed, get your communications, computer, and security teams together to meet with them. By tomorrow you can be running the game out of your worlds, colonies, ships, and outposts, throughout the Cloud, and we'll fleece them blind!"

"One question first," Bukha said.

"Anything at all," Zola replied icily. Never again would he tremble before this Koh. With Sigma and Gablona gone, most likely forever, this Gaf and his Xsarn friend were already putting on the airs of running the council of Kohs, but in forty-three days, he, Zola, would be the richest man who ever lived, and then they would see where the true power lay.

"Suppose somebody buys up a large block of winning tickets," Bukha said softly. "I'm not talking about the bets made in the last days or even the last weeks when the odds are only in the hundreds of thousand to one. I'm talking about the tickets bought now, at the start. If someone has enough tickets that pay back at that rate of odds, why it'll bankrupt the entire Cloud. And you can't simply not pay, for if you did, the Overseers would be all over you. I noticed in the contract that you've drawn up that the bet must be paid off or all members of your company will be held liable."

The room fell silent, and Zola sensed the bubble might just burst. The Overseer had forced that point of the contract, but they had both laughed over it, since the odds of such an event happening were in the millions to one.

"No problem," Zola replied smoothly. "In my prospectus, which I'll now load into your computers, you'll see the analysis worked up by my master theorist of probabilities; the odds are better than a million to one against such an event."

"Still," Bukha asked, "what if it does?"

"If someone does buy a large block of winning tickets?" Zola asked, and then he started to chuckle. "We'll just have to kill him, I guess."

There was a moment of silence and finally Zola broke it by laughing out loud, as if what he had said was just a joke, and one by one the other Kohs joined in, their laughter echoing throughout the cavernous room, even as Bukha and the Xsarn strode out, closing the door behind them.

The two looked at each other, even as the laughter sounded in the distance.

"The Overseers," the Xsarn said.

"So they talked to him, too," Bukha replied.

"I wonder what the hell their game is?" the Xsarn whispered nervously.

Losa looked out across the courtyard, which was his private place of meditation, and smiled inwardly.

The ambassador from the Xsarn had been the start of it all. He knew sooner or later that the Kohs would try to bribe those whom they called the Overseers, to make an arrangement to protect themselves. Oh, he had played that out wonderfully, expressing righteous consternation at their sinful ways, threatening the Xsarn with reeducation right alongside Gablona.

Then the emissary had broken the news that they wished to punish Gablona themselves, and would even help the Overseers in their task.

It had been so easy to suggest the Hole as a possible location, and then to let everyone think that Gablona had been rescued from his personal control.

The trap had been sprung, the trap he had thought about for centuries, to end this impasse with the interlopers who had come barging into their preserve.

Oh, he knew their ways. That "punishment" was nothing but a euphemism for their disgusting games, but that was all part of his plan as well.

But this other one, this Zola, with his scheming had been unforeseen. That, however, would fit wonderfully. It could so easily lay the groundwork to distract attention away from the true intent of what he dreamed. The chaos of the Al'Shiga could go hand in glove with the chaos that Zola would unknowingly create before this was finished. The Arch Overseer would not know till it was far too late to do anything but step aside to the one who had at last solved the great problem and eliminated the intruders without violating the code in the slightest.

If Losa had possessed hands, he would have rubbed them with glee as he floated across his private chamber.

chapter four

"You're dead, Larice. The moment I see your face, my men will kill you."

Aldin looked at Gablona with disbelief. How could this man be so insane?

"Listen, Corbin . . ."

"It's Koh Gablona to you."

Aldin strode across the chamber to where Sigma and Gablona were sitting, nursing their last round of brandy and cigars before going down to the Hole.

"Gentlemen, we can talk openly here," Aldin said, the desperation in his voice obvious to the two Kohs. "I'd like to suggest that we approach this in a logical manner. There'll be enough problems with the natives as is, each of us will be lucky if we even make it to our designated safe houses. Why make the situation any worse down there than it already is? All we need do is survive our forty days, all's forgiven, and we're free."

Gablona looked at Aldin with barely concealed disdain.

"Turning coward, is that it?" Gablona sneered. "The legendary Aldin Larice is now afraid of a little fight?"

Aldin turned to look at Sigma.

The old Koh merely extended his hands in a gesture of resignation and smiled wistfully.

"As long as he's like this, I've got to be ready," Sigma said evenly, his eyes boring into Aldin's. "And how am I to know you aren't simply playing the innocent here, and that you'll engage in a little knife work in the dark once the game begins?"

"But what's to prevent us from going together to the same safe house?" Aldin argued. "We'll hole up and sit it out, that would show all of them.

"Remember, I'm a vasba. It's my job to hunt out interesting combats to wager on. But even I wouldn't go near the Al'Shiga. They're the craziest bastards in the entire Cloud. They'll react to us like cats to a mouse. They'll play with us for a while and then finish us off, the slower and more painfully, the better. Damn it, the Hole's a place we send hardened convicts to as a death sentence. Men beg for execution rather than be sent down there. I tell you, if we want to live, we better team up."

"I'd feel safer on my own," Sigma replied.

"You'd feel safer?" Gablona snarled. "Why, you're the one that got me stuck in the reeducation center. It's me that should be worrying about you."

"Business, my friend, nothing more than business," Sigma replied.

"Well, you'll see some business from my assassins before this is done."

"Gentlemen, we're talking about survival." Aldin tried to reason.

A chime sounded through the room's intercom system and the three fell silent.

"It's time," the voice of the Xsarn intoned over the loudspeaker. "As you witnessed in the drawing of lots, Sigma will go down on the first elevator car. Your Gavarnians are waiting for you, Sigma."

The old Koh stood up and walked over to the window that looked down on the Hole. He drained off the rest of the brandy in his glass and with a flourish tossed the empty crystal into the corner, where it shattered. He gave his two companions a characteristic shrug of his shoulders and, without another word, stalked out of the room, cigar clenched between his teeth.

Aldin looked beseechingly at Gablona, but his old employer returned the gaze with murder in his eyes.

"The plan for the last game was foolproof. If you hadn't interfered, I'd be the richest man in the Cloud, and you'd be the richest vasba."

"And Alexander would have been murdered," Aldin replied quietly. "Sorry, Koh Gablona, but as a vasba, I was sworn to maintain a fair game, and fair game it was to the end."

Gablona looked at him with a hateful gaze.

"My only concern is that the Al'Shiga will get to you first," Gablona said.

He paused for a moment and inserted a beefy finger into his mouth to pry around his teeth. After finding the source of his annoyance, he pulled his finger back out with a chunk of food dangling on the end of his fingernail. With a flourish, he licked his finger clean and looked at Aldin with a disdainful smile.

Not another word passed between the two as they waited out the long minutes until Gablona was finally called. Nervously Aldin got up and walked over to the window. The Skyhook, what the natives call the "Seda," cut a straight line down toward the planet below.

The Hole was an apt name, he realized. The entire planet was shrouded in a thick cloud cover, except for one circular region some five hundred kilometers in diameter right on the equator, which was actually an escarpment that rose more than fifteen thousand meters above the shroud-covered lowlands. The greenhouse effect below made life impossible, but above the clouds there was a warm semitropical climate year-round. It was a unique oasis of life on an otherwise dead planet.

The Seda rose straight up from the middle of the habitable region, its white surface reflecting scarlet from the dull light of the red giant that was just breaking the horizon to the east. The structure was a source of amazement to all three races that had reached the Cloud, yet another bit of evidence of the technical prowess of the First Travelers.

Why they had bothered to build it here, on what was for all practical purposes a worthless planet, was beyond anyone's knowledge. Many felt that it was the same as the ringlike Kolbard, built it seemed just for the sheer fun of building it, and nothing more.

Some even theorized that it was done for nothing more than a visual joke. From farther out, the milky-white planet with the dark round spot looked almost like a giant eye floating in space, the Hole being the iris and the Skyhook a giant needle sticking straight out of the middle.

If there was one practical advantage the Skyhook presented, it was the fact that it enabled the Hole to be sealed off with little difficulty. All ships were strictly forbidden to land. The only contact permitted by merchants to the lower world was through this one tower and the elevator cars that came up to the geosync docking port.

Security thus was fairly simple. There was a clearing station below near groundlevel to prevent any of the Shiga from trying to come up. And even if they did take over that point, they'd still have to gain control of a ship at the top of the tower, something that all three races would never allow.

The floor swayed ever so slightly beneath Aldin's feet. For a moment Aldin felt a surge of fear—the tower must be moving! And then he realized that of course it would move, shifting with the rise and fall of the solar wind, atmospheric winds down below, the gravitational pull from the planet's two moons, or from occasional seismic activity. But the First Travelers had seen to that, as well. There was another surge that he knew would be from the tower's control system to dampen the sway, which if allowed to continue unchecked could quickly build and threaten the tower's structural integrity.

"Gablona Koh, your car is ready, your men are waiting for you."

With a smile Gablona rose to his feet. "You know, Aldin, I'm actually looking forward to seeing you down there."

He dropped his cigar onto the heavily carpeted floor, grinded it out with his heel, and then he was gone.

Aldin watched as a glass car, suspended on the outside of the tower, dropped away, falling toward the planet below. With mock gravity Aldin raised his glass in salute.

"Mind if we join you?"

Aldin turned around to see his old friends Yaroslav and Zergh standing in the doorway.

"The Xsarn said it was all right if we spent a little time together before you go down on the next car." And the two came into the room.

Aldin noticed that Zergh was no longer wearing the ceremonial tunic of the vasba but had changed instead to the robes of a samurai, with the traditional two swords belted about his waist.

"What the hell are you doing?" Aldin asked.

"Thought I'd come along for the fun."

"Damn it all, you could get killed down there."

"Ah, yes, guess I could," Zergh replied. "But those samurai kind of got to me, perhaps the first men I've ever met with a little honor to them. Now, I won't take any arguments. The Xsarn said fifty men, and since you were six short, I volunteered and he didn't object."

Aldin could only shake his head as he came up and clapped his friend on the shoulder.

"Here, I brought you this," Yaroslav said, pulling out a package that he had kept hidden behind his back.

With Zergh's help Aldin unwrapped the gift and looked at it with amazement.

"The ceremonial robes of an early eighteenth-century samurai," Yaroslav said proudly. "Took a bit of research on my part, but I think they're correct. After all, you want to impress your guards, don't you?"

"How are they?" Aldin asked.

"Good men," Zergh replied enthusiastically. "It took a little persuading, but I convinced them to come with me. Our tech folks then altered the humanbots, programmed them after doing a memory sweep of Oishi, and they were dropped down without a hitch. We slept the samurai as soon as they were jumped up to the ship, and they've only been awakened an hour ago. They've already received their tracking scanners and translator implants programmed for common speech and the Al'Shiga dialect. They're having some problems with the translators, claiming they're an affront to their dignity, but I convinced them that they'll need them to survive.

"For this situation, however, I'm still not sure they're the right choice," Zergh continued. "Sigma's berserkers look tough, and as for Gablona's assassins, they should fit right in down there. I'm afraid your samurai are going to stand right out. Racially for one thing—what with all your human races blending together, pure Orientals are a rarity. The other problem is their bearing. They're proud men, they carry themselves like warriors who fear nothing. It won't sit well with the Shiga."

"Do they know anything yet?" Aldin asked.

"Only what we agreed on earlier, that they've been sent to help a friend of their lord who is in trouble, nothing more."

Aldin nodded and then looked down at the bundle.

"How the hell do I get into this suit?" he asked.

Yaroslav laid the various garments out on the floor and helped Aldin to remove his coveralls. The diaperlike underwear struck him as absurd, and the three of them laughed when they finally realized Aldin had put it on backward. At last came the outer robe, which Aldin held up to admire. It was light blue in color, a white rose emblazoned on the back.

"Traditional touch," Yaroslav replied. "Your house needs a symbol, that's all."

Putting the robe on, he could not help but feel somewhat absurd, but at the same time he realized that he would gain easier approval from his new comrades if he appeared dressed as they were. With a final flourish Aldin took the long sword from Yaroslav's hand.

As a professional he had once looked upon such objects as collectables, works of art to be admired. It struck him with a cold chill that his very life might now depend upon this primitive device.

The code of the game was strict, as was the law in the Hole: only weapons powered by physical strength could be used.

As an added touch the Shiga strictly forbade any type of projectile weapon, thus bows were out. Some merchants did arm their premises with them, but if the Shiga found out, there'd be a riot. Aldin realized he could have tried to slip a microburster in by swallowing it, but the tracking scanner that had already been implanted into his body would have picked it up. Even if he got it past the scanner it wouldn't do much good. Use it once down below, and there'd be a mob of fifty thousand religious fanatics on them within the hour for having broken the rule of drawing blood only by hand. It was going to have to be swords or daggers. Or for that matter, garrotes, poison, snake baskets, the Shiga needle blade, or . . .

He tried to block it out for the moment.

Yaroslav helped him to adjust the two swords so that they balanced correctly.

"Not bad, Aldin-san."

"What?"

Yaroslav only shook his head and smiled.

The Xsarn appeared in the doorway, flanked by Bukha Taug.

"So, you two," Aldin said, trying to sound injured. "Loyal friends showing up to send off their comrade to the execution?"

"Now, Aldin," Bukha started.

"Don't now Aldin me," he shouted. "This is a hell of a note. You profited by the Alexandrian game as well as I, but now I take the fall, is that it?"

The Xsarn turned an inquiring gaze at Bukha, who extended his hands in a gesture of innocence.

"The man's overwrought," he replied coolly.

"Obviously overwrought," Zergh chimed in, the faintest of smiles creasing his features.

"It's only for forty days," Bukha said, quickly steering the topic away from any implications regarding the last game. "Get it over with, the finances here will be taken care of, and everything will be back to normal."

"Take care of yourself," Aldin said evenly, coming up to Yaroslav's side.

"Sure you don't want me to come along?" his old friend asked.

"Do you really want to?"

"Down there?" Yaroslav asked, a sheepish grin crossing his features. "Well, not exactly, not good for the health of someone like myself."

Aldin smiled and slapped his old friend on the shoulder.

"Let's get out of here," he said, looking over at Zergh. Without comment the two strode out of the room. As Aldin cleared the doorway Bukha stepped before him.

"I'm betting on you to win," Bukha whispered with a smile, his voice loud enough for the Xsarn to hear.

"Thanks for the confidence," Aldin replied coldly, and then pushed on, the Xsarn falling in by his side.

"You'll meet your guards in the lift chamber," the Xsarn stated. "Once the lift starts down you may brief them in any manner you choose. The lift will deposit you on the planet's surface in exactly four hours after departure. There, a bonded agent from the Rhee Trading Consortium will meet you once the lift is opened. His only obligation is to show you to your safe house. Once at the door of the safe house, you're on your own. Pickup will be at the tower at sundown after eighty days of Hole time. There'll only be two hours left to today, so they'll be counted in as part of tomorrow.

"The other two teams will already be down. Since there's only one entry point into the tower, it couldn't be arranged any other way, so technically the game starts the moment Sigma sets foot on the planet."

"A fine advantage for them." Aldin sniffed. "One of them could have already killed the other and then be waiting for me."

"I doubt that," the Xsarn replied.

"How come?" Aldin asked.

"You see, there's some sort of festival going on down there today. You'll see what I mean when you get there.

"Good luck," the Xsarn said, extending both right arms.

Aldin hesitated for a moment, then reaching out, allowed his forearm to be grasped.

"Never thought I'd be playing in one of my own games," Aldin said, trying to hide his fear.

"It was the only way to settle this dispute," the Xsarn replied.

"And who are you betting on?" Aldin asked, his professional curiosity getting the better of him.

"You know I can't, I'm the gamemaster."

Aldin gave him a look that said he wasn't fooling anyone. The Xsarn drew closer.

"Sorry, old friend," he whispered, his fetid breath washing over Aldin, "but the odds are on Gablona."

"Thanks for the confidence," Aldin snapped, and he shouldered his way past.

The doorway slid open and then closed behind Aldin and Zergh. As the door clicked shut, the assembled warriors went to their knees.

"Aldin-san, we are ready to serve you in your hour of need."

Aldin looked at the men before him and the fear that had gripped him faded away. He looked back at the closed door, and the thought of how all those on the other side had written him and his ronin off swept over him. Like hell, he suddenly thought.

The warriors were still kneeling, with eyes lowered.

"Oishi!"

"Yes, my lord."

"Stand up and look at me."

The samurai came to his feet, his eyes level with Aldin's.

He wrestled yet again with what he had done to Oishi and his companions. He had drafted them into almost certain death. But then again if he had not, it would not have been humanbots that had ripped their stomachs open, but these brave men. At least they had a fighting chance now.

"Come on," he said with a cold, even voice, and as the men fell in behind Aldin, they walked into the turbolifter that would drop them down into the Hole, thousands of kilometers below.

Hours had passed on their journey down, and the Hole loomed directly below them, the curve of the planet's surface spreading out farther and farther. Aldin looked straight up for a moment at the docking port they had left hours ago, which was no longer visible, and then back at the samurai. He had tried to explain the nuances of the Al'Shiga, and to explain, as well, how they had to survive not only threats from them but from two other "great lords." Somehow he felt as if the samurai had seen through him already.

They were strapped into chairs that ringed the wall of the lift car, with a clear view through the glass floor at their feet. The experience of free-fall during the descent down the side of the tower, with the destination directly below one's feet, was unnerving even for the most experienced of travelers; several of the samurai had simply fainted away, and most of the others, to their shame, had become ill.

For Oishi there had been wonders enough already. What had only seemed hours ago, he had been kneeling before the tomb of lord Asano, his task completed, ready to face the death he knew his emperor would decree.

Now they were falling out of the heavens, sliding down what looked like a great column to whatever awaited them below.

Something wasn't right, he thought. This Aldin was not his image of a powerful being from another world. If anything, he could sense fear in the man he was sworn to serve. Oishi struggled with his own fear of all that he was seeing, but at the same time he realized that for a being of the heavens there should be nothing to fear. So why did this Aldin seem nervous?

Aldin looked over at Oishi and could sense the doubt in the man. He felt a twinge of regret, knowing that Oishi had been told less than a half-truth, but for the moment he needed their unswerving loyalty, for it would be put to the test in a very short time.

How could he possibly explain all this to them? Aldin wondered, looking at the samurai. But he realized he had to say something, he could see Oishi wanted explanations.

"Everyone down there is crazy," Aldin said quietly.

"How so?" Oishi asked.

"Just believe what our lord Aldin said," Zergh interjected. "Let's just survive getting to our fortress. Stay close, don't talk to anyone, and most of all, no matter what the insult, ignore it."

Some of the samurai grumbled at this command; ignoring insults was not high on their list of proper behavior.

"Remember," Zergh continued, trying to placate them, "your lord Aldin is your first, your only concern. Your honor is pledged to protecting him. If you accept a challenge on the open street, you might suddenly face a mob of thousands ready to join in the kill. Do you understand me?"

Oishi thought for a moment and then nodded. Turning, he looked to his companions.

"You will obey," he barked, and the others were silent.

"Once we get to our safe house, we'll hole up," Aldin stated, "and then try to find out where the other two are hiding out. But for now the main problem is getting safely in; nothing else counts."

"What if we see your other enemies on the street?" Oishi asked.

Zergh looked over to Aldin.

Damn it all, Aldin thought. He now realized that he had been so preoccupied with survival on the Hole that he had not taken time to sort out any offensive strategy, an approach he was sure Gablona and Sigma had thought through.

"If we can take them, we attack," he whispered. He looked to Zergh for reassurance, and his old companion nodded with approval.

Oishi noticed the exchange of glances between the two, but said nothing. When he looked over at Takashi he saw that his brother and old comrade had noticed the exchange as well.

There was a sudden sense of weight returning. The free-fall period was over. They were starting to cut into the atmosphere and deceleration had started.

Aldin looked up and saw that already the sky overhead was starting to shift from the blackness of night into a deep, glowing red. The sense of weight increased as they crossed through one G and then pushed up to two. The samurai, unaccustomed to such a sensation, tried to hide their fear. Free-fall had been bad enough for them to adjust to; the sudden shift made several of them ill again.

Just great, Aldin thought. These men might be fighting in a matter of minutes and most of them were half sick.

Looking straight down, he started to pick out details on the surface below. Surrounding the Skyhook, a city was now clearly in view. From out of the base of the tower stretched five broad avenues that ran like ribs on a Japanese fan a quarter of the way out to the rim, and terminated in five more cities, the space in between being covered by thick, heavy growth, while the area beyond was sectioned off into orderly fields.

There was a final lurch as the descending car braked even harder and then the pressure eased off as they slowly started to drift to a stop.

With less than a kilometer to go, he felt as if he were looking down upon a writhing mound of insects that had been stirred into life. The western side of the Skyhook faced a huge open area more than half a kilometer across, and with a sickening shudder Aldin realized that it was covered with a surging mass of Humanity and Gafs, hundreds of thousands of beings, seemingly locked in bloody combat.

The turbolift door opened, and all conversation was drowned out by a roaring ocean of noise.

Even as they tried to exit the car, a mad crush pushed in around them, terrified Xsarns, Gafs, and Humans, most of them dressed in the multihued garb of half a hundred different trading houses.

The samurai elbowed their way around Aldin, attempting to set up a protective perimeter, while Zergh's bellowed commands were lost in the wild cacophony of screaming chaos.

Aldin felt frightened out of his wits. Was this a real riot, or was it something perhaps whipped up by Gablona or Sigma, who had the advantage of going down before him?

A sudden scream rent the air. Turning, Aldin stood transfixed as a Gaf merchant collapsed on the edge of the circle of samurai who stood around Aldin with drawn swords. A man rode upon the Gaf's back, his right hand moving back and forth across his victim's throat with a vigorous sawing motion.

There was an explosion of scarlet. The Gaf reared back up, staggered, and then fell forward again, showering all about him with a river of blood.

The blue-robed assassin leaped from the back of his prey and held a bloody saw-toothed dagger aloft.

"Al'Shiga of the Isma!" he screamed, his eyes wild with triumph.

"Zergh!"

Before Aldin could stop him, his old companion pushed through the protective circle of samurai.

Zergh's long, two-handed blade hissed out in a deadly arc. The severed head tumbled through the air and, driven by the impact, fell at Aldin's feet. With horror Aldin saw that the man's face was still frozen in a look of triumph.

A shout of approval went up from the samurai as several clamored to retrieve the trophy. Zergh stepped back into the ranks and could not help but grin at the admiring looks on the faces of the warriors around him.

Meanwhile, the panic-stricken merchants continued to push into the car. Several fell upon the bundle that the Gaf merchant had been carrying and with drawn daggers argued over the contents.

"Let's get out of here," Oishi roared, and leading the way, he pushed against the throng. Aldin and the rest of the group followed.

"A bad move," a voice suddenly shouted from the crowd, swarming around the encircled band of warriors.

Aldin looked up and saw a man dressed in the flowing burgundy tunic of the Rhee Consortium trying to push against the flood of refugees.

The man made it to the edge of the circling samurai and pulled back his face cloth.

"I'm Eda, with the Rhee trading group. The Xsarn contracted me to serve you," he shouted.

"Don't trust him," Zergh shouted, and as if by command, the samurai standing before Aldin snapped out their blades, ready to strike.

The man backed up a step, his hands up. With a slow, deliberate action he reached beneath the folds of his robes.

Oishi, not liking the move, barked a command, and the samurai nearest to the small man thrust out, his blade stopping but a fraction from the man's throat.

Eda, as if totally detached from any possible danger, nodded his approval at the samurai's skill. Cautiously he pulled his hand back out from the tunic's fold and held up a small portascreen.

"Get it," Aldin said. His first impulse had been to simply step forward and take it himself, but his nerves were on edge. Anything could be a trap here. The portascreen could actually be a bomb or, for that matter, the handle could have a poison clip.

He watched as the samurai with the drawn sword reached out with his other hand and snatched the small dictation pad away. Aldin exhaled slowly. He had just ordered, for the first time, a man to lay his life on the line. He didn't like the feel or it; it would take some getting used to.

The samurai stepped back while one of his companions took his place with drawn sword to guard the man.

With a bow, the warrior came up to Aldin's side. Gingerly he took the pad. Written upon it was the Xsarn's private identification code-name that he once used with Aldin for taking bets.

"Let him into the circle," Aldin commanded.

Oishi looked at his commander. The man was far too trusting, this could still be a trap. The samurai looked to Oishi, who gave a nod of approval. Aldin noticed it, as well. Though they might, at least for the moment, acknowledge him as their lord, they still looked to Oishi as their commander in the field.

The man stepped in behind the protection of the samurai and breathed a sigh of relief. Aldin suddenly realized that for the last minute his attention had been focused on this one individual while all around them was still chaos. Hundreds of merchants and offworlders clamored to get aboard the car, while from just beyond the doorway leading into the plaza came the wild, incessant roar of battle.

He shot a quick glance again to Oishi. He saw the man's eyes darting back and forth, taking in every detail, watching the clamoring flood of terrified merchants, scanning an individual for a second and then locking his gaze upon another. Aldin looked back to Eda.

"How do I know you didn't steal this?" Aldin shouted, trying to be heard above the roar of confusion around him.

"You don't," Eda shouted back.

The man was right, but there was no alternative to trusting him other than to stay here for the next forty days.

"All right then, what do we do?" Aldin asked, realizing he had to go along. If he hesitated, the men around him would sense it. Above everything else, he had to act decisively if they were to trust him.

"My orders are to escort you to a safe house. It's a small

fortress several hundred meters beyond the square, located in the foreign merchants' quarter."

"The other side of the square?" Aldin shouted. "There's a goddamn riot going on out there."

"Oh, that," Eda said, a smile crossing his features. "Scares the living Xsarnfood out of the green traders. It happens every ten days or so. It's just a religious festival. This one got a little rougher than some, a bit of a pogrom thrown in for good measure."

"Religious festival? What the hell are you talking about? It sounds like a riot!"

"To the locals it's one and the same."

Eda stopped and looked around at Aldin and his companions. "I saw the other two come down. I'm placing my money on the berserkers that Sigma fellow has. Why, you can cut off their heads and they'll still keep coming for you."

"Thanks for the confidence," Aldin shouted. "By the way, which direction did they take?"

Eda smiled and wagged his finger in a scolding gesture. "Can't tell, and even if I could, I wouldn't know. Now let's get you to your safe house."

"Couldn't we wait till things simmer down out there?" Zergh ventured.

"Till dark? Are you crazy? It'll only be worse then."

"I got plenty of time," Zergh replied coldly.

"But I don't," Eda rejoined. "Hell, my payoff for this job is worth a year's standard salary back home. I plan to get you there and then get the hell off this planet. I'm short on time, and you're my last assignment."

"I'm not moving till they quit," Zergh roared, and pointed out beyond the door.

Suddenly to everyone's surprise the noise outside died away, as if those on the other side had heard his wish and were now hurrying to comply.

Zergh looked around and then gave a weak smile, as if he had exerted some mystical power over the mob and was too shy to take credit.

"Let's go," Eda commanded, and pushing his way through the terrified merchants, he stepped out into the reddish glare of the afternoon sun.

Aldin looked around at his companions, who waited for his

command. Eda, without looking back, continued around the corner and disappeared from view.

There was nothing to do but follow.

Aldin pushed forward, and at the sight of the drawn blades held by the samurai, the merchants in the doorway gave back before the group.

They stepped out into the open.

The sight was simply stunning; the entire group drew up short. They stood upon a raised dais that completely surrounded the slender Skyhook. Before them the square was jammed with hundreds of thousands of beings and for a moment Aldin feared that the mob had turned out to give him a special greeting.

The square seemed to be cordoned off into sections, a massed grouping of blue robes to the right with what looked like Gafs in red robes, followed by white-, green-, and orange-robed groups proceeding around the tower. Around the base of the Skyhook stood a massed formation of yellows. Each of the groups was separated from the other by the broad avenues that spread out in a fan-shaped pattern from the square, with the yellows forming a ring around the base, their formation broken only by the avenues that cut through their ranks to terminate before the open dais upon which Aldin and his companions now stood.

This is going to be one very short game, Aldin thought as he looked out across the hundreds of thousands, expecting that at the sight of him the mob would surge forward and simply crush them underfoot. The eerie silence held and then suddenly a triumphant roar echoed from the white robes' section as half a dozen Gaf heads, still dripping blood, arched into the air over the avenue that divided the two groups.

A deeper growl of rage, from the assembled Gafs, thundered across the square. A contingent of half a hundred red-robed Gafs surged across the avenue toward the white robes. There was a confused flurry of action; the Gafs fell back to their comrades, bearing a struggling form. Seconds later a Human head was tossed into the air and now the Gafs howled with triumph—the riot was on again.

"Good time to move right now," Eda suggested. "The celebration is really hot and they might be too busy to worry about our passing through.

"Just tell your people to stay close, and no matter what, not to speak to anyone," Eda continued. "Your Gaf companion there's already incurred the blood debt of the Isma sect, the blue robes. Don't make it worse."

Before Aldin had a chance to reply, Eda started down the steps of the dais and onto a broad avenue that separated the Gafs from the Blues. The group fell in behind him, the samurai still forming a protective circle with blades drawn.

Aldin looked around and realized that the entire dais around the Skyhook was almost deserted, except for small knots of Shiga, mostly yellows, who looked at them with open hatred. Few in number, they offered no challenge, but it was obvious from the way they hung just out of range that they might be willing to take an opportunity if it were offered.

One of the Shiga dressed in light blue broke away from his group of a dozen onlookers and, racing ahead of the group, disappeared into the surging mob.

"Most likely going to tell his friends," Zergh stated. With a shout of defiance he raised his sword up over his head and shook it in the direction of the blue-clad assassins who warily followed the group.

Their gestures in response were universal and readily understood.

"Nothing like calling attention to yourself. And you were worried about the samurai," Aldin commented bitterly.

As they stepped off the dais and out onto the avenue, Aldin thought that the noise, dust, and horrific stench of hundreds of thousands of unwashed bodies would simply overwhelm him. As if to somehow touch back to his normal life, he paused for a second and turning, looked straight up. It was a sight that could have held him enthralled for hours, this miracle of First Traveler engineering.

The Skyhook tower cut heavenward through the dull red sky, a perfectly straight line that soared ever upward until disappearing in a distant point of light that Aldin realized must be the first docking station thousands of kilometers above.

But the more immediate concerns pulled him back to the situation at hand. The left side of the avenue was lined with thousands of Gafs chanting and roaring. Over their heads fluttered hundreds of red banners covered with the wavery Shiga script.

On the right side of the avenue were thousands of Humans,

most in blue robes, but scattered among them were occasional clumps of greens and oranges.

"Over here it's the Sutar cult, against the Isma, with some Bengada and Kuln allies," Eda roared, as if his comment would make any sense.

Eda edged over toward the Gaf side of the street, and his companions nervously followed. The middle of the street was covered with a scattering of bodies, some Gafs, but more Humans, all of them headless.

Suddenly a knot of Gafs with red bands of cloth knotted round their heads surged out of the crowd, rushing straight at the intruders. Most carried saw-toothed daggers, while several held glinting wire garrotes. The Japanese lowered swords, ready to meet the advance. At the last second the dozen Gafs flowed around them, barely noticing their presence except for a couple of angry snarls, and then pushed on across the street.

A wild shout went up from the Human side. The blues broke in a surging confused rush, backing away from the street, while here and there others leaped out, red cloths tied around their foreheads.

The press was so great that the mob's retreat was blocked and dozens went down, trampled beneath the confusion as the Gafs plunged into the swirling maelstrom of Humanity and disappeared from view. Awestruck, the party stopped to watch. Suddenly a Human head arched up into the air and a wild shout of triumph rose from the Gaf side. The mob surged and eddied as if it were a single living entity coiling in agony; another head went up, a Gaf's, and a cheer from the Human side greeted the sight. Suddenly the knot of Gafs broke clear a dozen meters away from their point of entry, blues scattering in every direction. Two of the Gafs held Human forms, still twisting and writhing, and they started to race back across the avenue.

The mob surged after them. One of the Gafs, obviously wounded, was swarmed over, and seconds later his head was tossed heavenward. His companions, without a backward look, pushed on across the avenue bearing their prisoners, who howled with terror.

The Humans surged after them, and for a second Aldin thought that a general riot between the two sides was about to explode with his group caught in the middle.

But at the midpoint of the avenue the chase was broken off

by the masses. Shouting with triumphant glee, the Gafs bore
their prisoners across the street and melted back into the red-
clad ranks of their comrades, who shouted with joy at the display. The mob surged inward around them and seconds later
two Human heads soared upward to be tossed back and forth
like balls, while torn fragments of still-quivering bodies rained
back out onto the street.

Throughout this entire display the two sides behaved as if
Aldin and his entourage did not even exist. Hoping that their
festival was taking all their attention, Aldin signaled for the
group to catch up with Eda, who had stopped merely to let the
Gaf attack party pass and was already pushing on up the street.
Running after their guide, they forged ahead, staying close to
the Gaf side, shifting in their path to avoid torn fragments and
bloody smears that littered the length of the avenue.

At the end of the great square, Eda suddenly turned right
and headed straight across the avenue toward the Human mob,
and for the first time he slowed, letting the outer circle of samurai surge around him.

"This is the hard part. We got to get through this mob, our
destination is on the other side," he shouted, trying to be heard
above the howling madness around them.

"Couldn't we just circle around this?" Aldin shouted.

"Too far to go. Believe me, the alleys are far more dangerous than the square during the festival. Now stay close!"

Suddenly a loud, piercing whistle rent the air.

"Side shift," Eda screamed. "Brace yourselves!"

The Human side seemed to explode into a wild frenzy, while
from the other side of the street the Gafs howled with joy. A
small knot of orange robes came surging out of the crowd,
those on the edge of the group slashing indiscriminately with
their blades at any Humans not dressed in orange. A dozen or
more heads were tossed up around the edge of the group. The
orange ranks closed and, chanting a wild paean of joy, they
surged across the avenue to the other side, where the Gafs
greeted them with jubilation.

"A masterful betrayal," Eda cried. "Masterful! Now, let's
move before the ranks close."

Pushing ahead, the group headed straight into the hole produced by the defection of several hundred orange robes to the
other side.

They plunged into the swirling mass of warriors. The circle

of samurai were up to a fever pitch of excitement with swords raised ready to slash out at any who dared to approach.

Oishi broke away from Aldin's side and darted around the inside of the protective circle, shouting for his men to remain steady.

The mob gave back defiantly, as if deeming to give serious notice to the outsiders for the first time.

After several minutes the group finally broke through the press at the far end of the square and rushed into a narrow side alley.

Eda stopped for a moment as if to catch his breath.

"What the hell is all of this?" Aldin roared, pointing back to the mass insanity just beyond the alleyway entrance.

"Festival. Happens every ten days, when the closer moon is new," Eda shouted. "All six clans live separately in their own cities. With the new moon, they all come to the great square of the Seda, to pray before the tower. Looking for a sign."

"A sign?"

"That the tower will open to them. See that?" And he pointed up to a platform that jutted out from the tower three hundred or more meters above the square.

"They call it the place of judging. Representatives from each clan enter the tower with the first car in the morning. In fact, it's a high honor. Anyhow," Eda continued, "they get to the transfer station. The servobot security system searches all the up-bound passengers. Since the Shiga don't have proper identifications and monitoring implants, they're culled out of the group. A hell of a lot of bots usually get busted up in the process. Quite expensive actually, but no one in his right mind would want the job."

"Then what?" Aldin asked.

"Why, they're taken to the platform and thrown out," Eda said matter-of-factly.

As if to illustrate Eda's point, a sudden hush fell over the crowd. A tiny yellow-robed figure appeared on the brink of the tower.

"Ema! Ema! Ema!" the hundreds of thousands started to chant.

"Ema?" Oishi asked, trying to be heard.

"The hidden teacher, the Ema," Eda replied. "A messiah fig-ure who will liberate them. If one appears on the platform and does not fall, then he is the great Ema. Damn fool must have slipped on to the last car up. Won't these bastards ever give up?"

The yellow-robed form suddenly pitched forward. For several seconds he looked almost to be flying, his robes fluttering about him, his arms extended straight out.

The body impacted headfirst at the base of the tower.

A loud roar went up from the crowd and the rioting continued.

"Every ten days," Eda shouted, shaking his head. "Of course, no Ema's revealed, then everything degenerates from there. Each clan feels the impurity of the others prevents the hidden teacher from being revealed. Those wearing red headbands are the Mukba, the elect, and are allowed to take heads. The rules are strict, otherwise they'd have wiped each other out long ago. It's a great honor to be a Mukba, the rest are just here for the fun of it. Sort of like the running before dragons that those damn fool Daks practice. Same damn thing every week. I tell you it gets on your nerves after a while.

"I think we better get moving," Eda said, looking back toward the square.

A group of blues had detached themselves from the crowd and were now looking in their direction.

"Once outside the square, it's open season on offworlders. Those young bucks might be looking for some fun. Let's move." And the party, following Eda's lead, started up the alleyway.

"Infidels, pork eaters, nonbelievers!" the blue robes shrieked, closing in behind them. As if a signal had been given, inhabitants of the narrow, refuse-choked alleyway started to peer out from the upper floors of their squalid hovels.

Within seconds a rain of garbage and chamber-pot contents started to rain down from above, and the Japanese, now wild with rage, started to shout their defiance back.

Young children jumped from rooftop to rooftop, some of them pulling up roofing tiles to drop, while others leaned over to relieve themselves upon the foreigners.

"Just keep moving," Eda shouted, "before they can cut us off. We're almost to the foreign quarter."

Suddenly there was a sickening crunch, and with a groan, one of the samurai tumbled forward, hit squarely on the head by a heavy rock heaved from above. A shout of triumph went up from the children overhead, who danced about with joy, while the Japanese shook their fists in impotent rage as they picked up their fallen comrade. Blood was pouring out from under his helmet. Oishi rushed over to his side, bent over, and then came back up, a look of cold rage on his features.

Stunned, Aldin realized that the man was dead—the first one to die in his service. He started to say something to Oishi but then thought better of it. He looked at the man and then at his outraged comrades. With a shudder Aldin realized that he didn't even know the man's name.

"Almost there, almost there," Eda cried, the nervous strain of it all showing on him as well. "Just turn left at the next corner!"

Picking up their pace, the group surged forward, and their tormentors, sensing a growing panic, pushed in behind them, shouting abuse.

The front of the column turned the last corner and came up short.

A wall of a dozen or more blue robes stood in their way. Aldin peered over the heads of his guards and saw that the tallest one in the middle of the group was the same man who had most likely observed the killing of his comrade back by the Skyhook. Beyond the waiting blues was the gateway into the foreign quarter, the barrier open, the iron-studded doors leaning back drunkenly as if they had been smashed open, while over the street hung a low pale of eddying smoke.

Eda's cool exterior finally gave way.

"Fanatical bastards," he cried. "I'm sick of them. Just sick of them. Some of the maniacs have started a fire!"

"Well, stop whining and get us out of this," Oishi shouted, sizing up the group ahead of them. Turning, he saw that with every passing second, the group behind them was being reinforced by new recruits pouring in from adjoining alleyways. Overhead the storm of debris was turning into a veritable blizzard of tiles, garbage, and excrement.

Eda, a look of fear in his eyes, took a deep swallow and stepped to the edge of the samurai ring. "We are willing to pay blood money, so that there is no shame. We still have his head and will barter it back." And so saying, he motioned for one of the samurai to surrender the trophy, which he had belted to his waist.

"Not enough amber in the Hole," the tall one shouted.

"Barter time not now," Eda replied, nervously licking his lips. "The dead one has already been lifted to paradise and even now rests in the arms of girls ever virgin. Rejoice for him and leave us pass. Blood money will be sent to you."

"We demand the blood of a servant to go with him," the tall one shouted.

"Better move," Oishi shouted, looking back over his shoulder, "they're working up for a rush!"

Aldin looked back. There was a cry from a samurai standing next to him, and with a shove the samurai pushed Aldin to one side. There was a dull thump and the man went down to his knees, knocked senseless by a roofing tile, which shattered against the side of his head.

"Charge!" Oishi cried, and with raised sword he pointed to the blues before them.

As one the samurai rushed ahead, eager to be at their tormentors.

"No! Stop, damn it, stop!" But Eda's words were drowned out as the samurai, shouting with joy at the prospect of battle, swarmed up the filth-caked alleyway. Stunned at the sudden onset, the assassins drew back, their short daggers and garrotes no match for the long striking swords of the samurai warriors.

Blood splattered across the alleyway, bodies went down, shrieks of agony rent the air as the group waded in to the attack. Zergh, giving himself over to the blood lust, pushed to the fore, two-handed sword held high, with Aldin following in his wake. Within seconds they were through the blue-clad ranks, most of the enemy falling where they had stood, while the few survivors fled into the stinking hovels and darkened alleys that lined the end of the street.

After pushing through the shattered entryway into the foreign quarter, the group came to a stop on the other side.

Oishi barked a series of commands and the group formed up again, turning to face the threat he expected from behind. But the alleyway was quiet now, except for the moaning cries of several assassin wounded left behind by their fleeing comrades.

The mob stood silent, and in its silence it was even more threatening than it had been but moments before.

"Now you've gone and done it," Eda snarled, coming up to Aldin's side. "They were just having some fun with you, that's all."

"Fun? You call one of my men being killed fun?"

"To them it is," Eda shouted. "They were testing your nerve, that's all. It's festival day. The Mukba fight for martyrdom. It should have been a one-on-one, your stupid Gaf friend and him fighting to settle the debt. You've broken the covenants of the law and now the entire Isma, the blue robes, will kill you on sight."

"Well, why the hell didn't you tell us?" Oishi roared, coming to Aldin's defense.

"Because you panicked and didn't give me time. Look at them back there, they'll never deal with you now, it'll be kill on sight."

"Goddamn crazies," Aldin snarled, and looked over at Oishi.

"You did what was right," he said, clapping the man on the shoulder. Oishi shot Eda a vicious look for having berated his lord before the men and felt an inner sense of relief for being supported in his decision.

"Any of our men hurt?" Aldin asked.

Oishi looked around the ground and saw that they had the body of their one comrade and the prostrate form of the one knocked unconscious before the charge. He then noticed that Tomoichi, one of the youngest of the band, was sitting on the ground trembling.

He went up and knelt by the youngster's side.

Tomoichi looked up at his leader and smiled wanly.

"It's only a scratch," he whispered, and held up his right arm to show where a ragged but shallow cut had sliced his arm for several inches above the wrist. The boy started to shiver, obviously from the shock of what had just happened. Oishi grunted sympathetically. The sight of one's first wound was enough to unnerve even the bravest.

"You're a man now, Tomoichi." And he clapped the youngster on the back.

"Somebody wounded?" Eda cried, pushing through the crowd.

"It isn't much, a couple of stitches will take care of him," Oishi replied.

"A sword," Eda screamed, "give me a sword!"

Confused, Oishi just stared at the little man as if he were mad. With a wild lunge, Eda reached down to Tomichi's side and snatched up his fallen blade and raised it high.

"Stick out your arm!" he shouted. "Stick it out!"

Tomoichi looked at him wide-eyed. Oishi pushed his way in front of Eda, his own blade up, ready to strike.

"His arm!" Eda shouted again. "Cut it off now, before it's too late."

Confused, Oishi looked back at the wounded youngster. The boy was still shaking, and even as Oishi looked at him he fell over, his body wracked with convulsions.

"It's too late," Eda whispered, and, dropping the blade, he turned away.

"What's too late?" Oishi cried, grabbing Eda by the shoulder.

"Don't you know they carry poison blades here? That's why they have saw-toothed daggers. The blades are dipped in a waxy solution that sticks between the teeth. I only hope your boy there was hit with a fast agent."

Wide-eyed with horror, Oishi looked back. Tomoichi's body arched and twisted as he thrashed upon the ground. A strangled cry escaped from his lips, and then with a sigh he fell back, his features relaxing into the stillness of death.

"It was the fast agent," Eda said.

Stunned, the samurai looked down at their fallen comrade, one of the youngest of the forty-seven ronin. The silent spectators down at the end of the street had witnessed it as well, and a shouting jeer went up.

"Pig's spawn, he'll burn in hell!"

Several of the samurai, driven to the edge of reason, turned and started back toward the crowd, but Oishi pushed in front of them.

"Not now!" he barked. "We'll take them, but when we're ready."

The men hesitated.

"You are samurai," he roared. "Now obey."

His words brought reason back to the ranks, and following Eda, the group retreated up the narrow street.

Wreathed in the eddies of smoke, the mob was lost to view, their shouts of defiance prodding the samurai who fought to control their anger.

"It's just around the corner," Eda said, "and then I'm done with you."

The street through the heart of the foreign quarter was empty. The shops looked like fortresses under siege. Not a single building had a window facing the street, other than narrow slits lining each floor. The single doorway into each structure was more often than not made of steel studded with heavy bolts, flanked on either side by narrow spy slits, and protected overhead by spouts out of which boiling oil or some such concoction could be poured.

As they approached the corner, clouds of smoke rolled up from the alleyway to greet them.

"I'm getting a very uncomfortable feeling about this," Zergh whispered, coming up to Aldin's side.

Trying not to appear too anxious, Aldin merely nodded in reply.

His worst fears, however, were confirmed when they reached the corner.

"Well, there it is; my contract is finished," Eda said coldly, while pointing toward the source of the smoke.

"What the hell do you mean, there it is?" Aldin shouted, coming up to the guide's side.

The building that Eda was pointing to was engulfed in flames, which shot out of the spy slits like blowtorches. The neighbors were out but were busy working the corner pump in order to throw water on their own threatened structures.

Even as they stood watching, the roof of the building caved in with an explosive roar, sending a shower of sparks heavenward into the damp air.

"That is, or should I say was, your safe house; my job is finished."

"Who the hell did it?" Zergh shouted, coming up to join the argument.

Eda merely shrugged his shoulders. "Maybe your competitors, since they got in here first. Then again, I told you killing that blue robe was going to cause problems. Perhaps his companions found out where you were staying and got there first."

"Well, now what are we going to do?"

"I've fulfilled my contract," Eda replied, his voice edged with contempt, "so it's your problem, not mine. You've made it difficult enough for me to get out of here as is, the blues might think I'm part of your group."

Feeling a touch of panic, Aldin looked around. He had thought that they'd be able to get into their safe house, barricade it, and hole up for a couple days till they sorted things out.

"Couldn't we buy your services?" he said hastily. "Look, we'll pay you what you want."

"You couldn't pay me enough," Eda said coldly. "You've got the smell of death around you. I've lived here long enough—I know it when I smell it, and I'm usually right. If I stick around, the smell will wear off on me."

"Look, back up there." Aldin pointed up toward the towering Skyhook that dominated the view. "I've got wealth, stock, I've even got my own ship."

The last part wasn't quite true, his ship was a wrecked hulk floating somewhere out in space, but neither he nor Zergh would tell it otherwise.

"Name your price," Aldin pleaded. "Just a standard day's service, that's all I ask."

Eda looked at him with contempt.

"Besides what the Xsarn's paying," he said, "I've got a hundredweight of fossil green amber. Your wealth is meaningless, and anyhow, once you're killed, your money will be confiscated and then I'm left with nothing but an I.O.U. from a dead man. You're worthless, Aldin Larice." And with a harsh laugh he started to turn away.

Oishi's blade snaked out, touching Eda on the throat. Without comment the samurai looked at Aldin, awaiting his command.

"Let him go," Aldin said, disgusted.

Eda merely smiled. "Wise. Kill me while under contract and even if you live the Xsarn will want answers."

"Get the hell out of here," Aldin snapped. "And you can tell the Xsarn for me that he can kiss my ass."

"I'm sure he'd love to," Eda replied with a laugh. "Some free advice though to you, the dying. You better find someone to let you in before dark—the Shiga love night hunts. I'll also tell you that your opponents are near, very near, perhaps hiding even on this very street, since this is the only foreign quarter in the Hole. Have fun."

With a sarcastic wave Eda turned and disappeared into the smoke and was lost from view.

"A cheery bastard." Zergh sniffed.

"Cheery all right, he's short time and getting out." Dejected, Aldin looked back at the flaming wreckage of what was to have been his safe house. "Well, I'm open to suggestions," he whispered softly.

chapter five

"My lord Gablona."

Wearily Corbin looked up at the black-robed assassin who stood before him. He hadn't walked so damn far in years. His legs still trembled from the exertion of running for cover.

Damned green robes, he thought angrily, a bunch of crazy fanatics all of them, and what a stench.

He eyed the assassin closely; barbarians, as well, he thought. But at least these were barbarians in his employ.

"What is it?" Corbin barked, leaning over to rub the knotted muscles of his beefy thighs.

"The master wishes to see you."

"Well, tell him to come in here then."

Had to keep these animals in their place, Corbin thought. This was his chamber and people came to him, not the other way around. He shifted his gaze around the room. Some chamber. It still stank from the Xsarns who had inhabited it before vacating it for the purpose of the game. All the damned furniture was oversized, making him feel like a child, and was crafted, as well, for insectoids whose lower limbs articulated backward, thus resulting in some rather unusual designs for chairs and such.

"But the master wishes for you to observe something that he's noticed."

"Damn it all, why didn't you say that the first time?" Corbin said wearily, and with a groan came to his feet. He left the room located in the central core of the house and followed the assassin down a narrow corridor to the front gate. Hassan was standing in one of the narrow defense slits that projected outward from either side of the door, his eye to one of the windows.

Hearing their approach, Hassan turned with a catlike ease

that Corbin found most disturbing, as if the man were ready to strike him down out of hand.

A thin smile creased Hassan's deceivingly gentle features. "I think there's something down the street that you'd like to see." He gestured for Corbin to look out one of the spy slits.

Sensing a possible trap, Corbin hesitated.

"Ah, a wise precaution," Hassan replied smoothly, not taking insult. "Rest assured, it's safe."

Corbin looked closely at Hassan. He'd only been with this man for less than half a day. Hassan had been properly correct before him, acknowledging him as his lord and commanding the others to instantly obey all commands on pain of death. The riches and titles Gablona promised seemed to have an effect at least, and Hassan had thanked him profusely, promising the best of service. The master of assassins had absorbed the briefing on the way down the Skyhook with a sharp, insightful manner, asking numerous questions about the two jinn they would be fighting and the natives that they would have to contend with. Thinking back on that, Gablona suddenly realized that the bulk of the questions had been about the beliefs of the Al'Shiga, and several of the other assassins had displayed more than a passing interest in what they were hearing. But not one comment was made about what they had heard.

He was a cold one, Corbin realized. When he had told Hassan that failure resulting in his death would mean instant condemnation to hell, the assassin looked at him unmoving, even while the others cried aloud in dismay, babbling that they would prevent such a thing from ever happening.

There had been one curious question to be answered. Hassan had inquired as to which direction was south. He was about to ask why, but some instinct warned him not to, and he pointed off at a right angle to where the sun had risen. He finally remembered the reason behind that question when the assassins had immediately knelt for prayer, the moment they were safely in their fortress.

Realizing that the charade had to be played, Gablona had knelt with them, mimicking their actions. He remembered enough from their history to realize that being a nonbeliever would lower his status. Inwardly he cursed his people for not briefing him thoroughly on this. Now, if it had been Aldin doing the briefing, he thought almost wistfully . . .

He suddenly noticed that Hassan was still waiting for him to look where he was pointing, a gentle, almost innocent smile on his face. Corbin leaned over to look.

A low chuckle escaped from Corbin's lips as he peered down the street. So that's where Aldin's safe house was supposed to be. So now Aldin was out on the street with nowhere to hide. Pulling back, he looked at Hassan and smiled.

"Is that one of the other lords then?" Hassan asked quietly.

"That's Aldin all right."

"I thought so. You could see by the way those men around him stood in the protective circle. I've heard of such men—they come from beyond the Mongol lands to the east."

Corbin looked at Hassan wondering where in his time he had heard of samurai.

"They have some men such as us—ninja, I believe they are called. The grand master above me had dealings with them from time to time. Good warriors, but bound too much by their honor."

Corbin nodded in agreement and smiled. He liked this Hassan, he was a man such as himself. He liked him but also knew that he'd have to be controlled, for men such as himself were always a threat in the end

"Should we try for them?" Corbin asked, realizing that he'd have to concede all tactical decisions to this far more experienced warrior.

Hassan pressed back up to the spy slit and watched for a moment. "If only we had a bow. He's not a hundred paces up the street. It'd be such an easy shot."

"What about a rush now, and get it over with?"

Hassan, his eye still to the slit, shook his head.

"No surprise. Always we must use surprise. Those look like good swordsmen, they're already on edge, waiting for a rush from any quarter. No, my lord, it is stealth, when your enemy does not expect it, that wins. First you intimidate, then you wear down through fear, then finally you kill."

"But what if they come up this way?"

Hassan still shook his head.

"Even if we rushed out, we can pass only two out the door at a time, and all their men would be there to greet us. We know where they are, but they do not know where we are. Whichever way they go, two of mine will follow. Wherever they finally hide, we shall know. Then time and darkness will be our allies.

"Besides, one of my men is already carrying the message of alliance to the lord Sigma, whom you saw moving into his hiding place on the next street. The agreement for the moment will be struck. Let him make the first move and then we shall follow up."

Hassan looked back at Corbin and smiled with a wolfish grin, and Corbin could only smile in return.

"Well, we just can't stand here," Zergh said impatiently.

"He's right, my lord," Oishi replied. "Your fortress is lost, the blue robes know where you are, and we must find shelter before darkness."

Aldin looked up at the sky and saw that the sun had shifted significantly toward what he figured would be the equivalent of west. These damn twelve-hour days were going to be difficult to get used to.

He looked up and down the street, which was now completely deserted, the neighbors having fled back inside once they realized that the fire no longer threatened them.

As if to add weight to Zergh's comment, a distant shouting echoed up from the direction from which they had come.

Oishi turned and nodded to Takashi, who leading several of the samurai, raced back up the street. After gaining the corner, they peered around the edge and then came running back.

"A mob," Takashi barked. "Hundreds of them coming up the street!"

"This way!" Oishi commanded, and without waiting to see if Aldin agreed, he started at slow trot on up into the foreign quarter.

Half a dozen samurai, Takashi in the lead, ran ahead toward the first side alley. They took a quick look around the corner and then motioned for the party to hurry up.

At a run, the group followed their lead.

Aldin kept scanning the buildings to either side, noticing the faint outlines of faces in the spy slits, sometimes Human, sometimes Gaf, and occasionally the triangular shape of a Xsarn.

Nearing the corner, they passed a house, and Aldin noticed that there were no curious faces looking out. It struck him as strange but then he pushed on. Oishi, beside him, was watching cautiously as well, ready in an instant to react to any attack, be it missile or an armed host pouring out of a building.

They reached the first corner and, turning, ran down the alley. The path was so narrow that only a thin crack of sky was visible from above, so that they ran in a dank semitwilight. One of the samurai stayed back for a moment, watching the corner they had just turned, then sprinted down after them.

"They've just turned the corner by the fire," he shouted breathlessly, coming up to Oishi to report.

The party had stopped for a moment in a small plaza with half a dozen streets to choose from.

"This way," Oishi barked, and started up a steep winding path, so that within seconds after they cleared the plaza they were lost from view. They knew the pursuit was still on though for a wild howling echoed up the street after them: the blue robes shouting their anger that the murderers of their kin had so cowardly run away and not stayed to face the hundreds wearing the red knot.

Gasping like an asthmatic in a dust storm, Aldin struggled to keep up, not wishing to accept the indignity of having some of the samurai carry him along. For long minutes they continued up the winding steps, until finally coming up short at a closed gate. It was obvious that the festivities occurring in the rest of the city were being enjoyed with particular abandon just on the other side.

"Damn, the other end of the foreign quarter," Zergh snarled. "We can't very well go back out into the main city."

"We can't retreat, either," Oishi replied grimly. Looking up and down the street, they saw no way out, other than to go all the way back down to the plaza and hope that the mob hadn't arrived there yet. But one of the samurai who'd stayed at the end of the retreating group came around the corner.

"They're fanning out from the plaza," he gasped. "Some of them are coming this way."

Oishi looked grimly around. Silently he pulled his right arm free from his robes, tucking the sleeve into his belt, thus leaving his sword arm freer for action. As one, the warriors around him followed suit.

Aldin looked at Zergh, who gave him a shrug as he pulled his two-handed sword free from its scabbard and then, with a gesture of bravado, imitated the samurai in freeing his right arm. The warriors around him murmured their approval at the sight of his powerful sword arm, not knowing that they were looking at a Gaf long past his prime.

"If it's time to die," Aldin said, his voice quavering slightly with fear, "I am honored to do so with men like you."

He knew the line was nothing but bravado, the type of thing one of his favorite generals from the past, such as Napoleon, or even Alexander, would have said to inspire the troops before battle. But what the hell, these were his troops, and this was going to be his first and most likely his last, battle. But instantly he could see the effect.

Oishi drew in a sharp breath; a look of respect crossed his face, and quickly spread to the others around him. There was also a brief glimmer in the samurai leader's eyes, the slight twitch of a smile. Was it that Oishi had figured out that this was a game? Aldin wondered.

Oishi formed his men into three ranks, covering the street from one side to the other as the roar of the approaching mob drew closer.

"I say there," came a booming voice. "Would you lads care for a drink first before the fun?"

Aldin whirled around to find a Gaf of tremendous build standing in a narrow doorway. He was dressed like all Gafs, no matter what their home world, in the gaudiest of outfits, which in his case was a green-and-orange-checkered jumpsuit. In his hand he held a massive decanter of wine, which he held up in a friendly gesture. Several of the samurai broke free from the line and, approaching the Gaf, lowered their swords, ready to strike at the slightest provocation.

"Whoever's running this crew, would you kindly tell these fellows to point their stickers in some direction other than my belly or my friends up above might get upset."

Aldin turned his gaze away from the bizarre-looking Gaf in the doorway and saw that the narrow upper-floor windows were occupied with Gafs, while more, with swords drawn, stood behind their leader.

In the distance the shouts of the mob grew louder.

"Turn those blades aside," Aldin shouted, and he pushed through his men to come up before the Gaf. With a cry of alarm Oishi followed him, to step in front of his commander.

Aldin quickly collected his wits.

"I could use a drink," he said smoothly, extending his hand to the Gaf. If this being was one of Sigma's berserkers, he thought, then this will be over with sooner rather than later, but he had to take the chance.

With a roaring laugh the Gaf gave him the jug, which held at least two dozen liters. Aldin struggled to bring it up to his lips.

It was a Gaf favorite, their sparkling muscatel, and he nearly choked as too much of it splashed down his throat.

Aldin took a deep breath and hoped that his nose was telling him right. "Smells like a tavern in there behind you."

"That it is, and I own it. Only one on this entire stink hole. Locals round here hate them, you know. It's a sin, so I've got to keep it quiet."

"Could we perhaps adjourn our toasting each other to the inside?" Aldin asked a little too hurriedly.

The Gaf looked at him and smiled with a toothy grin that set Zergh on edge.

The tavernkeeper craned his neck to look down the street and then shifted his gaze back to Aldin. "Table fees are awful expensive."

"We'll pay it," Aldin said, trying to keep from shouting.

"Hundred katars a man," he said, surveying the group. "My brother Gaf with you though can have his table for free."

Aldin did a quick calculation and realized that was four hundred more than the entire war chest given to them by the Xsarn.

"Ten, and that's a fair price," Zergh barked back.

"Negotiations are over," the Gaf said with a smile, and he stepped back to close the door. Oishi started to move forward, but with a warning wave of his finger the tavernkeeper pointed first up to his comrades in the windows and then to the heavily armed Gafs behind him.

"Twenty-five," Aldin cried in desperation.

"Seventy-five and it's a bargain," the tavernkeeper replied smoothly and slowly, as if he had all the time in the world.

That'd leave them more than seven hundred, Aldin thought, and was about to agree when Zergh stopped him.

"Not one-tenth of a katar over fifty," Zergh snapped back in peevish tone. "Otherwise before we die we'll kick your door down and let the blue robes come in after they've finished with us!"

Aldin shot his companion a look of anguish.

The tavernkeeper threw back his head and roared with laughter, but he was barely heard, so close was the mob in its rampaging approach.

"Sixty and not a tenth less!"

"Done!" Aldin cried, and dived for the doorway.

"Wait, wait, the color of your money first," the Gaf said, extending an open paw.

Frantically Aldin spun around and fumbled for the pouch that he had tucked into his shirt. After pulling it out, he started to count out the coins, all the time the shouts of the mob echoing around him.

Counting out the heavy coin that was the universal barter of the trading worlds of the Cloud, he found that he didn't have the right change. With a shout of exasperation he simply thrust the money into the Gaf's hand, who then hurriedly handed it back to one of his assistants.

"Your change will be returned momentarily," the Gaf said evenly, and then stepped aside.

In a mad rush the samurai stormed in, Oishi standing outside, urging his men to hurry. As the last man rushed inside Oishi leaped through the door and put his shoulder to it, while the tavernkeeper threw down the heavy steel bar.

He then pulled open a tiny peephole and offered the aperture to Aldin for a look outside.

They'd not been a moment too soon, and rather than feeling grateful he felt a maddening rage at the Gaf for having timed things so close.

The mob came storming up the street, stopping at last at the closed gate. They milled around, their angry shouts echoing in the narrow street.

"They must've come this way!"

"Maybe they're sorcerers, as we heard," a huge Gaf wearing a blue robe roared. "And used their magic to escape."

"Perhaps they ran down one of the other streets!"

"Let's tear these buildings apart anyhow," another one screamed, and some shouted their agreement. One of them looking threateningly straight at Aldin, who realized that his eye must be visible at the slit.

Instinct told him to step back, and not a second later a narrow stiletto poked through where his eye had been.

The Gaf behind him roared with laughter at his discomfort and then slammed the steel cover port shut, snapping the blade in half.

There was an angry shout on the other side and pounding on

the door. Finally the voices started to drift away as they went off to other quarters in search of their lost prey.

"Care for that drink?" the Gaf asked good-naturedly. "After all, you paid for it."

Aldin followed his host into a low-ceilinged room that stank from overripe wine, bad food, and the obvious effects consuming them had on some visitors' stomachs.

The Gaf and several of his burly assistants got behind the bar and pulled out enough mugs for his new clients. Several jugs the size of the one the Gaf still held in his hand were pulled up and uncorked.

The samurai looked around with a mixture of awe and disgust. Awe for the Gafs, whom they found fascinating. The somewhat canine look of the Gafs inspired them with the thought that perhaps these creatures were under the protection of heaven. The awe was there, as well, for the fact that the Gafs stood near nine feet in height and could obviously crush any one of them with a single blow. They had yet to realize that the strength was offset by slower speed and a coordination that in a Human would be considered clumsy.

As Japanese, the filth of the tavern repulsed them, and they made their disgust obvious by the way they gingerly picked up the heavy mugs and eyed them suspiciously before starting to pour their drinks.

All the while Oishi stood in the back of the room, watching everything, letting nothing escape his gaze. They'd been saved, to be sure, but this could still be a trap within a trap, the drink drugged to make the kill easier. He barked a single command in Japanese, overriding the speech implant.

The other samurai looked to their commander and placed their mugs down.

"Ah, poison you fear, is it?" the tavernkeeper roared, and with a laugh he went to each jug in turn and raised it to his lips, swallowing off a healthy swill.

"Come on, you paid for it," he said. Though the others could not sense it, Aldin picked up an offended tone in the Gaf's voice. The accent had the ring of Jurka to it, Bukha Taug's home world, where hospitality rites were held in the same esteem that all Gafs of the old had once honored.

He decided to take the chance.

"Most expensive cheap swill I've ever bought," Aldin said quietly, as he poured out a drink and held the mug up in salute.

He looked at Oishi out of the corner of his eye, letting him know not to interfere, and then he downed the drink.

It really was what Gafs thought was a fine wine, and he almost choked on the bubbly sweetness of it.

But Oishi would not relent and the samurai sat around their tables in silence, some of them casting longing gazes upon the heavy wine jugs before them.

"As you want it," the Gaf said, "but mind you now, you've paid for them and I've provided, so I don't want to hear any complaints."

"I was wondering what else you might be able to provide," Aldin asked, coming up to lean against the bar.

"Now, I knew it was a lucky day when I saw you fellows running up the street, straight to Maladi's tavern," the Gaf said with a wink. "Customers, I said to myself, and on festival day, no less, when most folks are home quaking behind their door for fear that the celebrations might get out of hand. They kind of did this time, heard some buildings got burnt, a couple dozen merchants killed. But that's life in the Hole, we say around here."

"We could use a place to stay for the night."

Maladi's eyes sparkled with delight.

"It'll cost," he said smoothly.

"Come on and just give them a break, will you?" came a voice from the swinging doorway behind the tavern. The door snapped open and a towering woman came out.

In a coincidence that was almost uncanny, the woman looked almost identical to Aldin's first wife, so that he gave her an obvious double take. Her hair was dark, almost black, showing an early streaking to gray along the bangs that covered her forehead. Her figure was slightly plump, but definitely not unattractive in the plain shirt and loose trousers that she wore tightly belted around her waist.

If there was one difference between her and his first spouse, it was with the eyes; they were a light blue, rather than green, and did not carry a look of snakelike cunning.

She scanned Aldin's face for a moment, noticing how he was staring at her, and then took in the rest of the group.

"I'm Mari," she said evenly. "Welcome to the Pig's Kiss. I'm half owner, along with him." And she pointed at the Gaf.

"The Pig's Kiss, what a name for this place," Maladi roared. "Why, if the Shiga knew that, they'd really go wild."

"You're the game players, aren't you?" Mari said evenly, ignoring Maladi.

"Ah, so that's it!" Maladi said. "I thought it might be you. You wouldn't be Gablona, by chance?"

"No. Aldin Larice," Aldin said coldly. "Why?"

"Too bad," Maladi replied, suddenly cooling a bit. "Got my money on Gablona living—five hundred katars cross-bet twenty different ways. Damn me, I even had a couple riding on your dying the first day, too."

How the hell did this Gaf already know about the games? Aldin wondered, but realized this wasn't the time to ask.

"What about lodgings for the night?" Aldin asked, coming back to his main concern.

"Now, knowing you're the gamers sets things different. In fact, I just shot myself in my foot, I did, by letting you in. Could say I lost my five-hundred-katar bet, seeing how Gablona's first rival would be a smear out on the street by now if I hadn't."

"I'll make good on your lost bet," Aldin said wearily.

"Ah, now that's the spirit. Now, beyond that your lodgings will cost—"

"Five hundred will buy 'em lodgings for the week," Mari snapped. "And that's still twice the going rate. Anyhow, you only bet a hundred, and fifty of that was mine."

Maladi turned on Mari with an evil look, but she stood her ground.

"I already heard what you charged them for their first drink."

"Business, purely business."

"Look at it this way," Mari interjected. "They're the gamers, you'll have the ringside seat and the inside track on the betting if they stay. They leave, and you lost out on the information you could sell."

Maladi suddenly broke into a grin again.

"Knew I went into business with you for a reason," he roared good-naturedly. "Second round of drinks and dinner are on me for tonight." And with a laugh he kicked the swinging door open and disappeared into the kitchen to get the cooks working.

Aldin could only shake his head. The money that was supposed to last them for the full eighty game days was almost gone in the first four hours.

The woman was the only one left as Maladi's guards followed their boss into the back, and she drew closer to Aldin.

"That was generous of him throwing dinner in," he said sarcastically.

"You could still be out on the street," she shot back.

Yes, he realized, he certainly could be.

"Let's just hope that he doesn't realize for a while that when your enemies make a move on you, this establishment might be in the way." And a conspiratorial smile flickered across her face and then disappeared.

Aldin found that he was still staring at her, completely unnerved by her resemblance to his ex.

"Something about me bothering you?" she asked evenly.

"Well, ah, you see . . ."

"It's just you look a lot like his damnable ex-wife." Zergh laughed, coming up to Aldin's side.

"Does that bother you?" she asked coldly.

"Ah, no. Well, actually, yes," Aldin said, fumbling for an answer.

"Reminiscing about your loving wife is all fine and good," Zergh interrupted. "First, though, how do you know about the game?"

"Why, everyone around here knows," she replied as if it were a fact they should have been aware of.

"This certainly screws the situation," Zergh cursed quietly. "If the money's running on Gablona, then it will be to everyone's interest to help him out.

"Were you aware of this?" Zergh asked, looking over at Aldin. "I was with the samurai the whole time and completely out of touch with what was happening."

"How could I? I was locked up the whole time you were away. Yaroslav must have known, but damn it all, he didn't say a word."

"Well, it's common knowledge around here," Mari replied, pouring herself a drink. "Most likely even the Shiga know about it, the way the foreign quarter was buzzing."

"And there's another thing," Aldin said quietly. "Maladi really spilled it when he called it a game. Oishi must have heard, and that sure as hell doesn't match up with what he's been told about this fight. He thinks I'm fighting mortal enemies, and then that loud-mouthed Gaf tells him it's a game. It's still a mortal conflict for us, but somehow knowing the details might not settle well with him."

Aldin looked over his shoulder and saw that Oishi was looking straight at him, as if reading his thoughts.

There was only one thing to do, Aldin realized, and that was to come completely clean and tell the whole thing out.

"It can wait for now," Zergh responded. "Let's get some food in us first, secure the guards, and then take a closer look at this place."

"Some advice," Mari interrupted. "Don't think about trying to doublecross Maladi about paying just 'cause you have all those armed ruffians. He's not a bad sort and usually keeps his word, but if he smells a double cross, he'll have more friends here than you can whistle up in a year, and they'll turn your heads over to the Shiga as a payoff to keep them from bothering us."

"Well, that's a nice way of putting it, but I've got a question for you," Aldin replied.

"Go on then. But I already know it. The reason Maladi brought you in was the profit. My reason for giving you a place to stay? Well, let's just call it profit as well—business's been slow lately. Something's been stirring with the Shiga, and most of the merchants have gotten out of here over the last couple of weeks. It's that simple," she said evenly, holding Aldin's gaze the whole time she spoke.

Aldin could only nod in reply.

"I hope the food's better than the wine," he said dryly, realizing it was best to shift the subject, even though his curiosity was aroused concerning this woman.

"It should be, I'm the head cook for this dump." And with a smile she turned and went back into the kitchen.

Aldin turned and motioned for Oishi to join him at a grease-covered table in the corner of the room.

The samurai sat down by Aldin's side, his back to the wall. Nothing was said, but Aldin could feel the tension.

"I have some explaining," Aldin began lamely,

"I have not asked," Oishi replied formally.

"But I owe you the truth. I've lied too many times, to too many people. I'm not going to now. I needed men with honor, men I could trust, and that is why I wanted you."

"But to a samurai life is honor, and honor the reason for living."

"That is why I wanted you. It is true some men are calling this a game. I shall tell you about that when time permits. But to me it is more than that. I've studied you, Oishi; I've studied warriors throughout history. If there is one thing positive I can say about some of them, it is that those who reached true greatness did so because they cherished honor.

"The men I face are without that. They believe that it is cunning, that it is deceit that brings power. True, it can, but it is a power that is chimerical, for in the end their deceit is revealed, and then their power fails. The friends of some of those men think what we are going through here is a source of amusement, a game, if you will, for them to bet upon.

"But there is more to this, Oishi. Far more. For me this is a question of honor. Can men of honor win against men of deceit? If there is a game in all of this, then that is it. A test to prove that we can triumph."

Zergh, who was sitting at the same table, could not help but give a snort of disdain. "Then explain how men of deceit usually win. You're an idealist, Aldin; that's why I came along, to protect you from your own idealism."

Oishi was silently watching the two.

"Then if this is a game," Aldin replied, "let this be the testing of it. I'm talking about the broader sweep of history, Zergh. There are times of darkness when deceit does win, but I'm convinced, as well, that the tide of Human, or Gaf, or even Xsarn nature wins out, and sets things back onto a path of progress, throwing down those who win by deceit.

"I want to prove that to those bastards up there watching this."

Aldin shifted and turned back to Oishi. "There's a lot more to explain about those who are watching this contest. But know for now that I chose you because I wanted men of honor around me, and in turn know that I will not deceive you."

He held Oishi with his gaze. For a long quiet moment the samurai stared at Aldin, probing, looking to see if there was a different answer hidden within.

"We'll need to talk yet more, my lord," Oishi said quietly.

"Something's up!"

Aldin looked up to see Takashi standing by the table. "What is it?"

"There's a Gaf outside who wants to talk to you, and to you alone."

"Who is it?" Oishi barked, coming to his feet.

"Claims to be an envoy from the lord Sigma and wants to arrange a meeting."

"How the hell did Sigma know where to find us?" Aldin asked.

Takashi could only shrug his shoulders, while behind him the doorway swung open and Maladi came strolling out to check on his guests.

Aldin and Zergh looked at each other.

"Word travels fast," Zergh observed dryly.

"I'll see to it. Then we'll talk more later," Oishi said, coming to his feet, and strode off to meet with the envoy who was still out in the alleyway.

Zergh looked at Aldin and leaned across the table.

"Looks like you're on probation," he said evenly.

And what if I fail? Aldin thought nervously.

chapter six

"He is unarmed," Oishi said, "but still I don't trust him, my lord. I've seen curious weapons here, and he might have something hidden on his body."

"He's right," Zergh replied. "A Gaf like that one—" and he pointed over to the messenger in the corner of the room "—could crush a man with a single blow. Remember, Sigma has berserkers; those warriors are convinced that dying in battle is the final glory."

"But he won't give you the message?" Aldin asked, looking back at Oishi.

The samurai shook his head. "Insisted that it must be to you alone."

"We could force it out of him," Zergh responded, his voice cold.

Aldin looked over at his friend. Zergh still surprised him at times. When need be, he could display an absolutely deadly cunning.

"If we tie him down, will you do the torturing?" Aldin replied. "Remember, we're no longer talking theory and academic questions of war, this is cold hard reality."

"If need be," Zergh replied, but to his relief Aldin could hear the doubt in his old comrade's voice.

"Zergh has just given the answer," Oishi replied, and with a bow he turned and walked away.

Minutes later Aldin came up to the table in the corner of the tavern and sat down. Across from him sat one of the legendary berserkers of Basak, perhaps the finest individual warriors in Gaf history, who were trained from childhood in the belief that the only moment of reality was the moment of death and the taking with you of servants to do your bidding in the next world. If the manner of death was considered exemplary, their comrades would sacrifice additional servants to go with them before their funeral pyre. Thus they actually had a rudimentary rating system classifying one's death as a one-servant death, or higher, depending upon how dramatic the comrade's departure.

Knowing the proper approach, Aldin stared at the warrior with a full display of teeth.

"You shall crawl before me, when I go to my ancestors," Aldin opened.

The Gaf spat on the floor and as he did so the samurai, who'd drawn back, reached for their blades, ready to avenge the insult. But Aldin motioned them to be still.

"In the next world you shall eat my spoors and consider it an honor."

Aldin laughed in reply and, pulling up a chair, sat across from the messenger.

The Gaf's hands and feet were bound. At first he'd almost refused, roaring that he would be at their mercy, until Aldin had finally pledged to serve him in the next world if he was betrayed. But he could see the berserker was still nervous with the arrangement.

"You've agreed to much," Aldin said, "to allow yourself to be thus bound."

"I swore oath to Taug Sigma to bring the message; if I failed, then there was but one choice left."

"A pity to waste your life on suicide with no servants to

wait upon you, your siblings to be shamed that their brother had failed in the leaving of life."

"The Gaf was silent.

"What is the message then?"

"Taug Sigma has charged me to arrange a meeting between you and him."

Aldin sat back. Sigma, as usual, did not waste time. But why the hell hadn't he talked before they came down, unless it was because there was no way they could hold a conversation without Gablona being present.

"And has he met with the other Taug, the one called Gablona?"

The Gaf only looked across at him and smiled.

"Foolish of me to ask a man sworn to die for his Taug."

"I expected you to be a fool. Your guards are puny; many of them will serve us before long."

"We shall see," Aldin replied evenly. "Tell Sigma that he is welcome to come here to meet with me at any time."

The Gaf leaned back and gave a short bark of disdainful laughter. "Rather you should come to meet with him."

"I am not that simple to fool," Aldin snapped. "Sigma knows that."

"Sigma is willing to arrange several alternate meeting places."

"Unacceptable. If he can select, then he can prepare the trap."

"Then we must have an intermediary," the Gaf replied.

Aldin sat back.

Of his two opponents, he trusted Sigma more than Gablona, and he suspected that Sigma felt the same. An alliance at the start would be to their advantage. He had to meet with him face-to-face in order to work out the arrangements though. He couldn't let this chance be passed up. And besides, Sigma already had a tactical advantage: he knew where Aldin was hiding but Aldin did not know Sigma's location.

"All right then, we'll meet," he said cautiously. "We'll let someone else select the place."

"Who then?" the Gaf replied.

Aldin realized immediately that the Gaf's ready agreement meant that Sigma had foreseen Aldin's thinking and had ordered the Gaf to agree. Could this be a trap within the trap? He hesitated for a moment, and then realized that this game was for real. It was no longer mere risks on money, he'd have to weigh the odds on every decision and then gamble—with his life.

Aldin looked back over his shoulder. "Zergh, go back in the kitchen and bring out Mari."

Aldin turned back to look at the Gaf. After upturning two mugs, he poured a drink out for the both of them. The Gaf eyed the drinks suspiciously.

"Tell me which one to take first," Aldin replied politely, and the Gaf pointed out one of the mugs, which Aldin brought up and then drained off. The Gaf reached out with his bound hands, clumsily grasped the mug, and finished his drink in turn.

"Did Sigma ever tell you what this was really all about?" Aldin asked cautiously as he poured another drink.

"What?"

"Why we're fighting."

"Ah, he told me about the gods who set him down to be tested against you and the other evil demon."

Aldin could only laugh.

"Did you want something?" a voice interrupted, and Aldin turned to face Mari, who stood before him with a slightly sardonic smile lighting her features.

"You are now ambassador extraordinaire," Aldin announced with a pompous tone.

"You've been drinking too much," she replied sarcastically.

"Ah, just like my ex," Aldin responded. "We need a go-between, a neutral who will select a meeting spot."

"A Human woman?" The Gaf sneered.

Mari shot him an evil glance.

"Then we'll ask her boss to work on this as well. The two of them will decide on a place in secret. She'll go with you to inform Sigma. He and six guards will then proceed to the meeting place, while Maladi over there," Aldin said, pointing to the hulking Gaf who was sitting behind the bar eyeing them curiously, "will guide us. Two of your guards and two of mine will first enter and agree the place is secure and then we shall meet. The woman will go with you, and the tavernkeeper will go with me."

"Why the hell should I go rather than Maladi?" Mari asked. "Not to say I'm willing to be part of this thing anyhow."

"Because I trust you more than I trust him. He could go

with this messenger and arrange a double cross if he saw enough profit in it."

The Gaf looked at him, a slight smile crossing his lips. "My Taug said you were crafty. All right then, it is agreed."

Aldin smiled inwardly, for through Mari he'd be able to find out Sigma's hiding place.

"You've agreed, but I sure as hell haven't," Mari snapped. "The blues are tearing the streets apart looking for you. It's dangerous out there."

"I'll make it worth your while," Aldin replied.

With a snort of disdain Mari turned and stormed off, but Maladi stopped her before she got back into the kitchen and after a brief exchange the tavernkeeper took her by the arm and led her back over to the table.

Aldin felt himself bristle at the Gaf holding her like that, and thought the reaction strange.

"Ah, my noble guest," Maladi started, "so my services are needed. Surely my partner and I would be more than happy to serve you."

"If we do, it's an even split," Mari snapped back.

"But of course," Maladi said offhandedly. "But my services will be steep for such a dangerous task. Shall we say, five hundred katars."

Aldin groaned, but after several minutes of spirited debate he got the Gaf down to two fifty.

"Of course, the fee is split," Aldin finished up. "I'll give Maladi his half, and Sigma will pay you before the meeting starts."

Aldin looked over at the berserker. He knew that talk of money to their class was considered dishonorable, but the Gaf did have to come back with an arrangement, and the berserker growled an agreement.

"Then we meet in one hour. My men will untie you, those two will privately decide on a place, and then you can be on your way."

"In the next world you shall lick the ground before me, so that it is clean for my boot to step upon," the berserker snarled.

"Your brothers and you as well shall carry me upon your backs and cry out that they are thus honored to be my servants," Aldin snapped in reply.

"You're all crazy," Mari growled, as the two spat on the ground by each other's feet.

* * *

"You know the blues are rampaging through this quarter looking for you," Sigma said, a cheery smile lighting his features.

Aldin settled back into his chair and looked around the narrow candle-lit room. The approach to the amber merchants' warehouse, owned by a customer of Maladi's, had been a nervous one. All his guards except two left behind to hold the tavern had started out and then been dropped off at an abandoned building a block away, while the six primary guards had pushed on to the place Maladi had designated.

Unfortunately Mari had not made it all the way to Sigma's hiding place, but instead had been held in the street by several Gaf guards until Sigma had returned with the rest of his followers. After a hurried conference he agreed to follow her to the meeting.

But Aldin realized she'd most likely be able to make some fairly good guesses as to where Sigma's fortress was located.

"And I suppose you've thought of selling me to the blues and currying their favor," Aldin replied.

Sigma leaned back and examined his manicured fingernails. Even while in captivity waiting for the game to begin he had somehow arranged to have his hairdresser, masseurs, and body scrubbers attend to him. Aldin wondered how he'd look after forty standard days on the Hole.

"With you gone in the first day, Gablona would turn his attention on me. I prefer you as the buffer."

"And I prefer you as the buffer," Aldin replied.

"Come, come, Aldin, you're only a vasba, and might I add a vasba who's made a lot of citizens angry over the last year. With the wealth and connections Gablona and I have, we can arrange certain advantages down here that you cannot. So, as a betting man, I'd put you on the low end of bets worth taking."

"On the planet of the Al'Shiga," Aldin replied smoothly, "I doubt that."

"With the right promises of money, Gablona and I will be able to buy support."

Aldin could only laugh. "Remember, Sigma, as you've just pointed out, I'm the vasba and your not. It's my job to arrange fights and to have a superior knowledge of military history. The Al'Shiga frighten me, and they should frighten you as well. They are perhaps the most potent political movement in the Cloud—if ever they obtained spacefaring capabilities, they could tear us apart."

"Ridiculous. The Skyhook security system prevents that, and that is why all the Kohs who trade here pay a heavy premium to provide security for this world."

"Don't underestimate them," Aldin warned.

"They're all insane animals," Sigma replied disdainfully. "I don't know what was going on when you came down, but it was sheer insanity when my people came through. That tossing of heads, really quite disgusting. Can't understand why they haven't wiped each other out ages ago."

"From what I could see today," Aldin stated, "the killings follow a complex ritual, otherwise they'd all run amok and wipe each other out in a couple of days. That's the curious part of it all. They're all on the razor's edge of mass murder, but somehow their leaders keep them in check.

"Most likely not more than a hundred or two died today. Thus in a typical year maybe five or six thousand die. Add in another ten or fifteen thousand killings a year, to keep their skills in practice, and you could call it social Darwinism if you like."

Aldin sat back in his chair and looked closely at Sigma. It was a shame, he thought, that they were being pitted against each other. Of all the Human Kohs, he had the most respect for this one. Many an evening they had sat like this, debating some point of military history. Sigma was not one of the true connoisseurs who had acquired a master's knowledge in one particular subfield—his sense of business kept him from that, for unlike many of the Kohs, Sigma still believed in having his hands on the family business rather than delegate it to underlings. Thus he didn't have the time that, say, Zola or Vol could devote. To him the games were an interesting hobby, when time allowed it.

"My point is," Aldin continued, "that the Al'Shiga are to me a terrifying power. Our information about them is quite limited, actually. No outsider has even gotten into their ranks. Hell, I didn't even know about this festival business till I got down here. It's one of the most closed societies in the Cloud. I did read though that for them assassination is a daily part of life. Every move, every action is taken either to complete a kill or in defense against it. Do you realize that when one is accepted as an initiate of the knife, he is given the name of a stranger from another clan? Nothing but the name, no photo, no vid, nothing. He must then find his prey and stalk him."

"To kill?" Sigma asked.

"No, that's the interesting thing. If he kills him outright, then he is still an initiate. If it was organized any other way, then half of all their people would be dead. Remember as well that I'm talking both male and female on this world. So it would be against the logic of survival for a group to have such a system that killed women before they bore the next generation.

"But anyhow, once he receives his ceremonial knife and endures the naming ceremony, the game, so to speak, has started for him. The initiate might spend years trying to track down his target—in fact, many never do, for the concealment of identity is obviously to one's advantage. But if successful in finding the target, the game has only started, for he must isolate his target. If he can succeed in catching his target, he is allowed to perform a single slash with a nonpoisoned blade on the victim's body and then must escape. Only then is one a full member of the clan."

"Madness," Sigma grumbled.

"Genius," Aldin replied sharply. "The body of the clan does not lose anyone, but all the stealth and training for the kill has been brought to bear. Also, if someone is thus struck, they may never be a master. And if they are a master, they lose their rank. Thus it is a ritual with serious connotations of rank and prestige. The game has its deadly side to it. One can defend to the death, and if a witness is present they can kill out of hand. Finally, if a master is cut, he can regain his honor and rank only by assassinating the initiate who took away his honor. Killing of foreigners is viewed as a side action. We're beneath their dignity as far as the games go, but if they feel the urge to try their garrote out some evening, then the attitude is 'boys will be boys.' That's why this place is so deadly. In self-defense, we might kill one of them, and since we are outside of the clans, then everyone in a clan turns against us, as I've so unfortunately already discovered.

"Killing of foreigners is practice to them." Aldin lowered his voice so his guards wouldn't hear. "The same way my own samurai would test their blades on convicts, to make sure the cutting edge was good."

Sigma looked over at Oishi and the other guards who stood by one wall of the room and saw the drawn swords glinting wickedly in the candlelight. He quickly looked back over his shoulder and gathered some reassurance by the sight of the Gaf berserkers with their massive axes drawn and ready if Aldin was considering a double cross.

"It's tied up in their worship of the Seda as well," Aldin continued.

"Yeah, that struck me as strange. Here they worship that thing, and yet only we can go up and down it."

"Precisely," Aldin replied. "It is their holy of holies. According to their tradition, when they were cast down from heaven, it was by us, the demons who took wrongful possession. But it is also their belief that we won because they had allowed themselves to be impure. They believe that those of us who come down do so in part to taunt them."

"So why do they allow it?" Sigma asked.

"That's just it. Because they feel they are not yet ready to return to the Cloud. They need this Ema, who they believe is in hiding. He'll come when one of the clans has purified itself."

"Purified how?"

"Through the proper blood sacrifice. However, we don't know when that will be. It's one of their hidden secrets."

"But what about this red headband business?" Sigma asked, still curious about the Al'Shiga. He realized that this conversation was essential and that, if anything, Aldin was giving away valuable information that could only help.

"I saw them slashing at anyone with glee," he said.

"The highest honor both for killer and victim," Aldin replied. "The festivals are a safety vent, a release, and wearing the red band means you can kill anyone with impunity. It is given to each master and the religious leaders, called ullas, during the thirty-odd festival days. Everyone turns out to see how many heads are taken. It's an honor, as well, if you're cut by a red band but escape. Sort of like the masculinity rituals of Lentra, where the Xsarns jump into the serpent pits and run before the vipers to prove their virtue, or those damn fool dragon runners we see on the vids.

"These people, Human and Gaf, might seem mad," Aldin

concluded, "but look at what they've set up. It's a vast training ground for warfare through assassination. They're all promised paradise if they die with blade in hand. To us it seems illogical, because all that killing is turned against themselves, but consider if they were ever taken and turned outward, with modern weapons put in their hands. They could shatter the social system of the Cloud in short order."

"You sound paranoid, Aldin Larice."

"When I look at the Al'Shiga, I have every reason to be. We allow contact because of the trade in precious ancient ambers, which they alone control. They understand the secret that warfare can be fought through other means and that one man can get to his target with enough skill and determination. If anyone, or any system, ever turned them loose on us, we'd be destroyed."

"But that's foolish," Sigma replied. "Besides the Overseers, it's our mutual understanding that conflict hurts business, which has held the peace between the various Kohs. Granted, we wage war against each other, but it is economic war, and all of us benefit in the end. If anyone was so foolish as to use the Al'Shiga, then we'd all suffer, and whoever used them would see that terror turned against him as well."

"But I wonder about the Overseers," Aldin said quietly, keeping his voice down to a whisper. "Why have they allowed us to use this place for our little conflict? Let's not fool ourselves. Setting up a game out on the edge of the Cloud, on the Kolbard, for instance, is one thing. But the Hole is damn near in the middle of the Cloud, with half a dozen major trade lanes intersecting in this solar system. The world where the monetary conference is taking place is in the same system. You know damn well that the Overseers must be aware of this. I can't help but wonder why they're sitting back. And I can't help but wonder, as well, if they might have something to do with the Al'Shiga movement."

"Just like you." And Sigma gave a snort of derision. "Here you are, facing me, Gablona, and those crazies out there, and you worry about something that doesn't even affect you. If I were you, I'd be thinking about how to survive till tomorrow, and to hell with the Overseers. Why, if anything, I'm praying the Overseers come in and break this game up so we can get out of here."

Aldin was silent.

"Enough of this," Sigma replied. "My guards are most likely hungry—" he dropped his voice to a whisper, "—and their leader has already told me that they can be most disagreeable if they don't get four full meals a day. Let's finish our business so we can get a good night's rest."

"Are you then proposing an agreement?" Aldin asked cautiously.

"If I didn't have that in mind, I wouldn't have asked you to come out and meet me," Sigma replied.

"What are the terms then?" Aldin asked.

"Nonaggression for the duration."

"Do you already have the same agreement with Gablona?" Aldin asked.

Aldin watched Sigma's eyes, but there was no waver. But he knew Sigma was too much of an old hand to give himself away.

"With that madman? You heard the threats he shouted at me before we came down."

There was no way he'd know for sure, but to be on the safe side Aldin had to assume that not only had there been an understanding, but that Sigma might be setting him up as well.

"Just nonaggression then?" Aldin asked. "I was thinking of shared information and daily contact between two of our representatives for the latest updates on Gablona."

"But of course," Sigma said.

Aldin settled back in his chair and eyed Sigma coldly. "For thirty years I've deferred to you, since you were a Koh, but there's no title, no rank down here. I'm going to give you a blunt warning. First, I won't come for you as long as you don't come for me. I think you know me well enough to know that I'm speaking the truth. But if you do come for me, then I'll not stop till I've taken you out."

Sigma bristled at the threat but didn't reply.

"And secondly," Aldin continued, "if you've made a deal with Gablona, I'll be betting on your being the first to die, and it will be by his hands. He wants you almost as much as he wants me. Don't trust him."

"I can imagine if I had met with him, he'd be saying the same about you," Sigma replied.

"No doubt, but the difference is I think you know who is the more believable."

There was a second of hesitation, but then the same dispassionate smile returned. And in that second Aldin knew that this meeting was a setup to lure him out.

"I think it'll be best if I leave now," Aldin said sharply, and he rose from the table. "And beyond Gablona, don't underestimate the Al'Shiga. Their part in this game, I fear, is more than just simple madness."

He motioned for his guards, who fell in around him. Maladi and Mari joined the group as well. Oishi stepped out first, checking the street, and then motioned for the party to follow.

The foul, filth-encrusted alleyway was silent as the party slipped out. One of the samurai stood by the door, acting as rear guard, while the group continued on up the path to where the rest of their guards waited.

It was Mari who suddenly grabbed Aldin by the sleeve, holding up her hand for silence, and pointed.

Oishi, noticing her move, started for her, suspecting the worst, but then, following where she pointed he froze as well.

The next alleyway up, and across the street, was as dark as the others, but somehow there was a feeling that a particular threat lurked there.

"Alarm!"

The shout echoed down the street, and at the same instant there was a faint flash in the dim light. One of the samurai leaped before Aldin even as he tried to back against the wall, in a desperate attempt to hide. There was a dull thump and a slight gasp of pain.

From up the street dark forms came surging out. For a moment Aldin felt a wild panic, then in the starlight he saw the flowing robes of the samurai, blades drawn, racing down the street toward the party. Oishi ran up the street, shouting a command, and some of the party turned into the side alleyway. Seconds later they reemerged and came back to surround Aldin.

But Aldin did not notice. Crouched over a body, he sat in stunned disbelief. The samurai lay before him, the hilt of the blade in his chest rising and falling spasmodically as life drained away. The blade became still.

Zergh pushed his way through the crowd and then saw Aldin.

"Thank the heavens," Zergh cried softly. "I thought it was you."

"No," Oishi replied, "it was only one of mine." And Aldin looked up to see the bitterness and rage on the samurai's face.

"He didn't have to." Aldin groaned. "He stepped right in front of it."

"He did what his honor demanded, what he would have done for any lord, at least for what he thought was his lord," Oishi replied coldly.

Aldin came to his feet and looked closely at Oishi, and then with a growing sense of shame he turned away.

"Definitely not one of the blues," Zergh said matter-of-factly, having not even noticed the bitter exchange.

"How can you tell?" Oishi asked, kneeling down alongside the body.

"If I may?" Zergh asked, and then without waiting for permission he pulled the blade out of the corpse and handed it to Aldin.

"Earth origin," Aldin whispered. "Looks to be medieval Persian."

"Gablona," Zergh said quietly.

Zergh took the blade from Aldin's hands and tucked it into his belt.

"If I may interrupt," Maladi said, his voice edged with nervousness. "You may discuss the worth of the blade when we're back at the tavern; I can even put you in touch with a collector hereabouts, but let's get off the street. You've just lost a man, the slayer is still loose, your friend Sigma's guards are not far away, and there are the blues, and your other rival, to think about as well. For reasons of health I think it best to seek a better climate."

With a grunt of approval Oishi came back to his feet and directed some of the men to help carry their fallen comrade home, and the party set off.

The group arrived at the tavern several minutes later without incident, the relief evident on all their faces when the door was safely bolted.

"Who called the alarm?" Oishi asked, once they were back in the taproom. "It was good work."

The room was silent.

Aldin looked over at Zergh, who sat in one corner examining the blade. He shrugged without replying.

"No one?" Oishi asked.

"We heard the shout, and that was when we charged out," Seiji replied. "We thought it was you calling."

"Then who?" Oishi asked, looking over at Aldin.

The attempt was by Gablona, that was obvious, so he was out. The locals certainly wouldn't have intervened, and Sigma wouldn't have warned him either. If there wasn't anyone left, then who had? Mari had helped, to be sure, but still there was someone else out on the street who had stopped him from being killed. If someone wanted him to live, who was it, and why?

chapter seven

"I'm glad you wanted to meet with me," Kurst said, as he came in through the door. "I've had some great ideas since we last met."

Zola couldn't help but smile at his probability analyzer. This man had made him tens of billions in just the first day of the game. The Kohs had begged for the stock in the gaming business, and now five days into the match, shares had nearly doubled in value as the full impact of the game started to take hold. Considering his own fifty-one percent share, the doubling in value had earned him yet billions more. He had every reason to feel expansive.

Behind him a bank of vids was monitoring the messages that were being flashed from one end of the Cloud to the other, and even on into the smaller Magellanic. The ad people had cost a bundle, over a billion up front, but within hours their campaign had swept every tech world within reach by transjump link. Ads designed to every species, culture, and eco-standing had filled the airways almost nonstop now for days, pitching the game and posting every move of the three players.

The pitches had to be tailor designed for each market. Mistakes could be costly. On the world of Ilm a single mistake showing a Gaf of the Obe class standing within a hundred meters of one from the Jiil class would have triggered revulsion and destruction of every vid transmitter that had dared to show such sacrilege.

The Ophet system required special care, for the covering of one's genitalia was considered a disgusting practice designed to draw attention. Religious leaders would be sure to howl at such sexually provocative material. Each of the worlds therefore had to have a system set up to match the particular cultural mores, and the ad execs were sharp with their calculations, for all could see that this was a short-term account that needed immediate and massive exposure.

Then there was the printing of tickets. This was the first major difficulty and had become acute, causing a serious paper crisis throughout the Cloud as tickets were printed out in the tens of billions every hour. On several worlds paper stocks had been completely depleted, triggering riots that had killed thousands when no more tickets could be issued.

Riots broke out, too, as lines, sometimes kilometers in length, formed up for the gambling opportunity of the millennium. Sales offices had been set up through the management firms, agencies, and government stations controlled by the various Kohs. But still there were not enough locations to handle the flood of buyers who were bombarded nonstop by the advertising campaign.

In some areas, those who successfully purchased tickets would be set upon the moment they left the office and torn apart by the mob, who'd yet to realize that just holding the ticket was useless. For to avoid fraud and the printing of bogus tickets, an elaborate system had been established whereby each ticket purchased was identified, and the purchaser's personal identity number printed on the stub, with the information stored in the local computer. Twice a day the local information was uploaded to the main systems on Ator, which created another crisis. So much data was flowing in that the systems were hopelessly overtaxed. The main offices were simply swamped with the backlog, and as a result, no one even bothered to run a betting analysis.

Then there was the crisis of computer capacity, which resulted in the sudden purchase of massive memory and data-handling systems. They had to be plugged in even while the system was running, all, of course, at triple overtime pay by the high priests of the industry, whose mysterious jargon was always a guarantee for yet higher prices.

There were other factors, as well, that the Kohs had not anticipated. For one, the commerce of the Cloud had suffered tremendously over the last five days. Billions of employees from their various business ventures were calling in sick, so they could stand on line to buy tickets. Millions of others had to be pulled off their regular duties in order to manage the game.

Ships were not being loaded, passengers and crews were staying close to the nearest betting gate, ready to place the next day's wager as the odds changed. It was not serious enough yet to start an economic panic, but the trend was disturbing. But for the moment Zola didn't care, as the man who first thought of it all pulled up a chair and accepted the brandy and cigar that he now took without asking—as was his right.

"Have you seen the latest reports?" Zola asked, waxing enthusiastic.

"It's already topped two point two trillion on the eighty-day tickets," Kurst shouted. "Considering the lag time on the machines and communications systems, I'm willing to project that by the end of this week ten trillion tickets will have been sold!"

"Ten trillion in the first ten days," Zola whispered, awestruck by what had happened. More than a hundred and fifty for every citizen of the Cloud.

"When I get an idea, I get an idea," Kurst said in a self-satisfied tone.

"Glad the three bastards lived this long," Zola replied. "If one of them had been so impolite as to have died, it would have screwed the odds and perhaps ruined our game. I almost feel as if someone were looking out for them."

Kurst looked up at Zola, hoping for some insider news. He'd been trying to crack into the com links that were carrying the raw information coming up from the Hole, but the Kohs had realized that any such information could affect the bet flow and had been sure to keep the insider news confidential. There'd been a flurry of action the first four days, with four known attempts on Aldin's life and two on Sigma. But somehow, as if someone had been watching over them, all attempts had failed and the stockholders had breathed a sigh of relief at the end of each day. For if one died, the odds would drop dramatically.

"Do you see any leveling off of bets?" Zola asked lazily.

"After about ten days the odds and the payoff are down by a third. I expected we'd see a dropoff by now. The key thing is a death by around the midpoint or so. It'll stir up the action— the psych people believe that a sensory overload will be setting in by then and interest will be diminishing. One death, and they'll flood the ticket agents again up till the cutoff point."

Zola listened closely and smiled while pouring another drink for his brilliant friend.

Kurst smiled in turn. There were some other permutations as well, but that could wait for the moment. After all, there was the idea his girlfriend, a broker in the stock and futures market, had come up with, but that was a deal best left outside of Zola's control.

"So, tell me about your ideas," Zola asked, and Kurst, looking across at the Koh, smiled openly.

"But how could you have bought in with him?" Bukha said wearily. "You've got an uncle on one side, and your family head on another, fighting to the death, and you throw in with that Zola who's turned it into a cheap blood sport for the mob. Being a Koh should carry more dignity than that; loyalty to blood should come before anything else."

"Blood has nothing to do with it," Tia replied. "The technicality of my being a Koh is a flimsy one at best. My dear uncle Corbin, if he lives, will be sure to eliminate me."

Bukha sat back with a sigh.

"I always thought a little bit better of you," he said, shaking his head. "Figured that some of Aldin's teaching would rub off on you."

"I learned from him," Tia said evenly. "Learned that nice guys finish last when it comes to living with Kohs, or anyone, for that matter."

Bukha looked closely at the girl. Was this a bluff, an angry retort, or had she really hardened to such an extent that the Gablona blood was coming to the fore?

"So why have you decided to get together with the two of us?" the Xsarn asked, stirring from his couch in the corner of the room.

"Just wanted to see a couple of old friends," Tia said evenly, "who've been sulking by themselves while everyone else is busy chasing profits."

"When the Xsarn and I figured this game out," Bukha replied sadly, "we thought it'd be a damn good lesson to those three." As he spoke he looked over to the Xsarn, who sat in the corner, noisily sucking on a feeding tube.

"And you were all so innocent," Tia replied sarcastically. "Or was the bet that wiped out Gablona based on playing on a little inside information yourself?"

Bukha looked at her evenly and did not reply.

"As I was saying," Bukha continued, "we never figured they'd truly get each other, that their fear of the Al'Shiga would cause them to hide away until the forty days were up. The betting then between us Kohs would be a minor amusement to help ease the tension of our accountants and lawyers fleecing us blind, and might help pay some of the expenses as well. I never should have let the three choose their own guards. Gablona threw the whole thing off balance when he pulled in some of the best assassins in history. It was a move completely for the offensive and he was out for blood."

"Come on now, do you really expect me to believe your plea for innocence?" Tia replied sarcastically. "You knew that this game would be ugly, and Corbin would grab hold of it with a vengeance. And besides, if one of them did die, it would help to defray the costs of the accounting as well."

Tia stopped for a moment and looked at the two closely. "And another thing, exactly why did you two pick the Hole? Or should I ask why did you agree to the Overseer's suggestion to use it?"

The two were silent, looking back and forth to each other like two conspirators fearful that someone else already knew.

Finally Bukha broke the silence. "It was suggested to us." He hesitated and looked over at the Xsarn.

"It's none of your damn business," the Xsarn snapped, coming to his feet.

"Curious, that's all," Tia replied smoothly. "No need to get excited."

The three settled back, eyeing each other cautiously.

"Well, anyhow," Tia said after a long, uncomfortable moment, "my other reason for dropping by is that I thought you might find a little piece of information rather interesting."

"And that is?" Bukha asked.

"Well, I was taking a close look last night at the incoming

reports, and I noticed something rather unusual coming out of the Livollen Consortium of worlds."

"I own the Consortium," Bukha snapped. "Some of Vol's agents set up ticket sales through their trading representatives, but I'm not involved with the selling, if that's what you're wondering about."

"I know that," Tia replied. "It's just that there's been a dozen large blocks of tickets bought. Twelve people have each purchased five million tickets all on the third day of the game. Each in a different city, and each purchaser did so with cash."

"Incredible!"

"Just the thought of that much money in hundred-katar cash coins is staggering," Bukha said. "And the printout. It must have taken hundreds of machines to churn out the mountains of paper."

"Caused several riots," Tia said, chuckling. "One whole province's betting system was clogged for the entire day just to handle it, and no one else could bet."

"Who were they?" the Xsarn asked.

"I don't know. I've got their ID numbers, but they're citizens of your world, so we don't have any records."

"Five million each, you say."

"Almost to the katar. I've quietly asked one of my people to run an analysis, but it'll take days. But just a quick random check of several hundred bets from each purchaser shows that so far there is no cross-lapping of bets."

"So you think they're working together."

"Just an educated guess, but I think so. I never would have even caught it, our system wasn't designed to flag such a thing, but the data came in on the riots so I called up the reports and saw that our line from that world was feeding in bets full-tilt. The bets coming in from each locale all had the same ID number assigned to them. If I hadn't thought to check, it would have been folded in with the trillions of others and never noticed.

"This whole damn game was set up on such short notice, no one ever thought to program for or even look at trends other than the gross numbers. Trying to sort through trillions of bets looking for patterns is damn near beyond us. It was just a lucky accident, I guess, but it just doesn't feel right."

"First off," Bukha said, "you know and I know that the

whole thing is a sucker's bet. Anyone with enough sense to own that much money wouldn't be laying it all out. Sure, the average mark'll buy five, ten, maybe even five hundred tickets if he's a complete idiot, but five million?"

"My thoughts as well," Tia replied. "You know, at first I thought it might be one of the Kohs, figuring to fix events with the game and then get the payoff. But that wasn't the case."

"Communications for the game both in and out are strictly under my control this time." The Xsarn sniffed. "If any Koh wants to go down there himself, let him, but I don't think anyone is crazy enough to even think about that."

"So why are you telling us this?" Bukha asked, looking over at Tia.

"Just thought you might be curious," Tia replied airily, but Bukha could see that the information had been troubling her and she definitely wanted it checked out.

"It's your lottery, not mine," the Xsarn replied coldly.

"They're your worlds," Tia snapped. "I think something's afoot here. I'm thinking, as well, that you're more involved in this game than you'd like to have known."

Bukha almost started to bristle at the accusation, but realized that it was useless. He was about to respond when a soft paging chime cut in.

"The latest game report," the Xsarn said, his voice showing his excitement.

Tia came around to the side as he punched the information up on his desk scanner.

He looked out of the corner of his eye and could see the concern on Tia's face as she scanned the report.

"FOR STOCKHOLDERS ONLY, GAME DAY FIFTEEN—ATTEMPT ON LARICE CURRENTLY IN PROGRESS, BY GABLONA. IMPLANT UNITS FLAT-LINED FOR THREE GUARDS WITHIN LAST FIVE MINUTES; GABLONA, TWO FLAT-LINES ON GUARDS."

There was a pause as the real-time data link waited for any changes.

The screen flashed again and Bukha felt Tia's hands digging into his shoulder.

"LARICE INJURED, NO REPORT IF BLADE POISON . . ."

Bukha looked up at Tia, a tight grimace creasing his face. "This could be it," he said softly.

Damn it all, she thought, and she turned away. That fat fool, why the hell wasn't he more careful?

"Worried for your uncle? Or the effects on the bet flow?" Bukha asked coldly.

"You bastard," she snapped, whirling around.

He raised his hand up.

"All right then, all right," he said softly. "I just had to be sure. So, you're playing something inside of this as well, is that it? Aldin Larice isn't just a number then, a bet to be won."

She stood eyeing him defiantly.

"You don't have to say anything more." He looked back at the screen.

"I'll check out those bets for you. It'll take a while to track them down, but my curiosity is aroused," he said quietly. "Perhaps there's someone who knows more about this game than we'd care to think. And if they do, then it affects Aldin as well."

The terminal started to flash again, and yet another report started to scroll across the screen.

"We're getting reports that it's absolute chaos out there."

Losa floated from the corner of the room, where he'd been meditating, and looked at the messenger.

If it was possible for an Overseer to feel emotion, then this must be it, he thought inwardly. He thought about the last such time, when the subject Gablona had escaped, or thought he had escaped. For a moment he had actually felt something; he was not sure what, but the look of malicious joy on the one called Gablona when he thought he was being rescued had stirred something within. It had taken days to purge out the turmoil that had brought about.

The Overseer looked at Vush. He could see that the younger, slightly rotund Overseer was clearly excited by what was happening. Most disturbing, all of this. Were the intruders somehow polluting them, after all? Was their desire for a finish to the charade in fact a defeat rather than the victory hoped for?

"Go on then," the Overseer said softly.

"Information is coming in about an attempt at termination," Vush responded.

"And?"

"It has triggered absolute chaos. Their economic activity has all but ceased, everything is at a standstill. Reports are indicating that within minutes after the first report, productivity started to curve downward. There are already reports coming in from agents of riots, as mobs attempt to buy tickets before this particular event affects the betting."

Losa nodded. "And is the situation covered?"

"Of course, in either direction," Vush replied. "I made sure of it myself."

"Then it is acceptable," Losa replied softly and, turning away, he floated back to the corner of the room to continue with the meditation of Inward Searching.

So disturbing, all of this, he reasoned, but, after all, it was a most cunning idea that he had created, and if he could allow himself to feel anything, it would be pride at his ingenuity.

"Takashi, behind!"

His old companion whirled in a blur of motion. There was the faint hiss, the sound of a sword arcing on a deadly path, and the soft thump as the blade cut through cloth and flesh.

Oishi sat crouched in the darkness, watching from the corner of his eye. Was it Takashi or the assassin who had just been hit? But his thoughts had to be elsewhere, for there was the faintest of flickers in the darkness to his right, a motion more felt than seen. It had to be another one. Darkness was their enemy now. If only he could get to one of the lamps and start it up again to see if Aldin was still alive.

The attack had been totally without warning. Aldin along with half a dozen guards had been up late; the rest were asleep in the converted barracks rooms upstairs. It had been a habit of Aldin's since their arrival to sit up into the night, plotting strategy with Zergh, or talking with Mari, staying awake for a day and a half of game time then sleeping for one night.

Oishi had warned him to vary every pattern to his life, to never sleep in the same room twice, to do everything different, at all times. But Aldin had laughed in his usual self-deprecating way.

Oishi could only thank the gods that some inner sense had stirred him from his sleep and brought him downstairs to check, for just as he had stepped into the taproom, half a dozen black-clad forms had burst out of the kitchen. Three had made straight for Aldin, and then the single lantern in the room had gone out, even as he leaped to Aldin's defense.

There was the movement again, while over in the corner where Takashi had dived he could hear the sound of labored breathing and struggle. The doorway to upstairs was closed, with the sound of fighting behind it. He was tempted to head for it and try to free the staircase for his men, but he had to get to Aldin first.

Again there was the flicker of motion, a shadowy form that was as dark as the night.

After releasing his long sword, he clenched the short blade in his hand and slithered across the room to place himself between the shadow and the corner where he had last seen Aldin.

The shadow moved again. There was a bounding leap. Oishi rolled backward slashing the air before him, even as he fell over.

Only a faint hiss preceded the blade that caught against his shoulder, laying it bare. The shock of the unexpected blow set him back.

The shadow was above him slashing, jabbing.

Oishi cut out with his foot, short quick jabs that hit nothing. He kicked again and felt bone smashing beneath his heel. There was a grunt of pain. The attacker dived forward, driving his blade into the floorboard within inches of his throat. Oishi slashed with his own blade, striking flesh, and then a desperate hand clamped over the blade, slamming it to the floor. A hot sticky spray splashed across his eyes as his opponent tried to twist the blade free with his bare hand.

Oishi drove his free hand up, catching his opponent in the throat. There was a terrible crack as he smashed the man's windpipe, and then a sickening gurgle. The hand on the blade loosened. With a quick even motion Oishi raised the sword and slashed with a horizontal motion. A river of blood washed over Oishi's face as the body above him went limp.

Suddenly a dagger was at his throat, and at that instant Oishi realized that death was upon him. This mystery that had extended his life but for a handful of days and shown him wonders undreamed of was finished at last. He would go into death and the realm where all should be as it should be, and the confusion of this strange world be left behind. He waited in that single extended moment for the cold kiss, but the dagger held.

"Samurai?" a voice whispered next to his ear. It was Aldin.

For a split second Oishi felt a towering rage. How the hell was he to protect this man, if he wouldn't protect himself? A proper lord would have simply cut, taking no chances. If a guard was killed by mistake, then that was the price paid to preserve the lord's life. Yet having stared in that second into the abyss and now to have it close, at least for the moment, caused a strange sense of release to wash over him.

"Oishi," he whispered, and he felt the blade draw back.

Oishi pushed aside the still-bleeding corpse above him, and Aldin crawled up to his side. Gently, so as not to frighten him, Oishi brought his hand up to Aldin and placed it over his mouth to signal that he wasn't to speak. Aldin nodded in reply.

Ever so slowly Oishi led Aldin back into the corner. The fighting on the staircase continued. In the darkness, he wasn't sure how many assassins had made it into the room, and for that matter, the door to the outside could still be open and another wave of attackers already infiltrated into the building.

"Oishi, don't move." It was Takashi speaking in Japanese. So, he'd gotten his man. Stealthfully Takashi rose up, his form barely visible. He started for the door that led up to the barrack rooms. Oishi was about to call a warning even as Takashi reacted. His blade hissed out again, this time cutting the body completely in two, and Oishi heard the grunt of satisfaction as his companion snapped his blade back, to slash the upper part of the body yet again before it had even hit the floor.

Takashi reached the door and with a wild scream yanked it back.

A shaft of light flooded into the room, and with a roar, Takashi charged up the stairs, striking the enemy force from the rear. A wild cheer rose up from the samurai fighting downward. Oishi ached to join the fray, but knew that he had to stay with Aldin. From the light produced through the doorway, the rest of the room was dimly visible. He could see several of his men, dead in pools of blood, the enemy that he had killed sprawled out on the floor not an arm's length away.

He looked over to Aldin, who sat with his back to the wall, an assassin dagger in his hand, stained to the hilt with blood. And for the first time Oishi saw the river of blood pouring down from Aldin's scalp. The man was still alive, and if the blade that hit him was poisoned, there was nothing he could do now. Suddenly Aldin's features grew tense and he came up to a fighting crouch.

Oishi looked back. One of the assassins had gotten by Takashi and for a split second was poised in the middle of the room. Oishi was about to spring, but then realized that though he could see the assassin, the assassin could not see him, for he'd been fighting in the light, and in the dim room his night vision had not yet adjusted. He had to stay next to Aldin, in case there was yet another attacker in the room.

The lone assassin turned and fled for the door back into the kitchen. Seconds later there was a gurgled cry and the door flung open again. Oishi braced to receive another rush, but there was only a lone form staggering out, the man who had just escaped the moment before. A butcher's knife was plunged to the hilt into his chest, the point of the blade sticking out of his back. He staggered and then ever so slowly, collapsed against the bar.

Behind him Mari came walking out, her right hand stained with blood, a look of grim satisfaction on her face.

"You better secure the back door," she said calmly. "I've been holding those bastards off for the last ten minutes while you children have been playing in here."

Incredulous, Oishi came to his feet. "Takashi, sweep this room first, then every inch of the building. Assign your men."

As his lieutenant shouted commands, Oishi turned to check Aldin.

Aldin came slowly to his feet. Oishi quickly wiped the blood from the man's face and saw the fresh flow pouring down from a wound that had nicked off part of his left ear and cut a sharp line from the back of his head down to his cheek. It looked ugly but as far as he could tell, it wasn't serious. He watched closely, fearing the start of the convulsions but nothing came.

Aldin stood looking at him as if in shock.

"This room is clean," Seiji shouted, and then, leading a group of men, he stormed into the kitchen, while other guards came up to circle Aldin. Zergh, who had stepped out of the room only moments before to relieve himself in the basement, came storming through the pack of men and up to Aldin's side. At the sight of blood he stopped, stricken with terror, but Oishi nodded reassuringly.

"It was obviously Gablona," Mari said, coming up to Aldin's side.

Aldin looked around at the bodies in the room. Five assassins were dead, along with three of the samurai who had been laughing with him only moments before. Slowly he walked over to the staircase and looked up. Two more of the enemy were dead up there.

"Why only seven?" he wondered out loud.

"Eight," Mari interrupted, and Aldin and the samurai turned to look at her. Taking his arm, she led him into the kitchen, where the eighth body stood, pinned to the wall with a carving knife.

"Who did that?" Oishi demanded.

"I took care of the bastard," Mari replied evenly, and she then nodded over toward a dead Gaf. It was Maladi, facedown in a bucket of grease, his throat cut from ear to ear.

"You killed him, too?" Aldin asked, incredulous.

"What? My own partner?" she cried, insulted at such an accusation. "I thought it curious that he gave his bouncers the night off. I was in the taproom keeping an eye on you when I heard three knocks, then three more. That set me on edge, so I slipped back into the kitchen and hid in the corner. Maladi was opening the door. The first eight assassins slipped in and Maladi closed the door behind them, and I thought, 'Uh-oh, Mari girl, this is it.'

"I couldn't give the alarm, they were between me and the door out to the taproom. It was then that one of your samurai must have suspected something and came into the kitchen.

"Well, then everything happened at once. They killed the man and seven of them charged in. The eighth turned on Maladi and, as easy as can be, he cut him an extra mouth. I heard the fighting going on in the next room, and that eighth fellow went to open the door again, I guess to let more of his friends in. So it was simple self-preservation, and I felt it best to sheath my carving knife in the source of my problems."

Even as Mari spoke she walked over to the corpse, gave him a curious sort of look, as if she were about to ask him a question, and then pulled the blade out of his back. The corpse slumped to the floor, and she wiped the blood off on her apron.

"I bolted the door shut again," she continued matter-of-factly. "They were sure mad out there, you could hear them hollering and yammering in their gibberish from one end of the quarter to the other."

"You saved us all," Oishi replied, his voice full of admiration. "If you hadn't bolted that door shut again, they would have overwhelmed us."

"They'd have had my throat cut like Maladi over there, that's why I killed the other one, too. I figured if I didn't, he'd get me, it was as simple as that," she said smiling.

The samurai stood around the woman open-mouthed with amazement. She talked about killing two of the dreaded assassins as easily as if she had been dispatching pigs in the basement. Even Takashi, who had just killed several in hard-fought combat, was shaking his head in amazement.

"I guess that means I own this dump now," Mari said quietly. "Maladi never did have any relatives; sometimes I thought nobody would be so stupid as to admit it for fear he'd hoodwink them out of something. I might as well tell you that I suspected he was playing you out against the other two for profit. But I couldn't prove anything, so I kept my mouth shut. Anyhow, I loaned him money more than once out of my own savings when he fell on hard times over some bad bets. So I guess you could say this dive was my collateral."

Oishi eyed her closely and then looked over at the dead Gaf in the corner, and then back to Mari. She merely smiled at him. Was it possible? he wondered.

She patted Oishi on the arm, as if to say that they were now sharing a little secret, and then stepped back into the taproom with the rest of the group in her wake.

"What a bloody mess," she said, looking around the room. The three dead samurai had been moved to the corner of the room, where their comrades prepared them for interment in the basement, since a pyre was not possible.

Mari came up to Aldin's side as he slumped into a chair and looked at him with concern.

"So what are you going to do?" she asked quietly, her hand slipping over Aldin's.

"Survive," he said bitterly, and then he looked over at Oishi, who sat next to the bodies of his fallen men. "Survive and outthink, outfight my enemies, so that my men survive. That's what it's all about. It's not causes, it's not bets, it's simply surviving so your friends can survive as well.

"It was Gablona who did this," he said coldly, motioning to the corpses of his men in the corner. "I was willing to sit back, to leave him alone, even after those other attempts that failed. Funny how I got warning on each of those, but not tonight. If my men are to survive, then it'll have to be Gablona who's eliminated, or kept so off-guard that he'll not be able to do this again. That Koh is still playing at war; it's time he learned what the reality truly is. If I don't teach him, Oishi and those who serve me will continue to die like this."

Aldin came back up to his feet, and Oishi watched him closely as if searching for his inner thoughts. The samurai came to his feet and then walked over to Aldin's side.

"We go for Gablona," Aldin said quietly.

The samurai looked at Aldin closely and realized that at last this man understood and felt the true essence of what it was to be samurai. For the first time Oishi felt, as well, that there might be a chance of surviving this after all.

"You should have killed me in the dark," Oishi replied. "You did not know if it was me or another attacker."

"I was willing to take the chance."

The faintest of smiles crossed Oishi's face. This man was not the typical lord, but in the end he might be one worth serving after all.

"So, the doorway was blocked before the second detachment could get in?"

"That is right, my lord."

Hassan looked the man over with disdain. In former times the answer would have been obvious. The two dozen who'd been sent would either have succeeded or not returned. But their numbers were too few, far too few. Thus he had made the one mistake in his plan. He'd not completely trusted the tavernkeeper's offer to open the door.

In his suspicion that it was a trap, he had ordered that eight men were to go in and secure the back room and only then were the rest of his precious men to be committed. Perhaps it was a trap, but he doubted that. Something must have gone wrong once the first group got inside.

"Dismissed. And as you lay upon your pallet tonight contemplate the pleasures of paradise that your far more worthy comrades now enjoy."

The door closed behind him.

So the fat one would not be pleased. Hassan gave a snort of disdain. Let him. For the moment it was to Hassan's advantage to serve him. But that time would pass. That the fat one thought him to be such a primitive as to believe in gods above was insult enough. If this Gablona was truly an initiate into the highest orders, then he would know the truth as Hassan knew it, that there were no gods, there was no Allah, there was only one thing—and that was power, unalloyed by sentiment or fear.

For that was the secret of secrets. He, too, had once risen through the ranks. As initiate, as Refik, as master, and then finally to grand master.

But as a master he was shown that religion was but a sop for the masses. That there was but one supreme rule, and that was the rule of power through fear and lies. A power he fully intended to seize yet again on this world made as if to his order.

He had wandered disguised in these strange streets, and had learned what the fat one had not told him, for the city was hot with rumor and beneath the rumor, truth, which any man of wisdom could divine.

At first his senses had reeled with the shock. The world he had known did not exist except in legend. Nearly two hundred generations of men had passed since his age. If Gablona was near godlike, then it was in the fact that he and his kind had somehow mastered the ability to race across time. The shock had almost overwhelmed his mind, that for a moment he doubted his own teachings, for surely only a god could do such a thing.

But in watching the fat one he had seen nothing but a man. A man consumed with lust, greed, and the desire for vengeance.

He had heard, as well, the other rumors, the truth about what this battle was about. A merchant from the tower in the sky had showed him blocks of paper, covered with strange script, and offered to sell them, claiming they were part of the game.

Hassan smiled at how easily he played that one. Drawing out the questions, even buying some of the paper, while the merchant had rattled on about the odds and how thousands of worlds were betting on the outcome of what he, Hassan, was now playing such an intimate part.

Then he had returned again to the city and the people who were a thread back into his own time. Though the translating device compensated for the different language, the words were sometimes strikingly similar to his native tongue; the rituals were hauntingly familiar as well, even to the bowing to the Seda. And he knew that these people looked to the first Old

Man of the Mountain, Sabah, though they did not know his name, as their first teacher of the truth about power.

Then at last he had met Ulsak, the leader, and the groundwork for the plan started to form in Hassan's mind.

But to this Ulsak he revealed nothing. He spoke not a word of how he was a destiny, it was for this that he had come forward to lead these people to their greatness, and the fat one would be his path to that dream. First there would be victory for his master of the moment, but later power far beyond the worthless rewards Gablona babbled about. For Gablona could not give him the one thing that he truly wanted: the power of life and death over others.

The door swung open behind him.

Hassan smiled to himself; the fat one was angry.

Fixing his features, he turned.

"I know," he said softly.

"That cuts our strength by nearly a sixth," Gablona snapped.

"And theirs as well, most likely," Hassan replied evenly. "My men don't sell their lives cheaply. But remember that you sneered at these men who carry the long swords and said they would fall easily. I think now that it is proven that they are good fighters. Let us not underestimate them again."

"This gives Sigma the advantage," Gablona shouted, not even realizing that Hassan had put the blame on him. "We haven't attempted him yet, planning to take out Aldin first. Sigma had promised to try for Aldin as well."

"Obviously he did what a prudent leader would in such circumstances, and has waited for us to eliminate each other," Hassan replied, the tone of reproach in his voice growing more evident.

"Are you saying that I didn't plan this correctly?" Gablona snapped. "After all, you approved it."

"For it was your plan," Hassan said. "And coming from such as you, I assumed it to be infallible."

Gablona glowered, not sure if Hassan was mocking him or simply showing the proper respect.

"So, now what do you suggest?" Gablona asked, realizing that he desperately needed this man, but in his heart feeling the first tug of fear, his inner sense that had always saved him in all his dealings with dangerous men.

"Take out Sigma now."

"Why?"

"Because for the moment he is the more powerful, and since he hasn't attacked Aldin as planned, we must assume that he has betrayed you. We can also assume that Sigma might very well be planning a strike against you. Therefore, strike first."

"But what about Aldin? Our attack might have stirred him to strike back."

"The blues are still looking for him," Hassan said evenly.

"I don't trust that rabble," Gablona said. "They could turn on us just as easily."

"I'll take care of that," Hassan replied smoothly. "I already know where Sigma is hiding. The rest can be planned out in several days."

Gablona hesitated for a moment.

"Trust me," Hassan said, a gentle smile lighting his features.

Sigma looked across the table to the head of his berserkers. The week had been quiet. The only problem had been simply feeding the Gafs under his command. He found that in a strange sort of way he was actually growing fond of these big, lumbering warriors.

They kept him up most every night, what with their shouting and brawling, but he did have to admit that when all fifty of them surrounded him and marched down the street, he did not feel the slightest fear, for even the Al'Shiga drew back at their approach and only pelted him with offal from afar.

Now, if only Aldin had the sense to have hired such guards. What a fight that would be. Why, he'd almost be tempted to arrange a set match, a hundred Gaf berserkers smashing it out. It would have been like the betting days of old.

It was too bad about Aldin, Sigma thought, shaking his head sadly. He had heard the report on the assassination attempt. He assumed it came from Gablona, and if it had, Aldin's forces were most likely weakened by the effort. And if that was the case, there was only one answer.

Aldin might be the more trustworthy, but Gablona was definitely the more cunning, thus the harder to take out. Most likely the old Koh had simmered down a bit by now and was ready to listen to reason. He'd offer him part of his Sulli Conglomerate as a payoff. After all, Gablona had wanted that particular venture for years. A deal would be struck, and they could sit out the game and then go home. After all, Kohs could talk to each other. In the end it was profit that counted more than vengeance.

But he'd have to make a good-faith gesture first. And Aldin was indeed nothing more than a tradesman, a vasba, when one got right down to it.

"I think it's time that you boys had some action," Sigma said evenly, and the expressions around the table lit up.

chapter eight

"Blackie, it's remarkable," Kurst exulted. "Simply remarkable what you've done."

Sisa Black leaned over and with a playful gesture ruffled Kurst's heavy mane of tangled brown hair. Like his glasses, his shoulder-length hair was also a dozen years out of fashion. Most likely Kurst hadn't even noticed the latest trend of quarter-inch cropping, with long bangs in front.

Her job required that she be smartly turned out, so she always followed the latest trend, which for this year was ankle-length dresses with a bustle and a neckline that plunged almost to her belt. Kurst and she had been students together years before, and, though never making their arrangement permanent, the relationship had held, even though separated by a thousand light-years of space. Professorships were hard to find on Ator, and Sisa had no desire to give up her job as president of a futures brokerage to live out on some provincial planet.

"Any word on hits brewing?" she asked softly, while pouring out her fifth caffeine jolt of the day.

"Looks like something's moving down there. I'm keeping close to Zola, and the moment I hear . . ."

The two looked at each other and smiled.

His fascination with what they were doing took hold, and after getting out of his chair, he walked over to the vid display that dominated one of the office walls.

The market was in full swing, and she came up to his side to watch.

"When we get an idea, my dear, we certainly get an idea," she whispered while nibbling on his ear.

The floor that she ran, which had once dealt in amber and precious metal futures, was now given over solely to gaming futures. It was a highly classified venture; no knowledge of it had yet to reach the Kohs. For they would be sure to muscle in, and besides, Zola would discover who the major inside contact was.

So it was trading on the sly, but trading that way was quite lucrative indeed. The tickets kept their original registrations, to be sure, but contractually any winnings were signed over to the current holder of an option.

Blocks of tickets purchased by investment firms would be bid upon. The final outcome was not important at this date, rather the potential of future outcomes is what mattered. Therefore, any tickets that had not called for a death before the fourteenth game day were now a valuable commodity with a potential of winning, and as such held a potential value, calculated on the various current odds.

Options could be purchased to hold tickets for as little as six hours, one-half of a day down on the Hole. Of course, if during those six hours an event occurred that the tickets did not cover, then the buyer was wiped out. But if the tickets were still viable after six hours or, even better, an event had occurred that the tickets did cover, then their value would soar.

The big board that filled one wall of the trading floor started to light up with buy orders, and the market, sensing a trend, started to go wild.

"Looks like buy orders for a Gablona hit on Aldin," Blackie said. "We've got some of those in our portfolio. What do you think?"

Kurst was awed by the power that he now held. In a matter of days he had come from being a forgotten professor in the outback to a financial advisor playing with millions, and all because of a barroom conversation with an old friend.

"I don't think so," he said softly. "Put out a sell order on those. Aldin survived the last hit attempt. I think if anything he'll be going for Gablona and not the other way around."

Sisa tapped into her phone link and in seconds the sell order went out.

Kurst laughed with glee as he saw tens of thousands of tickets changing hands every second. The potential profit of it all was staggering to contemplate. What had started out only days before as a venture involving tens of thousands of tickets now saw hundreds of millions of tickets changing hands every hour. Sisa had told him how only this morning a whole new trading consortium from one of the Gaf worlds had bought into the market, doubling their volume within the first hour.

Sisa's sell order was on the floor, and the trend kicked off as a Gaf consortium started to snap up all tickets dealing with a Gablona hit on Aldin.

Her pager rang and she tapped back into her floor dealers, spoke what sounded like a code, and then looked over at Kurst.

"We just cleared a profit of two hundred and fifty thousand on that sell order," she said, squeezing Kurst's hand. "My dear, I think we're going to be very rich before this is all over."

For a moment he wondered about that. They had to keep security on this little venture. If the Kohs ever found out and his insider leaked, there'd be hell to pay. But the big board was flashing like a machine gone berserk, and Kurst giggled as he watched.

The streets were empty. It was festival time again and the foreign community was in hiding, while the natives were busy over in their quarter whooping it up and trading heads.

Feeling that this was to be an all-out effort, Sigma decided to commit his entire force to the attack and not leave half his men behind as guards.

Stealthfully, as stealthfully as fifty heavily armed Gaf berserkers could be, the contingent wound its way up the narrow street to Aldin's hiding place.

The forward guard came back around the corner and motioned that all was clear.

Ura, the berserker leader, looked back at Sigma, who merely nodded.

A dozen Gafs surrounded each of the two heavy beams and picked up the knotted rope ends that extended out from each of the battering rams.

Ura raised his hand and then with a bellowing roar brought his arm down.

With a wild shout the berserkers hefted the rams and started out. The first group turned up a side alley leading to the back entrance, while the second group, with Sigma at the rear, charged up the main street.

The lead Gafs stormed up to the spy holes on either side of the door, slamming up heavy wooden shields to block attack from the inside.

The battering team slowed for a second as they turned and positioned the ram and, then with a shout, they ran straight for the door. The beam hit with a bone-shattering impact, the wooden and steel frame cracking and groaning.

Again Ura roared.

The attackers backed up and slammed the ram in again.

Peering around the arm of one of his guards, Sigma watched the building. At any second he expected Aldin's defenders to appear, but there was no response.

Again the ram hit the door still blocking their way. With a roar of rage the Gafs backed up and charged yet again.

As they started forward, the door suddenly flung open from the inside. One of the Gaf warriors, who had broken in through the back door, filled the narrow entryway, the ram coming straight toward him.

With a terrified squeal he fell backward, the heavy ram coming through the doorway like a bolt fired from a bow. The dozen Gafs running with the ram suddenly found no resistance as the ram shot through thin air where the door had been only seconds before. The mass of warriors went down in a roaring tangle as one after another they slammed into the doorsill to either side, each warrior's four hundred pounds of flesh and armor piling into one confused heap.

Ura shouted with rage at the tangle and, raising his heavy battle-ax, he ran straight for the heap of warriors, leaping over them, and charged on into the building.

Sigma's guards, inflamed with the prospect of battle, left his side and, screaming with delight, stormed on into the building, leaving the Koh standing alone on the street except for the dozen dazed rammers.

Beneath the head of the ram Sigma saw the Gaf who had opened the door, struggling weakly to lift the hundreds of pounds of dead weight off his body, even as his companions leaped onto the log in their mad clattering push to get into the building.

Sigma suddenly realized that standing out on the street alone was the height of madness. With a running leap he raced for the door, and jumped onto the log. There was a groan of protest from underneath, but he pushed on into the darkness.

It was roaring confusion inside. Peering into the gloom, he saw his warriors lumbering about the main taproom, shouting and growling for their foes to show themselves.

There were no Humans in sight.

Sigma actually felt a surge of excitement. What a story this would make once he got back with the other Kohs! A charge of sweaty Gaf berserkers, chanting their battle cries, he at the forefront. How the others would envy this.

Ura came up to Sigma's side and saluted, his anger visible. "The filthy cowards have all run away. The place is empty."

"What? But this is the right place," Sigma said, suddenly angry that the heroic nature of the raid had been ruined by Aldin not complying by being around.

"Kolda led the charge on the back door; it broke on the first strike, the beam was not in place. That's how the front door was opened for us. The place is empty. They've all run away, the miserable cowards," he said dejectedly. "And we were sure there'd be a good fight today."

The Gafs around him, who'd been worked into a fighting frenzy, were now venting their rage by shattering the tables with axes and chopping the bar apart in a shower of splinters. Several berserkers were already behind the bar, smashing off the tops of Maladi's horde of muscatel and draining the huge jugs off, half the contents spilling down their armor, while others eagerly snatched and growled for their share of the loot.

"You better get them under control," Sigma shouted in exasperation. "The last thing I need is a lot of drunken guards."

"Ah, let them have their fun. It'll take their minds off the disappointment of not finding servants," Ura replied happily. "You've kept us cooped up, what with your hiding and all. The lads need a little fun. Otherwise, they might vent their rage at missing a good fight in a manner you might not appreciate."

Ura looked over at Sigma, a strange glow in his eyes, and Sigma realized it was best not to argue.

"And don't worry," the Gaf said, slapping him on the shoulder with a blow that made Sigma's knees buckle. "If that enemy of yours isn't here, then he'll be back or we'll just go out and look for him. Anyhow, my warriors fight best after they've had a couple of drinks."

Sigma, shaking his head, walked over to the corner of the room and settled down, realizing there wasn't anything else he could do. Ura came over to the table and slammed down a jug of muscatel.

"Good stuff this," the Gaf roared. "Have a drink, you look like you need it!"

Sigma pulled the cork out of the jug, sniffed it, and wrinkled his nose with disgust.

"Too strong for you?" Ura asked, laughing at this strange Human's discomfort, and then, turning, he went back to join his comrades at the bar.

Sigma looked about the darkened room. The Gafs were getting louder with every passing moment. Several of them chanted their bizarre minor-key death songs, stopping for a moment to upend a jug before passing it on to their comrades.

There'd be no hope of surprise if Aldin and his samurai should come wandering back in, Sigma realized. But if Aldin wasn't here, and had left his place abandoned, the old Koh suddenly wondered, then where in hell was he now?

"It doesn't feel right," Oishi whispered, drawing away from the window slit that faced Gablona's fortress across the street.

Aldin came up and crouched by the samurai's side.

For several days they'd planned this move. Now that Maladi was gone, Mari had proved herself invaluable once again. Within a day after he had asked, she returned with the information as to Gablona's hiding place, and had already purchased a small warehouse directly across from Gablona as a base of operations. To Aldin's shock it'd only been several blocks away from Sigma's, and not a block away from the original safe house assigned to him.

She also told him about the catacombs beneath the city where it was believed the Al'Shiga buried their dead. It was a secret few outsiders knew; even Maladi had been in the dark about that. Unfortunately there were no entrances which connected the tavern to the warehouse, so they'd have to risk traveling above ground.

Aldin swore a silent oath. "Should we try for it anyhow?" he asked.

Oishi looked at him. There was a time for caution, but not now, he thought. Perhaps the enemy had been forewarned, but to withdraw would be bad for the morale of his men, who were aching to avenge the deaths of their comrades. Neither would it have the desired effect on the morale of the foe, who so far had struck with impunity.

"Do you want to withdraw?" Oishi asked, curious about the answer.

Aldin looked at him grimly.

"Let's try to get this damn thing over with," he said coldly, and his answer was greeted by the slightest of smiles on Oishi's face.

Oishi looked at the other men in the room and nodded.

The two crossbow catapults were small ones, rigged together by several of Oishi's men.

The samurai strode over to the closed doorway and, reaching down, picked up the first bottle. It was quite a remarkable weapon, Oishi thought, an idea mentioned by Aldin and the potential of which he realized at once. It was in violation of the Al'Shiga custom, but since they were all attending the festival, Aldin reasoned that the risk would be worth it. Taking the candle, Oishi lit the rag wick at the end of the bottle and then nodded to the two catapult crews to fire.

As he yanked the door open, the two machines fired, slamming their bolts across the street, the shafts disappearing through the two narrow watch slits to either side of the door. Oishi threw the bottleful of distilled alcohol, which shattered a quarter meter away from the intended window, the liquid igniting nevertheless and flowing down the wall like a river of flame.

Several more samurai stepped to the door, throwing in turn. The second and third bottles disappeared into the building, the men around Oishi barely able to suppress a cheer when they could see the crackling flames ignite within.

Two more bolts slammed out, sweeping into the upstairs floor. Within seconds half a dozen bottles had slammed into the building. In a moment of reckless abandon, Takashi dashed out of the door, three bottles in his hands, their wicks burning. Standing in the middle of the street, he aimed them for the upper floor; two of the three sailed through the narrow slits above, where they shattered into flames.

But nothing happened. No response or defense was offered.

Takashi stood in the street as if daring the enemy to strike. With a dramatic flourish he drew his sword and waved it over his head.

"We are the forty-seven ronin!" he cried in Japanese.

Then with a quick dash he ran up to the nearest spy slit and looked inside. A second later he dashed to the next one, and then the next. Turning, he raced back to his companions.

"It's a furnace in there," he shouted, coming through the door.

Suddenly from around the corner came Hideo, a short, extremely thin samurai who had been in command of the watch set on the back entry to Gablona's fortress, with his three companions racing behind him.

"Nothing," he shouted with disgust. "We tossed our bottles right in, even looked in the slits; there's no one there."

"It's empty," Aldin said quietly. "Somehow either Gablona knew or he has gone off elsewhere."

"For what?" Takashi snapped, his blood up for the confrontation.

"To hit either Sigma or myself," Aldin replied.

"I don't care where he is," Mari suddenly interjected, "but I think our welcome as the new neighbors has just worn out."

From out in the street came shouts of anger. Aldin went up to the window slit with Mari at his side. Across the street the building was a roaring inferno. But above the crackling flames could be heard a gathering roar of angry shouts. On either side of the building the neighbors were pouring out, some with large contingents of armed guards. More than one was pointing at the small warehouse and shaking their fists. Aldin noticed, as well, a scattering of blue robes suddenly starting to appear.

"You've broken the taboo down here on any weapon other than one that can be held or thrown by hand. You've got the Shiga going as well."

"Time to leave," Aldin said, looking back at the samurai, who nodded in reply. Several of the men started to pick up each of the catapults.

"We can build more. If you're seen on the streets lugging those things, then we're really in trouble."

Seiji, who had helped with the building of the machines, patted his catapult affectionately and then fell in with the others and started for the back door.

Weaving down side streets to throw off any pursuit, the group pushed on as twilight started to descend around them. Aldin struggled to get up to the front of the group where Oishi and Mari, as guide, were leading.

Nearing the block where Sigma's fortress was located, the front of the column slowed. Aldin pushed forward to where Oishi stood peeking around the corner, his hand held back in a gesture of warning.

As Aldin came up to his side, he could hear the sound of drunken yelling. Surprised, he realized that it was Gafs.

"What the hell is going on?" Aldin whispered.

The next street over was boiling over with Gafs, obviously drunk and roaring their defiance. And then he saw Sigma, not fifteen meters away.

Oishi looked at Aldin, who was completely taken aback by this sudden turn of events. To take out Gablona was one thing, but with Sigma it was not quite the same. Still, he was the enemy now as well, like it or not.

He had to decide, and quickly. Sigma was out in the open, his guards scattered up and down the street. Somehow it was almost ludicrous, the small, portly man surrounded by the giant, hulking warriors.

It was a question of honor to him. Somehow he found it hard to order an attack on the man who had yet to openly raise a hand against him. Would Sigma do the same if the opportunity was offered? In his heart he knew the man would.

He looked back down the street to where Sigma stood, and then to his astonishment the Gaf closest to the Koh staggered as if the alcohol had finally laid him low. But as the berserker fell, a river of scarlet flashed out from where his throat had been only seconds before.

Sigma had finally convinced Ura that with the uproar they had created, any hope of surprise was now lost. For a moment they had debated whether they should hide and wait for Aldin's return, but the approach of twilight had made Sigma feel uneasy. A trap could easily be turned on him as well. Their own fortress was far more secure than the now thoroughly destroyed tavern, and the party finally decided to leave.

One of the Gafs talked about burning the place, but no one had thought to bring along a striker, and fumbling about, looking for a means to become arsonists, they quickly grew frustrated and simply gave up on the idea.

The return was far less stealthful than the approach. If anything, the Gafs' blood was now so thoroughly worked up that they were almost aching for a fight.

Sigma walked in the middle of them, lost in thought. Had Aldin been warned? he wondered. He knew that the implant they all carried could locate them on the scanning systems in the Skyhook right down to the very centimeter. He could not help but wonder if the implant had a double purpose: to monitor not only his vital signs, and that of his companions, but also to pick up every spoken word as well. If so, could Aldin have gotten the information?

His musings were interrupted by a loud cry of delight from one of the Gafs by his side. Sigma looked up.

A crowd of green robes stood at the end of the street blocking the approach to his safe house, all of them wearing the read headbands of the Mukba.

"I think we're going to have some fun," one of the Gafs growled, raising his axe and testing its edge with his thumb.

Sigma's pulse quickened. Could this be a trap? But he also felt a rising curiosity to see how his berserkers would perform pitted against some of the locals.

The Gafs, laughing with drunken joy, started to spread out in the narrow street, tossing aside the remaining jugs of liquor. Their shouts echoed and reechoed.

Sigma watched the green robes carefully. There was something about them that just didn't fit. They remained still as the berserkers started to approach, until the two groups were only a couple of dozen paces apart. Suddenly one of the green robes gave a universal gesture of contempt that was understood by any being.

With a roar, several of the Gafs raised their battle-axes high and started into a lumbering charge. Their comrades around them, caught up in the spirit, rushed to join in the fun.

The green robes broke and, turning, fled back up the street. A Mukba wouldn't break, Sigma realized. Hell, they fought Gafs on this planet every festival day. The berserker's charge rushed straight past the safe house and kept on going.

Sigma turned to look for Ura to order him to call the guards back. But Ura was gone, rushing ahead with the rest of the mob. He suddenly felt a sense of foreboding.

"Ura!" Sigma shouted, his high, thin voice lost in the uproar of the Gafs.

A bellow of rage sounded next to him, and Sigma turned to see one of the few remaining guards around him stagger forward.

And then Sigma saw the blood.

The Gaf twisted and squirmed by his feet. Stunned, Sigma backed up from the dying warrior. There was another scream of pain. A guard on the other side of the street collapsed, a throwing dagger sticking out of his open mouth.

Confused now, Sigma turned in a circle. What was happening?

The safe house, he had to get in. He started for the door and saw that it was being pulled open. His guard on the inside, he thought.

Another Gaf on the street went down.

The door now swung wide to reveal Human men dressed in loose, flowing robes of black.

Gablona's assassins had taken his house while he was away!

Several of the Gafs who had started with the charge now saw the threat pouring out from behind as a swarm of assassins leaped through the doorway and out onto the street.

Sigma backed up against the far side of the street. One of his guards rushed past him, battle-ax held high, his death chant filling the air. An assassin headed straight for him. The Gaf swung low in a deadly sweep. With almost mocking disdain, the assassin rolled under the blade, came up behind the Gaf, and with one swipe of his scimitar cut the Gaf behind both knees, sending him tumbling to the ground.

The assassin did not see another Gaf coming up behind him, and as if splitting a log, the berserker's axe cut down, slicing the man nearly in half with a single blow.

In spite of his terror, Sigma doubled over, retching at the sight of the man's entrails spilling out in a steaming pile onto the pavement.

But the assassins had seen their target, and nothing would stop them now. The Gaf who had cut down the first assassin went down seconds later as a black-robed attacker hit him from behind, driving his blade into the berserker's back, cutting the spinal column.

Sigma looked up and saw two men coming straight toward him. One more Gaf tried to intervene, leaping before the two. He caught one on a downward blow, cutting him from shoulder to hip, but the other leaped past, driving straight for his target.

With a squeal of terror Sigma turned blindly, running up the street.

How could Gablona do this? They were fellow Kohs, they had an arrangement! And, after all, it was only a game!

Sigma barely saw the loop of wire as it snaked over his head.

There was only the cold shock as the razor edge of the garrote dug through flesh, severing tissue and nerves.

An explosion of light filled his sight.

It was only a game! And then he fell into the darkness.

Sickened, Aldin turned away. If only Sigma had turned up the alley instead of going the other way, he most likely would have sent his men out to save him. He had been tempted to intervene anyhow. But he knew that in doing so some of his own men would die, with little if any hope of success, so sudden had been the attack.

He looked up at Oishi.

"That's one less," Oishi said coldly, and numbly, Aldin could only nod in return.

Hassan bolted the door shut as the last of the attackers slipped back in. One of the acolytes stood before him, panting for breath, a bloody garrote in his hand.

Gablona came pushing through the crowd at the door and could tell by the look on Hassan's face what the news was.

"Who did it?" Gablona asked, and Hassan pointed to the wide-eyed youngster who held up the gory instrument of destruction for his inspection.

Gablona looked at Sigma's blood as it slowly dripped off the handles tied to either end of the wire.

"Good," he mumbled, as if to himself, and then without another word turned and walked away.

The plan had worked just as Hassan said it would. One of the assassins had managed to creep onto the roof of Sigma's building and had overheard the Gaf's excited talk about their attack. Suspecting that Sigma would strike with everything he had against Aldin, they had simply waited until the attack was launched and, after taking the fortress, had simply settled back and waited for the return. The ruse of dressing up some of his own as green robes had worked better than planned, scattering Sigma's guards from one end of the street to the other.

Just before the attack had come word that Aldin had attempted to take him and destroyed his hiding place in the process. He could only laugh now at Aldin's discomfort. Hassan had second-guessed that one as well.

They now had Sigma's hiding place and supplies. Next it would be Aldin's turn, and then they could wait out the remaining days and return up the Skyhook in triumph.

Out in the street the Gafs howled with rage. The green robes had disappeared, easily outrunning the heavier warriors. Ura quickly realized that the cowards had no intention of fighting, and as he slowed, he heard for the first time the screams of combat from behind him.

It was a trap! Turning, he called for his warriors to follow. Together they had raced back down the street and turned into the alleyway that led to their fortress. A score of his comrades were down, two or three still fighting with a knot of assassins that were withdrawing back into what was supposed to be their hiding place.

Bellowing with rage, Ura charged, but the door was slammed shut in his face. He and his comrades slammed on the door, trying to chop it down with their axes, and for several seconds he was oblivious to the fact that yet more Gafs were dropping around him as the assassins poured hot oil out of the murder hole above the door, while long spears were shoved out of the side windows.

Screaming with rage, Ura drew back and his comrades followed, the taunting jeers of the assassins ringing in their ears. It was then that Ura suddenly wondered what had happened to the one he was charged with protecting.

He scanned the street and spied several warriors standing in a circle farther up the street, looking somewhat mournfully at the ground.

It was Sigma.

Ura came up by the old man's side and knelt in the gutter. The slash mark of the garrote had cut clear to the spinal column and the Koh's head lolled back obscenely. Ura threw back his head and howled with rage.

For a Human, one without hair, he had found the old man to be tolerable, almost amusing with comments about battle and his obvious discomfort with the rough ways of the Basak. It was a wound to his pride that he had agreed to protect him and then failed. Ura looked at the body for a moment and then came back to his feet.

"Now what are we going to do?" Kolda snarled.

Ura looked around the group that had gathered. He looked back at their former hideout. And as he looked, yet another bitter taunt was hurled at the group.

More than half his comrades were dead. So thorough had been the surprise, many of them had been struck from behind as they pushed on up the street, oblivious to the threat from behind.

There was no place to hide now, and darkness was setting in—the time when mobs of Al'Shiga wandered the streets of the foreign quarter looking for victims. To rush the fortress was suicide, but he could see no other way. Raising his axe, he started to turn back toward certain death. At least then he could see the hairless one in the next world and apologize.

Kolda smiled as his leader walked away. At least this was one assignment that he didn't have to risk his life for. Maybe the one called Zola would pay him nevertheless. Then again, he realized, the game was still young, and perhaps there would be another chance to earn the riches that had been promised him.

"Come on," Oishi hissed, "let's get moving."

The last of the samurai slipped across the alley; in the darkness they were not even noticed by the knot of Gaf warriors standing over Sigma's body.

But Aldin, and Zergh standing by his side, did not move.

"They'll all be dead before morning," Zergh said quietly.

"There's not much we can do about it," Aldin replied grimly, still shocked at how vicious Sigma's end had been. There was a time when that man had been the most powerful Koh in the Cloud, and now he lay dead in the gutter, a victim of the so-called fun of combat.

"There is something you can do," Zergh said.

"Look, I know what you're thinking," Oishi interjected, ready to argue.

"And it's a damn good idea," Mari snapped quickly. "Those lumbering giants are fools on the defensive, we just saw that, but they would be murder to face in tight quarters on the attack."

Zergh came up close to Aldin.

"Let me do it," the old Gaf said. "They're savages, but honest savages.

"And besides," he said softly, "they're Gavarnians."

Aldin was about to stop him, but before he could say a word, the old Gaf broke free from the group. Oishi swore softly beneath his breath.

From out of the twilight Ura saw a shadow emerging. For a second he was ready to strike and then, to his amazement, realized that it was an aging Gaf, and not one of the Shiga, for this one wore a wonderful outfit of flowing robes, with two swords belted at his waist.

"I'm here to make an offer," Zergh said straightforwardly.

"What?"

"I'm a comrade of Aldin Larice."

With that several of the berserkers snarled and raised their axes, but Ura held them back.

"It was the other one, the fat one called Gablona that did this, not my man. We share the same enemy; we can share in his killing."

Ura hesitated. He was a fighter, not one to talk parley.

Zergh looked back at where Gablona and his men were now cloistered, and the taunts of the assassins could be plainly heard.

"You are good warriors," Zergh said. "Charge that fortress, and you'll die good warriors."

"We are not afraid of death, old one," a berserker snarled.

"Of course not," Zergh continued, "but all of you will die without taking a single one of them with you. You will go before your brothers without any servants to wait upon you in the afterworld. Your brothers will say that you are brave, to be sure, but that you died without bringing servants to honor them."

Several nervous minutes passed and then Aldin saw the Gafs coming back up the street, Zergh at the lead. Oishi swore even louder now.

"If they get into our midst and turn on us, it'll be difficult," Oishi snapped.

"But with them we have more numbers than Gablona," Mari argued.

Aldin looked at her and realized that for the first time she was speaking as if part of the group, rather than merely an outsider. She saw his look and shrugged her shoulders.

"We can barrack them in the basement," she continued, "and keep a guard up until we're sure. They just lost their leader, they're on a strange world—I think it's worth the chance."

Zergh came up to Aldin's side. "They'll join us. I think we can trust them, but it'll take a little time for their blood lust to calm down."

Together the two groups set off into the night, the Gafs being kept to the rear. At last the tavern was sighted. With a cry of alarm, Mari stopped at the sight of the back door, which had been torn clear off its hinges.

Oishi ordered Takashi and two others to rush the building. They entered and came out shortly thereafter and signaled that the tavern was empty.

The group rushed in, and with a cry of rage Mari surveyed the wreckage of her property. Lamps were finally lit, and while the group stayed in the kitchen, teams of samurai were first sent out to look for any deadfalls or traps.

"Who could have done this?" Mari shouted. "Look at this mess, just look at it!"

"Gablona perhaps?" Oishi ventured.

"I doubt it," Zergh said. "It would have been booby-trapped from one end to the other."

"It couldn't have been the Al'Shiga, the attackers were drinking like fish from the looks of it," Mari shouted, kicking the broken remains of emptied wine jugs.

Suddenly they all fell silent and turned to the Gafs, who still stood out in the narrow courtyard.

"Well, we were angry when you weren't here for a good fight," Ura said, a look of pained embarrassment on his face.

chapter nine

Out of breath, Kurst turned the last corner at the run. Blackie was already there to meet him.

He looked up and down the corridor—it was empty.

"Come on, let's move!" he shouted, grabbed her arm, and raced for the nearest lift that would send them up the two hundred stories to the hidden exchange office.

He punched the buttons, and the elevator kicked up, rocketing them skyward.

"What is it?" Sisa gasped, still trying to catch her breath. She'd been in her office when the personal com link that tied her to Kurst clicked on, telling her to meet him by the back service elevator.

Kurst looked around the elevator wide-eyed. It could be bugged. The information was so hot that he didn't even dare to call it in over their private link from Zola's offices across the street. It had been an incredible stroke of luck that he had been with Zola in the com center when word came up through the scramble system and was then decoded while they were in the room. With a shout of triumph Zola had raced from the center, leaving Kurst to fend for himself. And fend he had, covering the half kilometer to Blackie's office in what he felt must have been record time.

Damn, why hadn't he thought of a code?

Desperate, he fished in his pockets for a slip of paper and a pen and then started to dash off a note.

Sigma dead 20 min ago by G; 10 min, info goes public!

The door slipped open.

Blackie grabbed Kurst by the arm, and together they ran to her office.

"Stay here," she snapped. "You can watch through the hookup."

Blackie raced out of her office and down the corridor to the trading floor.

The big board was still going wild, the last hour's report having announced that Sigma had hit Aldin's hiding place. Odds had shot up for one of the two to be dead by the other before the day was out, and trading had been frantic.

Kurst adjusted the vid link and saw Blackie slowly and deliberately walking on to the trading floor, her traders and agents coming around her in a circle.

The group broke apart and within seconds the buy and sell orders went up for a primary kill/day buy, meaning that they were centering in on options for a particular event for a particular day, in this case for Sigma to be killed by Gablona on game day thirty-one, while at the same time unloading blocks of tickets that called for Sigma to live. Kurst felt a moment of panic. When the news hit the floor within the next five minutes, her jumping the market would be just too obvious.

But then he breathed a sigh of relief when he saw that she was masking the buy, mixing it in with other orders that would, in fact, be worthless.

Within minutes she had closed out on nearly a quarter of all tickets bearing the critical information regarding Sigma's death. However, several other firms still held the rest, steadfastly refusing to sell at any offer, and were now competing with her in frantic bids to snap up the blocks held by a number of the smaller firms. Among the hundreds of traders on the floor, this drama was but a minor scene in the far wider frenzy.

A siren sounded in the background. The hundreds of traders on the floor fell silent.

The big board, quoting the various options, went blank, and in two-meter-high letters an announcement started to scroll across.

CONFIRMED REPORT JUST ANNOUNCED BY GAMEMASTER XSARN TO ALL COM LINK SERVICES. SIGMA AZERMATTI DEAD DAY FIFTEEN, GAME DAY THIRTY-ONE, BY CORBIN GABLONA.

Pandemonium broke out. Only moments before there were still over seven million possible outcomes to the game. The number had now dropped to just under forty thousand. Over 99 percent of the options that moments before were worth billions were now nothing but worthless scraps of paper. The first cut in the market had been made.

Traders ran frantically, screaming. White-robed medical crews that had been waiting days for this moment came out onto the floor. Half a dozen traders were already down with cardiac arrests, mixed with a sprinkling of strokes and various fits. In a far corner there was the crack of an Erik 10, but the user had not been thoughtful, and after the bullet smashed through his head, it took out two other traders. Many others, however, had taken the far more customary path for such a moment. Swarms of traders raced off the floor to call their lawyers so that defenses could be prepared, since more than one innocent investor in mining shares off Oseabond would soon discover that his broker had looted the stock for "temporary working capital."

Ninety-nine percent of the market was gone, but there were still tens of millions of options on tickets that had increased a hundredfold in value.

Blackie finally managed to break free of the floor and slipped back up to her office.

"That was a close one," she said, slumping into a chair.

"Do you think it was too obvious?" Kurst groaned, now very nervous over what they had just pulled off.

"Discounting the bad tickets we bought as false leads, we still increased our investment by at least ten thousand percent. We can pay back the investments that I sort of, how shall I say, borrowed from, and the profit is all ours! I think that was worth the risk."

Kurst shook his head in amazement. The fear of being found out by Zola was washed away by the incredible wealth the futures market was creating.

"Besides," Blackie boasted, "I can out-con any con in the business. Hell, I got my start selling polyester futures to Gafs. Now let's set up that coding information so we can jump the next kill as well."

"They did what?"

With a shout of rage Ulsak, the Master Ulla of the yellows, rose up from the silk divan, a long-bladed knife poised in his hand, and strode across the room to confront the trembling messenger.

"Now repeat what you've just told me," he said evenly. All

who served Ulsak feared these moments when a message came that was contrary to his given orders and plans.

"All three tried to kill each other," the messenger, a young ulla, said slowly, staring past Ulsak as if he did not exist.

"And?"

"The one called Sigma was slain by the one protected by the dark robes."

Ulsak stood silent for long seconds, the dozen lesser ullas about him silent as well.

"And the men assigned to cover this moment?"

"They weren't there," the messenger replied, a slight tremble in his voice.

"They weren't there?" one of the ullas cried. "That was their assignment, and you were responsible!"

"Some blue robes came into the foreign quarter during the festival, a fight started, and my men left their posts to aid their brothers," the messenger replied weakly.

"Damn. Damn all the fools!" In his rage Ulsak was about to say more, and then, remembering that others were present, he turned away.

"Leave, all of you leave. And wait out in the hall," Ulsak roared.

He heard the door creak shut behind them.

Returning to the divan, he wearily sat down. He could understand in a way how it happened. All of the lower orders viewed the other clans with suspicion. It was as it was planned to be—constant training and warfare that only those of the inner order of ullas and masters understood. But nevertheless, this one foolish mistake could cost him everything that he had planned.

Rising up again, he went into the private room behind the audience chamber and pulled down a book of holy writ. As he opened the bound volume, several sheets of paper fell out. Taking them in his hand, he gazed upon them for a moment. They were of a texture never before seen on the Hole, pearly white, almost translucent, unlike the rough parchment used for the holy writings. Holding the sheets up, the memory of that moment of fear had come back.

Nearly forty days past, he had stepped alone into the Seda. The messenger had come in the morning, identical to the messenger that had come a half-dozen times before to speak of a plan so stunning that he at first had refused to believe it.

But the words of that first messenger had gradually weaved a spell, until he had finally spoken what had been hinted at throughout the previous meetings.

"It is the time for the hidden Ema to reveal himself," the stranger had whispered.

Those words had come to him as if the messenger had somehow looked into Ulsak's dreams. Dreams that had tormented his nights, and in recent years had danced at the edge of his every waking thought.

Could he, in fact, be the hidden Ema? The one promised to at last unite the Al'Shiga, to end their exile and return them to their destiny among the stars?

So the whisperings of the messenger had worked their way, until at last the stranger had offered him proof of his greatness.

"Come with me to the Seda, rise upon it into the heavens, and there meet with the archangel that shall give the Keys of the Cloud to you."

He had slain the man, in a wild moment of fear. In fact, the man had challenged him to do so as proof of what he said. So, drawing his blade, he had cut him apart. But strangely the man had not died, even with belly open. At last Ulsak had decapitated the creature, and, to his horror, still the severed head had whispered those words to him.

"You shall be the Ema. But first you must rise up to heaven to receive your mandate."

The next night another messenger had come, knowing all that had happened to the previous one and saying that still the archangel waited. But if he did not come, then another of the master ullas would answer the summons to greatness instead.

So at last, in the middle of the night, Ulsak had followed him to the base of the Seda. He felt somehow that he was going to his doom, for surely any of the Al'Shiga who dared to ascend the tower to the first level fell back to their death. But he knew in his heart that if he did not attempt this, he would be forever tormented in his mind, wondering if what the messenger said was truth.

Alone, they had stepped into the ball of glass and rose heavenward. The glass room slowed at what he knew was the place of falling, but strangely it did not stop, and then suddenly it raced upward with such speed that he had cried aloud with fear, for it felt as if his body were being crushed in upon itself.

As a master, Ulsak knew that such things as archangels, such things as heaven, were merely legends to feed to the masses, but as the Hole fell away beneath him and the stars shined with piercing coldness above, he feared for a moment that he might have been wrong.

At last the crushing eased and the room of glass slowed, rising into what appeared to be a great building hanging on the side of the Seda. Attached to the building was a strange shape, and then he realized that for the first time in two thousand years, one from the Al'Shiga was looking upon a ship that sailed the stars. And then the door from the glass room opened.

For the first time in his life Ulsak knew a moment of true terror. If there was such a thing as archangels, then he was gazing upon one.

The creature hovered before him, with long robes trailing to the floor and what he supposed were eyes gazing upon him with cold intensity.

"I am Losa," the creature had whispered. "Do my bidding and through me you shall be called the Ema."

The memory of that moment still struck fear into his heart. He had come to realize that what he had seen was no angel of the Unseen One, no being tied to the legends of holy writ. But at that moment all that he knew had been washed away in awe and terror.

He turned away from the memory, for even in the privacy of his inner musing Ulsak found it impossible to admit to himself that he was capable of fear. For in the end, had not this creature merely been part of his own plan and shown him the path to the Ema? The path that he had known in his heart was rightfully his.

He let the book of holy writ drop to the floor, and taking the sheets of paper, he walked over to the single lamp that illuminated the hidden room.

After opening the sheets, he spread them out upon the table. The instructions of Losa had been clear. The creature had been wise in that he had stated that not all events might be controlled. There were certain things that would be allowed to happen, but he must guarantee that specific proscribed events could not happen.

Ulsak scanned the notes upon the paper, and coming to the thirty-first day, he saw what was listed—and sighed with relief.

Turning through the sheets, though, he saw what would be allowed afterward and started to form his plans. There had been one mistake, but there could not, for any reason, be a second.

He would be the Ema. Was not the prophecy of his coming correct? All of this was no coincidence. Had not this Losa come in preparation of the Great Darkening that would occur in but five more festivals? The day before the messenger had first come, the sky watchers had told him of the coming celestial event with hushed awe. The soothsayers and shamans had whispered that the Great Darkening would be the proper time for the Ema to reveal himself. The masses were not yet aware of the portent, but he would declare its coming when the moment was right.

He scanned the sheets of paper yet again and smiled. The strange offworlder in the dark robes would have to be told now what to do, and Ulsak would find a way to work upon the other offworlder as well.

After returning to the bookshelf, he picked the book up off the floor, placed the papers inside, returned it to the shelf, and walked out of the room.

"Return to my presence," he shouted, coming back into the audience chamber.

The door out into the hall swung open and the ullas filed in.

"This shall not happen again, for I command it, and as I command, so it shall be written and done, for every word that I speak shall now be written as law. Soon the Great Darkening shall be upon us and then I shall be revealed," Ulsak said evenly, fixing each of them in turn with his gaze.

Nervously the ullas looked at each other. Only one could ever say that his words would be written as law—the one who would be the Ema, the one who would lead them back to the Cloud.

Ulsak looked at them and smiled.

"And I shall remember which ullas served me well in the days before my revealing," he said.

"There is a message to be sent," he continued. "Send in my writer, and one to carry the note. You may leave me now."

The ullas nervously looked to each other.

"And the one that failed me," he said softly, and the ulla who had brought him the message stopped and turned back to hear his fate.

"You shall go to the temple of our fathers where . . ." Ulsak stopped for a moment, staring into the man's eyes. He always felt a strange delicious chill when he gazed into the eyes of one he was about to kill.

". . . You shall impale yourself," Ulsak whispered.

The man's features went ashen.

He watched the eyes widen into terror. Some would cry out now, or even throw themselves to the ground, screaming for mercy. Ulsak waited.

The man started to sway, and then collapsed.

"Get him out of my sight," Ulsak snarled, disgusted with the display.

The door closed and he was alone.

Chuckling softly, the one who dreamed of being the Ema turned to the side table and, cutting a fragment of his favorite delicacy, contemplated what needed to be done.

"It's chaos out there," Bukha said, looking out over the stadium field at the thousands of lawyers and accountants working on the financial tangle of the Alexandrian game. Wild shouts echoed up from the open field, which had been sectioned off into thousands of office cubicles. Several in the crowd were already being taken away by the medical crews, and Bukha could only wonder if they would still be billing their services at eight hundred katars an hour even as they lay in the hospital.

Tia looked over at the Gaf.

"Ticket sales have skyrocketed again, just as Zola predicted," she stated even as she stirred the drinks and then offered one to Bukha.

"So, your stock is going up as well," Bukha replied.

"Zola just announced a doubling of shares, so of course I'm happy. Hell, I've just made more than a billion on paper in the last hour."

"On paper, and on the blood of Sigma," Bukha replied sharply.

"It was you and the Xsarn who thought it up," Tia snapped back in reply.

"I know, I know," Bukha said, throwing up his hands in a defensive gesture. "But at the time it was still just a game. Granted, a game with some danger to it, but I never thought it would come to this," he growled, pointing out to the thousands below who were still running about in a frenzy.

"Anyhow," Tia said, putting a hand on Bukha's arm in a gesture of reconciliation, "you sent me a message saying you'd learned something."

"Right, well, I managed to track down two of the individuals in question."

"And?"

Bukha left his perch by the window and settled in behind his desk. With a flip of a switch, the window overlooking the stadium was sealed off and the faint hum of an anti-bugging static field switched on.

"Can't be too careful," Bukha said.

"Then you're on to something," Tia said, coming up to sit across from Bukha.

"We're still hunting through the records for the others. Damn difficult. The ID numbers are valid, cross-referenced with retinal scan and printing at birth, but who they are now has been buried through name shifts and such. Most of my own security people go through the same procedure. But anyhow, we think we've got a lead on two of them. One of them is a Heta drone, so wiped on the juice he's a scramble. His story is that he won the cash in a massive gambling binge, bought the tickets, then sold them out to a dealer to buy more juice."

"Five million katars of juice! Who's he kidding?"

"Claims he got jumped and lost the shipment."

"Xsarnfood," Tia snapped.

"Exactly."

"So that leaves us nowhere. The juicer was a front, and we still don't know for whom."

Bukha shook his head slowly, and for the first time Tia saw a look of fear in the Gaf's eyes.

"The second buyer is a juicer as well, same story, but there's one key difference: his last job was working as a liaison officer for the Alma Consortium."

Tia's eyes grew wide with astonishment. The Alma was a board set up by the Overseers to coordinate the few business transactions that would from time to time arise between the Overseers and the other inhabitants of the Cloud.

"Then the Overseers are in the game!"

Bukha nodded his head in reply.

"But if they are, then what the hell for?"

It'd been an uneasy night for all of them. The Gaf berserkers had finally been convinced by Zergh that the basement
was the best place for them, so that both sides could get a
good night's sleep, and in the end he had agreed to go down
with them.

The doors were another problem. The Gafs in their enthusiasm had smashed the front barrier to pieces and, before leaving, had torn the back one off its hinges. There was nothing to
do but pile shattered tables and debris against the openings and
post triple guards of samurai on each.

The brief night of six hours finally passed, and the Gafs
were let up from below.

"It can't go on like this," Oishi whispered impatiently, as the
hulking warriors barraged into the kitchen, bellowing for food,
while Mari shouted back that the damn fools had destroyed
most of it the day before.

"Well, we've taken them in, for better or worse," Aldin replied wearily, still yawning from lack of sleep. "If we try to
turn them out now, we'll have twenty-six more enemies ready
to tear us apart. And besides, how the hell are we going to get
them out anyhow?"

"They can be useful," Takashi interjected.

Oishi looked at his old friend with a jaundiced eye.

"Remember what our emperor said about dogs—and to my
thinking they're nothing but overgrown fighting dogs."

"Don't let Zergh hear you say that," Aldin mumbled.

"They've got traits to admire: bravery in battle and absolute
disregard for self, to begin with," Takashi argued.

"Along with loudness, brawling, and drunkenness," Aldin
stated.

"If we could only be sure of their absolute loyalty to you,"
Takashi continued, "they'd be worth the trouble."

Aldin sat back in his chair. If only Yaroslav were here.
Yaroslav had been an absolute encyclopedia of arcane knowledge about such things. With such beings, to simply go up
and ask what would command their loyalty would be a loss
of face.

He tried to cast back through his memory. There were the
territorial rituals of dogs, which involved holding the lesser

creature by the throat or urinating on territory or even the body of the lesser being, but he didn't think that would go over too well.

"I wish we had some sake right now," Takashi said wistfully. "It'd clear my head for some action."

Then the memory came back to Aldin, from what seemed ages ago when he was still a student and Yaroslav was lecturing on the similarity of Gaf social customs across thousands of primitive worlds that were prefeudal, even though they'd been cut off for centuries.

Aldin caught Zergh's eye and motioned for him to come over, even as he gagged on the thought.

The circle of Gafs stood before Aldin, a look of reverent awe on their faces. Even the samurai were impressed and mumbled to themselves in the background. Ura was the last to finish, and coming up to Aldin, the Gaf raised the two-handed beaker up to where he stood atop the shattered bar.

Aldin looked inside and struggled to stop the churning of his stomach. If only pissing on their territory could have been the answer, he thought wistfully. He had to do it; to back out now would be the worst possible rejection imagined, and certain to trigger a fight to the death.

He closed his eyes and brought the beaker to his lips, and then raised it up. The hot liquid hit his lips. He forced his mouth to take it, and the salty taste made him want to gag it all back up.

Finally he swallowed. It had to be done. He swallowed again and then again, but still the beaker was only half empty.

The warm liquid coursed down his throat. He tilted the beaker up higher, cheating a bit as some of the liquid poured out either side of his mouth and ran down his robes. At the sight of it, however, the samurai let out a cheer of approval and the Gafs joined in, beating their axes on the floor, raising a shower of splinters.

The cup was getting lighter. He gulped again and then tilted up to the vertical so that the last splash of liquid washed over his face.

He opened his eyes and looked out at the Gafs. As one they raised their axes on high, bellowing their approval. Aldin smiled, and looked about the room. Even Oishi was impressed, shaking his head, a bemused smile on his face that turned to a wince of pain when Ura came up to the samurai's side and clapped him on the shoulder in a show of comradely spirit.

"You have taken part of our spirits into your flesh, Aldin Taug," Ura roared, "now we shall serve without question. Even our last lord had not offered to do such, to mingle his soul with ours."

Aldin heard that bit of news with astonishment. He assumed Sigma would have done so, but then realized that the old Koh, who had merely dabbled in primitive anthropology as a hobby related to the games, would not have picked up such an arcane bit of knowledge.

"Then hear me," Aldin said sharply. And the Gafs stopped their celebration.

"It is true I am a hairless one, and am honored that warriors such as you would agree to fight for me."

The Gafs roared at this, making ribald comments about how they would put hair on him one way or another.

"But you let your last master die, even if he was only a master of coin for you."

The Gafs fell silent, not wishing to be reminded of their failure.

"I say this not to shame you," Aldin said quietly, "but to promise you honors and the souls of many servants. But there is only one way you can win those honors."

He fell silent, playing a typical trick of oration, and the Gafs went for it, calling out for an answer to his riddle.

"You will listen to me, even in the heat of battle, and if not me, then Oishi or Zergh. Even if the enemy is before you and we say fight not, then you will not fight."

The warriors started to mumble, but Aldin held up the cup he had just drained, and at the sight of it they fell silent again.

"By what I have just done, I have taken in a small part of each of your souls, some of your strength and your wisdom. Trust me, turn aside from the small meaningless fights when I tell you, and in the end I shall give you the greatest fight that you have ever dreamed of as reward."

With that, the Gafs again roared their approval. Aldin stepped down from the bar and, with a ceremonial flourish, strode out of the room and into the kitchen, with Mari and Zergh following.

"What big fight at the end?" Zergh asked.

"I had to promise them something," Aldin said, "so I promised them what they wanted most."

"But if there isn't any fight at the end, then they'll be real problems, for one who has drunk of them cannot lie."

"I'll worry about that later," Aldin said wearily, desperately looking around the room. Then seeing what he was looking for, he sped to the far corner of the room and, leaning into the sink, promptly vomited back up the half gallon of Gaf blood he had downed only minutes before.

"So, the Overseers are into the game," Yaroslav said, as if it were knowledge that he was already familiar with and wasn't any cause for concern on his part.

"You act like you already know," Tia replied sharply.

"But of course, my dear. But of course."

Tia looked across at the old man, not sure if she should be angry at him for not saying anything before. She wasn't quite sure why she had even bothered to come see him. Since Aldin's departure, he had seemed to have withdrawn from all involvement with the game, or the possible negative effect it might have on his old friend.

"I thought you'd at least have some concern for Aldin."

"But I do," he replied evenly.

"Well, you certainly aren't showing any. He's been down there for seventeen days, and what have you done but sit here in this lousy one-room flat and read your damn journals on the com link?"

"What else can I do?" Yaroslav said quietly. "Research keeps me busy."

"Well, you could try to help Aldin."

"How?"

She couldn't find an answer for that, and exasperated, she sank into the one empty chair that graced the shabby little room.

"You really do care for him, don't you?" Yaroslav said softly, looking across at the girl.

"He may be the only thing I've got left," Tia replied, her eyes starting to brim over with tears. "I've been such a bitch to him. He tried to warm me about Gablona, and I thought he was just being an old prude. He's the only man that's ever shown me any kindness."

Yaroslav sat back in his chair and sighed. "You're lonely, dear. But it'll pass."

"I don't think so," she said. "I can't trust anyone. If any man shows an interest, I think right away that he's after me because, technically, I'm a Koh, or that I was once the mistress to that pig Gablona and might still have influence."

She spat the name Gablona with hatred.

"Remember, you're a Gablona as well," Yaroslav replied. "Your tie to the Gablonas is with blood; Aldin's only your uncle through marriage."

"But he's the only one that showed any interest in me for who I am."

Tia looked away for a moment, struggling for control. When she turned back again, the cold exterior was back.

"I just wish," she said softly, "that I'd never gotten involved in this whole thing."

"It was the only way," Yaroslav replied. "Corbin would have hunted Aldin down sooner or later. We had to bring it to a head where Aldin would at least have a fighting chance for survival. It's just that certain unforeseen things seemed to have come into play."

"You mean the Overseers."

Yaroslav smiled, and standing up, he shut down the com link system.

"I think I've found what I was after this morning," he said. "Had my suspicions from the beginning. I was presented with only half of a puzzle, you see. That's why I stayed behind. I couldn't tell Aldin, it'd just give him something else to worry about."

Yaroslav walked over to the one closet in the room, and, pulling open the door, he stepped back as clothes, books, and stacks of paper came tumbling out. A white, mangy-looking cat with mismatched eyes of blue and green leaped out as well, took one look at Tia, and then leaped back into the closet. Yaroslav stepped over the pile, waded into the jumble, and started poking around.

"I'll be going on a little trip, my dear," he shouted from out of the darkness.

"Where?"

The old man stuck his head back out of the closet and smiled. "Rather not say. Things might be getting a little heated before the end, and the fewer that know, the better. Just do me a favor. Drop by here occasionally and feed little Tanya for me. Found her or, should I say, she found me the other day, and we've become quite good friends.

"Oh, and by the way," he said almost as if by an afterthought. "When you get a chance, check up on any of your family's shipping firms. I have my suspicions—might be nothing, then again it might be everything. It's what I've been hunting for. That's why I've got to leave, make sure that certain things don't happen."

"What are you talking about?" she replied.

"Just a hunch, the other half of the puzzle, if you will. You'll know it when you see it."

A moment later Yaroslav reemerged from the closet, and shouldering a weather-beaten pack, he gave Tia a quick kiss on the cheek and headed out the door.

"When will you get back?" Tia cried, following him out into the dank, foul-smelling hall.

"Who knows?" he said, and turning, he disappeared down the hall whistling an off-key tune.

chapter ten

"This is sheer insanity," Oishi growled, looking warily from side to side. The north gate of the foreign quarter was behind them now, and as they turned the corner, it disappeared from view.

"We need food, we need other supplies, and most of all we need information. I plan to go to the Seda," Aldin replied.

"But you shouldn't be out like this," Oishi pleaded. "It's too dangerous."

"The Gafs are sworn to me," Aldin whispered. "I've got to demonstrate to them that I'm willing to take the risks as well."

Oishi fell silent at the response, not willing to admit to the logic of what Aldin was saying. The argument was far too true; he knew that his old lord Asano would have done exactly the same. Asano was no daimyo to hide within his fortress; if there was a crisis, he would stride forward to meet it head-on.

When Aldin had casually announced that he was going out on the trading venture as well, the Gafs had shouted their approval, and Oishi had seen his own men look one to the other and quietly nod their approval.

The addition of the Gafs was already paying off. Thirty of the samurai under Takashi had stayed behind to guard the tavern and work on defense, leaving eight men and all the Gafs to go with Aldin.

Not being festival day, the streets were crowded with Al'Shiga going about their daily business. Young men and women, dressed in their distinctive tight-fitting robes, wandered by in small groups, eyeing the passing strangers with open hostility. Mari stuck close to Aldin's side, guiding him and his followers toward the Seda.

So mysterious had the Al'Shiga been to Aldin that he had assumed that the city would somehow be like a badly made vid, with knife-welding assassins lurking in deserted alleyways, the streets empty except for furtive forms sneaking out of dark hiding places rushing to secret rendezvous.

But even on such a world as the Hole, people still had to fulfill the mundane tasks of living, no matter how exotic their beliefs might be.

Open-air market stalls lined the street, merchants selling a wide variety of wares. Finely woven carpets were spread out for display next to delicately worked silver jewelry, furniture carved from exotic woods, pottery, and finely painted prayer cards that, when burned, served as votive offerings.

Being a restricted primitive world, there were no tech devices, and Aldin found the change to be refreshing. Here were products still made by individuals who obviously took pride in their skills, and eagerly shouted to the passing offworlders to come and buy.

Heading down toward the main thoroughfare, the group passed the food markets, and Aldin was reminded that there were some negative aspects to primitive worlds as well.

They plodded through rotten castoffs, for when the produce had spoiled to the point of no longer being sellable, the merchants simply swept the refuse off their tables and into the streets.

The Shiga taboo against meat meant that only vegetable

products were available out in the open. There was a wide variety of tropical fruits and grain products from the cultivated fields beyond the cities. Some of the offerings were mushrooms and fungi grown in the geothermal-heated caves that honeycombed the world beneath their feet. Some of the growths looked truly gruesome in the daylight. One species and its dealers caught Aldin's attention, for he'd heard mention of it even before coming down to the Hole, and he slowed to take a closer look.

The fungi being offered was a huge bud nearly several meters across that looked like a decaying human corpse, known appropriately enough as "the rotting man." The plant had an elongated central pod with five tendrils, one rounded where a head would be, the other four corresponding to arms and legs.

The closer the plant looked to human form, the more valuable it became. Growers had found all sorts of tricks, such as crossbreeding and cutting the shoots while still young, to coax the plant to follow a desired form. Masters of the art, working with secret knowledge passed down for generations, would on occasion grow true masterpieces with fingers, toes, and even faces and pale white hair.

Of course, such masterpieces fetched the highest prices, sometimes trading on the market for equal weight in rare amber.

Aging was part of the process as well. After the plant was harvested, the interior would start to decompose into a green, pulpy liquid that fermented. Cut open too soon, the contents were still just sugar; too late, and the drink had gone sour. Consuming the liquid was the only infraction of the taboo against drinking that was tolerated in public, and thus was even more valued. To some connoisseurs of the rotting man, it was the bouquet when the plant was sliced open that was worth the price, the drink being merely an afterthought. Elaborate ceremonies had sprung up around the opening of a masterpiece. A full ritual could take a day or more to reach the moment when the knife finally punctured the skin, the invited guests honored beyond measure for the right to attend and inhale what to them was the delectable fragrance.

The samurai around Aldin watched with disgust as a deal seemed to come to completion at a vendor's stall. The haggling had been brisk, with several parties competing for a prime specimen, though not quite of masterpiece status.

Aldin's curiosity was aroused by the sight, and he slowed to watch the results.

The deal was finally struck, and with great ceremony, the successful bidder called over his kinsmen to pick up the coffinlike box that held the rotting man so that it could be borne home for the feast.

The merchant, now following tradition, brought out a smaller rotting man a half meter in length, and obviously of inferior stock. After reaching into the folds of his robe, he pulled out his dagger and, with a flourish, cut the fungi open from head to foot with one quick slice. The plant emitted a soggy, raspy belch as the air within was released. The bidders and their kinsmen leaned forward and, like true connoisseurs, exclaimed their judgments.

"Fine scent, rich and full-bodied," one cried.

"Richly sour. Perhaps aged too far past perfection." Another sniffed.

A faint stir of breeze carried the scent over to Aldin, and with a gag he realized yet another reason why the fungi was called the rotting man.

The merchant turned to a small tray of cups and, after scooping them into the plant one after another, offered a round of drinks to his clients. The pulpy green liquid had a faint iridescent glow of putrification to it, and trying to hide his disgust, Aldin pushed on, the samurai muttering darkly to themselves, while the Gafs laughed at their companions' discomfort, for they felt the entire show had been a display of crudeness equal almost to their own.

Leaving the street of the rotting men, the group turned into a narrow alley where no stalls were open. Mari explained that it was a quicker way to the Seda, bypassing the more crowded sections of the market. She assured Oishi there was no danger, but for a moment Aldin felt as if the bad vid he had imagined earlier had been filmed in this very spot. For indeed up and down the street doorways would come open for a moment, several individuals would peek out and then quickly scurry away with strange bulges under their robes, while others, waiting in side alleyways, would rush out, leap through the open doors, and then slam them shut behind them.

He looked to Mari with a quizzical, raised eyebrow.

"Meat merchants. The only native animal worth eating looks like a pig and is taboo. The damn things thrive here, living down in the caves. They feed them the cast-off mushrooms and fungi and turn out fertilizer. The meat gets sold here. Everyone eats it, but no one wants an elder or ulla to see them. That's why most of the Shigs eat in secret.

"It's not wise to stare, they might think you're trying to recognize them," she added, and with that, Aldin urged the group to push on.

"We're coming up on the merchants of the Hauchma Sul," Mari whispered, as the group approached a turn in the road.

"The what?" Aldin asked, curious about the sound of disgust in her voice.

"It's rumored that they somehow train a plant to grow over a human skeleton until finally the bones are devoured and only the roots are left."

Aldin tried to suppress a shudder.

"Like the rotting man plants, the Shiga have a near reverence for the things, hanging them as decorations to remind them of their mortality."

Turning the corner of the thoroughfare, the group came to a stop at the frightening sight that confronted them. All up and down the lane hung hundreds of vinelike forms, that appeared to be exact replicas of human and Gaf skeletons. Aldin paused for a moment to look closer, and as he stopped, a merchant came bustling out of a shop, eager to make a sale even if only to a cursed offworlder.

"Finest Hauchma Suls to be found on the Hole," the merchant started. "Every rib in place, look, just look at this one here, even the teeth are there. Count them, this one has all its teeth."

"How do you make these?" Aldin asked, thinking of what Mari had said.

The merchant looked at him and smiled, wagging his finger.

"The secret of the Al'Shiga," the merchant said. "If I told you, you offworlders would not buy from us."

"Just curious, that's all," Aldin said, and drawing back, he started to leave.

"Surely a small one, a child's form, might be more to your liking?" the merchant asked.

"Sorry, I'm not interested. Just looking."

"Pig spawn," the merchant snapped, spitting at Aldin's feet. The native hurriedly withdrew as the Basaks growled menacingly.

They moved off down the lane and at last came to the open boulevard that led straight as an arrow to their destination.

The Skyhook soared straight into the heavens above them. It could, of course, be seen from anywhere on the Hole, but it was only here on the main concourse that the view was unimpeded—the full magnificence of the First Traveler creation soaring above them.

To Aldin, who had seen many of the strangest sights in the Cloud, from the ringlike Kolbard to the remnants of the great supernova, the sight of the tower still left him awestruck. Like many of the other creations of the First Travelers, it had a permanence to it that transcended anything the Humans and Gafs had so far dared to attempt.

The Gafs and samurai looked at the structure, not able to quite understand its function as Aldin could, but nevertheless convinced that here was something that only gods could build.

"If we're going to make contact," Mari announced, "it'll be someplace around here." Following her lead, the group set out across the vast open plaza that surrounded the Skyhook.

The pavement was of the same material used by the First Travelers to face the Skyhook. However, the brilliant metallic substance was barely visible, for the square from end to end was coated with the remnants of thousands of festivals that had been held down through the centuries. Over the entire square hung the noisome stench of decaying blood, so that Aldin and his samurai companions covered their faces and struggled to hold down their breakfast with each breath.

A faint stirring of wind brought drifting clouds of smoke emitted from one of the clan temples that bordered the square, adding yet another overpowering smell of the fetid plaza.

With a shudder, Aldin looked over to the blocklike structure. A procession was weaving its way up the outside steps, dragging a yellow-robed form along in the middle. The thin, high cries of the victim drifted on the foul-smelling breeze.

Horrified, Aldin slowed to watch, but a cloud of smoke curled down from the top of the temple, obstructing the view; therefore he could only imagine what nightmare was being performed atop the temple stairs.

From out of the interior of the temple came more forms, carrying shroud-wrapped bodies upon their shoulders, and they, too, turned and started up the outside steps. While this drama was being enacted, others were crossing the square on their own business, not even pausing to take a second look, so inured were they to the harsh demands of their cults.

"I think we better push on," Mari whispered, grabbing Aldin by the arm.

At last they reached the base of the Skyhook and ascended the stairs that led to the wide platform that surrounded the structure.

The scene was one of chaos.

Offworld merchants stood behind their temporary stalls, trading with the natives for the precious green amber. Most of the merchants were day runners, as the offworlders who dared to live in the foreign quarter referred to them with disdain.

They'd come down the Skyhook on the morning run, do their trading during daylight, and then hop a car back up to safety at day's end. The Shiga, who hated all foreigners, at least had a small measure of respect for those who dared to live in the foreign quarter, but for the day runners their contempt was outright and without reservation.

Gangs of young Shiga thought it high sport to go down to the Seda and pelt the merchants with offal. Legitimate dealers of the Shiga felt it an act of high humor if, after striking a fair deal, they could still cut the merchant's throat after goods had been exchanged. However, their code did command that it was sinful to kill with intent of robbing, so after a merchant and his guards were dispatched, they would leave their amber in payment for the goods traded, and depart.

Of course, such an act would trigger a near riot, as the dead man's neighbors fell upon his stall. Such activities caused even greater disdain on the part of the Shiga, who would jeer such base activities.

At times the merchants' circle appeared to be the center of a mad feeding frenzy. A merchant would be killed, his neighbors would fall upon the loot lying in the street, and more Shiga would move in to kill the unwary, thus leaving more stalls open, until a bloodbath would be triggered, and the surviving merchants, their deep pockets stuffed to overflowing with green amber, would flee back to the protection of the Skyhook waiting room.

Aldin slowly walked the circle about the tower, the Shiga eyeing him with suspicion. Fortunately no blue robes were in the crowd, as Mari had foreseen, since today was a sacred day for their particular cult and, as such, all were in the temples.

"Aldin, Aldin Larice!" a voice suddenly echoed.

Aldin turned and saw a merchant waving and grimacing excitedly in his direction.

"Will Wedser!"

Shaking his head with disbelief, Aldin motioned for his guards to follow, and warily they edged through the crowd that backed away at their approach.

Wedser motioned for his half-dozen guards to back out of the booth, and as the samurai and Gafs set up a protective ring, Aldin stepped into the enclosure.

Wedser reached for a small lever underneath the table and the guillotine shutters slammed down. There was an angry cry from the samurai outside, but Aldin could hear Mari reassuring them.

With a grin he grabbed Wedser's one good hand. His friend, as usual, looked the worse for wear. It seemed that whenever he'd run into his old school and gambling friend, there was another part of his original anatomy gone, replaced by a shining prosthesis that would be embellished with fine gems or intricate carvings.

The right hand, of course, was a replacement, the original having been lost when the two of them were still students and had gone on a drunken hunting expedition against one of the smaller dragons of Maci.

Both of Wedser's ears were of the finest silver, and substitute for the ones hacked off in a barroom brawl. To Aldin's amazement, Wedser's nose was now made of gem-encrusted platinum, and he couldn't help but stare.

"Ah, yes, the nose." Wedser chuckled. "Remember my Gaf bodyguard Orklon? Well, he bit it off when he thought I'd cheated him on a little wager."

"But I saw Orklon standing outside!" Aldin exclaimed.

"We made up," Wedser said matter-of-factly.

Aldin shook his head, not even bothering to ask for the details.

Wedser, still chuckling, reached into his tunic and pulled out a flask, offering it to Aldin.

"You know, I've got several thousand riding on you," Wedser said while Aldin took a long pull on the flask.

"How the hell did you get into the betting?" Aldin asked. "That's a Koh privilege."

"Not anymore." Wedser chuckled. "The entire Cloud's betting on this one." And then he went on to explain the intricacies of the lottery and the underground futures market that had sprung up around it.

Aldin could only smile and shake his head.

"Seems like you already know about the lottery," Wedser remarked, looking at his old friend.

Aldin only smiled in reply.

"You know, the betting was rather heavy that you'd already be dead."

"Well, I'm sorry to disappoint the mob," Aldin replied bitterly.

"Anyhow, I got in on the beginning when the payoff was over five million to one," Wedser announced triumphantly.

"I hope you at least had the loyalty to bet on me," Aldin said.

Wedser merely shook his head and smiled.

"By the way," Aldin asked in an offhand manner, "is there any rumor as to who got this lottery thing started?"

"Word is around that Zola Koh had something to do with it."

Aldin leaned back, and for a moment a thin smile creased his features.

"Anyhow," Wedser asked, wanting information far more than wishing to provide some, "any tips for an old friend?"

Aldin, as if coming out of a reverie, looked over at Wedser.

"If you're playing the market," Aldin said, thinking aloud, "sell short."

"What was that?"

Aldin looked over at his friend and smiled. "Care for a little arrangement?"

Wedser smiled and drew closer.

"I'm all ears," he said, chuckling at his own joke.

"Two things then. First, I need a contact with the Al'Shiga. I need supplies, food, and, most of all, information."

Wedser thought for a moment before replying.

"Funny you should ask," Wedser replied. "There was a Wardi—yellow robe—who came through here not an hour ago, asking for you."

"Oh, really?" Aldin replied.

"Yeah, I told him to look for you in the foreign quarter, but he said he preferred to meet you outside of there."

"Who is he?"

"Didn't give a name, but my guards know who he is."

Aldin nodded his approval, and pulling open the steel shutter, Wedser shouted for Orklon to go find the yellow robe in question.

"And the second part?" Wedser asked.

"Just thought you might be able to find an old friend of mine." Aldin motioned for the shutter to be closed. With a smile he leaned forward and poured a drink for both of them.

"Come, offworlder."

The man before him was obviously a master; the silver trim on his yellow robes denoted his rank. The native was shorter than most, with a powerful stocky build. His face was as rugged and square-shaped as his massive body, his black hair cut even at the shoulders. The first thing that Aldin had noticed about this man was dark smoldering eyes, and he wasn't sure whether they held the look of a terrible purpose or of insanity. About his waist was a broad leather belt; a small sack and scabbards for several blades, which were ornamented with precious amber inlays, hung from his side.

For a second Aldin looked back at Wedser. Could Gablona have gotten through to him and arranged this meeting as a setup?

"He did give the ceremonial head bond," Mari whispered, sensing Aldin's hesitation.

As if hearing the woman's words, the master looked back. "I have bonded my head for your safety, or do you not believe my words?" There was a note of menace in his voice.

"All right then," Aldin said evenly, "we'll go with you."

The Gaf guards gathered around Aldin; the samurai formed an inner circle, and Oishi, as usual, put himself between Aldin and any possible sources of danger.

The Shiga looked over at Aldin with obvious curiosity over such precautions.

Let him think I'm cautious, Aldin thought. If this master ever thought he could get the upper hand, it would be murder just for the sport of it.

Without a backward look, the Shiga turned and strode through the swirling crowds, with Aldin's party following in his wake.

At the approach, the crowds of Shiga parted before them. After several minutes Aldin realized that they were parting not so much for his armed guards but rather at the sight of the master. All eyes were upon him. The Human Shigas backed up, mumbling to themselves.

The man looked neither to the right nor the left. He didn't swagger as some of the others did, nor did he slink along from doorway to doorway expecting attack at any moment. His stride was self-assured, purposeful, as if he were walking along a country lane without a care or fear.

The samurai mumbled to themselves in admiring tones, sensing the calm self-confidence of the warrior. After crossing the open plaza, they came at last to the tunnellike gate that led into the Wardi quarter of the city.

Without even slowing, he led the way into the darkness. The wide tunnel was packed with a shouting wave of beings coming in the opposite direction. In any other situation Aldin would have called his guards in and waited for the crowd to pass—the narrow confines of the tunnel was the last place that he'd want to be trapped—but the master simply continued on.

Oishi looked at Aldin and then with a shrug realized that they'd have to follow and hope this wasn't a double cross.

As before, however, the crowd parted at their approach, the master moving before them like the prow of a ship cutting through a sea of men.

Suddenly there was a quick flurry of motion, a muffled scream echoed in the semidarkness.

With fluid ease, the master swung about, his right foot catching someone in the crowd full in the chest. There was the dull snap of cracking ribs. Even as he kicked, a blade in his left hand slashed across the throat of another, who fell back howling, fumbling with his hands to stem the pulsing flow of blood.

The action was almost over before Aldin even saw that the two Bengada in green robes had drawn blades in their hands and wore the ceremonial red knots.

The samurai nodded their approval at the display, as the master, still holding his fighting blade, surveyed the dozen or so greens in the crowd with an almost languid disdain.

"Twice today you've tried," he growled. "Haven't you had enough?"

The greens backed up and without a word disappeared back down the tunnel, leaving their two dead companions on the pavement.

"This will only take a moment," the man said. He took the satchel from his belt and knelt by the first body. Aldin turned away as the bloody container received two more heads, doubling the day's take.

After leaving the tunnel, they went on into the city. Most of the travelers on the street were Human yellows, but here and there were small clusters of Gafs as well. Both Human and Gafs nodded at the approach of the master, raising their right hands, palm outward, in a sign of greeting, which he, as an obvious superior, did not return.

Finally he led the way into a small side street and turned at last into a narrow doorway that opened as he neared it. Aldin looked back to see several dozen yellow robes emerge from out of the side doorways, cutting the group off from behind. He looked over at Oishi, who merely nodded.

The group stopped at the door, and Oishi pushed ahead and stepped in first. His tension was obvious. If the man had wished to set them up, this would be the ideal place. They were near to the other end of the city; home was almost a league away. Thousands of yellows, who could obviously be aroused by this leader, could be on them in moments.

Aldin looked around at his guards, who were eyeing the building and the alleyway with suspicion. Every nerve seemed to be screaming at him to go back out of here and retreat to the safe house. But he knew that they were backed into a corner. They needed contacts with the Shiga, and if he wavered at all, there'd be a loss of face, not only in front of the Shiga but among his own guards, as well.

After pushing through his guards, Aldin came up behind Oishi, and together they stepped into the ulla's fortress.

He was stunned by the simple elegance of the place. The doorway led into an atrium, lit from above by skylights, the walls hung with bright tapestries, which were either ornately worked script from the Shigas' sacred text or curious representations of star fields and whirling galaxies.

The atrium led into an open courtyard, and he couldn't help but wonder if this was some architectural holdover from a distant past.

The courtyard even had a fountain in the middle, most likely fed by the hot sulfurous springs that welled up at a thousand different locations throughout the Hole.

The man beckoned for Aldin to sit on a low divan and motioned for Zergh, Mari, and Oishi to join them as well, while the rest of Aldin's guards settled down on the floor ·in the foyer.

"My name is Ulsak," the man said. "And you are Aldin Larice."

Surprised, Aldin looked at the Grand Master of the Wardi. He had heard, through Mari, of this man—most feared of all the masters of the six clans.

"So, you wish an understanding," Ulsak said lazily, even as he pulled the bloody satchel loose from his belt and tossed it to a waiting servant.

"Precisely," Aldin replied, thrown off guard for the moment by Ulsak's directness.

"Why?" And as Ulsak spoke, he fixed Aldin with his gaze.

"Because it could be to both our advantages."

Ulsak threw back his head and laughed. "Little man, little man, there is nothing among the stars you could offer me, yet there is everything that I could offer you. Your life could be one example."

Nervously Aldin looked about the courtyard and into the shadows of the half-dozen corridors that disappeared off into darkness.

"No, no," Ulsak said evenly. "There's no one hiding in the shadows. Such melodrama is for the young, or the inexperienced. But if I wanted you dead now, you would be dead. Such as you are of no account."

"It seems," Oishi interrupted, "that we could kill you now as well."

Ulsak threw back his head and barked out a short grunt of laughter. "Bravely spoken. Would you care to cross your blade to mine, here and now?"

Oishi stood up, ready to accept the challenge, but Aldin shot out his hand, restraining him.

"We're here in peace," Aldin commanded. "You gave your head bond to that. We seek merely an arrangement for trade and information."

Besides, he knew that if Oishi succeeded they'd never get out of the building alive. That was *if* Oishi succeeded. After the display in the tunnel he had doubts that even the best of his swordsmen could match the man in front of them. He looked up at Oishi, motioning for him to sit down. Oishi shot him a glance, and in that look Aldin realized that the samurai had nerved himself to die against the Shiga, all over what was merely an opening insult in the game of words.

"Best listen to him, little man," Ulsak said coldly.

Aldin fixed Oishi with his gaze.

"Another time," he whispered, and finally the samurai relented and sat back down, fixing Ulsak with a cold stare.

Aldin looked back at Ulsak and saw a faint look of approval in the man's eyes at Oishi's behavior.

"If we're done with threats," Aldin sallied, "then let us talk terms."

"What is it then that you can offer me?" Ulsak responded.

"Off this world, I'm a man of substance. When my time here is done, I could arrange exclusive trade to you for the finest metals of sword quality. Whatever luxuries you'd require, I could bring to you. Name the price and the goods and they are yours."

Ulsak leaned back and laughed again. "You offer me gifts and trade from a man who will soon be dead. You offer the promise from beyond the grave. You offer nothing."

"How can you be so sure that I shall die down here?"

"Come, come," Ulsak replied. "This is the world of the Al'Shiga, the brotherhood of the blade. This is our world, and you are merely an interloper here. Don't you think I know why you are here?"

"You tell me then," Aldin replied coldly.

"The games," Ulsak replied slowly, leaning forward and staring at Aldin.

"So you know?"

Ulsak could only shake his head in amazement.

"Then if you know," Aldin replied, "why do you even tolerate this action of those who sail the stars? You hate all of us, I know that. Why, then, let the Hole be a place where the star-rulers play their amusements?"

"Because it amuses us as well," Ulsak replied, a smile tracing his mouth.

"How so?"

"Because what you do here fits our own game," Ulsak replied.

"In what way?"

Ulsak could only shake his head as if talking to a child. "You know that the Ulman, the Great Festival, comes on the last day of your so-called game."

"The double eclipse," Mari said as Aldin turned to her in confusion. "Word of it's been going around the city. Both moons will eclipse the sun at the same time."

"So what does that have to do with us?" Aldin asked.

"You see, I wish to make you and yours an offer."

"Which is?" Aldin asked, feeling suddenly on edge.

"That when the sky darkens you come to me."

"And you'll do what?"

"Why, kill you, of course," Ulsak responded. "What else?"

"Thanks for the offer," Aldin said, "but I think I'll pass."

"You don't understand," Ulsak rejoined. "I like you. I like the way your men showed up the Isma and the look of your warriors. If you come to me, I'll make sure that you suffer not. You'll be drugged for the ceremony and your men will be spared, to be my servants."

Aldin merely shook his head.

"You don't understand," Ulsak replied. "We of the Shiga will not let you leave this place alive. We could kill you at any time."

"Then why not do it now?"

"I have my own private reasons," Ulsak replied.

"Oh, just that you want me to come walking in here like a lamb to the slaughter, that's all." Aldin stood up.

Oishi barked a command, and the samurai accompanying the group rushed out from the foyer to stand by Aldin's side.

Ulsak remained seated on his divan, but from behind him there was a faint stirring, and half a hundred yellows appeared from out of the shadows to stand on the other side of the pool.

"Shall we have it out here and now?" Oishi growled.

"No need," Ulsak replied lazily. "No need at all. I was just trying to be friendly, and you take insult."

"You've asked us to come to you begging for death, but know that we, the forty-seven ronin, will die sword in hand."

"Too bad," Ulsak replied. "Let me tell you your alternative then. Before the sky darkens our ullas shall proclaim that the hour has come and that a new sacrifice must be made. Then shall the hunt begin. As many of you as can be taken will be taken alive. Then shall you be brought to the great square."

He fixed Aldin with his gaze. "The ceremony is really quite simple. You'll be tied with a canvas sack strapped to your shoulders. Into the sack a pipe will be fixed, and with each passing second a drop of water shall fall, and another.

"Oh, it won't seem like much at first, but as the hours pass, liter after liter of liquid will drip in, weighing you down further and further."

"That doesn't seem like much," Aldin replied, and even as he spoke he wished he had not, for he suddenly had a flash of insight.

"Ah, but there is one little detail," Ulsak said dreamily, his eyes half closed.

"You see, you and all your men will be tied over sharpened stakes. Gradually the burden upon your shoulders will be too much to bear and you'll sag beneath the weight. But no, for the stake will jab into you, and you'll straighten up again. But then you'll sag again, and cut even deeper.

"Finally you'll try to nerve yourself, to force yourself down to end the agony. The stake will slide into your body. The hot stab of agony will cut through you, and with a shriek you'll rise back up again. I've seen it before, it's a wonderful show to watch. Some victims try to jam themselves down, but always the flesh rebels, and so they struggle on.

"Oh, and the screams, such wonderful screams, even from the strongest and bravest," Ulsak continued. "Some just scream, most whimper and beg. We love the beggars. Each cry for mercy is met with howls of derision. It's really quite funny sometimes. The victims will start bouncing up and down on the stake like a toy, trying to jam the stake through to their heart and finish it, but always they pull back, so exquisite is the agony."

Ulsak leaned over from the divan and picked up a fragment of a rotting man. He examined it in a detached manner before placing it into his mouth.

"So it will go for hours, as gradually you weaken and falter, sliding lower and lower, impaling yourself. Until at last the stake drives clear through your body.

"Oh, if it's done right, a stake can cut clear through a man's diaphragm and into his lungs before he finally dies. It's a wonderful thing to watch. You should visit our temples more often."

Aldin struggled to suppress a retch of fear. He was tempted to draw his own blade now, to fall upon the ulla and go down fighting.

"You're thinking of finishing it right now," Ulsak commented. "But I wouldn't do that."

"And why not?" Aldin asked, his voice husky with tension.

"For I need Gablona to die with you," Ulsak replied. "After all, you wouldn't want your fat friend to have the pleasure of dying after you, now, would you?"

"Why? How come the time of our dying is so important to you?"

"I've presented you with an enigma, a mystery." Ulsak chuckled. "Die now and you won't find out. You know that if you fight me now, out of your own fear, it will be cowardice that will condemn all your followers here to certain death."

Aldin spared a quick glance from Ulsak back to his samurai and Gafs and realized that the man was right. If they tried to fight, the alarm would be raised, and in moments everyone with him would die.

"Let's go for him anyhow," Oishi hissed.

Aldin looked back to Ulsak, who still sat unmoving.

"Why not just take me prisoner now?"

"If you were my prisoner now and for the days remaining before the Ulman, it would not be correct. That is for you to ponder. But I did want to tell you about your final reception. After all, it gives me pleasure to know the fear you'll live in. That is why I loitered at the Seda all these days, knowing that sooner or later you and your followers would come looking for information.

"I wanted to tell you this so that you had time to think upon it, and in the end would come willingly to me. It'll be so much easier than having to hunt you down and drag you out to such a painful end.

"There's nothing more to be said now," Ulsak said, putting on a show of being suddenly weary and bored.

"You may go. There is no need to worry now about food. Before you arrive back at your tavern, my people will deliver all the food and drink you require. There'll even be a purse of amber waiting for you, if you should need to purchase anything we have forgotten."

Ulsak saw the suspicion in Aldin's eyes. "Head bond I give that all I provide you with is wholesome."

"Why?" Aldin asked.

"To keep you safe until it is time for my people to fetch you," he replied, smiling. "Know that always my men will be watching you, and the fat one as well. We won't accept any more games between the two of you and shall find a way to warn either of you if something is amiss. I wish to keep you safe until you are needed for the sacrifice."

Ulsak rose from the divan and strode across the room to stand before Aldin.

"It is as if your fate were already ordained," he whispered. "Submit to what I have decreed, and die without pain."

Without a word Aldin motioned for his people to start for the door.

"The game is only beginning," Aldin said, feeling that the line was foolish but that he had to say something.

Ulsak laughed. "Sleep and dream of what I've told you, Aldin Larice. I know a great many things more, and I know, as well, that by the end, the nightmares you will have will bring you to me with open arms, begging for the peace I can bring you, before we drive the stake into your living body and like a broken toy you try to jam the sharpened point into your own heart to end the agony."

"You did what!"

Vush bowed low before Losa. For an Overseer, the outburst was something unheard of, for theirs was a society where calm detachment was the highest and noblest reaction to almost any news—good, bad, or indifferent.

"As I have just explained, I sold the tickets where either of them lives. We know your plan is reliable, the Shiga will not fail. Therefore, looking at the profit line, I thought it was a useless investment."

"You sold an option on all our tickets that dealt with the two of them or either one living through to the end of the game?"

"There was an aggressive bid for them, with a high profit margin," Vush explained nervously.

"How many did you sell?"

"All of them," he whispered nervously.

Losa turned away in exasperation.

"We both know they don't have a chance of surviving this festival," Vush replied. "Ulsak will see to that, so why waste the investment?"

"That's beside the point. We are dealing with probabilities here. There is a chance, small though it may be, that they might live. We've already soiled our destinies far too much with this venture. If my superior should discover our involvement . . ." He fell silent, not even wishing to contemplate what the council might say about such dealings.

"Who bought them?"

"We're not sure. It was a dummy corporation, and they picked up all five hundred thousand first-day tickets the moment I put them on the trading floor."

"Why did you do it?"

Vush could only shrug what would pass for shoulders. How could he explain that close contact to the game had seduced him as well? At first he'd been detached, but each passing day of watching the board and smelling out the trades had finally hooked him. The sell-and-purchase flurry just before Sigma's death had been the nail in the coffin. He was a market addict. The turning of billions in profits was a game that had become an obsession.

The lower beings had captured him essence and soul with the lure of betting the system and winning. Of course, he no longer even contemplated the fact that wealth held no meaning for an Overseer, since it was meaningless for them to purchase what they could not use or need.

"I saw the chance," he could only say lamely, "to turn five hundred thousand nonviable tickets into cash."

"And what the hell are we going to do with cash?" Losa asked, his voice rising to a shout.

Vush could only stand there, somewhat amazed himself at what he had just done. How could he explain the beauty of the profit they'd just made? An initial investment of a half million k's turned into two and a half billion.

"Let's just hope for your sake they don't live," Losa growled.

Vush showed his shock at such a comment. It was completely against all their training to wish such an ill event upon another being. Even the superior showed some shock at what had just escaped his lips, and he turned away in embarrassment.

"Everything else is at least ready," Losa whispered, changing the topic after his humiliating outburst.

"The moment the game ends, the claims will be presented. The holdings of every company in the Cloud, save for those belonging to the Xsarns and Gaf Koh Bukha, will be forfeit when GGC can't pay off its debt. The total collapse of the Cloud's economy will follow, and we'll be in control.

"The Shiga will be released and all evidence will point to a vindictive act by Gablona's heirs. Chaos will result from that, and in the end, their civilization will turn to us to restore order. Thus there'll be no resistance to our takeover.

"We can comfort ourselves in knowing that it was they who designed it, set it up, and implemented it. Thus we have no shadow on our destiny, and we can bring order to these beings once and for all. Let us hope that what you have done will not affect this."

No problem at all, Vush thought cheerfully, and we'll still make a fascinating profit.

"It's too bad about Gablona and Aldin though," the superior replied. "But of course we'll have nothing to do with their actual passing; that is in the hands of others."

"But of course," Vush said, nodding solemnly in agreement.

Losa turned away from his assistant. The message had come to him this morning from the Arch requesting his presence for an audience. So the old one had found out at last, Losa thought. Well, already it was too late for him to change anything, and lost in thought, he floated from the room.

chapter eleven

Stunned, Tia leaned back from the terminal and shut the system down.

So that's what Yaroslav was on to, she thought, having returned to check once again, still not quite believing the discovery she'd made earlier that morning. The parts of the puzzle meant nothing by themselves, but together they presented a dangerous picture.

It had been difficult tracing Yaroslav's path, but after several days of poring through his notes, she had at last found his access code word. From there it became a process of tracing system after system, looking to where he had cut into the com link files, since all links were recorded.

Then had come the stunning discovery. Several weeks before the game had started, a front company for the Alma Consortium had purchased fifty aging transport liners from one of Gablona's shipping firms. The document of transfer was signed by Gablona himself, while he was still in the reeducation center!

Now, why would Alma be interested in enough transports to carry nearly a million passengers?

And then the realization had come. Bukha had confirmed that the Overseers had invested heavily into the game. But why could they be so certain about some bets, and if so, what guarantees had they offered to make sure that such actions would indeed take place?

She had taken her suspicions to Bukha, and he had thought them to be so wild as to be beyond all logic.

"Granted they're betting on this," he had replied, "but the rest of your crazy ideas? Not even the Overseers would dream of such a thing. In fact, I have just sent a memo to the Arch expressing my curiosity as to their intentions, and he replied that he was just as surprised as we were."

"Do you actually believe the leader of the Overseers?" Tia had snapped.

"No, of course not. But what you're suggesting is wholesale genocide, something beyond the capability of any Overseer. And besides," he had said coldly, "how do I know you're not simply trying to implicate Corbin, or arrange for his disgrace, so that when he regains legal title to the Gablona holdings, you'll be in a position to challenge him?"

"You're playing the game as well. Remember our little purchase together, through that hidden futures market. We'd be fools not to know that it was the Overseers dumping those shares."

"You were sworn to secrecy on that," Bukha snarled, "and damn you, you'd better keep it. I pulled you in because we needed the capital. I find it interesting that you dumped your shares with GGC in order to buy the tickets, but that's your concern, not mine. Now, I don't have any more time for your insane stories."

And he had dismissed her as if she were nothing but a wild-eyed girl who had concocted a fabrication in order to get attention.

Damn them, she cursed silently. Where the hell was Yaroslav?

She knew there was only one action she could take now, since the damned Kohs, who gloried in their superior attitudes, would never listen. Turning the com link back on, she tapped into her office to relay a message to Bukha's private line.

After shutting down the unit again, she looked around the shabby apartment. From out of the half-open closet she could see Yaroslav's cat peering out at her.

Tia walked over to the kitchen alcove, pulled out the heavy bag of food she had just purchased that morning, and poured all the contents out on the floor. After jamming the filthy sink drain closed, she filled it with water.

"No litter for you," she said, looking over at the scrawny cat. "You'll have to find something in the closet, but I don't think Yaroslav will even notice."

The cat looked at her and retreated back into its hiding place.

If something was coming down from the Overseers, there was only one way to intervene now she thought, and walked out of the apartment.

"I tell you this whole thing stinks of fraud," Bukha shouted, looking down the length of the table to Zola, who eyed him nervously.

"My dear Bukha, we agreed to this meeting with you and the Xsarn to finalize the findings of our accountants. The preliminary reports are in at last. In five days all the final documents will be drawn, and all holdings from the Alexandrian game will be back with their rightful owners. That is the topic of this meeting, not your accusations."

The room seemed to be divided in half. Most of the Kohs, all shareholders in the Galactic Gaming Company, at one end of the table, with Bukha and the Xsarn at the other.

Tension had been high all morning, and for most, their attention was scarcely on the accountings of the last game but rather on the climax of the current one.

For over fifteen days there'd been no action. Both Aldin and Gablona seemed to have settled into a siege mentality, their fortresses barricaded, with no attempts made against each other. The Al'Shiga had been strangely quiet; reports came back from the offworld traders that the marketplace was empty, the locals almost in hiding.

For Zola, all was going according to plan. The following morning, the gates would be closed on all further betting, according to the lottery rules. But he was still worried. He was starting to suspect that there were information leaks within his organization, and a large block of tickets could be bought up overnight that could cause a loss to the company.

"Besides," Zola continued calmly, "you're talking about an accomplished fact. GGC Incorporated has taken in over five trillion bets so far, and there's a hell of a lot more yet to be reported into our main computer system. Over ninety-nine percent of them have already become invalid. Of course, statistically we'll have to pay some money back out, but current profit-line estimates run to nearly four trillion after expenses."

The Kohs around Zola nodded among themselves; those nearest to their leader patted him upon the back in an effusive outpouring of goodwill.

Zola leaned back while one of the Gafs next to him bent over to light one of the foot-long cigars he had taken to of late. There was the slightest of nervous twitches as he held his cigar, which he covered with a quick flourish of his hand.

"Shares in the company are now worth a quarter of a billion each per block of a thousand, a five thousand percent increase in investment. The final dividend and payout should exceed the value by over three to one. I therefore think, Bukha Koh, that you are nothing but a fearmonger, trying to frighten investors to a panic and sell out so that you can buy in on the game."

The other Kohs looked at Bukha with scorn, as if he had just made an obscene noise.

Zola turned and looked back at the group with a self-confident smile.

Bukha realized that any further comment was useless, and settled back in his chair.

"Well, there is one other problem," the Xsarn interjected, "which needs to be addressed."

"And that is?" Zola interjected lazily.

"Payment of the accountants and lawyers handling the Alexandrian case."

"I know a good payment." Vol snarled. "Once we're done

with them, let's take them all and drop them in the Hole, for the Shigs to take care of."

There was a chorus of affirmations, for as in any age, such beings were held in disdain by the more honest citizens.

"At least it'll eliminate all those damn vid ads of lawyers asking you to sue after every liner crash."

"Now, now, gentlemen," the Xsarn said, raising his upper and lower arms in an appeal for calm. "I admit to sharing the same sentiments, but it simply wouldn't be practical. They'd all file lawsuits that would keep us tied up for years. After all, they're like Dargonian lice: wipe out one crop and another will spring up to replace them."

"Wait a minute," Zola said, cutting off the debate. "You just said we've got to figure out the payments. I thought that you said the assets of the three game players would be used in the event that any of them died."

"I did," the Xsarn replied slowly.

"Sigma's dead; his holdings should be more than enough."

"But he had no holdings of any worth, and his legal team has already filed a brief to that effect."

"What the hell are you talking about?" Zola roared.

"It's simply this. I found out this morning that Sigma seems to have outguessed us all. Two days before he was taken prisoner for the game, he filed a document putting all his holdings into a trust for exactly one year. At the end of the year, if he was still alive, the trust would be turned back to him. If he was dead, the trust would be retained by the original holders."

"And who holds the trust?" Zola asked.

"The Alma Consortium."

"The Alma Consortium?" Vol roared. "That's an Overseer front!"

"Exactly. And their lawyers have already filed a brief declaring that all of Sigma's wealth is now theirs."

"This is impossible, it must be a forgery!" Zola said, coming to his feet.

"I've already checked. It's valid, and it predates the signed agreements for this game. Therefore, when Sigma signed the death waiver giving his property over to defray expenses, he was in fact signing away nothing. His money was already locked in a trust fund.

"Which brings me to the point, gentlemen," the Xsarn continued. "The heads of the accountants' and lawyers' guilds seemed to have gotten wind of this complication."

"They would, wouldn't they?" One of the Gafs snarled.

"I called this meeting to inform you that they want payment in advance before delivery of all reports and the legal signing of all documents returning our properties back to the original holders."

"In advance? Who the hell do they think they are?" Zola snapped.

"They've got us by our soft shells," the Xsarn replied. "Without payment, they'll sit on the reports, our companies will languish, and we'll lose billions more."

"The reports are already filed," Vol cut in. "I say we just seize the computers, hire different lawyers, and sort it out on our own."

"You know the code of their guild," the Xsarn said. "They'll never commit an act that could deny a brother of his fees. Every lawyer in the Cloud will be against us."

Zola threw up his hands in exasperation. "All right, how much do they want?"

"The bill comes out to twenty-one billion and some odd change."

"Twenty-one billion!" Zola choked, and for a moment everyone thought he was about to have a stroke. Gasping, he turned to the sideboard, and had to drink a triple brandy before he finally regained composure.

"But I thought it wouldn't be more than ten billion!"

"I've checked," the Xsarn said, shaking his head dejectedly. "They had a fine-print clause for quadruple overtime payments. Of course, they spent more hours on overtime than they did on the standard pay rate."

"Well, this is a hell of a mess," Zola mumbled dejectedly.

"A mess that's got to be solved now," the Xsarn replied. "Every day that the closing is delayed will amount to a loss of billions in trade."

"They want it now?" Zola asked, incredulous.

"In writing; today."

Zola looked around at his companions, who suddenly stepped back or attempted to blend into the walls.

"Then we'll just have to ante up the money from our companies," Zola said.

"But most everything we own is already locked into the last

dispute; the lawyers won't accept that," the Xsarn replied. "But they did have a suggestion."

"And that was?"

"Payment out of the funds of GGC."

Zola sat back for a moment and punched into his com link. The day after the game ended, the company would pay out the dividends based on winnings, and all the company's assets would be gone.

"We can't touch the assets until all bets have been paid off."

"They'll accept that as long as you personally guarantee a payment of ten billion up front and the remainder after the close of the game."

After dealing with the heady sums of the last two months, billions seemed like a paltry sum. At least it would keep the dogs quiet, Zola reasoned.

"Agreed," he said dejectedly. "Now tell those bastards I want the Alexandrian paperwork on our desks the moment the game ends."

The Xsarn nodded in reply and punched the prearranged message to the lawyers waiting outside, who brought in the contracts.

After they had left, followed by a variety of mumbled threats, Vol stood up and motioned for attention.

"Well, there is another alternative," he said quietly.

"And that is?"

"The game still has six days standard to go; Aldin, as we know, has next to nothing, but if Gablona should happen to die, then we'll still be able to attach his assets."

The group looked up to the Xsarn.

"I've checked his accounts," The Xsarn said quietly. "He didn't show the foresight of our dear departed friend Sigma, and all his property is still legally in his hands."

The Kohs fell quiet and looked from one to the other.

"It certainly would be a pity though if good old Corbin should die," Zola said softly, and all the Kohs around him shook their heads and mumbled in agreement.

Bukha looked around at his fellow Kohs. Could Tia have been right? he started to wonder. He'd yet to say anything directly about his concerns regarding the Overseers, for a variety of reasons. But could she have been right?

* * *

"I think you're insane, Aldin. Completely insane!"

"Yes," Mari snapped angrily. "Let's just hide here till it's over."

"Hide here?" Aldin could only shake his head in disbelief.

Ulsak's envoys had paid a visit that morning. The leader of the group was finally admitted and handed Aldin a missive from Ulsak, which stated in the politest of terms that the original deal still stood, and warning him as well that with the coming of the next dawn a special eight-day festival would start. The Ulman, the coming of the Great Darkening, had been revealed to the masses the week before, and the city would be packed with celebrants from the other five cities until the climax.

The party had left stacks of food outside the barricaded door and then departed.

Deliveries of food had come at regular intervals, just as Ulsak had promised. At first the samurai had refused to touch it, despite Ulsak's head bond, but Mari had finally reassured everyone that poisoning of food was considered the basest of crimes, fit only for cowards. In fact, what they had experienced was part of Al'Shiga tradition: the sending of food and gifts to one's victim before hunting him. All the natives did it, and great status was attached to the amount of wealth one lavished upon his intended victim.

There was even a rotting man, one that Mari assured them was of the finest grade, fit only for true connoisseurs. The Gafs, as if a challenge to their crudeness had been offered, finally snatched it up and, bearing it down to their quarters in the basement, tried it out.

Half of them had come staggering back up, retching and gasping. Those who endured the ritual swaggered up later, and fell to taunting their weak-stomached comrades, but most of them seemed a bit pale, by Gaf standards, for the rest of the morning.

"Look, Ulsak knows our hiding place, and undoubtedly so do the other groups," Aldin argued. "Ten minutes after the festival starts, we'll be under siege."

"We've been working on this place for weeks," Mari countered. "They could throw hundreds against us."

"My lord does have a point," Oishi replied, coming up to join the two behind the bar.

Aldin nodded to his bodyguard.

"This Ulsak has acted first and foremost to frighten. He hopes then that we shall be like rabbits, frozen in fear, ready to be plucked up and thrown in the sack. That was the meaning of this morning's action and the threats at the earlier meeting."

"What would you do then?" Aldin asked.

"Go on the offensive."

"What!" Mari hissed. "There are only sixty of us; there's a million of them."

"All the more reason," Oishi replied gamely, a smile lighting his features. "For it would never be expected. Always do what your foe does not expect."

"Behind these walls we could last till the game is up," Mari argued.

"They have no doubt thought of a way to get to us, and you have not thought of something else."

"And that is?"

"The game, as you call it, ends shortly. But that is only up there." Oishi pointed upward. "Down here the situation will still remain the same. You'll never get from here to the Sky Tower alive."

"And there is the other problem," Mari countered.

"That is . . ." Aldin ventured.

"Your friend Gablona."

Aldin could only grumble to himself. No matter what his plans, Gablona was still the unknown factor.

"Someone coming," Hideo barked, coming in from the guardpost by the door.

"Now what?" Aldin cursed silently. He could only hope it wasn't more Shiga with their damn rotting men. The whole place still stank from the last one.

Following Hideo, he slipped up to the door and peeked out.

A single form came up the street, slipping from doorway to doorway in the lengthening shadows of early evening.

There was something familiar about the person. Aldin watched as the stranger suddenly stepped out and started to rush up the street, and then he saw other forms step out behind him.

"Let's go!" Aldin shouted, pulling up the bar to the doorway.

Before his companions even had time to ask, Aldin was out the door, Oishi and Hideo behind him.

The stranger saw him and hesitated.

"Run!" Aldin screamed.

"Aldin!" It was a woman's voice, and she started toward him.

Then the shadows following her closed in, joined by half a dozen more from a side alleyway.

"Ronin, to me!" Hideo screamed, drawing his long sword and rushing forward.

It was over in seconds, before Aldin could even react. The dark-cloaked attackers swept in on the woman, who, seeing the threat too late, tried to rush toward the tavern.

A thin rope coiled out, the weighted end snaking around her. Hideo charged in, but suddenly more attackers materialized. With a vicious cut, Hideo dropped one, and then a second.

Aldin came forward to his aid.

"No!"

A form came up beside him and, with a vicious blow, knocked him to the ground. Aldin, terrified, started to kick out, and then saw that it was Oishi holding him down.

"Hideo!" Oishi screamed.

But it was too late. The old samurai turned and turned again, but in an instant he was swarmed under, and the blades of the assassins flickered as they slashed in the pale light of early evening.

There was the pounding of feet about them, the wild cry of more samurai pouring out of the tavern, the heavier Gafs trying to shoulder their way to the front.

But the attackers were gone, already disappearing into the side alleyways.

Aldin came to his knees. He looked over at Oishi, but already the samurai was on his feet, a look of anguish on his face.

He rushed forward to the body of his friend, a dozen feet away. With a cry, he knelt down by Hideo.

"Oishi made his choice," Zergh said, coming up to help Aldin to his feet.

Dazed, Aldin looked at his old friend.

"He might have been able to save Hideo," Zergh said quietly, "but he had to stop you from rushing in where, if recognized, you would certainly have been killed. He chose obligation over friendship." And then Zergh turned away.

Stunned, Aldin stood in the middle of the street as Oishi

came past him with unseeing eyes, bearing the body of his old comrade back into the tavern.

"Why the hell did you rush out like that?" Mari demanded, facing Aldin as he came back through the doorway.

"Because I knew who was out there. It was Tia, my niece."

Startled, Zergh turned around. "What the hell was she doing down here?"

"I don't know, but for her to try to seek me out, it must be important. But now the Shiga have her."

"Those weren't Shiga," Takashi said, the last to return from the foray.

Aldin looked down at what the samurai held in his hands. It was a strip of black cloth.

Tia was in the hands of Gablona.

"There was a moment when the one called Larice was in danger," the messenger said, trembling before the presence of Ulsak. He had been part of the ceremony that had dispatched the last ulla who had displeased the master, and he had no desire to be the next.

"And?" Ulsak asked, looking up at the man through half-lowered eyelids.

"He was stopped without harm," the messenger continued, not elaborating on who had done the stopping.

"Very good then," Ulsak replied.

"And this offworlder?"

"She was taken by Gablona's men. The one called Larice was obviously distraught—she called his name."

Could it be Larice's lover? he wondered. Perhaps there was a way this could be used.

For days he had contemplated how to take this Aldin and Gablona unharmed. Gablona was as good as in the net already, but the envoys to Larice had returned with reports of the intricate defenses that had been built. Many would die in the attack. That did not bother him though, he would expend ten thousand of his followers if need be. His only fear was that Aldin himself might die in the process. He had underestimated the man, expecting in the end that he would be resigned to his fate as any of the Al'Shiga would have been. Among his own people, if one realized that a master of the knife was hunting him, more often than not he would simply go to the great square and there await the man.

Tradition demanded then that the deathblow be a painless one, with the sharpest of blades, for one who accepted his fate. To hide would mean that a slower death was permitted. He had expected Aldin to take the painless death.

Killing him now in a tavern fight would not fit his plans at all. After all, Ulsak was the Ema, and a fitting sacrifice must be made to sanctify the moment when the two darknesses appeared. Two lives offered for the two lights—that had to be the way.

"And you say the fat one now has her?"

"Yes, Oh Great One."

Ulsak looked up at the ulla and smiled. All about him had started to call him that of late. Already they were accepting the revelation of his destiny.

He had learned one thing of this Larice. The man had the foolishness to be compassionate. Ulsak saw how concern for his own men had stayed Aldin's hand. Such a thing was weakness, and perhaps that weakness could be used.

"I want a messenger sent to those who guard Gablona. You know the man in question?"

"Yes, Oh Great One."

"Give me several moments, and then I will summon you."

The messenger, breathing an inner sigh of relief, left the presence of the leader. Out in the hallway the other ullas looked at him with some surprise, expecting that they had seen the last of him when he entered the room.

The messenger saw a stranger in the back of the group, and then had a vague recollection of having seen him before. It was the mad shaman who had suddenly appeared before the Seda some days past.

Two of the ullas, dragging the man between them, went into the audience chamber.

Ulsak looked up at them and cast a curious gaze on the ragged bundle between them.

"Why do you bring this filth into my presence?" Ulsak demanded.

"He has been making a nuisance of himself," one of the ullas said, releasing the old man and pushing him to the floor.

"In what way?"

"We keep finding him prowling about the base of the Holy of Holies, the inner sanctuary beneath the Seda."

Curious, Ulsak looked at the ragged bundle at his feet.

"Then just kill him," Ulsak said lazily.

"We can't. He is a madman, a shaman, and thus protected. Only a master may have a madman killed, and then, only in private," the ulla replied, trying not to sound dogmatic in the presence of his leader.

The old man rose to his knees and gave a long, penetrating look at Ulsak, then immediately fell flat upon his face.

"I have seen the eyes of the Ema, and thus shall I be saved," the shaman cried.

Ulsak, who had been about to order the quiet strangulation of the annoyance, stopped.

"How do you know that?" he asked. Only to those among his inner circle had he revealed his true identity.

"Is not the Seda the way of the Ema? I have come to pray before the Holy of Holies, for soon the greatness of he who shall rise upon it will be revealed," the old man cried.

"Only you as our leader can order his dispatch," one of the ullas whispered. "He's proclaimed that you were the Ema to not only our own but to the other clans as well."

Ulsak smiled softly. Did not the Ema need a prophet to call his name before the arrival? His own ullas could not do it, for it would be suspect.

Ulsak turned to the side table and sliced off the hand of a rotting man.

"Come, old man. You must be hungry." And he held forth the morsel.

The old man looked up at him with ravenous eyes and snatched the delicacy, consuming it with obvious relish.

"Get out of here," Ulsak roared at the ullas. "To think that you would even dream of harming the messenger of the Ema!"

The ullas nervously retreated, and as the door closed, Ulsak leaned over and cut open the stomach of the rotting man.

"Join me for a drink, old one," he said enthusiastically, not even noticing the suppressed retch of the shaman as the smell of the rotting man filled the room.

"So, if it isn't my darling former mistress," Gablona said lazily, looking up at Tia with half-closed eyes.

Tia turned and looked back at Hassan, who smiled knowingly at her.

"I was going to come to you next," Tia snapped, "but I couldn't find where you were hiding."

"Of course, but of course," Gablona said softly, signaling that Hassan could leave.

The assassin stood in the doorway, wishing to hear what was about to be said, acting as if Gablona's command did not matter.

The Koh looked up, and Tia, her eyes shifting from one to the other, said nothing.

"You may leave us, Hassan."

"She could be dangerous," Hassan replied smoothly. "Perhaps a guard should stay with you."

"I said you may go."

There was the faintest of smiles on Hassan's face as he bowed low, the look of defiance still on his face. Tia watched with interest, saying nothing. The door closed behind Hassan.

"I haven't seen you since the end of the Alexandrian game," Gablona said smoothly, picking up a thin sliver from a small rotting man that rested upon a side table. He speared another piece and offered it to her, and she wrinkled her nose in disgust.

"An acquired taste. Turned my stomach, too, at first, but really it's like an aged, full-bodied cheese."

He ate with his eyes closed like a true connoisseur, as if all his senses were concentrated on the repast.

"After this game is ended and I am back in my rightful place, I intend to export this delicacy. I think there's a market for it with some of the other Kohs."

"That's if you survive," Tia said.

"But of course I'll survive," Gablona replied. "I would think, my dear, that given the present circumstances, you should be more worried about your own survival."

"Come now, Corbin," Tia said meekly. "Remember, I'm also part of the Gablona clan. I was merely holding your assets until everything blew over."

"Xsarnfood!" Gablona roared. "You betrayed me to Sigma, and you threw in with that damned uncle of yours. I ought to have your ass dragged down to a Shig temple, but frankly I think I want to kill you with my own hands!"

Gablona stood up, kicking the side table over so that the rotting man fell to the floor with a sickening thump.

Tia struggled to remain calm. "Kill me now and you'll never find out why I came down here."

"Ah, yes," Gablona said. "Of course I was thinking of that

as well, so first we'll talk and then I'll kill you, unless your answers convince me otherwise."

But he still remained on his feet, his fat, chunky hands resting on the sword strapped to his waist.

Tia eyed the sword and suddenly found it difficult to suppress a laugh. Somehow the fact that Corbin Gablona had been reduced to wearing a sword seemed totally ridiculous. He was a Koh, a year ago he had hundreds of paid guards surrounding him, and now he was reduced to this. But she could see, as well, the murderous look in his narrow, slitlike eyes, and all thought of making a light comment fled.

"I came to warn the two of you that the game is fixed."

"Fixed," Gablona said, a smile lighting his face, and with a deep chuckle he sat back down.

"Fixed, you say?"

Tia nodded in reply.

"But of course it's fixed," Gablona roared. "Do you think me to be that stupid? I had it fixed from the beginning!"

Incredulous, Tia could only shake her head in disbelief.

"How do you think you fixed it?" she asked softly.

"I promised Zola an even billion up front. I also pointed out to him that if he could make certain arrangements regarding my safety from the Shiga, that such information could help with the betting."

"What could you possibly use to bribe the Shiga?" Tia asked.

"Ah, now that was a fine stroke," Gablona said. "And quite frankly, none of your damn business."

"And I suppose you really trust Zola," Tia said.

"Of course not," he snapped. "But it's more profitable for him if I live than die."

"Not anymore."

"What's that?" Gablona asked, stirring from his complacency.

"Sigma outwitted all of you. You and Zola figured that with Sigma dead, the lawyers would be paid from his estate, and then there'd be no reason for you to be hunted. But Sigma signed his holdings over to a blind trust before he was captured. He died penniless. The Kohs need twenty billion, and if you die, that debt will no longer be their concern."

"The bastards, they wouldn't think of it!"

"If there's a way, they'll do it," Tia said coldly.

Gablona's eyes suddenly grew narrow. "If you knew this, then why were you going to Aldin first? You don't give a damn about me, you never did."

"I was going to come to you next."

"That's a lie," Gablona roared. "There was something you were going to tell your precious uncle, and you were going to keep me in the dark!"

"All right," Tia snapped. "We've got evidence that the Overseers are arranging the game as well!"

Gablona was silent for a moment. "To what end?"

"If certain events came to pass down here, they'd clean up on the bets, bankrupting GGC."

"That's Zola's company, not mine," Gablona growled. "If they bankrupt him, that's fine with me. In fact, I'll cheer them on."

"You don't understand," Tia shouted, frustrated with his self-centered interests. "Almost all the assets of the Cloud have been tied into the company. They agreed to sign a financial liability clause stating that if there wasn't enough money in the pot, that additional winnings would be paid for by the shareholders' personal fortunes."

"So what?" Gablona laughed. "Damn fools were crazy to do it. If the Overseers clean them out, then more power to them."

"But the Overseers are playing the bet that either one of you, or both of you, will die!"

For the first time Gablona looked concerned. For a moment he sat in silence. Turning away, he reached down and yanked one of the feet off the rotting man that lay splattered on the floor and munched the delicacy in a detached, thoughtful way.

"Are they bribing the Shiga then?"

"It's the only conclusion we could reach. They seem to be gearing up for some sort of festival."

"Ah, yes, the festival. Something about an eclipse. One of the blues already told me about it. They'll take Aldin then for the sacrifice, and the game is over! But I've made my arrangement for that as well, through Hassan."

"How's that?"

"Hassan has been my contact to one of the Shig masters; we've got a guarantee. Part of the deal is that one of my men gets to strike the deathblow."

"Why should that matter?" Tia asked wearily, not believing what she was hearing.

"Because, my dear, the biggest betting arrangement in history is being played out. I've brought several hundred thousand tickets and a major block of them call for me to kill Aldin. If Hassan strikes the blow, I get the credit and win several hundreds of billions as a result!"

Gablona actually beamed with pride as he revealed the foresight behind his planning.

"Of course, with Aldin dead, everything will be finished— the game's over, and I go back up the Skyhook to claim my winnings and start afresh. If the Overseers have wiped out my other Kohs in the process, what concern is it of mine? The game will be over, and I'm a free man."

"The game is not going to be over, damn it!" Tia snapped. "This is why I was going to Aldin first. He'd at least listen to logic. The Shigs will take him, and you as well."

"I've already paid them off," Gablona said smugly.

"With what? Money? They don't give a damn about money. It's power only they're after, and somehow the Overseers have offered them far more than you'll ever be able to scrape up."

"First off," Gablona said, "I can outbribe any damn Overseer in the Cloud, I made my deal with them as well. They asked me to sign a trade agreement for some of my ships the day before I was sprung from the reeducation camp. They said it'd be a goodwill gesture of trade between us. You know and I know they don't do business with us. I'll simply threaten to blackmail that bastard Losa with the information that he's dabbling in our financial concerns. I did business with them once, I'll do it again. As for the Shiga, I'll just send Hassan back out and he'll match anything those do-gooders can come up with as a counteroffer."

With a sigh of exasperation Tia sank back in her chair. So the damn fool *had* signed over the ships. He didn't even realize they were going to frame him with it.

"Go ahead," she grumbled, "let them kill you. Frankly, I really don't care at this point. This whole damn thing has gone totally insane."

Gablona eyed her carefully, and Tia, remembering her former days with him, realized that already he was plotting something else.

"What is it?" she asked wearily.

"Oh, something really quite simple. Knowing your uncle,

he's a man who places honor and family above most anything else."

Tia suddenly felt a cold chill.

"Look, Corbin dear," she said quickly, "we can work something out between us. After all, you always did say I was the best mistress you ever had."

"Past tense, my dear, past tense," Gablona said. "I was just wondering though what Aldin might say if I offered to meet him in order to exchange you for something else."

"Such as?" Tia whispered.

"Himself."

chapter twelve

"This is madness," Oishi hissed.

Aldin looked at his companion and shook his head.

"She's my niece, I've got to do it," he said.

"I don't care about her," the samurai replied evenly. "It's you I'm responsible for."

"And in the end I'm responsible for her. If you were me, would you do any different?"

"I would remember my obligation to my clan, to those who serve me."

Aldin turned with a smile and, reaching out, rested his hand on the samurai's shoulder.

A faint smile crossed Oishi's lips, and he lowered his head, not able to argue with this man.

"Your men are in place?" Aldin asked.

"Don't worry, we'll still get you out of this," Oishi said gruffly.

"You better," Aldin said, trying to put on an act of bravado.

He started to walk out into the street, but a hand came up, grabbing him by the arm. Turning, he saw that he was looking into Mari's eyes.

"Come, come," Aldin said quietly, "time for us to be off."

The woman drew closer, and Aldin suddenly realized that her hair was freshly washed, a light scent of lavender wafting on the air. Her eyes held his for a moment, and for the first time, he admitted to himself that he was somehow drawn to her. For so long now she had just been Mari, quick to argue with him or anyone else who came near, so that even the Gaf berserkers had learned to give her a wide berth. But now he saw the vulnerability underneath it all. A vulnerability that he realized was caused by him, and the danger he now faced.

They stood silent for a moment, their hands lightly touching. The samurai drew back, while the Gafs coughed and growled self-consciously.

"Take care of yourself, you stupid bastard," Mari whispered.

"Is that it?" Aldin asked with a mild tone of self-pity. "You certainly have a way with words."

"You damned fool." She drew him close, wrapping her arms about him. Aldin felt the lightest of kisses on his neck, and then the brush of lips across his.

"We'll get you out; I'll bash that fat bastard if he so much as touches you."

"Certainly a romantic send-off." Aldin laughed self-consciously.

Mari smiled up at him, her eyes damp, and then abruptly turned away. With a curse she pushed one of the hulking Gafs aside. Zergh drew close to her and she buried her head in his chest.

"Here goes," Aldin whispered to himself, and he stepped out of the alleyway and started for the door. Never had he felt so alone as he did at that moment.

The street was empty, wrapped in shadows and fog. Sound was muffled by the swirling blanket of gray, but still he could hear the deep, steady rumble of the drums, as in the distance the Al'Shiga gathered in the Great Square before the Seda, the drums calling the faithful on this first morning of the ceremony. The fog had been a help at least. After slipping out of the tavern, Oishi had dispatched the yellow robe that had been watching the back door, and thus they had gotten by the guards unseen, taking out the one who watched Gablona's place as well.

There was a deep, almost primordial feeling to the twilight before the dawn. The fog was all-encompassing, as if the entire world were a grayness, the void before the coming of light, while the drums were not only heard but felt, matching the pulsing of his heart.

The shadows of buildings loomed to either side, and Aldin felt as if from every window slit unseeing eyes were watching, judging, and deciding if here was someone worth the time to kill.

A deeper darkness stood to his left, the walls of the black house reaching above him, and he knew that here there was no fevered imagination stoking his fears. He was being watched. A shadow fluttered in a window and drew away.

Would Corbin simply strike him now? He found himself almost wishing that he would, ending the suspense and the fear. For if he feared anything, it was that after nearly two score days on this world, Corbin had been seduced by its naked brutality and would prefer the techniques of the Shiga to the simpler brand of murder practiced by the Kohs.

The door was open; they were waiting for him.

Aldin realized at that moment that if ever he was performing a courageous act, it was now. But if it was so courageous, he wondered, why was his heart thundering and his legs turning to jelly? Suddenly he was afraid not only of Corbin and what might happen, but also of the far more mundane fact that in another couple of seconds he might lose control of his bladder, or just simply pass out.

Hoping that the cloak he wore to keep off the morning chill would hide his trembling legs, Aldin made for the door.

Ominously the entry corridor was empty. Nerving himself, he stepped inside.

"Bravo, Aldin," a voice called out of the darkness. "Bravo indeed, worthy of a vid performance."

Corbin stepped out of the shadows. "Heroic uncle comes to save innocent niece from the clutches of the villain."

"I've met my end of the deal," Aldin said weakly. Try as he could, his voice was pitched too high, so that his words sounded like the squeak of an excited adolescent.

"Now, now," Corbin replied, beckoning for Aldin to follow him into the back chambers, "all in good time. But for the moment let me again be the gracious host to my old vasba and my former mistress."

"Let her go now," Aldin replied, trying to sound forceful, "or the deal is off." And he took a step backward.

"I don't think you have much choice," Gablona growled, and he pointed to the door behind Aldin.

An assassin had slipped in from the street behind Aldin. A naked blade in his hand was poised at Aldin's back.

"I think that if you tried to back out, you'd find one more orifice than your body was designed for."

Gablona stopped for a moment, chuckling at his own wit. "Come, I think for health reasons it would be better to follow me."

Aldin felt the blade nick through his cloak. He stepped forward and followed Gablona into the heart of the fortress.

"What the hell is going on?" Zola shouted, punching up the viewscreen. The drink he'd been about to offer his visitor lay spilled upon the floor. He'd expected yet another unpleasant meeting with the Koh everyone had now nicknamed Cassandra, but before their conversation had even started, a paging report had sounded, diverting his attention.

Bukha came around the desk to stand behind Zola.

Zola called in a screen command, and instantly the printed text gave way to a grid coordinate. On the screen were two blips of light side by side.

"Aldin and Gablona are together," Bukha said quietly.

Zola punched in another command and the scale of the screen shifted. Still the two blips were right on top of each other. "Damn it," he said, "they're practically sitting in each other's laps!" He watched the screen and saw no shifting or movement. "Obviously they're not fighting. What the hell is going on?"

"I'd say offhand," Bukha commented lazily, picking up a bottle of muscatel from the sideboard and pouring a replacement drink, "that they seem to be talking."

"Impossible," Zola snapped.

"Impossible, maybe, but nevertheless they aren't moving about, the way they would if there was a fight. But what about the others?"

Zola nodded and punched in another command. The scale of the screen shifted, zooming back to cover an area of several blocks.

"Aldin's guards and Sigma's Gafs seem to be spreading out around the building, but curious . . ."

Zola's voice dropped off.

"What is it?"

"Just that I see only ten guards for Gablona."

"Curious indeed," Bukha said quietly, and walking past the screen, he settled back into his seat.

"Well, I did come here to discuss a certain situation."

Zola, with his eyes still on the screen, merely grunted.

"Do I have your attention?"

"Of course, of course," Zola said absently.

"I just wanted to warn you that from my latest information, you, and in fact the entire economy of the Cloud, will be bankrupt."

"What, what was that?" Zola replied, his attention still fixed on the screen.

"Damn it, listen to me," Bukha suddenly roared, and standing up, he swept the screen off Zola's desk, so that it fell to the floor and shattered in a sizzling shower of sparks.

"Now what the hell did you do that for!"

"You've got to listen to me!"

With a snarl of defiance Zola swung around in his chair and punched the paging button. "My monitor just got knocked out," he snapped. "Damn it, find another one and bring it in here right away."

Releasing the button, he looked up at Bukha.

"My people will bill you for the damages," Zola said briskly. "Now state your business, then get the hell out of here."

Exasperated, Bukha slammed his drink down on Zola's desk, spilling the contents. "You've been had," he snarled. "I don't give a damn about you. But I've got to stop this, otherwise, come next week, the Overseers will control the economic wealth of the Cloud. I'm not tied into it, but if they hold the majority, they'll be able to squeeze the rest into their fists before another year standard is out. And damn it all, it's your fault!"

"What? What are you talking about?" Zola demanded, his attention finally fixed on what Bukha was saying.

"Listen closely," Bukha said with deliberate slowness. "The Overseers are playing your game!"

"Playing the game? You mean the lottery?"

"Exactly."

The color drained from Zola's face. "How?"

"They set up some dummy companies. Now tell me, how many valid tickets are still out there?"

"What kind? There're tens of millions of tickets floating around that can still pay off. Hundreds of billions were sold after Sigma died, but payoffs on those will be low, only in the thousands."

"You don't even know!" Bukha shouted.

"There was never a cause for worry," Zola said defensively. "My probability expert pointed out that the more tickets sold, the greater the chance that the results would fall into the probable average."

"So you haven't kept track of those tickets sold on the first day."

"How could we, there were trillions sold!"

"Well, I'll tell you then," Bukha snapped.

"That's privileged information. Only the stockholders had access and you're not a stockholder."

"But one of your ex-stockholders did some research for me."

Zola sat back in his chair.

"That bitch," he said. "Well, it serves her right to have sold short. I thought she was a fool selling that stock back to me, and now I know it."

"She's the only one who will ever get any profit out of this venture. Did you ever stop to think *why* she sold short?"

Zola fell silent. He had been gloating that Tia had sold her shares to him for ten billion. She was giving up a dividend of fifty billion as a result. No matter that he had used company assets to pay her—that could be buried easily enough with a couple of false entries about payouts once the game was ended.

"Because," Bukha continued, "in ninety-six hours GGC will be belly-up."

"Tell me," Zola said, his nervousness suddenly apparent.

"As near as I figure, there are still a couple of hundred possible outcomes over the next four days."

"Correct."

"The full payoff will only occur, though, if tickets also show a bet that Sigma would die on day fifteen."

"Of course, of course."

"Well, at this very moment there's a block of tickets out

there held by several betting syndicates. These tickets all show Sigma dying on day fifteen."

"How many?"

"In the tens of millions. Now, if your so-called probability norm was followed, there should only be a couple of hundred thousand probable winning tickets still out there."

The reality started to sink in.

"Tell me the rest," Zola said meekly.

"Tia managed to figure out that these syndicates hold blocks of tickets ranging from a quarter of a million up to five million on one of the probable outcomes that could happen over the next several days."

"I think I'm going to be sick," Zola whispered.

"Sick? You better start thinking suicide," Bukha snapped.

"But we've got trillions of katars in assets!"

Despite what he was hearing, Zola could not help but show some pride when he mentioned the amount. It was ten times what any Koh had ever controlled before.

"Well, you're going to need all of it," Bukha snarled. "The syndicates are fronts for the Overseers. If one of several of these probability outcomes occur, the ones the Overseers are betting on, your little firm will owe them an amount ranging from three trillion to ten trillion katars."

Zola sat in the chair with a numbed, glazed-eyed look.

"And remember," Bukha said with an almost vindictive tone, "any stockholder at the time the game ends, or after the seventy-fifth game day, will have his personal assets made liable if the company should not be able to meet its obligations. The Overseers insisted on that clause in the agreement not to interfere, and in your rush for money none of you ever thought about the reasons behind it."

"They'll own the Cloud," Zola whispered hoarsely.

Bukha fixed Zola with a vicious stare. "You walked right into their trap."

"If you had told me yesterday, we could have dumped out of the company before the clause took effect."

Bukha was silent.

"Why didn't you tell me!" Zola screamed.

"Because you would have turned it to your advantage and not acted for the benefit of us all."

"What can we do?" Zola asked weakly.

Bukha leaned forward and smiled. "Make sure that the two below live, or die in an unexpected way."

Zola swung about in his chair and punched the pager.

"Get Kurst now!" he screamed. "And damn it, where's my other screen?"

Zola turned back to face Bukha, and already the self-assured look had returned. "Now I guess we should figure out which probability would be best to our advantage."

"Brilliant, absolutely brilliant," Blackie mumbled. Kurst could only beam with pride. The information he had brought was simply priceless. With a smile she rose from her desk and took the short walk down the corridor and out onto the trading floor.

The buy orders were out in seconds. Apparently the market already knew that Aldin and Gablona were together, in the middle of Gablona's lair. Trading was brisk, with six-hour options on first-day tickets calling for Aldin to die by Gablona fetching up to five hundred thousand a share. But when Blackie's order went out, the representatives of the Alma syndicate were nevertheless quick to notice and to counterbuy in turn.

Within minutes, tens of billions in options were exchanging hands on the trading floor.

"So nice of you to drop by," Gablona said, settling into the chair across from Aldin. "Just like old times, Koh and loyal vasba getting together for a drink."

Aldin was silent, nervously watching the assassin who stood to one side.

Gablona, noticing Aldin's discomfort, waved for the assassin to step out of the room.

"So, have you been enjoying our little stay down here?" Gablona asked smoothly.

"Look, Gablona," Aldin said, "get to the point."

"Gablona Koh," Corbin snapped back coldly. "Remember my title and your social rank."

"Corbin," Aldin replied slowly, "the title goes to those who deserve it. For generations the word Koh was linked to men of honor, to men who understood the code that only through integrity could we keep the economic system of the Cloud intact. You've debased it, cheapened it. My father served your father, as did his father before him. But you've changed all that forever."

"Are you quite done?" Gablona laughed.

Aldin suddenly realized to his surprise that his nerves had been steadied by the outburst. Finally after all these years he'd spoken his mind to Gablona, and the release had made him feel strangely cold, as if detached from what he knew might occur in the next few minutes.

"You realize of course that we're both being played by the Shiga."

"You perhaps," Corbin replied smoothly. "Ever met Ulsak?" Aldin could only shake his head with disgust.

"He introduced me to their delicacies," Corbin said, "and to some of their other practices as well."

"What did he want with you?" Aldin asked.

"Oh, only an offer. A guarantee, if you will. Deliver you to him, and I get their agreement to have this place unhindered when the game is finished."

"And you actually believed that?"

"I made it worth his while. Oh, there was quite the bidding for you. Now, my friends the blues are still enraged over that foolish little incident on the first day. I had quite the bidding war going between the two. But finally Ulsak made a little sweetener for the deal."

"Go on, enlighten me."

"He agreed to let me kill you and thus make a rather interesting profit on the side."

"How could your killing me affect . . ." Aldin began, then fell silent.

"Exactly," Gablona said with a grin. "I don't have any tickets with you dying by the Shiga. But I did have someone buy up blocks of tickets with my killing Sigma and then you. Now it's all a question of when. I've only got fifty valid tickets for you dying on this game day or the next. But if I hold off for four days, I'll have a thousand. Hold off till the next-to-last day of the game, and I've got two thousand. And finally I own ten thousand tickets calling for your death on the last day. So, you see, I stand quite an increase in the profit line by keeping you alive for just three more standard days. I'll come out of this little affair with billions in profits, and Ulsak agreed to it all."

Aldin could only look away with disgust.

"So eat hearty, my friend," Gablona said, laughing while pointing out a table spread with a variety of Shiga delicacies. "Ulsak even provided me with some confiscated brandy. Fine stuff. I suggest you make yourself at home. The festival should be starting about now, and our friends will be by to pick you up."

"Release the girl," Aldin said coldly. "At least fulfill that promise that you made to me. You said you'd let her go if I surrendered."

Gablona settled back into his chair, a broad smile lighting his features. "I lied."

"He's been in there nearly an hour," Mari whispered, looking around apprehensively, for the fog was starting to burn away.

"He said not to move till the girl was out," Oishi replied.

Suddenly the distant rumble of the drums fell silent, there was a faint brightening to the sky, and the sun broke through the early-morning haze.

A horn sounded in the distance.

Mari grabbed Oishi by the sleeve. "Damn it, do something, now!"

"Now let me guess," Gablona said. "I don't think that you'd be so stupid as to walk in here without a plan for your people to get you out."

"What makes you think that?" Aldin replied nonchalantly, as he picked about the tray of meats Gablona had offered, trying to find something that didn't look too disgusting.

"It's what I would have done."

"I doubt that. You wouldn't have done what I just did, not even if it was your own mother held prisoner."

"My mother," Gablona barked. "Let me tell you about my mother. If the Shigs had her, within a week she'd have turned them around and been made their queen. But as I was saying, I wouldn't suggest that your people come in here and try to cut you out. For tickets or no tickets, you wouldn't get out of this room alive."

"I assumed that, but what about Tia?"

"Still the girl. The way you're acting you'd think she was your mistress rather than your niece."

"You're disgusting," Aldin snapped.

"I know," Corbin replied, his one-hundred-and-thirty-five kilo frame shaking as he laughed.

"All right, I think it's about time anyhow. Let's fetch her."

Corbin picked up a small bell by his chair and rang it. Seconds later the door behind him opened, and Tia, looking rather worse for the wear, was pushed into the room by one of Corbin's guards.

"I think you better stay," Corbin commanded of the assassin. "After all, we wouldn't want the odds to be two to one in here. Might upset the betting upstairs."

Aldin rose to his feet and went over to Tia's side.

"What the hell are you doing here?" Tia cried, and without being told, she suddenly realized what Aldin must have done.

For the first time since her childhood Aldin saw his niece's eyes start to fill up.

"You stupid idiot," she said, wiping away a tear. "You know whatever he offered would be a lie."

"I know," Aldin said quietly. "But if I hadn't, I never could have lived with myself." And he put his arms around her.

"Did he hurt you?" Aldin asked.

"Who, him? He wouldn't have the guts to touch me."

"Now, now," Corbin drawled. "There was a time when you rather enjoyed the way I touched you."

"Filth," Tia snapped. "I had more fun playing with a block of ice than I ever had with you."

For a second Aldin feared that she had pushed him too far. There was a flaring of anger in Gablona's eyes, but he merely turned away, struggling visibly for control.

"Rather than simply have you poisoned," he said slowly, "I think I'll give you to the Shiga instead."

Aldin felt as if he were going to lose control, that he would simply have it out here and now and, with luck, take Gablona with him. The Koh, as if sensing his mood, stepped back several paces.

Suddenly the doorway that led back out to the front of the building swung open, and one of Gablona's assassins entered the room.

"Ah, my friend." Gablona laughed. "Are the Shiga here for their package?"

The assassin nodded in reply.

"Where's Hassan?"

"Detained," the assassin replied. Suddenly Gablona realized that he did not recognize this man.

The double door was pushed open and a file of yellow Shiga entered the room, all of them cloaked in the robes of their order.

Without a word they surrounded Aldin, pushing Tia aside.

"Oh, take the girl too," Gablona said nervously, not sure of what was happening, still looking at what he thought should be one of his assassins. "Tell your lord Ulsak that she's a gift from me, a little extra dividend to show my friendship."

"You bastard," Tia screamed. "If the Kohs ever hear of this, that a family head murdered me, a Koh in my own right, they'll never forgive you."

"Memories can be erased with enough money," Corbin said, trying to hide his fear. From out beyond the doorway he heard the sound of struggling and a muffled cry in the barbaric tongue that his assassins still used among themselves.

Several of the yellow robes surrounded Aldin and then the girl, while Gablona stepped back into the corner of the room.

Four of the men broke away from the group and started toward Gablona.

"Where are my guards?" he shouted.

"Dead," one of them whispered. "Ten of them were nothing for us."

With a movement so swift that it was almost a blur, one of the yellows reached to his headband and pulled out a coil of wire. The wire snaked out, looping over Gablona's head.

Screaming with terror, Gablona fell to his knees, desperately struggling to pull the razorlike strand loose from his throat. The steel bit in, the skin about his jugular pulled so taut that the slightest pressure would cause the skin to rupture, spilling out his life.

"You're going on a journey as well," one of the yellows snarled. "It's time we all visited Ulsak."

Aldin and Tia were pushed to the door. Coming past Gablona, Aldin almost felt a touch of pity. The man was half choking, his eyes bulging in their sockets from the strain and the terror.

"I tried to warn you," Aldin said coldly, but before he could say another word one of the yellows cuffed him with the back of his hand, nearly knocking Aldin to the floor.

Down the darkened corridor they were led, and then out into

the brightness of early dawn. The air was still cool, faint wisps of morning mist drifting past overhead.

Around them were several dozen yellows, who looked nervously up and down the street.

"Let's move," the one leading Aldin commanded. "The blues still want these two."

At a near run the party started out. Gablona staggered in the middle of the group, his captor having attached a long pole to the garrote handles and then passing his prisoner off to one of his men.

The group made its way down the street. The two yellows leading the way suddenly slowed, as if sensing that something was not right. Several shattered barrels lay in the middle of the alley, the paths covered from one end to the other with the spilled contents. The reek of liquor filled the air.

"These weren't here when we passed," one of the Shiga said cautiously, going over to kick one of the barrels aside.

Suddenly there was a flash of light and a thunderclap roar.

The lead warrior, screaming, staggered back, his robes drenched with flames, half his companions on the ground, writhing in agony.

"Tia, down!" Aldin screamed, diving for the pavement.

As he rolled into the gutter, he looked up and saw his guard turning, blade drawn, coming straight at him.

The man was going to kill him now, Aldin realized, trying to kick himself backward out of the Shiga's reach. The warrior took another step and then was slammed backward as the snap of a catapult was heard. Another half-dozen bolts cracked out from the corner building. With a wild shout the door was flung back, and, with Oishi in the lead, the samurai swarmed out.

Their blades flashed in the morning light, sweeping and cutting as they advanced.

A Gaf berserker leaped over Aldin and, with a backhanded blow, finished off the yellow that had been brought down by the bolt.

There was another explosion, this time to the rear of the column. Aldin sat up and saw a dozen Shiga down on the ground, their shattered bodies pouring blood from half a hundred wounds.

Aldin looked up, and from an upper window another projectile, a heavy, five-gallon jug, arched out, a sputtering fuse marking its path.

"Down," Aldin screamed.

The jug disappeared in a blinding flash, knocking the rear of the column flat.

From out of a side alleyway farther up the street, more Gafs appeared, screaming hysterically, Zergh at their head.

The narrow street was aswarm with men and Gafs. Aldin felt hands grabbing him by the armpits, and he came back up to his feet, several samurai standing about him, beaming with delight. He saw Tia crawling out from under a Shiga corpse, her cloak and trousers soaked with blood, a dagger in her hand, which she had obviously used. As quickly as it had started, the ambush was finished. The last of the assassins were stunned by the flame, explosions, and surprise, and had died without inflicting a single casualty. One Gaf had been lost, but the rest were elated and now danced about, shouting with glee that their blades had tasted blood.

But there was a new component to the plan that he had not thought of.

"Gablona! Get him!" Aldin cried.

The Koh lay in the middle of the street, floundering about like a fish out of water. The assassin who had been leading him lay slumped against a wall, a catapult bolt driven clear through his body.

Seiji approached the Koh and, grabbing hold of the staff, pulled Gablona to his feet. The skin about his throat had been cut from the pressure of the garrote and a trickle of blood started to run down the front of his silken shirt.

Gablona, feeling the warmth, felt about his neck and, with a strangled gurgle of fear, raised his bloodied hands up before his eyes.

Aldin came up before Gablona.

"More than we bargained for," Oishi said grimly, looking with disdain at Gablona.

Aldin was silent, as if making a decision.

"Twist the garrote but a bit more," Oishi said coldly, "and you're rid of him."

Aldin looked from Oishi to Tia and then back to the Koh.

"What should we do, Tia?" he asked.

"I'm tempted to choke the life out of him myself," she replied with a chilling laugh.

Corbin extended his hands, gurgling pitifully.

"I remember Kira, the coward. He had that same look before I took his head," Oishi snarled with contempt.

Aldin continued to stare at Corbin without moving.

"We better get moving," Mari shouted, coming up to join the group. "Takashi just came in and reported that the blues have stormed the tavern, and now they're really mad. They'll be coming here next."

"Do you wish the pleasure of the kill?" Oishi asked, pulling the garrote handles free from the pole. "Or should I twist the life out of him now?"

Tears coursed down Gablona's face, and he held his hands up to Aldin, imploring him for mercy. The act drew jeers of contempt from the samurai. Without a word Aldin stepped forward and took the garrote handles from Oishi. Gablona's breath came in short wheezing gasps.

"It would take but half a twist," Aldin said. "And when I think of what you'd given Tia over to . . ."

He turned the handles ever so slightly, and Gablona let out a half-strangled shriek of fear.

With a snort of disgust Aldin turned away and let the handles drop.

Gasping, the Koh fell to his knees and pulled the garrote free. Sobbing, he fell forward, his breath coming in deep, shuddering groans.

There was a murmur of disappointment from the samurai and Gafs.

"I don't understand," Oishi said in confusion. "He's been trying to kill you down here; moments ago he betrayed you and your niece. And now you do this. It's not wise, my lord, to let such an enemy live."

Gablona looked up at Oishi, his eyes filled with hatred.

"I have my reasons," Aldin snapped. "Now let's move!"

With a barked command, Oishi turned away, pointing the way back to the building that they had taken earlier at swordpoint and from which they had launched their surprise attack.

Aldin looked quickly around. The ambush had gone off perfectly. He had counted on the fact that Gablona would betray him and not release Tia. He had counted, as well, on the belief that the Koh would not kill him outright and either sell him to Ulsak or keep him alive for later use. The barrels and bombs were to be used in storming the citadel. What had surprised them all was the arrival of the yellows, but Oishi had obviously adapted the plan to take care of them. In fact they had made it easier by bringing Aldin and Tia out into the open. The broken barrels had been ignited with the first bomb, and the possible retreat backward was shattered with the others.

It had taken days to boil off the hundreds of gallons of sulfurous water for the first ingredient, and digging in the tavern's privy provided the saltpeter. They had used half their stockpile in this the first attack.

They'd broken all the rules of the Hole, using projectiles and explosives to kill Shiga. If they had not been united against them before, they would most definitely be so now. But already he was thinking on that path as well.

"Let's go," Mari shouted, anxiously pulling at Aldin's sleeve.

"Someone's coming," one of the samurai warned, and pointed up the alleyway.

From around the corner a single man appeared, blood pouring from a slash across his cheek.

It was Hassan.

"You damned fool," Gablona roared. "What happened?"

Hassan approached the group, walking right past the samurai, who held their blades up, ready to strike.

"We were betrayed," he said, speaking to Gablona as if the rest were not even there.

"By whom?" Aldin asked.

"Who else? Ulsak. I, and the twenty men you sent with me for a parley, were met just outside the foreign quarter where they jumped us. All my men were killed. I alone fought my way out and tried to get back here to warn all of you."

Aldin looked at the man. "The Shiga use poison blades." He pointed at the wound. "You should be dead."

"Oh, this," Hassan replied smoothly, reaching up and dabbing the blood as if aware of the injury for the first time. "A yellow picked up one of our blades and tried to use it on me."

Hassan looked about the group.

"I guess I should surrender to you," he said evenly, and reaching into his belt, he pulled out his blade and handed it hilt first toward Oishi.

"I'd rather be your prisoner and get out of this alive than wait for the Shiga to get me."

Oishi looked coldly at Hassan, not believing a word he had heard.

"Take him with us," Aldin said. "His skills might be useful. Now let's get out of here." And planting a kick on Gablona's backside, he pushed the Koh.

"For what you've done, the entire Shiga will be after you." Gablona gasped.

"They're after your ass as well," Aldin snapped.

In the distance a horn sounded, and then another, and another. The Shiga would soon find out their sacred laws had been violated, on this, the start of their festival, and Aldin felt a cold wave of fear. If they were worked up before, he could only imagine the frenzy that would come now.

"So this is the price of your agreement?" Aabec of the Isma said coldly, his blue robe fluttering as he gazed about at the carnage.

Ulsak was withdrawn, almost distant, as he walked among the corpses of his followers. After rolling one over with his foot, he squatted down to examine the wounds.

"Blast wounds," Ulsak said softly.

"How?" Tores Ser of the Bengada sect shouted. "We've never allowed explosives on the Hole, everything coming down is monitored in agreement to that. We train without such things in order to prevent those above from ever suspecting or learning to fear us."

"They made it themselves," Ulsak replied.

"And look at this," Aabec stated, pointing to the catapult bolt that protruded from a Gaf body.

Ulsak nodded grimly. "They've brought their little game down here and brought their own rules as well."

"Our followers will ask questions," Aabec whispered, coming up to the other rulers. "They've been taught that such things bring instant death."

"We'll think of something," Ulsak replied, and the others nodded. After all, wasn't that what their religion was all about, a game of deception to keep the faithful in line?

"Then we agree on the rest?" Ulsak asked.

The others fell silent.

"You should have just killed them out of hand," Aabec suddenly stated, and the others nodded in agreement. "We could have had them both dead a hundred times over."

"But I did not want it so," Ulsak snapped in reply.

"And why not?" Tores Ser inquired.

"Because the two could not die until the final ceremony."

"I suspect you haven't told all," Tores Ser said menacingly.

"Suspect all you want, but in this we must be united."

Tores Ser said nothing, but Ulsak could see the suspicion in his eyes—a suspicion the others obviously shared.

"We've heard the ravings of this shaman," Aabec said coldly, looking over at Ulsak. "Heard a rumor as well that you actually met with him and did not stop his mad ramblings."

"Tell me," Nargla of the red Sutar sect asked quietly, "do you intend to call yourself the Ema?"

Ulsak merely looked at the other masters and smiled.

"Follow me in this. Soon I can reveal the rest to you. I asked you to hold back your men from killing the offworlders, and you agreed as we always have when a master makes a request of another," he said evenly. "If there is failure, I shall take the blame."

There was a murmur of interest from the others. They had their various rivalries for power, to be sure. But the tradition of a hundred generations had shown the masters that it was through cooperation with each other that their own power was maintained in balance. But Ulsak had been different, trying to somehow grasp for something more.

They all shared the same thought—undoubtedly this man was going to proclaim himself as the Ema, and as such demand their allegiance to him. But of course such a thing was impossible, since only a madman would dare to claim the title.

The other masters looked one to another and then back to Ulsak, and nodded in reply.

"We start the hunt at once," Ulsak stated, fixing each in turn with his gaze.

"I shall section off the foreign quarter first, and then the city around it. Your people are to be pulled out of here and back to your own cities. I then want a cordon set up completely around the outer edge of the wild jungle region, so that if they try to slip out, they can't get past you and then on into the cultivated regions beyond. We haven't much time, they must be found before the Ulman."

"There're a million places they could hide in this city alone," Aabec replied.

"If need be, I'll burn the entire region to the ground," Ulsak snarled. "For in a brief time none of us shall have need of it, ever again."

And those around him looked back and forth to each other. So the rumors were true; perhaps there was a way off the Hole, after all. He had asked their cooperation with a vague promise of power undreamed of, but if he could indeed get them off, then that meant he was the Ema, and they in turn would have to submit.

One by one the masters turned away without further comment until only Ulsak stood alone gazing at the corpses about his feet.

chapter thirteen

Aldin came up to the window and looked out to where Oishi was pointing.

It was a scene out of a nightmare. The night sky was illuminated from horizon to horizon with flames. From their vantage point overlooking the great square, streams of foreign refugees filled the side streets, their few possessions lashed to carts, wagons, and overladen wheelbarrows. Others staggered beneath the weight of their packs, struggling to move forward.

The flames that had started late the day before in the foreign quarter had quickly spread even into the yellow section, but the inhabitants, if anything, seemed to revel in the destruction. Aldin had actually seen some of them, carrying torches, toss the burning brands into buildings in their own quarter.

The air was rent with the roar of the conflagration; explosions, as houses and fortresses burst into flames; and the high, thin screams of the terrified merchants.

There was an insane randomness to it all. Groups of merchants would finally work up the nerve and rush out from the shelter of an alleyway about to be engulfed in flames. Approaching the perimeter of yellow Shiga, they would slow. Shiga warriors would surround the group. After several minutes most would pass. But others would be cut down on the spot, while still others were herded away.

Some groups of merchants would try to charge through, but none ever made it to the Skyhook, a trail of bodies the only sign of their passing. Perversely, as quickly as they fell, other merchants would fall upon their bundles of goods, even as their comrades were being dispatched.

"Anyone they even suspect of being us is singled out," Oishi said.

"I never thought it would ever sink to this," Aldin whispered.

"Gablona, come here and look at this," Aldin hissed, and stepping back, he pushed the Koh up to the window.

Gablona was silent, his pale face drawn with fear; he had yet to recover from the fright of his capture and the subsequent chase.

The route Aldin had planned for their escape into the countryside had been blocked. They'd nearly been trapped when a group of yellows picked up their trail. It was almost like a hunt. The group that stumbled upon them sounded a horn, and it seemed as if from every alleyway bands of assassins came pouring out to close the net.

Mari had led them on a mad dash, leaping fences, crawling over refuse heaps, and skulking in abandoned buildings until finally they had shaken off the pursuit—a feat that had cost the lives of two more samurai, who without Aldin's knowledge had stayed behind to slow the searchers.

Rather than heading for the outer edge of the city, Mari had led them inward toward the center, reasoning that such a path would throw off the yellows. For the moment it had worked, and finding an abandoned warehouse next to the great square, they had crept in, to wait out events.

"This is your fault," Gablona said, looking back at Aldin. "If you had come along quietly, none of this would have happened."

"And you'd be dead, too," Aldin snapped back in reply.

But still the words hit hard. Aldin looked back out to the square. Hundreds of innocents were dying out there, and the entire city seemed to be given over to an insane pillage as the yellows appeared bent on destroying it all from one end to the other.

Mari, as if sensing how deep Gablona's words had hit, came up to Aldin's side.

"There's more to it than what we think," she said soothingly. "Even the Shigs wouldn't destroy their own nest unless they had a reason. They could hunt for us just as easily without this. It's as stupid as rioters burning down their own homes and shops to protest some imagined grievance. Once they're done with this, no merchant will ever dare to live down here again. Without the merchants the supply of metals will dry up overnight. This place will be worthless. It's almost as if the Shigs are burying everything, since they no longer need it."

"Damn it all, that's what I came down here to tell you about," Tia said, coming up to join the group by the window.

"What's that?" Aldin asked. They had been so busy with their escape, he hadn't even found the time yet to ask her why she had taken the risk to come down to this madhouse.

"Remember, I'm still the acting Koh of the Gablona holdings," she stated.

Corbin turned and fixed her with an icy gaze but said nothing.

"It's just that I found a report that fifty of my dear lover's heavy passenger transport ships had been contracted from one of the shipping firms our family still held."

"So what's so important about that?" Gablona asked. "I already told you about that."

"I thought it to be rather curious, since all the ships were hired without a filed port of destination, with an open-ended contract."

Gablona fell silent.

"So what does that have to do with this?" Aldin snapped, pointing back out toward the destruction outside the window.

"The ships turned up in orbit around the Garn system. I found the information on Yaroslav's files just before I came down here. That's why I came. I felt the only way to stop this was to get to you two and hope to arrange a truce. If you two live, it throws off all their plans. The Overseers won't win, and most likely they'll just leave the Shiga alone then. It seems at least that my coming here kind of worked anyhow," she said almost in a self-congratulatory manner.

"What's the Garn system?" Mari asked.

"Just a worthless hunk of real estate, the next star over from here," Tia replied. "By jump, it's not even an hour away.

There's nothing there, no resources, no colonies, nothing, just a scorched rock orbiting a dying star. We only found out because even as I was tracking down those ships, one of our prospecting vessels that was in the Garn system reported the ships as they jumped in, then all contact was lost.

"Here are fifty ships," Tia continued, "worth millions a day in leasing payments, orbiting in the middle of nowhere."

"As if waiting to pick something up," Aldin said slowly.

"As if waiting for something to happen here," Tia replied.

The enormity of it was stunning.

"Why didn't you tell the Kohs?" Aldin asked.

"I tried, but Bukha wouldn't listen. The rest of the damn fools were so caught up in their game, they wouldn't have believed me anyhow, figuring I was just out for my own gain."

"The Shiga are destroying all this because they no longer need it," Aldin said, astonished. "They'll be leaving, on Gablona's ships. By the heavens, they're planning to get off this planet, and somebody is helping them!"

Gablona backed up from the group, which turned to face him.

"I had nothing to do with it!" he squealed.

Aldin grabbed hold of Gablona and started to shake him.

"I ought to throw you out there to the mob. If the yellows don't kill you, the merchants will!" he screamed.

"I didn't do nothing! The Overseers wanted the lease, I gave it to them, that's all," Gablona cried.

"So that explains all of it. The archaic tactics, the destruction of everything they own. You were going to bribe them with transport off in exchange for your miserable hide. The Shiga have been preparing all along to leave this world and spread their cult throughout the Cloud, in service to their dark and hungry God."

"Honest!" Gablona shrieked. "I had nothing to do with it! I promised them some modern weapons, that was it!"

"I hate to say it," Tia said, "but I think for once he's telling the truth. It was Alma money, and they were going to frame Gablona as the fall guy!"

"That's it!" Gablona gasped, looking gratefully at Tia. "That's it, they were framing me!"

"Shut up, all of you," Oishi said.

Aldin looked over at the samurai who had crouched back from the window. As if dropping a piece of trash, Aldin let go of Gablona, who fell back gasping, and, bending low, came up next to the samurai.

"All your arguing drew some attention," Oishi whispered.

Ever so cautiously Aldin crept up to the window slit and peered out.

Directly beneath them a group of yellows stood, looking up straight at the window.

Aldin quickly ducked back down.

"Damn it all," he cursed, "I thought we'd be safe here for a while. Let's get the hell out of here."

"But where?" Tia asked.

"This is a warehouse for a food merchant," Mari replied. "I was checking it out; down in the basement I saw a door that must lead into the catacombs beneath the city."

Turning, they scurried out of the room and down the staircase to the ground floor. Before they had even reached the landing, there was a pounding on the door.

"Let's go," Oishi barked, and the rest of their companions, who had remained hidden on the ground floor, fell in behind Mari's lead.

The pounding on the door behind them ceased. Suddenly there was a splintering crack, and the door bulged back on its hinges.

Oishi, Seiji, and Ura fell to the rear of the group, letting the others push past.

There was another crack, one of the hinges was ripped out of its mount, and the door leaned back. The last of the group cleared the steps to the basement.

"Fall back!" Oishi ordered, but the two with him refused to budge.

Another crack and the door crashed inward. Half a dozen Shiga standing on the other side dropped the heavy beam they were using for a ram and started to rush in.

Oishi leaped upon the door, his sword arching out, taking the head off the first attacker. With a backhanded flourish he swung his blade up on a diagonal cut, slicing the second yellow open from hip to shoulder.

Ura waded into the fray, his two-handed axe raised high, dropping the third yellow who had turned and was coming in low beneath Oishi's guard.

The three stepped back from the door, as if taunting the remaining attackers to press in.

The three remaining yellows hesitated. One of them barked a command and then, turning, ran back up the street.

"Coward!" Seiji screamed, and pushing through the door, he closed with the remaining natives.

"Don't," Oishi shouted, but Seiji, taken up with battle lust, ignored him.

Seiji feigned with a stab and a quick sidestep. The first yellow jumped to one side, while the second came straight in.

Recovering, Seiji slashed low and then, in imitation of Oishi, attempted a backhanded sweep upward that caught his opponent in the same way that Oishi had.

The assassin to his side closed in, and his dagger sunk home into Seiji's back, even as the young samurai shouted in triumph.

Wild with rage, Oishi leaped over the falling body of his nephew and, with a downward slice, finished the last assassin.

"That's them!"

A group of frightened merchants stood across the alleyway, having witnessed the entire fight, and now, screaming, pointed at the three. The one remaining yellow, who had broken away, was already out in the square, screaming for help.

His vision blurred with tears of rage, Oishi looked around and barely noticed Ura grabbing him by the shoulders, pulling him back through the doorway.

"Now they've seen us!" Ura roared.

"Seiji!"

"Forget him, he's dead," Ura shouted, and grabbing Oishi by the arm, he dragged him back into the warehouse and toward the basement door.

Aldin, along with several of the samurai, noticing that Oishi had stayed behind, were coming back up the stairs in search of him. Ura, bellowing for them to move, pushed Oishi into the group.

"Where's Seiji?" Takashi asked.

"Dead," Oishi said weakly. "I failed, I should have stopped him."

Stunned, Takashi stood on the stairs and then with a wild cry started back up.

Aldin reached out and grabbed him.

"It's too late, my friend, your son's dead," Aldin cried. "Now stay with me!"

Tears of anguish formed in Takashi's eyes, and he was torn

between service to his master and to his son who lay in the doorway.

"You must live for me!" Aldin cried.

Oishi, forgetting his own anguish, came up to Takashi's side and, grabbing hold of him, looked into his eyes.

"He's gone," Oishi whispered, "but we must still live."

Trembling, Takashi nodded in reply, and, turning, they started down into the darkness.

Stumbling down the stairs, Aldin urged the group forward.

Aldin gagged as he stepped into the basement and covered his mouth with his sleeve.

The room was a long, deep cavern, sloping downward into the dark. Mari was right. It was a food storage room, a room filled from one end to the other with rotting men. Hundreds of coffinlike containers lay on the floor, each of them filled with the human-shaped fungus in various states of decomposition. Hundreds more of the rotting men were stacked like cordwood along one wall. The stench was overpowering. It was even too much for some of the Gafs, who were joining a number of the samurai who had staggered off to one side, retching.

The only light was a single lantern up ahead, which cast long wavering shadows so that the corpselike forms seemed to shift and waver, as if hundreds of decomposing bodies were twitching and jerking.

Aldin looked around and saw in an instant that no one was moving. With an angry shout he pushed his way through to the head of the column.

"What's wrong here?" Aldin shouted. "How come we're not moving?"

"Because the bloody door's locked, that's why," Mari snarled.

"Locked? What the hell do you mean, it's locked!"

"Look at my lips," Mari said slowly, "and listen. I said that the door is locked. The catacombs are on the other side; a lot of merchants lock their entry, afraid thieves might slip in."

"You mean you led us down here into a trap?"

"I knew we couldn't trust her," Hassan said, his voice icy with sarcasm.

Aldin wanted to turn and lash out, but there wasn't time. "Can we knock it down?"

"How? Throw rotting men against it?"

"Well, let's blast it then!" Tia suggested.

"It might look good in the vids, but not in real life," Zergh replied. "That door's solid iron. You'll need something on this side to contain the blast, otherwise it'll just blow away from the door and destroy everything in here."

"Then we gotta get back out of here," Aldin cried, suddenly overwhelmed by a terrifying wave of claustrophobia.

The sound of footsteps echoed above them.

"They're in the building," Zergh whispered.

"Then we'll just fight our way out," Ura said, patting his bloodstained axe.

"They'll just swarm us under," Aldin said, his voice edged with desperation. "Get out in the street, and even the merchants will riot against us."

"Then it is time to chant our death songs," one of the Gafs said, an almost dreamy quality to his voice.

"Yeah," Tia commented coldly, "in a couple of days though we're gonna look like these damn plants."

"That's it!" Aldin shouted.

"I think it'll be over any minute now," the Xsarn said, looking at the display screen that dominated the far wall.

One-half of the monitor provided a sensor-implant reading, showing Aldin, Gablona, and their companions clustered close together. The second half of the screen showed a close-up shot from one of the sensor mounts on the tower. It was zoomed straight in on the warehouse, and showed hundreds of yellows swarming into the building.

"We can't let word leak out," Vol shouted. "Remember, there's the other market as well. The stock market's taken a bad enough beating as it is. The day after the Alexandrian fiasco went public we took a twenty-two percent loss. If word gets out the Overseers are planning a hostile takeover, it'll go insane."

"From what we're seeing on the monitor, it won't matter in a couple of minutes," one of the Kohs remarked. "They'll own the companies anyhow, and damn it, we can't even get our assets out!"

Several of the Kohs were in near-catatonic states. The crowd that had at one time so eagerly gathered around Zola had now abandoned him, the seating having shifted to the opposite end of the big table, so Zola now sat alone, while Bukha had a circle about him.

"It's Bukha's fault," Zola shouted. The logic was so outrageous that immediately the room fell silent, ready to hear what he had to say.

"Bukha himself admitted that he suspected this trick, as early as game day thirty. Why didn't he say anything then? If he had, we could have dumped our stock, or . . . or . . ."

"Rigged the results," the Xsarn interrupted.

"Exactly."

There was a low murmur of agreement from the assembly. With a smug look Zola sat back.

"Because I still only suspected," Bukha replied coldly. "In this volatile a situation, even a rumor could have set off a panic."

"We're businessmen," Vol said. "We would have approached it like businessmen."

"And panicked," Bukha snapped.

"Now it's too late," Zola replied. "They're only three and a half days standard, or seven gaming days, left. You said earlier that there were alternatives. What are they?"

"By your own admission, there are nearly fifty million tickets covering the bets of Sigma dying on day fifteen, and Aldin and Gablona dying by the natives some time in the next seven days."

"Damn Gablona and Aldin both," the Xsarn said, a cold anger in his voice, so that those sitting next to him backed away. "They've both had the chance to kill each other for the last day, and neither one has acted. If they had, the Overseer bets would have been worthless and we'd be out of this mess."

The rest of the Kohs growled in agreement.

"What held them back?" one of the Kohs asked.

All of them could see where Aldin and Gablona were huddled together, within inches of each other. Just the flick of a dagger from one or the other, and the Overseers' plot would be ruined!

"Damn it, Aldin, kill him," Zola hissed, "before the Overseers win it all!"

"Do we have any other alternatives?" the Xsarn asked, looking at Bukha.

"There is one," Bukha said slowly. "If either Aldin or Gablona dies by a source other than the natives. The Overseers' holdings of bets in those areas is next to nothing."

"So we'll still get the profit!" Zola cried.

"There are one or two possible outcomes that could prevent that, since a large block of tickets is still outstanding on both surviving."

"What's the best payoff?" Zola asked eagerly.

"One dies by the other, or by Sigma's Gafs, since a kill by them would still be credited to Sigma."

"Is there any chance to arrange it?" the Xsarn asked.

"But that would be against the rules," Zola said with an innocent smile.

"By the way," Vol asked, looking around the room. "Where's Tia?"

"Oh, went back home, something about family business, I heard," Bukha finally replied.

"This is horrifying," the Arch whispered, looking first at the two Overseers who stood before him and then back to the screen.

"It is a destiny that is now beyond our intervention," Losa replied softly.

"A destiny that we are aiding nevertheless. The Al'Shiga are killing hundreds of innocents."

"Innocents? I think not," Losa responded. "They are of the merchant classes. By its very nature the merchant class must exploit to derive this thing they called profit. Profit is derived at the loss of that whom you deal with. Therefore they have taken from the Al'Shiga, building upon their debt to existence, and now the Shiga vent their rage at this, their first act of rage upon all who live in the Cloud. We must try to understand their violence and hope to be able to help them better relate to themselves."

"But we are helping them nevertheless."

"We are merely letting the balance return," Losa stated. "First, they are about to wreck them economically with this lottery. In a very short time, and by their own rules, we shall have control of their economic system. Second, the Shiga shall be loose. Such a movement will sweep across the Cloud for years, until there is nothing but chaos. We are letting the natural forces play themselves out, as we should have done when the three races first arrived, rather than intervening and stopping their war."

The Overseers fell silent. The action they had taken once before was still a source of controversy to them. They had been appointed as guardians by the First Travelers, to hold the Cloud until such time as their unseen lords return. Never had they expected the onslaught by the other beings.

What they had done was nothing more than a bluff, a bluff that had stopped the wars, before one power had become dominant and unified the Cloud. Thus had a status quo been maintained.

Their one demonstration of power had awed the primitives, but never had the primitives realized just how tenuous the Overseers' hold over them really was. For the world-shattering demonstrations had in the process destroyed the very machinery that brought them about, and the Overseers had no idea how to re-create the mechanism, since it was a First Traveler device.

"Whether the decision was right or wrong," the Arch said, "still I made it, and it has at least kept us in a semblance of power. But now you have taken it upon yourself to force the issue."

"And force it I have," Losa said coldly. "We will soon have control over their economic system. If we had attempted to take that alone, they would have rebelled directly against us. The Shiga are the other ingredient. The day their game ends and it is announced that we own most of the assets of the Cloud, the Shiga will break out."

"But it will be chaos," the Arch replied.

"And it will ruin our own economic ventures," Vush said, an edge of panic in his voice. "The profits we will lose will be astronomical!"

The other two turned and looked at their companion with disdain.

"It seems, friend, as if you have been seduced by these outsiders!" the Arch commented.

Vush fell silent and looked sullenly at his two companions.

"We are not concerned with economic systems," Losa said, "but rather with controlling these vermin. If we merely took their economic system, there would be shock at first, but rather quickly the Kohs would unite against us, and in any such confrontation we would be quickly eliminated. Do remember we are not more than several hundred in number, while they have tens of billions."

"So, the Shiga?" the Arch asked.

"The day the game ends, the Shiga will be allowed off their

planet. The Kohs have only a mechanical security system there, no living being wants the job. It will be easy for us to bypass them with our own system.

"The fifty ships I mentioned earlier will arrive at that time. They belong to Gablona, and it will be made to look as if Gablona bribed the Shiga to save himself. Each of those ships can carry twenty thousand. That first wave will spread out—in fact, it will hit the planet that is the economic nerve center of the Cloud and where the Kohs are currently meeting. That wave will then be followed later by others. They shall be like an epidemic, spreading from planet to planet.

"The chaos resulting from our control of their economy will paralyze the resources of the Cloud, and we will merely say that what we now own cannot be used for violence.

"Within half a dozen years, the Cloud will be in anarchy. The people will blame the Kohs."

"But could not the Shiga themselves become a threat? You yourself have had contact with them. Could they not then point to us and tell the people what we have done?"

"We have had contact with only one of them. He alone knows the full extent of our involvement. It would indeed be unfortunate if his ship should meet with an accident, and thus he could not speak. He is their unifier, and with him gone, the rest will merely spread like chaff in the wind. The center lost, the Shiga will play themselves out. If another unifier rises up, we can arrange for him as well."

"You are talking about murder," the Arch said coldly.

"Your definition, from another time," Losa replied.

Losa looked up at the Arch, who hovered before him. The Arch was old, with a memory stretching back eons before the barbarians had come. And his ways, too, were old. From this confrontation the others would see that the Arch had not met what needed to be done, that he was not willing to risk the path of his destiny for a higher good—the preservation of the Cloud. After this was done, the consensus of the others would shift away from the oldest and come to rest on someone else, and Losa knew who it would be.

"It is still intervening too far."

"When the Shiga have expended their energy, reducing the remaining spacefaring worlds back to primitive states, it shall be complete. The barbarians will be trapped on their planets;

the few that are left, we can control, and thus we will have done what the First Travelers asked.

"Through holding their economic forces in check and letting the violence of the Shiga play out against it, they will render each other impotent."

"And if this fails?" the Arch said evenly.

"Then you will still be the Arch, and I—" Losa laughed smoothly "—well, then I shall be in your hands for punishment. I did this on my own. If successful, it will be my success; if it fails, then I am sure you will be quick to blame."

The Arch looked down at Losa, his features creased with a look of contempt. Losa had played the game all too well. There was nothing the Arch could do. If he tried to stop it, the involvement of the Overseers would be revealed, and then the barbarians would unite.

"But what about my profits?" Vush cried.

The other two ignored him even as he turned and floated from the room, lamenting the possible destruction of his new-found game of economics.

"I do not know whether to thank you or to curse you," the Arch said coldly.

"If what that screen indicates is true," Losa replied softly, "the Al'Shiga will soon have them, and then there'll be time enough for thanks."

"They must have gotten through the door and locked it from the other side," a Shiga shouted.

"They couldn't have," Ulsak whispered. "I think they're still here." He gazed about the room of rotting men. Somehow his prey was near, very near.

He looked again at the iron door. The heavy locks would take time to smash. To open them would have required a key; the scum must have had one and gotten through.

He again looked about the room. A thought started to form in his mind when a shout came from the end of the corridor.

"My lord, some of our men have set fire to the building. We'd better get out!"

"Damn them all!" Ulsak roared. A day and night of uncontrolled arson was starting to take its toll on discipline, and some were now burning anything they could set a flame to.

With a curse he turned away.

"Is there another way in there?" he roared, pointing to the door.

"There should be another entrance in the next building, behind this one," a yellow answered.

"Let's go then and send a party out through the back alley, in case they got out that way. Then find the man who set this building aflame. I want him tied to the door frame and left as an example."

With a cold snarl Ulsak turned and started for the exit. He stopped in the doorway for a moment and turned in hesitation. He looked to the corner of the room, where the thousands of rotting men were stacked, and then stormed back up the stairs.

There was a stirring in the corner.

Gagging, Aldin tried to push away the rotting man that lay on top of him. His hand went straight into what would be the stomach, and the foul gases within escaped with a soggy rasping sound, the slimy green-brown juice within cascading in a gurgling torrent straight into his face.

With a groan of disgust he pulled his hands out, now covered with a slimy brown-green coating.

Not now, he thought, struggling to control his stomach. He pushed up again, this time grabbing the plant by the throat. The head came off in his hands. Kicking out, he pushed the rotting man aside, the head still in one hand, and stood up.

The room was alight with the faint phosphorescent gleam of the plants, giving a strange, eerie glow to the cavern. Overhead there was the sound of crackling flames—the yellows had put the building to the torch.

His heart was still pounding with fear. The act had been one born of desperation and several minutes of hard arguing. The Gafs had wanted to storm back outside, and the samurai were in agreement, stating their desire to at least die out in the open. Finally he had convinced them, and they had crawled into the pile of rotting men, pulling the plants over and around them.

"It's clear," Aldin hissed.

All about him, it seemed as if corpses were rising up from their graves, to suddenly be shaken aside, revealing the slime-covered fugitives beneath.

As one, the entire group started to cough and gag, kicked the plants aside, and reassembled in the middle of the room. Aldin nodded with approval toward Ura, who had stayed with

Hassan throughout. If there had been trouble with that man, having the Gaf's hands on his shoulders would have stopped it. Hassan might be useful yet, he thought, but that did not mean he trusted him.

Only Gablona, out of the entire group, seemed calm as he absently munched on the remains of a rotting man. What was worse, it instantly became obvious that Gablona was drunk, having swallowed a good portion of a liquid meal from at least one of the plants.

"Now we're even worse off than before," Gablona said, his voice slurring. He pointed straight overhead. The growing sound of the conflagration was clearly audible.

"This whole building will collapse in on us," Tia cried, her voice edged with panic.

Aldin looked around at the group. The samurai and Gafs were not pleased at all, and he could feel their anger.

"Better to have died in the open," Ura growled, "rather than be roasted like sholts in a flame."

"What are we going to do?" Tia shouted.

Without comment Oishi unsheathed his sword and started for the exit, but even as he reached the opening, a flaming beam collapsed across the doorway.

Wide-eyed, the samurai turned back to face the group.

"I have no intention of dying by fire," Oishi said softly, coming back to Aldin's side. "It's not the best of ways to go; I've seen it before."

Aldin looked straight into Oishi's eyes.

"Let me do it for you," Oishi said softly, "and for Tia and Mari as well. One of the others will take the fat man, but I wish the honor for you. It will be painless."

Aldin had brushed with death so often in the previous days that he thought he would be used to it. But still he could not control his trembling. And he realized now, as well, the courage of the samurai around him, who had willingly faced death not only for him but also for their dead lord, three thousand years ago.

"At least your killing us will ruin the betting," Aldin said, trying to force a chuckle.

What an irony, he thought, turning away. In this madness of betrayal and counterbetrayal, it would be an act of loyalty and compassion that would ruin all the plans of the powerful Kohs.

Whatever happened, Zola would likely make hundreds of billions out of it, he thought, shaking his head.

Aldin looked back at Oishi, and trying to force a smile, he merely nodded in reply.

"Give me a moment," he said softly.

"We don't have long." And as if to add force to the argument, there was an explosive roar. The far end of the cavern caved in with a shower of sparks and a wave of smoke and searing heat.

Aldin stepped over to where Mari and Tia stood huddled against the wall.

"Oishi asks to help us leave here," he said softly, taking the two with either hand.

Tia buried her head in Aldin's shoulder, crying.

Mari looked down at Aldin, trying to force a smile. "Damn it all, Larice, I was hoping to bed with you at least once." And leaning forward, she gave him a passionate kiss. Pulling back she wiped away her tears and smiled.

"Let's go," she said softly.

Aldin looked back at Oishi, who stood with drawn sword, and nodded. Taking the hands of the two women, Aldin went to his knees, facing the wall, Mari and Tia to either side.

"The Basak die fighting!" Ura roared defiantly.

Screaming with rage, the berserker ran up to the iron door and slammed his axe against it.

He stepped back to give another blow.

Almost on the edge of hearing, Aldin detected the faint jingle of metal striking the floor before him. As if in a dream, he looked down.

A key was lying on the floor.

"Wait!" Aldin screamed.

With a surge of terror he looked back. Oishi had already started his swing on Tia. The blade came to a stop, inches from the girl's neck.

"It's the key, the goddamn key!" Aldin screamed.

He reached forward, snatched the cold metal object up in his trembling hands, and came to his feet. Fumbling, he stepped to the door and stuck it into the latch. He turned it as he held his breath.

The door clicked open.

Laughing hysterically, he looked up and pointed to the sill above the door.

"It was resting on top of the doorsill! Ura's blow must have knocked it down."

"Well, let's get moving!" Ura roared, looking around triumphantly as if he had somehow reasoned out their escape, rather than stumbling upon it in a blind rage.

Grabbing hold of the door, the berserker pulled it open.

Aldin held his breath. Ulsak had ordered his men to enter the catacombs through the next building. Were they already in there and waiting? Even if they were, Aldin reasoned, at least now he could go down fighting.

The door swung back. Silence.

Ahead there was the phosphorescent glow of yet more rotting men, but nothing else.

With a shout of joy the Gafs rushed forward, the samurai falling in behind.

Oishi came up to Aldin's side, and the two stopped for a moment to gaze upon each other; nothing had to be said, for both understood.

chapter fourteen

"Which way do we go?" Oishi asked, looking back at Mari.

"How in hell am I supposed to know?" she snapped back. "This is my first time down here, same as you. All I know is the catacombs go for kilometers beneath the entire foreign quarter. Rumor is it even leads into the other cities."

"But you lived here, I thought you'd know," Oishi replied, trying to be patient and deferential to the person he now considered his lord's chosen lady.

Ahead lay a narrow corridor, with an immediate branch off to the right. The party stood in silence, still stunned by the narrowness of their escape, as the rest of the building caved in behind them with a shuddering roar.

"Do you hear something?" Aldin asked after a moment.

Directly ahead there was a distant, rhythmic pounding.

"Ulsak's boys trying to get in, I think," Tia whispered.

"Well, that settles it then," Aldin announced, and pointed to the right.

Holding the lantern rescued from the cavern, Oishi took the lead and the group set out behind him.

The tunnel went on for several hundred meters and then doglegged to the left, where several turnouts greeted them.

"Now what?" Oishi asked.

"Like I said, how the hell am I supposed to know? Where we're going, they don't give road maps."

"We could be running in circles then," Gablona announced.

"Better than frying to a crisp," Aldin retorted.

"Why not simply hide down here?" Zergh asked. "It'd take them days to find us."

Several of the samurai turned about at the suggestion, and more than one nodded his approval.

Aldin shook his head. "Two reasons. First off, we don't know this place. They undoubtedly do. If ever we are discovered, they'll call in their friends, and that's it."

"And the second reason?" Oishi asked, watching Aldin closely.

"Old military axiom. 'In open country, do not bar your enemy's way; on dangerous ground, press ahead; on desperate ground, fight.' "

"Sun Tsu," Oishi announced, a look of admiration crossing his face.

Aldin merely nodded. "We are on desperate ground. Our enemy expects us to run, to hide. He'll never expect us to attack, and I plan to take the offensive. If we don't, not only will we lose our lives, but the Cloud will sink into chaos. They know we're in the catacombs; they'll expect us to hide here. So let's give them a surprise—let's move and get out of this city."

He looked at the choices ahead of them, did a quick mental toss of the coin, then pointed to the right.

Another hundred meters brought them into another cavern, and the party came up short.

It was a garden of rotting corpses, and for the first time, those not of the Al'Shiga discovered how the plants were grown.

The entire corridor was filled with garden beds, and from each a dozen or more of the plants sprouted. Gablona took one look, paled, and dropped the remnants of the rotting man he had been so blithely munching on.

The rotting men were fertilized with Human corpses.

Bodies filled the garden beds, covered only with a scant layer of dirt, their outlines clearly visible. Here and there the soil cover had been washed away, so that cadavers in various states of decomposition stared out at them, the fungi growing out of foreheads, sunken chests, and protruding limbs.

The stench was overpowering. Trying not to look to either side, Aldin strode down the middle of the cavern, his companions nervously following.

When they reached the end of the cavern, a corridor curved off to the left, and there another horror awaited them.

Now they could see, as well, where the baskets of men came from. Skeletons hung suspended down the length of darkened halls, illuminated only by the faint glow of the plants growing in their fertilized beds. Each of the skeletons was encased in a filigree web of vines that traced about the bones, feeding off their calcium and finally crumbling them to dust, leaving nothing but the outline behind, encased in wood.

"Pull half a dozen of those things down," Oishi commanded. The men looked at him in confusion but complied.

Leaving the corridor of baskets behind, they met another three-way junction. The group stopped for a moment to rest.

"We could be going in circles down here," Gablona repeated drunkenly.

"Well, do we have any damned alternative?" Aldin snapped.

The Koh merely smiled and shrugged his shoulders.

"Noise to the right," Ura hissed.

Aldin looked up. Suddenly there was the faint glow of a torch in the distance. "Move!"

They pushed straight ahead.

"They're on to us," Ura shouted, and from behind all could hear the shouts of pursuit.

"Keep moving!" Aldin cried. "If we stop to fight, they'll get word out to block us."

The group took off at a run. Oishi fell to the back of the column and ordered his men to stack the baskets. Sticking his lantern into the middle, he waited till they were ablaze before withdrawing the lamp and racing to rejoin the group. Within seconds the tunnel behind them was engulfed in fire, the baskets looking like writhing skeletons in the flames.

Shouts of rage echoed behind them as they raced on into the darkness.

Horror after horror was passed: fungi shimmering with green phosphorescence; hundreds of baskets, which Oishi knocked down, torching them as he passed; and pens of blind, white sholts, which the party drove out of their cages to further confuse the pursuit.

Twice more they ran into search parties, one running straight into them from a side corridor. The fight was sharp but brief, leaving three yellows and two Gafs behind. One enemy survived, and with a shout disappeared into the darkness.

For nearly a day and a half they pushed on, no longer taking the time to stop, until finally two Gafs had to carry Gablona between them, lest the overweight Koh slow them in their desperate retreat.

At last Zergh, who was at the head of the column, signaled a halt.

"There. There, do you smell it?" he whispered.

So long had they been breathing the stench of the catacombs that Aldin felt as if the reek of decomposition had seeped into his very soul. He came up to stand by Zergh.

"What?"

"There. Smoke."

Then he smelled it. Smoke from a wood fire and, mingled with it, the scent of fresh air.

"To the right!" Aldin cried.

The party pushed after him, desperate to breathe clean air. There was a faint light in the distance, glowing red. The group rushed forward and spilled out into the forest.

It was nearly as bright as day, though overhead the stars shone dimly. To their left the city was in flames, a firestorm that swept from end to end. The pall of smoke, roiling low, dipped down in vast eddies, cloaking them in its choking darkness, then rose back up again.

The wind roared about them, sucked in toward the vast heart of the inferno.

"Now where do we go?" Oishi asked.

"To stir up some trouble," Aldin replied, looking about.

"How?"

"If I know Ulsak, he's lost tremendous face already by allowing our escape. There'll have to be a hunt for us out here, and he'll be under pressure; there must be less than five of their days to go now. By now he must have figured we've gotten out of the city, and there's just too much territory to cover without the help of the others. Let's clear the city and see what we can stir up."

The group stopped for a moment and looked back again at the city, the Skyhook rising up out of the flames, reflecting the firelight so that it looked like a pillar of fire rising into the heavens.

"They're insane, totally insane," Mari shouted. "There'll be nothing left but ashes."

"Perhaps they wish it that way," Tia replied softly.

"We think they made it out of the city, master."

"You think? Did I hear you say you think they made it out?"

Ulsak turned on the messenger, his features contorted with rage.

The messenger bowed low before the master ulla.

"I want an answer; I cannot act on assumptions, on 'I think.' Did they or did they not escape?"

The messenger, trembling, raised his head from the floor.

"They escaped, tracks were found leaving a hidden entry between the west and north gates," he whispered.

"Did your men do what I told them? Seal off every possible entry, and then search corridor by corridor?"

"It was impossible," the messenger cried. "The catacombs run for dozens of kilometers, with half a hundred known exits, and perhaps as many unknown. They must have stumbled on an unknown path and followed it out."

"If I recall," Ulsak said softly, "not less than a month ago I foresaw the chance of this happening and suggested that you prepare for such a likelihood. Did you?"

"To the best of our ability," the messenger replied softly, not daring to say that such a conversation had never happened.

"Your ability is lacking," Ulsak said, and then turned away to face his aides.

"They must be between us and the whites," Ulsak said, looking at his staff. "Send a messenger over to them now, I want the other four sects alerted immediately. We've got to find them and kill them with all proper ceremony, otherwise our plans are for naught. And let my commanders tell every man that if they slip by again, all who are responsible will suffer as much as the two we plan to capture."

Ulsak turned and looked back at the man cowering on the floor.

"Impale him," he said, the slightest of grins lighting his features. "Make sure it's the slow way."

"Will the traitor come through for us?" an ulla asked, coming up to Ulsak's side, even as the condemned ulla was dragged out of the room.

"He knows what to do," Ulsak replied coldly.

"We did find one man down in the catacombs though."

"Who?"

"Just that mad shaman. He was by the door of the ancients, peering about and shouting incantations."

Ulsak stopped for a moment, half wondering.

"Should I bring him to you?"

"I don't have the time. Whip him out of the city and tell him to go live with the Sutar. I have no further need of him. He has been my prophet, but now the time of prophecy is at hand."

The ulla bowed low and scurried away.

About the doorway of the ancients? Why and how could that old madman have found his way down there? But there was no time now to dwell on such matters, and he pushed the thought out of his mind.

The starlight barely silhouetted their target, who rested easily against the tree.

Aldin felt an almost wolflike thrill. Since coming down to this place, he'd been the prey, with all the disadvantages of the defense. No matter how vigilant, one was still gripped with fear, not knowing when or where the attack might come. For a day and a half since emerging from the catacombs, they had been hunted by the Shiga, but now the tables were about to be turned.

A twig snapped directly behind him, and turning, he saw Hassan freeze in midstride. The samurai accompanying him mouthed a silent curse at the assassin, who looked about as if embarrassed by his mistake.

Instantly the guard was alert, dagger drawn.

Aldin froze, watching the man from the corner of his eyes. If the man shouted, they'd really be in it.

Oishi lifted his head up from the ground, and cupping his hands, he gave the call of an owl, a signal they had noted was used as communication between the Shiga guardposts.

The guard relaxed and started to lean back against the tree.

He never saw, and barely felt, the blade that a second later slashed his throat open.

Takashi grabbed the body and quietly lowered it to the ground.

The attack party swept forward, Aldin staying back with the reserves at the edge of the woods.

The enemy encampment was plainly in view.

Oishi tied his own sword behind his back and swept up the blade from the dead sentry. He looked about at his men.

The sky to the east was starting to brighten, so that the pale yellow robes they had taken from the last group they surprised were barely visible.

"Ready," Oishi whispered.

The dozen men nodded.

"Now!"

The dozen samurai rushed forward and within seconds were in and about the first campfire. A dozen of the whites were slain before the alarm was even given, but by then the samurai had already turned about and were rushing back into the woods.

"Ulsak, Ema Al'Shiga!" Oishi roared, waving a bloody head in his hand as the party melted back into the woods.

The reserve of samurai and Gafs were already pounding down the trail, rounding the first bend. They reached the first of four warning stakes tied off with a red cloth and gave the trail a wide berth; as they ran deeper into the woods, they passed the three others.

The samurai dressed as yellows rushed behind them with Oishi in the rear. When he reached the first stake, he pulled it from the ground and flung it into the woods.

The pursuit was closing fast.

After turning the next corner, he pulled at the second warning stake as he had the first.

From behind he could hear the shouts of rage. There was a thunderous crack, and the screams of rage turned to cries of terror and pain as the first man tripped the spiked deadweight that swung down from an overhanging branch.

Laughing grimly, Oishi pushed on into the woods, the pursuit left behind.

Stopping at last, the group fell to the ground, breathing hard from the exertion and excitement.

"Well, that ought to stir things up a bit," Aldin said grimly. "No matter what Ulsak says, some of the white Shiga will still think that the old ways haven't been given up, and some yellows have gone off to hunt a couple of heads."

While they talked, Takashi scrambled up to the top of a tree to gain a better view. Minutes later he was back down.

"What'd you see?" Oishi asked.

"They're still drawing the net, keeping a continuous line all the way about the five cities, closing in at a slow, steady pace."

Aldin sat in the dust and drew a circle on the ground.

"A good five hours of light left," he said quietly. "They'll most likely close half the distance into the city by then. We've got to keep stirring things up and hope for the best. If we can punch a hole and get out, or, better yet, turn them against each other, we'll make it through the next three days. And then Bukha can get us out of here."

Aldin looked over at Gablona, who sat quietly, and as Aldin's gaze turned upon him, the Koh smiled softly.

"But of course," Gablona whispered, and Hassan, by his side, merely nodded his approval.

"Let's move across the whites and hit the blues next," Aldin said, and the samurai growled their approval at the mention of the blues.

As the sun crossed the zenith, the group settled down along the edge of a marshy stream and waited. They could clearly hear the beaters, pushing closer, and the excited shouts of the Shiga racing up and down the line as the men shouldered their way through the brush.

Suddenly, not twenty meters away, the dense undergrowth parted and a face peered out.

Aldin froze and raised his hand to those waiting on the opposite slope, signaling that the enemy had arrived.

More and more appeared along the edge of the stream and hesitated.

Finally, what appeared to be an ulla pushed forward and with a hearty curse stepped into the stream. Within seconds he was nearly neck deep and, with feeble strokes, beat against the lazy current. All up and down the riverbank the men started in after him. The ulla finally reached the other side, and dripping mud, he slipped and splashed up to the edge of the riverbank. His hand reached up to grab a root, in order to pull his way up onto dry land.

"Ulsak, Ema Al'Shiga!" Oishi rose up out of a bank of rotting leaves. The ulla's head flipped from his body, and with a wild shout, Oishi snatched it from the side of the bank before it tumbled back down into the stream.

For a moment the blues stood there stunned, all eyes turned on the yellow-robed warrior, only his eyes visible; about his head the red cord of the Mukba. With a wild shout, Oishi turned and scrambled up the slope, a dozen more yellow-robed samurai rising up, some striking at those who had drawn close to the bank, the rest simply falling back, taunting the blues.

They all disappeared over the hill.

With shouts of rage at such base betrayal, the blues surged forward, eager for revenge. After reaching the bank, they started up; one, then another, and suddenly a score fell in the high grass. The grass-covered traps were only a half-meter deep, but it was enough to drive the sharpened stakes clear through the foot of a victim.

As Aldin and his companions disappeared down the trail, pulling back from the closing circle, they could hear the shouts of the blues in the distance—and the name of Ulsak screamed with rage.

"But I tell you, my men had nothing to do with it!" Ulsak roared.

"That is beside the point," Orphet of the white snapped back in reply. "My men are convinced that your people have everything to do with it: that you yellows have not put down the dagger of the ritual, and are taking advantage of the hunt to harvest some more heads, and that this is part of your plan."

"That's madness. Do you believe that?"

"Of course not," Orphet replied evenly, but Ulsak and those around him could see that the answer was more diplomatic than truthful.

"Well, do you doubt my word?" Ulsak roared.

"For two thousand years we've lived with the dream," Tores Ser of the greens replied. "The dream of returning to the stars, of ending our exile and purifying the Cloud to the One Faith.

Now today you've told us that you, Ulsak, shall make the dream come to pass. That the tower shall be open, that ships await, and we can sweep out to the stars. Only the hidden Ema can have such power. Do you therefore intend to claim before all that you are the hidden Ema?"

Ulsak looked about at the other leaders of the Shiga. They would see—in three days they would see him as he was meant to be revealed.

"Yes, I claim that title. I am the hidden Ema of the Al'Shiga, sent to liberate, to guide us on our destiny to the stars!"

His claim was greeted with stunned silence.

"And by what signs do you thus reveal yourself? For the Ema shall have the power to unlock the tower, to guide his people upward, where the ships of God shall await us, so that we shall do His bidding and slay all who oppose Him," Nargla of the red Gafs stated.

The others looked at him. Though the inner circle knew that what they taught to the masses was merely legend, Nargla had not rejected his faith when raised to the inner ranks.

"Bring to me the two that are hunted," Ulsak replied. "They must be brought to me no later than the night before the Ulman. Upon the square they shall be staked, and the moment that is done, the doors to heaven shall open wide for us."

"The doors open for any man or woman," the leader of the white Janinsar sect replied, "but only those from above may return. If the Shiga dares to enter the tower, then he is cast back down."

"But by that you shall see," Ulsak announced, "and thus it will be revealed that I am the hidden prophet. From above I shall watch the sacrifice, and when it is complete, and I have not been cast down, you shall see that the way is open for all. I have been promised that, by those called the Overseers."

"You're mad," Nargla said coldly. "You are no hidden prophet. If we gain the tower, it should be by the hand of the Unseen One, not by these politics. We are doomed here, and nothing more. We all believe that, at least we who rule should."

"You shall see. Perhaps this is how what you call the Unseen One has decided it shall be, through the foolishness and greed of those we wish to overthrow," Ulsak said, a distant look to his eyes.

"But it all rests on these two," Orphet replied coldly. "That means to me that you don't have this power of the Ema unless those are delivered."

"It is the sacrifice," Ulsak stated quickly. "With their blood I promise you the stars."

"Our own people don't understand this. They don't understand why you burned the foreign city, and even your own homes, they think you've gone mad. It was to be a time of taking heads and general festivities. Instead you've called us to merely hunt these two. Our people have always been taught that only when the Ema comes will the six tribes be again united as one, answering then to the tribe that has raised up the Ema."

"You fools," Ulsak roared. "All I want is those two alive; nothing more. Then you shall see that what I speak is the truth. If not, I offer you my own head in sacrifice."

The other ullas fell silent.

"You offer your own head?" Orphet asked craftily.

"Yes! Just tell your people that the attacks upon them are not by my men, that it is a deception. Tell them that the two must be taken alive and brought to me. My head I shall then offer as debt, along with the heads of my entire clan, if what I say does not come to pass."

The masters looked from one to the other and smiled.

"Then your word is bond," Orphet replied softly, and turning, he strode out of the room, all but Nargla following.

"And if these two are not captured?" the old Gaf said softly.

"They will be. But remember, I want them alive."

"Why? If you simply want them dead in payment, then we should kill them on the hunt and be done with it."

"No!" And Ulsak turned away.

He wanted those above to see that it was he, Ulsak, who did the kill, not someone else who might then claim to have been the bringer of the liberation.

He turned and looked back at Nargla. "Because they have offended me. And those above demanded that their deaths not be hidden, but out in the open, in the great square for all to see."

It was a lie, but Nargla could not know any different.

"The circle was half closed today; tomorrow by sundown your people shall be to the walls of the city. My own have formed a perimeter about it. The only ones in between are those we hunt, once you and your escorts return to your men."

"But if they are not captured . . ."

"They must be," Ulsak said, and in the strain of his voice Nargla understood what was to be done. The kill would be his before the night was over, but it would not be the kill Ulsak expected.

"There. The only spot not covered by watch fires," Aldin said, pointing off to the south.

"A part of the red sector," Mari said quietly.

In a broad arc from horizon to horizon the fires of the Shiga surrounded the city, the noose drawing in ever tighter. Aldin looked back over his shoulder. Parts of the city behind them still burned, the outline of the town now marked by another circle of flame, the watch fires of the yellows, preventing return back into the catacombs.

"Why is that one spot unlit?" Aldin asked, thinking out loud.

"It could be a trap to lure us in," Mari commented.

Aldin looked back at the city and judged the distance back out to the outer perimeter.

"Damn, if only we had one more day. Damn it all." He lowered himself down from the tree limb from which he and Mari had been watching the position of the hunters.

"Is that one spot still dark?" Oishi asked, coming up to join them.

Aldin nodded.

"It's worth a try. Could be our little strikes of today had their effect and some of the Shiga are dropping out of the hunt, leaving a hole open. If we could break through, we'll be out on the other side and can run them all the way to the escarpment. By then your game will be over, and hopefully your so-called friends will pick you up."

"I still don't like the smell of it," Aldin said.

"Do we have any alternative?" Oishi asked softly.

Aldin realized that the samurai was right and could only nod his head in reply.

Within the hour they were off, moving single file down the narrow trail that one of the Gafs, scouting ahead, claimed moved straight toward the darkened area. As the stars wheeled overhead, the party pushed forward, wary of any traps that might be set, not knowing that now there was no one between the two perimeters, so nervous were the six clans of betrayal by the other.

As they drew close to where they felt the position to be, the group slowed its advance. Ground that could be crossed in a minute at a pleasant walk now took a long, agonizing hour to cover as samurai and Gaf scouts drifted ahead, signaling to the rest when all was clear. They'd move up a hundred meters, then wait until the next hundred meters were cleared.

It was during one such wait that Ura crept up to Aldin's side and whispered the news. "Hassan is gone."

"What! I thought your people were watching him and Gablona."

"We were," the hulking Gaf said lamely.

Aldin felt as if he were about to burst with rage, but realized that Ura was mortified at his failure—no reproach could make him feel any worse. "Gablona?"

"Still here. Claims he knows nothing."

"Damn him, I almost wish I *had* cut his throat."

"Can I?" the Gaf asked, his features lighting.

"Damn it, no," Aldin snapped. "Now go back and keep an eye on him at least."

Crestfallen, the Gaf disappeared back down the trail. When Oishi came back to report the next sector cleared, Aldin broke the news.

"Damn him, I wanted to kill him and you wouldn't let me."

"I know, I know," Aldin said, cursing himself for not following his instincts.

"We'd better move," Oishi announced. "For whatever reason, he left. It can only hurt us."

Following Oishi's lead, the party quickened its pace.

"They're heading toward the red perimeter." Hassan gasped, still out of breath from the run through the forest. He'd nearly met his end at the city wall, when a yellow, nerves on edge with rumors that the whites were out hunting heads, had taken a swipe at him, and only through instinct had he managed to roll beneath the blow even as he shouted that he was a friend.

"Where?" Ulsak asked.

"The darkened position."

"Damn him. Nargla is offering them a way out, I know it!

"Let's move," Ulsak ordered.

* * *

"There's the line," Oishi whispered.

"It just isn't right," Aldin replied. "No fire, no guards, just a gaping hole waiting for us to walk through."

"Or into."

"Or into," Aldin echoed softly. His heart was thumping like a trip-hammer. If this is what men talked about, the thrill of the ambush and the stalk, he resolved never to step outside a building again after dark should he get out alive. He felt as if every bush had eyes; that this was a dark, foreboding whirlpool, sucking them in to certain destruction. Through the brush, a couple of hundred meters to either flank, they could see the roaring blaze of the perimeter, but here it was as dark as the grave.

"What shall we do?" Aldin asked.

"Draw swords and move straight in," Oishi replied. "The only alternative is to sit here till dawn, which isn't too far off, or retreat back into the net they're drawing closed around us."

The word was passed down the line. Sheathed weapons were drawn and shimmered softly in the starlight.

Oishi stood up and started forward.

"Drawn blades aren't necessary, offworlders," came a voice out of the darkness.

Oishi froze. Startled cries of alarm echoed down the line.

"I said, drawn blades aren't necessary!"

A single torch burst into flame not a dozen meters ahead. Oishi, lowering his blade, stepped before Aldin.

"If we wanted a fight, my people would have taken you long ago." A single figure stepped forward.

Aldin put his hand on Oishi's shoulder. If this was a trap, they'd walked straight into it. At least delay might give them time to find a way out.

"Who are you?" Aldin shouted.

"Nargla, Master Ulla of the Sutar."

"Mari!"

The column behind Aldin parted as Mari pushed her way forward.

"He claims to be the master of the reds," Aldin said as she came up to his side, not daring to take his eyes off the Gaf who stood on the trail before them.

"It's him," she whispered.

"I wish to strike a deal," Nargla said.

"A deal for what?"

"Safe passage through for you."

Aldin didn't know whether to shout with relief or order Oishi to attack in the hope that at least they could take a Shiga leader down with them.

"I know you don't believe me," Nargla said.

"And why should I? I'd be mad to trust what you say."

Nargla barked softly. "Well said."

"Then what is it you propose?"

"If I wanted you dead, I would have simply ordered an attack on you, without this parley."

"We might have caught him by surprise, and he's stalling till his people move up," Oishi hissed.

"Also well said. That is how I would react."

"Enough of the compliments. Get to the point," Aldin snapped.

"I want some answers first, before I let you through."

"And that's it?"

"That's it. There's no love lost between Ulsak and me. You're the path to his goal. If I can eliminate the path, then I have hurt my foe. Ulsak wants you taken alive, for a sacrifice. I intend to wreck his plans."

"And eliminate us in the process," Oishi argued.

"Is that it?" Aldin asked, motioning for Oishi to be still.

"But first there are some things I need to know," Nargla replied.

"Ask."

"You have my honor as an ulla of the Shiga. You have my head as debt if I betray you."

Mari mumbled a surprise at this.

"It's a bound oath," she whispered.

"I merely ask that we talk first, then the path will be cleared."

"We can talk just like this," Aldin replied, his mind on edge with caution.

"Our shouting will only draw attention," Nargla reasoned, "and things that will be said are best not heard by even my own. I merely want you and the fat one to come to me. We'll sit and talk and then you are free to pass my lines, as I have sworn."

Aldin hesitated.

"You are free to come into our lines," Oishi called.

Nargla laughed harshly. "I am the one offering life. I have

the power but to shout, and my men on the other side of the stream will swarm over like flies to carrion. If there is any walking to be done, it will be done by you two, not I."

Aldin looked first at Mari and then Oishi.

"Don't, my lord," Oishi begged.

"It might be the only way," Mari reasoned. "He gave his oath on his head. It means that if he lied, any of our clan is free to claim it without retribution at any time. It also means he can't call one of his clan to harm you."

Aldin still hesitated.

"Oishi!" he shouted in a voice loud enough for Nargla to hear. "You still have that bow that you made down here?"

"Yes, my lord."

"Then nock an arrow. Draw it straight on that Gaf. If he moves to harm us, kill him."

And then he looked back at the Gaf for a reaction.

Nargla stood still, a slight look of disdain lighting his features.

"The weapon of cowards," he barked. "But draw if you will, I won't harm you."

"Bring up Gablona," Aldin shouted.

A minute later the Koh was at the head of the column squealing with fear when he realized what Aldin was proposing. After drawing a dagger, Aldin nicked Gablona in the back, pushing him forward.

"So, you are the two," Nargla said almost matter-of-factly, looking each of them over closely as they drew closer.

"If you mean the ones that have avoided capture by the entire Shiga nation," Aldin said, "then the answer is yes."

"A successful avoidance of capture is successful only when the hunted is safely beyond pursuit. If I were you, I would not be so boastful," Nargla said softly.

"Still, we've given Ulsak and his friends a run," Aldin said.

"For what reason is all this madness?" Nargla asked.

"You wouldn't believe it all if I told you," Aldin replied wearily.

"Most likely I would not, coming from the lips of an unbeliever."

"Then why are you bothering to talk with us?"

"Because I wish to know why your death will bring Ulsak power. For if what he said is true, then the Seda will be opened at midday the day after tomorrow when the sky grows dark. Who would be so mad as to allow us off this world merely for the sake of killing you two?"

Aldin shot Gablona a look of contempt, and the Koh tried to avoid his gaze.

"It's a long story," Aldin replied.

"Don't move!" Nargla suddenly hissed.

There was the crack of a twig to Aldin's left.

Turning, he looked off into the darkness beyond the light of Nargla's single torch.

There was the sound, as if someone had blown on a pipe barely heard. Something nicked his shoulder.

Stunned, he looked down. It struck him as almost being too absurd to be believed. He'd been hit in the shoulder with a dart the size of his finger, the sharpened point already stinging his shoulder, as if he'd been jabbed by a bee.

"Ulsak!" Nargla shouted, throwing his torch to the ground.

As if he were suddenly looking down the length of a long, dark tunnel, Aldin started to turn. Everything seemed to be happening in slow motion.

He heard Oishi's bow snap and the sound of impact as the arrow lifted Nargla off his feet, smashing the heavy Gaf to the ground.

Gablona staggered before him, looking somehow comical with several darts sticking out of his fat stomach, his face contorted. The terrified Koh was shouting, but Aldin could hear no sound.

Suddenly forms leaped past him; around him, dozens of them.

Distantly he saw two faces peering down at him. One was Hassan; the other, Ulsak. He tried to scream even as he fell away into darkness.

chapter fifteen

"Are you sure about the information?" Blackie asked, still not quite believing what she was hearing.

"I had it from Zola himself. The rest of the Kohs are in total panic. It seems that there's a block of two million tickets calling for the death of Aldin and Gablona on the last day, which starts in just another six hours standard."

"Two million," Blackie whispered, sitting down across from Kurst. "And these are first-day buys?"

"Exactly."

"That comes out to a payoff in the trillions," she whispered. "GGC will be completely wiped out."

"There's more," Kurst said softly. "In the papers of incorporation for GGC they waived the liability clause. If GGC can't pay off all debts, the stockholders must forfeit all personal assets. In other words, a majority of the corporate assets of the Cloud will go to the winners."

"Who holds the tickets?"

"Alma," Kurst replied. Several days ago he hadn't even heard of them, but now he could think of little else. The Overseers were to everyone but the Kohs a vague entity of semilegend. If the game was merely going to be ultimately a transfer of funds from one consortium to another, it would be of no concern. But as the news leaked out, a tremor was felt throughout the marketplaces of the Cloud. If the Overseers owned everything after tomorrow, what would happen?

"Surely they can't allow this," Blackie said.

"Certainly not. Zola and some of his friends are talking of open rebellion, refusing the transfer of funds, and planning to keep right on running things."

"But these Overseers—legend has it that they have awesome power in their control."

Kurst could only shrug. "As long as the social order stays

intact, there isn't much that can be done. Surely these Overseers won't start smashing entire worlds just to gain their winnings."

"Let's hope, but what is your information?"

"There's still a plan afoot. I overheard Zola's conversation with another Koh. Really, as this thing gets worse, they're getting more and more slipshod in their security. Anyhow, Zola's claiming that he still has someone down there, and an arrangement for Sigma to kill Aldin and Gablona."

"What! But Sigma's dead, his Gafs going over to Aldin."

"But if one of Sigma's Gafs kills those two, then the credit still goes to Sigma, even though he's been dead for nearly a month."

Blackie looked away from Kurst and punched up the latest market flow on the screen.

Trading had slowed off significantly the last five days. Options on some tickets had been running at almost full payoff value, five million katars for what had originally been a one-katar investment. All tickets regarding the death of Aldin and Gablona by the natives had vanished from the market days ago, their holders now hanging on for the final payoffs.

"There aren't many tickets out there," Blackie said.

"Buy them," Kurst snapped. "Zola's been right so far. This is the final insider move."

"They're going for fifty-three thousand a ticket right now for a full option till the end of the game."

"Buy 'em all," Kurst replied.

"Look, we've made several hundred million," Blackie argued. "Let's keep what we've got and get out before this market collapses."

"Several hundred million can buy over six thousand options," Kurst said, quickly running the calculation in his mind. "We could turn that into thirty billion with this kind of information. We'd be Kohs if this works out, think of it!"

Blackie looked up at Kurst, amazed at the transformation. A month before he had been an archetypal professor, locked up in his probability studies, playing his imaginary numbers games. But now he was as rabid as any shark on the trading floor, smelling yet one more deal, the final big one that could bring him all that he ever dreamed.

"I still don't feel good about this," Blackie said softly.

"Do it!" Kurst shouted. "Do it and we'll be Kohs, with wealth beyond imagining."

Blackie sat back, looking at him closely. Finally, with a quiet nod, she got up and left for the trading floor. Within minutes the shares of a Sigma kill had climbed to sixty thousand, and kept on rising.

Oishi sat alone, bathing his wounds in the gently swirling water of a stream. The field about him was a riot of color covered with deep orchidlike flowers as wide across as a man's reach, the scent an intoxicating fragrance that made him think of the cherry blossoms of home. The early-evening light drifted across the sky, as if taking the red of the flowers and using it to paint the clouds.

But he did not see it. Alone, lost in thought, he cleaned each of the cuts and then, rising, returned to the riverbank. Taking up a thread and a needle that one of his men had carried, he set to stitching the long dagger slash that had laid open his shoulder.

The pain was barely noticed; long ago he had learned to control such things, turning his thoughts to something else. But what he thought of cut far more deeply than the sting of the needle.

He had failed his lord.

He had stood ready, bow drawn, and watched his lord walk straight into the trap that he feared. With the snap of the first twig, he'd tensed the bow, aiming straight at the red-robed Gaf's heart.

The onset had been stunning and complete.

One moment, the path was empty except for the two offworlders and the Gaf. The next moment, half a hundred yellows had swarmed out, engulfing Aldin and Gablona. In that first instant he thought that in spite of Mari's comments about head bond Nargla had betrayed them anyhow. But Nargla never had a chance, Oishi had seen to that.

With a cry of rage he'd fired, then, tossing aside his bow, raised the others to charge, with the desperate hope that still the situation might be saved.

But maddeningly, the path was blocked by a squad of yellows who seemed determined to do but one thing, to die so that the others might escape.

Oishi's full attention returned to his wounded shoulder. The last rough stitch went in. He twirled a knot into the line and bit the thread.

When that first blade had hit, he thought himself dead, for surely the poison would bring him down. That first cut drove him to a wild frenzy, and he waded through the yellows, bellowing with rage, slashing again and again with his long sword.

Yet the yellows did not give back before him. As quickly as one died, another leaped to fill the gap. And all the time, over the heads of the assassins, he could see the knot of men dragging Aldin and Gablona off into the darkness.

At last, with a wild shout of rage, he downed the last assassin, the man's blood splashing into his eyes as he took off his foe's right arm with a single upward slash, and then kicked the screaming yellow to the side of the path, for the rest of his men to finish off.

Coming up to Nargla, he stopped.

Aldin and Gablona were gone. Off to his left he could hear the captors crashing through the bushes in retreat, and with a shout he ordered his men to pursue, expecting that at any second he would fall at last to the poison, not only from the first wound but from the half-dozen other slashes he had picked up in his wild, frenzied attack.

To his right he could hear shouts of alarm as well; the reds were stirring from their hiding place and coming up to the rescue of their leader.

There was one last act to perform, he thought, his mind suddenly cleared from the first wild, explosive rage.

He turned back up the path and, grabbing the first yellow body, he carried it up and dropped it next to Nargla. He put his foot on the Gaf's chest, yanked the arrow out of the ulla's heart, and then, taking the dagger out of the yellow's hand, he plunged the blade back into the hole. At the very least it would give the reds something to think about. Then turning, he crashed into the woods, even as the first red assassins appeared on the trail, racing to the rescue of their master.

He paused in his thoughts and, leaning over, examined the still-oozing wound on his thigh. Then he set to work on that one as well, the needle rising and falling, stitching the gaping cut together. It was funny, he hadn't even noticed that one until they'd finally given the pursuit up within sight of the city walls.

Every step of the way it seemed another yellow had leaped out at them. It would only take a moment to dispatch the assassin, but each moment put Aldin another step farther away, and finally the pursuers no longer even heard them, but could merely follow the trail until at last it had come to the clearing. The shattered city was before them, the gates shut. He was tempted to give over to his rage and simply charge straight ahead, but it was Mari who stopped him.

"He's already in the city," she whispered, her voice choked with tears. "We'll simply be throwing our lives away without any hope of saving him."

Trembling with exhaustion and despair, Oishi agreed, and the group had retreated back into the woods and camped by the small, flowing stream.

More than half were injured, four more samurai and five Gafs dead, ironically leaving him with exactly forty-seven warriors, including Mari and Tia. Gradually they had come to realize that the enemy had not been using poison blades. Most likely out of fear that one might accidentally be used on Aldin or Gablona, so intent was this Ulsak on capturing them alive. Without the poison, the assassins had fought at a disadvantage, accustomed to a fight where even a scratch was as good as a blow to the heart.

Finished at last with the wound, Oishi stood up and stretched. The dark red sun was on the horizon, sinking faster than what he was used to, on wherever his own world now was.

Standing, he looked along the bank. Several of his men had been doing the same as he, cleaning their wounds, tending to their weapons, or simply sleeping the sleep of exhaustion.

Sentries were posted, but somehow he knew there was little need for that now. The circle had advanced no farther, for what they had sought was taken. A day ago, all those with him had assumed that they would fight, and fight well, before going to their deaths. Now, but a day later, they rested along the quiet riverbank, knowing that after tomorrow, the game would be ended. Already Tia had promised them wealth, titles, and what could be called the ranks of daimyos for their loyal service to her uncle.

The sun's disk flattened out and disappeared. The seventy-ninth day had ended. With a sigh Oishi realized that if they so desired, this time tomorrow they would be free to leave.

And Aldin would be dead.

After putting his loincloth back on, he picked up the tattered robes of his old uniform he had once worn in service to Asano. The sleeves were caked with dried blood, the stains already set into the silk. He looked at the garment closely. Mingled somewhere in there were the stains of Kira's blood as well. How far away was it really from that world? Oishi wondered, looking up at the sky. He could remember the night when Aldin had taken him up to the roof of their hideout and pointed to the swirling light that sparkled in the midnight sky, and told him that there was home, the world that but months before had been the only world he'd ever known.

With a sigh he searched again for that speck of light. Where was Asano, his old lord? For by now he had come to realize that where he now walked was no spirit world, this was a world of living, breathing men, and other creatures as well. And like his own world, it was a realm with all the deceits, all the betrayals that men carried in their hearts. All except for Aldin, who in so many ways reminded him of Asano, right down to the gentle laugh and the desire to treat others with honor. So out of date, Oishi thought sadly, out of date even in my world, for what did honesty in his refusal to bribe Kira get his lord but betrayal, humiliation, and death?

Oishi put on the bloodstained robe and reached down to pick up the two blades that he had laid out on the grass. Replacing the weapons at his waist, he smiled inwardly at their touch. They were living things, his companions on the road of the samurai, with a lineage dating back to the great master Matsumasi, who had forged them with his own hands, imbuing them with his sense of honor and truth.

There was a faint cough behind him. He knew it was Takashi, who always did this when he wished to speak but did not wish to interrupt Oishi in his thoughts. He turned to face his brother and could see the grief in Takashi's eyes as well. The loss of the warrior's only son had cut into his soul, but he would hold his mourning in check till this was over.

Till this was over, Oishi thought. Zergh had lied to them, that fact Aldin had finally revealed. Even if they had survived there was no going back to their own world ever again. It was a world thousands of years past, and others had died, in their place. But somehow that didn't seem to matter at the moment.

"I was speaking to Tia Koh," Takashi said, and as he spoke

Oishi looked past him to see that the other samurai had drawn about him, the Gaf warriors standing on the edge of the circle.

"And?" Oishi asked softly.

"She said that we shall be named daimyos in her kingdom, with an entire world to call our fiefdom. She blames us not for Aldin's capture and says that it is senseless to do more."

Oishi merely nodded, and saw Tia standing on the edge of the group, Zergh at her side. She smiled wanly at him, the anguish of what she had been through still written on her features.

"As she said to me as well," Oishi replied.

Takashi was silent.

"So why are you telling me what I already know?" Oishi asked.

"For though honored, I must respectfully decline."

"To do what instead?" Oishi asked, looking at his brother who, though older, still acknowledged Oishi as the leader.

"I shall die with my lord Aldin," Takashi announced.

"But there is no way we can possibly reach him in there," Oishi said.

"Nevertheless, I swore to protect him. I have failed. At least I shall die sword in hand, and in the next world my lord Aldin shall greet me, standing beside Asano, and both shall know that I died a samurai—with honor."

Oishi felt tears in his eyes, and looking to the others, each of them nodded in turn. For once the Gafs did not bellow in their crude way but instead silently lifted their axes on high in agreement.

He watched as Tia gazed in amazement, and bracing her shoulders back, she nodded to him as well, Mari at her side.

"Then I shall not die alone," Oishi whispered. "I could not ask this of you. But know that yet again the forty-seven ronin are one. And though our lord will see us not, still in the end he shall know he did not die abandoned."

The group relaxed, as if they had already passed the great barrier, and now that it had been crossed, they hid their fear, choosing to enjoy the last moments of comradeship. Several of the men and Gafs fell into light banter, patting their weapons and boasting of accomplishments past and to come.

Tia came up to stand by Oishi's side, and nervously she reached out and took his hand.

"Why?" she asked.

"Because I am samurai," he replied, as if that simple statement explained all.

"You must not go with us," he said, looking her straight in the eyes.

"Sexist," she snapped, a smile tracing her features.

"What is that?"

"Never mind," she replied, and from her look he knew there was no sense in pushing the point any further. "When do we go?"

"I was thinking in the middle of the night. We'll get into the city, push as close as we can to where this Ulsak lives. If we can get through, we'll get Aldin out."

"But you don't believe that for a moment, do you?" she whispered.

He knew there was no sense in lying. "They made a mistake once, and thus we escaped. Such a commander as Ulsak will not allow it again. He'll have thousands of guards out, but at least they shall know we tried—and died as samurai."

Oishi sat down on the grass by the riverbank, and kneeling down, Tia joined him, her hand still in his. Around him the other samurai had drifted away, some to sleep, most to talk with old friends or new friends found among the big furry Gafs whom they still deferred to, remembering the old edicts of their emperor. Others, like Takashi, simply sat by the bank of the river, watching the reflection of the starlight as they inwardly prepared to say good-bye.

"Tell me of your worlds," Oishi said softly. "And how all this came to be."

"Ah, where do I start?" Tia laughed gently.

"Wherever you wish."

With a sigh she drew closer, her lips close to his.

"How you came to be here, I'll start there, and then tell you of the history of men, back to a place once called Earth," she whispered.

Smiling, she looked into his eyes.

"There is a legend that has been carried across ten thousand worlds," she said in barely a whisper, her eyes gazing into his, "to all the worlds where men have walked. Across three thousand years still it is remembered, the story of the forty-seven ronin, who would die for their lord, already dead . . ."

So the stars wheeled in their course, the great Magellanic

Cloud, in all its splendor, lighting the sky above them like a silvery band.

"I hope you go first," Gablona said weakly, looking across the room at Aldin, who stood chained to the opposite wall.

"Pleasant of you," Aldin replied. "And considering what they plan to do, I must say that I agree."

The door into their cell creaked open and Ulsak strode in, his face alight with an evil grin. Stopping in the doorway, he looked from one to the other, gloating over his catch.

"I must say, your hospitality is not quite as good as the last time," Aldin snapped, pleased with himself at his defiance. He'd been planning the line for hours, feeling that it was certainly better than groveling before the man who was about to bring about his death.

"Ah, yes, the accommodations," Ulsak replied, looking about the cell. "One of the few buildings spared the conflagration just so happened to be my private dungeon."

"How convenient."

"Yes," Ulsak replied, playing along with the game. "You see, my personal fortress was caught in the fire when an errant breeze blew some embers on the roof."

"How sad," Aldin retorted, happy with the momentary diversion the banter provided.

"So I thought it best to house you here, with a safe roof over your heads till dawn."

"Which is how long away?" Gablona cried.

"Oh, the night passes slowly for you, does it? How callous of me. It is near the middle of the darkness. But for your convenience I'll have a guard come to you every quarter of the hour for the rest of the night to inform you of how much time you have left.

"Have a pleasant evening, my friends." Ulsak laughed, and turning, he strode from the room.

The two were silent for a moment, until finally Gablona raised his head to look at Aldin.

"I hope you suffer worse than me," the Koh screamed.

"And then Aldin said good-bye to Alexander, known as the Great . . ."

Oishi reached out and touched her lightly on the cheek.

"I think it's time we started," he said softly.

She stopped, self-consciously, and laughed gently.

"I wish this night could go on forever," Tia said, and sighed.

"But in a short time it will," Oishi replied. "And then you can tell me yet more, for as long as we wish."

Before he even realized what he was doing, he leaned forward, his lips brushing against hers.

Eagerly she sought him out, her hand still held by his.

Finally he pulled back, their one kiss fading away. The two smiled like children who had kissed for the first time in a darkened corner.

Oishi came to his feet, and as if knowing that he was again the leader of his comrades, she released her hold on his hand.

"It's time," Oishi said, and all about him the others stirred, coming out of their reveries, their quiet thoughts, or the final snatches of forced bravado shared with comrades who understood what in fact each was trying to hide.

"What is your plan?" Ura asked, coming up before Oishi, his Gafs forming up in a knot behind him.

"Plan?" Oishi lowered his head and started to laugh. "Plan, you ask? Find a low spot or break in the wall, go through it, and then head into the city."

"What about the catacombs?" Mari asked.

Oishi shook his head. "It's a miracle we ever found our way out of them. We could go in there and be lost for days."

The others nodded in agreement.

"Then let's go," Oishi announced, drawing his sword, he held it up to the starlight.

"Bravo. Bravo, I say," a voice called from out of the shadows. "I wish I could have a social realist painting of this moment, I'd call it 'the forty-seven ronin march again.' Absolutely heroic!"

The group stopped, weapons lowered.

"Who is it?" Oishi shouted.

"Lower your voice, my good man. Please lower it, or they'll hear."

The shadow drew closer. Beneath the starlight, a bent, wizened form took shape; leaning on a staff, a man stepped before the group.

"What the hell do you want, old man?" Mari snapped.

"Just a little talk between friends."

"No tricks from you, old one, or we'll cut your throat and be done with you," Ura growled.

"You Gafs, always such a bloodthirsty lot."

"I know that voice," Tia snapped, and pushing through the crowd, she came up to the old man.

"Well, I'll be damned," she said with a laugh. "Yaroslav!"

"Yaroslav it is." The old man chuckled, and extending his arms, he threw aside the staff and danced in a circle.

"Had all those bastards fooled, did it for weeks. Got a little flogging in the end, but at least they didn't impale me. Shows you what can come from being a good anthropologist. I was their mad shaman, and they ate up every word I said, like Xsarns in a shit bowl!"

"You know this man?" Oishi asked, coming to stand by Tia.

"Ah, yes, you and Tia," Yaroslav said, wagging his finger at the two. "Been watching you for some time, really quite touching."

"You old goat," Tia snapped, even as she hugged Aldin's old friend. "You mean you were watching us?"

"Watching you. Damn my eyes, the moment I heard that Aldin had been taken, I knew I had to find you before you folks ran off and did something rash and got yourselves killed. I have a little trick up my sleeve. There was a small chance I could pull it off alone, but with your help the odds are increased. Some good detective work on my part, to be sure, but I figured you'd be near the gate where Aldin was brought in."

"You know where they have him then?" Oishi asked hopefully, his features alight with joy.

"Nope."

With a sigh Oishi turned away.

"Then step aside, there's something we must attend to," the samurai said sadly.

"Now wait a minute," Yaroslav said, rushing up to the head of the group and standing before Oishi. "This whole thing is ready to crack open. Whatever trick you played against the other clans had its effect. Those young bucks of theirs are hot for some yellow blood, their ullas are barely holding them back."

"That's no concern of ours now," Oishi announced.

"Why, the reds are in an absolute frenzy, claim that Ulsak murdered their ulla to get Aldin. Even the discovery of one of your men dressed in the yellow didn't quite persuade them; they think Ulsak dressed the body up as a ruse."

Oishi smiled at that one.

"Ah, I thought your hand might have been in it. Not even Ulsak would kill another ulla—a bad precendent for masters to kill masters. The only thing that's keeping them together is the sacrifice of Aldin and the promise of what comes later."

"You mean their getting off this world?" Tia asked.

"How did you find that out?" Yaroslav shouted with surprise.

"A little deductive reasoning, that's all. Gablona tried to make a deal for his life, the Overseers manipulated it, and fifty ships are now slated to dock at the tower tomorrow. Why the hell didn't you tell me before you left?"

"Girl, there's hope for you yet," Yaroslav announced. "Sorry I couldn't say anything, but to be frank, I still wasn't sure of you. Blood is thicker than water, they say. You are only Aldin's relative by marriage."

He paused for a moment and looked at her again. "I guess I was wrong.

"But anyhow," Yaroslav continued, looking back to the rest of the group, "we can still have our say in this thing."

"By trying to turn the clans against each other?" Mari asked.

"I thought of that. It could help, but there's more important business to be done. I plan to bring down the whole damned thing, but I need you people to help me bring it about. You can run about and raid if you wish, but the damage has already been done, and in the few hours remaining, you won't do much more. Now, come dawn, the gates will be opened, then all the Shig fighters from the other five clans will march in, all of them hot already. There'll be more than a million of them in the great square. The slightest spark ready to set them off. Now if Ulsak delivers as promised, all will be forgotten. But if he fails . . ." And his voice trailed off as he looked around excitedly, bursting with anticipation for what he had planned.

Oishi hesitated.

"We were going to die in the name of our lord," he said quietly.

"When all this hits, you most likely will," Yaroslav stated.

"What are you thinking then? And be quick about it," Ura demanded.

"First, back to the catacombs."

"What? To crawl about down there, while our lord dies above?" Oishi shouted. "Never!"

"Just trust me," Yaroslav said excitedly. "I'll try to explain what we need to do on the way. With your help I'm sure of getting past the guards Ulsak has set up."

Oishi looked over at Tia, realizing that she alone out of the group knew this insane old man.

"He's Aldin's closest friend. Him and Zergh," she said quietly. "I'll go with you, Yaroslav."

Oishi looked at the man closely and could see the excitement, and also the pleading, in his eyes.

"All right then," Oishi announced, "but this better be a damn good reason."

"Oh, it is, it most certainly is." Yaroslav began to cackle. "Why, it'll be the biggest damn display in history. Now let's go."

And following the old man, the party disappeared into the darkness.

chapter sixteen

The roar of the multitude thundered over them, so deafening that Aldin could not even hear the screams of terror from Gablona, who was standing right next to him.

A million voices cried out in anticipation, their factional differences forgotten for the moment, united at the thought of watching the death of those whom Ulsak had promised.

Aldin looked over his shoulder to where Ulsak stood above him on the dais. The ulla looked out upon the multitude with arms extended, a glint of savage delight in his eyes. For a moment his gaze dropped to Aldin.

The old vasba turned away. The Shiga leader was completely mad, one could see it in his eyes, and Aldin trembled inwardly with the thought that in a few short hours that madness would be unleashed across the Cloud.

"Hear me, O my people!" Ulsak screamed, but his voice was carried away, like the cry of an infant before the thunder of a maelstrom.

Four guards stepped up to Aldin's side, and grabbing his chains, they pulled him forward. Together they stepped off the high dais and started down the steps to a lower platform that was constructed so that all in the great square could see.

No matter how hard he had tried to nerve himself for this moment, Aldin felt his knees go to jelly when he saw the sharpened spike rising up from the platform floor.

Swooning, he sank to the ground, so that the guards had to drag him forward.

At the sight of his collapse, the howling of the Shiga rose to a thunderous pitch, and Aldin felt as if his ears were about to burst.

With rough shoves and curses the Shiga dragged him to the stake. Trembling, he looked up from the ground. The steel spike glistened evilly in the morning sun. Aldin turned his head aside and vomited, which caused the crowd to roar once more with delight.

Lying on the ground, gasping for breath, he saw Gablona rolling on the platform beside him, his shrieks for mercy carried away by the roar of the crowd.

Rough hands grabbed Aldin by the shoulders and pulled him to his feet. Another hand forced his mouth open and pushed a flask between his teeth. Cool liquid poured down his throat, and he drank, thinking that this would be the last time he would ever do so.

Seconds later he felt a tingling in his fingers and his heart started to race, as if he had suddenly downed half a dozen jolts of coffee.

"It'll keep you from passing out," one of the guards shouted in his ear. "We wouldn't want the fun to end too quickly."

Suddenly the crowd started to fall quiet, their faces uplifted toward the heavens.

"The smaller darkness," a guard shouted, and Aldin looked up toward the pale red sun.

The edge of the sun's disk, partially obscured by high thin clouds, showed a thin sliver of darkness, as if the edge had been nibbled off. A hush fell. After the thundering roar, the silence was almost as frightening.

The sea of faces gazed upward and then looked down to where Ulsak stood. Aldin looked over his shoulder and saw that Ulsak had walked up to a high pulpit constructed atop the dais.

"Hear me, O my people," Ulsak roared. His voice echoed across the plaza. Farther out, criers mounted small platforms scattered throughout the crowd, and hearing Ulsak's words, they shouted them once again so that even in the farthest corner of the square the words of the leader could be heard.

"Today is the day of the Ulman," Ulsak shouted. "And now I reveal to you all what shall come to pass. Today shall be the day of uniting. Our six clans shall become one."

His words echoed away, and a low murmur arose, so that Ulsak held his hands up even higher to call for silence.

"For the uniting has been prophesied since our beginning. By the sacrifice of these two, the Unseen One has decreed that the time has come.

"Now at last I am allowed to reveal to you who I am."

He paused with a dramatic flourish, and as his words were carried out, an ugly murmuring rose from the crowd. The yellows fell silent, as if in anticipation, for if their ulla was raised up, then the Wardi would be the first within the one clan.

"Hear me, O my people. At last I may reveal all. For I am the lost Ema, sent to guide you back to the stars!"

A wild shout went up from the assembly, the voices raised up in either triumph or rage at such sacrilege. Around the base of the tower dozens fell to the circle of yellows, as some of the reds, driven by wild fanaticism, drew blades and rushed forward. For a moment Aldin thought that a general riot was about to break out, and for the first time in years, he silently prayed.

But suddenly an awed hush fell over the crowd as again they looked to the sky. For the first time in their two thousand years upon the Hole, the inhabitants saw the beginning of a double eclipse.

The shadow advancing to the right had already slipped farther in, but to the left of the sun the thinnest sliver of another shadow had appeared, moving in the opposite direction.

Hushed with awe, the crowd looked back to Ulsak.

"This is our sign. The two shadows, represented here by the two about to die. At the moment the two horns of light disappear, they shall die, and the Seda shall be opened to you, my people, and together we shall go to the stars and kill in the name of the Unnamed!"

His words were met with stunned silence—which held a power as frightening as the thunder of the multitude.

"In promise to you and as a sign, I go now, to above—there to cast open the doors. Look to the Platform of the Fallen, and there you shall see me. And when I fall not, then you shall know that I am indeed the Ema revealed. And when next you see me face-to-face, we shall be among the stars."

With a dramatic flourish Ulsak turned from the pulpit and strode down the stairs. A dozen Wardi warriors stood at the base, a platform held high, covered with the finest of yellow silks. Ulsak stepped upon it, and shouldering their burden, the twelve carried their leader across the dais and to the entry of the tower. One last time Ulsak turned to face the Al'Shiga, and then he disappeared through the entryway and on into the tower.

"Impale them," an ulla commanded, coming up to the guards.

The four men picked Aldin up, and after moving forward, they positioned themselves about the upraised stick. Then, ever so gently, they lowered him down. Aldin's feet touched the ground, and as they did so he felt the nick of cold steel slice through between his legs. Instinctively he rose up on his toes, and at the sight of his struggling, laughter rang out across the square.

The guards grabbed the four chains that were hooked to a steel belt about his waist, extended them out, and hooked them to four curved spikes extending up from the platform floor.

Ever so gingerly Aldin tried to move. The steel belt held him in place, and try as he could, it was impossible to move himself off the deadly spike scant inches beneath him.

He heard something being rolled up behind him, and turning his head, he saw a large copper urn, a single spigot extending out from the container that was hooked into the canvas bag on his back.

The ulla came up to the spigot and then looked up to the sun, as if judging the time. He turned the flow open and leaned forward to look inside the bag.

"That should bring you down just as the horns disappear," the ulla said with a grin, and then he turned to the guards.

"If either of them are still standing by then, just push them down and finish it." He looked back at Aldin, the same merciless grin still lighting his features.

"You're lucky. The water flow is quick, and you'll be dead

in a couple of hours. Usually we take a full day to finish the job."

"Your mother takes carnal pleasure from pigs," Aldin snapped.

The ulla's face darkened with rage, and Aldin started to laugh hysterically. After all, there wasn't anything worse the swine could do to him now.

Several of the guards turned away with smirks as the ulla stormed off the platform.

Aldin looked over at Gablona, who stood just three meters away.

"This is a fine mess you've gotten us into, Larice," Gablona cried.

"I've gotten us into? You cheated on the last game; you even tried to fix this one. You made Ulsak that deal. You're insane."

"Well, at least those bastard Kohs up there'll have nothing left after I'm gone," Gablona cried.

"Just shut up and leave me alone," Aldin said.

He stretched up on his toes again and then, ever so slowly, lowered himself down. The edge of the blade nicked him again.

The crowd before him had fallen silent, except for occasional taunts and jeers. He gazed out over them. A million madmen, he thought, shaking his head. Their women and children back in the cities, almost as insane. The Cloud would become a charnel house when these people were let loose. For two thousand years there'd been no organized military, so there would be little if any organized defense. The wolves before him would slaughter with glee.

He shifted his shoulders slightly. Already he could feel the first faint tug of weight as the canvas pack on his back started to fill with water.

He lifted his gaze up. A most incredible sight, he thought wistfully, a double eclipse, and he watched as ever so slowly the sun began to disappear.

"We've lost all contact with Skyhook," Vol shouted, bursting into the room.

"We know," the Xsarn screamed. "It went down ten minutes ago."

The Kohs were in wild confusion. All afternoon there'd

been a funerallike despair. Aldin and Gablona were obviously in the hands of the Shiga, and the vid hookup had shown the preparations—and the impaling platforms. Throughout the entire Cloud all commerce had stopped. Here and there a lucky ticket holder sat in a tavern or in the public square, watching the printout reports, already counting the millions he'd win if he was lucky enough to have bought the winning combination on the first day, not knowing the disaster that was in the making.

One of the minor Kohs of GGC had already been found dead in his office, a liter bottle of poison in his hand.

"Zola, is this a repeat of last time?" Vol screamed. "Switch the vid signal, then tell everybody something different happened."

Zola could only shake his head. His hoped-for agent was lurking somewhere down there in the catacombs, hundreds of meters away from the two. With that mob it would be impossible now for him to get through.

He looked up at Vol.

"Are you mad?" he whispered. "The only com link directly to the tower is down. All signals from the game, however, are still being routed through."

"Then why?" Vol roared.

"Because, my fellow Kohs, I think the Overseers are about to pull something else that they don't want us to see."

Suddenly by Bukha's desk a paging signal flashed on. Picking up a headset, he hooked in, and all about him fell silent.

A quiet moment passed, and a look of stunned disbelief crept over his features.

He dropped the headset.

"So, Tia was right after all." Bukha gasped.

"What? What about Tia?" Zola asked.

"She tried to warn me, but I simply wouldn't believe it."

"Warn you of what, for heaven's sake?"

"I just had two reports come in. The security system on the tower was shut down an hour ago, when a dozen Overseers boarded the structure. The damn thing's wide open."

"And what's the other?"

"It was just reported that fifty primary transports just down-jumped and are in orbit around the Hole, already maneuvering to dock with the tower."

"Fifty ships?" the Xsarn asked, still not comprehending, and then the truth finally dawned.

"I think I'm going to be ill," the Xsarn whispered, and rising, he staggered from the room.

"That's it," Yaroslav whispered.

Directly ahead they could see a half-dozen yellows standing in the open corridor, and beyond that, what appeared to be a door, made from the same substance as the Skyhook.

"We're directly under the foundation of the Skyhook," Yaroslav whispered.

"Be quiet, old man," Oishi whispered. He'd heard what was planned but still could not quite believe. But there was nothing else that could be done but to follow through with this madman's folly.

The party approached the six yellows and slowed.

"You're relieved," Yaroslav announced, drawing up to the guards. "My men here have been sent down to replace you."

"By whose orders?" one of the yellows growled suspiciously.

"By my orders."

"You're the mad shaman. You can't order us."

"Oh, yes, I can," Yaroslav roared, waving his hands about as if drawing up a mystical curse.

The six stepped back slightly but still refused to move away.

"Leave us now."

"When our ulla tells us and not before," one of the yellows barked defiantly.

"Oh, that's it?" Yaroslav snapped, and he started into waving his hands in earnest while drawing up next to the leader.

The guard pushed Yaroslav back with a curse and then doubled over with a grunt, a dagger sticking out of his chest.

Oishi flung aside his yellow robe, and in the same movement his sword snaked out, catching the second yellow before his look could even change from astonishment to pain. The rest of the samurai closed in and finished off the others.

"A good kill," Oishi announced, clapping Yaroslav on the shoulder.

"Still have the old touch. I told you I would," Yaroslav snapped.

He strode up to the door and gazed about.

"Seven keys," he said softly, and his fingers traced out the outline of seven squares set into the wall.

"Took me a while to even figure that out. I was down here for days prowling around, right under their noses. They thought I was mad, and after meeting with Ulsak, they left me alone. Then heaven knows how many hours I spent on these keys. Pushing them, and pushing them. Figured that a certain sequence would do the trick to let us in. But by Jove, which seven? Finally stumbled on it a couple of days back, and then it was 'open sez me.' "

Yaroslav stood up on his toes and touched the seven inlaid squares.

Nothing happened.

"Now don't tell me I've forgotten it," he mumbled crossly.

Exasperated, Oishi turned away to avoid screaming with rage.

"Now let's try it again, one, two, four, six, three, five, seven."

There was a faint click and the doorway opened.

"Figured those First Travelers would have a logic to the sequence, otherwise I'd still be out here punching. Well, what are you waiting for?" Yaroslav snapped, looking back at his companions, and he strode into the room.

Oishi waved, and from the darkness at the end of the corridor, the rest of his party appeared, each of them laden down with earthen jars that Yaroslav had directed them to pick up earlier.

As Oishi stepped through the door he fell silent with awe. The room gleamed with the same strange whiteness of the tower. Overhead, lights without flame, like those he'd seen when aboard the sky ship, snapped on dimly, so that several of the men gave startled cries.

"Quickly now, quickly," Yaroslav called, guiding them onward.

Down the long corridor they followed the old man until at last the pathway broadened into a single room.

"Stack the jars along that wall," he commanded.

Momentarily confused by what he was seeing, Oishi went up to the wall Yaroslav had pointed out.

Strange lights glowed along the length of the room, while here and there strange figures danced across boards of glass. And then one of his men screamed.

From out of the far corner it emerged. It towered twice the height of the startled samurai—a strange metallic-looking thing with a hundred arms that wavered back and forth as it approached, floating as if suspended by invisible hands.

"I'd like to introduce you to a First Traveler," Yaroslav announced, pointing to the creature that hovered before the terrified group.

"Quite harmless actually," Yaroslav announced. "Lets you wander about, do what you please. I don't even think it's aware we're here. Just busy with doing its job, that's all.

"When I finally broke in here, its presence confirmed what I'd suspected of this room. Figured that such a location would have to be down on the planet, since being located in space made it vulnerable to all sorts of mishaps. Quite ingenious of them, really. Any seismic activity, the sensors pick it up, a dampening system switches in, cancels it out before anything can go wrong. It even compensates for the solar wind fluxes, with tiny rocket bursts.

"Now we got a wonderful moment here. Two large moons aligning sets up quite a tidal force, along with that huge sun above us. Oh, quite a gravitational pull indeed. These controls here should dampen it out, since the force is not distributed equally, with a greater pull farther up the line than down here."

Yaroslav looked over at the samurai and saw he'd lost them.

"Oh, never mind. Just put those jars there. Carefully now, nitro and ammonia nitrates are a bit finicky, not like your black powder. Took me days to make the stuff."

The last jar was finally placed, and Yaroslav looked around the room.

"I think you better get out of here," he said, a smile on his face as he stuck a roll of fuse into the single jar of black powder and then placed it into the middle of the explosives.

Stepping back, he grabbed a torch from one of the Gafs. For a moment he hesitated, looking closely at the warrior, and then he turned away.

"Let me do it?" Oishi asked. "The rest of you get out of here."

"Not on your life," Yaroslav roared. "And give you all the fun? Now get the hell out of here!"

The samurai looked at the old man, and with a nod he turned and raced from the room, following the others.

Yaroslav looked up at the First Traveler that hovered impassively above him. It had created itself to build, to maintain, but in its world, a concept to defend had never occurred, and so it watched and did nothing.

"Sorry, old man," Yaroslav whispered. He touched the torch to the fuse and with a wild shout of glee, like a boy who'd just let off a firecracker in school, he turned and raced out of the room.

Most of the sun was gone now, and the pack dug into his shoulders. Beads of sweat ran down his face, the salt stinging his eyes.

As the sun slowly disappeared between the closing disks of the moons, a low chant had started from the yellows, which gradually had built and swelled, the plaza echoing with the noise.

"Al'Shiga, Al'Shiga, Al'Shiga!"

Maddeningly it was timed to the beat of his heart, each word a thundering roar that pulsed as the blood thundered through his veins.

He tried to shift the weight, and as he did so, his knees buckled and the steel slipped ever so slightly into his body.

With a grimace of pain, he straightened, and his agony was apparent, so that the Shiga roared the louder.

Finally he decided. He would do it. In one cold thrust he'd simply lift his feet and fall. It could certainly be no worse than this. For surely it would come anyhow; to draw it out, for even another minute, was madness.

Shaking his head, the sweat fell away from his eyes. He wanted somehow to scream a curse at them all, but knew they could not hear.

And then he raised his head up, to gaze at the wonder in the sky, the two horns starting to form between the closing disks, the Skyhook bisecting the sun now as it rose to the midday sky.

All this he was leaving, he thought almost wistfully, while another part of his mind steeled him for the fall.

He raised himself high onto his toes, to add the extra inch or two, as if it would help to speed him into oblivion.

Good-bye to it all.

He let his knees buckle, and he tried to drop.

With a wild shriek of pain he shot back up. For a moment he felt off balance, as if he were going to fall again, and he tottered, still shrieking, knowing that the blade had cut in not more than a centimeter at most.

Down he started to slip. Desperate, he fought to regain his balance and shot back up on his toes. His balance wavered and he slipped downward again, the edge of steel slipped into the now-open wound.

In his mind he remembered Ulsak's taunt—how the impaled would bob up and down like a toy, screaming their anguish. He looked over at Gablona and saw the Koh was doing the same, and for the first time in weeks he felt pity for the man, even while shriek after shriek was torn from his own lips.

Suddenly he heard the taunts and chants die away to a hushed silence. Thousands of arms were pointed toward the tower. Steadying himself, Aldin looked up, and there, far above, on the side of Skyhook, was a tiny yellow dot.

For a moment he thought he felt the ground beneath him buck, and he danced for balance, bobbing up and down again, and then the tremor died away.

Soon the horns would close, the north and south ends of the sun shrinking away to nothingness, and at the thought of what was coming, Aldin shrieked with pain and rage.

The platform trembled beneath his feet, so that with a fearful gasp, he stepped back. Wide-eyed, Ulsak turned and looked to the Overseer.

"It is nothing," Losa whispered. "The tower moves because the moons draw upon it. But there is nothing to fear."

Trying to control his rising terror, Ulsak turned back and stepped out.

For millennia, whenever a Shiga had attempted to escape back up the tower, he was met here, three hundred meters above the square, where all passengers going up were checked before continuing their journey to the stars. Those of the Accursed then stepped back into the cars of glass and ascended. The faithful were dragged to this doorway and thrown out, to fall back onto the Hole.

But never again, Ulsak thought triumphantly, mastering his fear.

He stepped to the edge and gazed out.

Below him, filling the city, were his people. And suddenly, as if on a distant wind, he could hear them calling, chanting.

"Ema, Ema!"

Beaming with triumph, he stood there for long minutes, basking in the adulation of the multitude.

Craning his neck, Ulsak gazed up the long length of the Seda, which now pointed like a needle straight into the eye of the disappearing sun—the horns growing smaller and smaller.

It was all his; he would soon be master of the stars.

And then his eyes narrowed.

The needle was no longer straight!

He saw the faintest of bulges, like a ripple running down a string held taut. The bulge loomed larger, racing downward.

With a startled cry, Ulsak leaped back into the room behind the platform. A growing rumble, a creaking and groaning, snapped through the Skyhook, and like a ship riding a wave, the tower shifted, slamming Ulsak into the wall.

Wide-eyed, he looked at the Overseer, and even on such an alien face, he thought he saw fear.

Another ripple snapped them yet again; the two were tossed against each other.

With a cry of alarm, Ulsak stepped back out onto the platform. A wave was racing straight up, returning back to the heavens, but another was rippling down, twice as big as the first. The tower shuddered. A dull rumble barely on the edge of hearing echoed through the room, growing louder and louder. The floor bucked up to meet him, then instantly dropped away.

Crawling, Ulsak dragged himself back to the platform, and sticking his head out, he peered up. Wave after wave was rippling downward, each one bigger than the last.

"It's falling," Ulsak screamed. He turned, with blade drawn, to confront the Overseer. But the room was empty.

"I forbid it!" Ulsak cried. "As the Ema, I forbid it!"

He dragged himself out onto the platform and stood erect. Below, the multitudes shifted and moved, as if he were gazing down upon insects beneath his feet.

"I am the Ema!" he roared to those below, and to the heavens above. "Stand and believe, for I command it!"

A thundering roar echoed louder and louder.

He turned his gaze upward once again, and as he did so, the horns shimmered and disappeared in the clear noonday sky. A blazing red crown engulfed the dark spot where the sun had been, while from horizon to horizon the stars shone out in all their splendor.

"It is the time that I foretold!" Ulsak screamed.

The thunder grew louder and a wave of darkness came racing down from above.

"I am the Ema!"

And as he screamed, the platform fell away beneath his feet.

Suddenly Aldin was aware that the roaring of the crowd had died away.

All faces were lifted upward, and in his agony, he raised his eyes.

For a moment he thought his vision had deceived him: the Skyhook had a bulge in it.

Amazed, he watched as the wavelike motion raced groundward, growing larger and larger. A distant rumble slapped through the soles of his feet as the wave snapped into the ground. Instantly it recoiled and raced back up the other side of the structure.

A deadly hush fell over the Shiga.

Another wave came down, and as it passed the first one going back up, the two seemed to combine, doubling the bulge for a moment, so that it looked as if the entire tower should snap in half.

"Aldin, what's happening?" Gablona cried.

"Something wrong with the tower. It's setting up a wave motion."

The second wave hit the ground and Aldin felt the ground shake beneath his feet, so that he struggled for balance.

"Here comes another one," Gablona cried excitedly.

"The damn thing's going to collapse!" Aldin shrieked.

His words drifted out over the crowd, and an excited murmur started to rise.

Aldin realized the moment had to be seized.

"Ulsak blasphemed!" he screamed. "He is not the Ema, our deaths displease the Unnamed One!"

A wild shout went up from the reds closest to Aldin.

The fourth wave hit and, rebounding back up, rose past the fifth traveling downward. A thundering crack echoed across the plaza.

Aldin looked up and at that moment the sky darkened as the eclipse went total. He drew in his breath, for he should already be dead.

He looked to the guards about him. Three of the men stood

back, their eyes wide with terror, but the fourth one strode forward and, reaching out, grabbed Aldin by the shoulders and started to push down.

"Ulsak!"

A roar went up from those nearest the platform.

The guard, who had been looking into Aldin's eyes with grim hatred, turned his gaze upward and stepped back with a startled cry.

Aldin looked back up.

In the half-light he saw a shadow racing down, robes fluttering in the wind.

With a sickening crunch, Ulsak hit the pavement, his body bursting open by the gate into the tower.

"Death to the Wardi, they have blasphemed!" a voice rose up from the reds.

The guard turned away from Aldin and fled, while all about the dais a wild frenzy of killing erupted. Another wave hit, with a mind-numbing roar.

Aldin watched gaping in amazement as wave after wave raced up and down the length of the Skyhook, so that it tossed and turned like a ship upon a storm-driven sea.

A light rain drifted down around him, and confused, he suddenly realized that it was flecks of material wrenched off from the tower. The rain turned into a shower, and then into a torrent, as larger and larger chunks of facing ripped free, plummeting into the crowd. First one man fell, then another, and then two or three went down as chunks several meters in width fell upon the crowd.

Amazed, Aldin found himself laughing.

"Looks like the choice is impaling or being crushed," he roared, looking over at Gablona, who stood open-mouthed, gazing at the crumbling tower.

Suddenly he felt hands upon his shoulders, and in a flash of panic he braced himself, knowing that some enraged yellow still wanted to finish him off.

There was the tearing of canvas, and the water sack behind him ruptured, the weight splashing away so that he felt as if he were floating.

In the semidarkness, a Gaf stood before him, a man in a tattered samurai robe by his side.

"Pull these chains up!" Oishi roared.

Fumbling, the men around him fell to with a will, and Mari

broke through the press, throwing herself into Aldin's arms with a scream of relief, so that he momentarily sagged.

"I'll be damned if I'm able to sleep with you now!" Aldin shrieked, struggling for balance.

The chains fell away and gingerly he rose up on his toes and stepped back.

A samurai came up to either side and prevented him from collapsing.

"What about me!" Gablona screamed.

Aldin looked over and saw that the Koh was still chained to the spike.

"A billion katars," Aldin roared.

"Anything, anything," Gablona pleaded.

"Tia, you witness as fellow Koh!"

"Done," she cried, coming up to Aldin's side.

"Anything, I'll make it one point one billion. Just let me out!" Gablona screamed.

Aldin nodded and several Gafs pulled Gablona loose.

"How do you like my show?" Yaroslav cried with glee, coming up to Aldin's side.

"Magnificent, how did you do it!"

"Later . . . but right now, let's get the hell out of here."

Yaroslav waved for the group to follow, then started back toward the tower.

"Back there?" Aldin screamed.

"It'll be an hour or more before it really starts to come down, and there's no way we'll get across the square alive. Let's head for the catacombs and get out of this madhouse. There's an entry down through the tower."

Aldin looked back over his shoulder.

Beneath the eerie light of the eclipse, the Shiga were falling upon each other in a wild frenzy of murder and revenge. Color surged against color, while those closest to the tower desperately tried to claw their way out from the hail of doom raining down from above.

"You're all fucking crazy!" Aldin roared, and following Yaroslav, they raced into the tower entrance.

"We're still too close," Tia shouted, gasping for breath as they climbed a low hill outside the city walls.

"We could walk for a week and not get away from the debris," Yaroslav announced. "That thing's forty thousand kilometers up. The top parts will simply go into orbit, lower sections in decaying orbit, while the rest will collapse back in on the world. You could be a thousand kilometers away and still get hit."

"Anyhow I did some rough calculations as to how it would fall and found a cave just ahead where we could get some cover and still watch the show."

"Hope your math isn't too far off," Aldin said anxiously as he turned his gaze heavenward.

Just below the crest of the hill they found the shelter Yaroslav had been leading them to. Beneath the lip of the cave, the group turned to watch the madness in the city below.

From every gate, the Shiga poured out, different color robes mingled together, slaughtering each other on the way—the general pogrom against the yellows giving way in minutes to an all-out frenzy against all other sects. Few yellows seemed to be left. Here and there they could see knots of them holding off against several other sects, and as soon as the yellows went down, the comrades of moments before would turn against each other.

"Look at that wave," Tia cried, pointing back to the tower.

A massive pulse came racing downward, clearly illuminated now by the hourglass-shaped sun that had crossed into the western sky.

"This might be the one," Yaroslav whispered. "Once that imbalance started, it would just keep feeding on itself, growing and growing till it came to this."

The air about them rumbled, as if from an approaching storm.

With an earth-shattering jolt, the wave hit the ground. The tower started to torque from the effect. A loud crack echoed across the Hole, and ever so slowly, the tower twisted in its moorings.

Another even larger wave hit as the tower base was still twisting from the previous blow.

To everyone's stunned amazement, the structure actually lifted into the air, ripping free from its foundation. For long seconds it hovered fifty or more meters in the air, pulled up by the momentum of its mass rising upward. And then a downward pulse hit, smashing the Skyhook into its foundation with such force that the entire city seemed to leap from the impact, so that for a moment even the Shiga broke off their frenzy of killing and lay upon the ground, wailing in terror.

"It's snapped!" Gablona cried, pointing upward.

Aldin looked up and saw where the tower had parted, kilometers above, so that it seemed like a mere thread had been cut.

"Twenty, maybe thirty kilometers up." Yaroslav chortled. "Oh, this is going to be simply marvelous. And I did it, I did it!" The old man danced with glee.

For a minute or more it seemed as if the thread had barely moved, and then ever so gradually, it started to shift, racing out eastward, the narrow filigree line broadening out.

A faint shriek filled the air, growing in volume as it dropped in pitch.

Louder it grew, and closer the line came toward the ground. The base, again resting on the ground, leaned over, the angle dropping lower and lower. A plume of dust rose up from around it, and then the structure started to hit.

It was as if one long string of explosives had been laid out in a line from the center of the city, all the way to the edge of the Hole and beyond.

With a thundering roar, the tower smashed downward, the explosive impact rippling straight across the city, sending rubble hundreds of meters back into the air, to rain down again and cast up yet more destruction.

The ground shook beneath their feet as the line of impact swept past, not more than a kilometer away, and then thundered off into the distance.

"And look at that!" Ura screamed, pointing up.

A section of tower, several kilometers or more in length, was plummeting straight down like an arrow.

"Magnificent!" Yaroslav shouted, still capering about.

It hit the south edge of the city, the three-kilometer-high length telescoping in on itself, sending out a deadly plume of debris that soon covered the entire city beneath its pall.

The Gafs roared with delight, joining Yaroslav in his mad dance.

"Thousands, tens of thousands of servants for our brothers in the next world," Ura exulted. "We'll be the most famous Basaks that ever lived and died!"

They watched as the sun drifted away before them, until finally only a small span of sky separated the hourglass-shaped disk from the horizon.

"You know, I wonder whatever happened to that bastard Hassan," Gablona said, coming up to stand by Aldin's side.

"Knowing him, he'd survive even this," Aldin replied, feeling almost good-natured toward his old employer.

"You weren't serious about the billion, were you?" Gablona asked, as if joking with an old friend about a half-forgotten debt.

"One point one billion, to be precise," Aldin replied with a tight-faced smile.

"Well, at least we've survived. In another couple of minutes it'll all be over."

"Aldin!"

Something slammed into him, and he staggered back and rolled.

Looking up, he saw the Gaf named Kolda lying on the ground, a samurai blade in his chest.

Takashi stood over the body, a strange look of detachment on his face, and then he fell away, his stomach sliced open from hip to hip.

With a cry of panic, Aldin crawled up to the fallen samurai.

"The Gaf came up behind the two of you and drew his blade, but I stopped him," the samurai whispered. "Something about that one's been bothering me for days."

Yaroslav and Oishi came up and knelt by Takashi's side.

"Can you help him?" Aldin cried, looking at the old man.

Yaroslav looked at the wound and shook his head.

The samurai looked up and smiled.

"Ah, what a fight it was today, best battle I ever saw. My son shall enjoy hearing of it," he whispered, and then he fell away.

Horrified, Ura came up and looked at what one of his comrades had done.

He turned to Oishi, an imploring in his eyes. "Kolda was a traitor. May he never gaze upon his brothers in the next world. May he be the servant of demons, to torment him ever after."

"And of the blood debt of my brother?" Oishi asked coldly, snapping his blade half-way from its scabbard as he stepped before Ura.

"He shall be the servant of your brother in the next world,"

Ura said evenly, eyeing Oishi's blade, "but if you want more, you are welcome to try."

"My brother is dead," Oishi roared, swinging his blade free and raising it on high.

From around the group, weapons were leveled as humans and Gafs came to the support of their leaders.

"Damn it, hasn't there been enough?"

The two sides hesitated.

"Hasn't there been enough killing?" Aldin asked again, his voice a choked whisper as he stepped between Ura and Oishi. Turning, he looked into Oishi's anguished eyes.

"Your brother is dead," Aldin whispered, "he died with honor to save me. Your brother's blood debt is upon me as well." And as he spoke tears started to course down his face.

"He was my brother as are you and I ask you, let there be no more killing."

Aldin looked over his shoulder at Ura, who stood with blade held high.

"As you are my brother as well."

The Gaf lowered his blade and turned away.

Aldin looked back again to Oishi and held him with his gaze.

"My friend," Aldin said softly, "I will help you to bury our brother."

Oishi's shoulders started to shake, and, as tears ran down his cheeks, he slowly sheathed his blade and went to kneel by his brother's side.

Aldin looked over to Gablona, who merely shrugged.

"That is honor," Aldin snapped. "He took an oath and died by it. While to you, you think honor is something to be bought and sold."

Gablona looked at him with silent contempt.

"You didn't learn anything, did you?" Aldin said.

Gablona didn't reply.

"That's what all of this was about. That's why the Shiga failed, that is why you failed." He turned away to look back at Takashi.

"And that is why he died," Aldin whispered as he stood up and walked away from the group.

The sun was touching the horizon, and as he watched, it slipped away and disappeared.

"The game's over," Yaroslav said softly, coming up to Aldin's side. "It's over."

Gablona came up to Aldin, and the old vasba looked at him with contempt.

"Why did you save me?" Gablona asked.

"Business," Yaroslav said with a smile. "You see, Aldin and some of his backers have several hundred thousand tickets riding on the two of you coming out alive."

"You bastard," Gablona roared, "and here I thought you were saving me out of loyalty to an old employer."

"Correction," Aldin said softly, looking up at the Koh. "When we're done collecting our winnings, maybe I'll be offering a job to you."

"Better I died back there than to suffer this," Gablona roared.

"Oh, we can still arrange that," Tia said, joining the group. "I'm sure Oishi would love to escort you down to what's left of the Wardi."

With a bellow of rage Gablona strode away.

"What'll you do with your winnings?" Yaroslav asked.

"Pay off some old debts, I guess," Aldin said softly. "I guess some of them I'll never be able to pay off though." As he spoke, he looked first at Takashi and then at the Gafs and samurai who stood around the body of their fallen comrade.

"Saved. I don't know how, but we've been saved," Zola cried, collapsing back in his chair.

All about him the other Kohs were in wild celebration, raising toasts to good old Aldin and Gablona for having been such sensible fellows and coming through the game intact.

"Ah, gentlemen," Bukha shouted, pounding on the table to get attention.

"What is it now?" Zola laughed. "Old doom and gloom. I told you we'd come through it."

His disappointment about the failed assassination of Aldin and Gablona was almost forgotten. The seduction of the one Gaf had been a plan within a plan. It'd been easy enough, taking the berserker aside before the trip down, impressing him with a little flashy trickery, a levitation or two with lift beams, and then the promise of undreamed-of wealth. Anyhow, the Gaf was now conveniently dead, so no one would ever know, even if the botched attempt had lost him billions.

At least the Overseers hadn't wiped him out, and he could only guess at how much GGC had won.

"Gentlemen, please," Bukha said. "I have one question."

"Go on, what is it?" Zola asked.

"Are all the stockholders of GGC present in the room?"

Zola looked about and did a quick count.

"Not counting Petir, he was a little too quick with the juice."

And the other Kohs shook their heads and laughed at the foolishness of their old friend.

"Good then," Bukha said smoothly. "There are two orders of business left to attend to, then we can adjourn this council and return to our worlds and the business of business. The reason for calling this extended council has been fulfilled as of this morning. All our properties tied into the Alexandrian game have been sorted out, all our lawyers and accountants have accepted the findings, and the paperwork needs only our signatures. But let us discuss the more pressing concern first."

"And what, pray tell, is this pressing concern?"

"First off, we can start to arrange the payout of winnings," Bukha announced softly.

"Yes, the winnings," Zola said offhandedly.

Several of the Kohs fell silent. So intent had they been upon the threat the Overseers presented that the other possible outcomes had become secondary.

"Fine, then," Bukha said, and he nodded to the Xsarn.

The Xsarn rose up to his full three-meter height and looked over the room. "Two hours have passed since the setting of the sun on the Hole, officially closing game day eighty. I therefore officially decree, as moderator of this contest, that all tickets bearing the bet Sigma dead by Gablona game day thirty-one, Aldin and Gablona survive, are winning tickets, paid at odds as represented on said tickets."

"Right, go on, then let's get this over with. There's only a hundred thousand first-day tickets with those combinations throughout the entire Cloud." Zola chuckled. "I've already checked."

"Then you officially accept those results?" the Xsarn asked.

"I do."

"And attest to them as chairman and majority shareholder of GGC?"

"I do," Zola replied, and leaning forward, he pressed his thumb to the monitor before his desk, and the scanprint

was taken, officially marking the document the Xsarn had
called up.

"Excellent," Bukha said.

"Why are you so enthused?" Zola asked.

"It's just that there are other blocks of tickets," he replied
smoothly. "You were so intent on first-day buys with full odds
that you never bothered to check out tickets bought between
the fifth through thirty-fifth days. It seems as if there is a block
of over a million tickets purchased on those days, and all held
by one firm. Oh, some of the tickets had been held by others,
but they were bought up on, shall we say, a little side venture."

Zola paled.

"I've taken the liberty of running some calculations," Bukha
continued. "Of all possible winnings on your officially accepted results. You'll see them on your screen now."

Zola squinted at the screen, and then, with a scream of anguish, he stood up, knocking over the chair.

"They got it all!" he shrieked. "There's only nine billion left
after payout!"

"Exactly," Bukha said softly, a self-satisfied grin lighting his
features.

"Who did this?" Vol asked, collapsing in the chair by Zola's
side.

"Oh, a little holding company—a bit of venture capital some
people pulled together."

"Who?"

"One of the shareholders is coming up now. One of my
ships just picked him up, and he'll be here in a couple of hours
to claim his earnings. An old vasba friend of mine."

He neglected to mention that he had been one of the major
venture capitalists, but they'd find out soon enough.

"Aldin Larice?" Zola whispered.

"The wealthiest man in the Cloud," Bukha roared, pounding
the table as if he had told the funniest joke of his life.

"Busted, completely busted." Kurst groaned. The massive
display board had gone dark; the trading floor was empty.
Around him the servobots swept by, sucking up the thousands
of pounds of shredded paper and broken bottles, and carting
away the occasional suicide found beneath all the trash.

Kurst cradled the Erik 10 in his hand and tried to nerve himself to look down the barrel. "Three hundred million lost. We could have been Kohs!"

Three hundred million, all of it gone. The downpayment on the new ship was as good as gone, the mortgage on his time-share pleasure world cost more in a month than his old salary could pull down in ten years. There was a half million outstanding on his credit. All of it gone.

He cocked the Erik 10 and brought it up to his temple.

"At least let me step out of the line of fire before you pull the trigger."

Kurst looked up.

"Hi, Blackie," he whispered, suddenly feeling rather foolish. It was like a bad vid, the girlfriend coming to talk the fallen financial king out of finishing the job.

"Just leave me alone for a couple of minutes, will you?" he asked, his voice shaking.

"You know, the genius who thought up this venture shouldn't be wasted," she said soothingly.

Kurst groaned in reply. If only he hadn't gone out for a drink with that crazy old man, he thought wistfully. He never would have heard about the game or have been given the idea for the lottery, and none of this ever would have happened. Damn that Yaroslav, he thought darkly.

"Well, all I wanted to do was show you something before you pulled the trigger," Blackie said.

"What?"

She knelt down by his side. She fished through her pockets and pulled out a creased, coffee-stained slip of paper, holding it up for him to see.

He held the paper up in the dim light, looked, and then started to hand it back to her.

With a startled cry he suddenly snatched it back and looked at it again.

"It's a winning ticket, a first-day winning ticket!"

"Used to have five hundred of them, but sold the option on four hundred and ninety-nine. But for the hell of it, I figured I should hang on to one, just in case."

"You're a wonder, Blackie." And dropping the pistol, he grabbed her by the arm and started for the door.

"I've been thinking on some probabilities!" he said hurriedly. "This last lottery thing could be just the beginning.

Now listen to this idea . . ." And the door swung closed behind them.

The Arch floated into the room, the dozen Overseers already assembled bowing low at his approach.

"Are you all satisfied?" he said, the slightest trace of anger rippling through his voice.

The others were silent.

"Can we control the damage?" he asked, looking over at Vush.

"Already done," Vush said in reply. "There are no written records, no evidence. The story of the juice heads who originally bought the tickets will hold. The ships were officially contracted through Gablona's company, so that lead is closed, and already they are making their way back to port."

"And Losa?"

"Dead, along with the dozen others who went with him. The security system on the tower had been deactivated and then went down with the tower. Losa and the others tried to escape, but the car was knocked off its tracks and fell back into the Hole. All possible evidence was destroyed when the tower went down."

"A dozen dead," the Arch whispered. "Nearly five percent of our numbers." And shaking his head, he looked out over the assembly.

"The case then is closed. If need be, we shall have to cover any traces of evidence as they come up. Oh, the Kohs know, to be sure, but they won't dare to say a thing, since their reputations are on the line as well. But I tell you this, the next time we shall have to be subtle, far more subtle." And with a nod of dismissal he floated out of the room. No one would ever know, he thought. No one would ever suspect that he had been aware of it all from the very beginning. So those under him took the blame, and he, as was fitting of any leader, could always prove his innocence.

Finally only Vush was left. The others might be downcast, but he most certainly was not. Dumping the Sigma killing Aldin and Gablona options had netted him a fortune, and if he had hands he would certainly have rubbed them with glee as he floated out of the room, contemplating what investments to play with next.

* * *

Showers of debris still rained down, the sky above traced with brilliant streaks of light as sections of the tower, some of them hundreds of kilometers in length, dropped into the atmosphere and fell white hot on the blasted landscape below.

Wild shouts of rage and anguish still echoed in the streets of the doomed city, but he did not hear them.

Stepping over the mounds of dead, he traced his way up to what had once been the Seda, the focus of veneration that had been their doom.

Kicking through the rubble, he searched, guided by the flames about him and the broad streaks of light in the heavens above, as if the sky itself was being torn asunder.

The street bucked beneath his feet, slapping him to the ground, and long seconds later a distant rumbling boom washed over him, the blast sucking the breath from his lungs.

He turned and looked to the west. Over what had once been the city of the reds a massive fireball, thousands of meters high, raced skyward, its top already spreading out in a dark, malevolent cloud.

He pushed on into the rubble, and then at last he found what he sought.

The head was gone, smashed beyond recognition most likely, or carried away by someone still taking trophies. Most likely by a red, he reasoned, it'd give them some comfort. But from the cut of the robes, he knew who it was.

He spat upon the corpse.

"You were not the Ema," he hissed coldly, "for never did you have the cunning."

And Hassan looked out over the ruin, and then raised his eyes upward.

"But some day I shall be!" he whispered coldly.

chapter seventeen

"I wish you could have seen the look on his face." Bukha laughed and poured himself another goblet of sparkling muscatel.

"Here he is, barely recovered from the shock of finding out our little company had snatched all the winnings. So he's settled down a bit on that thought.

" 'After all,' he said," Bukha whined, giving a fairly good imitation of Zola, " 'we still won nine billion out of it,' and then in walks the lawyers' and accountants' guilds, handing him a bill for twelve billion, wiping him out and leaving all of them in debt besides. Then, it turns out, he borrowed from the company as well, to buy out Tia. And now he's even deeper in debt than before!"

Roaring with laughter, Aldin lay back on the silk divan and took another drink from the tray that the servobot offered.

"I think you've had enough," Mari announced, taking the goblet from his hand.

"Enough, is it?" Aldin shouted, a mischievous smile lighting his features. "My dear, you are talking to one of the richest beings in the Cloud." And he nodded deferentially to Tia and Bukha. "If I want a drink, I shall have it."

"Doctor's orders," she replied, handing the goblet back to the servobot and shooing it away.

"Your little injury still isn't healed, and you heard him say 'no alcohol and plenty of rest for a month.' "

"Which ends tomorrow," Aldin announced defiantly.

"And then your payoff to her as well." Yaroslav laughed.

The two looked over at the old man, and both reddened in self-conscious embarrassment.

For the evening's festivities Yaroslav was again wearing his shaman outfit. Ever since their return, he could hardly refrain from again describing how he'd brought down one of the larg-

523

est structures in the Cloud, and given the slightest excuse, he'd quickly launch into a full technical rundown on the forces involved, his hands waving back and forth to show how the mounting oscillations finally tore the tower apart.

"I heard Gablona gave you a call. What did that bastard want?" Tia asked.

"Yes, yes. What did the old fox want now?" Bukha interjected.

"I still can't believe this," Yaroslav responded. "A short time ago Aldin and I were being hunted from one end of the Cloud to the other. Through Bukha we planted the idea for this game, feeling it was our only hope of living out the year and getting Gablona off our backs. Oh, we threw in a few flourishes—the lottery, for instance. And now Gablona's actually calling you!"

"That part with the Overseers though," Bukha countered. "You must admit that was a close one. We never expected that."

"But still we came out of it all right," Yaroslav replied.

"Barely," Aldin said, his voice not more than a whisper.

"Anyhow," Bukha asked, looking over at Aldin, "what did that man want?"

"The usual, can't pull the working capital together to pay off his debt."

"So what did you say?"

"I offered him a job," Aldin said, laughing. "And the damn thing was, he actually hesitated for a second before telling me to go to hell! But he did have an interesting counterproposal."

"And that is?" Bukha asked, suddenly alert.

"He's interested in a game," Aldin replied matter-of-factly.

"By heavens, a game," Bukha roared, slamming down his drink.

The group fell into a fevered excitement, and within seconds Yaroslav was holding forth on an interesting part of the ring-like Kolbard that held potential.

With a sad shake of his head, Aldin rose to his feet and slipped out of the room.

As he walked down a broad open corridor, the doors at the end parted.

Before him was his favorite spot on his new yacht, which he had named *Gamemaster*, in memory of his old trade.

From one side to the other the forward hull was transparent, revealing the entire Cloud in all its splendor, the starry heavens a vast sea of light sprinkled across the darkness of space.

And he saw the one he was looking for, standing alone, gazing out upon the universe.

"Thought I'd find you here," Aldin said softly, coming up to his friend's side.

"Ah, my lord," Oishi replied, bowing low.

Aldin came up and put his hands on Oishi's shoulders, forcing him to rise up.

"Oishi, I am not your lord. I never was."

The samurai smiled, shaking his head. "It gives meaning to what I am, a samurai in service."

"If that is how you wish it," Aldin replied. "But in service to a friend, in the same way that I shall forever be in service to you."

Oishi was silent.

Aldin's hands still on the samurai's shoulders, he looked into the man's eyes. "Do you miss them?"

Oishi nodded his head ever so slightly.

"Takashi, and Seiji, and all the others," Oishi said softly.

Aldin could only nod.

"But they died as they wished, as warriors," Oishi quickly said, turning back to look at the stars.

"They died for me, for all the foolish vain reasons that brought us together. And the burden is more than I wish to bear."

Oishi looked back at Aldin.

"You tried to explain how we came to this strange place," Oishi said. "It is hard to understand, but what I think it means is that if you had not, I and those of us who are left would already be dead. So in that you gave us life. You did lie to us in the beginning, for I have heard it is impossible now for us ever to go back to the exact time that we left."

Aldin was silent.

"So I shall not die for Asano," he said quietly. "And I met the lady Tia instead." And a smile creased his face.

Aldin nodded. The two had been inseparable and he felt nothing but pleasure with the Tia he now saw, who in the presence of Oishi was at last carrying herself with the dignity befitting a Koh. And for the first time he saw her truly happy as well.

"I am glad of that, and thankful," Aldin replied softly, "but still the others haunt me."

"Then perhaps you did not learn, as you said Gablona had not learned," Oishi continued. "For some rare people honor is above all else. I pledged my honor to help you. I pledged it first not knowing who or what you were, believing something else. At first I felt cheated, but honor held me to my sworn course. But then I came to see the honor within you as well. That you would give all, including your life, for the sake of a friend. That you treated others with respect, expecting nothing less in return.

"Oh, such actions often as not can bring deceit from men of no honor. But after all, Aldin, to speak in terms your world understands, life is nothing but a game, and it is not the winning of it but the playing of it with honor that counts in the end.

"Those who died for you believed that. If you wish to honor them in turn, then live as they would live and mourn them not."

Aldin gazed at Oishi and smiled with a sad, wistful look in his eyes.

"And, yes," Oishi said softly, "I am honored to call you my friend."

"Larice, where are you?"

The two turned around and saw Mari towering in the doorway.

"Come on back in here, Yaroslav's cooking up some great ideas."

"Coming, dear," Aldin said, and turning, he suddenly winced with pain.

Oishi, a look of concern in his eyes, came up and took his friend about the shoulders.

"Your wound! Are you all right, Aldin?" Oishi asked.

Aldin could only look to the doorway where Mari waited.

"I hope so," Aldin said softly, "I sure do hope so."

And together, arm in arm, the two friends left the room, rejoining their friends as the *Gamemaster* soared into the sea of night.

THE NAPOLEON
WAGER

For Professor Gunther Rothenberg and Rick Schneid, Napoleonic Historians, who hopefully just might be amused that their hero was finally given a second chance.

Prologue

To: Retuna and the Third Circle of Overseers
From: Vush of the Fourth Circle of Overseers
Subject: THE GAME!

The companions of my circle agree to your wager as stated. Results from the first "hit" as the lesser beings call it shall be in shortly. We accept your bid in support of the Larice circle against that of the Gablona circle. Odds of 3.7 to 1 for success by Gablona for the first attack agreed.

Actually, I'm rather hoping that the intended strike is unsuccessful, since failure will mean an extended "war game" that will certainly prove to be most entertaining. Retuna, do remember, my brother, that things like this on the commlink or in writing could be most embarrassing. As Overseers we do have our reputations to think of, so in the future I suggest that all such transactions be, as the lesser creatures say, "face-to-face." Peace be with all of you.

Island of St. Helena, Longwood Estate, midnight, June 18, 1820.

It had been a bad day. Today of all days always was a bad day. Memories of other dates, though now bittersweet in their recollection, did not hold quite the same poignancy. How different it all would have been if that damnable Grouchy had only marched to the sound of the guns. It was all so clear now. He should have put Ney in charge of covering the Prussian advance. Ney would have come; Ney never would have lost the Prussians the way Grouchy did. And Grouchy in Ney's place. Grouchy never would have charged so recklessly and thus wasted his cavalry.

Five years ago today—Waterloo.

The thought stirred him from a restless half sleep, the thought, and the intermittent pain. He listened to the night noises. He could hear the sentry in the small garden outside the window. A pause in the footsteps, a muffled conversation—damned English, just the sound of the words grated. There was a soft laugh—a girl's. Of course, she was resisting slightly, honor demanded it. Not much could happen, the sergeant of the guard would be by soon, but the rendezvous would be arranged for later.

He smiled a bit, he could not begrudge a soldier that, even if he was a damned Englander.

He lay still on the sweat-soaked sheets. This day was hard; it was always hard to remember, especially when there were so many others. They marched in order through his still so well-organized mind—June 14, 1800 . . . Marengo. The legend of Marengo. The victory march composed to commemorate it, he could hear it again, the slow steady beat, then the wild flourish of trumpets. His fingers tapped out the beat, his eyes shining with pleasure and with tears.

Austerlitz, December 2, 1805. The crown jewel of his score of triumphs. The victory march of Marengo playing as the Imperial Guard advanced, storming the central heights. The thundering cannonade. And the cheers.

They echoed even here. How they had thundered in the cold winter air, how they echoed now in the stillness of the night. And only he could hear.

Prometheus.

Someone had called him that. "They will chain him to a rock, where the memories of his glory will gnaw and torment him."

It will never come again.

He closed his eyes, as if to hide himself from his own tears.

"I lost the battle of Marengo at five o'clock, and I won it back again at seven."

He remembered that, shouting it once when his staff started to panic. But when? Borodino, Leipzig, Waterloo? It must have been Waterloo.

He couldn't remember. It was true; he had heard it whispered and he knew it to be true. He was slipping away. He had already felt the first faint tugging of mortality even in the glory of Austerlitz. A flash memory of what he had learned in school, how when a Roman general was given a triumph an old man would stand behind him on a chariot and whisper, "Remember, all glory is fleeting."

As the sun set upon Austerlitz he remembered that, knowing somehow there would never be a moment like that ever again.

And then knowing that the body was betraying him. The weight coming to his slender frame, the eyes failing, and now the pain in his stomach, the ghastly pain.

"All glory is fleeting."

Is it really ending like this? he wondered. A shabby little room, chained to this rock. He listened in the silence as if half expecting a voice to reply with a denial, a warrior angel to appear to take him from this. And again to be arrayed, to walk the field late at night, to sit with his old grumblers about the fire and speak of the coming victory that he had dreamed and they would now create. Was this the final fate?

The victory march of Marengo. He could hear it again, and the cheering, the guard cheering on the fields of so many victories, *vive l'empereur, vive l'empereur*. Oh, but one more time, he prayed weakly, grant me just one more time, one final chance to know it all yet again, and he wept in lonely bitter silence.

chapter one

"Come, come, my friend, there's nothing to worry about out here," Bukha Taug said expansively, while pouring himself another round of sparkling peach wine.

Leaning back in his floating pleasure couch, the richest Gaf of the entire Magellanic Cloud glided back over to Aldin Larice's side.

"This pleasure world of yours is on the far side of the Cloud," Bukha continued. "Why, hell, it's not even on the charts."

Lifting his feeding tube out of his meal trough, the Xsarn

politely wiped off the last traces of excrement, a Xsarn's primary diet, before leaning over Aldin.

"Bukha's right you know," the Xsarn stated, his fetid breath washing over Aldin in a nauseating wave. "Corbin Gablona is most likely dead by now if those reports we heard are true. Anyone crazy enough to go back down to the Al'Shiga Hole most likely would be killed on sight. Those bastards are still in a frenzy over what you and your friends did . . ."

Aldin Larice, former gaming vasba, and now the richest Human in all the Cloud, held his hand up for the Xsarn to stop. The insectoid was almost as bad as his old friend Yaroslav when it came to talking about the last game.

Aldin looked around at his companions.

Mari—he really didn't even want to think of her—was off in the forward section. It amazed him how adversity could throw two people together, maybe even make a couple out of them for a while. But once affluence came, it would all hit the old legendary fan. He suspected that down deep she was far happier as a barmaid in that godforsaken watering place back on the Hole, where knocking a customer out to roll them, or—though he did not like to think about it, either—to drag him upstairs for some entertainment, was considered high sport. Now, as his wife, the second one that is, she was the richest Human female in history and her tastes had run amok. Before going into hiding for health reasons, she had actually gone so far as to buy an entire planet, because she felt it looked kind of pretty. The damn place was absolutely worthless, but the real estate dealer still convinced her to sign on the dotted line.

It's not that I really don't like her, he thought dryly, at least as far as a wife goes. The first one, a blood relative of Corbin Gablona's, had been a raging nightmare. It's just that Mari's nagging tone sounded at times like screeching chalk on slate. They had stayed loyal to each other, though; he felt anything else was rather tasteless. In some ways she was still a rather good friend, but as for the rest, he would rather not.

A muffled sob sounded in the far corner of the room. Zergh, his partner of nearly thirty years of gaming, was mindlessly watching an old holo of a Gavarnian operatic romance, *Trag and Vula* for what he guessed must be the fifteenth or twentieth time. Twenty hours of nonstop Gavarnian singing, chest thumping, and the obligatory death arias while committing double suicide at the end was enough to turn any non-Gaf stomach. The more sentimental, the more gaudy, the better for a Gaf. Their love of incredibly bad wine, polka-dotted and striped polyesters, and gooey operas made him wonder how such a race had ever had the reputation of also being some of the most fearless warriors that had ever lived.

Zergh, as if sensing that he was being watched, looked over his shoulder at Aldin, motioning him to come over. The Gaf's facial hair was soaked with tears. Aldin smiled, waving his hand in refusal. The last thing he wanted was for the seven-foot-tall Gaf to use his shoulder as a sobbing towel. At least he wasn't as overblown in his sentimentality as some Gafs. There'd been a craze a generation or so back to hang oneself at the end of the thirty hour epic *The Return of Trag and Vula*. Zergh had threatened to do so on several occasions but had never seriously followed through on it, always arranging for someone to stop him at the last minute.

"Damn opera," the Xsarn snapped. "Zergh, they really aren't killing themselves. The poison turns out to be a bad batch sent by the matchmaker to fake their deaths so he won't get sued. That way we can endure that damned sequel."

Zergh looked over darkly at the Xsarn, who thought better than to continue.

Thirty years with Zergh; where had it gone? Aldin wondered. In their younger days they had climbed to the top as the best damn vasbas—arrangers of staged battles on primitive worlds and holo simulations for the wealthy class of Kohs. He figured he'd retire on that, getting at least a reasonable annuity from his old employer, Corbin Gablona. Damned time travel had changed all of that. Before, all he had to do was design computer simulations of famous ancient battles, or occasionally sneak down to a primitive planet, evaluate a war, calculate the odds, and then arrange the betting on results. But no, Corbin and the others, when they first realized time travel was possible, immediately latched onto the idea of going back into history to retrieve famous generals and bring them forward for entertainment and high-stakes bets on the results.

Gaming on warfare had been the one true passion of the ruling class, the Kohs. It had helped them to relieve the tedium of the unrelenting peace that the Overseers had imposed upon all who lived in the Magellanic Cloud. Everyone, down deep, had to admit that the Overseers were right, when several millennia back they had suddenly appeared and stopped a bitter three-way war between Gafs, Xsarns, and Humans who were locked in a deadly struggle for control of the Magellanic Cloud. The instantaneous and total destruction of half a dozen planets by the Overseers had convinced everyone that the mysterious beings held the upper hand and were not to be trifled with.

Gradually, a certain camaraderie had developed between the oligarchy of barons of the three species; they were linked together by education, class, good breeding, and their mutual love for gambling on nearly anything, especially warfare, either simulated or real conflicts that were occurring on primitive planets not observed by the Overseers. Occasionally, the Overseers would get word of a "little wager" and break the affair up, hauling a couple of the miscreants caught in their net into a reeducation school for peaceful coexistence.

A good vasba, a true gaming master, knew how to arrange a damn good simulation, or pick out a primitive war under a tight security net beyond the paternalistic eyes of the peaceful-coexistence police. Such an individual had to have a gutterbreed cunning and an instinct for survival mixed with a superb historical education and a certain panache that would enable him to float in the erudite world of the richest beings in history. It had been a comfortable living, until they all started breaking the rules that had kept their little sporting ventures lucrative and entertaining for thousands of years.

Alexander the Great had started all of this. Honor had prevented Aldin from screwing over the legendary Macedonian when Corbin and some others wanted to fix the game and see Alexander take the fall. The fact that Aldin had cleaned up with a couple of side bets, which was rather illegal for vasbas, really wasn't all that serious. But when the extent of his game fixing, and Corbin's cheating, had become apparent, he had suddenly found himself on the legendary Hole, fighting for his life.

He looked over at Bukha Taug, who was lounging on a hover chair, consuming yet another bottle of sickly sweet peach-flavored champagne. Bukha's plan had been beautiful, and he had at least been honest. They had cleaned everyone's clocks, coming out of the Hole game as the two richest beings who had ever lived, owning damn near 53 percent of all the corporate assets of the entire Greater Magellanic Cloud.

And for what?

Frankly, he was bored silly. The problem with living on the edge was that you got rather used to the view. It made life exciting, it made a goal. But when you finally achieved the goal, then what?

Aldin Larice sighed almost melodramatically and looked around at his companions. They were good company to be sure, true friends who had been close to him when he was nothing but a vasba. But was this the end of it all? he wondered. I'm rich, I can buy anything I want—and I'm sick to death with boredom. I no longer have any dreams, he realized sadly, no dreams but uselessly spinning out whatever time I've got left, indulging myself, and doing absolutely nothing that can offer a challenge. He remembered childhood, when for months he had anticipated a gift for his birthday. The gift, which must have cost his mother most of a week's wages, was beautiful—but even at nine he had come to learn that the anticipation was far better than the owning.

And besides, though he found it hard to believe, he was now one of the most hated men who ever lived. Just because he and Bukha had legal title to all those assets didn't really mean that they actually controlled them. The other Kohs had worked on every stratagem possible to tie things up, and in the process had triggered the worst economic depression in centuries, worse even than when the Bank of Hovde had announced that a ship bearing nearly all the precious specie of the Cloud had had a little accident—and run into a sun. It was a hoax, a little attempt to manipulate the precious-metals market, but it still had upset things for twenty years or so, until the ship was finally found in the bank president's private hangar.

This was far worse. The other Kohs had used their commlink systems and holo news stations, with their damnable "we're on the people's side" reporters, to paint him as a greedy exploiter of the common folk. The assassination attempts had finally gotten outright monotonous.

As for Corbin? Frankly, Aldin couldn't care less at this point. His old, obese employer had, of course, welshed on the 1.1 billion katars owed in payment for freeing him from the Al'Shiga's impaling stick. He expected that, and anyhow it was kind of hard to collect on a deal made under such duress. But there was vengeance in the old man's heart, of that he was sure. The reports that Corbin had actually gone back to the

Hole were disturbing. The damned fool was too shrewd to go there just for the fun of it.

"If he's playing with Shiga," the Xsarn said, looking over at Aldin as if he had read his thoughts, "they'll cut his heart out and use it for a game of catch."

"My dear bloated cousin isn't that stupid."

Aldin looked up as Tia, his niece, came into the room, Oishi Kurosawa by her side. The young woman came around and playfully mussed Aldin's thinning hair.

Aldin took her hand and looked up at her. She at least had gained something out of all their adventures. After three years with Oishi, the transformation from spoiled little rich girl to charming lady with a regal bearing had been remarkable. Oishi looked down at Aldin and tried to force a smile of agreement.

"We've got a new security report," Oishi said quietly.

The others groaned. The old leader of the forty-seven ronin was now one of Aldin's most trusted friends and in charge of all security. The samurai had adjusted and mastered with glee all the changes from eighteenth-century Japan to life in the Cloud a millennium later.

"About what this time?" Bukha asked.

"A 'we are there for you' news report. Corbin Gablona's body is a seedbed for a Shiga rotting-man mushroom," the Xsarn said lazily, while motioning for a servobot to bring in his dessert.

"It's about Corbin Gablona, at least in that you are right," Oishi said, his features now fixed with purposeful intent.

The Xsarn shook his head. Oishi of late was considered by some as a bit too cautious, ready to see a plot behind every flutter of a window curtain.

"This was supposed to be a vacation, a chance to relax," Aldin Larice said quietly, attempting to suppress a retch as the Xsarn slipped his feeding tube back into his foul dinner and slurped up the rest of his meal.

To relax, simply to relax, was something Aldin found to be completely impossible.

Trying to stabilize the crisis had been a nonstop job for Aldin, consuming every moment from wake-up to collapse eighteen hours later.

Yet each effort seemed to disappear into a myriad of Byzantine laws governing trade, unyielding bureaucracies, and what he knew was outright obstruction. It never ceased to amaze him that some low-level government or corporate servant, who simply could not be fired, could derail desperately needed reform simply because a form wasn't filled out in just the proper way.

Dozens of planets that had once been major hubs of trade were now ghost worlds, visited only by an occasional tramp cruiser. Billions were out of work, tens of billions more living on the edge waiting for the good times of corporate expansion and trade to return.

He was the richest Human in the Cloud, yet he didn't dare show his face anywhere in public for fear it would be shot off. So this was living, he thought sadly, pouring himself another drink. Richest man in the Cloud, and before he could even bathe someone had to sweep the shower head for detonators and check the water for trace poisons.

"Come on Aldin, don't worry, be happy," Mari said, settling down by Aldin's side.

The group groaned inwardly at her inane comment.

"Well she is right in a way," the Xsarn said. "I dare say this is the finest pleasure world I've ever seen. Climate is perfect, it's isolated, and this palace has every convenience ever created."

Aldin looked around the feasting room and nodded glumly. The Xsarn was right. The palace had been created half a millennium ago by a Gaf Koh and forgotten until Aldin had picked it up and poured in several tens of millions to reactivate the servobots who maintained it and replaced the thousands of panes of glass. The main palace covered several acres, all the exterior walls made of glass that at the touch of a button could become transparent to reveal the tropical splendor outside. Every possible amusement imaginable was here, from holo theaters and floating beds to fountains of wine and giant whirlpool baths big enough to hold several hundred at a time. There were even half a hundred of the highly illegal Human and Gaf replicated bots in the gaming room in the basement to make the casino a little more lively and also to add a little sense of happy crowds enjoying themselves. They also kept several of the samurai and Gaf bodyguards happy in other ways with their remarkable talent to perform actions that were more than a bit impossible for a real female. Since one could not really call it cheating, Aldin did find a couple of the experiences to be rather interesting, though he would be far too embarrassed to let anyone know he had tried them out. One of the female bots went scampering by outside, a samurai bodyguard in happy pursuit. The bot jumped into the ocean, the samurai, peeling off his robes, jumped in after her, and they drifted away with the current.

The oceans were luxuriously warm and free of anything that might view a swimmer as dinner, but since Aldin had never learned to swim they held no real interest for him. The mountains were covered in a lush growth of trees that had such a bizarre combination of reds and purples that they almost looked like a Gaf clothing designer had taken inspiration from them. Best of all, the planet was completely uninhabited, covered by orbital surveillance and thus about as totally secure as any place could ever be.

It was here, with his retinue of a dozen friends and samurai and Gaf bodyguards, where he was supposed to feel safe and conduct business.

Bukha rolled his eyes.

"Damn it, Aldin, unwind a bit. This is supposed to be a vacation. The hell with that latest report."

"It is only when we stop worrying that we become vulnerable," Oishi replied quietly. His tone was as always polite and courtly, but there was an insistence to it that indicated he would not be ignored.

Oishi stepped rigidly before the group. Though Aldin had argued with him for years about etiquette, Oishi still insisted upon bowing to Aldin before addressing him in public.

"An intelligence operative reported the sighting of Corbin Gablona, five former Kohs, and a hundred or more dark-robed men on the world of Parduki seven days ago. Sogio personally arrived with the report less than an hour ago."

"Which means it took that report almost as many days to reach us here, since the operative decided to hand deliver this rather than put it out on the open wave," Tia said quietly, coming up to stand by her husband's side.

"One of the dark robes purchased a derelict cargo ship on its last legs and the group left. As they pulled out, Sogio decided it was best to come straight here with the information."

"So what?" the Xsarn replied. "We know that madman Gablona is out there on the edges of the Cloud, but the bastard is powerless. Too bad the Shiga didn't get him, if that's where he really went."

"It's just that a conversation was overheard between two of the dark robes. Sogio said that one of his operatives reported that they are definitely members of the Al'Shiga cult."

That statement caused a moment of stunned silence.

"That bastard," Bukha roared, coming to his feet. "Are you telling me Corbin somehow managed to spring some of those madmen off the Hole?"

Oishi nodded.

The room was quiet.

"That's not good at all," Zergh said darkly, tearing himself away from the holo. Wiping the tears from his eyes, he switched off the opera, while Vula was shrieking out the famed, "My lover's eyes are like pools of sparkling muscatel." The contra-soprano's voice warbled in midcry and faded away, much to everyone's silent relief.

Zergh came over to settle by Aldin's side, the floating leisure chair struggling to readjust to the added weight.

"He's violating one of the major laws of the Cloud by bringing those buggers off planet. Second, he must be as insane as the psych profiles indicate. Playing with the Shiga is like lying down in a nest of snakes. They're hopping mad for revenge after the loss of their Skyhook tower."

"So he must have made some arrangement with them," Aldin said evenly. "I won't be seeing any amateurs coming after me anymore. Those people scare me to death."

Absentmindedly he rubbed the part of his body where the Shiga's impaling stick had left it's mark. That little escapade still had him waking up screaming. At least on the Hole, he knew where they were—which was all around him. Out here the Shiga could blend in, and wait. Heaven only knew how many of the crazy religious fanatics Corbin was now sprinkling around the Cloud.

"You haven't told us everything yet," Aldin said, looking up at his self-appointed protector, able to see at a glance that Oishi was more than a little worried.

"The rest is that our informant also overheard one of them joking how 'the fat one' had cooked up a surprise but he was disappointed that there wouldn't be any blood on the Shiga knives as a result."

"Is that it?" the Xsarn asked.

Oishi nodded in reply.

"So why all the fuss?" the Xsarn growled. "You had me so

worried there for a moment that you almost put me off my food.

"All your samurai are here, and I dare say are rather bored and would like a little fight," the Xsarn said, as if talking about a betting game rather than his own shell being in jeopardy. "And I bet those dumb Gaf berserkers would love a little amusement time with the Shiga."

The Xsarn looked up to see that Basak, the leader of the "dumb Gaf berserkers," was standing in the doorway, listening in on the conversation. The warrior said nothing, but a simple hand gesture that implied the cracking open of a Xsarn carapace was sufficient for the Xsarn to mumble an overhasty apology and turn his attention to his steamy dessert.

"So let him kick around out there," Bukha interjected, chuckling over the Xsarn's discomfort. "We can always arrange an accident."

"I suggest we evacuate this place at once," Oishi said coldly.

More than a few of Aldin's entourage groaned.

"What in heavens for? We just got here yesterday," the Xsarn replied defiantly.

"There is no such thing as perfect security. Security can be reasonably attained by always altering your schedule. Thousands of sources must know that our group would be away for thirty days, and from some of our purchases it wouldn't take much to figure out it's to some tropical resort, a very private resort. Conversations are overheard, schedules checked. I suspect Corbin might know where you are at this very moment. Thus we must leave within the hour. I've already alerted the ship's computer to start powering up."

Wearily, Aldin got to his feet.

"You heard him, let's get the hell out of this dump. Besides, this place was starting to get on my nerves."

He looked around the group. These were his friends, the only ones that really counted in this universe. Those he had made after his rise to Koh status didn't count. For Aldin had quickly discovered two things about wealth. The first was that anyone who put value in it was a self-deluded fool. The second was that the friendships of wealth were about as reliable as the promises of a suma drone looking for a vial.

"Well, I for one am staying," the Xsarn Prime announced. "I've heard a lot about the fine cuisine produced by the local carnivores, and I fully intend to sample it first."

"You do seem to be overreacting a bit, my courageous husband," Mari announced, coming in behind Basak, her voice edged with disdain.

"If you want to stay, that's your business," Aldin replied sharply.

"I'll run away with you," Mari snapped, "but I thought I'd married a man, not a boob afraid of his own shadow."

With a sniff of disdain, Mari stalked out of the room. Aldin's friends looked the other way to spare their henpecked friend further embarrassment.

"Let's get packing," Aldin said quietly. "I've got the wrong feeling about all of this."

"Jump-point transition in ten seconds."

Chortling with delight, Corbin Gablona settled back in his chair to ride out the turbulence. The blackness of the jump hole snapped away, and instantly the stars of the Magellanic Cloud formed in their myriad glory before the viewport.

"Target acquisition on line. Five degree deviation in axis rotation due to late arrival. Strike will impact 452 kilometers from primary target."

Corbin cursed silently, punching in a command for a simulation display.

The holo field simulation showed the planet Culimir floating in the darkness, the image magnifying down to the single continent surrounded by turquoise seas. The computer traced the impact line in, and he watched with satisfaction as damage calculations and pressure overloads raced alongside the computer-generated shock waves.

"Fifty p.s.i. overload still calculated for primary target," the computer whispered. "Total destruction assured."

Corbin rubbed his fat, ring-covered hands with delight. Pushing away from the console, he floated his chair over to the forward window, joining a knot of black-robed figures who had gathered to watch the show. The image before them was not real—Culimir was sixty million kilometers beyond—but the telescopic systems made it seem as if they were hovering just several thousand kilometers away.

Jump points rarely got closer. Any attempt to travel at translight speeds so close to a planet or star was suicide with the random bits of dust, boulders, and even the gravitational effects attendant with all planetary systems.

"Now watch this," Corbin said, laughing. "Damn my eyes, I wish I had thought of it sooner."

"There it goes," one of the black robes whispered.

The cargo ship, which had followed them through the jump gate, snapped past, decelerating out of translight. The ship, however, did not kick in its sublight retro thrust but continued to race straight in toward the planet at a significant portion of light-speed, a maneuver that was all but suicidal. Which was exactly the intent.

Haga, the Shiga pilot, could now be heard over the comm-link, laughing out his death prayer to the Hidden Ema, calling upon him to prepare the hundred virgins for his arrival in the afterlife, an event that if all went to plan would occur in not much more than a few minutes. Forward of the ship there was a flash of light from the lone gunner, Kcuf'ha, Haga's brother, whose job was to lock onto even the tiniest particle of dust and vaporize it before the ship hit it. A thousand ton cargo vessel traveling at 0.1 light-speed would make one hell of an impact on whatever was in the way. The same could be said for a one gram cinder that happened to be sitting in the flight path.

"Just a question of mass and velocity," Corbin replied smoothly. "Take an old cargo ship of a thousand tons mass. Accelerate it up to its maximum sub–light-speed of 0.12 and aim it straight in. The result, an explosion of several million megatons on impact. Everything within a thousand kilometers totally destroyed, the atmosphere ripped away, varying levels of destruction as far as five thousand kilometers away."

Corbin signaled for a servobot to bring a drink over. He nodded to the man standing next to him, beckoning for him to help himself to a brandy. The robed figure shook his head.

"Ah, yes, of course, against the rules," Corbin said with a chuckle. "Honestly, you don't know what you're missing."

"There are other pleasures far more enjoyable," whispered Ali Hassan, once of the dreaded order of Assassins from ancient Earth and now of the Al'Shiga. "Far more enjoyable pleasures." He turned to look back at the screen, eager for the show to begin.

"It'll look like an accident," Corbin said, as if trying to re-assure his fellow conspirator. "A cargo ship, out of control, smashed into the planet. No one will ever know."

"Magnificent," the hawk-faced man said evenly. "Never in

my wildest fantasy did I dream of unleashing such destruction."

"I told you to trust me, Ali," Corbin replied expansively. "Trust me, and you'll see destruction never before imagined."

"It doesn't really seem fair somehow," a quiet voice, almost at a whisper, said from the opposite end of the cabin.

Corbin looked back over his shoulder while Hassan gave a snort of disdain.

"Weak stomach, my fellow Koh," Corbin said, his voice harsh.

"Zola Faldon does have a point," Vor, one of the minor Gaf Kohs, said, coming to Zola's defense. "Aldin, I don't care about, he's vasba, lower class. But Bukha Taug's down there, and the Xsarn Prime. They're like us."

"Were like us," Corbin snapped. "After all, they did cheat all of you out of your holdings."

Several of the Kohs feebly nodded in agreement.

Trying to act expansive, Corbin guided his float chair over to where his old companions were gathered.

"The opening sneak attack in war is a time-honored tradition. Remember Yarmir at Alpha Sigma. And did Caesar send an embossed scroll to the senate telling them he was going to cross the Rubicon? Like hell, he just crossed it and marched. So my friends, let's just say that cargo ship is hitting the Rubicon."

He chuckled at his display of military historical knowledge as if it were the old days, when Kohs gamed in military simulators over brandy and cigars, as good gentlemen should, debating the finer points of history. He motioned in a jovial manner for the servobots to circulate and refill the drinks all around.

"But gentlemen don't attack gentlemen without warning," Zola said weakly, looking around the room for support and finding precious little.

"You were the one hopping for revenge," the tertiary Xsarn said quietly. "Corbin offered a solution."

"It's all my responsibility," Corbin said, not mentioning that the whole affair was being secretly recorded, and that unbeknownst to Zola the cargo ship was, through a long paper chase, ultimately registered in his name.

"All of it my responsibility." Corbin chuckled, and the others forced out a low series of laughs in reply, several of them mumbling about a need to get back to the good old days, to restore things as they were.

The group stood around self-consciously, barely paying attention to Corbin, who launched into a long monologue about the finer tactical nuances of the military reforms of the Enlightenment on Earth, which had so foolishly attached a negative value to assassination and first strike without proper warning. Several of the Kohs noticed a number of mistakes in his delivery, especially regarding Frederick the Great's lightning attack into Silesia, which he placed in 1730, but none dared to correct him; no one was in the mood for a debate, and besides, the expert in all such things, the being who could have settled the argument, was one of the targets down below.

"Impact ten seconds," the computer voice whispered. The gathering looked up from their drinks.

"Three, two, one . . . impact."

The group stood staring at the screen. There was a delay of several seconds, and Corbin silently cursed the cargo ship pilot who was supposed to drop a translight message relay to beam the image back out. The damn fool had most likely forgotten and was too busy getting worked up in anticipation of the virgins in Paradise Ali had promised him.

The image on the screen suddenly shifted. The camera zoomed in. There was a blinding flash that filled the room with a harsh white glare, dampened down a hundredfold from the reality that would have instantly blinded anyone who was looking.

Long seconds passed, the computer filtering the image down again, and then yet again. A glaring white light was rising up from the planet's surface, millions of tons of vaporized rock shooting straight up, punching out above the atmosphere, the column a hundred kilometers across.

The shock wave was already spreading out at transsonic speed, literally ripping the landscape up from the rocky surface. The widening circle hit the ocean, instantly vaporizing it into superheated steam, pulling the water straight up from the seafloor, raising it up into a mountain a thousand meters high, the back end of the tsunami boiling away, to be replaced by the billions of tons of water further out. The landside shock wave continued outward, slamming into a high range of mountains, which in an instant became so much bare rubble.

The image of a planet dying filled the screen—soundless,

accompanied only by the gasps of the Kohs and the delighted cheers of the Shiga assassins, several of whom wept with joy for the fate of the two brothers who surely would be the envy of all in Paradise for having sacrificed their lives for such an ultimate act of destruction.

The image suddenly became distorted, the planet rushing toward the screen, and then went dark, as the relay drone, which had been jettisoned astern of the cargo ship with a retro system, followed its parent down into the storm and added its own mass and velocity to the Ragnarok of destruction.

"Should we go down to check for survivors?" Zola asked quietly, looking around lamely at his comrades, as if his little display of humanitarian concern would somehow exempt him from responsibility for what they had just done.

"From that?" Corbin laughed, pointing to the now darkened screen, showing only the openness of space before them. The view was ironic somehow. Culimir still glowed a tranquil green in the emptiness of space, a single world orbiting an aging red giant. It would be another couple of minutes yet before the image of its destruction reached them at light-speed, to suddenly flash far brighter than the sun that gave it life. The delayed view of the planet, sixty million kilometers away, still looked peaceful.

"He's dust now!"

"What have we done?" Hultan asked, his voice breaking.

"Why, started a war of course, you damn fool," Corbin snapped. "And we've won it already. Aldin and his friends were down there—" Pausing for dramatic effect, he pointed to the steady green light of the planet. "—and now at least part of him is coming straight up here! Let's get the hell out of here before some damn Overseer ship shows up!"

Laughing, Corbin stalked out of the room.

The assembly of fellow Kohs looked anxiously one to the other and then back to the planet. Long minutes passed, and then as bright as day there was a blinding flash of light, the light of destruction reaching out to them at last.

"We've unleashed a nightmare," Kulma Koh said evenly.

"And we'll spring it across the Cloud," Ali announced gleefully, surveying the Kohs with disdain.

The group had been slow, far too slow for Oishi's liking. The hour deadline he had fixed had long since passed. All of his samurai and Gaf berserkers, except for Sogio, were already aboard the ship, but at the last minute Aldin's friends had started an argument outside the ship remonstrating with him to stay for just another day.

And then the alarm had been triggered, a hidden sentry beacon parked near the jump gate showing a single vessel coming through the primary jump point and rapidly decelerating.

Back in his former life he had trained for years to master the art of protecting his daimyo. In the three years since that life ended, he had dedicated himself to mastering all the complexities of this strange new reality with the sole purpose of protecting his new daimyo and friend.

One unannounced ship was cause enough for alarm, but then another one had appeared, coming straight in. Dropping its jump impulse, it had instantly shifted to the maximum 0.1 light-speed, which was still far too fast for anything inside a solar system. He had sent Basak to hurry the group along, watching the monitors as the ship just kept coming in, not slowing.

"What the hell is going on?" Tia whispered, coming to stand by his side to watch the screen. Any traffic to this world was suspicious, that was exactly why he liked keeping Aldin here. Other worlds might have a hundred or more ships a day coming in, any one of which might be bearing an assassin. But out here, nothing could come in without drawing an awful lot of attention.

The one ship came to a complete stop, as if to try to block the jump gate back into the administrative heart of the Cloud. But evading that was simple. There were three other beacon-marked jump points from this system out to other worlds. And even if they were blocked, one could always do a blind jump from damn near anywhere and just hope for the best. Blocking one gate was useless.

Mystified, he could only shake his head.

The minutes passed, and still the second ship kept straight on, the computer softly whispering at last that if it continued there would be a rather nasty little impact on the western edge of the continent.

"Almost like the dumb-ass pilot wanted to commit suicide," Tia said nervously.

And then the terrifying reality hit him full force.

"Al'Shiga," Oishi shouted.

"Energy release at impact?" Oishi shouted to the computer. Several long seconds passed.

"Your voice indicates stress," the computer replied laconically. "There is reason to feel that way. Energy release of one thousand plus tons instantly decelerating from 0.1 light-speed cannot be immediately calculated with software provided, but it will be rather large. Suggest that you consider moving."

Leaping from his chair, Oishi raced to the entrance ramp of the pleasure yacht.

Aldin turned away from the argumentative group at the front entrance to the pleasure dome, led of course by his wife, who was bitterly denouncing his decision to follow Oishi's request to leave, and started toward the hangar.

"Move it!" Oishi roared.

Aldin looked up at his friend, somewhat confused.

"Oh, stop the hysteria," Mari snapped peevishly. "I've still got to pack my wigs."

"Forget the damn wigs!" Oishi screamed, leaping down the ramp. Even as he raced toward Aldin he cursed inwardly. A couple of rail guns placed in orbit could have prevented this. Hit the damn thing ten thousand kilometers out and there'd be a flash, a bit of sunburn, and nothing more. Damn it!

"It's coming in now!" Tia screamed. "Cover your eyes!"

Aldin, still somewhat confused, was looking straight at Oishi, who felt as if he were running in slow motion. Looking straight at him—westward.

With a shout the samurai didn't even bother to slow and with a leap he jumped on Aldin, pushing him to the ground, groping to pull his robes up over his friend's face.

There was a flash of light across the heavens, turning the early twilight into a dazzling blur. In an instant, the world turned into the heart of a sun.

Oishi climbed on top of Aldin, shielding him with his body. Even through tightly closed eyes he felt as if the light were striking him blind.

From a great distance away he heard a thin high shriek, as if the brilliance could somehow sweep even sound away with its intensity.

There was the pungent smell of burning, and though there was no pain, Oishi realized that his hair was on fire, as well as his silken robes. He waited for the heat of this new sun to consume his body into dust, but then, ever so gradually, the radiant brilliance started to fade away.

They didn't catch us with a direct one, Oishi realized. Maybe we can still get out.

"Get in the ship!" the samurai roared, coming to his feet.

Opening his eyes, he dared a glance to the west and thought for an instant that he'd been struck blind. From horizon to horizon there was nothing but a stunning sheet of whiteness, as if he were staring into the heart of a sun gone nova.

"Move it!" Oishi screamed, reaching down to pull Aldin to his feet.

Stunned, the old gamemaster looked about.

The rest of the party stood about in silent disbelief, their clothes smoldering. Fortunately, all of them had been facing Aldin and away from the burst.

"Get in the ship!" Oishi repeated as he raced past the group.

One moment he was running; in the next instant he was down, as if his legs had been swept out from under him.

The shock wave surged through the ground beneath him with a mind-numbing roar. Behind him he could hear the ten thousand windows of the crystal palace exploding into a hurricane of flying shards. In seconds the thirty million katar building stood naked, tons of glass showering down, leaving a bare skeleton frame.

"My clothes!" Mari shouted, turning to look back at the palace, which was silhouetted by the stunning diamond-white radiance that still dominated the western sky.

"We'll buy a new wardrobe!" Zergh roared, coming out of the palace, bleeding from dozens of lacerations, his yellow and lavender pin-striped robe dangling in shreds from his massive frame. From inside the now-bare structure, dozens of servobots hooted in distress, racing about to sweep up the broken glass. Several of the illegal Humanbots staggered up from the casino below, twittering merrily, pointing at the angry sky as if it were a holo display.

"Anyone left back in there?" Oishi shouted.

"One of the Gaf berserkers," Zergh said mournfully. "Bastard was threatening to cut his own throat at the end of the opera; the shake up did it for him. I guess it's all the same. Tragic, but in a way rather artful and poetic."

Oishi ran through the group, pushing them toward the ship, the samurai within spilling out to help, and getting in the way, while Basak and his friends, hearing of their comrade's death, sent up a loud keening wail.

The ground kept tossing and bucking, and with a shuddering groan the yacht slowly settled down on its port-side landing skid, which splayed outward with a groan, the metal twisting and snapping.

The ship leaned drunkenly over to one side, its port-side landing gear collapsed beneath its massive frame. Oishi prayed silently that the ship's hull had not been breached.

Several samurai stood in the doorway and, reaching out, pulled Oishi in, while Aldin screamed for them to seal the hatch.

Oishi raced forward to the flight engineer's cockpit, and Tia looked up anxiously from the copilot's console.

"Port engine is winding down," she shouted.

Aldin gained the pilot's console and strapped himself in. Zergh, following him, was tempted to raise a protest, but Aldin's look stopped him. Aldin was finicky about anyone other than himself piloting *Gamemaster II*, and in this situation he wanted to be at the controls.

"Get us out of here now and the hell with the port engine," Oishi shouted.

The ship leaped straight up, slamming Oishi into his seat. Climbing above the palace, Aldin pivoted the ship straight west for a quick survey of the damage.

From horizon to horizon, the entire sky was a column of white-hot fire, soaring upward, obliterating the heavens.

"Too big for a pulse bomb," Aldin whispered. "What the hell did he create?"

"A cargo ship coming in at a damn high part of sub–light-speed."

"The mad bastard," Aldin whispered. "It's been joked about, but no one's ever done that, even in the ancient wars."

"Well it's happening right now," Tia gasped.

Awed, the four watched as the devastation of an entire world unfolded, while they continued straight up, going supersonic, the ship shuddering under the strain of climbing at half power inside the atmosphere.

"Here comes the blast wave," Aldin shouted.

From over the horizon it seemed as if the entire surface of the planet were being peeled away. Trees, rivers, lakes, even the very soil down to bedrock, were tearing loose, soaring outward at supersonic speed, exploding into a miles-high wall of fiery Armageddon.

"We better get the hell out of here," Aldin sighed, swinging the ship about and hitting the throttle up to full.

An instant later the first red warning light snapped on, and then an entire row started blinking wildly.

"Airtight integrity lost," the computer announced dispassionately. "Engine three shut down, number two in caution state. Repeat, airtight integrity lost in passenger section, attempt to go outside atmosphere will result in serious discomfort and/or death of all passengers. Suggest that you set down at nearest friendly authorized-dealer repair facility. Repeat, airtight—"

Aldin snapped the audio off and looked over at Oishi with stunned disbelief.

"The ground shock hit too hard, the landing skid must have punctured the hull." He sighed.

Zergh scrambled over to the emergency control station and started punching up damage control.

"Keep us ahead of the shock wave," Zergh shouted, even as Aldin swung the ship about and started to race eastward.

Groaning inwardly, Aldin surveyed the damage as it flashed across the screen.

One of the landing struts had indeed smashed clear through the hull, wiping out one engine and damaging a second, and the gear could no longer be retracted. Even the main access corridor was losing pressure; moving everyone forward was useless. He punched up the comm channel. Mari was screaming at the top of her lungs, and he pitied his friends and bodyguards who were shouting right along with her. He cut the channel off.

The caution light on the number two engine shifted to red, and Aldin immediately shut off the power feed before it went critical.

Oishi looked over at Aldin and shook his head.

"We don't have enough power in number one for escape velocity," Aldin said.

"Hell, we can't go up anyhow."

"We won't have enough to escape the shock wave either," Tia shouted, looking up from the navigation and tracking screen.

"Maybe it'll finally slow down," the samurai said grimly,

punching up a rear view. The storm was continuing behind them with an unrelenting fury, drawing closer by the second.

Aldin raged inwardly. An attempt on his life, that he could accept; ever since he got into the Alexandrian game he'd been living with that chance. But to destroy a world and all the creatures that lived on it? That was genocide. At least the poor things that lived here would never know what hit them.

He hooked into a monitor back at the shattered remains of his palace. The servobots were still racing about mindlessly, sweeping up the glass, throwing it down incinerator shoots, and going back in for more. Several of the Humanbots were now out on the lawn, the ones programmed for more provocative activities dancing shamelessly, their clothing gone, somehow keeping their footing as the ground bucked and shook, most likely thinking the roaring thunder was music. One of his favorite models was loudly declaiming poetry, an ancient Icelandic saga about the end of the world, inspired no doubt by the horrifying storm that, if one was dispassionate to the damage, held a remarkable beauty to it.

The shock wave raced in. There was a final brief image of the bay rising up, the Humanbots clapping appreciatively, and then the screen went blank. He switched back to the main screen view astern. The storm was coming up over the horizon and closing in.

"There's too much drag from the landing gear, it's going to catch us," Aldin stated. "I'd try for height and pray."

The ship surged upward, accelerating clumsily as the atmosphere thinned. Though the computer controls were rock steady, it felt as if the entire vessel were about to vibrate itself into a million pieces.

Mari appeared in the cabin doorway.

"You idiot," she growled. "You should have listened to Oishi and left immediately."

Aldin wanted to turn on the woman and scream. If it hadn't been for her damn procrastinating, they would have been long gone. But then again, it was impossible for her to ever accept any blame, no matter how wrong she might be. That was one of her more remarkable traits: to somehow, and to her most logically, figure out a way to trace the blame for everything back to someone else. Yaroslav more than once had said that if degrees were given out for transferring guilt, she should have earned a doctorate.

"It's closing in," Aldin said, ignoring his wife, his eyes glued to the aft display. "Get the hell out and strap yourself into your seat!" he shouted.

Her eyes widened as she suddenly saw the display screen, and in an instant she was gone. Aldin hit the collision alarm for the benefit of anyone astern who was not buckled in.

"There's nothing we can do," Aldin said, looking over at Oishi. "Put the ship on automatic."

Oishi hesitated for a second. Aldin reached out and patted him on the arm.

"Aldin-san," Oishi whispered, trying to keep his voice steady while he turned over controls to the computer, a system that he still viewed with the deepest of suspicions.

"Ten seconds until disruption of flight," the computer announced calmly. "According to my calculations, we crash in—" Tia slammed the computer voice off.

She looked over at Aldin and forced a sad smile.

"I always figured Corbin would think of something," she sighed. She leaned forward in her chair as far as her restraining belts would allow, pecked Aldin on the forehead, and settling back took Oishi's hand in hers.

As usual, the computer wasn't quite up to par and the storm hit at 9.91 seconds, but nobody noticed the mistake.

chapter two

"There is no confirmed kill," Vush of the Overseers announced solemnly.

A groan went up from the assembly of Overseers, Humans, Gafs, and Xsarns.

"So how the hell do we get our payoffs," Nugala, Xsarn Secondary of the Tala Hive, shouted dejectedly.

"I'm sorry," Vush replied sanctimoniously. "Our hidden observation drone did detect lift-off by Aldin's pleasure yacht. The vessel was then lost in the interference created by the shock wave that encircled the planet. Until we have a confirmed corpse, we have to hold on the primary bet."

"Xsarn food," Ubur Taug snapped. "Nothing could have gotten out of there. You bastard Overseers are just trying to tie up the assets on the bet so you can draw interest. Nothing could have survived that blast."

"My dear friends," Vush whispered, rising up to hover above the angry crowd. "It simply wouldn't be fair to pay off the bets when we can calculate that there was one chance in two thousand, one hundred and forty-three that the vessel reasserted hull integrity and achieved space, or one chance in eighty-nine that they found safe haven on the far side of the planet."

At least several in the crowd, those who had bet on Aldin's survival, were happy with the pronouncement. But the mood of the three dozen others was less than friendly toward Vush and the half-dozen Overseers who were running the betting pool.

"Come, come, my friends," Vush said soothingly, "we can at least pay off the side bets for Corbin successfully hitting and destroying the palace. A nice bit of astro-navigation, that. And the computers are open for a new side bet that Aldin, Bukha, the Xsarn, and/or Zergh survived. Odds on Aldin are now eighty to one, with various multiples for any combination of the others."

"Wait a minute," Ubur growled. "You said the odds were one in eighty-nine that they found safe haven, and now suddenly it's eighty to one."

Vush looked around, a bit confused by all of this, his gaze at last fixing on Hobbs Gablona. Hobbs, who ran this gaming and pleasure planet, floated into the center of the room aboard his float chair. He looked almost like a twin of Corbin, topping out at over one hundred and eighty kilos, a characteristic that was common to most of the males of the Gablona clan, but there the comparison ended between him and his cousin. Hobbs's features were fixed in what appeared to be an almost perpetual leering grin of earthy delight. He was noted among the upper set of the Cloud for running a gaming palace second to none for exotic betting situations, luxurious treatment of guests, a tacky sense of vulgar showmanship, and a blind eye to some of the more unusual activities that his customers sometimes indulged in, especially when they were willing to pay well for his arranging of entertainment.

"House odds," Hobbs announced taking over for the thoroughly confused Overseer. "After all, there is a bit of an overhead in running these things." Laughing, he pointed to the fountain in the center of the room, filled with sparkling burgundy in which several of the Gafs were now bathing, and to the covered feeding trough in the corner around which the Xsarns were happily gathered.

"And the only damn game in town," another Koh sighed as he bellied up to his terminal to bet on a straight ticket of all four players surviving.

There was a sullen murmur of agreements to that point at least.

"Come, come, friends, another round of bets to liven it up for a bit longer before the game finally ends. And remember, gentlemen," Vush said, "the visuals, food, and drink are free after all."

The show had indeed been spectacular. The masked remote unit placed in geosynch had relayed the most spectacular explosion to have been witnessed in the Cloud since the end of interstellar warfare nearly three thousand years before.

Connoisseurs of fine explosions who were not invited to the private gaming party had eagerly paid the Overseers' asking price of a hundred thousand credits to be hooked into the live vidlink. Some of the Kohs addicted to explosives had occasionally crashed a derelict ship into an uninhabited moon for the fun of it, but never at a speed of much more than one one-hundredth of light. No one had ever witnessed a cargo ship slamming into a life-supporting planet. The group had been awestruck by the sight, forgetting even to cheer as the explosion tore away half a continent.

Even as they grumbled at the Overseer, most of the crowd was still glued to the monitors, going over the instant replays and pointing out to each other the finer points of what was still going on. A betting pool had been quickly set up on the exact time that the shock waves would collide on the far side, and Xsarn Secondary had regurgitated excitedly when he had picked up half a million on that bet.

Several of the Kohs were already in the holo simulation rooms, where the computer could analyze the data from the blast and re-create a wide variety of vantage points from anywhere in space, or even down on the planet's surface. Wild shouts of delight could be heard from the rooms to be drowned out by the wall-shaking rumble of the shock wave blasting over the viewers.

"Gentlemen," Vush announced, looking around the room in what he thought was a facial gesture that could be interpreted as a smile, "after all, there are still other bets to be played in this game. Do remember that though Aldin and Bukha might be dead, Aldin's estate is still the largest in the Cloud."

There was a murmur of excitement as the various Kohs and other nouveau riche beings looked expectantly at each other and started to break up and head to the wagering computers.

Though old fortunes had failed with the last game, numerous new ones had been made as well in the wild economic chaos that had followed. If Aldin was dead, and even if he was not, there was a vast economic empire waiting to fall into eager hands.

"My staff has prepared a full betting portfolio listing several hundred different options to be played against, so settle back gentlemen, all accommodations, food, and entertainment are yours here at the Overseer betting palace."

The crowd, though still angry about the delayed payoff from the attack on Aldin, could not help but give a halfhearted cheer of approval. There was no denying that the Overseer Vush had thought of everything when he had chartered Hobbs's world for the game.

"More profit for everyone," Vush said to Hobbs as he floated past, believing that this Gablona was undoubtedly delighted by the situation of additional betting.

Hobbs looked back at the screens replaying the blast, the fuzzy image of Aldin's ship staggering ahead of the shock wave and then disappearing. It gave him a slight knot in the gut. After all, in his early days he had even been a vasba for a while, and the old guild had some set rules about looking out for fellow members. A discreet tip-off was all he could offer, but it seemed as if that was now far too late. The thought of Corbin winning was disturbing enough; the thought of Aldin losing permanently was far worse.

He looked over at Vush and smiled, saying nothing.

As Vush floated from the room he gazed around benevolently at the group he had suckered into his game. However, as the door closed behind him the look of benevolence changed in an instant to horror.

"So are we enjoying our little game?"

In an instant Vush was on the floor, kneeling before the Arch Overseer, feeling like a youth who had been caught by his parents while performing some sinful and very disgusting act.

Vush looked up at the Arch, trying to read his four multifaceted eyes for some sign of what was to come.

"Oh, I knew about your little arrangement some time ago," the Arch said evenly.

"How?" Vush whispered.

"Let's just say that at the end of the last game I could see the infection of greed had been passed by the lesser barbarian races into you. I figured sooner or later you'd succumb to the sins of violence and gambling."

"I plead temporary madness," Vush said quickly. "Too much contact with their inferior breed has unsettled my mind. I'll be happy to retire to a meditation world if you will ever find a way to forgive me."

If an Overseer could have laughed, the sound coming from the Arch would have been a fairly close approximation.

"Do you really expect me to buy that rubbish?" the Arch replied, falling into the language of the Humans.

Nervously Vush looked up at his master and judge.

"Tell me, what are the odds on Corbin Gablona succeeding?"

"If Aldin is dead, then I dare say there are no odds. Corbin's Al'Shiga, and his control of several dozen ships to be used as planet rams, will hold the rest of the Cloud in terror. Even if Aldin lives, which is a serious long shot, the odds are still 6.7 to 1 against him."

The Arch turned away and floated across the room.

"I tremble to think what would happen if Aldin lives. The entire Cloud might fall into civil war as the disgruntled old Kohs fight against Aldin and those still loyal to him. It would be a terrible bloodletting. It could wreck the civilization of the three outside species who now inhabit this realm of space."

The Arch turned back to look at Vush, and what passed for an Overseer's smile crossed his lips.

Vush breathed an inner sigh of relief.

"I have contended with this infection from the next galaxy for far too long," the Arch snapped out, his voice filled with loathing.

Vush floated excitedly to his feet.

"You are not forgiven," the Arch said, and Vush was immediately back on his knees.

"You've presented me with a most interesting problem, most interesting indeed."

"I was simply trying to spare you the details, and prevent the equanimity of your soul from being disturbed."

"I never knew you to be that considerate," the Arch replied sharply.

"But as I was saying. If Aldin should live, there'll be open interstellar war across the entire Cloud." The Arch looked back at his underling.

He never had agreed with the intervention to stop the last war three thousand years before. Granted he was horrified at the overt violence, but he had always felt that they should have let these noisome creatures burn themselves out completely, and then they could move in and establish order and control.

But moral arguments had won out, they had used the devices left behind by the First Travelers, and through a demonstration of sheer power, and the destruction of half a dozen planets, they had terrified the lesser species into a peace that had lasted down through the centuries.

And at what price? he thought bitterly. It was like trying to maintain order between a vast family of bickering, spoiled children. The quiet peace of the Cloud had been destroyed forever by their presence.

In the now-legendary past, beyond the memory of any living Overseer, even beyond the existing memory of the vast machines, which through the millennia had gradually lost their recall, the First Travelers had roamed the Cloud. They had created the great monuments to their power, the Rings, Skyhooks, and the vast, all-encompassing Sphere, which to them were nothing more than amusements to pass the long eternity of existence. He had often wondered who the First Travelers were. Were they simply the machines that still existed scattered throughout the Cloud, aged and worn after countless ages, or was there something even before them, endless layers of creation nestled within one another like onion skins?

The Overseers, their numbers always so small, had arrived to behold such wonders, and the machines had bowed to them and asked them to be the protectors of the monuments created. So they had settled here, curators of the entire Greater and Lesser Magellanic Cloud as the Humans called it. They were so few in number, but that had always been the way of their species, to replace one of their number only when finally, after countless time, a spirit finally slipped away to the void.

There had been two galaxies to roam in quiet contemplation, forever seeking the knowledge of the one true light. Entire worlds could be the home of a single being living in solitary meditation.

Now the Cloud was aswarm with these quarreling brawling mobs, who cluttered the space lanes, soiled the planets, and shattered the quiet of the universe.

At first the Overseers had viewed it as some great mission, to teach these creatures the ways of peace, the joy of contemplation, and the total release of nonaction. But may the Eternal damn them all, it was simply wearing too thin, he thought angrily.

And then finally they had destroyed the Tower to the world of the Al'Shiga.

The near-total destruction of the race on that planet had not bothered him in the slightest. Funny, he thought, there was a time when the Overseers had debated for centuries over the morality of eating nonsentient life-forms. Most had gone totally synthetic as a result. That, he realized, was yet another sign of their corrupting influence: now he didn't even get upset when they slaughtered each other.

But the destruction of the Tower, that was simply too much to bear. It was a sacred monument, a true artifact of the legendary First Travelers, and the Humans and Gafs had destroyed it and, in fact, had even exalted over the destruction. Holo movies showing the collapse were one of the most sought-after items now by the mob.

"Disgusting, absolutely disgusting."

"Did you say something, my Arch?" Vush whispered, looking up at his ruler.

"What? Oh, nothing, nothing at all," the Arch hissed, his voice edged with annoyance.

"Will you punish me?" Vush asked nervously.

"But of course," the Arch snapped angrily, and Vush bowed his head. Most likely he'd be sent to contemplate his sins for ten centuries on some forsaken rock. No betting for a thousand years, Vush thought dejectedly. I'll go crazy without some action.

"Oh, get up on your feet," the Arch growled. "Float with some pride, damn it."

Stunned by his leader's decadent vocabulary, Vush rose up into the air, mindful to keep himself a head lower out of respect.

"Here is your punishment," the Arch said softly, fixing Vush with his gaze. "You are to continue running this game."

Vush could not contain his exuberance, and so quickly did he rise that his head slammed into the ceiling.

"Your enlightened wish is always my desire," Vush replied ceremonially.

"There's something else," the Arch said evenly.

"Whatever it is your enlightenment wishes," Vush said, forgetting any form of decorum so that his voice was near breaking with excitement.

"We never had this conversation."

"Never had this conversation?" Vush asked quizzically. "How can that be? We are speaking this conversation at this very moment."

"A Human concept," the Arch replied sharply. "It means that in your mind you will establish a logic system that denies the reality of what we have exchanged and replace it with another reality that states you and I never discussed these things."

"Oh." Vush wrestled with the thought. His exposure to Humans had exposed him to this strange logic. But it surprised him that an Arch would be so worldly as to request such a thing.

"As you wish," Vush said quietly.

"As I order," the Arch snapped back. "Also I want you to create a situation wherein the events of the game may be altered from time to time as I see fit, especially if Aldin is still alive."

"You mean rig the results," Vush replied smartly, feeling a surge of pleasure over knowing the correct term.

"Yes, that is how they call it. This war must go on. I want these creatures to get a complete scare thrown into them in the end, if need be to push their technological prowess back to a more manageable level by the time they are done."

"You mean a real, full-blown, planet-busting war?" Vush replied.

"Yes, that," the Arch said, amazed somewhat that he had finally voiced his secret desire of centuries.

Stunned, Vush looked at his leader.

"Do the other Overseers know this?" Vush asked guardedly.

"That is none of your damn business," the Arch snapped. "We've got to weaken these creatures a bit before we can bring them back into line. Let them do their destruction on each other for a while. It's not our fault or our sin. In the end they'll come rushing to us for peace, and as the brokers of that, we'll bring better control. We thought we could rule them through the organization of Kohs, and look at what that has finally resulted in. The Koh system will be finished by this war, and then we'll simply rule directly, and those swarms of creatures out there will beg for our guidance. Maybe then we can have a little peace and quiet around here."

Vush was stunned by the extended outburst. Overseers were supposed to be reticent and above all discreet, to communicate crisply and without emotion. For an Arch, the last outburst was the closest thing to a tirade Vush had ever heard.

Even the Arch suddenly seemed embarrassed by his comments and turned away.

"I'm leaving now. I need to find a place of solitude," the Arch said softly. "I find being anywhere near those creatures has a most disquieting effect on my soul."

Vush, bowing low, backed out toward the door.

"Keep this game going," the Arch said coldly, and then the jump-down beam encompassed him and he was gone.

"What the hell do you mean there's no confirmed kill?" Corbin yelled.

Hassan stood dispassionately by the entryway into Corbin's cabin. How he had ever found himself back in this man's employ was beyond his understanding. He had sworn to drive a dagger into Corbin's bloated belly if he ever had the pleasure of meeting him again.

But two years of struggling for survival in the wreckage of the Hole had tempered that rage. He had managed to organize a cell of new followers, and even held some sway in the power struggles that had rocked the Al'Shiga. But there was simply no way to get off that forsaken rock.

No way until a smuggler ship had alighted almost directly on top of his encampment. The offer had been straightforward and simple. Service in return for rescuing Hassan and his followers.

He had accepted; only a madman would refuse the chance to practice his craft among the unsuspecting billions who lived their fat easy lives throughout the Cloud. Yes, the fat one still had his uses, but there would be a reckoning. For the moment patience would have to do until the intricacies of travel through space had been mastered.

"That was the report issued by the Overseer. All bets are closed until it is confirmed that Aldin is either alive or dead."

"What the hell does he want," Corbin roared, "a bottle full of that bastard's dust?"

"It seems their observation remote detected a ship lifting off from the palace seconds before the shock wave hit."

With an angry snarl Corbin stalked over to the control board that dominated an entire wall of his bedroom suite. With a wave of disdain he dismissed the several girls who had been waiting for him, and as they exited the room, they eyed Hassan fearfully. A rumor had gone through the entourage that Hassan had only once succumbed to the temptations of the flesh since he had joined Corbin. Her body had been found afterward, at least most of it: the guess was her head was floating somewhere out near the last jump portal.

The screen lit up to show the revelers on the gaming deck below. The ship was still in orbit over Aldin's pleasure world, and the passengers were continuing to observe the death throes of the planet. It had been nearly a standard day since the hit, and firestorms now engulfed nearly half a hemisphere. An entire world was dying down there, and it held a strange, perverse fascination. Even the more fastidious types who viewed real violence with disdain were engrossed by destruction on a scale so vast, it took on a certain degree of unreality.

"It is possible that they raced ahead of the shock wave, the turbulence blocking our monitors from so far out," Ali ventured. "Once on the far side they pulled straight up and away, using the planet as a shield from observation."

"Or they could have crashed on the far side," Corbin said slowly. "We've been in geosynch over the blast site watching the show."

Corbin settled back in his chair.

"Damn you, you should have thought of this possibility and suggested a sweep around the world just to make sure," Corbin snarled.

"You have lived in this universe far longer than I," Hassan said coldly, "and thus you are more familiar with such things."

Corbin was about to snap back a reply, but the look in Hassan's eyes stilled his words. He knew he needed this master of intrigue and assassination as an ally. The mere presence of the Al'Shiga on his side struck fear into all around him. But of late he was starting to wonder if he was indeed riding the tiger, and if, when the time came to eliminate the tiger, he would be able to get off his mount alive.

He forced a smile of reconciliation.

"You are correct, my friend," Corbin said warmly. "Let's take a look at the far side. If we detect a ship down there, maybe you and your friends can have a little fun with your blades."

Hassan smiled in reply, a smile that chilled Corbin's blood.

If there was one thing Yaroslav truly hated, it was space travel. He let out a groan of anticipation as the computer announced jump-point transition. Jump-point transitions turned his stomach inside out. He was pumped with enough motion-sickness juice to put a Gaf to sleep, but still he felt his bile rising as the forward screen suddenly washed out, went dark, and then an instant later snapped into focus.

"Merciful heavens," he whispered. Switching the forward screen to maximum magnification, he quickly surveyed the firestorm consuming the continent where Aldin's pleasure palace had been. Even from the distance of the jump-point, the monitor was able to pick up a nightmare of chaos.

"If he was down there, he's dead," the old scholar said mournfully.

The tip-off of a strike had come ten days' past. He suspected it was Jorva Taug who had passed it along, or just maybe Hobbs Gablona. The warning had ruined all of his fun.

The visit to the Ring of Alexander, and the pleasure of the conversation, had to be cut short. Ever since the Hole game, he had found it to be a rather unhealthy occupation to be one of Aldin's friends, and hanging around on remote pleasure worlds had grown a bit too boring, especially with carping from Mari about Aldin's "smelly old friends." In the end there was no place else to go but the Ring.

Alexander—now there was somebody to sit up late with and talk to. His recollections of Aristotle were revealing and most amusing. Kubar Taug's knowledge of the lost books of the philosopher Varnag were worth several articles at the very least. The only problem was that the existence of Alexander and Kubar in this time frame was something of a secret. If he published, the Ring would soon be swarming with tourists and another great spot would be ruined.

Their plans for a campaign against the Lagara over in the next continent were most justifiable, and he had been offered a staff command position, complete to the military panoply of a Macedonian general. It was most tempting. He could image a bronze statue of himself, helmeted, shield up, spear in hand. It was all going so comfortably, until the incoming message.

What had been even more disturbing was the emergency beacon flash, using Aldin's private code, that he had picked up twelve hours ago, causing him to cancel a quick side stop at Irmik for a friendly visit with an old and most interesting former student and instead push the ship to maximum speed.

He now regretted wasting the half a day on debating whether to go on what was most likely a false alarm anyhow. Now he truly regretted it.

"We've got something!" Corbin shouted. Excitement rippled through the room as the various Kohs and fellow conspirators pushed around the screen.

In an instant, odds of fifty to one against survivors were offered and millions were wagered. Side bets started to spring up as well on the possible outcome if Hassan's assassin team had to go in to finish the job.

"There's a ship down there, and it matches the profile," Corbin said, scanning the board.

"Any signs of life?" the Kohs shouted excitedly.

"Can't tell, atmospherics are going crazy down there."

Corbin spun around in his seat and looked at his companions.

"It's in the middle of a swamp, and there's no place to land this ship. Jump-down beams aren't the healthiest thing with atmospheric conditions like that—you might materialize with a bucket of hail in your chest."

He fell silent for a moment.

"I'll go down on the docking ship to check things out," Hassan said. There was a strange look in the assassin's eyes.

Though trying to act jovial, Corbin was deeply embarrassed that he had not thought to do a simple sweep of the far side, just to make sure. In the excitement of a possible ground fight the others hadn't noticed, but later there would be comments about this lack of efficiency, and there was no one he could possibly pass the blame to. He could see that Hassan was fully aware of this. He half suspected that Hassan had thought of this alternative even while the primary shock wave was encircling the planet but had kept silent to embarrass his master.

"Take him alive," Gubta Koh shouted gleefully, interrupting Corbin's thoughts. "Then we can space the bastard and place bets on how long it takes him to die in vacuum."

"Droll, but childish," Umga, Xsarn of the Polta Hive, announced. "A lot more fun it would be to shoot him into that black hole over in the fourteenth quadrant. His going over the event horizon would be worth quite a few laughs."

The group broke into a round of good-natured joking, even though with Aldin technically still alive bets worth millions were riding on this. If he got off the world, and even if they later caught and killed him, it would be ruled that Corbin had not destroyed him as a result of the first attack.

"Well, let's send Hassan down. If there's anything left, we'll take him alive," Corbin said expansively.

"And your beautiful cousin?" Hassan asked softly.

Corbin looked over at his master assassin and the room went silent.

He had written her off long ago. She was still a distant blood relative, though, and in what little corner of his heart still had feelings for her, he had simply hoped that she would be vaporized with all the others.

"Kill her," he said quietly, and the room went silent. There was something about his pronouncement that disturbed even those who had been his companions of late.

"But make it swift and painless," Corbin added, as if in an afterthought and, standing, he stalked out of the room.

With a sardonic smile Hassan surveyed the assembly, many of whom looked away as his gaze fell upon them, and turning, he followed Corbin out of the room.

"Aldin, I think I hear something."

Groaning, Aldin Larice opened his eyes and saw Oishi kneeling over him. Sitting up, he rubbed the walnut-size lump on the back of his head. For that matter nearly every square inch of his body was covered with bruises. The last hour of his once-priceless yacht's flying time had been the ride of a life-time. All inertia dampening had been lost when the shock wave hit, so every toss and turn had thrown the occupants about the cabin and rolled them into a tangled jumble.

How the nav system had ever managed to set them down was to him a miracle. The salesman had told him that the Vax 8 autopiloting and emergency backup controls, designed to deal with one hundred and twenty-two types of emergencies, was the latest thing on the market. The manual actually did declare that it could handle surprise black holes and acts of God such as random asteroid impacts on planetary surfaces, though no legal liability was intended by such claims. His frugal nature had almost dismissed the pitch, but Oishi had agreed with the dealer, so to shut the polyester-clad Gaf salesman up he had signed for the six hundred thousand katar system, which at the time he felt was nothing more than a frill to keep Oishi happy. If he ever saw that Gaf again, he swore that for the first time in his life he would actually get on his knees and kiss the boots of a space-yacht salesman.

Aldin came to his feet and moved aft. The stench of unwashed bodies living in the emergency shelter area was near overpowering. Fear and excitement, especially for Gafs, immediately triggered an incredibly strong musky smell. It was possible to go outside, but the storms of hurricane proportion outside were simply too dangerous to venture into.

Going over to Tia, he knelt down by her side.

"How we doing this morning?" he whispered, taking her bandaged hands in his.

"Like cooked Xsarn food," she replied, forcing a smile through cracked lips. "Is it daylight out there?"

"A bit stormy, but the sun's up," Aldin said cheerfully, trying to hide his concern. She'd taken a cut in one eye, and Zergh had insisted that both of them be bandaged up.

"Sun's up?" Mari snapped peevishly. "We're stuck here for the rest of our lives, and now the climate on this place stinks. You realize how much money you lost in this world? I figure it'd be at least a hundred and fifty million . . ."

Aldin looked up at his towering wife, and for once the anger in his eyes silenced her tirade.

Somehow, he thought inwardly, if he had simply stayed

poor, this woman would have been perfectly happy to buy another tavern on a safer world than the Hole. They could have settled in and undoubtedly been completely happy.

The problem was that Mari was an incredible financial manipulator, having already gained the reputation as a class-one money shark, but her taste was worse than any Gaf had ever dared to display. Within Gaf circles she had gained quite the reputation for haute couture and had even opened a fashion line that was famed for its swirling paisleys intermixed with mauve and yellow polka dots.

"There it is again," Oishi whispered.

Aldin came to his feet and went through the airlock to stand next to the outer door.

There was the sound of the storm outside, but there was something else as well, a high-pitched whine growing louder by the second. There was a booming throaty roar, and a vibration ran through the vessel. It was a ship going into a full reverse thrust.

In an instant his entourage of samurai guards was on its feet. Most of them now carried the modern accoutrements of a guard—Erik 15s, and the favored heavy weapon of the Gafs, the Ulman Scatter Sweeper, which put out a beehive cluster round that could knock over anything in a sixty degree spread for more than a hundred yards. The only problem with that weapon was that it couldn't differentiate between who was friendly and who was not. Oishi still held to the old form, even though there was an Erik tucked into his waist. Sweeping out his sword, he approached the door cautiously.

"If it's Corbin's people, we better go out to meet them," Oishi stated, as if merely discussing some minor point of strategy rather than an issue of life or death. "In here they could simply place explosive charges on the hull and be done with us."

Aldin cursed silently. There had been a hold full of armaments on board, including a highly illegal ship-to-ship laser cannon; all that was now buried under thirty feet of muck in the collapsed stern of the ship.

Oishi grabbed hold of the door with one hand and held his blade poised with the other.

"Let's go!"

The door slammed open. A bent, shriveled form stood in the

doorway. With a backhanded sweep Oishi brought his blade up for the kill.

"For heaven's sake watch that damn thing!" Yaroslav roared, tumbling over backward to avoid the blow.

The samurai behind Oishi leaped through the doorway, weapons poised to be confronted by a wiry old man who came back up to his feet and then doubled over with laughter.

"Scared the hell out of you, didn't I," Yaroslav chortled.

Aldin didn't know whether to curse him or knock him off his feet with an embrace. Finally, he chose the latter.

The now-ecstatic group piled out of the ship, and despite the near hurricane-force winds and driving rain gathered around their rescuer, barraging him with questions.

"We don't have time for it now," Yaroslav yelled, trying to be heard above the commotion, "there's another ship that'll be here in ten minutes, and the occupants are less than friendly."

"Corbin?"

"I think so, he was closing in when I shot by. He'd be blind not to pick me up and follow me in."

"That fat slob," Mari roared, standing in the doorway. "I want to stay here and give him a piece of my mind. Look what he did to our ship. He's gonna pay for this! I'll sue the bastard for damages. Our lawyers will eat his lawyers alive."

For just a brief moment Aldin was tempted to leave her. She'd most likely be more than a match for Hassan.

"Let's get moving!" Oishi shouted. He rushed back into the ruined ship and quickly reemerged, carrying Tia.

Aldin looked around the impenetrable swamp.

"Just where did you land?" he shouted.

To his amazement, Yaroslav pointed straight up. Resting directly on top of the wreck stood the old man's tiny personal transport.

There was no time to argue whether there was room for everyone or not. Scrambling up the side of the shattered yacht, the group started to pile in through the airlock.

Rushing into the control room, Aldin slipped into the copilot seat and started punching in the lift-off commands.

"Looks like company," Zergh suddenly announced with a groan, coming in alongside of Aldin and pointing forward.

Looking through the forward viewport, Aldin saw a heavy ground shuttle hover into view.

"Everyone's aboard," Yaroslav announced.

"Punch us out now!" Aldin shouted.

The ship lurched off the ground, standing nearly on its tail to avoid smashing into the landing craft. For an instant Aldin found himself staring into the control booth of the other ship, not a dozen feet away.

"Hassan!"

The hawklike eyes gazed into his, and he felt a cold shudder of fear. Oishi snapped out a curse in Japanese and brandished his sword. But Hassan did not respond, his remorseless eyes still locked on Aldin.

Zergh started to spin the ship on its axis and hit the emergency jump-out engine into life.

Unable to resist the impulse, Aldin leaned over and flashed a universal gesture of contempt at the assassin, and then the vessel disappeared from view.

Within seconds the planet was dropping away. Punching up through the atmosphere, the ship quickly gained escape velocity.

"There's Gablona's yacht," Yaroslav announced, pointing to a converging blip on the screen. "When he saw me swinging in, you should have heard him rage. This little ship always was good for getting in and out of tight corners quickly."

Aldin leaned over and hit the commlink.

"Corbin, are you picking me up?"

There was a moment of silence, and then the screen before Aldin lit up to reveal Corbin Gablona at his angriest.

"What the hell did you do it for?" Aldin asked.

"Why not?" Corbin replied, his angry features suddenly relaxing into a show of outward calm.

Aldin could only shake his head in disbelief.

"You should have left me to die back down on the Hole," Corbin said smoothly, a smile lighting his features. "But then again compassion always was one of your weak points."

"I'll see your head lying in the dust!" Oishi roared, stepping up to the screen.

Corbin recoiled in mock terror and started to laugh.

"As the old tradition must still hold," Corbin replied, "do consider my little present to your world as a formal declaration of war. All your holdings are now fair game. Since it seems I failed to eliminate you in this first strike, I'll simply have to stage a repeat on some of your major holdings as a result. I've got a dozen more ships ready to crash at selected points around the Cloud."

Aldin simply could not reply.

"It'll make a hell of a vid," Corbin continued. "I'll title it, *A Study in Destruction: Holos of Worlds Being Destroyed.*"

"You're sick," Aldin roared. "Let's just settle it here. Your people and mine back down to the planet. You're killing millions of people who have no part in this is even beneath you."

Corbin started to laugh.

"Oh, we'll get around to that eventually, but how do I know what weapons that little rescue ship's got on board? No, it's been three thousand years since this Cloud's had a good gut-busting war, now I'll give it to them and simply declare myself ruler when everyone is thoroughly intimidated."

"What about the Overseers?" Aldin cried. "They'll never allow it."

Corbin leaned back laughing, his mass shaking in great convulsive waves. Wiping the tears from his eyes, he looked back at the monitor and smiled.

"You figure that one out. You know where to reach me when you want to surrender. My terms are simple, the ceding over of all assets to my name, recognition of my rightful place as ruler, and my confederates as Kohs and cabinet members in my government. Finally you, Yaroslav, Zergh, Bukha, the Xsarn Prime, and Tia will face punishment by my hand. Think about it." The screen went dead.

Stunned, Aldin looked over his shoulder to the group that had gathered to watch the exchange.

"Do we have any ship-to-ship weapons?" Aldin asked.

He already knew the answer, but he could always hope that one had been concealed on board, despite the three thousand year injunction against such devices.

The cabin was suddenly illuminated with a blinding light.

"He sure as hell has one," Zergh roared, as the nav system automatically sent the ship into evasive maneuvers. At any distance greater than twenty thousand kilometers, ship-to-ship weapons were next to useless, since a good navigation computer could punch in a dozen lateral shifts per second. At anything more than a tenth of a second between radar pulse to lock on, firing was simply pure chance. Only the luckiest of shots would have an effect. Corbin had made the key mistake of hovering in geosynch rather than coming in low behind the landing craft for the kill—or he feared that Yaroslav might be armed after all and didn't want to take the risk.

Aldin thought about that for a moment. Both he and Corbin were masters of archaic warfare, but space combat was something they had never toyed with before. It was a lost art. An art they were all going to quickly learn.

Within seconds it was obvious that the lighter mass and maneuverability of Yaroslav's ship, even with sixty refugees crammed aboard, would quickly outrace any attempt at closing.

Aldin turned away from the conflict to look at his friends.

"I'd even suggest ramming the bastard," he said evenly, "but we'd get fried first."

Oishi nodded in agreement, even though the contemplation of it implied suicide for Aldin and everyone on board.

"Look, I didn't volunteer for another nick-of-time rescue just to get suicided for my efforts," Yaroslav replied.

The old man, however, breathed a sigh of relief at the rejection of such an idea.

"What are we going to do?" Aldin asked.

"Fight a war," Bukha said grimly. "He's taken the gloves off, so now we'll take them off as well."

Disgusted with only this alternative, Aldin settled back into his chair.

"The Overseers?"

"You heard him," Zergh interjected. "They're standing back."

"I find that hard to believe," Aldin said. "Sure, I know they're secretive, that they're most likely weaker than we ever realized, but if they don't nip this in the bud, they'll get fried in the end as well. If Corbin can destroy us, he'll turn on them next."

"Maybe they want us to fight it out," Yaroslav said, examining the quality of his manicure even while the ship continued to weave and bob, the inertial dampening all but dissipating the rapid movements. The nav system was already locked onto the nearest jump gate and was rapidly closing in, with Gablona more than fifty thousand kilometers behind and falling away.

"I think we need a drink," Aldin announced, wanting to take the time to contemplate what had just occurred. A servobot quickly appeared toting a tray of drinks, and everyone was glad for the round of brandy.

"I'm just glad someone got your emergency beacon going, otherwise I would have really been late this time," Yaroslav said, leaning back in his chair and holding his snifter up to examine its contents.

"What beacon?" Oishi asked, leaning forward. "We never set it out. If we had, Corbin would have definitely come looking for us earlier than he did."

Amazed, the group looked at each other.

"Maybe it was the Overseers, triggering one outside the system so Corbin wouldn't detect it," the Xsarn announced, shaking his head. "They wanted all of us to live."

"So the game could continue," Aldin said in stunned disbelief.

chapter three

"I don't like this one bit," Yaroslav whispered grimly.

"It's too late now," Aldin snapped in reply, and he pointed forward to where the fifty-meter-wide boulder tumbled in on its trajectory.

The battered ship they were riding in continued to shake as the reverse thrusters rapidly slowed their approach to the planet.

"Damn inertia dampening is shot to hell," Aldin mumbled to himself.

He had to confess that being the most powerful Koh in the Cloud once had its advantages. His yacht had been a finely tuned masterpiece. He had even been able to afford the standard fifty jump overhauls, and the always-outrageous costs of jump engine tune-ups. But that was gone now. In the last six months, since his escape from Corbin's first raid, nearly every ship, repair port, and terminal once under his control had been smashed to oblivion. And as for independent stations, the mere sight of him approaching sent them into near convulsive fits, with much battening of hangar doors. No one was crazy enough to want to service anything belonging to Aldin the Hunted, as he was now referred to.

The Hole had been bad enough; now the gaming field was the entire Cloud. Corbin had not really needed to kill all that many, just a couple of service station managers found on Shiga impaling sticks had convinced everyone that doing business with Larice, or even allowing him landing rights, was a sure method to get a visit from the "black robes."

At least he could be thankful that after the planet-buster of the opening round, Corbin had toned things down. Some of the operations had been drop-in assaults designed to take out important personnel in Aldin's organization. Others had been surgical strikes designed to take out key locations. So far noncombatant casualties had been kept to a minimum, except for the murdered station attendants, landing-field operators, parts suppliers, and any banker willing to allow a credit transfer, but Aldin feared that most likely after today that would all change.

To be sure, he had wanted to strike back, but the problem was where to strike? Zola pleaded all innocence, as did every other Koh, and despite Oishi's demands, he could not bring himself to do a raid in those areas. Being a vasba, he found, dragged with it a certain code of honor about innocent people never being used in games. Even the supposed proof of a badly reproduced holo tape of Zola and a dozen minor Kohs being aboard Corbin's ship was not evidence enough. The damned problem of it all was that Corbin's operation was wonderfully designed to be clandestine. Having lost all his assets in the last game, the man really had nothing to lose, no place to really call home. There was occasional evidence of a temporary base in some outback region of the Cloud—he had even used the Kolbard Ring for a brief stay—but other than that, the bastard was simply a rumor, a ghost, hiding out in some unknown bolthole in the untraveled areas of the Cloud; yet always possessed it seemed with the uncanny ability to figure out where Aldin was.

At least until now.

"It's hitting the atmosphere," Oishi announced, a flicker of triumph in his voice.

A brilliant streak arched across the evening sky of Hobbs's Pleasure and Amusement World Emporium, followed by a sharp snap-flash of light at the impact point.

"All right, let's get down there," Aldin snapped.

The forward thrusters were kicked in. Aldin felt his stomach turn over, and swore he'd get this bucket fixed at the first opportunity.

"On the mark," Oishi announced, looking up from the radar screen. "It took out the rail gun they were mounting beyond the port. There's some shock wave damage but collateral effects are nominal."

Aldin looked over at his samurai companion and smiled. Oishi on most any other occasion would still voice his opinion in the formal speech of a Japanese warrior from the late seventeenth century. But in this new form of warfare, he had quickly mastered the technical skills and jargon necessary for command.

The *Survivor* swept into the atmosphere, riding through the shock wave, and then swung out over the ocean for final approach on the base and amusement halls.

"Ground-assault team make ready," Oishi commanded. Leaving his seat, Aldin went aft to watch final preparations.

Basak and his berserkers were beside themselves with joy, now that the first offensive was about to be launched. Almost all the berserkers and samurai were armed with modern weapons and battle armor, but Basak still preferred his massive two-handed battle-ax, claiming it would create the proper mood for the occasion, while Oishi, still in the tactical battle seat, was wearing both swords. As Aldin looked the towering Gaf over, he could only agree.

The aft cabin switched to red light, and joyful shouts of anticipation emanated from the group.

Oishi came aft, and like his Gaf companion drew his blade.

"Remember," Oishi commanded, "we hit the repair sheds, and set charges to blow any ships, though if there's something in there undamaged and better than this bucket we'll swap. Remember to hit the repair equipment. If we get Corbin here, all to the better. If not, this is one of Corbin's hidden repair bases for this section of the Cloud. We destroy this and we might have a chance to get some control back in this region."

Oishi looked over at Aldin, ready to say something, but the look in the old Koh's eyes was enough to end the argument. Oishi had gone near insane attempting to talk Aldin out of coming on this strike, but no argument would prevail. Aldin wanted to be in on the raid.

"I'll be with Aldin for the hit on the gaming center and re- sort facilities. Remember we have fifteen minutes to place our charges and to get out. Who's ever down here already sent out an alarm."

A warning Klaxon sounded through the ship.

"Final approach," Zergh called through the intercom. "Ten seconds."

Aldin felt his knees going weak. Some insane pride had pushed him into doing this little adventure. Now there was no telling what would come of it.

A jarring *thud* ran through the ship, drowned out by the wild shouts of delight from the Gafs. The airlock popped open.

What Oishi had called collateral damage stunned Aldin with its magnitude.

The entire landing area was a shambles, even though the hit had slammed in nearly half a kilometer away. An old cargo ship, caught out in the open, was blazing with a hot white heat, lighting the tropical evening like a beacon. The dozen flimsy hangar sheds lining the field had caved in from the blast, the delicate ships and personal yachts within reduced to twisted piles of rubble.

The Gafs swarmed past Aldin, shouting with glee at the de- struction already created. Teams swarmed out across the field, rushing toward the repair sheds.

"Let's go," Oishi shouted, drawing his blade and pointing toward the infamous Hobbs's Pleasure and Amusement Palace.

Within seconds Aldin was regretting his decision as he pumped his spindly legs to keep up. The glass walls of the pal- ace were riddled with gaping holes and glass was still tinkling down, adding an almost cheery counterpoint to the explosions rocking the field. It flashed back a memory of his own palace disintegrating, the demented servo- and Humanbots wandering around before the shock wave hit. It was the same here. A dis- traught servo was outside, attacking a pile of glass with a near- demented fury, loading up, and then pausing to look around, wondering where it should deposit the mess.

The lead element of samurai hit the front doors, which slid open at their approach. The entire portcullis of the castlelike structure suddenly lit up in a gaudy display. Thousands of lights flashed on, forming a single word, HOBBS, though the second *B* and most of the *S* were missing. Wild calliope music filled the air, though the computer that controlled it must have had a couple of links jarred loose, for the music was pumping out at at least three times normal speed.

"Welcome to Hobbs," a booming voice echoed, so that the assault team slowed in bewilderment.

The shifting lights on a massive billboard over the entrance clicked into a wild exotic show. Couples appeared to be dancing, dice and playing cards flickered across the screen, roulette wheels spun merrily, while female Humans and Gafs appeared in a chorus line that quickly degenerated into a most unusual interspecies erotic display.

Oishi charged through the group, pushing it forward, and the team disappeared into the cavernous maw of Hobbs's shattered glass castle.

The gaming tables were empty, chips worth hundreds of thousands of katars littering the floor.

"Aldin, you son of a bitch." Oishi whirled around, blade drawn, the other samurai pointing Erik 15s at the protesting form that floated into the room, the Gafs leveling their cluster round launchers.

At the sight of an old comrade from his early days as a vasba, Aldin almost felt a touch of nostalgia. Hobbs was yet another distant cousin through his first marriage into the Gablona clan. And as was typical of the Gablona line, to call this man portly was an understatement. The owner of the amusement resort floated into the center of the room, riding a lift chair, which groaned under a mass that made Corbin look like he had been to a reduction clinic. The chair, a gaudy model with genuine gold gilding, carried Hobbs across the room.

Hobbs's piglike eyes squinted out through roll after roll of flesh, his head so massive it was impossible to discern where his jowls ended and the rest of his body began.

Several guards came out, flanking their boss, but at the sight of the heavily armed samurai and Gafs confronting them, their resolve weakened. Hobbs, with a wave of his beefy hand, dismissed them.

"I'll sue you," Hobbs shouted angrily. "I'll sue you blind."

Wearily Aldin shook his head, coming up to stand beside an old acquaintance he had not seen in years.

"Sorry you got in the way, Hobbs," Aldin said in an almost self-deprecating manner. "It had to be done."

"What in the name of the Cloud does my innocent emporium have to do with your little squabble?"

"Corbin, is he here?" Oishi barked, coming up to face the giant who floated before him.

"Check my register, you imbecile," Hobbs roared. "He left yesterday! So why did you have to smash my place up?"

Oishi went over to the desk and punched up the guest register. He scanned the list, saw Corbin's coded entry, and angrily smashed the keyboard with his fist.

"Damn, we missed him."

"I'm just a poor cousin, the same way you were when you married into the family," Hobbs shouted, his voice taking on the whine of an injured child. "I got my life savings in this joint, and now because of the two of you I'm wiped out."

"I'll make good on it once this is over," Aldin said, trying to calm the man down. "You and I both know Corbin's been using this place to refit his ships with weapons. I had to take it out even if he wasn't here."

Hobbs fell silent. He knew that protesting his innocence on that point was useless, the shattered evidence lay everywhere out on the field. Corbin had offered him far too good a deal, to slowly cut back the entertainment business and then use the amusement center as a cover.

"And besides," Oishi interjected, "we heard how you threw a gaming party the day the war started."

Hobbs looked around guiltily.

"Family pressure," he replied lamely.

"If the Overseers ever found out about what you were covering for here, you'd be in reeducation and weight loss," Aldin said coldly.

Hobbs leaned back and started to roar with laughter.

"What's so damn funny?" Aldin inquired.

"I can't say," Hobbs said, a touch of mirth in his voice.

"All right, sweep the place," Aldin commanded, looking back at his warriors.

The samurai moved out, storming up to the second floor where the guest suites were located.

Seconds later shrill cries filled the gaming room, as dozens of entertainment girls came rushing in, circling around Hobbs as if their boss could actually offer some protection from an armed assault team. Aldin eyed the Human and Gaf females with interest. He thought back to the night he had first met

Hobbs, and what they had accomplished at a little entertainment dive on Luxot, and as if the purveyor of amusement had read his mind, the two smiled.

"Bit too old now for those days," Aldin said wistfully.

"Damn me, Aldin Larice, come back when your little skirmish is over with my cousin and I'll show you you're never too old."

Aldin chuckled softly.

"I'm married, you know."

"Yeah, I heard about her. Miss Amazon. It'll never last."

Aldin nodded sadly.

His reverie was suddenly shattered by the angry bark of an Erik 15.

Screaming, the crowd of girls scattered in every direction. Aldin ducked low, drew his weapon, and scanned the cavernous room.

"Upstairs," Oishi roared, moving up alongside of Aldin.

"I guess you found my guests," Hobbs said, trying to feign a superior boredom. "I didn't think they'd be so stupid as to start shooting."

Wild shouts echoed from the next floor, and moments later Zola Faldon appeared at the top of the stairs, flanked by several samurai.

"How dare you come barging in here like this," Zola shouted, clinging to a towel around his waist. His cry of protest was broken off as the samurai pushed him down the stairs.

Aldin looked over at Hobbs, who gave a weak smile.

"You ain't gonna like what else you'll find up there," Hobbs said quietly.

"Aldin-san." One of the samurai beckoned.

Ignoring Zola's shouted protest, Aldin raced up the stairs, Oishi by his side.

A cluster of samurai stood around a doorway out of which steam was pouring.

Entering the steam bath, Aldin gasped for breath. The far wall of glass was blown wide open; shards of glass had sickled the length of the room, all the occupants within having sustained a bloody range of injuries. Med servobots were already at work, patching up the dozen or so occupants.

A Gaf body lay spread-eagled by the door, a gaping hole in the middle of his chest. It was Kulta, a minor Koh of the Gaf-dominated Nagamak sector.

"He had a weapon under his robe," one of the samurai said. "There was nothing I could do."

Now it was really going to hit, Aldin realized. A Koh had finally been killed.

At the sight of Aldin, the half dozen other Kohs in the room broke into wild taunts and threats. Aldin looked around the room with disdain.

"So how much have you made off the gaming so far?" he snapped angrily.

"Not as much as I'm going to collect when you're dead," Zola shouted from out in the hallway. "The Overseers are going to send you up for life on this one!"

Zola barged back into the room and pointed to the now faintly visible far corner.

Aldin saw the second body and his heart froze.

The glass beneath his feet crackled loudly as Aldin nervously approached the body. He had never seen one face-to-face before, and now at last he was looking at an Overseer. A dead Overseer.

The room became as quiet as a tomb. The being had been decapitated, his multifaceted eyes looking up at him a half dozen feet away from the rest of the body. Aldin looked back at the Kohs who gazed at him accusingly.

"They won't stop till you're hunted down," Zola hissed excitedly.

Aldin looked at the group with disdain.

"You helped to let the genie out of the bottle," Aldin snapped back. "We gamed for hundreds of years as a gentlemen's sport. Then Corbin got greedy and cheated on the Alexandrian affair. So all of you in your wisdom put us into a fight. Now Corbin is triggering an interstellar war and you damn fools are gambling on it! Now we're all involved. Just what the hell was that Overseer doing here?"

The group looked back defiantly, but stayed silent.

"Gambling with you, is that it?" Aldin shouted.

Several of the Kohs looked nervously at Zola, and in that moment Aldin understood.

"Larice!"

The shout was from outside the building. Going over to the shattered wall, Aldin looked out to see Basak. On the far side of the landing field a hangar boiled up in a fireball of light, illuminating the berserker in a sharp red glare, and showing all too clearly the struggling form that he was holding up with a single hand.

"Caught him trying to sneak aboard an undamaged yacht," Basak roared. "Should I throw him back in the fire?"

Aldin stood frozen, unable to respond. The grinning berserker was holding the kicking, struggling form of an Overseer up in the air with his one hairy paw.

"Oh, gods," Aldin groaned. Now they were really in it for certain.

"Go ahead and play your damn game," Aldin snapped, looking back at the other Kohs and figuring that since he was in it so deep he might as well try to bluff them into intimidation.

"Overseers here proves one thing beyond doubt, those bastards are in it, too. That stiff in the corner won't talk, but the other one didn't get away."

The Kohs looked nervously at each other.

"Now I wouldn't go blowing this out of proportion," Zola said in his high-pitched whine, coming up to Aldin's side even as he stalked out of the room.

Aldin looked over at Zola.

"Look, Zola, the other Kohs never gave you any respect in the old days, but I never did anything wrong to you. I even arranged a couple of games for you at discount, which was strictly against my contract with Corbin."

Zola nodded, obviously torn between fear of the dead Overseer, the captured live one, and what Aldin might be getting them all into.

"I want the truth from you, just this one time, and I'll never ask again," Aldin said softly, drawing Zola down the glass-covered corridor and away from the other Kohs. "Just answer me this: are the Overseers in this game against me?"

The diminutive Koh looked nervously back at the steam room.

"You tried to rig the last game to your own advantage and I lost a good samurai and a friend as a result," Aldin whispered. "I've never told my friend Oishi that." He nodded significantly to where his bodyguard stood in the corridor.

"If I blow that to him now, that you were instrumental in killing his brother, I think he'd kill you out of hand."

"You wouldn't do that, would you?" Zola whispered.

"Watch me."

Zola licked his lips nervously, still clutching the towel

around his skinny waist, and motioned for Aldin to follow him over to a corner of the hallway.

"The game was the Overseers' idea," he whispered. "We all know Corbin's nuts. All of us were just hoping he'd run into an uncharted rock during a jump outside of the lanes or something like that. Hell, Aldin, we all hated you for wiping us out, but in a good-natured way, if you get my meaning. We cheated you, you cheated us; isn't that what business is all about?"

He smiled woodenly, and Aldin forced a smile in return to hide his disgust.

"Then we heard that Corbin had sprung some Al'Shiga. Now that got us nervous."

"And you never bothered to tip me off about Corbin or the Overseers, damn you."

"Honestly, I was getting set to pass a message along. But then a small group of us was suddenly visited by an Overseer. He proposed to us a little betting venture"—Zola shrugged his shoulders—"and the offer was just too good to refuse."

"A little excitement, is that it?"

"Well, you must admit we've never seen a game anywhere other than on a planet. This had all sorts of exciting permutations. The only time we've ever bet on space combat was back in the old days when Yaroslav made up a couple of those historical computer simulators of the war of the three races. This Overseer promised us the real stuff, and at house odds with only a 2 percent commission. Hell, Aldin, that's even better than your old rates."

Zola looked up at him as if he should of course understand the logic of it all.

"I suppose a gentleman really couldn't pass up such a chance," Aldin said, his features creased by a thin smile.

"Exactly!" Zola said eagerly, clapping Aldin on the back as if he were the most understanding of fellows and that all was forgiven.

"And now it's out of control," Aldin roared.

Zola drew back fearfully.

"We figured you'd get hit in the opening round," Zola said nervously. "Nothing personal intended, of course, or given your resourcefulness you'd knock him out inside of a couple of weeks."

"And, of course, you bet on my winning."

"Oh, but of course."

"At last count, seven worlds have been hit by asteroid shots, another twenty-five by ground landings, and one entire planet damn near wrecked," Aldin said sharply. "Things were bad enough with you and the other Kohs ruining the economy; this on top of it all is creating chaos. You make me sick to think you're betting on this."

"Don't give me your holier than thou," Zola retaliated. "We saw thousands die on primitive worlds during the arranged matches of old. Easier when it's primitives dying, is that it?"

Aldin fell silent. Suddenly he felt very, very old. Wearily he turned away.

"It's got to stop," Aldin said softly. "Try and arrange a set match with Corbin. We'll meet on a planet, his people against mine, winner take all."

"Always the romantic," Zola replied haughtily, the whine of a true upper class gentleman returning. "Corbin's insane. I half think you're nothing but an excuse for him to run rabid through the space lanes."

"So how do we stop him?" Aldin asked.

"Kill him," Zola replied sharply.

"And the Overseers?"

"That's your problem to figure out," Zola replied, a malicious grin lighting his features. "In all our recorded history, no one's ever killed an Overseer. I wonder what they plan to do about your little precedent-breaking act?"

Aldin was at a loss for words. Turning around, he started down the stairs. Hobbs waited for him at the bottom of the sweeping staircase, surrounded by his entourage of exotic performers.

"So now you know what you've done," Hobbs said, a genuine touch of pity in his voice.

Aldin looked around at the wreckage.

"Hobbs, I suggest you get out of here," Aldin said. "The Overseers might not like witnesses to this little transgression of theirs."

The man's jowls quivered nervously.

"What about my place?"

"Put it on my tab," Aldin said, a thin smile creasing his face.

"How can I get out of here?" Hobbs moaned. "You've smashed every ship."

Aldin looked around the room. If the Overseers had gone so

far as to actually instigate a game, the last thing they'd want would be witnesses, now that one of them had been killed and another was in the hands of his berserkers waiting outside. His plan of action was already being formed by the turn of events, and Hobbs could be a witness that just might help.

He owed the man at least that for all the free meals the impresario had placed before him at one time or another.

"All right then, damn it, come along."

Hobbs let out an excited cry.

"Been years since I've been up," the amusement director said. "Maybe seeing space will do me some good. Come on girls, let's get moving."

"Oh, gods," Aldin groaned. If Mari ever heard about this, the screaming would go nonstop for days.

Aldin looked up the staircase to where Zola and the other Kohs stood.

"The rest of you bastards can stay here," Aldin snapped.

"You're taking the girls with you?" Zola whined.

Aldin grinned wickedly and turning, strode out of the palace.

The outside grounds were as bright as day. Dozens of ships and all the docks and repair sheds were awash with flames. The Gafs were streaming back to the ship, ecstatic with the destruction and arson that they had helped create. They were in such an exuberant mood that he suspected they would even forget their demands for pay, which had been rather in arrears since the start of the war.

Basak came around the side of the building, still holding the kicking Overseer.

"No casualties," Basak reported. "They all ran away and wouldn't fight." His voice was full of disappointment.

A flash of explosions rippled through a hangar, and the building collapsed, crushing a magnificent yacht in a tangle of broken beams.

Basak smiled approvingly and then looked ruefully at the struggling form that he was so easily holding aloft.

"Just what is this thing?" Basak asked curiously.

"Put me down, you oaf," the Overseer said evenly. "Such action is a guarantee of reeducation for all of you."

"Ah, shut up!" Aldin snapped.

The Overseer turned his attention back to Basak.

"I'm an Overseer," he said icily.

Startled, the Gaf let go, dropping his captive to the ground, where he crumpled up in a heap. Full of superstitious dread, Basak let his ax drop from his other hand, and reaching down solicitously, he helped the being back up, nervously dusting him off, all the time mumbling incantations against unseen evils.

Furious, the Overseer looked back at Aldin.

"You murdered one of the select, you'll be reeducated until you die," the Overseer hissed.

"And you, my dear Overseer, have been caught in the middle of a gambling arrangement around our little war." There was a note of disgust in Aldin's voice. "Now everything will break down because of this, the peace of three thousand years shattered by your greed, so don't even try your damned sanctimonious threats."

"What are you going to do?" the Overseer asked nervously.

Aldin was at a complete loss for words. In his hands were a responsibility and power he never imagined possible. All because of this damned raid. If he let the truth out to the entire Cloud, any hope of the Overseers intimidating everyone back to a semblance of peace would be lost. Yet if he did not reveal the truth, he'd be branded a murderer of an Overseer and hunted from one end of the Cloud to the other, not only by Corbin, but by every citizen of the Cloud eager for the reward that would be on his head.

"You're coming with me till I figure it out," Aldin whispered.

"You're a dead man for this," the Overseer hissed.

Aldin looked back at what had once been the symbol of peace and order for the three races.

"Just shut up and listen to Basak here, or I'll find a juice suit and wrap you up in it."

Horrified, Basak looked over at Aldin, and then, still mumbling his incantations, he nervously beckoned for the Overseer to follow him, so intimidated by the responsibility that he completely forgot about his precious ax and one of his warriors had to bring it along.

"Now what are you going to do?" Yaroslav asked, coming out of the ship to join his friend.

"Damned if I know," Aldin replied, shaking his head in confusion.

* * *

"I say kill him."

Stunned, the other Overseers who had gathered together for the emergency meeting of consensus looked at the Arch. Never had such words been uttered by the master of a race allegedly dedicated to contemplation and the insurance of peace.

"How have we come to this?" Yu, oldest of the ageless, whispered sadly. "We came to this magnificent Cloud to find quiet contemplation, escaping from the teeming of life in the mother galaxy. And then they followed us here, behaving as they always did, like brawling children. So we came to realize that we must teach them our ways, to control them if we were to survive. It was either that or try the impossible, an uncharted trek to a galaxy far distant, where we would, without doubt, meet the same experience yet again. We knew the task to bring peace to their hearts would take millennia, but it was the only way."

His voice trailed off, and if it were possible for an Overseer to weep, he would have done so.

"Yet, instead, it seems as if they have triumphed over us, polluting us instead of our saving them from themselves. I am saddened that our Arch would contemplate such a thought as violence."

"It's time to be realistic," the Arch snapped back peevishly. "The death of Loysa was easily covered up, but the killing of Retuna, and the capture of Vush on that disgusting game world, is known by hundreds, perhaps thousands."

"Perhaps we can still negotiate something," Yu replied, but his words were met by looks of disdain from the hundreds of Overseers gathered in the audience chamber.

"The myth of our infinite power and our shield of invincibility are gone," came a soft voice from the back of the room. The Arch looked up to see that it was Mupa, one of the younger Overseers and a meditation companion of Vush.

"We must establish our dominance again, immediately, otherwise these lower creatures will run roughshod over us," Mupa continued, his voice rising in a tone of self-assured insistence.

"Mupa is right, they'll hunt us out in our private meditation worlds and make sport of us," another replied. "We'll have no respect."

There was a loud chorus of agreement.

The Arch nodded slowly as if weighted down with some

great burden. Yet inwardly he was near to rejoicing. Throughout the millennia the numbers of the outsiders had increased at a relentless rate, while of the Overseers there were never more than five hundred in number. Only half a dozen had been born since Mupa, to replace those who, after tens of thousands of years, finally grew weary of life and either "spaced" themselves or just simply disappeared. Control had only worked through the order of Kohs, an arrangement he had never been comfortable with. The arrangement was by accident as much as by design, both sides finding an accommodation with the other, a status quo maintained by the illusion of invincible power and underneath it all the conservative nature of the Kohs, who realized they had a good thing. Their gaming had been viewed as a safe outlet, though a certain decorum had to be maintained, and occasionally one of the Kohs was sent to a "peaceful reorientation" center to keep the rest just a little off balance and fearful.

But it was, after all, a hoax they had been perpetrating, presenting an aura of limitless power to keep the Kohs in line, who in turn kept the peace and made sure the Overseers and their private meditation worlds were never trespassed upon.

But the Arch had become enough of a student of these distasteful species to know that the bliss of changelessness was anathema to them. Though they could be held in check temporarily, sooner or later the latent pressures of their social system were bound to trigger change. The Xsarns, as a hive species, were somewhat manageable, but as for the Gavarnians and especially the Humans, such hopes were impossible. The old monied families of the Koh class had been facing ever rising pressure from the emerging classes of the nouveau riche, who would not have the tradition of hundreds of years of social breeding to keep them in check.

Gablona had been one such case, as was Zola, never content to simply retain their vast holdings, but always grasping for yet more. Out of such individuals conflict would eventually come. Once there was conflict, sooner or later the mask of unlimited power would be pulled back to reveal just how thin was the true range of power the Overseers controlled.

He knew Vush's idea of triggering a fight was a risk of the first order. But he had hoped that such an action would generate chaos and then the Overseers could come in, offer some minor demonstration to awe the natives, and in the aftermath reestablish an order of Kohs that could again be controlled.

But then again he knew in his heart that he had harbored a darker fantasy: that the war would simply explode in an orgy of destruction that would cripple their economic system and technological base for space flight, so that once again the infinite reaches of the Cloud would be hospitable to the silence and loneliness so eagerly sought by the Select.

Now the plan had gone in a completely unforeseen direction. What little he understood of Human military theory—a subject that the mere contemplation of inevitably created an upset stomach—should have warned him that one of the fundamental principles of war is that whatever has been planned will usually be transmuted into paths unforeseen.

And, as if in some dark accordance with that fundamental principle, events had evolved into something no Overseer could ever imagine—one brother of contemplation killed by the outsiders, another prisoner. It was true that Loysa had died in the collapse of the Skyhook. But his body had never been found, and to reveal his death would have also revealed their complicity in those events.

Vush as a prisoner, he thought darkly, was far different. It was Vush who had first been seduced by the gaming of the Humans and who had found in the acquisition of money a sense of joy. Most all the others were totally mystified by that one. What good was money? No Overseer ever had a need for physical objects. What the mysterious First Travelers had left was sufficient for them, the creation of new things anathema to their beliefs.

All had been stunned when Vush had appeared at a meeting for contemplation wearing a robe of Gavarnian fabric, riding aboard a yacht of Xsarn design. So unlike the quiet simplicity of their own ships, this one was far too overpowered, and filled with the gadgets the lesser species took such perverse delight in. There was even one of their replicated machine Humans aboard, designed along the exaggerated lines of a Human female wearing a most strange costume of leather. It was not even possible to formulate the words to ask what that was for, and for his own sense of tranquility he found it simply best not to ask. And now Vush was in the outsiders' hands. What could they do to him, to corrupt him even more—and for that matter, what might he say as well?

They must reach Vush. For even though he had been seduced halfway, no one could imagine what he might finally
turn into, or whom he might turn against after undue exposure
to the noisome influences of the outsiders.

The room had fallen silent while the Arch floated before
them, lost in his thoughts. He looked down to see that all were
waiting for his pronouncements, which would guide their final
consensus.

"We must create an object lesson," the Arch finally said,
controlling the mounting anger he was feeling. The mere fact
that he was feeling anger made him angry. As an Overseer he
had spent tens of thousands of years in contemplation just to
control such feelings; the outsiders were ruining all of that
work.

"First a reward for the capture and presentation to us of
Aldin Larice must be posted."

"There is a problem," Yu whispered in reply. "So far there
has been no public announcement as to the capture of Vush."

The Arch nodded in reply. Thank the Unseen Ones that at
least the Kohs and their distasteful vasbas had kept that fact secret. All were terrified at the prospect of one of their brethren
being dragged before a public tribunal, thereby shattering forever the mythical aura the Overseers had granted to them in relationship to the masses. Even though Aldin was a vasba
upstart, and as such of no real concern, he could still spill far
too many secrets and implicate others, including one of the old
school—Bukha Taug, who though an ally of Aldin's was nevertheless a Koh of the highest breeding.

"That leads me to the second consideration," the Arch replied.

"And that is?" Mupa asked, the slightest note of anticipation
in his voice, as if he could already imagine what was to be
said.

"We shall announce that Aldin Larice and his confederates
have kidnapped one of our brothers."

"That will make us look weak," Yu said, shaking his head
in disagreement.

"No it will not," the Arch replied forcefully. "For at the
same time I shall announce that there will be a demonstration
of our wrath for this heinous crime."

"A demonstration?" several of the Overseers asked, curious

and excited, but not yet quite sure if what they heard was what he was truly suggesting.

"Exactly," the Arch said.

"What do you have in mind?" Yu interjected.

"Oh, I don't know yet. Blow up a planet, smash a star, some such thing to get our point across. That ought to get their attention."

Mupa, breaking a decorum that had not been shattered at a meeting of consensus in thousands of years, floated up and let out a whoop of delight, while Yu, shaking his head and mumbling a curse, floated out of the room.

"You mean a First Traveler device?" Tulbi, third assistant to the Arch, asked nervously, bobbing into the air excitedly as he spoke.

"We have no more of those terrible devices that can destroy planets," another voice called. "I was on the team that retrieved the device from the sacred Sphere of the First Travelers. When we destroyed the worlds three thousand years back, we used everything we had except for some small tracking missiles that can make themselves disappear. They have not the power for what you are considering. We have nothing, which has been the fortunate bluff that has maintained our position of awe over the barbarians."

"Yet there are other devices," the Arch replied, looking over to Mupa for support.

He knew that most of his brothers were now totally out of their depth with this issue. All but a handful of them eschewed the technology and miracles of the First Travelers. Very few across those thousands of years had ever had the slightest glimmer of curiosity to study the wondrous creations.

The creations of the First Travelers were, to a certain degree, held in reverent awe, even at the same time the Overseers' antitechnological minds had recoiled from the very devices that had given them intergalactic travel, an unending supply of physical comforts, and the myriad of machines to serve them in their isolated meditations. Yet they were material things, and, of course, all that was material must be illusion in the pursuit of inner knowledge and the dreamed-for mindless consciousness that all sought.

The Arch looked over to Mupa, his first assistant, and nodded.

"There is a device I have managed to decipher, and brought

back with me thousands of years past," Mupa said, floating up to join the Arch upon the platform.

Mupa was viewed with some slight disdain by his brothers, for he had, like Vush, become somewhat captivated by knowledge other than the search inward. Vush and he had on several occasions even journeyed across the sacred Sphere. Their last visit of nearly four thousand years past had lasted for centuries. They had explored the vast holding bays and storage vaults of the First Travelers that stretched for hundreds upon thousands of miles. If he could have smiled he would have done so with the memory of that time.

The last visit had been slightly unsettling, something had not seemed quite right with the Sphere, as if the machines that were still building it were not working in unified efficiency. That had been a puzzlement, as had been the two small boxes they had brought back with them, along with a number of other curious artifacts. He had offered the boxes when they had smashed several planets to scare the barbarians, but then Arch Yu had deemed them to be too unreliable and had opted instead for the planet-busting devices that they better understood. Now at last he would have a chance to try out his curious toy.

"I have come across a device of the First Travelers," Mupa continued, "which has properties I do not completely understand. It appears that one can place it at a given position in space. Then one removes himself from that area, after carefully pointing it at an intended target. Upon activation, using the control box, which you keep with you, it opens a tear in what I would crudely call the dimensional fabric of time and space, sucks the chosen object through, and then instantly places it somewhere else."

The assembly looked at each other in confusion, staring at Mupa as if he were speaking an unknown language.

Not even noticing their responses, he continued, warming to his subject.

"It is really quite remarkable. I just hit these buttons, it turns on, and in that moment an entire planet disintegrates, travels, if I wish, light-years away, and then shoots out the other side. It appears as if the First Travelers used it to transport matter to be used in the building of the Kolbard ring-world and the Sphere.

"Is the planet that is moved thus still intact?" Tulbi asked, unable to contain his curiosity.

"Oh, I don't think so," Mupa replied innocently. "I would guess that such a quick trip, for something the size of a planet, would crunch it into dust. But it sure would be something to see."

He fell silent and cleared his throat nervously, ashamed for having become excited.

"Thank you, brother, you have given us our solution," the Arch interrupted, motioning for Mupa to return to his proper position beside the platform. "So you see it really is quite simple," the Arch said. "We take this device, point it at some uninhabited world or a star, and disintegrate it.

"The barbarians will be properly impressed by our power. We can then simply position our ships near their major banking worlds and threaten to do the same. I promise you, my brothers, that within a very brief period of time they will come to us begging for forgiveness. I therefore propose for consensus that within ten standard days we pick an appropriate planet or star as a demonstration to all the inhabitants of the Cloud that we are not to be trifled with."

And this time, the Arch thought, we'll settle it right, by getting rid of any Koh that had grown too upstartish, and above all else that would mean Gablona, and the gamer Larice.

"You sure this device is easily managed?" the Arch asked, looking down at Mupa, ashamed to ask the question in public but nevertheless feeling a need for reassurance.

"Oh, my, yes indeed. Just push all the buttons in the control box for on, and push them again for off, it's as simple as that, and good-bye to a planet. Though I believe that using it on a sun would be far more dramatic and exciting."

If the Arch could smile, he would have.

"Come on," Basak said in an almost begging tone, "try some, you'll like it."

Vush turned away with revulsion at the proffered hunk of meat that the Gaf berserker offered him on the point of his knife.

"Can't you get it through your thick skull that they don't eat meat," Hobbs said wearily, even as he leaned over, scooping the nearly rare steak off the knife point and into his mouth.

"Poor things, just skin and bones," Basak said in a worried tone, looking over at Vush with open concern.

"Why, when I hoisted him into the air I thought I was picking up an empty doll, I did."

Vush, struggling to control himself, in what was an increasingly vain effort to remain aloof, turned away and started for the door.

"Now, now," Basak said, coming to his feet. "You know as well as I do that Aldin said you weren't to leave this room."

The Gaf berserker grinned good-naturedly at Vush, but it was evident from his voice that he'd enjoy hoisting the Overseer into the air again with one hand and holding him aloft for an hour or so for the fun of it.

Hobbs looked over at Vush, and with a nod of his head motioned for the Overseer to rejoin them at the table.

"This is absolutely humiliating," Vush whispered, trying to keep the growing despair out of his voice.

"Ah, so he can talk," Basak roared delightedly. "Seven days we've had you as our guest, and finally you decide to speak. And I'm the one who brought you around."

There was a look of triumph on Basak's face like that of a little boy who had finally solved a puzzle. The half-heard legends of the Overseers had caused him to build up in his Gaf-warrior mind the image of a towering foe who could smash entire planets at the snap of a finger. He had heard Aldin speak of them often enough with awe. He had to confess to himself that his warlord Aldin had been a disappointment the first time he had laid eyes upon him. But by the time Aldin had finished with those damned Al'Shiga, the old man had grown in Basak's thinking to someone at least as powerful as a good Gaf with an ax.

He was still waiting for this Overseer to demonstrate something to put him in awe, but so far he had been disappointed. The eight-foot stature of the being had some promise, but he was nothing but skin and bones, covered in a long white robe that clung to his diminutive frame. The only thing that was unsettling was the multifaceted eyes, sort of like those damned inscrutable Xsarns, Basak thought darkly.

Looking over at Vush he gave him a friendly grimace, revealing his twin rows of sharp yellow teeth, and at the sight of Basak's smile Vush backed around to stand behind Hobbs.

With a snort of disgust Basak went back to his meal. Slicing off another hunk of meat from the leg joint of some unidentifiable creature, he set into eating with the obligatory grunts and smacking noises that those of his clan felt any gentleman should use to express his appreciation for a damn fine meal.

At least the food stocks they had taken from Hobbs's kitchen before beating a hasty retreat had managed to fill all tastes, even this delicacy, whatever it was, Basak thought dryly as he set to chewing.

"I am hungry," Vush whispered.

"Ah, so you do eat!" Hobbs cried excitedly.

"I will not do so in the presence of barbarians," Vush replied indignantly. "I wish to speak to your preparer of foods in private."

Vush gave a shudder of revulsion for this admission. To the Overseers, all natural functions were viewed as being somehow unclean, and were to be practiced in the utmost of privacy. To even admit to having to eat was traumatic; how could he ever admit that for the last four days he had to fulfill another function that was driving him to absolute distraction?

Cheerfully Hobbs brought his chair around to face Vush.

"Aldin said you'd talk sooner or later. Now, let's see, would you care for some boiled lassa, a wonderful delicacy, fit for only the wealthiest Kohs?"

"What is lassa?" Vush asked, unable to contain his curiosity.

"Centipedes found on Odak. The meat comes out all fluffy pink—served with drawn butter it's a delight."

Retching, Vush turned away.

Basak roared with delight at the Overseer's discomfort, but Hobbs shouted for him to be quiet. Sulkily Basak returned to his meal. Balefully he looked over at Hobbs, still not sure if he liked this blotted hairless one; such decisions usually took time. But at least the Gaf females who traveled with this hairless one had proved to be a fitting diversion, so as such he would not insult him too much.

"All right my friend," Hobbs said, propelling his chair to the corner of the room where Vush stood. "Listen, one of my girls is a real charm with near any dish you can imagine. You just tell her what you want, and she can mix it up for you."

"But she's a female," Vush blubbered.

"So?"

"It is not proper," Vush replied. "We have no females among us."

"Damn, what a bore. I'd go mad," Basak roared. "How do you make little Overseers, then?"

Horrified, Vush could not even reply. Female Overseers had left for another galaxy eons ago, claiming a need to remove themselves from the presence of "exploitation," as they put it. He could barely even remember them. As for reproduction, far more sanitary methods of cloning were of course preferable—at least he thought so.

Vush looked over at Basak beseechingly, as if begging him not to pursue this line of the conversation.

"What the hell do you mean no females?" Basak continued. "Or do you fellas only like each other?"

"That is enough!" Vush shouted. "All of you disgust me, absolutely disgust me." And with a wild cry he fled to another corner of the room, curled up in a ball, and started to rock back and forth.

Hobbs gave Basak a sharp look of rebuke.

Basak merely shrugged his shoulders in reply.

"Well, it does seem kind of strange to me," he said defensively, and picking up the hunk of meat off his plate he walked over to the door, punched the access code, and stepped out into the ship's main corridor.

Hobbs gave a quick scan of the room to make sure there were no sharp implements left behind by the Gaf, and guiding his chair he floated to the exit.

"I'll tell you what," Hobbs said. "I'll whip up something without any meat in it, no fish, no nothing that moves. Just some nice greens, how does that sound?"

"It can only be harvested after it has died or has fallen," Vush whispered, raising his head.

"Count on it," Hobbs said soothingly, and leaving the room, he made sure to rescramble the code on the door before proceeding up to Aldin's stateroom.

"Well, did you hear that little exchange?" Hobbs announced, coming through the door without knocking.

Aldin looked up from the viewscreen and smiled.

"At least it got him talking."

Punching in for a servobot to bring a double brandy, Hobbs guided his chair into the center of the room.

"I feel somewhat sorry for him," Oishi said gently, rising from the shabby divan facing the forward viewport and coming over to stand alongside of Hobbs.

"I find that surprising," Aldin said.

"Oh, I know," Oishi replied. "If it hadn't been for their

damn meddling, or perhaps lack of meddling, Corbin never would have gotten as far as he did in starting this war. In some ways he reminds me of the holy monks of my old world who removed themselves to hidden places and attempted to find release from the world. I feel more empathy for him than for some others present."

Oishi looked over at Hobbs with a jaundiced eye.

"I already told all of you, I had nothing to do with it. Corbin simply asked me to jack my rates up so the usual clientele would go someplace else, and he'd make up the difference. Hell, I was so busy running the damn place I wasn't even having any fun. Corbin's offer gave the girls and me a chance to relax for a while.

"Why, I never even saw my dear cousin until after he started the war and it was too late to get out of the deal," Hobbs said quickly. "Yaroslav flushed my systems' memory banks, they'll confirm it. It was all done through one of Corbin's old lawyers, curse the damned breed. It was only in the last couple of standard months that those ships dropped in with their damn Al'Shiga, and that gun was emplaced and the supplies started to come in. Next thing I knew I had an illegal military base in my backyard. Light transports would come in, and a couple of weeks later would leave, rearmed with laser weapons and tracking missiles.

"So what was I supposed to do, go out there and chase 'em all away? I'm not even that crazy. They stayed on the base, I just hid in my pleasure house.

"Then that damned Zola and his confederates show up, to evaluate the base, have a good time, and meet with those two Overseers. Then you people drop in and wipe me out."

Hobbs's face started to crinkle up, and there was a groan of disgust from the others in the room. The last thing they felt like listening to was another breast-beating on how his life savings had been wiped out in the hit.

"It's all the truth, Aldin. I know you uploaded my memory systems before you took off, it's all in there." He looked over at Yaroslav for support.

"Hobbs, I've known you for nearly forty years," Yaroslav sniffed, "and from the first day I was convinced you'd charge admission to your own mother's funeral if you thought you could make a katar out of it. When we were teaching together at the university, you were accepting bribes from students in your literature classes to jack up their grades."

"Well, they paid, didn't they?" Hobbs said defensively. Looking injured, he sank into his chair.

"But your records were clean," Yaroslav finally admitted, "even the coded access ones I finally managed to crack this morning."

"You cracked my private files?" Hobbs asked, looking slightly embarrassed.

"It's a good thing Bukha isn't in this room," Yaroslav said with a wicked grin. "Your little holo vid journal with that Gaf delectable, Peaches I think you call her, would definitely outrage his sense of morality."

Guiltily Hobbs looked around the room. Interspecies sex did occur—at least between Gafs and Humans; if anyone had ever tried something with a Xsarn there was no record of ever admitting to it—but to the vast majority of puritanical Gaf males, such actions were an outrage.

Basak stopped his meal in midbite.

"Peaches," he growled quietly. "You mean my Peta? Did you say something about my Peta?"

"I think it's the one and same," Yaroslav whispered, leaning over Basak's shoulder.

With a growl Basak started to come to his feet.

"Now, now," Aldin said, extending his hand. "Remember, Basak, different people, different customs, you've got to honor that when you're with me."

Basak shot Hobbs a nasty look and then sulkily settled back into his chair.

"At least your little idea worked," Yaroslav said, looking over at Aldin and shifting the topic.

"Yeah, it was a fairly good one at that," Aldin said, a grin lighting his features. "Just stick Vush in a locked room for a day with the two most disgusting beings aboard this ship and he'd be bound to crack."

Basak's mane, trapped beneath the folds of his Day-Glo yellow jumpsuit, bristled up with pride at the compliment Aldin had paid him, while Hobbs, caught now between his anxiety over Basak and a sense of being outraged, simply was too confused to respond.

"Interesting comment about no female Overseers," Yaroslav said, as if almost to himself.

"Sounds like they have a problem, if you ask me," Basak interjected as he noisily sucked on the remnants of the bone he had been chewing on.

"It is a point," Aldin replied. "Now that we at least got him talking about something, perhaps we can loosen him up further and start pumping for information about the Overseers."

"So you've decided to give him a free passage out?" Oishi asked with a note of concern.

"Call him a guest for right now, but first chance that we can get him back to his people, I'm letting him go," Aldin replied, coming to his feet and walking over to the forward viewport.

The Overseer had been a point of contention between Oishi and Aldin. The samurai felt the best possible way to handle the situation was to hang on to him and use him for a bargaining chip. At first Aldin had felt the same way, fearing a massive manhunt across the Cloud the moment he no longer had Vush as a shield. But on the other side it was the first direct exposure he had ever had to the hidden power-holders of the Cloud, and he could be a possible source of information, and at least could tell their side of the story if he felt he had been treated fairly.

Lost in thought, Aldin gazed absently at the panorama outside the forward viewport. The great Core Cluster of the Cloud filled the entire window with a swirling mass of brilliance. The jump-out had taken several long days into this almost-unknown transit point going outward toward his favorite spot, the Kolbard Ring of Alexander the Great. The next jump point could take them straight in, or by swinging over to the one other track would simply lead them out into unexplored reaches of empty space. It was, Aldin hoped, the safest place he could find for the moment. He knew that the Overseers would respond to the death of one of their comrades and the kidnapping of another. When the time came, he did not want to be anywhere in the Cloud, for though he had lost all fear and respect for them, still he was not quite sure of what technology they had up their sleeves for locating someone they really wanted to find.

He knew as well that Corbin would be scrambling after the hit, and that even though Corbin was innocent of the death of an Overseer that perhaps there would be a backlash against him as well.

"Aldin, something's coming in through the commlink," Tia

said, looking up from the console set in the far corner of the room.

Aldin, his joints cracking, went over to join her.

From Aldin's expression while he looked at the screen, Oishi and the others saw that the news on a general broadcast channel was less than pleasant.

After a long moment Aldin turned to face his friends.

"Well," he whispered, "I guess we're really in the fire now."

chapter four

"Of course, you must understand the shock, the disgust I felt when his horrifying actions were made known to me," Corbin Gablona said silkily, his face a mirror of humble piety.

Tulbi, envoy of the Overseers, the voice of the Arch, struggling to control his inner feelings, said nothing. He knew this barbarian was inwardly gleeful at the discomfort the Overseers were now experiencing. He wished as well that somehow the tables were back to where they should be, with this barbarian groveling in fear before a representative of the Arch.

"Do you have any suspicions of where this Larice person and his fellow conspirators might be hiding?"

"Upon my word as a gentleman, believe me if I even had the slightest hint, I would most certainly have rushed to get word to you immediately and sortie out personally in an attempt to save your comrade from any further indignity," Corbin replied almost breathlessly, while holding up his bejeweled hand, as if examining the thirty carat stone on his pinky for a flaw.

"You've heard the broadcast that went out to the entire Cloud?"

Heard it? It had turned his stomach with abject terror. At first he had thought the Overseers would lump him in as an offending party as well. But when the full details came in, branding Aldin as the sole culprit, he relaxed. Though it was rather curious, Bukha was not mentioned at all. And the part about one of them being sliced up at Hobbs's in front of that squealy-voiced Zola and half a dozen other Kohs—no mention of that at all. Just the "kidnapping" of Vush, and nothing else. He half suspected they were playing a divide-and-conquer game, but if it eliminated Larice, then let them demonstrate their power; he could play along for now. And it seemed that in their stupidity they were actually offering him a pardon for the war, and would act as if everything had been Larice's fault. Their demonstration would shake everyone up to be sure. And if he played his cards right, when everything settled down they'd make sure he was back in as one of the leading Kohs.

The thought filled him with anticipation. That's how they'd have to play it out. Smash a planet, scare the Xsarn food out of everyone who would then come groveling. Then they'd point out some of the old trusted leaders and reestablish order. It'd be just like the old days again.

Of course, Larice would be gone, and he would get back all that was taken by that upstart. And then the others would go as well. Oh, I'll bide my time, Corbin thought, not allowing his expression to change into one of anticipation. Hassan and the others would have to be put on ice for a while, if need be an accident could be arranged to get rid of them and make himself look respectable. But after a time, he could let Hassan, or his replacement, take care of all the others, one by one, starting with Bukha, Zola, and the Xsarn Prime. The art of revenge had to be upheld, Corbin realized; it was, after all, a family tradition.

"A righteous response and well called for. Yet again a demonstration of your infinite wisdom," Corbin said, allowing the right tone of fawning awe to creep into his voice. "I knew that gutter-bred Larice would be the downfall of the Koh system. That is why I tried to resist him for so long.

"Oh, he is a skillful one," Corbin continued. "His people made it appear as if this conflict were all my doing. But believe me, I have the evidence to prove that he started it all."

"Of course you do," Tulbi sniffed in reply.

"So what do you want of me?" Corbin asked, knowing they were now at the real heart of the matter.

"In three standard days we will make our demonstration of power. If you wish to be in the same system to witness it, you may be my personal guest."

"I wouldn't miss it for the universe," Corbin replied with an almost childlike joy.

It was going to be a real planet smash, and to his jaded senses such an event couldn't be missed. What they were promising was going to make his cargo ship "accident" look like a child's firecracker in comparison. Granted, the event would be broadcast live throughout the entire Cloud, but it was never as good as being there. Anyone who wished to maintain his reputation for being on the in at exotic events simply had to attend.

"In fact we command that you be there, along with all the other Kohs, so that all of you can see what can be done if our ire is provoked."

"As you command," Corbin replied, going so far as to incline his head as a token of respect.

"There shall be an investigation," Tulbi continued, "and if I do remember correctly, there is the little matter of your breaking out of a reeducation seminar just before that disgusting business on the planet of the Al'Shiga."

Even though he was in a heavily-armed ship, Corbin felt a twinge of fear. The Overseer had arrived alone, aboard a Xsarn-piloted yacht, with a guarantee of noninterference. But the thought of being back in an Overseer juice suit made his skin crawl.

"I ain't got nothing to do with that. Hell, I wanted to stay, that damned Zergh and his friends kidnapped me. I'm innocent, I tell you."

"I just want to remind you that you still owe us something like three thousand standard days of reeducation."

"Now you aren't thinking of sending me back there?" Corbin growled, his tone suddenly belligerent. " 'Cause if you are, I ain't going."

Tulbi looked coldly at the creature seated before him, amazed at how quickly, and childishly, he could shift from simpering to threats. Typical of the species. He was inwardly disgusted with having to deal with this renegade, or for that matter any of the three species. But for now it could pass. They already had their plan within a plan to deal with him when the time came. At the present it suited their purposes to act as if they were going to overlook his multitude of transgressions. For one thing, it would completely unsettle the other Kohs to see Corbin apparently forgiven, if he performed the necessary acts of obeisance. They could use him then as the spy to keep the others in line, and, if need be, eliminate other Kohs. In the end, of course, they would have him in the juice suit for the rest of his life, if he was lucky enough to survive.

"Come, come, I was not even considering reeducation," Tulbi whispered soothingly.

"So why the threat then?" Corbin retorted.

"Just a reminder that we are willing to overlook certain little mistakes if you demonstrate a new understanding of our needs and are willing to cooperate in our new universal order."

"Who said I wasn't willing to cooperate?" Corbin snapped back.

These barbarians, Tulbi sighed inwardly. When all of this was done, he knew he'd need at least a hundred years of complete solitude and meditation to wash their filthiness from his soul.

"It's just we want to recover our brother intact," Tulbi said quickly, trying to steer the conversation back to its original point.

"So why didn't you say so in the beginning?" Corbin laughed. "That'll be easy to arrange."

"That's all we ask of you in return for certain considerations."

"Like washing my slate clean."

"Washing your slate?"

"You know, letting me off the hook."

"That sounds horrible. We would never put someone on a hook," Tulbi said in the most sanctimonious of tones.

Corbin sighed. "Forgetting about my sentence."

Tulbi nodded at last in understanding.

"Yes, the slates will be clean."

"I would be remiss if I did not offer my services in other ways as well," Corbin said, his voice silky.

"And what additional services are you referring to?"

"Larice's financial management has left the Cloud in chaos. It will take a lifetime to straighten out," Corbin said, with a heavy tone, as if the responsibility of it all were already weighing him down. "Now as for myself, I have had a lifetime of experience in such economic concerns, which, besides creating prosperity, also builds harmony and understanding.

"Since most of those corporate concerns were mine to start with, before this upstart so vilely cheated me out of them—"

He paused for a moment, his features reddening, and then re-gaining control he continued. "—I know that it will help the cause of peace if I assume control of what I ruled before all this unpleasantness started."

Trying to keep from gagging, Tulbi continued to nod.

"That was our intention, but it is important that our brother be returned intact to us, otherwise we will be most deeply dis-tressed, and in such a moment I cannot say what the consensus of my brothers might be.

"You do know how such things can be," Tulbi said, as if speaking now to a close friend of such superior intellect that it was almost not worth bothering to say. "Perhaps the wrong people might get blamed, perhaps even all the Kohs might be found at fault."

He smiled, if such a thing was possible for an Overseer, and Corbin felt as if the temperature in the room had suddenly dropped.

"When you said intact, I assume you mean you want Vush back alive and unharmed."

"How did you know his name?" Tulbi asked, unable to hold back his curiosity.

"Oh, word gets around," Corbin said, chuckling at the Over-seer's discomfort. "Remember there were a couple of dozen witnesses to his abduction, along with the security holo cam-eras that Hobbs forgot to erase."

The fact that Vush had given his name to barbarians, the fact that he had even met with them in secret to gamble on the war, was shocking to Tulbi's sense of orthodoxy. Surely Vush himself might wind up in reeducation, something unheard of for an Overseer in a score of millennia. But before the barbar-ians it must never appear that a brother had actually strayed from the path.

"I heard he even had a couple of shots of liquor at the party just before the strike on Larice's planet, and then there was that scene with his Humanbot, but good taste prevents me from elaborating on that, the code of gentlemen you understand," Corbin interjected, guessing that little lie would surely cause a reaction.

He struggled to control a grin at the obvious shock of Tulbi, who nervously ran his hands up and down the sides of his robes, struck speechless by the thought of an Overseer behav-ing in such a manner.

"And this is on holo tapes?"

"I heard there's copies floating all over the place."

Tulbi actually twitched, and Corbin sat back, examining his curled fingernails for a long minute before pressing on.

"Some of the Kohs said that given a couple of more days your Vush would have been one of the boys, indulging in all sorts of delightful vices."

"Enough!" Tulbi roared.

"Now, now," Corbin cried, holding his hands up in a soothing gesture. "Just thought you should know that one of your boys was maybe out making a little hay on the side."

That phrase had Tulbi thoroughly lost, but he did not even wish to inquire, fearful of what "making hay" might really mean.

"Don't worry though," Corbin quickly continued, "his little mistakes are safe with me. My boys are tracking down the tapes and destroying all of them. Gentlemen, after all, don't keep such information on other gentlemen. It's terribly embarrassing for everyone if that type of scandalous material gets into the hands of those damn news people." He gave Tulbi a conspiratorial wink.

Completely lost at the significance of certain barbarian phrases and body gestures, he floated into the air and drifted to the door, signifying the interview was at an end.

"Just one question though, your excellency, before you leave."

"And that is?"

"What do you want me to do about Aldin Larice, Bukha Taug, and his other hangers-on? After all, if we do manage to find your brother Vush, chances are the others will be there as well."

Tulbi still could not believe the orders the Arch had directly given to him regarding this question. He had hoped it would not be asked, that the unspoken implication would be message enough, and thus he would not have to carry its burden upon his destiny.

"Whatever you wish, we will not interfere," Tulbi replied, using the Arch's exact words.

"I was hoping you would say that," Corbin said cheerfully, and Tulbi shuddered inside as he drifted from the room. Turning in his chair, Corbin looked up at the holo camera lens, no bigger than the point of a needle in the wall, and smiled.

* * *

"I can't believe this, they're mad!" Vush cried, bursting into the forward cabin, holding his head bobbing up and down in an agitated manner, with Hobbs and Basak following behind him.

"If Mupa's doing it, it's insanity."

Shocked by the sudden emotional display of an Overseer, Aldin remained quiet, glad that his guest had finally broken at last. After Hobbs had told Vush about the Arch's announcement, Vush had emitted one loud shriek and then curled up in the far corner of his room, rolled into a tight ball, and started to shake—until now.

Stunned, the group looked at the Overseer. Yaroslav, in a most nonchalant manner, poured out a tumbler of brandy and offered it over. Somehow the Overseers could manipulate objects within very close range with a remarkable dexterity. The tumbler drifted out of Yaroslav's hand, floated up, twirled several times to coat the inside of the glass, and then tilted up to Vush's lips.

"Remind me not to play roulette with you ever again," Hobbs growled.

Still floating, Vush looked around the room, coughing slightly from the drink, which he downed in a single gulp.

"The announcement said that my brothers were going to smash a planet?" Vush asked nervously.

"Forty-eight standard hours from now."

As if disbelieving what he was hearing, Vush violently shook his head.

"They don't know what they are doing," Vush whispered nervously.

Aldin could sense that he was treading somehow into completely unknown areas of Overseer powers.

"Why do you feel they don't know what they are doing?" Oishi asked, trying to keep the nervousness out of his voice. "You chaps have done this thing before."

Vush looked down at Aldin, fixing him with his gaze. He knew that he was in deep enough trouble as it was, and upon his return to his brothers would be viewed as an outcast for millennia to come. Though in his age-long pursuit of inner knowledge and contemplation he had grown used to the self-imposed isolation of the Brotherhood of Searches, this was somehow different. Now he truly was alone, rejected most likely by the only social system he had ever known.

"You must get me in touch with my brothers," Vush said, with a decided note of pleading in his voice.

Aldin was on the edge of rejecting the request out of hand, but some inner sense stopped him. He could actually sense fear in this one.

Oishi shook his head and gave a snort of disdain.

"Oh, most certainly. There's a price on Aldin's head and all of us are in this up to our necks. The announcement claimed we kidnapped you from your ship and are holding you hostage. The moment we allow you to make a commlink transmission, every fortune hunter in the Cloud will flock to where we are."

"If I put you in touch with them, I'd be placing myself at risk," Aldin said. "I'm way the hell out here to give me a little breathing room. If I drop a transmission for you, it'll be like a beacon advertising my presence."

"You could always jump out right after you sent my signal," Vush said.

"Look, you might not know the translight jump-point system, but I do. There's only one line out this way, and heaven knows how far out it continues."

Without asking permission, Vush floated over Tia's shoulder and looked down at the nav screen.

"Why did you choose out here?"

"Seemed safe," Tia replied, a bit testy at the Overseer's tone. "No one comes out this way, and if they did we could jump to the next gate and then turn into the Kolbard Ring.

"The next jump gate out will take you straight to the ring-world or off into nothing."

Aldin, though his face-to-face contact with Overseers was limited to this occasion, sensed that there was something behind Vush's curiosity. A probing as if Vush were trying to find out if Aldin knew something more than he should have.

"Oh, of course," Vush replied, looking straight at Aldin with his unfathomable eyes, the sight of which made Aldin feel as if he were a specimen on a dissecting table.

"I need to send a message, it's essential," Vush said, and again there was a pleading to his tone.

"I send the signal, everyone knows where I am. It'll take me a day and a half to jump down to a major nexus point, and what'll I see? Either your people or Gablona's waiting for the kill as I come out of null. Thanks but no thanks."

"You'll regret this, all three of your barbarian species will regret this," Vush replied, without any threat in his voice.

"Why?" Zergh sniffed. "Because you're going to bust a planet? Hell, I know your species well enough now to realize you'd never have the moral turpitude to smash a planet with any type of life on it. So you'll blow some lifeless rock apart. All us ignorant savages will shake in our boots. The war between Gablona and us will end simply by the pressure the other fearful Kohs will finally exert. This is exactly what we want. Once things cool off, we'll let you go."

"You were going to do that?"

Aldin shook his head.

"What the hell do you think we are? Barbarians?" He looked at the Overseer, not sure if he should be angry at the insult to his own integrity.

"Finding you down there was an accident," Yaroslav interjected, "so don't go inflating your ego by thinking that we blew up Hobbs's place just to get at you. Isn't that right, Hobbs?"

Hobbs, who sat in the far corner of the room, roused himself from an alcohol-induced daze long enough to nod in agreement.

"He was after my cousin Corbin, the shipyard, and supplies. You were an accident and I got caught in the middle."

The Overseer looked back over at Aldin.

"You mean you didn't really want me?"

"It was an accident." Aldin sighed. "The death of your fellow Overseer an accident I never wanted. We dropped the rock in to destroy the automatic ground defenses. If we really wanted to kill everyone, we would have landed the rock square on the pleasure palace."

Hobbs nodded in agreement, a sentimental tear streaking his face at the memory of his home.

"You'd have never hurt your old friend, would you Larice?"

Aldin smiled and shook his head.

"Knowing my dear cousin," Hobbs said dryly, "if he had arrived after the raid and found you there, he might have killed all of us and then blamed it on Aldin, so consider my vasba friend there as having perhaps saved your life."

Vush, thoroughly confused by the logic of individuals who

almost kill him and then claim to have saved him, was silent, looking back and forth around the room.

"Look," Aldin said, actually reaching up and patting the Overseer on the side, an action that caused Vush to recoil in horror. Aldin held his hand out in apology.

"Once things cool off, and I can figure out a way to get you back to your people, I will. If I just let you go, chances are Corbin might knock you off so I can be blamed for it. It's that simple, so why don't you just relax and enjoy yourself."

"Oh, the holo tape I have of him will show you just how much he can enjoy himself." Hobbs chuckled, and several of the girls with him laughed in a decidedly lewd manner.

"The only thing I'd ask of you is that when you get back to your people that you explain my side of things," Aldin continued. "None of us is going to accept reeducation, that's for sure. Just leave us alone, make sure Corbin and his murderous cutthroats are kept off our backs, and we'll just quietly disappear."

Even though the war would be over, Aldin thought, he was finished anyhow, and would be the scapegoat for everything that had gone wrong over the last several standard years. At best he might be able to sneak back to the shattered remains of his pleasure world, where he had had the foresight to stockpile a fair supply of portable assets. At least his old days as a gaming vasba had taught him to always keep a little cold cash hidden away in case he had to get out of town on very short notice.

There were enough gems, gold, and credit units there so he could at least live out his retirement in some comfort. The only question would be where to go. No space-faring world would be safe, since wanted postings and that twenty million katar reward were enough to have almost anyone turning in his own grandmother. Perhaps the Ring where even now Alexander the Great still lived would be the place to go. There at least, he and his friends could live comfortably, and the company of Alexander would be interesting to say the least. And besides, he realized somewhat sadly, he actually didn't want the old life back anymore. He had achieved everything, and found that without any interesting challenges it was far too boring. Life had simply become a process of trying to hold on to what he had already won. In a perverse sort of way the war had actually given him something back. Mari, with a couple of Gaf guards, had been disembarked, so at least there was quiet. As for the rest, he pushed the thought aside—there was no use go-ing over his own angst of existence yet again—and looked back at Vush.

Amazed with what he had just heard, Vush nodded his head in agreement, having learned that was a signal to Humans of agreement.

"But will you send the signal now? I must talk to my Arch," Vush asked, a note of pleading creeping into his voice.

"What do you want to tell him?"

Vush struggled with the temptation to tell the full truth. If his guess was right, this little demonstration would be engi-neered by Mupa. As one of the youngest of the brothers, he had expressed interest in First Traveler technologies, which the others used but never really attempted to understand. If an Overseer could have a friend among his comrades, Mupa would fill such a position. There had been a time, in the very beginning when the five hundred of them had first come to the Cloud, that he and Mupa had been enthralled by the great workings of the First Travelers. They had spent several millen-nia together, walking about the Ring. And then it was Mupa who discovered the Great Sphere, and the Ring had then paled in comparison.

The sheer magnitude of the greatest edifice ever created by the First Travelers, or any sentient beings, had come very near to seducing him with its technical wonders. The fact of the matter was that in his heart he knew it had indeed seduced him. The Great Sphere was over two million kilometers in di-ameter, with literally billions of kilometers of corridors, living areas, and, curiously, abandoned cities that might have housed trillions. It had been a quest for him and Mupa. The other five hundred had wandered off to uninhabited worlds, unsettled by the sheer magnitude of something beyond their power to cre-ate. Mupa and he had been alone, claiming the entire Sphere.

It had been a most haunting, chilling reality. Two alone in a vast structure, the greatest in the entire Cloud, and not once in their millennia of exploration had they encountered another sentient living soul. They had indeed met what they believed was a First Traveler machine, but it had expressed no interest in either of them, other than a strangely feeble attempt to get them to indulge in some foolish pastime that they had of course ignored, looking instead for more insightful experi-ences. Other machines, vast arrays of them, quietly traversed the labyrinth world, repairing, and in many areas, still building, for nearly one-eighth of the great structure was still open to space, like a piece of fruit with a section of it peeled off. In one of their last visits something had seemed wrong with it all, here and there a machine working at cross-purposes, but that visit had been too brief to contemplate the significance of this anomaly. The devices to destroy half a dozen planets were found in a great storage building.

The unsettling question beneath it all was why? Just why had the First Travelers set about to build such things, and then disappeared? He knew that the Ring was older, perhaps a test structure before setting out to totally encase an artificially created star. They had started the Sphere, it was still not finished, but there was no one there.

When technical questions regarding a First Traveler artifact forced their way into the attention of the Overseers, Loysa, who was far more of the scholar, was usually consulted. It was he who had used the devices for the first demonstration to overawe the three barbarian species. But Loysa was now dead in the collapsed Skyhook. Only Mupa was still around. And Mupa was an immature fool who held even less knowledge than Vush did.

When confronted by First Traveler technology, Vush felt, at best, as if he were gazing at some vast and impenetrable mystery. He knew that their machines ran flawlessly, and at times he could occasionally push a button to perform some task, but as to the hows and whys, that was simply beyond him.

The Arch had finally ordered them away from the Great Sphere, claiming that it was having a detrimental effect upon their spiritual quests. Yet in the nearly three thousand years of contemplation that followed, still he found his inner curiosity harkening back to the great corridors, and the awe-inspiring sight of standing on the inner surface of the Sphere, looking up at the tiny sun that filled the vast inner room. How strange that had been to him. A sun artificially generated, contained within a vast metal ball. Ascending into the great towers that punched above the atmosphere, he could gaze in wonder at the magnificent panorama of the interior surface of the Sphere.

No wonder it had seduced him, Vush thought quietly. The three barbarian species had thought the Kolbard, or the now-destroyed tower, to be the epitome of First Traveler wonders. The Sphere was something so far kept hidden, it was a wonder beyond their imagining. If they had looked more closely, and gone several dozen more jumps down this very lane Aldin was now on, they would at last detect an infrared emission, the dissipation of heat from the outside of the jet-black surface of the Sphere. But no one had ever thought to push onward, the Kolbard Ring always diverting them. He had been tempted at times to remove the navigational buoys that marked the jump lanes, yet another accomplishment of the First Travelers, and thus hide away the Sphere forever, but he was always afraid that if he did so he himself would never find a way back.

Vush knew the place had seduced him, but he knew as well that Mupa had been completely captivated heart and soul, like a Human Soma-addicted drone, by the power it represented. When the barbarians had first gotten out of hand, it had been Mupa who had suggested the planet-smashing devices found in the Sphere, which had then been turned over to the steadier hands of Loysa. That had indeed made Vush uneasy, even though he had agreed with the others that only through such a raw display of power could they gain their ascendancy over the barbarians.

Yet there had been that other device that they had deciphered, or at least thought they had deciphered, which now had him truly frightened. Mupa had found it, a remarkable tool. Both of them had agreed to leave it where they had found it, frightened by the power it contained. And now? Mupa must have taken it back with him after all and offered it to be used. There were no more planet smashers, they had set all of them off and had been bluffing ever since. If Mupa thought he could effectively play with the machine, and had convinced the others, then they had all gone mad.

"If you tell me what it is you wish to share," Aldin said, interrupting Vush's contemplation, "I'll take it under consideration."

"They're making a mistake trying to smash a planet," Vush said cautiously.

"Well that certainly is pressing news," Aldin retorted, unable to contain the irony in his voice.

"I must try to present to them that certain—how shall I say it?—mistakes might be undertaken."

"How do you know this?" Aldin asked cautiously.

"I just know."

"You'll have to do better than that."

Vush took a deep breath and tried to center his thoughts. Among his comrades a conversation of this great an importance could take months, even years, with pauses of weeks or more as both considered the most precise way of communicating. That he felt was the greatest hindrance in dealing with these barbarians. If you stopped speaking for more than several minutes, they grew extremely agitated. A six-month conversation would drive them to the point of insanity.

The beauty of words was to find the precise one. Across the eons the Overseer vocabulary had grown to tens of millions of terms. A simple Human utterance such as, "A scarlet sunrise above an azure sea," could of course conjure up a mental picture of an event worthy of contemplation. But it was so crude, so imprecise. After all, there were a thousand worlds where such an event could happen, each one with shades of nuance, of smell, of particular wavelengths of light. To search for exactly the right description to fully convey all the essence of an event like that took time. The state of the observer was crucial as well, his health, his length of silent contemplation before observing the event, even the type of clothing he wore to reflect his mood. All of that could be formed into one word, which by its power would fully impart the entire experience, but to find that word took infinite care. It was an art, and the three species were totally artless.

"I think I know the device they plan to use; it is not stable." He felt entirely frustrated. There was so much urgency to what he felt, and yet also so much that he had to conceal, and their damned language was not up to it. If it were, a single utterance would convince them.

"I do know something of history," Aldin replied. "You fellows used some form of antimatter detonators the last time, balanced to the mass of the planets you were destroying. What could be more simple than that?"

"This one is different."

"In other words, you ran out of antimatter detonators, and now your people are using something untested," Yaroslav interjected.

Taken aback, Vush fell silent, afraid he had already given away far too much.

Aldin came to his feet.

"I'm not going to allow you to contact your people just on the basis of that little tidbit. I want the full truth."

Torn, Vush was unable to speak. He could never reveal that their power was based simply on the cannibalizing of First Traveler technologies they barely understood.

"It's just untested," he replied, trying not to reveal anything else. "I have perhaps a better grasp than my brother Mupa as to its operation. I wish to consult with him."

"Oh, now it's not just a signal, it's a consultation," Oishi replied, growing more suspicious.

"It is the only way," Vush replied, a pleading tone coming into his voice.

"I'll think about it," Aldin stated, heading for the door.

"You'll all regret this if I can't speak to my Arch," Vush replied.

"Is that a threat?" Oishi snapped.

If Vush had been capable of cursing, he would have done so at that moment. How cumbersome this language of the barbarians was. The slightest mistake, or the improper mimicking of tonal inflection, could convey an entirely wrong meaning.

"It was not intended as such," Vush replied hurriedly.

"At least head into a jump-point intersection," Vush continued. "With any good fortune there might be a delay. If you then agree with me and allow me to contact my Arch from such a point, you could jump in any number of directions and no one will be the wiser as to where you have gone."

"I'll consider it," Aldin replied.

"And that's it, you'll consider it?"

"Exactly," Aldin said, as if weary of the whole conversation.

Rising back up, and setting his body at the proper angle to display angry disdain, the Overseer floated out of the room, the door sliding shut behind him.

"Head us back in," Yaroslav said quietly, coming up to Aldin and offering him a drink.

"You know if that son of a bitch hadn't caused so much trouble I might actually grow to like him," Aldin said, slipping into his chair with a sigh of exasperation.

"Why should we head back in at this time?" Oishi asked. "Going to an intersect point we might meet someone that could report our location."

"I never liked the idea of our skulking out here beyond reach of any action to start with," Yaroslav stated. "Gablona could be doing all sorts of trashing about."

"That strike of ours pretty well destroyed his facilities, and there hasn't been any indicator of a response since," Zergh replied.

"Go back in, pass any ship, even give the slightest whisper of where we are, and everybody in the Cloud will be out after us," Oishi responded.

"Just look at the holo tape of that conversation between Aldin and Vush." And so saying Yaroslav went over to a console, punched in a series of commands, and what appeared to be a solid image of Vush appeared in the middle of the room.

"It's hard to read a voice-stress analysis on these creatures, but even a cursory examination will show Vush is half out of his mind with anxiety."

"He's a prisoner of us so-called barbarians," Hobbs replied, drifting over in his chair to hover alongside the image of the Overseer. "Of course he'd be nervous. Good heavens, you should have seen him and his companion when they first showed up at my pleasure world. A couple of the girls came bounding over to them, wearing not much more than their birthing suits, and I thought the poor creatures were gonna die." Hobbs chuckled at the memory.

"But the stress indicators shoot out the roof once he starts talking about this planet smashing," Yaroslav said, pointing to the image in the holo and then to a computer screen that was punching out an analysis even while the tape played.

"Something big's going down here," Yaroslav continued.

"More than he's willing to discuss," Aldin said softly, watching the holo image. "All right, we go back in."

"It's about time for a little action," Basak growled from the back of the room. "My boys have been getting a bit bored drifting around out here."

"How long to get down to the first jump point with at least three alternate lines running out?" Aldin asked, looking back at Yaroslav.

"We'll get there approximately six standard hours before this little demonstration."

"If nothing really serious has happened as a result, we'll simply come back out here and settle back in. If not, we'll at least have some options to work with."

"What options?" Tia asked quietly.

Aldin could only smile and shrug his shoulders.

Oishi came up to the holo image and studied it carefully.

"I think we are all going to get a lot more than we bargained for out of this."

chapter five

Mupa could not help but feel amazement at these barbarians.
Hundreds of ships, ranging from vast cruise liners packed with
tourists, to the elaborate pleasure barges of the Kohs, had come
from every direction of the Cloud, like flies to honey in order
to watch the show.

He could easily remember the last time they had blown a
planet. Then the action had created abject terror throughout the
Cloud, causing a near-instantaneous cessation of hostilities. Either these barbarians had become jaded, Mupa thought, or they
were insane. At least all the Overseers who had shown up were
showing some modicum of decorum, just as he was.

The object of this exercise, a cold gas giant, hovered before
him, several million kilometers away. Beyond it Beta Zul, a
vast and highly unstable red giant star, filled the darkness of
space with its red orb.

The giant had been a cause of some concern when the Arch
had first selected the location, but Mupa had felt it best not to
raise any real objections. The proximity of Beta Zul to the
Core Cluster, which was the inhabited heart of the Cloud,
made the demonstration, if anything, a little more immediate
rather than out at the fringe of the Cloud. Somehow it implied
that with the mere flick of a finger such destruction could be
visited on any of the space-faring worlds filled with the three
barbarian species.

Even as he did a final run-through on what he hoped was an
accurate checklist, Mupa could hear his brothers exclaiming
about the hundreds of ships that were still pouring in through
the dozen jump points that converged in this particular system.
An hour before there had been a most unfortunate accident
when two ships had consummated certain statistical probabili-

ties by jumping down in the same spot at exactly the same instant.

The flash of instantaneous destruction had been most impressive as five hundred Gaf tourists, who had won their privileged seats in a hastily conducted lottery, and a hive ship of Xsarns suddenly got far more than they had bargained for.

*Ooh*s and *ah*s had echoed across the commlinks, as some of the witnesses assumed that the brilliant flash had been an opening warm-up for the show. Tourist ships were already scrambling over the area, picking up tiny bits of wreckage as souvenirs of the big event.

"I do hope that everything is in order?" Mupa looked up to see the Arch hovering over him.

Mupa swallowed hard and nodded.

"The triggering device that will activate the opening of the transfer gate can be launched whenever you desire," Mupa replied nervously. "Once it is dropped into the planet's atmosphere, all I need do is flick these buttons." He let his hand touch the small protrusions coming out of a golden box that rested in his lap. "That will open the gate. As I understand this system, the gate will instantly attach itself to the primary gravitational body within its region and quite simply devour it."

Mupa paused. What a wormhole or transfer gate was remained a mystery to him. Even the term was beyond his understanding, picked up back when Humans had first come to this region of the Cloud. One of their great scientists from their ancient world had somehow managed to replicate the process, but he was now, of course, long dead. The name they had for it conjured in his mind the image of an actual worm reaching out to devour the great yellow-green planet before him. He knew the Human term was not quite accurate, but the effect seemed the same and it had somehow stuck in the public's mind as well to describe what was going to happen.

"And where does it go?" the Arch asked, as if seeking reassurance.

"Into another dimension. If the wormhole is rotating at a significant portion of the speed of light it will even go into another time."

"But where?"

"Oh, somewhere out beyond the Cloud," Mupa said vaguely, and he fingered the golden box nervously.

The Overseer looked at how casually Mupa's hand danced across the device.

"I'd rather if you didn't touch it until we were ready," the Overseer said, trying to keep his voice even.

"Oh, nothing to worry about," Mupa replied, and with an audible click he threw the trigger over.

In spite of himself, the Overseer backed up.

"I've got to push these keys on the side first," Mupa said, holding the box up.

"How do you know that?" the Arch snapped testily.

"Just figured it out, that's all." If a lie was possible for an Overseer, Mupa had just committed that heinous sin. By "figuring out" he simply meant that he and Vush had discovered the box and the small instrument pack that actually activated the wormhole. A First Traveler machine, a most annoying thing actually, had been nearby when they had found it. It didn't seem to be working quite right, had pestered them a bit at first, and then left them alone. The machine kept replaying a holo projection of the operation of the device. However, it insisted upon shocking them whenever they attempted to pick it up, until he had, in a rare display of Overseer impatience, screamed at it to leave them alone, and it had drifted away.

"Don't worry about it, everything is under control," Mupa said, trying to sound as self-assured as possible.

"Well get the thing launched," the Arch retorted, trying to decide whether he was furious or frightened. The mere thought of either emotion made him ever angrier.

"Damn these barbarians," he cursed under his breath as he stormed from the room.

"We're not going to make it," Yaroslav said, coming up to stand beside Aldin as they pulled through their fifth jump-through in as many hours.

"Well, I never expected us to," Aldin replied, swinging his chair around to look at his old companion. "Don't tell me that Vush has made you nervous as well with his dire predictions."

"Absolutely yes," Yaroslav retorted.

"Even if we did get into a safe place to transmit, and even if I were then willing to break commlink silence, do you actually expect that anything Vush said would change what they plan to do?"

"The display of our intention might make a difference later on," Zergh said.

Oishi swung his chair about to look back at Vush.

"You will tell them of our effort, won't you?"

Vush, who had remained silent since his outburst of two days past, did not reply.

Zola and most of the other Kohs, who were aboard a yacht escorted by several of the small Overseer vessels, could not help but look nervously at a distant ship hovering on the far side of the gas giant, parked in among several hundred sightseeing cruisers. It was Corbin Gablona's battered yacht, escorted as well by half a dozen Overseer craft. Both his own vessel and Gablona's had been inspected by Overseers before departure to insure that no contraband weapons were on board. The fact that he was defenseless made him decidedly uncomfortable, especially with Corbin less than half a light-minute away. If anything, it showed him how much Corbin had changed everything, thus necessitating this demonstration.

A heavy Xsarn cruise ship drifted by in front of his vessel and came to a stop.

"Damn Xsarns, always pushing ahead of others," Zola growled, and punching up a commlink, he soundly cursed at the pilot of the bulky vessel. Seconds later it moved on, parking a kilometer to his port side. With all of space to choose from, it was getting rather crowded in the area as everyone hugged up close to the safety line set by the Overseers. Thousands of ships were jockeying for position on the equatorial line so that both hemispheres would be clearly visible.

There was a brilliant flash several hundred thousand kilometers above the northern pole of the gas giant, and everyone let out an excited shout, expecting that the show had begun. Tracking cameras swung onto the point and quickly jacked up the scale, projecting it onto forward viewscreens. The room filled with groans, and then with several appreciative chuckles when the image resolved into a glowing sign, an advertisement for a chain of space yachts manufactured by one of the usual characters who took delight in portraying himself as a madman who would give away his ships at below cost. The commlinks chattered with inquiries from angry Overseers attempting to ascertain who set off the display, an action that only caused additional hilarity and ribald responses, as if the pilots of the hundreds of ships that had gathered were covering for a school-boy who had pulled off an entertaining prank.

Zola made a mental note to buy stock in the man's company; sales were certain to go up since what was going to happen here would certainly prove to be one of the most-watched broadcasts in all the history of the Cloud. Tens of millions of katars had already been made on commemorative drinking mugs, souvenir shirts with an imbedded holo of the gas giant imploding into a shocking chartreuse that the Gafs were going crazy over, and even Xsarn food trays were being decorated with stenciled images of the planet that shrunk and disappeared when the owner sucked on the feeding tube.

It certainly was helping to maintain the decorum of the situation, a fact that, if it were possible, annoyed the Overseers to no end, and Zola could not help but find the whole thing vastly amusing.

"This is not supposed to be funny."

Zola looked over his shoulder and saw the Overseer floating in the middle of the room, and he immediately wiped the smile from his face and nodded in serious agreement.

"Shockingly childish," Zola said, and, of course, all the others agreed.

Feeling a flutter in his stomach, Mupa watched the monitor as the instrument pack that would open the transfer gate moved down toward the gas giant in a long tightening spiral. He wasn't sure if the flutter was from fear, excitement, or just simple hunger, for, after all, a proper Overseer spent thousands of years learning to suppress any and all emotions and direct contact between one's bodily reaction and the higher planes of intellectual contemplation.

The monitor flashed green, and on another linked display a tracking camera showed the instrument pack's retro system firing, stabilizing the machine in orbit around the giant, barely skimming above the swirling atmosphere of poisonous chlorine and ammonia. There was a ripple of excitement as dozens of his brothers all tried to float ever so much closer to the forward viewport, feigning disinterest and yet unwilling to move aside as more Overseers came into the room to watch. Even old Yú, who had stayed in the far corner of the chamber, rose up ever so slowly, his body turned as if looking in the other direction, yet tilting his head just enough to be able to watch out of the corners of his eyes.

Mupa looked over at the Arch and nodded. A holo camera, controlled by a Xsarn crew member, was flicked on, and the Arch started into a brief sermon that was going out across the entire Cloud, explaining the sinful ways of the three species, the heinous crimes of Aldin Larice and his compatriots, and the sad necessity of having to destroy a planet as a demonstration of their ire, closing with the promise that if order was not reestablished, the instrument of destruction would next be turned on some of the banking planets.

All the time the Arch was speaking, Mupa nervously held the box of control switches. He was barely aware of it when the Arch finished his hour-long preaching and the light of the camera swung onto him.

With a start he looked up, almost letting the focus of his thoughts on the firing box drift away. Behind the camera, the Arch was bobbing up and down as if motioning for him to get started. There was an expectant hush.

Mupa floated up, the box floating with him. He looked straight at the camera.

"Behold the power of the Overseers," he announced in the deepest voice he could muster.

He reached out to the box, and with grave deliberation pressed down on the first golden button as he had seen it done on the ancient First Traveler holo record. There was a barely audible click and the button popped back up, a small light alongside of it flashing white. He pushed the second and the third, the lights flashing beside each. And then with a melodramatic flourish, he poised his finger—or what passed for an Overseer finger—over the fourth button on the side of the box. He pushed down. It didn't move. He tried again, and still it refused to budge. Nervous, he looked up at the Arch, who started to bob up and down in a most agitated manner. Feeling totally ridiculous, he slammed down hard on the button, muffling a yelp of pain. He suddenly had the strongest of feelings that all the members of the lesser species were howling with delight, and he wasn't far wrong.

Floating back down to the ground, he placed the box on the floor, and then kneeling over it he rose back up into the air and willed himself to drop. Coming down full force, he slammed the button with extended arm. There was an audible *snick* as the button slammed down, the sound of which was hidden by the louder crack of his finger breaking and a most Human curse of pain escaping his lips.

All four lights on the box started to blink in unison, shifting through a broad spectrum of colors. Nursing his broken member, Mupa sat on the floor staring at the box and then at the holo screen.

"Nothing," one of his brothers whispered. "Absolutely nothing."

Wiping the tears from his eyes, Zola rocked back and forth in his chair while the other Kohs raised mock toasts to the gallant Mupa. The lone Overseer aboard the ship shouted in a shrill voice for respectful silence and was greeted with hoots of derision. Yet even in his mirth, Zola felt worried. If this was a show of Overseer power, then the mysterious power they claimed to hold was a sham. And if that was the case, then the last three thousand years of peace that they had been able to enforce was a sham as well, a paper cutout without substance. He didn't know whether to be furious or frightened by all that this implied.

And then suddenly all of it was driven from his mind.

Above the surface of the gas giant, there was a flicker of light—nowhere near as impressive as that of the yacht salesman's sign—just a tiny flash. Completely unnoticed at first, since the field of the effect was barely a meter across, the wormhole transfer gate opened, and the photons of starlight streaming past the field were twisted into a spiraling loop. It was a remarkable event, since the instrument pack that should have been crushed within a millionth of a second into the size of a single hydrogen atom nevertheless maintained its structural integrity. It fell. After all, that is what it was designed to do, to plummet into the heart of whatever it was expected to alter, burying itself into the very core of its gravitational field.

The chlorine and ammonia atmosphere of the gas giant offered not the slightest resistance. The hard molten surface of liquid chlorine and the compressed solid chlorine beneath it posed not the slightest problem for the field as it punched straight into the core and pulled along with it anything that was encompassed within the meter-wide band of the wormhole effect.

Yet there was something missing; within its own system of memory and logic the First Traveler package could not sense the proper connections. A signal of inquiry raced outward, back to its control station. A microscopic servo and computation unit acknowledged the inquiry, calculated that there was a mistake in the entire operation, and rolled a switch. And that micro-size switch broke, coming up against the unyielding bottom side of the fourth button.

Its creators had made things to last for eternity, but even the most simple device, such as a simple button, can corrode ever so slightly after millions of years of waiting to be pushed, or worse yet, hammered down. It was now firmly locked in place, which to the logic system of the controlling unit meant that the creator of this miraculous device was simply overriding the command to disengage. It took but thousandths of a second for the system to call up the alternate program for such a contingency. And yet the program was not quite as it should be. Several million years of waiting while random X rays bounce through space might nick and damage a dense-packed system that moves its commands on through circuits built around systems the size of single molecules.

Or in simpler terms, the machine hiccuped and then sent a rather unusual signal back: to run full bore until there was no more material left to take. The problem was that there was no command to send that material anywhere; the necessary part of the unit was missing, therefore it would have to just feed on whatever was available and pack it in around itself.

The instrument pack now received its command, a most unusual command. It had found a place to nest, now it had to find something to feed upon. A tentaclelike finger of spacial distortion, a wormhole in search of another end to anchor upon. Not even a millimeter in diameter, it snaked out and away in the opposite direction from the gas giant, and as if it were a living creature tracking down a scent, the tentacle of distortion raced toward the gravitational center of the great red giant star. In its outward track it deviated ever so slightly, like a wave running down a tautly drawn string, drawn to the mass of a Xsarn cruise ship of ten thousand tons, drilling a hole through it not much wider than a pinhead. If it had had time to even observe what was occurring, a Xsarn tourist, who was busy slurping on a feeding tube of a souvenir tray, would have seen the wormhole distortion pop through the hull of the ship, straight through his tray and the contents within, then through itself and out the other side of the vessel. Within one ten thousandth of a second two thousand Xsarns, tons of Xsarn haute cuisine, two thousand souvenir trays, and ten thousand tons of ship were sucked into the wormhole and flashed out of existence.

The tentacle of distortion snaked onward, almost drawn in by another ship, but overridden by the stronger gravitation anchor of the sun. Straight as a laser beam it dove across space, its event horizon bulged now by the churning hyper-compressed atoms of Xsarns and their ship. Already functioning in the other dimensional reality that was the same used for jump transition, an instant later the probing end of the wormhole punched through the chromosphere of the sun and leaped straight into the core of the helium-fired inferno.

It had all taken less than the time of half a dozen heartbeats.

"What the shit was that?" Zola gasped, coming to his feet. The other Kohs, who but several seconds before were laughing hysterically, had stopped; the sound of drinking glasses shattering on the floor echoed in the room, counterpointed by the angry hoot of a servobot, which was instantly responding to the mess.

The Xsarn cruise ship, whose pilot he had soundly cursed not an hour before for parking too close, was gone. It just disappeared. The effect had been startling, disorienting, reminding him of a picture on a flat commlink screen at the instant it was turned off; the picture would drop in upon itself to form a tiny point of light before disappearing. It was as if the Xsarn ship had suddenly compressed in upon itself and then winked out of existence. There had been a momentary streak of light that he thought had curved toward him before going over the port side of the ship.

"Look at that!"

One of the Gaf Kohs was pointing to a monitor to one side of the main screen. In the center of the monitor was the red giant, and what appeared to be a string going straight into it. It was not a string of light, it was not even really visible, rather it was a distortion, almost a sensing that something was wrong with the fabric of space.

"Get us the fuck out of here!" the Overseer cried.

* * *

It was, after all, nothing more than a moving machine, a play toy of its creators, designed to take entire stars and move them in a godlike manner. It was how they had transported the tremendous mass necessary to build the Kolbard Ring and later the Sphere. It was also a play toy used to combine one star with another for the mere entertainment such an act might provide. When the jump lanes were first being cleared, it was a simple means of moving out unwanted and dangerous material, consigning it to a cosmic dump yard where it could do no harm. Or, when more godlike activities were desired, it could heal an aging star with an infusion of new matter, simply to save an orbiting planet that they found appealing, or for the act of saving a star for no other reason than to save it.

It could be a work of art, the altering of suns for no other reason than to do it. Or, if in a mischievous mood, to pump a star so full of mass as to cause it to collapse upon itself and then detonate it into a supernova, to set off the biggest firecracker in the universe for the sheer spectacle it might provide. Such an event had been one of the First Travelers' last playful acts more than a hundred thousand years ago.

When one could engineer the design of an entire galaxy, such things were necessary to relieve the tedium. All one needed to do was place the proper instrument pack at the destination point and place a companion piece at the star to be moved and stand back and throw the switch on the control unit. But no one had ever been foolish enough to use the one instrument pack without the other, compounded by a little overenthusiastic hammering upon a sticky switch.

The link was not complete, and like a cosmic garden hose transporting the raw matter of stars, the pump was activated down the wormhole line. Matter that was compressed into thousands of tons per cubic centimeter was compressed yet further as it fell into the event horizon of the suction end of the wormhole. In an instant it snaked up the line, traveling far faster than light-speed, bulging the wormhole line out, the mass expanding the diameter of the event horizon and in turn generating an ever-increasing range of distortion, pulling in yet more matter from its surroundings. Racing up through the surface of the star, it flashed on up the line, snapping across space and then plummeting down into the very heart of what had been a cold gas giant. Within the first second, a million tons of active thermonuclear matter was deposited into the gravitational core of the planet. Though the gas giant was indeed cold, its center, under tremendous gravitational pressure from its own weight, was a chain reaction waiting to happen. Like superheated steam shot into a block of ice, the emerging mass of the sun, compressed to millions of tons per cubic centimeter, underwent two simultaneous experiences, rapid expansion when the gravitational pressures of the wormhole were behind it, and a rather interesting experience created by a thermonuclear reaction suddenly inserted into the heart of a planet.

Barely a dozen seconds had passed since Mupa had finally managed to push the button down. For long seconds he looked up at his Arch, expecting a berating unlike any experienced by an Overseer in ten thousand years. After all, he had managed to make all of them look like fools in front of all the barbarians. How could he ever explain that testing these types of devices was rather impossible, since testing them meant actually using them.

Suddenly he heard a squawking voice on the commlink, and then a rippled gasp go through his brothers. Floating back up, still nursing his injured limb, he looked at the main viewscreen. The instrument pack should have been above the planet. It was gone. Another screen showed an empty stretch of space, an ever so thin streak of light cutting straight across it.

"What is going on?" Mupa whispered.

The Arch looked back at him, his eyes showing confusion.

"I thought you were supposed to know."

How could he ever admit that he wasn't really sure?

"Replay that one!" somebody shouted, pointing to the screen with the line going through it.

The image went into reverse.

"Hold it!" several cried.

The image snapped through several enlargements. A ship was there, it looked like a Xsarn design.

The image started forward again, this time slowly. In the span of less than a single frame the ship disappeared, replaced by the line.

The Overseers all started to look back at Mupa for an explanation.

Other commlink screens were showing where the instrument pack was supposed to be—emptiness. Several showed a straight line emerging out of the planet, one of the cameras tracing it all the way across hundreds of millions of miles toward the red giant. Another link, the one hooked into Zola's ship, was showing complete pandemonium, panicked screams, and Zola hysterically calling for the pilot to jump them out, the hell with collisions and gravitational distortions.

Something was unraveling here—but what?

"Put the forward screen on real time!" Mupa shouted.

An instant later the vast forward viewscreen dropped all the other images to show what was actually in front of them, rather than signals that were jumped at translight speed. With the planet nine million kilometers away, it was thirty seconds until a real time view of the planet would arrive. Just about now, he realized.

The high-gain cameras mounted aboard the ship were superb Xsarn workmanship and could pick up every detail.

There was the flash where the instrument pack was supposed to be, and then nothing. Long seconds passed, while from the jump commlink images everything seemed to be going into chaos. He could sense the panic building.

There was a flash to forward, a ship accelerating up to jump velocity passing a dozen kilometers in front of their own vessel, a streaked blur of light, and a crackling voice screaming obscenities.

In real time the image of the planet filled the entire forward screen.

"What is that?" somebody whispered.

It appeared as if an arrow of distorted light were cutting straight from the surface of the world, driving across space to the sun behind them.

The flow through the wormhole was increasing at a near exponential rate, driving up to its peak load, for that given transfer distance, of trillions of tons of mass a second. What pulsed through its narrow corridor was in a highly compressed state not much more in volume than that of a Gaf's body, though a Gaf's body that would be very heavy indeed. In its own environment, inside the heart of a red giant star, this mass would be reasonably stable, but in the far less dense heart of the gas planet, when released, it would not only create tremendous gravitational distortions but would also explode outward, like superheated steam uncorked from a jar, while at the same time releasing a stunningly large nuclear pulse of heat and light. It was enough to give any planet a serious case of indigestion. Sooner or later it was bound to get sick.

One moment the surface of the planet looked just about like any other gas giant with its swirling poisonous clouds. The surface of the planet seemed to bulge outward with a certain slow-motion majesty at its poles, the energy of internal events first racing up the magnetic lines. The top and bottom of the planet peeled back, exploding into light.

Mupa, far more excited than he could ever remember, started to bob up and down.

"It's working, it's working!" he shouted triumphantly.

As if his words were a cue, the other Overseers let out a cheer, forgetting all sense of comportment and dignity, an event that made the Arch glad that he had, at least for the moment, shut down the link.

"Dignity my brothers, dignity!"

The room fell silent.

The Arch nodded to the Xsarn operating the camera, and it was flicked back on and turned toward the Arch, who floated before the forward viewscreen, the image of the erupting planet behind him.

"What you are witnessing is the destruction of an inhospitable planet," the Arch said solemnly.

He paused for a brief instant.

"By the mere flick of a finger this is what we can accomplish. If certain terms are not agreed to, we can arrange the same thing to happen to any of the worlds you now inhabit, or for that matter, all of them."

He floated in silence, letting his words sink in as they instantly flashed across the Cloud. Yet in the background, other commlinks were conveying a rising sense of panic from the hundreds of ships, news stations, and yachts that had gathered to watch the event. Good, it was having the proper effect, the party atmosphere of moments before now dispelled.

A shudder raced through the ship, the gravitational pulse arriving without warning, giving no time to the inertial dampening systems to compensate. A number of Overseers were knocked head over heels. The Arch, though floating, was slammed against the forward viewscreen and slumped down, the wind knocked out of him.

* * *

The explosions were rippling out across the entire planet's surface, vast plumes of star fire racing straight upward, the total mass of the gas giant not yet sufficient to turn the plumes back in upon themselves. Within the heart of the dying world position was everything. The instrument pack, contained within its field, was still very much intact. Around it, density was so intense that even light itself was near to coiling and looping back upon itself. But meters away the outward explosion of energy was pushing matter straight up at the speed of light, while up upon the surface vast eddies of chlorine and ammonia were plummeting straight back into the core, drawn downward by the vast gravitational forces now being generated. Long streams of icy gas would strike the upward currents, flash into nuclear incandescents, and be flung straight back up again.

The planet was a star forming, but unlike anything that normally occurs, this was the birthing of a billion years compressed into seconds. A balance had yet to be reached between the outward thrust of the thermonuclear furnace within and the gravitational forces that held the star stable and together. It was simply a writhing mess that was not quite sure what it wanted to become.

But for the moment, at least, exploding seemed like a good idea.

The gravitational distortions were continuous, the dampening systems of the lurching ship unable to compensate. Mupa looked about, reminded of bad holo films made by the Gafs that showed crew members of crashing ships flinging themselves back and forth across a set, while the recording camera gyrated to simulate a ship out of control. It was decidedly unpleasant, though.

He looked back at the planet. Streams of material were ejecting straight outward, the clouds on the planet's surface churning, some of them looking as if they were turning into whirlpools sucking straight down into the planet's core.

Of course the device had to be responsible, but since he had never actually seen a planet swallowed by a wormhole transfer gate he wasn't quite sure if what he was seeing was what he was supposed to see.

The dampening system ejected a sensor to be positioned ahead of the ship and thus relay warning of the approaching distortions. The lurching of the ship gradually steadied, though there were still occasional rumbles, the ship echoing to the creaks and groans of stressed metal.

"What is that line?" someone finally asked, disturbing Mupa's rapt attention upon the phenomenon on the planet surface.

"The wormhole, of course," Mupa said with a superior air.

"Oh." There was a pause. "Why is it going to the sun? I thought this was supposed to dump things into another dimension."

"I don't—" he stopped himself. "I don't believe that it is necessarily going through the sun," he replied, realizing that his words were being broadcast across the Cloud, and that the response didn't quite have the authoritative tone of an expert.

There was another pause.

He started to worry. Just what was actually going on here?

Another commlink line flashed into life, a distant voice talking. It took several seconds to register.

It was Vush!

Startled, Mupa turned to look at the screen, the sight of the kidnapped Overseer turning the attention of nearly everyone from the spectacular display of the planet.

He could barely hear his friend's voice above the insane chatter of the dozens of other monitor lines.

"You damned idiot, it's only half the machine . . ." was all they heard before another gravitational pulse rocked the ship and distorted transmissions, drowning out Vush's words.

Mupa looked forward. The entire surface of the planet was glowing, churning, and then started to lift outward.

Outward?

The wormhole was supposed to be eating the planet, collapsing it inward, not outward.

The rather unique sensation of queasiness coursed through Mupa. Too much was happening, and he was starting to feel overloaded. Voices on the commlink shouting, Vush yelling, the Arch turning toward him trying to say something, and a Xsarn crew member pointing at a monitor that showed that the gravitational pull of the planet was in fact increasing at a rather alarming rate.

A steady pump was now operating, running at maximum design load. Already a minute but discernable fraction of the red giant had coursed through the line, and the star's core was beginning to collapse in upon itself. It would take long minutes for the gravitational variation to take effect out at the outer edge of the chromosphere, a hundred million miles away, but red giants were balancing acts: the outward pressure of their internal reaction balanced with the gravitational effect. If enough reaction mass is lost at the core, outward pressure decreases and gravity takes over—the star collapses.

As for the wormhole, a tremendous amount of mass was now pumping down the line, enough to set up its own gravitational field. The Xsarn ship had been unfortunately in the line of its creation, and trace elements and all the component atoms of two thousand Xsarns were now blowing up through towering columns of radioactive bursts, leaping far above the planet's surface. The wormhole was spinning upon its long axis, bulging and twisting in a sinuous motion like a tornado weaving across an open prairie. Within the effect of its field even smaller wormholes would occasionally twist out from the main trunk, lasting perhaps for a millionth of a second, in a highly unstable state, and fall back in or disconnect. Some might run rampant for as long as a second or two, either bouncing across a hundred thousand kilometers of space and shooting matter back into the mother of all wormholes or existing a brief moment in total freedom. Of course, whatever these free-agent wormholes caught, even if disconnected from the main line, would fall in one end, and emerge out the other in a rather disorganized and thoroughly pulped state.

A pleasure yacht of half a dozen Gafs, who had told their wives they were at a business meeting, making no mention of their female companions for this trip, were more than a thousand kilometers from the main wormhole when they received a short visit from a disconnected line, which in its brief tenth of a second of existence never measured more than ten centimeters in length and barely a millimeter in diameter. The entire Gaf yacht fell in one end, and popped out the other, the ship turned inside out and backward, with Gafs, their ship, polyester clothing, and muscatel all churned into an unpleasant soup and sprayed with such velocity that another Gaf ship, fifty kilometers away, was hulled by the puree, resulting in a disconcerting decompression experience for all aboard.

* * *

For a brief instant it appeared as if the planet was racing in upon itself.

Mupa felt a momentary surge of reassurance at the sight. Of course that's what would happen. And then there was the snap of light, the blinding sight of a star being born. And in that instant he knew.

The Xsarn crew members were already reacting, screaming in panic, spraying the ingredients of their last meal upon anyone within range. One of them was pointing at the monitor, shouting that the wormhole was out of control and rather than sucking the planet up it was, instead, sucking the heart of the red giant straight into the planet.

Mupa barely heard shouted comments about novas, supernovas, black holes, and radiation.

The Arch was before him, holding the control box, shouting at Mupa to do something.

Numbly he took the box. The lights were flashing wildly, the fourth button still jammed down. And it was absolutely flush with the surface of the box. Typical First Traveler engineering, so finely crafted that unless someone knew the button was even there, it would be invisible. It was jammed and there was no way to get it back up.

Mupa looked up at the Arch.

"It's broke," he said weakly.

"What do you mean 'it's broke'?" the Arch roared, no longer even aware that the commlink camera was still running, broadcasting the entire event live across the Cloud.

"It's broke," Mupa whispered, unable to say anything else.

"Then fix it!"

Mupa studied the box intently, barely aware that the light in the room was shifting, growing brighter.

Rather clumsily he tried to pry the button back up, going so far as to bring the box up to his mouth and then try to suck it back up.

It was thoroughly and completely jammed.

"I can't."

He looked back up, and at that instant the planet made its transition into a star, flaring into a brilliant and, from a purely objective viewpoint, beautiful flood of light.

"I suggest we leave," Mupa said. "I think something very bad is going to happen."

He handed the box back to the Arch, as if somehow show-ing that he was washing his hands of the entire affair.

The Arch let the box drop.

"Oh, shit," he whispered, and then floated out of the room.

Zola, still sweating with fear, poured another drink to steady his nerves. He was out of danger, at least that's what the ship's navigator claimed. It was the first time in his life he had ever experienced a full transition jump from within the close grav-itational field of a planet, and worse yet, a blind jump through totally unmarked space. He had always been told that such an experiment would always produce one of two events: either you came out the other side, or before your nerves could even register the moment, you were vaporized. He was still alive and able to pour the drink, even though his hands were shaking violently. Most of the drink was spilling onto the carpet, to the dismay of a servobot that was holding a tray with one tentacle while trying to mop up the spill with another.

That was half of his fear. The other half was the thought of how the Xsarn ship had simply winked out of existence, not much more than a kilometer away, and the impression that whatever had hit it had almost hit him as well.

The jump had taken them a tenth of a light year out, drop-ping them back into a main jump line back toward the Core Cluster. The commlinks, with their near-instantaneous trans-missions, were jammed. A "We Are There for You" news crew was running several images on the same screen. The gor-geously coiffured main reporter—who allegedly could not even read a cue note but nevertheless managed to somehow project an image of infinite wisdom—was openly weeping while de-scribing the destruction of the Xsarn ship, which their cameras had recorded. The reporter looked absolutely sincere and was obviously angling for a major award. The tears streamed down his angular and well-tanned face to dangle on the edge of his mustache. An instant later the signal died and was replaced by a rival news system, with another emoting reporter showing footage of the "We Are There for You" ship being pierced by an errant wormhole. An ultra-high-speed camera replayed the footage in fascinating detail: the ship looked like a balloon that was slowly being sucked into a straw.

"Anyone wanna place a bet on what's going to happen next?"

Zola looked up to see that his fellow Kohs were recovering from the shock of their narrow escape.

"Ten thousand katars that ten to thirty ships are destroyed," someone shouted, and his bet was quickly covered at four-to-one odds.

Though the Overseer on board shouted his protests at the impropriety of gambling on such a tragedy, he soon fell silent with the realization that he was now being totally ignored.

Hassan smiled. He looked into Corbin Gablona's face and saw that the fat man was smiling as well, but underneath it all he could also see the fear.

"Why did you do that?" Corbin whispered.

"I wanted to see what it was like," Hassan replied, wiping the blade on his sleeve before sheathing it.

"You know what you've done?"

"They're powerless now. All of you people have been shaking in your boots for three thousand years."

He pointed to the monitors, which showed the planet exploding into a sun, the destruction of several dozen ships, the cries of panic, and most important of all the mad pandemonium aboard the Overseer ship, which had already turned about and was racing toward the nearest jump gate in order to escape, even as the Arch's last words reverberated across the Cloud.

"If we were close enough, I'd say destroy them in that ship and be rid of them forever."

Corbin Gablona felt an inner quaking of fear. Far worse than all that had happened outside the ship, it was what was happening inside it, and all that it implied, that terrified him far more. The Overseers were powerless, they had no understanding of what they had done, they could not control it, and, from what little he understood, there appeared to be a disaster of monumental proportions in the making.

It also meant that the entire structure of power as he knew it was forever altered. Though he had broken the bounds, there was still the question of dealing with the Overseers, even if some of them had been corrupted into the playing of the games. But this was different.

The Overseer Tulbi lay at Hassan's feet, the body still twitching spasmodically from the knife blow to the base of the skull. It finally grew still.

"You've killed him," Gablona whispered. "You've killed an Overseer."

"An Overseer?" Hassan laughed, his voice harsh. "I killed nothing, absolutely nothing, as I would kill any insect that boasted that it had power and yet could be crushed by the back of my hand. The old order is dead."

He paused for a moment.

"And I am the new order."

He looked at Gablona and smiled.

"In service to you, of course. Do you have any problems with that?"

Gablona looked around the room. All his guards were Al'Shiga, led by Hassan of the ancient order of Assassins of Earth.

He looked back into the man's hawklike eyes.

"You still need me if you want to survive," Corbin said, trying to hide the fear in his voice.

Hassan smiled.

"Of course I do, my lord Gablona, of course I do."

Hassan started to turn away.

"You saw that commlink message of the Overseer Vush. He is obviously still with your old friend Larice. You have the means to trace that signal; I suggest we do it now, and perhaps we can run him down."

Corbin could tell instantly from the tone of voice that it was not a suggestion—it was an order. And he did not hesitate to comply.

chapter six

The commlinks had been jammed with the news for three standard days. The plan had been forming, but the thought of it gave him a cold gnawing in his stomach. A strange sensation, that—to be cognizant of one's stomach, such an unpleasant sensation for an Overseer, and he found it deeply disturbing. The door to his room slid open, and Vush looked up expectantly as Hobbs came into the chamber, a servobot behind him toting a tray of wilted salad.

"Dead before it was plucked," Hobbs said.

"Thank you."

Vush swung around from his sleeping pallet and, taking up one of the Human eating instruments, forked a piece of dried fruit and chewed on it meditatively, a bit shocked that he was actually enjoying the taste of food.

"Been watching the news?" Hobbs asked.

Vush nodded.

"What does it all mean?"

"Something's broke and Mupa doesn't know how to turn it off."

"Well I think that's kind of obvious," Hobbs sniffed.

It was more than obvious. No one was quite sure yet, but somewhere around twenty to twenty-five ships had disappeared, not counting several that collided in the mad panic to get away.

The former planet was now a highly unstable yellow star, which was continuing to grow; its companion red giant, linked by the wormhole line, was collapsing in upon itself. The more disturbing question was, what would happen when there was no more mass from the draining red giant? Would the wormhole shut off, or would it snake out to look for yet more items to devour?

Vush finally worked up his nerve.

"I'd like to talk with Aldin again."

"Well, it's about time," Hobbs said cheerily. "And then afterward how about a good stiff toddy to take the edge off things?"

"How about one before?" Vush said nervously.

"So what are we going to do?" the Arch asked, for what he knew was at least the hundredth time.

Mupa, if he had shoulders, would have shrugged them.

"Nothing we can do," he finally admitted.

"What's going to happen?"

"The barbarians' news reports are most likely right. First the star will disintegrate when its gravity can no longer hold the chromosphere. Anything within a quarter of a light-year would be in trouble when that happens. Fortunately there are no worlds that close by."

"Oh, yes, most fortunate."

The Arch looked away for a moment.

"When will it happen?" the Arch asked.

"Days, maybe ten or fifteen at most. It might even get to the point that the gravitational force of the new star will even start to pull the side of the red star closest to it in on itself. It should be a beautiful sight," Mupa said with a sigh.

"And then?"

"Once the red star dies, one of two things. The wormhole will lose its anchor and collapse back in on itself and that is it."

"Or," the Arch prompted him.

"It will just snake outward. There are half a dozen stars within half a light-year or less, several of them have mining outposts. There are no major barbarian centers, but you know how it is, if there's something to be mined on a world, they'll be there."

Damn Humans and Gafs were everywhere, the Arch thought dryly. The First Travelers had accomplished so much, but they had committed one terrible sin: their demand for various metals, the exotic ones beyond the ever-plentiful iron and nickel, had led them to harvest nearly every vein of metal on all the planets of the Cloud. Perhaps, he mused, that is why they eventually moved on, they had simply run out of certain key components for building, for though they could make nearly anything, the creation of raw elements was a rather laborious process. As a result, there wasn't a world that didn't have some prospectors on it, looking for a precious vein of gold or lead or copper. It was impossible to ever feel any real sense of privacy. You could go to a world, think you had solitude, and then some Xsarn prospectors would wander into your encampment.

He looked back at Mupa.

"So it will attack another sun?"

"It'll lock onto one of those suns and suck it dry, and then on and on. Beyond those six suns we go straight into the Core Cluster, the red giant is right on the edge of it and could be called part of it as is. Hundreds of worlds there, including the banking centers of the barbarians' civilization. But chances are it wouldn't go that far."

"And why not?" the Arch asked, as if almost hopeful.

"There are two black dwarfs nearby."

"And pray what are those?"

"Suns that have burned themselves out. Their rather large mass is condensed into an incredibly small area. We've always avoided them since their gravity is thousands of times standard. Anyhow, they're almost solid compressed iron. Once the wormhole hits one of those, it's all over."

Mupa fell silent and the Arch looked over at him in an agitated manner, waiting for the rest of the information, not willing to admit to his own ignorance of such things.

"The core of a sun can burn every element up to iron. Start pumping in trillions of tons of iron and it shuts the nuclear furnace down. This dampens the outward pressure that holds a star up. Everything rushes into the center, pressure builds to an unbelievable rate, and then we have an exciting explosion."

"Supernova?"

Mupa nodded. "Poof. A supernova. The last one in these parts was well over a hundred thousand standard years back."

The Arch nodded—the one that many suspected the First Travelers had triggered.

"I can't make an accurate projection," he admitted, "but the lesser species' news reports are full of it. The shock wave from the supernova will slam into the galactic core, it might even tear some stars apart. It'll definitely douse everything within fifteen odd light-years with a lethal dose of radiation. It will shatter their civilization. Their key worlds of finance and the intersection for hundreds of jump points converge there. They'll never recover and billions will die."

"What I thought I'd hear," the Arch replied.

Mupa looked up at him fearfully, fully expecting that after this particular confession of just how far he had truly managed to bungle things, that he would be banished for the full extent of his natural life to some barren rock.

The Arch looked at him and then drifted out of the room without a word.

Mupa sat in stunned silence. He was positive that for the briefest instant the Arch had actually smiled.

"So you're telling us that it'll just keep going on until the damn thing blows and then the Core Cluster gets the blast?"

Aldin sat back in his chair and exhaled, his cheeks puffing

out. Every one of his group was present, filling the small room: the surviving samurai and Gaf warriors, Oishi, Zergh, Tia, Hobbs and his companions, Yaroslav, and even Mari, Bukha, and the Xsarn Prime, whom they had picked up when the Xsarn's private yacht had managed to rendezvous and drop them off.

Vush nodded his head, already learning to fit in somewhat better with these creatures. He took another sip of the steaming toddy that Hobbs had cooked up for him, and he actually found that he enjoyed the sensation of it going down his throat, warming his stomach, relaxing his mind.

Vush bobbed his head in reply to Aldin's question.

"As we surmised," Yaroslav said. He looked over at Aldin. "How do you think everyone will jump?"

"Gablona will have the time of his life," Hobbs interjected. "If it all goes to chaos, he'll tear out whatever pieces he can from the dying beast. He went outcast when he started this war. He'd be a fool not to know that even if he won, and everyone put up the front that he was one of the boys again, it'd never be the same. Now he has the breakdown that he wanted."

"And the other Kohs?" Aldin asked, as if looking for a reassurance of his own dark beliefs.

"They'll grovel to whomever is the strongest," the Xsarn said, his mandibles clicking in a display of extreme anger. "The Overseers have shown themselves to be fools, and beyond that, the truth of how they've controlled events is finally sinking in with my brother Kohs. We've been trembling in front of a hoax ever since we arrived in the Cloud. Gablona and his like will never allow them to run things again."

"Simply put," Oishi said, his voice cold, "it means war."

"The Overseers, what are they really doing?" Aldin asked, putting his hands together, fingertips touching, almost as if he were praying.

He looked over at Vush.

"Do you really believe it was an accident?"

It was, of course, impossible to read this one the way he could so easily read another Human, a Gaf, or even a Xsarn. He had no experience in this, to be able to pick up the slightest nuance or gesture that could reveal far more at times than words.

"If they listened to Mupa, it was certainly an accident."

"How is that?" Hobbs asked, smiling and prompting Vush along.

"Because he is immature, foolish, everyone knew that, especially our Arch."

"Yet you claim that this Mupa was your closest friend, if such a thing is possible among the Overseers."

"That is why I can say what I said." He paused for a moment.

"Go on," Hobbs said quietly.

"I was with Mupa when he found the wormhole device."

A bit surprised, everyone in the room stirred.

He then went on to spill it all, the hidden Sphere, the decrepit First Traveler machine guarding the device, and his own suspicions of its faultiness.

The room was silent as he finished, and Vush looked around nervously, suspecting he had told far too much, but no longer really caring. Upward of ten thousand beings might have died when the machine was set off and the various ships were swallowed. Billions more might get it in the not too distant future. He was fed up with all of it.

His back started to convulse and he lowered his head. Crying was impossible for an Overseer, but he was doing as close an imitation of it as was possible for his race.

"The Sphere?" Yaroslav asked, his eyes shining with excitement. "I've heard legends of it, fragments. An artificially created star completely encased inside a hollow ball millions of kilometers across."

"It dwarfs the Ring of Kolbard," Vush whispered. "The most magnificent creation ever rendered by the First Travelers, only the Prime Mover could have done more."

"Where is it?" Yaroslav asked, fidgeting in his chair like an excited child who had just been told that a long-dreamed-for gift was waiting on the doorstep.

A bit startled, Vush looked at Yaroslav and then around to the others in the room, all of them leaning forward.

"I can't," he whispered, half curling up into a ball. Hobbs motioned for the servobot to bring another toddy. The machine glided over to Vush and held the drink up. The Overseer ignored it, and the bot, not sure of itself, just waited patiently.

"I could make you talk easily enough," Basak growled, and as he spoke he stood up, stretching out his arms, the muscles rippling under his shaggy, matted hair.

Vush looked at him wide-eyed, while Oishi cut across the room and quickly shoved the Gaf berserker and his comrades out of the room.

Vush again curled up into a tight ball.

"Perhaps we can find an answer there," Aldin said, in the most soothing voice that he could muster. He knew that just a little part of him was lying. The Ring had held him in awe. There had been rumors of the Sphere, but he believed them to be nothing but rumors. Such a thing was impossible, requiring thousands of times the mass of the Ring. Gods, to be able to see it!

He suspected that Vush could see the avarice in his eyes and he looked away.

"You are pledged to nonviolence?" Oishi asked, coming back into the room, breathing a bit hard and stepping around in front of Aldin.

Vush looked up at the samurai. He had seen him before wearing his swords, but this time the man had no weapons. He found him somehow pleasing. There was a masterful bearing and grace to him. For this occasion he was dressed in the ceremonial garments of his old world, a simple robe of white silk decorated with a stylized blue flower. It was vaguely reminiscent of the flowing robes of the Overseers. He suspected that the man was wearing it because it might be familiar, but it disarmed him nevertheless.

"It was obvious that not one of your people understood how to operate the machine," Oishi said, just the slightest tone of accusation in his voice. He had mastered the common language of the Cloud in a remarkably short time, no longer needing the translation implant, but the hint of Japanese was still there.

"Do you honestly believe that Mupa could go back to this Sphere, discover his mistake, and thus prevent a catastrophe?"

Vush hesitated, and taking up the toddy that was still waiting, he downed a long drink.

"No," he whispered sadly.

"One of us can."

Vush looked back up, staring straight into Oishi's eyes. It would not have been all so long ago when such a gaze from an Overseer would have had one of the three lesser species blubbering in fear, ready to confess to whatever sin he had committed. He sighed inwardly. Those days were obviously over with.

"I could take you to the Arch; it should be he who decides this," Vush replied, trying to find some sort of fallback position.

"Do you honestly think he would agree to that?" Yaroslav interjected, trying to force down his excitement about the Sphere.

Vush hesitated. He did not want to truly confess his darker fear, and he buried it.

"I don't think so," he finally whispered.

"Will you show us then?" Yaroslav asked, his voice becoming insistent. Oishi looked over his shoulder as if to silence him.

"Remember, a nonaction that creates evil and violence is as reprehensible as an action that creates the same. If you stand by and do nothing, the tens of thousands of years of cleansing your soul will be for naught. You might as well start all over again and take a million years while you're at it. A billion deaths on your soul, and you who worry if the salad you eat is dead before plucking."

"A million years trapped in the Hole of the Shiga would not be enough to atone for all the deaths," Hobbs whispered, even as he smiled and leaned back in his floating lounge chair, motioning for one of his young ladies to rub the rolls of fat around his neck.

Vush started to shake again, and if he could have curled into an even tighter ball and simply disappeared from existence, he would have willed it so. He did in fact try to will it, but nothing came of the effort other than a pulled muscle in his back.

He finally looked back up at the silent gathering.

"I'll do it," he sighed.

Yaroslav grinned, slapping his knee with delight. There was an audible exhaling of a collectively held breath.

"But . . ." Vush whispered.

They all stopped and looked at him.

"I will tell only one person," Vush said, looking over at Hobbs. "He will navigate the ship. He must swear a solemn oath never to reveal his knowledge, and all ship memories are to be purged."

"I'm honored by your friendship," Hobbs replied with a good-natured grin.

"But of course," Yaroslav said.

"Not him," Vush said. "Oishi."

"Damn it all," Yaroslav groaned. "He'll keep his word, too."

"Precisely," Vush replied, feeling relieved. He looked up at Oishi.

"Swear on what you honor most that you'll agree to these terms."

Oishi, his eyes shining with pride, bowed low, and then hesitating, he looked over at Aldin and bowed again.

"Am I released to make a pledge that I cannot reveal, even to my daimyo?"

"Of course," Aldin said, feeling a wave of relief.

"Then excuse me for a moment."

He left the room and returned a minute later, reverently carrying his swords, the Gaf berserkers crowding in behind him, hoping that there was going to be a fight of some sort or, better yet, a beheading.

Oishi unsheathed the two swords and placed them on the floor in front of the Overseer and then knelt down before him. Reverently he bowed to the blades.

"These were fashioned by Marimosoto, master of blades; his spirit, the spirits of my fathers, reside in them. In front of them I now pledge my word to keep secret whatever you reveal to me."

Without hesitation he took the short blade and cut open his arm, letting the blood drip on the long sword resting before him. A servobot, disturbed by the scent of the blood, turned to look and started to move over to wipe the mess up. Sogio reached out and grabbed the machine, which struggled and hooted weakly.

"I swear by my blood, the blood of my sires, the spirit of my blades to honor my word to you, and if I fail, to die by my own hand."

Vush was impressed and appalled by the ceremony. Still barbarians, drawing blood, swearing oaths. Yet there was a dignity and power to it that convinced him. He looked about the room and saw the respect that the others held for this Human.

"I will tell you as soon as you wish to speak with me," he said, and rising up unsteadily, not sure if it was from the heavily spiked toddies or from a more disturbing phenomenon of emotion, he floated out of the room.

He paused at the door and looked back nervously.

"By the way," he said sheepishly, "there is one other condition."

"What is it?" Yaroslav groaned.

"I have exclusive right to arrange any gaming possibilities that come out of your little expedition."

"Well I'll be damned." Hobbs laughed, slapping the side of his chair. "An Overseer vasba."

Aldin, taken aback, could only grin and nod his head in agreement.

Vush tried to manage a graceful turn, bounced against the door frame, and drifted out of the room.

"Damn it, Oishi, you would have to go and promise like that," Yaroslav snapped peevishly.

"Well at least you'll get to see it," Oishi replied good-naturedly, coming to his feet.

Approaching respectfully, Sogio picked up Oishi's swords and with head lowered held them out to Oishi, who took a silk cloth from his robe and wiped them down before resheathing them. Tia, coming to his side, started to fuss over the cut, but a look from him was sufficient to tell her that she was to stop.

The Gaf berserkers, their respect for Oishi going up yet higher, gathered around him, several of them furtively touching his wound or bloodstained robe and then withdrawing hurriedly to their private chambers to touch the blood to their weapons and thus give them more power.

"It'll be tough getting there," Bukha said, his voice cold.

Oishi looked over at him.

"The Arch."

"They don't have any weapons, other than some disabling equipment on some of their ships," the Xsarn replied.

"But Corbin does," Aldin said.

"Why, Corbin, he'd never figure out how to get there. Hell, we've lived in the Cloud for three thousand years and no one has ever stumbled across it."

"The Arch will tell him," Yaroslav replied.

Aldin looked over at his old friend, a bit sad to realize that both had come to the same dark conclusion.

"And when we do get there, just how the hell are we to figure this thing out?" Tia asked. "I mean, if Vush spent thousands of years prowling around the place and couldn't figure out this wormhole machine, or any of the other things of the First Travelers, how are we suppose to?"

"It's simple," Aldin replied. "We can't, but someone else can."

"Who?" Yaroslav asked, caught off guard, not willing to admit that when it came to trying to master how to shut down the wormhole, that he was as totally confused as everyone else.

"Yashima Korobachi," Aldin said quietly.

"But of course," Yaroslav said, ashamed to admit that there was someone better than him at unraveling mysteries, but thrilled at the prospect of what this implied.

Oishi looked over at Aldin, not sure why Zergh, Yaroslav, and his daimyo were excited.

"The name, I do not know it," Oishi said.

"Oishi, we're going back to Earth. We're going to jump down to the twenty-third century, using the same machine that Zergh flew to bring you through time."

"Earth? You mean back home again?"

"Japan, A.D. 2220," Yaroslav interjected. "Just before the beginning of the great wars. Korobachi cracked the secret of control of the event horizons of black holes and wormholes. He supposedly even generated a wormhole and successfully navigated through one. No one knows how he did it; the information was lost in the wars when the Gafs bombarded Earth."

He paused for a moment, looking over at Bukha.

"Don't blame me," Bukha said wearily. "I wasn't even there, and remember, you did it to us first."

Aldin could sense an argument coming and held up his hand for the two to stop. After three thousand years, whenever the topic came up, tempers usually started to flare. Ancient history could still rub a sore spot, even now.

"Yeah, but your grandfathers were," Yaroslav mumbled.

"And so were yours," one of the berserkers growled.

"Enough, damn it. After all, we are civilized gentlemen," the Xsarn interjected hotly, and everyone backed down, not willing to be subjected to the spray from a Xsarn made angry.

"Even though both your ancestors did the same to mine," the Xsarn whispered underneath his fetid breath.

"We go back, snatch the guy, bring him with us to the Sphere, and let him figure it out," Yaroslav said excitedly. "Damn, I'd love to see him at work. Heaven knows what he might be able to figure out inside that thing. He'll shut down the wormhole in no time, and then we can take over the First Traveler stuff for ourselves."

"There's just one problem," the Xsarn said.

"What's that?" Yaroslav asked.

"There're only two ships to go back in time, one of them parked on my home world."

"Well, we'll just have to sneak down there and get it," Zergh said. "I've flown it before."

"You forget you're outlaws and Alpha Xsarn is in the center of the Core Cluster."

"I guess sneaking us in is up to you," Aldin said. "There's no other way around it."

"We'll have to abandon this ship and pile everyone aboard mine," the Xsarn said.

"Gods, a Xsarn hive ship," Hobbs groaned. "The stink will kill us!"

Aldin found himself hesitating. It was going to be hell.

"There's no other alternative," the Xsarn said. "We blow this ship up to cover your traces; it should throw the pursuit off for a while."

Several of the Gaf berserkers fell into making retching noises, but an angry look from Oishi silenced them.

"It will have to be that way," Oishi announced as if the argument were closed.

"Let's get started moving our gear," Aldin finally said, his mouth going dry at the thought of being aboard a Xsarn ship.

With a clattering shrug of his six arms, the Xsarn nodded and walked out of the room.

"So who has the other time-jump ship? We can always get that if going to Xsarn prime is too dangerous," Hobbs said as if offering out a hopeful alternative.

Aldin chuckled sadly and shook his head.

"The other one is most likely in the possession of Corbin Gablona."

It had been twenty years or more since he had been to the Prime Hive World of the Xsarns. He was not looking forward to it.

The traffic patterns through the jump points in were not at all what he expected. Interstellar fares had quadrupled for any passage originating from those planets closest to the runaway wormhole to any that were further out. There wasn't a yacht, freighter, cruise ship, or junk scow that wasn't converging in to pick up passengers who would pay damn near anything to get out. Most of the old corporation ships were busy pulling out their upper-level management people and giving a high priority to valuable office equipment. Traffic control had broken down, with ships leaping through holding patterns and the automated sentinels handing out tickets at a record rate.

One Xsarn yacht, heading in the opposite direction, needed only to worry about the congestion and the possibility of somebody running on the wrong side of the lanes, thus creating a head-on collision, an event that would for a brief instant glow as bright as the convulsing new star.

The Prime Hive of the Xsarns would, at least for the moment, be a fairly safe place, at least as long as the Xsarn Prime was Xsarn Prime. Aldin had never been able to quite figure out all the nuances of Xsarn rule and society. There were times when they appeared to experience a collective mentality, something he was almost sure happened when they gathered into one of their mating balls and for their various religious ceremonies that took up a good part of their yearly cycle. There were other times when their behavior seemed erratic in the extreme. There was a very strange phenomenon that would occur at times when one of them would form a large ball of mud and Xsarn food and roll it along whatever magnetic north line was handy until it dropped from exhaustion. Then another would roll it back to the original spot. The first would revive, go back, and push the ball north again, endlessly repeating the cycle until one or the other died of exhaustion. The Xsarn Prime, when asked about this, would only repeat one of their favorite lines, which appeared to be universal to all three species but had a special appeal to Xsarn humor: "Shit happens."

Lining up for final approach behind several food import ships, which he half believed he could smell even through the vacuum of space, Aldin finally turned the con over to the Xsarn Prime. His mandibles clicking excitedly, the Xsarn guided the ship in, swooping down through the atmosphere, breaking the final approach line to dock directly at the main terminus of his own private hive.

As the hatch was released the Xsarn strode out, waving his antennae high, thousands of identical-looking Xsarns swarming about the ship. Following behind him, Aldin took one deep breath and gagged at the overpowering stench that he suddenly believed was a full magnitude worse than the stench within the ship.

"Ah, home," the Xsarn sighed.

"Not exactly what I'd call it," Yaroslav growled, putting a scented handkerchief to his face, while most of the others donned gas filter masks that were filled with various scents to block out the smell, a convenience Aldin and Bukha had to do without due to diplomatic niceties.

Stepping off the ramp, Aldin followed the Xsarn, nearly deafened by the rhythmic banging as the members of the reception committee started to beat on their carapaces with all six arms, a drumming that thundered and rolled over them like a storm. Then came the part that he was dreading—the ritual of the communal sharing of food. Five thousand Xsarns, acting as if one, sprayed up the contents of their last half-dozen meals, the air turning instantly into a dark shadow of foaming mist. The Xsarns now started to roar with delight, dancing under the rain of food, turning their faces up to catch the shower, rubbing it over themselves, the Xsarn Prime being covered from the top of his antennae to his clawed feet in a single instant.

Exuberant Xsarns ran up to the Xsarn Prime's companions and treated them to the same friendly greeting. For a brief instant Aldin could hear Mari's high shrill laugh coming from the ship as she hid within, witnessing her husband's greeting. The laugh was cut short by a wailing shriek as a Xsarn clambered aboard and gave her a similar treatment. The servobots aboard the ship hooted in high-pitched distress as the gallons of regurgitated Xsarn food sprayed across shag carpets.

Unable to contain himself, Aldin leaned over, adding his meal to the ritual, his companions whipping off their gas masks to join in. The Xsarns, delighted at such a gesture of friendliness, redoubled their efforts to make these rare guests feel right at home. Several of the Gaf berserkers, however, delighted with the absolutely overwhelming display and laughing at the spectacle, set into dancing and waving their weapons. The Xsarns, deeply moved by the good manners and enthusiasm, surrounded the Gafs, lifting them up in the air so that those pressing in from the back could project their meals onto these remarkable friends.

"Your guards are making an excellent impression," the Xsarn Prime shouted, trying to be heard above the clattering, roaring, and retching.

Aldin, almost down on his knees from the convulsions, could not even respond as he was pushed through the crowd.

"No wonder this place is so low on the tourist circuit," Yaroslav groaned.

Aldin sniffed at his clothes. He knew that they had been stored aboard the ship, and as such had not received the Xsarn greeting treatment. Though highly insulted, the Xsarn Prime had at last relented and allowed him, along with Zergh, Tia, Basak, Yaroslav, Vush, and Oishi, to depart in secret and thus avoid the even more disturbing farewell ceremony, which, if it were possible, was even more disgusting. Hobbs finally managed to get aboard ship as well with an emotional and most likely correct argument that Corbin and the Overseers would kill him on sight and that there was no place to hide until this war was over.

"In close fighting, they'd always win," Oishi said, sitting pale beside Aldin. They've got natural armor against arrows, and when it came to sword fighting range, they'd only have to greet you." He shuddered slightly, an exhausted servobot looking over at him anxiously.

"I hope you enjoyed your stay," the Xsarn Prime said, a light tone of amusement in his voice, his face filling the commlink screen.

In the background Aldin could hear Mari cursing wildly.

"Take good care of the guests," Aldin said, not able to hide a slight chuckle.

"Larice, this is it!" Mari shouted across the link. "I'll divorce you for this, clean you out for everything you've got, dumping me in this damn shit hole planet."

Though it was impossible to read emotion in a Xsarn's eyes, his drooping antennae were signal enough that he was not amused with Aldin's decision to leave Mari behind. There was simply not enough room in the ship, Aldin had argued, truthfully enough. Except for his chosen companions, Vush who was hiding in his room, and the replacement Humanbot stored below deck, everyone else was being left behind. Bukha would depart later, along with the Xsarn to try to link back up with some of the other Kohs. The samurai guards were none too happy, but the Gaf berserkers were delighted. He suspected that down deep they were most likely struggling for control, but after the riotous reception given to those who had thrown themselves into the ceremony, the others, no matter how their stomachs might feel, had to best their companions or suffer the shame of it. They were already boasting to each other how they would outdo each other in the departure ceremony, and several, to the shock of the Xsarn, had requested the honor of joining in a mating ball. Disgusting crudity was a badge of honor to a Gaf berserker.

"We'll be back in twenty days," Aldin said, nodding a farewell to the commlink screen.

"If there's anything to come back to," Yaroslav quipped.

As they gained escape velocity and turned toward the first jump gate that would start them on their long journey back into the old galaxy, Mari's cursing could be heard in the background. With a smile Aldin turned the switch off and settled back for the long journey back to the Milky Way, which shone brightly off the starboard side.

At jump-point terminus MW1, the only jump transit back to the Milky Way, a lone ship poised for acceleration. There was no need to bring others in to try to block anyone who followed. For that matter he was hoping he'd be followed, for there would certainly be a surprise at the other end.

With a nod of command, Corbin Gablona signaled the ship to accelerate up and head into the jump point. He looked over cautiously at Hassan. At least in this type of situation Hassan still needed him, could not survive without him. For the moment, at least, he was back in control.

Hitting the jump point, the vessel leaped through the translight line and disappeared, heading straight down toward the Milky Way, a hundred and fifty thousand light-years away. This single jump line back to the old system was also the only door into the past.

chapter seven

Bracing for the gut-wrenching jump-down transition, Aldin Larice checked the calibration for what he knew must be the hundredth time.

It had been a laborious run down the jump line back to the Milky Way. Most other leaps were near instantaneous, but those were rarely for more than several hundred light-years, the longest within the entire cloud being out to the Kolbard Ring, a twelve thousand light-year leap. For some as yet unexplainable reason, part of the mystery of just how or why jump transition worked, duration of flight grew at an exponential rate. Given the incredible amount of energy required to maintain jump, any run much beyond that distance was totally out of the question.

How the First Travelers had ever managed to chart out the lines, discover the null points, lay out the markers and danger buoys, was beyond him. The discovery of jump was, in itself, shrouded in mystery for all three species, who appeared to have discovered it nearly simultaneously, thus triggering the outward leap from their respective solar systems, and the Great Wars for control of interstellar space, which eventually devastated most of the inhabitable planets of the old galaxy.

He had to give the damn Overseers their due. If they had not broken the cycle of violence in the Magellanic Cloud, the wars would most likely have resulted in the annihilation of all three species, the few survivors stranded on remote planets, reverting to prespace civilizations.

Granted, the Overseers were overbearing in the extreme with their holier-than-thou preaching, their constant seizure of the moral high ground from which to moralize. They reminded him far too much of the damned professional cause-seekers, who raced from moral issue to moral issue, weeping one month over the rights of criminal psychopaths being so cruelly mistreated by exile with their own kind to orbital prisons, the next month lamenting the insensitivity of someone laughing about Gaf trisexual cross-dressers. Anyone who disagreed with such individuals was branded insensitive, barbaric, incorrect, and Neanderthalishly phobic. He didn't mind someone telling him he might be wrong, but when someone told him he was definitely wrong, especially for daring to disagree with an accuser who knew he was morally superior, it simply grated on his nerves. The Overseers had been doing that for thousands of years. He knew he'd miss the order they provided, he'd do anything to bring it back, but he could only hope that at least in the future they'd shut the hell up.

He was surprised that there hadn't been an Overseer ship blocking the jump point back to the Milky Way. There must have been some sort of security system to reveal that he had hopped right into the Core Cluster and then back out again.

It was all going a little too easily.

He looked over at Zergh and Yaroslav, who were checking the calibration of the time-transit system. This was going to be the hard part.

"Not to worry," Yaroslav said, though it sounded as if he were reassuring himself as much as he was trying to put Aldin at ease.

A shudder ran through the ship and, with a spectacular Doppler shift, it went through jump transition. They were back in the Milky Way.

He had only been here once before, and he looked over his shoulder as Tia came into the forward room, Oishi by her side.

"Last time was when we came for Alexander the Great," she said with a grin.

"And you were one royal pain in the ass," he replied with a smile.

She laughed playfully and kissed him on his balding crown.

"Where is home?" Oishi asked, his voice betraying his eagerness to see Earth once again. Cherry blossoms, unfortunately, were something unknown in the Cloud, and he had finally convinced Aldin that if there was time he could go down and try to get a couple of shoots.

"Somewhere right over there," Yaroslav said, pointing out the window. Oishi pressed himself against the forward viewport.

"So far from the center," he said, as if almost disappointed.

"The Gavarnian homeworld is closer in," Zergh interjected with a faint touch of superiority. It was a point of Gaf pride that Humans were definitely from the outback and thus of lower breeding.

"At least we don't have the Xsarn along," Yaroslav said. "They get so damn touchy about the war and what it did to their home planet, he'd most likely puke on all of us before he was done."

"Well, they did start it," Zergh said.

"Like hell, it was you Gafs," Aldin replied, sounding professorial when the topic came to military history.

"From the viewpoint of a neutral observer, you're all to blame," Vush said, floating in to join them. "After the incident at Vak, all three of you started shooting within microseconds of each other, the rest is history until we so foolishly stopped you."

It was the first time he had come out of his cabin since they had left Alpha Xsarn, and Aldin found he was almost glad to see him. The secret location of the Sphere was locked up with this one individual, and his health had suddenly become a very important issue.

"Ever been here before?" Oishi asked.

Vush tried to shake his head, but since Overseer necks did not articulate well, his entire body turned back and forth.

"If you mean to this particular vantage point, I have not. Though I did come—"

He stopped himself.

"So there is another jump point!" Yaroslav said triumphantly. "Come on, if you weren't here, there's got to be another jump point."

"I've said too much already," Vush said sulkily.

"It's all right. Now don't say another word," Oishi interjected, feeling a sort of friendship toward Vush ever since making his pledge of secrecy to him.

Vush nodded and floated over to the window. Yaroslav was tempted to ask him some more questions, but a look from Oishi stopped him.

"I'd almost forgotten how vast it all is," Vush whispered, as if speaking to himself. "So limitless, all of space. So quiet, just the four of us, the three of you and us, all that is self-aware, except for the First Travelers, wherever it is they now hide."

He looked back at the group.

"Your language is so limited, so pale to all of this," Vush said softly. "Even the ten million words that shape my thoughts cannot give justice to the grandeur of eternity."

He silently floated out of the room, the door sliding shut behind him.

"A damn philosopher no less," Yaroslav growled, though obviously moved by the poignancy in Vush's voice.

"Actually, I kind of like him," Oishi replied.

Ten days after the wormhole was activated, the inner layers of carbon-oxygen of the red giant were long gone, exploding out of the new star at the other end of the link. The next layer up of helium burning at well over one hundred million degrees K now funneled into the wormhole, coursing in an instant into the heart of the new star, boiling up through the material already there, the star shifting in an instant into the beginnings of a red giant that was already nearly two times the mass of a standard yellow sun. A flat spiral of glowing hydrogen was, at the same time, spinning down the outside length of the wormhole, pulled along by the intense gravitational field induced by the tremendous amount of mass moving at translight speed through the dimensional pipeline. Occasional flickers were still giving birth to independent wormholes, some of which ejected matter into other dimensions and even other times.

A minor footnote of Gaf history could thus be explained, when three thousand years before a yacht, carrying the lover of a Gaf princess, disappeared in the region, the incident being blamed on a Xsarn exploration ship, thus triggering the seventh Gaf-Xsarn war. The mourned lover was, in fact, now percolating inside the new star, pulled through by an errant wormhole that had jumped time. Another wormhole, flung completely out of the system, popped through a jump-transit line, crossed time, and by sheer chance drilled through a distant Earth, causing the mysterious disappearance of an ancient union leader, of dubious moral character, involved in the business of moving goods on land with internal combustion machines; it popped him, complete with smoking cigar and Cadillac, back into the boiling sun.

Inside of it all, at the very core of the event, the well-crafted First Traveler wormhole-maker chugged along.

* * *

"Time-transition jump." Aldin and Zergh gazed intently at the instrument panel, both of them holding their breath.

"Now!"

For a fraction of a second Aldin thought the machine had malfunctioned. An instant later there was a rapid Doppler shift. Unlike jump-point transitions where there was a tiny cone of visible star patterns straight ahead, everything went totally blank.

"June 18, 2220," Aldin called, double-checking the panel, "the day before the Great Wars start."

A curious vibration ran through the vessel, one that set his teeth to chattering. If jump transitions were tough on the constitution, this was far worse, and he inwardly cursed the day, so long ago, when he and Zergh playfully suggested the possibilities of time travel to their old employer—Corbin Gablona. Several billion katars later he had actually pulled it off, one of the most expensive construction and research projects in history, all to be able to bring back various generals and warriors to support the games. The theory of exactly why it all worked was still a complete mystery, even to those who had made the system.

He had chosen the date with care. Less than a day later the Vak incident would occur, and with it the conflagration that would sweep across the entire galaxy. Yashima's work had been completed, and he was living in retirement at a remote villa on the northern island of Hokkaido. The timing was such that there was no chance of disturbing history. The Humanbot could be altered to replace him and away they would go, a full day before a crazed assassin would burst into his villa and gun him down.

They soared inward, hitting the time-jump line, and with a sickening lurch the backward count of the system started to click through with blinding speed.

"Just a couple of more seconds," Yaroslav said, and Oishi stood up excitedly, moving toward the forward viewscreen, which would suddenly fill with Earth.

Before he was even fully aware of it, everything seemed to go wrong at once. The ship somehow managed to pull a full inverted roll, the inertial dampening system a full second behind, thus spilling everybody to the ceiling before sucking them back up again into their old positions. Zergh, tumbling through the air, roared a quick string of Gaf imprecations before slamming into the control panel. Like a chip of wood on a storm-tossed sea, the craft bobbed and weaved and then finally settled down.

"What the shit?" Aldin shouted, looking over at Zergh, who was slowly sliding down the side of the control panel and dropping back into his chair.

The door flung open behind them, and Vush floated in, moving horizontally rather than vertically, a trace of yellow-green blood pouring down from a cut head.

"Something's jumbled the field," Zergh shouted, cursing as he tried to mop a spilled cup of coffee off a set of monitors, a servobot shouldering him aside to do the job.

"What?"

"I said something jumbled the field ahead of us."

Aldin groaned and sat back, nursing a bump on his head.

"I think we've got a problem," Zergh whispered, pointing to one of the monitors.

Aldin looked over at it.

"How, damn it?" he roared.

"I guess I bumped into one of the dials," Zergh said weakly, trying to force a smile.

Yashima Korobachi, overwhelmed with sadness, stepped out onto the porch of his villa. A weak sun was breaking through the morning clouds, glinting off the high-cresting waves of the cold Pacific. Angry gulls circled overhead, distraught that he who was always so free with gifts was this morning ignoring them.

Waves. He could remember as a small boy when his grandfather would bring him to this place. When the tide was rushing out, there was a small pool down in the rocks where a whirlpool would on occasion form. Perhaps that is where it all started, the fascination of a small boy squatting on a rock, throwing chips of wood in, watching them swirl around and disappear.

He smiled.

The news, damn them. Couldn't they see where his thoughts could now lead them? Infinity, the limitless universe, all dreamed of in his mind and now made within reach. And they were going to end it all.

He reached into his pocket and pulled out a crust of bread,

and breaking it into pieces, he fed his friends who wheeled overhead.

He did not even hear the crackling of the beam, nor see the coalescence of the hooded man who appeared behind him, nor hear the crack of the Erik 10 that sent him into the long sleep.

"Someone jumped through ahead of us," Aldin said, cursing and slamming his fist on the console. "Once someone does a jump into a particular time, it's impossible to do it ever again through that entry point. The disturbance wake almost killed us."

"So find another time-transition point," Vush said hopefully.

"We don't know of any," Yaroslav said coldly. "Gablona got to him ahead of us. We've only got enough energy for this one jump and we just did it."

"Whatever for? Why would Gablona come here?" Vush asked, still not understanding the confusion around him.

"To keep us from getting him, stupid," Yaroslav snapped.

Oishi, straightening out his clothes, struggled back to his feet and looked out the forward window. Earth hovered before him, and he felt his eyes cloud with tears; it was far more beautiful than he ever imagined possible. He looked back expectantly at Aldin, the needs of their mission, at least for this brief moment, forgotten.

"It's home, Oishi," Aldin said, forcing a smile. Then he looked over at Zergh.

"Just when the hell are we?" Aldin asked.

"Well the date is right at least," Zergh said quietly, "It's still June eighteenth."

"But what year?"

Zergh chuckled and scratched his head.

"Either the wave disturbance did it, or . . ." His voice trailed off. "When I fell back on the panel I spun the entry date a little bit."

"To?" Aldin asked peevishly.

"A nice round change it was, we're only off by exactly four hundred years."

Yaroslav looked over his shoulder and sighed.

"June 18, 1820. Just what the hell good is that when we're looking for a wormhole physicist?"

"Well it's better than nothing," Zergh said lamely. "At least I got us here."

"This is a fine mess we've gotten into," Yaroslav said, disgusted.

"Anyhow, now that we're here," Zergh said, a sudden smile lighting his features, "there's no sense in going home empty-handed."

The sounds in the garden had finally died away. The sentry had managed his rendezvous with the serving girl, and together they had their brief moment. He was tempted to stir from bed, to pull back the shutter, lean out, and tell them to be quiet. Soldiers could be like children. He remembered when they were his children, the finest soldiers ever to march across Europe, who would look at him with adulation, their eyes damp, joyfully offering their deaths for his glory.

He could not begrudge a soldier, even an English soldier, his brief moment of living.

Living.

He sighed and swung his legs off the bed, letting them rest on the cold wooden floor. The room was dank, a slight scent of damp mold in the air. In the dark, at least, he could forget the shabbiness. How many palaces had he slept in, the poor son of alleged Corsican nobility. Paris, Madrid, Cairo, Vienna, Berlin, and the cold rooms of the Kremlin. Even his campaign tent was better—the whispers outside of it that of his old grumblers, Imperial Guard of a dozen campaigns, silencing the camp when they thought him asleep, his children watching over him like hovering parents. The night before battle he would come out of the tent, showing the outward calm, the quiet self-assurance that would then flood through his army, convincing them that live or die, in the morn victory for France was assured.

Sleep would not come. Funny, he thought, I never really needed it before, it was the robber, sent to steal the precious hours when so much needed to be done. Now he longed for it, when the stillness of the last watch of night was at its deepest. Now it would not steal upon him and drown the pain, the memories.

Napoleon Bonaparte sighed heavily, leaning forward slightly, tucking his hands over his bloated stomach to try to hold in the pain, to prevent it from sweeping outward. Should he call his servant?

No. Let him sleep awhile longer. How many countless times

had he seen men sitting like he now did, clutching their stomachs, looking up at him with watery eyes, trying to hold their lives in, knowing that the darkness was coming. Some would force a smile—"just a scratch my Emperor," "long live France," "did we win?"

He had lost all sense of pity long ago and could look upon the thousands dead and dying and not feel a stirring. If a general ever did, he could no longer be a general. Now he knew what it must feel like, the pain, and he pitied them all, and himself.

I'm dying. He wanted it to come, the pain gnawing up inside him. I've been dead for five years already. They should not have stopped me. I should have gone back up to the guard as they covered my retreat, I should have picked up the flag, as I once did at Arcola. He smiled for a brief instant with that memory. How legends had been built around that, the wonderful painting by David—his picking up the fallen flag, leading the charge across the bridge. It was hard now even in memory to separate the truth from the legend . . . the legend was better, of course.

I should have died within my legend, not lingering here. There would be no more paintings by David, no *Victory at Marengo* marches, no return to the palace, Josephine, damn her, waiting, unwashed as ordered, or so many of the others who joyfully slipped into his room. He thought for a moment of the maid out in the garden with the soldier. He had flirted with her and she had smiled at him only the day before, and he heard her whisper later how he was a charming old man. Just an old man now, he thought with a sigh. Dying from a fire within, dying chained to this damnable rock.

Five years ago today . . . Waterloo, and now this.

He tried to stand up, his spindly legs trembling, his stomach, bloated, burning, the pain cutting through. Never again would there be what was. If only there could be the release, to dream, to once again be as it was.

"To die." The words were a sigh.

"France," he whispered, "France . . . *armée* . . . *Tête d'armée* . . . Josephine."

A shimmer of light began to form in the center of the room, which until the coming of the exile had been a pigsty. For a brief second he was not even sure if it was real, an illusion, or the summoning of the angel of death.

The light took shape, a human shape, growing brighter. The air that was within the cylinder of light rushed out with a gust, fluttering the worn curtains. Napoleon tried to straighten up, to face the end standing. He smiled; there was no fear, never such a low thing as fear, though for the first time in years, and not even aware of it, he made the sign of the cross.

The light shifted through a dazzling display of colors, and then with an audible pop the shape became real.

"Are you an angel?"

"Hardly, my emperor."

The accent was atrocious. But it had called him emperor! He was willing to forgive just to again hear the sound of the words.

Aldin Larice felt a surge of joy and yet also one of painful disappointment. He was standing in the presence of the emperor, Napoleon Bonaparte. Yet such a difference from the first time he had seen Alexander. Though dying, Alexander had still retained an almost godlike beauty, a power even at the edge of death. Napoleon looked like a man defeated, an old man who was waiting for but one final appointment. And he felt a surge of pity. In this musty room languished the greatest mind of the revolutionary age, the dreamer of empires, trapped by his own ambitions and defeat.

In a perverse way this was nothing but a tourist stop. There was no use for Napoleon in the crisis of his time. What use was this dying man, when it was a wormhole physicist that he had sought? Accident alone had brought him here. But as a vasba he could not be in this time without meeting him. Before all the madness of the games had started, bringing Napoleon into the future would have been viewed as a coup, as spectacular as fetching Alexander had been. And yet Zergh, who had a fascination with Napoleon, had said it all—that while they were in the neighborhood it would be impolite not to drop in, and perhaps offer a hand. Yaroslav, however, had come close to throwing a tantrum, denouncing Napoleon as a brutal murderer, and when outvoted by the group, he threatened to stay on Earth rather than ride in the same ship with the emperor.

"If you are not an angel," Napoleon asked, "then tell me, who and what you are?"

There was a wonderful command to his voice, instantly relayed and translated through Aldin's voice implant.

"Well," Aldin said, not quite sure where to start, "we were

passing through the area, and thought you might like to come along for the ride."

"A ride?"

"Call it a little trip, Excellency. A chance to get off this god-forsaken rock and live again."

The last thing Aldin Larice ever expected to see was Napoleon Bonaparte cry.

"He's a hell of a mess," Tia said, coming back into the room. Though everyone else except Yaroslav was awed by the fact that the emperor was in the next room, Oishi could barely contain himself from taking Tia over to the far corner of the forward cabin where he proudly pointed out a dozen tiny saplings. Napoleon, a hundred years in Oishi's future, meant nothing. The cherry trees were far more important.

"It was still the same," Oishi said, his voice choked with emotion. "The grave of my first lord Asano still honored. A temple is nearby and monks pray near his remains. There were even fresh flowers upon it."

His eyes filled with tears and he shyly brushed them away.

"Then I walked through the town, and would you believe it, I saw a Kabuki play, a play about us, me, *The Forty-Seven Ronin*. He chuckled. "I brought the cherry saplings. Little did that woman know how precious they truly were, to a time when no such things exist.

"And then I could not help it, I had to see. If only they knew the real truth of what happened to us. I asked a man to show me the grave of the Forty-Seven Ronin, and he took me to it. There was my name." He paused. "And yet so many of us are gone," he continued, his voice quiet. "Takashi. Only thirty of us left."

"Thirty who would be dead otherwise," Aldin said, looking over at one of his closest friends with deep-felt emotion. There were times when he wondered about the morality of all that he had done. But if he had not, Oishi and the other samurai would be dead. Alexander would be dust. And the man in the next room?

"How bad off is he?" Aldin asked.

"The medbots are finishing up the examination right now."

"Those damned things," Yaroslav sniffed. "I'd be damned if I let myself get treated by one of them."

"Corbin spent a bundle on them," Zergh replied. "When we

planned to bring Alexander back we figured he'd be in bad shape. There was no sense spending billions on this and then scrimp a million or two more only to let him die."

"Well, they better be good," Tia said. "He's got arteriosclerosis, some minor neural deterioration that must have been affecting his thought process, a hell of a nasty dose of tapeworms, advancing rheumatism, astigmatism, and damned if he isn't suffering from arsenic poisoning."

"Ah, yes, your typical ancient Human," Zergh said, with an air of superiority.

"Poisoning?" Aldin asked, looking up with professional curiosity.

"Damn stuff was eating right through him. His stomach was chewed to hell. The medbots will be working flat-out for a couple of days to bring him back on line. I figured we should let him rest up a little bit, tell him what's going on, before going to work on him. The guy was just going crazy with questions, especially when it finally started to sink in that we're from his future."

"The replacement unit integrated in all right?"

"He was dropped in a couple of minutes ago," Tia said. "It was a quick programming and change job, remember we thought we could just drop him off for our physicist friend who was going to get killed when the war started. This one had to be perfect, able to withstand an autopsy. It was a near thing. A guard peeked in the window just when we finished the transfer and ran off. Fortunately he'd had a couple of drinks, and his sergeant cuffed him around and then led him away."

"I heard a story about what they did to him at the autopsy. How a little something, a very little something was taken by one of the doctors as a souvenir. So thanks for letting me do that final check-over of his body before it got taken out of the mold," Yaroslav said with a smile.

"So that's why you wanted to make that change," Aldin said.

"I think it's disgusting," Tia interjected.

"He's got enough of an inflated ego as is," Yaroslav replied. "I'm glad history will think he was indeed small, indeed microscopic in at least one aspect of his life."

Zergh, at last catching on as to what Yaroslav had done to Napoleon's replacement unit, growled angrily.

"Well, now that we've got him, what the hell are we going to do with him?" Hobbs asked, his voice flat with dejection.

"Why, send him to the wormhole and let him figure it out," Yaroslav replied.

Zergh sniffed disdainfully and looked away.

"Look, as Zergh said earlier," Aldin interjected, "while we were in the area it wouldn't hurt to pick him up. You know, if ever there's a future game, it'd be great to have him around."

"It's still not going to help us any," Yaroslav said.

"You talk like he's a toy or something," Aldin replied sharply. "He's the Emperor Napoleon."

"All right. So now we have the Emperor Napoleon. We've failed to get the help we needed. We've got to go back home. It'll take months to get this bucket ready for another jump to look for someone else, say Einstein or Pradap Singh, for instance."

"Einstein," Aldin corrected him.

"As I said. By that time heaven alone knows what the wormhole will have eaten. Gablona obviously has the man we wanted, and the Overseers still have a price on our head. Civilization is about to collapse. What the hell are we going to do?"

"It sounds like you have a problem."

Startled, Aldin turned to the door. Napoleon, wearing a baggy hospital robe, stood before him. It was obvious that the man was badly shaken, and somewhat frightened by the disk of the Earth floating in the forward window. Yet, in a masterful display, he came into the room, hands behind his back, the only signal of his nervousness the twitching of his tightly interlaced fingers.

"Aldin Larice?"

His voice was slightly raspy, not quite catching the uplift of the final syllable to signify a question. He had already received the microscopic neural translating unit and had been instructed in its use, but the unit was still adjusting to the idiosyncracies of early nineteenth-century French, laced with a Corsican accent.

Aldin stood up, feeling a bit satisfied that here was someone to whom he could speak eye to eye.

Napoleon came forward and in a gracious gesture extended his hand, which Aldin took.

"I do not understand the hows of all of this." He looked

around the room, giving a bit of a start at the sight of Zergh, who stood up to his full seven-foot height.

"An intelligent being from another world, sir," Tia said, poking Zergh in the ribs.

"Looks almost like an overgrown dog," Napoleon said.

Zergh growled softly.

"No insult intended, of course."

"That's quite all right, Humans are noted for such mistakes," Zergh replied, grinning with a full display of sharpened canines.

Napoleon, not missing a beat, chuckled, and releasing Aldin's hand he went over and offered it to Zergh.

The Gaf vasba smiled genuinely this time and shook it warmly.

"Would you care for some muscatel?" Zergh asked.

Oishi, clearing his throat, stepped past Zergh and snapped his fingers to a servobot.

"Napoleon brandy," Oishi ordered.

The bot put a snifter beneath the universal dispenser and rolled forward, offering the drink up.

"Napoleon brandy," the emperor said, smiling with delight, looking closely at the bot.

"Why don't we offer him some beef Wellington," Yaroslav whispered, a comment that Aldin was glad their guest did not hear.

"What is this?" Napoleon asked, looking down at the bot.

"An automatona" Aldin said. "A machine to serve us and to clean up the place."

"Ingenious."

He looked back at Oishi.

"Japan?"

Oishi smiled and nodded.

"Good warriors, I heard; the best swordsmen in the world. Samurai I believe you are called?"

Oishi grunted with approval and bowed low at the compliment.

Next he turned to Tia, and smiling, he approached her; with a slight incline of his head he took her hand and kissed it lightly.

"Mademoiselle, I am honored to be in your company."

Tia, a bit flustered, looked over at Aldin, who smiled warmly, and at Oishi, who remained silent.

Napoleon, catching her eye movement, looked over at Oishi and nodded his head again.

"You are fortunate to be married to one of such beauty, and she to be married to one of such bravery."

"And you are the philosopher Yaroslav," Napoleon said, graciously dropping Tia's hand and looking over at the old man sitting in the corner.

"Philosopher?" Yaroslav sniffed. "Did Tia tell you that?"

"A compliment to disarm you," Napoleon replied, still smiling and coming over to offer his hand.

"Such familiarity from an emperor," Yaroslav said, his tone ever so slightly ironic.

"To command in this situation?" Napoleon said, looking around, letting his confusion show for the briefest of moments. "Would it do me much good?"

"I doubt it," Yaroslav replied.

"There you have it then. You see that I have made a tactical withdraw in order to be able to gain a strategic advantage."

"Like you did in Russia?"

Aldin could sense the bristling between the two. There was the slightest of flickers, and then ever so gradually a smile crossed Napoleon's features.

"I am told that this is the future, at least for me," he said, looking back over at Aldin.

"By several thousand years, once we return."

Napoleon nodded.

"And yet still I am remembered."

"Next to Alexander, as one of the greatest generals of history."

"Ah, yes, Alexander, a worthy rival for glory and fame."

"And better looking than you, too," Yaroslav replied.

Napoleon looked back at the old man.

"You are picking a quarrel with me, sir," he said slowly.

Yaroslav smiled. "But of course."

"Someday, maybe later," he said softly. "But not now. I will confess to be in your debt. I sense there is a crisis. Such things I have faced before. I am eager to face them again."

Yaroslav was silent, Aldin looking over at him with barely suppressed rage.

The door slid open again, and Vush entered the room. Napoleon could not help but step backward in shock at the sight of an Overseer.

"They are a bit unsettling at first sight," Yaroslav said, loud enough for Vush to hear.

"Is this the Human scientist of wormholes?" Vush asked.

"Not exactly," Yaroslav replied, a trace of a grin crossing his face.

"Then what is it?"

"Oh, only a damn good killer, one of our best."

Vush looked at Napoleon, and with a groan turned and floated back out of the room, the single word "damn" floating on the air.

"You delight in annoying everyone, don't you," Napoleon said, looking back and smiling.

"It can be one of the best things in life. The more self-important they are, the bigger the bubble to burst."

"You do it well," Napoleon replied. With a flourish he downed the rest of his brandy.

"An excellent drink," he said with a smile. "And now if mademoiselle will be so kind as to show me back to the hospital, I will confess that the pain is starting to master my composure."

Nodding to each in turn, he started for the door, Tia coming up to him solicitously to take his arm, surprised by how much he suddenly needed to lean upon her for support. Yet he stopped for a moment and looked back.

"I suspect that you are indeed in serious trouble. It is easy to surmise by your need to travel into the past to find help and by the behavior of that being who came in here. You came to find someone else you needed more, and I am just a substitute that was not intended, nor I suspect viewed as any use other than a nostalgia. Fate has her reasons for casting me here. My star is not yet ready to set, and I will be of service as you need it." He nodded again and slowly, struggling for a graceful exit, left the room.

"Well, I'll be damned," Yaroslav said, smiling and shaking his head. "Before it's done, I bet that son of a bitch will get the better of all of us."

"Why don't you like him?"

"Oh, of course, I just love him," Yaroslav said. "Who couldn't, once you get past the fact that the bastard killed somewhere around a million men by the time his wars were done."

"Alexander did the same," Zergh said.

"Maybe the further back in history, the less the pain comes through. It's just I always thought Alexander was driven by a desire to unite our entire world, much as Kubar Taug did yours. To bring about a universal peace under Hellenic enlightenment."

"Napoleon started out believing the revolutionary ideals of the Enlightenment," Aldin said. "It was a dream of uniting the western world two hundred years ahead of its time and ending the reign of nobility over that of ability."

"I never quite saw him that way," Yaroslav replied sharply. "Did you see how he worked each of us in turn? He's masterful."

"And you can't quite tolerate two such individuals in the same room," Zergh replied, "especially when one of them isn't you."

Yaroslav looked over at Zergh and replied with an obscure Gaf hand gesture that was nearly impossible for Humans to make and thus elicited a roar of delight at the absurdity of it.

Tia came back into the room, a worried look in her eyes.

"That little show of his was incredible, considering the pain he must be in."

"A showman of the first degree," Yaroslav replied.

"Well, he's out of action for the next couple of days. The medbots have their work cut out for them; purging out heavy-metal poisoning is a bitch."

"And just wait for the tapeworms. Too bad we don't have a Xsarn along, they'd love it, might even see them as a distant cousin," Yaroslav interjected.

"You're disgusting," Tia snapped.

"Always a pleasure."

"Well, let's head for home," Aldin said. "We'll try and figure out what to do on the way back in."

Punching the ship around, he quickly lined up on the time-jump line, and with a forward surge, the ship accelerated, hitting its maximum speed within minutes. Three thousand years were leaped in a matter of seconds.

Pushing through the next two transition points, Aldin spared a quick break from the controls to sneak back into the med room. The medbots hovered over their charge, half a dozen working at once, the body of Napoleon covered in a maze of monitors, wires, and control units. Though it played with his all-too-weak stomach, he could not help but watch, fascinated.

It was almost as if they were taking him apart from top to bottom, cleaning, repairing, draining, patching. A kidney too thoroughly impregnated with the arsenic was pulled out and replaced with a synthetic substitute, grown in the same manner as a Humanbot's organs. It was a treatment that, so unfairly he thought, only the richest of Kohs could afford, thus far extending their lives by repairing the ravages of their dissipation. He had snatched Napoleon only months from his demise; when the man again awoke his body would be as fit as it was at the height of his glory, in the heady days as first consul. Even the neural system would be revitalized, agility of thought returning from the cloudiness. Yet what will we do with him? Aldin wondered. Yaroslav, hiding his admiration in cynicism, was all too right. This was not another Alexandrian game. Civilization was on the point of a catastrophe. He had set out to find the cure and was returning with an anachronism.

"Aldin?"

He looked back at Oishi, who had silently entered the room.

"A problem."

"What?"

"Company's coming."

Stirred from his contemplation of Napoleon's fate, he returned to the forward control room and looked over Zergh's shoulder at the main nav screen.

"Someone's pushed through here; there're traces of unburned antimatter still kicking about, an engine slightly out of tune. The long jump point back to the Cloud is ten minutes ahead."

"Corbin?"

"I think so," Zergh replied.

"Damn it."

"Do you think he's armed?" Aldin asked, looking over at Oishi.

"We're not, and in such a case, I'd suggest that we assume that he is."

"Get Vush in here," Aldin said quietly.

If he's blocking the path back home, Aldin thought coldly, we can either try to run past him or wait it out.

"I'm picking up something," Zergh said quietly.

Aldin looked back at the screen. Six dots appeared, spreading out from the demarcation line of the jump point.

"Whatever it is, it doesn't look good," Yaroslav said, motioning for a drink from one of the bots.

Aldin heard the door open behind him, and there was the faint rustling of Vush's robes as the Overseer came into the room.

The six dots started to accelerate, and several more appeared behind them.

Vush looked down at the screen and then over at Aldin.

"Your brothers?" Aldin asked.

Vush hesitated.

"If Gablona came here, I think it fair to assume that they would be here as well, believing that you would come on the same errand."

"Well, that bastard Gablona got to him first," Oishi said coldly.

"That does not matter. The issue is you and the wish to rescue me."

Aldin looked up at Vush.

"Do you want to be rescued?"

Vush hesitated, looking back at the screen, and said nothing.

"Your Arch will certainly love to have you back," Yaroslav said with a light chuckle. "He can throw you in with your friend Mupa, and together you can watch everything go to hell. A million years on some forsaken rock at least. He's got to blame someone for all of this, and as they used to say, 'you're taking the fall.'"

"Turn left," Vush said quietly.

"What?" Aldin asked, looking up at Vush in confusion.

"Left, port, whatever—just aim at that star over there, the second one to the right." He pointed to the side of the forward viewport.

Aldin punched the ship around, not even bothering to ask why. According to the charts, there wasn't anything in that direction but empty space for nearly three light-years, and at the present speed they just might escape in roughly thirty years of running.

"Everyone out of this room," Vush said, looking nervously at the nav screen, which showed the unidentified ships still closing in.

Everyone looked at him in confusion.

"Oishi stays; he promised. The rest of you get out. I know another way."

"Well, I'll be damned," Zergh said. "It takes us hundreds of years to find this one jump point, we lose it for nearly three thousand years before we find it again, and then this one looks around and says there's another way out."

"Get out of here now!" Oishi shouted, and Vush looked over at him with relief.

"Well, you heard the boss," Yaroslav snapped. "An emperor in one room and a dictator in another."

Aldin and the others filed out, Yaroslav motioning for the servobot to follow.

Oishi swung into the command seat and looked over at Vush.

"I'm not sure, it's been so long, but I think we head a bit more to the right," he said, and with a sigh Oishi punched in the commands. Long minutes later he was suddenly startled when without warning the ship hit an unmarked jump point and accelerated into translight.

"Just where the hell are we heading?" Oishi shouted.

"If I'm not mistaken, I think it takes us straight to the Sphere," Vush replied with a self-satisfied tone. "A little secret Mupa and I stumbled on about ten thousand years back.

"Either there, or to the other side of this galaxy, I'm really not quite sure which."

"Just where did he go?" the Arch asked, barely able to contain himself as the first ship reemerged through the jump point back from the Milky Way.

"They turned about and then just disappeared," the pilot of the Overseer ship replied.

The Arch looked over at Mupa, who sat curled up in the corner.

"Well?"

"Vush must have been on board."

"Did you follow them?" the Arch asked, looking back at the screen.

"Where? It was an unmarked jump gate, we could have blundered around for years before hitting it."

The Arch looked back again at Mupa.

"Can you explain this?"

"Like I told you before," Mupa replied, his voice nearly whining, "the two of us wandered through there once."

"Without my knowledge or permission."

Mupa lowered his head even further.

"It's a confusing path. The wrong turn could take you all the way over to the far end of the galaxy."

"Or?"

"Straight to the far side of this Cloud and to the Sphere."

Repeating a habit he found all too distasteful, the Arch cursed to himself once again.

"And what about Gablona?"

"He claims they killed this Human who understands wormholes, took the new weapons we offered to him, and then disappeared," the pilot replied.

The Arch shut the screen off and drifted out of the room.

Too much was happening at once. Events were spinning out of control, and he had to find some means to reestablish it. They'd have to go to the Sphere, that was obvious. He'd point Gablona in that direction as well. By the simple fact of Aldin's escape it was obvious that Vush was now helping him. A brother Overseer was now in league with the barbarians. It was disgusting. He would have to be punished, as all of them would have to be punished.

At the end, there was no final bang; more like a sigh. The outer shell of the red giant, no longer held together by the gravitational mass from within, simply started to race outward, driven by the dying nuclear furnace. It was a most unusual phenomenon, a star sucked dry from within, the outer shell simply rupturing in a small novalike explosion. And then darkness.

Yet there was already another light beside it, now burning fiercely, vast explosions roaring up from below.

The vast wormhole pipeline for the briefest instant went dry. An inquiry raced out from the instrument pack buried deep within its heart. Was the job done? Should it continue? But the control system was now thousands of light-years away, and besides, the button was still jammed down, even if the message could reach it.

If an overworked machine could shrug its shoulders and with a philosophical sigh get back to work, this would have definitely done so. A quick scan probed surrounding space. There was the brief flicker of a gravitational center, and the wormhole snaked over to it. In a thousandth of a second, a shipload of Humans, who on a bet had come out to watch the show, were swallowed up. The tidbit could not possibly satisfy the need for more matter. The wormhole leaped across a quarter light-year and latched itself to a white dwarf star. At least that would satisfy the machine's requirements for a while, and then there were others beyond that. The line was now pointing straight into the Core Cluster, where hundreds of worlds and stars would serve as meals yet to come, one of them a vast ball of condensed iron, hundreds of trillions of tons worth, the burned out hulk of a dying star that had not gone supernova or collapsed into singularity. Fed into the heart of a star in convulsion, it would most certainly shut down a nuclear burn in short order, with the most interesting of results.

chapter eight

It was all rather disconcerting and yet so miraculous. He felt as if he had awakened from a cold, distant dream filled with phantoms of memories. How could he even begin to explain it all, as if fifteen years of living had been peeled away from his body, and his soul. The memories, were they even real? The biting cold of the retreat that he felt he would never get out of his soul. The numbed realization of the last defeat, the musty dankness of that damned island. Was it even real? The pain?

The pain, where was it? There was none! He felt his stomach. Strange, it felt flatter than he remembered. So strange. What was the dream and what was real?

He sat up. As he did so the room was illuminated by a soft diffused light and he looked around. This is real then, and not the fevered dreams of approaching death. The room was small, neatly arranged. Some drawers set into a wall, a door without handles. And the light? He looked around; there was no candle, no lamp, yet still there was the light. He felt a shudder, and he almost slid off the bed. That's what awoke me, like a carriage lurching to a stop. The ship—that's what they called it—a ship flying through the ether of space was moving beneath him.

He stood up. He felt light, a coiled vibrancy, just the way it used to be—out of bed after four hours and ready to work twenty more. And his eyes. Everything was so sharp, so clear. And hunger! My God, real hunger, not the dull ache, the dread of eating, knowing the agony it would create.

In the soft light he looked down at himself. He was naked, and yet it was real, his body had changed; it looked, and felt younger. He chuckled to himself, looking about the room, stretching. Clothes?

A faint clicking disturbed his thoughts. In the corner of the room a servobot waited patiently, its electronic eyes and sensors aimed at him.

"You are an ugly thing," Napoleon said.

The machine remained silent.

"So, my iron friend, shall I walk about naked?"

The bot moved to a side wall, pushed a button, and a closet slid open.

"Delightful!" Napoleon exclaimed. Hanging in the closet was a blue military jacket faced with white, epaulets of gold, sleeves and collar trimmed with red. The trousers were buff, the calf-high boots freshly polished till they seemed to glow.

Admiring himself in the mirror, the uniform on, he felt as if the years truly had slipped away. The uniform was tailored to perfection, though the material felt strange, almost silky.

It is something Aldin would have thought of, a friendly gesture.

And why the friendly gesture? he wondered. Admiration for his skills? Of course. But what was to be his part in this strangeness of ships that passed through the ether between stars, the hint of political strife and strange beings? Everything he knew was gone, if what they said was true. The English, the Bourbons, St. Helena, even France, as distant now as Babylon and Sargon.

"Soldiers of France, remember forty centuries of history look down upon you today." That was a moment, arrayed before the pyramids, waiting for the Mamluks to charge. *My world, my time, as distant to me now as the pyramids were to their builders.*

Who was that damned English poet, Shelley or Byron?

"Ozymandias." He half suspected it was a barb directed at him. So now I am ancient history for an Earth that does not even exist. And yet they mentioned Alexander. How did they meet him? he wondered. Did they collect the greatness of history? But for what purpose? To help them, to use us, or simply to collect us like a bored noble collecting antiquities?

The ship lurched again beneath his feet, causing him to nearly lose his balance. For a brief second he felt as if everything around him had gone into a blurred distortion, and a mild nausea enveloped him. He felt a brief shudder of fear. It was like the old symptoms, the dizziness, the nausea. Was it all an illusion, was he about to wake up and again be fat, dying, and vomiting in his own bed? He heard a distant cursing, and then shouts of excitement. No, this was real, very real indeed.

He looked toward the door. There was no sense hiding in here. A chance had been offered; the dream of old men, to suddenly have strength and youth returned to them. To be given the chance to do it all over again. Yet for all that he had built, there was no security now, the playing field was leveled again, and fresh. He could fall, not living up to the legend of what was expected of him.

It would be like beginning again as a young major of artillery, angling so sharply for the first command, the chance for glory and for power. Offensive, always the offensive, that was the path to victory. Fixing his features with a confident smile, he looked down at the bot, which sat quiet, impassively waiting for him to clear the room so it could make the bed. He patted it lightly on the side and, turning, strode out of the room, the door opening silently for the emperor.

Aldin burst into the forward cabin, Tia behind him.
"Just what the hell was that?" he shouted.
"It seems we've finished our jump," Yaroslav announced, as if it were he who had been piloting the ship. The old man, however, barely noticed Aldin. Eyes gleaming with delight, Yaroslav looked back to the forward screen, which was showing the real-time view in front of the ship.

Aldin stared at it intently for a moment, not quite sure of what he was seeing. Then he realized that the fact he was seeing nothing at all was actually quite significant. The scattering of stars and far-distant galaxies had a hole in the middle of it, a black circle of what appeared to be emptiness.

He looked over at Oishi and Vush sitting at the control consoles.

"The Sphere of the First Travelers," Oishi said quietly, as if standing in the foyer of a temple.

Vush looked at the forward viewscreen, his head bobbing nervously.

Aldin came up to Oishi's side and looked down at the nav screen. A close study of the system would help him to figure out where they were, but a look from his friend convinced him to honor their pledge, and instead he studied the dark circle in the middle. There was mass there, an infrared signature, most likely heat exhaust, similar to the backside of the Ring. It had a very slow rotation, barely noticeable, enough to create an artificial gravity on the inside. They were still twenty million kilometers out, but closing in at 0.1 of light.

Zergh came into the room and, immediately realizing where they were, let out a triumphant whoop. Within seconds the servobots were busy filling glasses for a toast. Oishi, with Vush's vague directions, initiated a shallow curving approach in toward the Sphere, and seconds later a gasp of astonishment swept through the room.

A pie-shaped section of the northern hemisphere was incomplete and open to space. As they dove in toward the gap, the interior of the Sphere came into view. From the distance of ten million kilometers it reminded Aldin of a crystal ball, veiled in black except for one small section, which revealed the mystery and brilliance within. The small artificially created sun hovered in the middle, as if dangling from a thread, its light illuminating the interior of the hollow ball.

The doorway of the control room slid open again, and Napoleon entered. He stood still for a moment, as if expecting a fanfare of greeting, and then seeing how his companions' attention was fixed to the forward screen, he quietly entered. To his untutored eyes the object before them held no real meaning for a moment; it looked like nothing more than a pie-shaped sliver of light with a glowing ball within. Yet it must be a great wonder, he realized, to hold their attention such.

He approached the screen, gazing intently at it.

"It is a sun, contained within an artificially made hollow ball, several million kilometers across," Oishi said, looking over at the emperor and attempting to interpret what they were seeing. Oishi could well understand the confusion, the awe over things trivial and the incomprehension of things magnificent. He had stood dumbstruck as well, when the reality of what the future was had finally started to settle into his heart and mind. It was a ripping away of the old world and replacing it with a new. It created heartsickness, almost a madness at times, and yet it was a constant wonder. He could only hope that this man would learn to live in a new reality not of his own creation.

"Then it is hundreds of times bigger than our Earth," Napoleon whispered, looking over at Oishi in confusion.

"Billions of times," Yaroslav said.

"The works of man pale to insignificance," Napoleon said with a sigh.

Aldin looked over at him and smiled.

"Made long before us by an unknown race we call the First Travelers. Everything of Human hand is insignificant to what they created."

"Go straight into it," Vush said, pointing toward the open section.

Zergh looked over at Vush for a second and then moved to occupy the copilot chair. Oishi might be good at his work, but everyone knew that few could outmaster the Gaf vasba when it came to piloting in what might be a difficult situation.

The dark Sphere now filled the entire heavens before them, the blackness of its exterior revealing no sense of depth, so that it felt as if they were coming up on a flat circle with a slice of light on the upper side.

"The opening is nearly a million kilometers across," Oishi said, "but it's latticed with beams." As they closed to within a hundred thousand kilometers, the sense of the depth of the Sphere started to be apparent, the blackness of the outer shell curving away.

Inside the Sphere, the far side was three million kilometers away, glowing with a reflected yellow light, silhouetting the small star in the middle. The vast open space started to resolve itself into a latticework of support beams that interlaced and cut across hundreds of thousands of kilometers. The opening was not truly open at all; there were tiny spots of darkness, which were in fact partially completed sections, some of them tens of thousands of kilometers across. Support structures a hundred kilometers wide cut a crisscross pattern that in places was partially filled in by a filigree of smaller lines and yet smaller between them, as if a spider were gradually weaving its tenuous web into a solid mass.

The distance shrank to ten thousand kilometers and then five, as Zergh bled off speed, adjusting for the unusual gravitational effects created by the massive structure.

Napoleon went over to one of the servobots and returned to the screen with a brandy to stand meditatively watching the show.

"You look good in uniform," Aldin said.

"My thanks."

"Tia's the one who thought of it," Yaroslav said, not bothering to look back, "though I threw in the historical details, and it was the bots that actually made it."

Napoleon smiled and decided to say nothing.

Any sense that they were approaching a sphere was gone, the vast open area filling all of space in front of them. Pulling the ship up slightly, Zergh maneuvered to avoid a hundred-kilometer-wide beam. The forward nav screen revealed a jumble of debris, interlocking structures, and cables. There was movement as well, something Aldin had not expected, and he looked over inquisitively at Vush.

"Could someone be there waiting for us?"

"They're still building it," Vush replied.

"Who?" Yaroslav asked excitedly. "The First Travelers?"

"Their machines. They've been building it for millions of years. It'll be hundreds of thousands more before they are done."

Zergh slowed to a near stop a dozen kilometers out and looked closely at the nav screen before slowly picking up speed again.

From behind one of the beams a massive shiplike vehicle appeared, several kilometers in length, trailing a long filament strand behind it.

Vush rose up, unable to contain his excitement.

"I haven't been here in thousands of years. Yet you can barely see the progress, so vast it is."

The ship laying out the long filament of a support beam moved directly in front of their ship, not a kilometer away. Zergh suddenly punched in reverse thrusters.

"The damn thing's got its own gravitational field," the Gaf cried in amazement. "It's got the mass of a small planet. It's laying out the same material that they built the Ring out of."

He looked over darkly at Yaroslav. "And the Skyhook as well."

Yaroslav shifted uncomfortably.

"I think that inside that ship, the building material is compressed at an atomic level," Yaroslav speculated in a professorial voice. "The matter is contained in a field to keep a nuclear reaction from igniting, and then it's trailed out behind the ship, like a spider dumping silk to form the ribs of the sphere."

The ship moved majestically on, the newly laid beam glowing briefly before cooling in the vacuum of space. Smaller objects, that looked like crosses between space vessels and pieces of multiarmed construction equipment, darted back and forth. Space suddenly seemed alive with movement.

Zergh nudged them in past the outer shell.

Awed, he brought the vessel to a stop. The entire inner Sphere was now almost completely visible.

"It is like gazing at heaven," Napoleon whispered.

The darkness of space was banished. The vast interior glowed with a golden light, the blackness of the outside replaced with a blue-green softness. All sense of scale was lost; it was simply too vast for the human mind to comprehend that what they were looking at covered an area of billions of square kilometers, all of it shaped and crafted to perfection. When he had heard of rumors of the Sphere, Aldin somehow imagined it cold, lifeless, an interior of gleaming icy metal. Foolishness. The Ring was beyond description in its magnificence. This made the Ring pale into nothingness by comparison.

He looked over at Vush.

"It is good that you kept this secret from us," he whispered. "At least let one small part of heaven remain beyond our grasp."

"Why didn't all your kind choose here to live?" Yaroslav asked, wiping the tears from his eyes.

"We believed it wrong to make our place of contemplation something made by others," Vush replied softly. "I think though it showed us our true insignificance and made us feel too humble to know that others had created perfection and we could never obtain it, either through the strength of our hands or the power of our minds."

To either side of the open section, walls hundreds of kilometers high had been constructed as barriers to keep the atmosphere in, and as the ship slowly drifted in, the view to the starboard side started to expand, the vast, limitless view gradually taking on detailed form. Mountain ranges, some punching clean through the atmosphere and soaring hundreds of kilometers high, dotted the landscape, their green slopes giving way to snow, and then finally to bare black crystalline rock. Several of the mountains had necklaces of bridges that soared across vast reaches of empty space, to anchor like a descending halo to a range on the far side of a sparkling turquoise ocean.

Spindly towers, a dozen times the height of the Shiga Skyhook, soared up from the surface, apparently constructed for no purpose other than the joy of creating them.

"One expects to hear angels," Napoleon said quietly, sipping at his drink, feet braced far apart, unable to contain the emotion of wonder from dancing across his features. A vast hexagonal-shaped section of framework a hundred kilometers across hovered to one side, a variety of multiarmed machines and what appeared to be tugs slowly moving it down, as if to lock it onto a bed of support beams.

Aldin watched it intently, awed by the manipulation of what must have been hundreds of millions of tons of mass with seemingly effortless ease.

What appeared to be a small beam layer, coming straight in from the sun, approached the hexagon. Zergh barely had time to call out a warning, when in the lonely silence of space there was a flash of light. A massive chunk of metal blew through the side of the hexagon, the beam layer continuing straight on, its side torn open, the contents from within spilling out, exploding into a flash of blinding light.

Zergh spun their ship over and accelerated, dashing in the opposite direction as the shock wave of the explosion leaped out.

"What the hell was that all about?" Yaroslav asked, gazing intently at the aft viewscreen, as the hexagon slowly started to tumble out of control. A number of ships streaked past, heading in toward the explosion, and to Aldin's disbelief, one came straight at them, causing Zergh to maneuver violently as the vessel shot past, tentacles and tool arms flailing. Two of the machines a kilometer to port smashed into each other, one of them vaporizing, the other continuing on. Yet smaller machines scurried out, apparently bent on retrieving the damaged equipment and fragments that were careening off in every direction.

The situation seemed to be compounding by the second; several of the smaller machines started to circle in on each other, as if they were dogs chasing each other's tails. They spiraled in faster and faster until finally three met, one of them bouncing out of the spiral, the other two then taking off in pursuit.

"I think there's trouble in paradise," Yaroslav sniffed.

Oishi looked over at Vush, who was obviously deeply troubled by what they were witnessing.

"They're working at cross-purposes," Aldin interjected. "It looked like some of the machines can't even sense the presence of others."

Zergh continued to pilot the ship out of the confusion, dodging through a forest of towers and converging machines.

Approaching the starboard barrier wall, Zergh spun straight up toward the sun, accelerated, and a minute later cleared the top. The confusion, at least for the moment, appeared to be left behind.

"Let's pull over here and take a break," Aldin announced.

Zergh nudged the vessel forward and finally settled it down on the lip of the barrier, thus granting them a view straight down to the Sphere's inner surface five hundred kilometers below. So smooth was the wall's surface that rotational movement of the Sphere caused the ship to slowly start to slide across the top until a final nudge of a docking thruster put them into synch with their surroundings.

It was as if they were now looking down on a planet's surface, however this surface just continued on forever, sweeping out, up, and away in all directions, until all details were lost in the vast eternal distance. Directly below, an ocean of bright blue-green glinted with reflected sunlight, a tower on a small continent in the middle of an ocean rising up clear through the atmosphere to top out at nearly the same height as the great barrier wall. A mountain range, which Aldin guessed must be at least ten thousand kilometers away, marched in a straight serrated line of snow-blanketed ridges, disappearing in the direction of the equator.

"Still going crazy back there," Tia said, breaking the awestruck silence, and pointed to a monitor that was tracking the hexagon that was starting to break into two halves, while hundreds of tiny dots appeared to be converging in upon the disaster.

"That," Vush interjected, his voice weak, "is not supposed to happen."

"Kind of what I thought," Aldin replied. "I mean, after all, this is First Traveler stuff. Nothing is ever supposed to go wrong."

"Well, that sure didn't look like a planned festivity to me," Yaroslav stated. "What's going on, Vush?"

"Something is not right, to be certain."

"If the pilot leaves the wheel," Napoleon ventured, "a ship might sail for days, but in the end it is bound to strike disaster."

"Not a bad metaphor," Zergh said.

"But that's impossible," Vush interjected. "You are talking about the First Travelers."

"Hey, you yourself said that when you and this Mupa fellow found the wormhole device, the machine that was supposed to run it appeared to be out of order," Yaroslav countered. "Well, what we're looking at here might be the First Traveler machines screwing up in a major way."

"Everything else looks so perfect, though," Tia whispered.

"It's a big place," Aldin said. "It's taken them millions of years to build it. It might take even longer for it to run completely amok."

"That should be the least of our concerns at the moment," Oishi said, looking over at Vush. "Right now we need to find the place where you found the wormhole device. So where is it?"

Vush hesitated and looked around the group. With a deliberate slowness he floated up and went over to the forward viewscreen and looked at the vista for several long minutes in total silence.

Napoleon could already see what was coming. Going to the bot, he got another brandy and took it over to Aldin.

"You're going to need this," Napoleon said with a knowing smile.

Vush turned to look back at the group.

"It's been so long . . ." His voice trailed off.

"Don't tell me you've forgotten," Zergh growled.

"It will come back to me. It's just the place is so big."

"So now what the hell are we going to do?" Yaroslav asked.

"I don't know," Vush replied, as if offended. "How about if

we just drive around for a while? Sooner or later I'll get my bearings."

"So where do we start?" Oishi snapped, barely able to control the rising temper that was about to explode.

"Oh, I don't know. That way," Vush replied, waving vaguely toward the equatorial region.

With a muffled curse, Zergh shot the vessel off the wall in a shower of burned skids and smoking wall, nearly knocking everyone over with the suddenness of the maneuver. With head bowed, Vush stayed by the screen and didn't look back.

"Rather an interesting situation," Zola said, smiling for the first time in days.

He gazed intently at the screen, which displayed a complex jump-route schematic.

"Where did you get this?" Zola asked.

Xsarn Tertiary clattered its mandibles in an agitated manner.

"It took a little digging. We knew from Xsarn Secondary that Larice dropped off most of his people, picked up the time ship, and went back to the home galaxy."

"Go on."

"Some of our old gaming-net people started, shall we say, a speculation as to where Aldin was going and why."

"And?"

"The betting was eight-to-five that he was going back to old Earth to get that Japanese physicist."

"Yashima Korobachi," Zola said.

"Ah, so you do know of him?" the Xsarn asked.

"Who doesn't?" Zola replied absently, examining the crease on his purple and green striped trousers.

"He went in and he hasn't come back out," the Xsarn continued.

"Ah, well, the vicissitudes of time travel," Zola said.

The Xsarn hesitated, but Zola nodded for it to continue.

"If he was after Korobachi, then he was looking for a way to defuse the wormhole. Overseer security has been lax, they've been running like scared children. Several of them were actually killed when one of their ships touched down on a pleasure world and a mob tore them apart."

"Delightful," Zola chuckled.

"One of our people gained access to the ship's computer, and this chart to a place called the Sphere was stored in it along with some notations concerning an Overseer called Mupa and the wormhole. It wasn't too hard to put two and two together."

"Excellent work," Zola said. "I think we can safely surmise that Aldin has fantasies of saving everybody by getting this scientist chap and then going to the Sphere and trying to get an answer on the wormhole and how to stop it."

Zola looked over the Xsarn and smiled craftily.

"You didn't just drop in for a friendly visit," Zola said. "Everything's going to hell. The entire western side of the Core Cluster is in chaos."

"And?"

"There are significant marketing potentials in all of this," Zola replied coldly.

"Such as?"

"Come, come, my old friend, you know as well as I." Zola Faldon laughed, his voice high and whiny.

Shipping rates out of the side of the cluster closest to the wormhole were up over 400 percent. That was short-term and most lucrative. However, there was an even grander consideration. If this new star should eventually explode, some computer models were speculating that nearly a hundred heavily settled worlds in the outer edge of the cluster closest to the explosion would be in danger. Those that were closest would most likely be rendered totally uninhabitable. Projections were running that over one hundred and sixty worlds would be in this band of destruction, a further three hundred requiring at least temporary sheltering for all inhabitants. Even if the star went supernova immediately, it would still take a couple of years before the blast of radiation and debris hit the nearest prime-level world, but panic was already spreading.

Of course, the chance was always there as well that the runaway wormhole might very well sweep all the way into the cluster and start devouring planets, a speculation that had already triggered the filming of several Gaf disaster films, thereby helping to fuel the panic.

Billions of beings would have to be resettled, hundreds of corporate headquarters and their staffs moved. One of the worlds run by the lawyers' guild was in the path of destruction, and some had suggested a boycott of ships to that world, thus leaving them to their proper fate—a concept that Zola found himself in complete agreement with.

There was barely a prime planet left in the Cloud that was not fully controlled by some corporation or guild, but as for second- and third-rate worlds, there were hundreds on the marketplace for next to nothing.

Zola smiled even as he thought of the possibilities: billions needing to move; desert, swamp, and ice planets to be bought for a song; and, with proper advertising, katars uncounted to be made providing new homeworlds for the refugees. What a chance for a killing.

"A consortium of investors, a very limited number of investors, could certainly come out well because of this," Zola said, looking up at the Xsarn.

"Precisely. Of course, it would all go awry if a certain vasba managed to shut the wormhole down."

Zola nodded in agreement.

He knew that Corbin Gablona and the Overseers were both after Aldin, along with a swarm of bounty hunters still after the Overseer reward. But Aldin had a propensity for survival against difficult odds. Odds. The mere thought of how much Aldin and Bukha had taken from him in the last game was reason enough to want Aldin taken care of.

"Don't worry, he won't get back," Zola replied.

The Xsarn Tertiary nodded, arms clicking, and he stood up to leave.

"Our assistants shall meet and draw up an investment plan. We can start purchasing planets almost immediately then; some of my field people have already scouted out a number of prospects."

"I'll get my media team to make them look like paradises," Zola replied. Gods, how he loved scams like this. It brightened his whole day.

The Xsarn left the room, knowing that the game within the game was working as planned. Zola, watching him leave, felt exactly the same way.

"You know that the Overseers will be behind us," Corbin said, looking over at Hassan, who sat in the darkened corner of the room.

"But of course they'll follow. This Sphere is after all their precious little secret."

Corbin sat in silence. He felt like he was trapped in a pit with a snake. As long as he could convince the snake that he served a purpose, he would continue to live. But already Hassan was learning to master ship's navigation and piloting. The nuances of the political and economic webs that governed the rather haphazard management of life in the Cloud he viewed as a joke, openly wondering how for three thousand years no single agent had not simply taken control with an iron fist. As for the Overseers, he had expressed contempt from the beginning, seeing before all others that their threats and their power were a charade. Corbin felt as if he were gazing into the pitiless stare once again, an unblinking gaze that from moment to moment toyed with the idea of granting continued life or death in an infinite variety of disturbing manners.

The fat man could be jovial, even charming in a disgustingly effete sort of way, Hassan thought, looking over at Corbin, who gazed at him warily. He could always have his uses as a front—at least until something better came along.

Something better. He hoped it was soon. He had once been a servant of Corbin's, had even been in awe of him in the early days, when this universe was still all too new and disturbingly frightful. The memory of that subservience did not sit well. And the whole time that he contemplated this thought, his features did not change in the slightest.

"We can expect Zola, maybe the others to follow as well," Corbin said. "After all, the person who sold us the navigation charts most likely did the same thing for anyone else who might be interested."

Hassan nodded as if he had ascertained such a fact long before Corbin had even begun to contemplate it.

Hassan let his gaze turn back to the forward viewscreen. A thin, pin-shaped sliver of light floated before them. It was hard to grasp the size of what he was looking at; his experiences had never prepared him to even contemplate such scale. Surely, if Allah even existed, this would have been a creation that would challenge even His skill. It would be a worthy place to rule from as the Hidden Ema—remote, distant. A place to return to when he had not only stopped the Overseer device, but learned how to use it for his own ends.

Hassan smiled as the ship started its curving descent in toward the Sphere.

chapter nine

"I think that's it."

Everyone stirred. Aldin, asleep on the floor, sat up with a groan. Oishi, who was stretched out between two chairs, sat up, his joints creaking.

The only one who had been awake throughout it all was Napoleon, sitting by Vush's side, nursing a brandy that he had poured for himself a dozen hours ago, while refilling Vush's drink at regular intervals.

It had been an illuminating twenty hours; he barely felt tired, and hunger was hardly noticed. The Overseer, who hovered beside him, intent upon watching the viewscreen, occasionally floating over to a control panel to alter course and then back again, had been reticent at first.

There had been several inquiries about his role as emperor, and his frank answers, especially regarding the executions he had ordered, had obviously upset Vush, who for several hours had launched into a nonstop sermon on the sanctity of life. Napoleon had sat patiently, barely disputing the Overseer, but in the end he terminated the line of thought with an offhand reference to the billions who would die due to the wormhole unleashed in part by Vush's own actions. It was a statement followed by a long and well-crafted reassurance of how fate can sometimes cast one into roles not anticipated, and thus, by extension, remove the onus of later tragedies created by what were initially good intentions.

Much had been learned. He felt at times as if he were hearing the fantastic tales of Baron Munchausen or Cyrano. Yet it was real. The fantastic being beside him would have been greeted either as an angel or a devil if it had appeared suddenly in the aisle of Notre Dame. Here it was just a lonely creature trying to hide its fear, its pitiful weakness, behind a mask of well-cultivated superiority. It was difficult to sit and listen, an art he had known in his youth when first introduced to those who thought themselves his betters. The early days in Paris, during the Revolution, when Robespierre held the reins, that had been a time to listen, to form plans alone, to wear the masks one needed if one's head was to stay attached. It was an art he had almost forgotten.

St. Helena had never forced him to this level of self-contemplation; it was as if he were almost removed from himself, detached to gaze at his strengths and his faults. Defeat had burned too deeply to admit all the mistakes. Too much had to be defended when in front of the mocking gaze of those perfidious English. Here, here it was different. He had to know what he was, what he had done, what he now could be in order to understand. Or was it the change in myself? he wondered, unable not to sneak a sidelong glance at the reflective surface of a viewscreen in order to reaffirm the changes Aldin had brought about to his body.

Thinking was so clear again, the body tireless. I have an opportunity here, he realized, even while still listening intently to Vush. I am almost youthful again, and so painfully aware of all that has been lost, and all that might be gained. He remembered the nights alone, fully realizing that there would never be a rescue, that no French frigate would arrive offshore to whisk him back to France and to glory. At those moments, when the true realization had settled in that it was over, there had been one last dream of consolation, that in the next world it would be like the warrior legends of old. Valhalla, a gathering together of his old comrades, the grumblers, all those lost in Spain, Russia, Leipzig, Eylau, coming to his banner, and again the old battles would be fought.

And now this instead, another chance after all, a chance unlike anything even a madman could have dreamed.

Vush paused for a moment to look over at the Human who seemed lost in thought and then back at the screen. He quietly continued on, almost absently, with his lecture regarding the barbarity of Humans, Gavarnians, and Xsarns, when suddenly he stirred, bobbing up and down and shouting.

Aldin, wiping the sleep from his eyes, came up to the forward viewscreen.

"Down there," Vush announced, the conversation with Napoleon forgotten.

Napoleon, who had ignored the remarkable scenery below to

concentrate instead upon Vush, looked out to where the Overseer was pointing.

The landscape below was rather remarkable, even for such
a remarkable world. A vast series of concentric rings seemed
to be carved into the landscape. It took him several seconds to
remember the perspective from which he was looking down at
this strange world, to realize that they were, in fact, a ringlike
series of towering mountains, as if planted as a painted target.

"Five thousand kilometers across," Tia announced, settling
into the nav chair. "The formation is perfectly circular, the
mountain ranges nearly three hundred kilometers high."

Aldin noticed that there were smaller rings set further out,
the landscape between each of the rings a barren, black surface, each ring a circle of light in a region that must have measured several hundred thousand kilometers across.

"It almost looks like a symbolic representation of a solar
system," Yaroslav said, looking over at Vush intently.

"I should have remembered this," Vush replied. "Mupa said
the same thing. In fact we spent several days running comparisons to systems in the galaxy, hoping maybe to find the
homeworld of the First Travelers, but it never came to anything."

"So where is it?" Zergh asked.

"The central one. The central mesa, the eye of the circle, is
one vast control complex. It was there that we found it."

"Well let's go in then," Yaroslav announced, barely able to
suppress his excitement.

Napoleon, like the others, found himself pressed up against
the forward viewscreen. They had been weaving back and
forth above the surface of the Sphere at over twenty thousand
kilometers while Vush tried to figure out where to go. The
land below had been a curious pattern of what he thought must
be green fields or forests, oceans, mountains, and then tremendous open spaces of blackness or polished silver, regions that
Vush announced were yet to be completely formed.

The ship went into a steep dive, pointing straight down at
the surface, Aldin taking the controls alongside Zergh. The exuberance of the moment showed in them as well, as they threw
caution aside and let the speed build. The mountains, which
punched up through the atmosphere, glinted in the perpetual
noonday sun, and as they dove past the top peaks the retro sys-

tem fired and sent a shudder running through the ship as it started to plunge into the atmosphere.

Napoleon felt like an eagle spiraling down from a mountain aerie and laughed aloud with the pleasure of it, as the ship started to flatten out its dive, swinging in between two razor-sharp peaks and passing above high alpine meadows. A light covering of clouds whisked by, their undersides dark with showering snow that flashed into steam with the heat of their passage. Through holes in the clouds the sun shone, the world a glaring crystalline white, as Aldin guided them into a pass and weaved down it, dodging and turning, while Tia clung to her chair, cursing the pilots. Oishi laughed aloud, his teeth glinting like the snow, a faint tear barely discernible in his eyes, for it had been long years since he had seen snow and it conjured a memory of home.

The pass opened out into flower-strewn meadows so that they appeared to rush above a carpet of burgundy and violet that swayed in the cold breeze coming down out of the high hills. The meadows in turn gave way to stands of high trees, unlike any they had ever seen, the trunks soaring upward hundreds of feet before the first limbs branched out, the leaves bright green and lavender. A cliff shot by beneath them, a cascade of water tumbling over it, plummeting in an angel-haired plume. The falls plunged a thousand meters into a circular pool that was of the deepest blue, the white foam dancing down upon it like a shower of diamonds, surrounded on the shore by a cathedral grove of elmlike trees.

The beginning of a river coursed down out of the hills, tumbling over falls, other streams coming down to join it from now-distant peaks. Though there were other things far more pressing, Aldin swung the ship about and brought it to a hover above the falls, pools, and tumbling river. Punching a button, he opened the outside hatches and let the air circulate in.

The room was suddenly awash with a fresh pinelike scent, mingled with a sharp vibrant chill of cool damp mountain air.

"Eden," Napoleon whispered, finding that for the first time in years he was moved by a sight not of his own creating.

After a few moments, Aldin reluctantly shut the hatches, turned the ship about, and raced on. The forest rolled down before them, the sharp mountain ridges and slopes giving way to a succession of gentle hills that seemed to go on forever. The ship picked up speed, racing across the open landscape, a sinewy river weaving back and forth beneath them, growing broader, turning at last toward an ocean, which was its final destiny, shining in the distance.

Aldin found it remarkable just how far they could see. It was like the Ring, of course. The horizon did not curve downward, rather it slowly curved up, so that sights thousands of kilometers away could be seen. In some ways, the Ring was more dramatic, for it curved up and away, rising straight into the heavens, with darkness to either side. But here the true scale of the First Traveler creation was far more overwhelming. As they moved across the landscape, the distant ring of mountains, five thousand kilometers across, were clearly visible, and beyond, the bowl of the world curved outward in every direction. Low to the horizon it was somewhat hazy, looking as he was through thousands of kilometers of atmosphere. But if he raised his gaze higher, the vastness of the Sphere was more clearly in view, stretching on forever it seemed. Dark places of bareness alternated with the patches of green and blue where the First Travelers had planted life, while directly overhead the sun shone, now somewhat more dimly inside the atmosphere. Its construction was the same as the sun of the Kolbard Ring, a variable artificial star with a high rate of shift, thus dimming down to a dull glimmer and ten hours later shifting back up to a pleasant warmth.

Aldin looked over at Napoleon and smiled, and neither one felt the need to speak, to disturb the thoughts of the other.

Zergh pulled the ship up slightly, gaining enough altitude to cut down on atmospheric drag. The woods had given way to a pleasant patchwork quilt of forested glens, meandering streams, and then vast open stretches of high prairie. Occasional areas of darkness seemed to move on the land, which were numberless herds of a bisonlike creature.

The sight of them startled Napoleon. He had come to think that this place was not inhabited at all, but then again he realized it already was, planted with trees and grasses, and why shouldn't there be other things here as well? As they passed over a vast open canyon, the air below was black with millions of winged creatures, some with black bodies and wings, others multihued, who seemed to be engaged in a war, towering formations of them spiraling up on rising columns of air to then swing out and pounce upon those below.

The canyon disappeared astern, the war, if it was that, gone from view.

What first appeared to be a central bluff started at last to resolve into a gentle upslope that as it climbed in a series of undulating hills, each slightly higher than the one before, some tree-clad, others covered in grass, and yet others strangely bare, revealed the black rocklike subsurface of the Sphere. The ship dove back down, the end of the journey near, all desiring to get a closer look. The upward slope suddenly flattened out, and they closed in upon it. And all stood in silent awe.

For the first time since they had entered the atmosphere, it was again impressed upon them that this was an artificial creation. The plain in the center of the five-thousand-kilometer circle was nearly a hundred kilometers across. The cone at the center at last resolved into a black volcanolike mountain that rose up for nearly a dozen kilometers, its peak torn and jagged.

Clouds swirled around the summit, the tops spiraling up to the top and then disappearing.

"A puncture hole," Zergh said quietly. "Asteroid impact from outside."

"The damn thing must be sucking air like mad," Tia said.

"It'd still take thousands of years to have much of an effect in this region," Aldin replied, "but curious that they haven't fixed it somehow."

Aldin looked over at Vush, who said nothing, as if he had never considered the implication of this scar.

Across the vast circle on the near side of the mountain was an unending array of buildings. Some were simple upright slabs, others cylindrical, others hexagonal, pentagonal, and yet others a bizarre free-form of sharp lines and then sweeping curves. The randomness of their design when viewed as an entire system, or city, however, was strangely pleasing to the eye, almost childlike in its whimsy, as if every possible design were to be tried and then in the end fitted together into a whole. Thus no one place looked quite like any other, each vista different, and yet all seemed to fit together. The wreckage of a number of buildings was strewn up the sides of the mountain created by the impact.

"Was it like this when you were here last?" Oishi asked.

Vush nodded, still silent.

Slowing the vessel, Aldin looked back over at Vush.

"Well, I guess we're here," he said expectantly.

Vush looked around nervously.

"I'm not quite sure," he whispered.

There was a universal groan.

"It was fairly near the center, but off to one side."

"Well, that gives us a hell of a lot to go on," Yaroslav sighed.

"How about over there? It looks rather familiar," Vush announced, pointing to what looked like a small overgrown park.

"As good as any place," Aldin grumbled, and guided the ship to a soft touchdown, dust swirling up underneath the vessel.

"Comfortable temperature and air's good, a little high on oxygen content," Tia announced. "Gravity is 0.8 standard."

"Same as the Ring," Aldin announced as he swung his chair around and headed for the airlock, the rest of the group eagerly following, anxious to get outside and stretch their legs after ten days of being cooped up inside the ship.

Napoleon fell in behind them, ever so slightly miffed that they had not waited for him to go out first. Then he smiled philosophically. After all, he was not an emperor any longer, and hard as it was to bear, his participation in this little adventure was quite simply an accident.

It was like a comfortable spring day in Paris. The air was just the right temperature, a gentle breeze wafting past the hatchway. Following the others, he stepped out into the parklike setting. It had the appearance of a city to be sure, but unlike anything he had ever imagined. The buildings were vast, blocklike affairs soaring hundreds of feet into the air, where several spires broke the monotony. A number of the structures seemed worn, fissured with great cracks, and one of the spires was shattered, its rubble lying around the base of the building. In the distance, the great black mountain punched straight up into the heavens, the clouds that masked its summit roiling and twisting into streaming plumes.

Vush looked around, hesitating, Aldin and the others looking at the Overseer with barely concealed exasperation.

"Well?" Oishi asked, his voice set as if coaxing a confused child.

The Overseer floated up and turned slowly, his gown rustling and swirling out around him. Napoleon wandered off while the group waited.

"Ghostly, isn't it?"

Tia came up beside him, smiling.

"I was just thinking that," Napoleon replied. He found a memory of Moscow filling him. Marching into the city, the dream of youth reached at last, the gateway to the Orient, an empire to reach across the world—and it was empty.

The same here: empty, dead, and a vague sense that something was all wrong.

"These First Travelers," Napoleon said, "they sound to be like gods. Perfection, masters of all the universe. A mystery beyond our understanding."

"I guess you could say that. We certainly couldn't have created all of this," Tia replied, and gestured toward the incredible scale of the Sphere, which swept upward in every direction. He looked up.

A world without night, a vast room floating in space. That was how the ancient Egyptians saw the universe, the Earth inside the bottom of a bowl, the heavens the top overhead. The gods created that, and yet here, he looked around critically.

In the distance there was a glint of light and a machine floated by; looking almost like one of the servobots, it moved in an erratic pattern as if searching for something. It continued across the plaza and disappeared into a pyramid structure. Tia followed it with her gaze.

"A First Traveler machine. We found them on the Ring of Kolbard and in the Skyhook tower. They're a mystery, as is everything else about their creators."

"If they could build this, why would they allow a hole to be in it?" Napoleon asked, gesturing back toward the mountain.

"Your guess is as good as mine."

"I think of a finely crafted clock. Shooting a musket ball into it is bound to damage the inner workings."

"What I've been thinking, too," Tia replied quietly. She looked back toward Vush.

"I think the damn fool's decided," she said, and the two fell in behind the group as it started across the plaza, moving toward the pyramid that the machine had disappeared into. The pavement underfoot changed dramatically, from the seamless black stone upon which the ship had landed to a checkerboard pattern of alternating blue and white squares. The far side of the plaza was dominated by the pyramid, which soared upward for nearly half a thousand meters and was sheathed from base to top in what appeared to be gold.

"Bring back old memories?" Aldin asked, looking back at Napoleon.

"The mamluks had already stripped the polished limestone surface off by the time I got there," he replied. "If I had held on to the place, I was tempted to restore them back to their original glory. But this . . ." his voice trailed off as he looked up at the building.

"So is this it?" Zergh asked, looking over at Vush.

"You've got to remember," the Overseer said, his voice a near whine, "I've been to hundreds of worlds and all over this Sphere. It's been thousands of your years since I was last here. These things tend to blur a bit in memory. But these blue and white squares, facing the golden pyramid . . . I do remember searching a pyramid, and we saw the machine outside of it. It might be this one."

"Just how the hell could you forget something as awesome as this?" Tia interjected angrily. "This is incredible."

Vush's voice almost sounded like it was chuckling.

"There're billions of square kilometers to this Sphere, and several hundred levels beneath it. So just shut up and let me think."

Aldin roared with delight over the Overseer's display of temper.

"Keep it up and we'll make you Human yet," the vasba said. Vush gave a shudder of disgust.

Vush paused for a moment, looking intently at the pyramid and then at the surrounding city, which was silent except for the everpresent whisper of the wind as it swept toward the mountain.

"This is it," Vush finally said with a self-satisfied air.

"Well, let's get inside, find the other half of the machine, and go out and save the Cloud," Zergh said.

Four more suns had disappeared up the wormhole, along with the seven worlds that had orbited them. The last one had been inhabited, the Xsarn mining population moving out aboard a fleet of Zola's ore carriers, hired, of course, at 1,100 percent the prewormhole rate. A small fortune was lost by a Gaf consortium that had gambled at most favorable odds that the second rather than the third planet in the now-destroyed system would be swallowed first. It seemed like a sure bet, except for the simple fact that the wormhole curved slightly as it bored in on the system and simply knocked off the third planet first before going on into the sun. The mass of the new star was nearly half that of Beta Zul, and it continued to grow, relentless in its appetite, the intake end of the wormhole cutting in closer and yet closer to the Core Cluster.

"It appears as if all of this is ruled by chaos."

Corbin Gablona turned his float chair to look back at Hassan standing behind him.

The presence of the assassin in such a position had always given him a chill feeling in the back of his neck. There was a time when he would have told him so.

He looked up at Hassan and knew that the assassin sensed his discomfort. The thin lips were curled in a disdainful smile.

"The machines, they work against each other," Hassan continued, the slightest note of surprise in his voice. "Those who made the Sida, the great tower of the Hole, they made this thing as well?"

Corbin nodded, as surprised as the assassin.

"All things descend to chaos," Hassan said, "even the creations of Allah, if ever there was such a being."

Slightly surprised, Corbin looked over at the assassin.

Hassan, seeing the surprise, smiled.

"Allah, God, the First Travelers—all children's legends to be used to instill fear, to manipulate those too afraid of the darkness."

Hassan chuckled softly. That had been the ultimate secret of his order, to promise a nonexistent paradise to the fools of the lower ranks who would thus gladly throw themselves to their deaths to fulfill the wishes, the dreams of their masters.

"You've made gods of these First Travelers, and now you tremble when what they created appears to be ruled by madness."

"It has never happened before. The Overseers used the First Traveler weapons to rule us. Therefore by implication the First Travelers were almost beyond perfection."

"The Overseers." Hassan sniffed. "Frightened children like all the other beings of the Cloud, of all the universe. You saw how easy it was to kill the one named Tulbi, and then to cover up its death by what you called a jump-beam accident. They are weaklings."

"And you alone are without fear," Corbin said, frightened to challenge with such a statement, but unable to contain his curiosity.

Hassan smiled.

"Where do we go now?" Hassan asked.

"The directions said that there is only one place in this entire Sphere where there are buildings, all the rest is wilderness. We scan till we find it."

"Scan quickly," Hassan said, the command in his voice cold and imperative. "I look forward to trying out those new tracking missiles. It should prove to be amusing."

Annoyed with the squabbling of the group, Napoleon Bonaparte stood by in silent exasperation.

The entry into the great pyramid had been easy enough; the doors had slid silently open at their approach. The interior appeared to be nothing more than a vast foyer, the floor a highly polished silver surface, the room springing into light the moment they entered. A maze of corridors went off in every direction, some up and others down to subterranean levels. Vush had stopped, looked around for several long minutes, and then quietly announced that this indeed was the building. A sigh of relief had gone through the group, until he softly admitted that though this was the building where he had discovered the wormhole machine, he wasn't quite sure where inside the cavernous structure he and Mupa had finally managed to come across it.

Napoleon found himself tempted to exert command—to give an order for the group to divide up responsibility, to start a systematic search for whatever useful military stores could be found, to bring the ship inside the building for safety and to set up a patrol. He watched them shouting and arguing and, with a philosophical shrug of his shoulders, he turned and strode away.

The room was so big that it took him several minutes to return almost to the doorway through which they had entered. He paused for a moment and looked up. The ceiling vaulted upward more than a hundred feet into the air. A dozen Notre Dames could easily be deposited in this one room. What did they use it for? An audience chamber? A place for pageants?

It all looked too cold, dead. A single room, silvered floors and walls, ramps leading off. No ornamentation, no stained glass, not a single painting to relieve the daunting space, to make it somehow Human. Grandness had always appealed to him, but this was a grandeur without life.

A stairless causeway led up the side of one wall, and he ventured upward. If the ground floor was a gathering place, then the upper rooms must contain the stored secrets of these First Travelers the others spoke about with such awe. The ground floor dropped away, the thin voices of argument echoing in the chamber. He laughed softly, amused that they had not even noticed his wandering off. The causeway turned and plunged into the heart of the building.

He stopped, a thrill of fear coursing through him. A machine floated before him, tentacled arms hanging limp, an array of blinking lights apparently looking at him with soulless intent.

He took a deep breath.

"So, are you the master of this palace?"

Nothing.

"What are you?"

The machine remained motionless, silent.

"As inscrutable as a Russian."

A faint breeze stirred from a side corridor, carrying with it a pleasant scent of flowers and fresh air. With a curious gesture the machine turned and waved one of its arms, as if pointing down the corridor.

"So do you want me to go that way?"

The machine's arm was rigid, pointing, and it started down the corridor.

He turned to follow it and entered into a broad passage suffused with the reflected light. He had a sudden flash of memory—it was of Brienne, school, sitting in the shade of an arcade facing the square and playing chess with Brother Louis, who taught there. It was one of the few happy memories of that place. What triggered the memory? he wondered.

The side corridor widened out, and he suddenly found himself back outside, standing on a balcony that looked out over the open square. It had a good feel to it, twenty meters up from the ground, the perfect place to stage a grand review. The machine followed him, floating to come up by his side.

The view was magnificent, the sun straight overhead, the inside of the Sphere glowing with yellow light, the buildings in the vast plaza reflecting it like burnished mirrors, the strange black mountain dominating the sky, the clouds about its summit coiling and spiraling upward.

Below, the blue and white polished squares stood out like a chessboard, twenty across and twenty deep. Chess: the memory in the corridor and now this. He looked over at the machine, wondering and then dismissing the speculation.

Napoleon leaned against the chest-high railing, his arms draped over the side.

He looked back at the machine that floated beside him, as if waiting.

"So, my mechanical citizen, you appear to rule an empty world."

The machine did nothing.

Sighing, he looked back out at the square.

"Like a chessboard."

He looked back at the machine.

"I once saw a mechanical Turk who could beat even the masters, but I suspect they had a dwarf hidden within its bowels. So, my soulless companion, could you play such a thing, a game perhaps, or at least whistle a steam-powered tune?"

A flicker of light caused him to turn with a start.

The empty square below was filled with forms. The first three rows of squares closest to him were now arrayed with geometric forms, the back line a mixture of pyramids, pentagons, hexagons topped with three-sided pyramids, and two octagons that tapered up to a point. Each form, nearly twice the size of a man, filled an entire square, yet they appeared to be translucent, the squares beneath ever so slightly visible. The second row was lined with tall narrow rectangles, the third row with short round cylinders. The far side of the square was matched with similar forms, white to his blue.

"A game?"

He looked back inquiringly at the machine.

The air between the emperor and the machine appeared to take on a solid form, a small representation of the board floating before him. With a speed too fast to comprehend, a white piece, a cylinder, moved forward three squares, a blue cylinder on the opposite side matching the move. Out on the plaza the corresponding pieces moved as well. A tall rectangle of the white slipped out through the gap created by the cylinder, moving in a diagonal line; a blue pentagon leaped over both lines and came down ten squares forward. Faster and faster they moved, and he struggled to follow, to gather it in, to understand the moves, the tactics, the goal to victory.

A blue rectangle disappeared with a flash; another move by white in the same turn then followed. A blue hexagon leaped forward and then turned, like a knight; a white hexagon crowned with a three-sided pyramid moved in what appeared to be an erratic pattern, a zigzag.

"Slower, I don't understand, damn it," Napoleon growled.

The pieces on the board floating before the machine disappeared. A single piece was now in the center. He watched its movement. It vanished, and a different-shaped piece took its place, moving differently. Pentagons, hexagons, pyramids, it was getting difficult to follow. He felt somehow as if his mind were being drawn outward.

"I don't like these pieces," Napoleon snapped. "Machine parts, a Greek philosopher's playthings."

The board disappeared, and the machine drew closer.

"Wait a minute," Napoleon growled, lapsing back into French, forcibly overriding the translator implant.

The silent machine stopped, hovered, and he felt as if somehow it were reaching inward, into himself.

A form appeared again, miniature, elegant, floating in the air, so real that he reached out to touch it, but his hand drifted through it.

"Yes," he whispered excitedly, "that is it."

The machine drew back slightly and the board reappeared, what he had just seen now floating as a playing piece. The piece moved.

"No, no, no. That one should be a fast-moving piece."

Napoleon held his hand up and pointed at the machine. "This, what I am thinking, this should be the slower one for straight lines. Yes, that's it. Now for the next one."

"Your majesty?"

Damn it all, he felt foolish calling for a man with the words "your majesty," but shouting out, "hey, Napoleon, where the hell are you?" seemed equally absurd. He did, however, make sure there was enough of a sarcastic tone in his cry to annoy the man.

Yaroslav, with Basak in tow for protection if it should be needed, heard a chortle of delight, turned, and started down the corridor. The others were still arguing, cajoling, and threatening Vush back down in the middle of the room. The Overseer had finally floated a dozen feet into the air, as if to escape them, and was simply turning in slow circles, as if trying to figure out where to go next.

The hell with the stupid bastard. If need be, he'd find the thing on his own. They had seen the First Traveler machine when they had first entered the building. Vush had tried to approach it, but the machine had turned away and disappeared up the ramp. And now Napoleon had disappeared as well. So he had to go look for them, and the thought of running as an errand boy looking for Napoleon was ever so slightly distasteful. At least it gave him a chance to explore a little bit rather than hang around at the edge of the argument.

As he wandered off, he realized that Napoleon had most likely thought the same thing and set out on his own initiative. The thought of that man finding something important ahead of him was troublesome.

"Napoleon?"

There was no reply.

"Damn Corsican," Yaroslav mumbled.

He turned down a side corridor, the floor lighting up dimly to guide his passage, the hallway ahead suffused with the outside light. He turned a final corner and came up short.

A master machine of the First Travelers, the same that he had met in the Ring and inside the base of the Skyhook tower, was ahead of him—and Napoleon was by its side laughing. Now, how the hell did that bastard find him first?

Yaroslav edged out quietly onto the platform.

"All right, you could call it the queen," Napoleon said, looking up at the machine. "Lower cut to the dress, Imperial style, make it 1806, breasts barely exposed. I rather liked that year."

Yaroslav edged around the machine and there, floating in front of Napoleon, was what appeared to be a miniature of a woman, dressed in a high-waisted gown, her exposed breasts spilling out of the top.

"Make them a bit larger," Yaroslav said quietly.

Napoleon looked over at him and smiled.

The woman's breasts swelled in size.

"Does that suit you?"

"Perfectly," Yaroslav replied with a lascivious grin.

The figure disappeared, and an instant later a heavy field piece floated in the air.

"Just what the hell is this?" Yaroslav asked.

"A game," Napoleon replied, as if stating the obvious.

Yaroslav went past him and looked out on the plaza.

Two armies of chess pieces were arrayed on the blue and white squares in the plaza.

"I think I have it now," Napoleon announced, and he turned away from the machine to look out at the square.

"It can read my thoughts," Napoleon said, looking over at Yaroslav. "I guess I should find that to be disconcerting, but for some reason it doesn't bother me. It's teaching me to play something like their version of chess."

From the far end of the playing field a front-rank piece, dressed in the uniform of a British Highlander regiment, moved forward three squares.

Napoleon, with a dramatic flourish, held up a finger and pointed. A front-rank piece, outfitted in the uniform of the old guard, moved in reply.

"No, not like that," Napoleon snapped.

The piece disappeared and rematerialized in its original square.

"More realistic, bayonet fixed and poised for attack. Smoothly now."

The piece, which was standing at attention, lowered its musket, bayonet glinting, and it marched forward three paces and snapped back to attention again.

"That's it."

Yaroslav settled back, fascinated.

The soft whine of a float chair crackled behind them and Yaroslav looked over his shoulder to see Hobbs floating out onto the porch.

"A game," Yaroslav announced, as if he were somehow refereeing it.

Hobbs surveyed the scene, watching intently as the machine moved a Prussian lancer out of the second rank, advancing at a gallop to the center of the field. Napoleon countered with a hussar leaping through the air over the two forward ranks, zigzagging down the field, and finishing by cutting down a Highlander in a realistic splatter of blood.

Frustrated, Napoleon suddenly looked over at the machine.

"I can't move twice? You did it, damn you!"

The board reappeared in miniature in front of Napoleon, who watched it intently for a moment, pieces moving and flashing in midair.

"Damn your soul, you cheated me, you didn't tell me that you only get an extra move with kills from the first two ranks."

He muttered darkly while an Austrian field piece moved forward and with a puff of smoke obliterated the hussar.

He took off his hat, slamming it down on the railing, and looked over at the machine, his eyes glinting.

Another guardsman advanced, a match made by the other side.

"I'll give you five-to-one on the machine," Hobbs said. "A hundred credits."

"Done," Yaroslav replied.

Napoleon looked over at Yaroslav and smiled.

"Just to make the game exciting, but I fully expect to lose my money on you."

Napoleon grinned.

"I didn't expect you to show any support for me."

Yaroslav shrugged his shoulders.

"It's worth it to say I bet on Napoleon and lost."

The game moved yet more rapidly, additional touches slowly being added in, explosions sounding when the guns were fired, hooves clattering when the hussars, chasseurs, lancers, and cuirassiers charged, bayonets flashing when the foot soldiers took another piece.

A marshal from the white side, dressed as a Prussian general, swept through Napoleon's left flank. He pulled a gun piece to counter, destroying the marshal. An alluring queen of the white then rushed forward, taking the tricolored flag in the middle. The plaza flashed with light as if fireworks were bursting in the air, "Rule Britannia" playing in the background. The pieces disappeared, and the machine tilted forward ever so slightly, as if bowing.

Napoleon looked around darkly at his companions, who watched him expectantly, a thin trace of a smile on Yaroslav's face.

Throwing his head back, Napoleon laughed.

"Well done, you trickster, well done indeed." He saluted the machine, then extending his hand Napoleon grabbed hold of one of the tentacle projections of the machine and shook it.

"Curious."

Yaroslav looked back to see Aldin standing behind them.

"I know. A game. Something of the First Travelers, like chess in a way. Napoleon here modified the pieces, though."

Napoleon leaned back against the railing and looked at those around him.

"Is this typical?"

"You mean a machine that plays games?" Aldin asked.

"Exactly. I knew I could not win; if it could create this, then it undoubtedly knew the rules far better than I. A chess master takes years to learn his craft." He hesitated for a second and then smiled. "That is why I never played one."

"I heard that you loved to cheat," Yaroslav interjected.

Napoleon looked over at the old man and wagged a finger at him.

"Your history books lie." He paused, and then broke into a grin again. "At least most of the time they lie. When they report my victories, that is the truth at least."

"Play it again," Hobbs asked.

Napoleon nodded, and turning, he beckoned to the plaza. The pieces reappeared, and within seconds the forms were moving again.

"Any luck so far?" Yaroslav asked, looking back at Aldin.

"Everyone's wandering about. It'll take months to search this one place, though, if we do it at random."

Yaroslav nodded.

"And we've got days at best."

"Besides, Vush can't even really remember what the hell it looks like."

"Well, he did say that there was a machine like this one next to it."

Aldin walked up to the machine and looked up at it.

"We're looking for a device that makes wormholes," he said.

The machine continued to face the plaza, intent on moving a hussar that destroyed an imperial guardsman.

"The Overseers Vush and Mupa came here and found part of it. Could you show us where that was? Could you show us other parts of that machine?"

Napoleon moved a battery out that blew a marshal apart.

"Damn your eyes," the machine whispered.

Napoleon laughed with delight.

"Could we hold this game for a second?" Aldin asked.

Napoleon looked over at him and then held his hand up to the machine.

"My friends here would like to talk to you."

The machine turned slightly.

Aldin posed the same question again.

The machine turned back slightly and then moved one of the queen pieces to the middle of the field.

Napoleon shrugged his shoulders in a typical Gallic gesture and, looking back, waved his hand. A guardsman leaped forward to bayonet the queen.

"Such a waste, she was radiant," Napoleon said quietly.

Yaroslav, watching intently, looked back at Aldin.

"It's obvious the damn thing has more important things to do."

Aldin thrust his hands into his tunic pockets and settled back to watch. The battle was played out swiftly, the machine's defense crumbling after losing one of its two most important pieces. Napoleon sliced in hard through the middle, sacrificing most of his front rank but thus gaining additional moves to bring up his rear. Just when victory seemed assured, a shimmer of light appeared above the entire plaza and an entire second playing level formed, floating translucent, several meters above the first. Above the second, a third level formed. The machine leaped its remaining queen upward and far to Napoleon's rear.

"Damn me, you scoundrel, you cheated again," Napoleon thundered.

"Another level of play," Yaroslav replied, while Hobbs cackled with delight.

Napoleon went up to the machine and half-playfully but half-seriously he shoved it, but it did not move. A miniature playing field again appeared in front of Napoleon, showing three levels and pieces moving up and down between them.

"You should have told me earlier," he snapped.

"You never asked," Yaroslav interjected.

The queen swooped down the following turn to kill a marshal. All of Napoleon's forces were far forward, the enemy in his rear. He moved a battery upward to threaten the machine's final defense, but it was too late, as his tricolor fell the following turn. The fireworks sparkled, "God Save the King" playing on what sounded like a full brass band.

"Bloody good show. Never did the English soldier fight so

well as he did today," the machine whispered, its voice reverberating slightly as if projected from a dozen different sources. The figure of the marshal down on the playing field rode up to beneath the platform and with a flourish drew his sword. His horse reared back, and he saluted smartly, before vanishing into thin air.

Napoleon, his hands clasped behind his back, stalked around the machine.

"You stole my own quote. It should be, 'Never did the French soldier fight.' You're as perfidious as they are and just about as heartless as Wellington."

"I am Wellington," the machine whispered.

Hobbs could not help but break down into a quaking laugh, his entire float chair jostling back and forth as his rolls of fat quivered.

Napoleon looked up at the machine.

"I am Wellington," it said, its voice cold.

"All right then. We play again."

"Could I interrupt?" Aldin asked.

Napoleon wheeled about.

"Can't you see we are busy, this oil-stinking Wellington and I."

"We do have other business to attend to here," Aldin said soothingly, "just a little emergency involving a couple of hundred planets."

"Ah, yes, there are priorities," Yaroslav interjected.

"All right, then," Napoleon replied. "Wellington, do give your attention to my friend. Let the game wait for a minute."

The playing field was again arrayed with figures, the machine turning its back on Aldin.

"Gentleman from France, you may fire first," Wellington announced.

Napoleon looked over at Aldin.

"It seems our host has different priorities," Yaroslav said, unable to keep from laughing, filled with a secret delight that Napoleon was being suckered into another game that he would undoubtedly lose.

Aldin watched the game unfold for several minutes and then quietly turned away. Zergh was waiting for him in the shadow of the corridor, and the two went back into the pyramid.

"Curious," Zergh said softly. "We've encountered those machines twice before, but this is the first time one's ever interacted with any of us, or demonstrated even the slightest concern. Hell, the last time it stood by impassively while Yaroslav blew it apart along with the Skyhook."

"According to Vush it ignored him while he and his idiot companion were playing around with the wormhole machine," Aldin added in. "So why now, why Napoleon?"

They reached the corridor by which they had ascended into the pyramid.

"Vush and the others went up this way," Zergh said, and Aldin followed his lead as the causeway spiraled upward. A small machine rolled past them, going in the opposite direction, dragging yet a smaller device with several dozen arms flailing, a thin beeping protest echoing in the hallway. Seconds later half a dozen devices similar to the captive scooted past and turned the corner in pursuit. There was a clattering of metal, and a moment later the mob of machines returned, this time dragging back smashed parts of the captor, some of which were still twitching feebly.

"I think this place might be going amok," Aldin said.

Reaching another level, they paused for a moment while Zergh looked around to gain his bearings.

"Let's not get lost. There must be hundreds of levels to this thing."

"If it's even the right building," Zergh replied.

Distant voices echoed in the hallway, and the two followed the sound. A huge doorway, more than ten meters high and just as wide, opened to one side, and they ventured in.

"The junkyard of the gods," Aldin whispered in awe.

"So, you think then that Vush has revealed the secret of the Sphere?"

Mupa nodded sadly.

"He has obviously gone off with them," Mupa replied. "I always did have my doubts about him. He was not of the Select in all things. That is why I spent so much time with him—"

"Shut up," the Arch snapped, cutting Mupa off and reducing him to a quivering silence.

The Arch looked down coldly at the youthful Overseer of but twenty thousand years who had gotten them in all of this trouble. He had yet to find a sufficiently remote punishment planet where, alone, Mupa could double his life span in contemplation. It had to have the right combination of factors, freezing cold, or boiling hot, to start with, he wasn't quite sure which one he wanted yet; ideally there should be a desert world with both, and nothing in between. The problem with desert worlds was that they could make one wonderfully crazy from their stark beauty, and he would not give Mupa that opportunity.

"If they should find this thing, could they use it from there?" the Arch asked.

"They would have to bring it back," Mupa replied, "to where the runaway star is, or at least nearby."

The Arch nodded.

"Let Corbin chase him at the Sphere. If he should escape, we can meet him on his return and take care of things in the appropriate manner," the Arch announced.

Of course, it would mean eliminating Corbin as well once this was over, but he had gone this far—a little further in degree of eliminating was hardly troublesome to his soul at all at this point.

chapter ten

Exhausted, Aldin Larice collapsed on top of a broken-down, spindly machine that sagged beneath his weight.

"Careful, that could be it," Yaroslav said, even as he wiped off a thin patina of grease and dust from a multilegged machine that looked like some sort of cross between a Xsarn and a turbo jack for a Brusarian pleasure yacht, and plopped down beside Aldin.

The cavernous room seemed to stretch on forever, the insides of it a mad jumble of broken parts, twisted machinery, and what looked like remarkably advanced holo computers, some with lights still blinking. A slow but endless procession of other machines wandered in and out of the room, ignoring the presence of the intruders. Some of the machines entering were dragging other devices; occasionally their burdens were twitching and struggling. They would deposit their burdens and leave, and more often than not the "junk" would crawl back out of the room, or be rescued by similar devices and carried back out.

"If it wasn't so maddening, it'd almost be humorous to watch."

Aldin looked up to see Tia standing beside him, her face covered in grease and dirt.

"How's it going?"

"Oh, he's sure that this is the room. I think he's right. Apparently this is some sort of repository for broken machines. The only trouble is that it's been several thousand years since he and Mupa were here. Supposedly the room was damn near empty then except for one of the master machines.

"And now this," she sighed, pointing to the chaos around them.

A ratlike machine scurried past, followed seconds later by dozens more, and disappeared into the insides of what looked like a servobot, the crew reemerging a minute later with small pieces of holo crystal, memory units, and strips of wire.

There was a thin yet persistent cacophony of screeches, grindings, scrapings, and beepings echoing through the room, reminding Aldin of what some Gafs called deconstructionist music. He caught a momentary glimpse of Vush floating up, looking about, and then drifting off again.

"Oishi still with him?"

"I think quietly contemplating beheading," Tia sighed.

"This is obviously a junkyard," Zergh said, sticking his head up from behind a pile of bent pipes. "But most curious. It's inside to protect valuable machinery, what looks like workshops line the far wall, and tools are scattered all about. When Vush was here, the place was nearly empty; now it's packed to the gills."

"And everything working to cross purposes," Tia said. "I've seen things dragged in here, and then others come in of the same make and drag them back out again, even when they're obviously dead, if you could call a machine dead. It almost seems like a machine clan loyalty."

"An interesting philosophical consideration." Yaroslav yawned.

"Oh, spare me," Aldin snapped, realizing his temper was far too short.

Aldin stood up, stretched, and headed over to where he had last seen Vush.

The Overseer bobbed up again for a second and then drifted back down. Oishi, seeing Aldin's approach, gave him a grimace of frustration.

"Say, Vush, you got a moment?" Aldin asked.

Vush turned and looked down at him.

"It depends on the definition of a moment," Vush replied. "To some species it might be a mere nanosecond of an all too brief existence. To one such as me, a moment could stretch into one of your centuries."

"Just shut up and come down here to eye level."

Vush floated down to hover in front of Aldin.

"Making any progress?"

"Well by a process of elimination one could define it that way."

Aldin nodded.

"Do you know what you're looking for?"

Vush hesitated.

"Go on."

"Not really."

Aldin nodded, restraining himself from calling on Oishi to pull out the sword and start threatening.

"So what is it that you are doing?"

"Well, I'm just sort of floating around, figuring that sooner or later something will come up."

"I see."

"And how long might later be?" Oishi inquired.

Vush hesitated. "A thousand years, maybe more in an extreme case."

"By that time the entire cloud will have gone down the hole," Zergh snapped, coming up to join the group.

"Oh, that is most certainly an exaggeration. There are quite a few million stars; even at the rate of one a day it'd take several thousand years before even a sizable dent was made."

"Most reassuring," Oishi growled.

Aldin stepped closer, knowing that he was violating the ten feet of personal space that Overseers felt was the closest they'd want another being to approach. Oishi, who was behind Vush, did not budge when the being backed into him. Aldin drew closer.

"Think of something else," Aldin whispered.

"Like what?"

"Well for instance, something other than prowling aimlessly through this junkyard."

"This is where we found the device to start with."

"Ah, excuse me," Tia interjected. "Just one question."

"And that is?" Vush asked, as if relieved to be able to turn away from Aldin and Zergh.

"It's obvious this was a place for broken machines. And yet you took the wormhole device out of here."

"You know Mupa and I debated that point for quite a few years. The First Traveler machine was here. At one point after a lot of prodding and poking it projected a holo image of how the thing supposedly worked. Now for myself I believed that this was an in-processing point, where things were brought for repair. Mupa argued that it was an out-processing, where things were placed once they had gone through the work-stations. He took it without my even really knowing."

"Fifty-fifty," Aldin replied, "a nice safe bet when playing with wormholes."

"So what are you suggesting I do?" Vush asked, an actual note of exasperation in his voice.

"You could try and talk to the First Traveler machine for starters," Zergh said.

"We're not even sure it's the same one," Aldin replied, "and besides it's busy playing with Napoleon."

"How about accessing into some of the computer systems?" Tia said.

"How?" Vush replied.

"Well, damn it, think of something, anything!" Aldin snapped, and turning he stormed off, kicking another rat machine out of the way. The machine squealed and skidded across the narrow path that weaved in and out through the piles of junk and disappeared.

Cursing, Aldin made his way through the heaps of broken parts, and gaining an access corridor he went up it, glad to be away from Vush. The causeway did a sweeping spiral turn upward, curving out over the cavernous junk hall, which finally disappeared from view.

Aldin stopped and cursed.

Another room, acres in size, was before him, this one piled almost as high with junk as the one below. He turned away and strode up the next causeway. The room above was the same, and then the room above that one as well.

Just where the hell did they get all of this junk?

He felt a stab of pain, and hopping up on one leg he looked down at the ground. A tiny rat machine was at his feet, a pinching talon extended, holding in its claw a thin slice of his trousers. It scurried forward to pinch again, and leaping up he came down hard, nearly losing his balance, the machine scrunching underneath his heel.

Another one came around the corner, claws raised.

"Oh, shit."

Turning, he started back down the causeway, the tiny machine in pursuit. Zergh, who had followed him up, stopped for a moment and started to laugh, until the machine darted toward the Gaf while Aldin ran past. The Gaf leaped upward, the rat turning and retreating, triumphantly waving a torn piece of purple trouser.

"I think they're upset," Zergh snarled, hopping and cursing as the two ran back down the corridor.

Gaining the next level, they paused for a moment to look back. The corridor was empty.

"Damn place," Aldin sighed. "I think we're on a fool's errand. We couldn't get Korobachi, and chances are Corbin killed him. We come here without someone to tell us how the machine works, and we run into a junkyard. Vush doesn't know what the hell to get, and I've got a bad feeling about the whole damn thing. It was a nice dumb-ass altruistic idea that by saving the Core we'd get off the hook, but I think it's a washout."

"Let's go back to the ship and get a drink," Zergh said, reaching down to rub his ankle, which was bleeding from the pinch.

Agreeing, Aldin followed him, shouting to Oishi, who was still with Vush, to join them when the Overseer finally decided to take a break.

Gaining the vast empty main floor, they stepped aside for a moment while a long line of machines rolled in, each of them bearing another machine, most of which were twisted and broken, some of them still sparking, others waving feebly.

Stepping out of the pyramid, Aldin came up short. The square seemed to be alive with forms—guardsmen, hussars, marshals, artillery pieces—moving back and forth.

"Well, at least the emperor is having a good time."

"Are you heading back to the ship?"

Aldin looked up to see Napoleon leaning over the balcony.

"Thinking about it," Zergh replied.

"Good. Get one of the servobots to bring out a bottle of brandy or a good wine. Also, something to eat."

"Beef Wellington perhaps for myself." Yaroslav was by Napoleon's side.

There was a low curse from above in French.

"Chicken Marengo will do," Napoleon shouted.

"What the hell is that?" Zergh asked.

He shouted down the ingredients as if passing an order to a waiter.

Zergh turned and walked away.

"Did you get that?" Aldin asked.

Zergh, obviously insulted, said nothing.

Munching on a chicken leg, Napoleon leaned over the balcony as the playing field was cleared after his twentieth defeat.

"It's not nice to lose, is it my emperor?" Yaroslav said, chuckling while pouring out two more brandies.

"It keeps advancing the rules," Napoleon replied.

The playing field was crosshatched with light. The sun above was down to the bottom of its variable phase, and the white squares of the field had in turn become illuminated to break the semitwilight.

Napoleon stretched and rubbed his hand over the stubble of beard.

"Aren't you tired?"

"No. Actually remarkably refreshed."

Yaroslav looked at him narrowly, wondering if the man was putting on an act of bravado. They had been at it for over half a standard day, and except for a brief pause to eat two meals and wandering inside to find a convenient spot to relieve himself, he still seemed almost as fresh as when he started.

Though he hated to admit it to himself, he found that he was actually admiring the man's stamina and ability to concentrate.

"Why don't we quit for a while?" Yaroslav finally suggested.

"Whatever for?"

"Well, for starters, I wouldn't mind a little rest."

"No one is stopping you," Napoleon replied, the faintest of

contemptuous smiles on his face, as if this admission of fatigue was a victory in a contest of endurance.

"You're always competing, aren't you?"

"That's what life is. To see a challenge, to formulate your strategy, and then to win."

"But this is only a game," Yaroslav said.

"Is it?"

Yaroslav paused and looked closely at the man before him. "Go on and explain," he finally said.

"Nine of us came here on a mission, a quest. It is obvious that none of you actually know what it is that you are looking for. Will you admit to that?"

Yaroslav nodded in agreement, though he hated to admit that even he was stumped this time.

"Have you ever seen anything like our friend here before?"

"I am Wellington," the machine said, its voice a whisper.

"Twice before. You know that."

"And from what I heard over these last days in talking with Vush and with others, this machine and others like it are capable of thinking; they are some form of sentinel of the creations of the godlike First Travelers."

Yaroslav nodded. "That's what we kind of assumed."

"Assumed or knew? Be precise."

"Is this an examination?" Yaroslav snapped.

"Humor me," Napoleon replied, smiling in a disarming way and looking straight into Yaroslav's eyes.

Damn him, Yaroslav thought. He has the presence, the self-assuredness. His own image of Napoleon had never really been all that positive. Now Alexander, there was someone he had taken to immediately. After all, he was Alexander the Great. But Napoleon, that was a character of history he had never really cared for. Alexander had endured the march back from the Indus with his troops, had carried a full panoply of equipment on his back through the mountains of Bactria, had ridden in the vanguard in the charge at Gaugamela and at Granicus. Napoleon had always been pictured as abandoning his troops in the retreat from Moscow, riding away and issuing proclamations that the emperor was safe. The etchings of Goya came to mind, the cynical drafting of sixteen-year-olds to prop up his collapsing empire, the killing of the sick soldiers at Acre, the choked fields of dead at Borodino, Austerlitz, and a hundred other places.

This Napoleon didn't quite match it, though he sensed that such ruthlessness was indeed below the surface. Yet how had he done it? Yaroslav wondered. He could sense part of that answer as he looked at him. There was a Napoleon before the legend, a man of flesh and blood, who could imbue others with his dreams, and in the imbuing convince them that there was a higher ideal worth dying for. He had wrapped himself in the glorious dreams of the Revolution, lifting it out of the ugly squalor of the Terror and firing a generation with the dream of sweeping all of Europe into a new order of equality.

"You don't like me at all, do you?"

Yaroslav looked at him.

"Most of the time, I don't."

"Because of what I did?"

"You and so many others like you," Yaroslav said, boosting himself up on the balcony to sit. "People like you might start out with a dream, but in the end millions die. Such madness is usually started by idealists."

Napoleon laughed softly, and refilling an empty tumbler he offered it over to Yaroslav, who took it with a nod of thanks. He looked over at Basak, but the Gaf was curled up in the corridor, fast asleep. Hobbs, however, was more than happy to join them in another drink and then settled back in his float chair to nurse the brandy and listen.

"This I find to be interesting. To meet my own historian, thousands of years after I supposedly died. And I hear in your voice that history was not kind to me."

"Oh, there are many who would disagree, but they forget the price of glory."

"Ah, yes, glory." Napoleon sighed. "And how would you define it?"

"A lie, a trick, a dupe to get others to die, a hunk of metal dangling from a piece of cloth in payment for a life. 'With baubles such as these I can lead armies.'"

"So they did remember that quote," Napoleon said with a sigh.

Yaroslav was silent.

"The medal is nothing but that, a bauble. Ah, but what it represents," Napoleon said, looking down, his hand brushing the Legion of Honor medal that rested on his left breast.

"But it is so much more. Certainly there are fools who see the medal and it becomes all, the way some would go to Notre

Dame, when it was restored to the church, and grovel before a statue of marble and believe that the saint resided within. There are far too many such as they.

"But it is so much more. It is a dream, a vision, a belief, a goal. For what is man if he does not dream? I believed in the Revolution. I dreamed of the glory of it, a people raising their heads out of the dust and declaring themselves free. Even if the Revolution had never existed, I would have dreamed it into being."

"Yet you created your own nobility."

"Yes, yes, I know. Yet who were my nobles? Ney, a cavalry sergeant, for one. A nobility of skill, of intellect. It is always that way. For some, the baubles of nobility gave a legitimacy of a higher ideal. Men will fight and will die if you offer them something to believe in. Even you, my cynical old friend, for I suspect that like most old cynics you were an idealist in your youth."

Yaroslav shook his head.

"Xsarn food."

"What is that?"

"Shit."

"Oh, *merde.*" He laughed.

"Tell me," Yaroslav said, unable to contain himself. "Is that what your guardsmen really said at Waterloo?"

"It's a good story, is it not?" Napoleon said with a smile. "And that is precisely what I am saying to you. They were offered life, and yet their honor was more important, such that they could die with a crude jest. If they had not, would their memories be recalled now? If those men had lived quiet lives and died old in bed, who would sing their songs now? It is the spirit such as that that impells men to greatness. There are things that transcend life itself. It is that which I dreamed of, and that which gave a nation into my control, willing to shape that dream. We would have united Europe nearly two hundred years before it finally happened, from what I heard. And from what little I have learned of the years after my time, I doubt it would have been worse for the uniting, and most likely would have been spared much agony in the years to come. Is that so bad a thing?"

"Yet it is men like you who create the suffering."

"There will always be men like me. There always were, there always will be. But I defend myself with the claim that at least I dreamed of a world of justice, freed from the old regimes of greed, spoiled nobility that starved its own people, and a society based upon birth rather than upon courage, intellect, and the spirit to reach beyond one's station."

Yaroslav leaned forward, his face shadowed by the twilight. "Do you honestly believe what you've just told me?"

Napoleon merely smiled.

"You've managed to divert things away," Napoleon finally said, breaking a long moment of silence. "There are more pressing issues than the fulfillment of your curiosity regarding myself."

"Such as?"

"What have you learned by watching Wellington here and myself playing all these hours?"

"A look into your logic. A game of chess can reveal an awful lot about the type of person behind the board. You for one are impatient, aggressive almost to folly, yet terribly cunning."

"Learning such about me is useless given what it is you came here for."

Yaroslav smiled.

"Regarding our friend then?"

"The victory at Waterloo was won on the playing fields of Eton," Wellington said, and Yaroslav turned to look at the machine with surprise.

"He never said that, you know," Yaroslav said.

"I never heard it," Napoleon replied. "Sounds typically English though, pretentious and trite."

"Curious," Yaroslav said, looking closely at the machine.

"Where did he get it then?" Napoleon said.

The two were silent for a moment.

"It obviously can read my thoughts—a clairvoyant machine. The shapes and forms of the pieces were in my thoughts, and it made them for me. I assumed when it named itself Wellington, it took that from my mind, too. But that foolish quote."

"I knew it, though," Yaroslav said.

Napoleon looked at the machine.

"Josephine," he whispered.

In a glimmer of pale yellow light, a holo image floated before him.

"A close enough proximity of her," Napoleon said with almost a wistful sigh, "at least when she was younger."

"Melinda," Yaroslav said.

Nothing happened.

"He obviously doesn't care much for your thoughts," Napoleon said, obviously pleased that the machine would do his bidding alone.

"Why, though?"

"Because I am Napoleon." There was a note of pride in his voice, as if the answer were all too obvious.

"Please spare me the false hubris. So, why?" Yaroslav said, ignoring the flashing look of anger. "If it can actually read thoughts, it must know why we are here, what it is that we seek, the crisis we face."

"Because it simply doesn't care," Napoleon replied. "You attribute altruism to a steam-driven machine of cogs and wheels. If a man should come up and cut your arm off, he would be wrong, a criminal, and all would say that he is evil and must be punished. But if one of Watt's machines should catch you, and crush you in its gears, one would simply turn the machine off until you were free, and then turn it back on again to do its labors."

He paused and looked back at Wellington.

"Isn't that right, you haughty boiler?"

"Another game?"

Napoleon sighed.

"And you'll change the rules again."

"A progression, my emperor."

Napoleon looked over at Yaroslav.

"Do you think you'll actually find whatever it is this Vush is looking for?"

"I doubt it," Yaroslav replied. "I didn't expect much to start with, and even less now. It was a vain hope. A desperate last stand, if you will."

"Desperation can breed insight."

"The machine doesn't give a god damn about Vush, you saw that. It only wants you."

"It showed good sense, then."

"It isn't helping us."

"Oh, really?" Napoleon said with a smile.

"Go on and play it again."

"I'm bored with this game. Let's play something different if you like, something more challenging," Napoleon said, looking back over at Wellington.

A flash of light enveloped him, and for the briefest instant he inwardly cursed, believing that the machine had killed him. He felt a falling away, a terrible sense of disorientation, as if he had been turned and turned upon a spinning platform.

There was an open field before him; a low declining slope dropped away. Half a kilometer down an enclosed farmhouse was on his left, stout walls surrounding a small courtyard, home, outbuildings, and barn all joined together. A similar, though smaller structure was straight ahead on the road that ran past him and then continued on up the opposite slope. Fields of wheat, golden and thigh high, swayed in a gentle breeze. Several orchards dotted the landscape. He felt his heart start to race, and his knees felt loose, rubbery.

His senses reeled.

"Waterloo," he whispered. "Yaroslav?"

"I see it," the old man whispered. "Damn it all, I hate those jump beams. Didn't know the old machine had one in him."

Basak, who had been asleep, came to his feet, looking around, confused, and with a growl drew the double-headed ax out of its sheath.

"Shall we play?"

Napoleon looked over at Wellington, who floated beside him.

He looked overhead, as if to reassure himself. The pale sun was straight overhead, the vast sphere enclosing the sky.

"*Mon Dieu,*" Napoleon gasped.

"How close is it?" Yaroslav inquired.

"Identical. Damn identical. There—" He pointed down the slope. "—Hougoumont, which held me up, the road to Brussels, the woods to the right, which hid the Prussian advance. All of it."

His hands shaking, he clasped them behind himself to hide the trembling and paced across the field, the high wheat swishing aside. He stamped the ground and then looked back at Wellington.

"It rained, you know."

The sun overhead went dark, and looking up he saw a small cloud hovering at the zenith that rapidly started to expand.

Napoleon nodded.

"Did you ever dream of doing something over again? A young lady lost by foolishness, a choice incorrectly made, a war lost?" he whispered, and looked back at Yaroslav.

The old man could not help but smile.

"Do you accept the challenge?" Wellington asked.

Napoleon smiled and nodded.

There was another glimmer of light, and a member of the old guard materialized, as if conjured up out of the dust.

The image saluted.

Basak stepped backward, growling, holding his ax up, ready to swing.

Yaroslav laughed and motioned for him to lower the blade.

"Come, come, my hairy friend. I think there's going to be a little war."

Basak grinned in anticipation.

"But there are risks," Wellington said.

Napoleon walked over to the guardsman, and, hand trembling, he reached out and touched him. His hand did not go through. He looked closely at the man.

"I remember you," Napoleon said, his voice trembling. "Jean Paul, you were with me from Egypt to Borodino."

"Where I died," the guardsman whispered, his voice sounding as if it were conjured from beyond the grave.

Napoleon stepped backward.

"It's just a transformation of matter, the clay of this sphere, into this," Yaroslav said, as if trying to reassure him. "A hell of a lot of energy to do that."

Napoleon passed his hands over his eyes and looked back at Jean.

"It is you?"

The guardsman looked at him with crinkled eyes.

"But of course, my emperor."

Napoleon looked back at Wellington.

"From my thoughts you took this?"

He hesitated, looking back at the guardsman.

"I had not thought of him in years, yet you pulled him from within my soul."

Another guardsman appeared, and yet another, until, within seconds, an entire company was formed. Wide-eyed, Napoleon gazed at them, whispering names, the forms smiling each in turn, coming to attention, saluting. He walked down the line, looking up at them.

"Pierre, I lost you at Wagram, and Claude, you died of typhus; O'Rourke, you were decorated at Austerlitz for taking that gun, and then you let a whore stab you in the back."

And they smiled, some saying a brief greeting back, a pledge of loyalty, an affectionate smile.

Tears in his eyes, Napoleon looked back at Wellington.

"Memories of the dead, your dead. He pulled them out of you," Yaroslav said, going up to the company, poking some of them, taking hold of a jacket to feel its weave.

"My dead," Napoleon said.

"Only a million, more or less," Yaroslav sniffed, looking over at Napoleon with a casual air.

Napoleon turned on the old philosopher.

"You know nothing of it," he snapped, "nothing. You write your histories and spin your lies. You know nothing of what is in here." And he thumped his chest.

Yaroslav said nothing, and going up to Jean he motioned for the form to hand over his musket. The guardsman, with cold lifeless eyes, looked over at Napoleon, who nodded an assertion.

Yaroslav took the musket and balanced it in his hands.

"I've always wanted to try one of these," he said. "Seen them on some of the more primitive worlds." He walked away from the line, and fumbling with the piece, he cocked the hammer. He turned back at a range of half a dozen paces and raised the musket. He pointed it at Jean.

Before Napoleon could shout out a protest, Yaroslav squeezed the trigger. An explosion snapped off. Jean, nearly lifted off his feet, crashed backward, knocking over the man behind him.

Yaroslav looked through the curling blue smoke, unable to hide a momentary astonishment at what he had just done, and looked back almost guiltily at Napoleon.

"You bastard," Napoleon shouted, going up to the company line, which remained motionless except for the one fallen guardsman.

The man was still, a neat hole in his chest, a pool of blood spilling out beneath him, staining the golden stalks of wheat. Napoleon knelt down by his side.

"He was just an illusion," Yaroslav said, though from the catch in his voice it was obvious that he was trying to reassure himself.

Napoleon looked up coldly at Yaroslav.

"It will be real," Wellington said quietly. "That is the risk."

Shaken, Napoleon came back up to his feet.

"I didn't really kill him," Yaroslav whispered. "Your Jean died over three thousand years ago. It was a creation of your memory."

Yaroslav hesitated.

"I'm sorry."

Napoleon nodded, looking back at the body.

"I needed to test something," Yaroslav said. "This is bloody insane. This thing—" he motioned toward the machine "—can actually transform things at will. We can do it, the jump beam is a form of it, but the energy involved, the sophistication of the programming that can take raw matter and change it to simulated flesh, wool, leather, iron, and powder, it's incredible. It even can kill its own creations, knowing just what a lead ball from a musket will do, all of it taken from your memory, or some store of knowledge."

He turned away, looking back at Wellington.

"Incredible."

"Absolutely," Wellington replied. "Now, gentlemen, I have picked my field and it is here."

"You mean a battle then, a replaying of Waterloo."

"In every detail. The Brown Bess musket, of .72 caliber, has an effective range of less than eighty meters, but can kill at three hundred. Everything is as it was."

"Why?" Yaroslav asked.

"Because," Wellington replied.

"Everything?" He looked around for a moment. Behind them a battery of nine-pound fieldpieces formed, first the guns, several seconds later the crews, then the caissons, the horses, and the guidons stirring in the breeze. The horses did not look quite right, the detail of muscles seemed flat somehow, the faces of the men indistinct, like the face on a coin that had worn down somewhat with time and usage.

A squadron of hussars came into sudden focus, another squadron behind it, the beginning of a regiment. Staff started to appear, sometimes the faces clear, others indistinct as if a blending of memories. A table came into existence, maps spread out upon it, log books, muster rolls, blank sheets ready for orders, a collapsed telescope with a set of worn gloves beside it. An ornate but battered field kit was on the ground, several bottles of wine inside, and a sudden scent of fresh bread and meat wafted up around them.

"Well, I think I'll find a safe spot somewhere back up there to watch the show," Yaroslav said, nodding toward the low hills to the rear.

"You are chief of staff," Napoleon announced.

"Ah, thanks, but I'll decline the honor."

"You are chief of staff. That was one of my mistakes last time. Soult was fine at the head of a division, even a corps, but here, today, he failed me. You know the historical battle, I want you by my side."

"Thanks but no thanks. I'll see you later."

Yaroslav, smiling wanly, turned to walk away. Napoleon looked over at Wellington.

Yaroslav suddenly turned back, his face wrinkled with a slight grimace of discomfort.

"Literally a pain in the ass," he hissed, rubbing his backside, a thin curl of smoke coming up behind him.

Napoleon could not help but laugh at the old man's discomfort.

"So much for desertion."

"I take it that there'll be a lot of lead and shot flying about," Yaroslav said, looking over at Wellington. "Will this stuff be real?"

"But of course."

"Oh, great."

He looked over at Napoleon, whose eyes were beaming with a sudden excitement.

"Again. To actually be able to do it again." He started to pace back and forth with nervous excitement.

"To victory," Wellington said, and he inclined himself forward as if bowing in salute.

"To the victor the spoils," Napoleon said quietly.

The machine did not reply.

"It takes two to play. To the victor the spoils? A free France, an empire, and I as its emperor?"

"Of course," Wellington said. "The play's the thing."

"And all the rules of war apply if we win?" Yaroslav asked.

"The rules of war? I'm a gentleman, of course the conventions will be observed," Wellington announced, its voice haughty as if it had been insulted.

Yaroslav nodded and smiled.

The machine turned and in an instant was moving at high speed down the slope. Within seconds it was past Hougoumont and curved back up the opposite slope to stop where the center of his line would be, barely visible in the twilight that was starting to shift back up toward full day, though still obscured by the gathering storm directly overhead.

"Aldin, something's up."

Tia shook him awake and he mumbled a curse, thinking at first that it was Mari waking him up to complain that she had another one of her headaches and that he should fetch her medicine from the night table.

Grabbing a robe, he stumbled out of his cabin, cursing at the servobot that followed, Tia, Vush, the rat bite, everything.

Oishi, sleepy eyed, looked up from the main console.

"Tia noticed it first," Oishi said, fighting down a yawn.

"What is it?"

"A hell of an energy spike," she said. "It's like the disturbance from a jump-down beam, the initial energy pulse that creates the vacuum and moves all matter out of the way. The same signature, but it's thousands of times stronger."

"Somebody jumping in?" Aldin said, now suddenly full awake.

"What I'm thinking," Oishi said grimly. "We're getting one hell of a lot of company."

Aldin looked over at the holo screen and the stream of information running across it.

"Nobody's got a jump system like that," Tia said. "It'll move hundreds of men a second."

"Well somebody's doing it, and I think we better get ready to get the hell out of here quick," Aldin said.

"They're gone, just gone."

Aldin turned to see Hobbs, his float chair laboring on a nearly depleted battery, drift with a lurching motion into the room.

"Who?" Aldin asked, looking back at the agitated impresario.

"Yaroslav, Basak, and Napoleon. I was half asleep; they were talking about doing another game. Napoleon said something about being bored, and poof, they're gone."

"Damn it all," Oishi growled.

Hobbs, pulling out an embroidered handkerchief, wiped the sweat from his face.

"We're still getting the spike," Oishi said.

Aldin leaned over his shoulder to look at the screen.

"It's not directed from above," he said, suddenly confused. "It's surface-to-surface."

He punched up another screen and studied it intently for a moment.

"A couple of hundred kilometers from here."

"Think they might be there as well?" Tia asked hopefully.

"Well we can't leave them in the lurch." Aldin sighed. "We'll go in cautiously, check it out."

Within seconds the ship was secured, and turning it about, Oishi plotted a course to where the energy flux was located. Stirred awake by the movement of the rest of the crew stumbling about, Vush came into the room and nervously voiced a fear that perhaps his comrades had shown up and were coming down to the surface.

"Then why the hell two hundred kilometers away?" Zergh asked.

"Perhaps they aren't sure where to land."

"Just about as sure as you are then," Zergh snapped, and Vush fell silent, looking nervously over at the Gaf vasba.

The city behind them, they raced out across the open, gently rolling fields, the black mountain to their right, slowly moving upward and away. The land was undistinguished, open fields, groves of trees, meandering streams, sections of it very artificial looking and laid out in regular block patterns, as if imagination had somehow failed. A shimmer of light started to appear, flashing beneath a strangely isolated cloud that flashed with lightning, a shower cascading beneath it.

"Whatever's going on, is underneath that thunderstorm," Oishi said.

Aldin nodded, easing their speed back. The jump beam was cutting down from a distant source several tens of thousands of kilometers away, traveling inside the sphere, and thus coming across the surface at a very low angle. Aldin maneuvered to safely avoid the beam, since it could have a most unpleasant result.

He checked the monitor again. The power being generated was phenomenal. Moving just one or two people was a major drain on even a more powerful ship; this thing was pulsing at a remarkable rate, hundreds of times a second, each pulse carrying enough power to move several hundred kilos of mass.

"Enough energy being shot there to power a couple of hundred liners from one end of the Cloud to the other," Zergh said.

The beam shut down and Aldin waited, hovering low to the ground.

"Should we go in closer to look?" Tia asked.

"Whatever was doing that undoubtedly could detect our ship moving out here," Zergh said, "so what the hell, let's go take a look."

"Why don't we just hang back awhile longer," Oishi said.

"It's not like a planet here," Aldin replied. "Wherever you are, everything else curves above you. If someone wanted to fry us from further up, we're down here in the bottom of a bowl. We haven't been hurt, and I'm curious to go take a look."

He nudged the ship upward and started forward.

"Looks like a road," Tia said, standing up and going to the forward viewscreen, the landscape rolling by several hundred feet below.

Aldin stood up from behind his console, leaving Zergh to pilot the ship. Something was moving down there.

The road just suddenly appeared, starting out in the middle of an empty field that was barely covered with splotches of dirt; most of the surface was of the black sublayer of the Sphere. Gradually the terrain started to form into low, undulating hills, covered with the rich grass of late spring. Square fields appeared; the dirt road weaving through them. And then, suddenly, to his amazement, moving up the next low ridge line he saw a long column of blue, moving slowly, undulating like a long centipede, flashes of metal gleaming.

An infantry column.

"Zergh, get over here," Aldin whispered.

His vasba companion joined him and pulled on his facial hair, stroking his chin and watching with silent intent as the ship gained on the column and then whisked over it. The ridge cleared the long open road and turned off to the left, its entire length packed with troops.

"Infantry, Earth, musket period," Aldin whispered.

"Napoleonic," Zergh replied.

They crossed up over another low rise clad in a heavy forest, the column half a dozen kilometers behind. An open field whisked below them, blocklike formations of men drawn up, their uniforms black.

"Prussian, at least I think so," Aldin said, his voice edged with excitement.

"Definitely," Zergh interjected with the voice of authority of one who knew more about late ancient Earth warfare than his human companion.

"We're being scanned," Oishi announced. "A heavy spike of energy."

Aldin turned away from the viewport and went back to the controls.

The ship shuddered beneath them. For a second Aldin thought they had hit something. But no, they were still moving, but slower. It shuddered again, speed bleeding off.

"Almost like a force shielding."

Oishi brought the ship to a complete stop, and the energy dropped down to a barely perceptible scan. He nudged forward and the energy shot up again.

"Whatever it is, they don't want us flying into this," Oishi said.

"All right then," Aldin replied, sitting back in his chair.

"This terrain looks vaguely familiar," Zergh said, pulling up beside Aldin and punching in the access code to their old vasba gaming files.

"Take us up higher," Zergh said, and Aldin responded. There was no further resistance from whatever had wanted to slow them down, and within seconds he had them a kilometer above the surface.

"Sure," Zergh whispered, smiling as he overlaid a holo simulation map onto the radar sweep of below.

"We just crossed over the Prussian column moving out from Wavre. I bet if we angled over further, we'd go over Grouchy."

He stood up and went forward to look back out.

"And Waterloo is about five kilometers out there," he said, his voice edged with excitement.

Even as he spoke, the cloud that had been dropping a light but steady rain started to dissipate away, curling in upon itself. Within seconds the sky above them cleared.

"Look at it!" Zergh cried excitedly. "There, that must be the rear lines of Napoleon, the three guard infantry divisions, those buildings, that's Plancenoit!"

Aldin sprang out of his chair to join him.

"It's better than any holo sim we used to cook up for the Kohs," Zergh gasped.

"Because it's real," Aldin said with a sigh of envy. "That machine must have built it out here."

"Well, Napoleon said he was bored," Hobbs interjected.

"Now that we know where they are, I'm ready to continue my search," the Overseer announced.

"Not now," Aldin said, waving his hand behind his back as if to shoo an annoying companion away.

"Aldin!"

"Damn it all, Tia, it's Waterloo down there," Zergh said. "This isn't some damn holo, or dressing up a bunch of primitives, this is some sort of reenactment of it."

"We should be searching for the wormhole device," Tia insisted.

"What? You've got to be kidding," Hobbs said, pointing back at Vush. "That damn idiot doesn't know where to look for it. It's a fool's errand, and besides I want to watch this."

"If we don't find the wormhole machine, a hell of a lot of worlds are going to get cooked," Tia argued.

Aldin looked over at her as if she were a teacher who had broken up some guilty little game behind the school building. He looked over at Oishi, who he could see was bitten by the bug of curiosity as well, even though Waterloo meant nothing to this samurai who had lived a hundred years before the battle was even fought.

"We could search that building for years and stumble across the damn machine and not even know it," Oishi finally said, coming up with a quick defense.

Aldin looked back at Vush.

"Ever see a battle before?"

He could almost sense that the Overseer was filled with curiosity.

"I don't think they're real," Aldin said. "Most likely simulationbots—artificial people—so there really isn't any blood being spilled."

"I'm relieved, even though this does seem like an evil thing to find amusement in."

"Come on," Aldin said, "be honest, do you even know what it is that you're looking for?"

Vush hesitated for a long moment.

"No. I barely remember even finding the first machine."

"There, the truth at last," Hobbs announced. "Now settle back and have a drink."

"But we should be looking."

Oishi stood up and went over to look out the window.

"If anyone or anything can guide us to it, it's that First Traveler machine," the samurai said while pouring himself a cup of sake.

He looked back over at Vush, motioning for him to take the drink. The Overseer took the cup and downed it, his multi-faceted eyes flickering for a moment. Oishi poured another drink for himself.

"Something is broken on this world. We all saw that. Most likely when that mountain back there was made." He pointed to the black volcanolike peak still clearly visible.

"It hit near the control center and scrambled something up. Everything started to work at cross-purposes. Those First Traveler machines I suspect are the daimyos of this creation. It is no longer controlling, it is letting everything fall apart while it plays games.

"The game has become everything to it, and it picked Napoleon as its rival. There's nothing we can do now until it is willing to acknowledge that we even exist. You saw how it behaved, ignoring all of us. For some reason it found something in Napoleon, and I half suspect this game is a test."

He downed his sake in one gulp, his eyes watering. A smile lit his features.

"So let us settle back and just wait for it to finish. Napoleon is down there, so is Yaroslav. When the battle's done we'll see what happened."

He hesitated for a brief moment.

"Is that acceptable, my lord?" he asked, looking over at Aldin as if he had momentarily forgotten himself.

Aldin smiled his thanks, as if he had been relieved from having to make a decision that he knew was futile and thus take them away from this spectacle.

"Power up the cameras," Aldin said. "Let's get some close-up views."

"I'll bet one hundred thousand on Napoleon," Hobbs said happily, moving his chair up closer to the screen.

"There's an incredible energy flux down there, almost identical to a jump-down beam," Corbin said, looking up at Hassan, who stood beside him.

"What is that?"

"It means that something is moving matter, a lot of it, from one place to another."

"How long to get there?"

"Twelve, thirteen hours. It's slow going inside this Sphere, there's too much junk and machines floating around inside here and it's way over on the other side," Corbin said cautiously, feeling a tickle of fear whenever he was now forced to say something that he knew Hassan would not want to hear.

"Make it faster," Hassan said, and all Corbin could do was lower his head and nod an agreement.

chapter eleven

"What do you think!"

Yaroslav looked around in stunned disbelief. For nearly an hour the formations had materialized, one after the other. Nearly a hundred guns of the Grand Battery appeared inside a prepared position, gunners, caissons, horses arrayed around the bronze guns. Blocks of men—regiments of the line, light infantry, and the vaunted Imperial Guard—were formed in columns, ready for the assault. The wide variety of cavalry units were last—light hussars in their splendid skintight trousers and dangling peacock-hued jackets; lancers, ulans, chaussers, and dragoons; and finally the heavy-assault horsemen, the cuirassiers with burnished breastplates and plumed helmets.

He had stood by watching in stunned silence, barely noticing that after the first few minutes Napoleon had gone over to the field table. As if conjured from his own will, a staff started to appear, the array of uniforms dazzling, some dressed in the skintight doeskin breeches and sky blue jackets of hussars, others in the resplendent finery of Imperial Guardsmen, high bearskin caps dripping with the light rain that came down from the clouds overhead, forming where clear blue sky had been only moments before.

The rain passed, the ground wet underfoot, the sun, building in its variable phase, becoming brighter by the moment. Several marshals were now present, along with a bevy of officers. The features of most were clear, distinct, and almost imbued with all the nuances of genuine life; others had that slightly vague look of not being fully formed, like indistinct extras standing in the background of a holo drama.

He kept thinking that this must be what it all was, a computer-generated holo drama. But no, it wasn't. A horseman, galloping off with a dispatch splattered him with mud, a marshal, shouldering his way past, actually pushed into him, almost knocking him on his back.

"Yaroslav!"

He looked up, and Napoleon was gazing straight at him.

"Stop gawking. You're supposed to be chief of staff, now get over here!"

Feeling self-conscious, the old philosopher and onetime historian went up to the table, realizing that the circle of men around Napoleon was looking straight at him. He suddenly felt decidedly underdressed for the occasion. He was wearing a loose-fitting tunic of silk in a design that could almost be Gaf, a pale yellow with red borders, his trousers red, offset by the latest craze of a broad sash of mauve-colored polyester, rather than a far more sensible belt.

The men about him were truly elegant, and he could see the sense to it, the decking out in finery for war; it lent it all a martial bearing, and he suddenly found himself wishing that he too could have a cocked hat and a broad-shouldered jacket with gold epaulets.

"You're familiar with the battle?" Napoleon asked.

Yaroslav nodded. "The history that's been handed down, that survived the destruction of Earth. Several good military histories of you are still around, written by the likes of Rothenberg, Chandler, and Schneid, which are considered to be the best."

Napoleon hesitated for a brief instant, a slightly aghast look on his features, but then he pushed the questions aside.

"And what did they say?"

Yaroslav looked around at the men who were waiting.

"Several mistakes were made. Jérôme should not have allowed himself to be drawn into Hougoumont, the battle on your left should have been a screening action to pin down the Alliance right, which was your original intent but not executed as you wished. Just threaten the right to make him use his best troops to cover the line of retreat to the coast. Hougoumont was a deathtrap that should have been avoided."

"Go on," Napoleon said, and he looked over meaningfully at a man who Yaroslav realized bore a resemblance to the emperor. The whole thing was now remarkably strange. He imagined that across a thousand nights Napoleon had, in the sleepless hour of midnight, replayed what had happened here and was now acting on it.

"But these aren't the real men," Yaroslav said softly.

"I know what they are!" Napoleon snapped. "But they are real to this moment, they need to understand, they will act as they really did. For the purpose of what is happening they are real. Now tell them!"

Yaroslav gulped hard, looking over at Jérôme, and could see that this man, or reproduction or whatever he was, was definitely not pleased to be told of a mistake in the presence of the emperor.

"Most importantly of all, though, you must take direct control of the battle," Yaroslav said sharply, looking first at Napoleon and then over at a red-haired marshal whom he suspected was Ney.

"You might have thought Wellington to be of small account, and thus Ney could handle him while you looked to your right flank, but Ney made too many mistakes."

"This is outrageous," the red-haired marshal snapped. "Who is this pajama-clad old goat?"

"He is my chief of staff for this battle," Napoleon said, his voice full now with a cold dark power.

"But . . ."

"No buts," Napoleon said, and he raised his gaze from the maps on the table.

"You might be Ney, you might not be Ney. But I suspect that you will act as my old comrade once did."

Napoleon came around from behind the table, and walking up to the marshal, he reached up and put his hand on the man's shoulder.

"We lost the last time. You were wrong, and I should have seen that. Now we do it again, and this time we do it right.

"I can assume—" He pointed out across the field, to where on the low distant ridge could be seen the deployed army of the British, Dutch, and Hanoverians. "—that the Wellington over there will do it different this time as well, attempting to anticipate my changes. And thus our own orders will be changed."

He smiled up at Ney.

"I should have put you in charge of the pursuit of Blücher and not Grouchy, he was always too slow. I need the Prussians stopped; you are the one to do it. I trust you enough to do that for me. Ney, I need you for this victory."

Ney's features softened.

"It is good to be with you again, my emperor."

Napoleon hesitated, looking back at Yaroslav.

"Is this real?" Napoleon finally asked. "All of this, it is too much, all too much."

"It is as real as it can be," Yaroslav replied, as confused by everything as Napoleon, but not willing to admit it at this moment when he sensed that the emperor above all else needed some reassurance in this strange world. There had to be a purpose behind this battle that could later be used to their advantage. He half suspected that the machine had clicked into an aberrant line of logic; if it was defeated, the defeat might shake it loose.

From the corner of his eye Yaroslav saw a puff of smoke. He turned to look, and from the direction of the enemy line, less than eight hundred meters away, another puff of smoke snapped out, and then all down the line. Seconds later a high moaning passed overhead, a plume of mud geysering up not fifty paces away. Within seconds sprays of mud and dirt were kicking up all around them. An orderly not a dozen feet away suddenly disappeared in a spray of blood, his decapitated body tumbling end over end.

"By the gods, this *is* real," Yaroslav screamed, his cry cut short when a twelve-pound solid shot hummed past, the concussion staggering him.

A howitzer shell burst overhead, fragments humming down; a mounted messenger started to scream, holding what remained of his left arm that had been severed at the elbow.

Replica, holo, or real, the arm lying on the ground sent a wave of nausea through Yaroslav.

"It certainly feels real," Napoleon said calmly, turning away to look back at the enemy line.

"So he decided to start things off instead," the emperor said, looking back at his staff.

"Ney, you have your orders, now ride like the devil. Skirt the south of the Paris woods and go cross-country; Grouchy will be south of Wavre. Take command of his corps, detach one division to pin the Prussian corps there, take the rest of your men and move west, and leave the artillery behind if need be to support the one division at Wavre. I want you back here with the rest of Grouchy's corps supporting my right at Plancenoit. They'll have to move twenty kilometers and be ready for action before the day is done. Do that, and the glory of this victory is yours!"

Ney, saluting, turned and called for his horse. A cluster of staff closed in around the marshal as he mounted.

"Sire, I'll see you at sundown on the field of victory!"

Rearing up his mount, he set off at a gallop, leaping his horse over a fieldpiece that had been upended by the British barrage.

"This time, by God, we're going to do it!" Napoleon shouted, looking back at the others.

Yaroslav could almost feel the electric charge of excitement gripping the men around Napoleon. He felt it as well, and for a moment he forgot the terror of the shelling they were experiencing.

Napoleon called Yaroslav over to the table and pointed at the map.

"Wellington's changed things already. I opened the barrage before; now he has done it instead. But he'd be a fool to try an assault. Less than a third of that army of his is reliable; a fair part of them were on my side only a year ago. They don't want this fight and will get out of it if we break the British."

A shell screamed past and burst directly behind the group, bowling over several more staff officers.

"And he's trying to kill us in the opening move," Yaroslav said. "Might I suggest we pull back a bit out of range."

Napoleon looked at him as if he were mad.

"And let the troops see their emperor run from a little rain?"

Yaroslav looked back up at the others, who were gazing at him disdainfully.

Basak growled at Yaroslav.

"First fun I've had in years," the berserker snarled. "When do we attack?"

Napoleon laughed, slapping the Gaf warrior on the back.

"Can you ride a horse?"

The Gaf growled as if insulted and nodded, even though it was the first time in his life that he had seen one.

"You can go in with the guard when the time comes. What time is it?" Napoleon asked.

"Ten-thirty, sire," an orderly replied.

"I started at eleven. It was too late, I realize now," he said. He looked down at his boots, which were caked in mud. "We can't move the artillery up closer yet."

He looked back at the British line.

"Tell the Grand Battery to open up and to concentrate to the left center of the British line."

An orderly galloped off, and several minutes later a deep-throated roar rolled across the field.

Napoleon stood impassive, while Yaroslav tried to avoid ducking whenever a shell or solid shot passed within fifty meters of their position.

"All right then," Napoleon finally said. "Jérôme, skirmish on the left, one division, not a single man more. We want him to think that is where the main assault will hit, so act as if you are screening something bigger to come. Do you understand me?"

The slight man standing with a sulky expression nodded in reply.

"Do not get drawn into Hougoumont, but let them think that if they do not cover it well, we'll sweep past their right and threaten their communication to the sea."

He turned away from his brother.

"D'Erlon, to you falls the hard task."

"Whatever your command, sire." The portly marshal came up to salute.

"In one hour, at eleven forty-five, you are to go in there." He pointed across the field.

Yaroslav looked up and saw the emperor gesturing to the right of a small chateau that he assumed must be La Haie Sainte, a building that marked the center of the Alliance line and rested alongside the road to Brussels.

"You will advance in columns of battalions on a division front; you are to go straight in."

D'Erlon nodded, looking across the field. "My support?"

"Milhaud, Jacquinot, their divisions of cavalry will be in support on your right flank."

"And my left flank, sire?"

"In the air, but flanked by the Grand Battery."

"They'll hit me there on my left; it's exposed," D'Erlon replied, unable to keep from ducking when a shot winged by so close that his cape billowed out.

"Exactly, let him. But you've got to hold. Bachelu's division will remain here on the crest and hold my center and left. At the same time, I want a second Grand Battery of guns to move forward toward Hougoumont; the ground should be drier by then. The battery is to suppress that chateau so it will not threaten our flank in the center, but it must not be done until he is moving to protect his left. Once he has committed his reserves against you, D'Erlon, Lobau and the entire sixth corps will advance by the oblique with you masking them. They will deploy to your right and we will have them flanked, while they have committed to your left!"

He looked over at Yaroslav.

"That will be the key moment. Lobau will swing into their left, Wellington will be shifting to counter, and then the Imperial Guard will sweep straight up the middle," he said excitedly, pointing out the movement on his map. "The secondary battery will cover the guard's left, the main battery firing overhead to continue pounding their center. That will be the moment he breaks!"

Yaroslav looked out across the field and could not help but feel nervous.

"Looks a bit like Pickett's charge," Yaroslav said.

"What?"

"Oh, nothing, I guess you know best though."

"Of course!"

A solid shot plowed in, striking the muddy ground just in front of the knot of officers, spraying Napoleon with mud.

"Now go!"

The men, with excited shouts, saluted and ran to their mounts, their staffs cheering as they wheeled and galloped off to their respective commands.

"Shall we inspect the line?" Napoleon asked, and without waiting for Yaroslav's reply he went over to a horse, allowing himself to receive help to be boosted up into the saddle.

"I haven't ridden in years," Napoleon confessed, nervously edging the horse around as if to judge its temper. A howitzer shell exploded behind them, a second later an entire caisson going up with a thunderclap. The horse shied away, fidgeting, but he held in a tight rein till the animal calmed down.

Yaroslav looked up at Napoleon.

"Well, are you going to follow me on foot?"

"I can't ride," Yaroslav confessed, ashamed at the snickers that sounded behind his back.

Napoleon gave him a look of exasperation.

"Then someone can lead your mount. Now let's get going."

Driven primarily by a desire to get away from the uncomfortable shelling, Yaroslav allowed himself to be boosted onto the back of a small mare, a hussar taking hold of the reins and falling in alongside Napoleon, who started down the slope to where the Grand Battery of nearly a hundred guns was methodically at work, bombarding the Alliance positions across the valley. The field was already choked with smoke, but through the billowing clouds he could clearly see the other ridge, the guns winking with a flash of light and a puff of smoke.

Everything was pandemonium, the whistling moan of shot winging by, the terrified screams of horses that had been hit, the cries of the wounded, the cheers of the men as Napoleon rode past, the units drawn up in battle-line formation, taking off their caps, waving, calling out the emperor's name.

Napoleon's eyes were ablaze. He reined up in front of a formation, stopping by the regimental colors, and leaning out grabbed hold of the stained silken folds of a French tricolor.

"Men of the Thirty-second, I remember you!" he shouted.

Yaroslav looked closely at the unit. Almost all the faces had that hazy indistinctness to start, but as Napoleon looked out upon them, more and yet more of them suddenly started to take on a sharper form, as if the First Traveler machine were still reaching into his memories, and with a light stroke of an imagined brush, now painted in the fine details.

"You gave me victory on half a dozen fields; I am certain you will do so again today."

The men cheered as he kissed the folds of the flag, and he then continued on to stop at the next regiment down the line and grabbed hold of their flag.

"Men of the glorious Twenty-eighth, you were with me at Austerlitz, you were among the first to break their line. Will you add a new legend to your crown of glory today?"

The men roared their approval, several of them breaking

ranks to come up to his mount, reaching out almost reverently to touch his horse or his mud-caked boot.

He looked out at the men, and Yaroslav could see the tears in his eyes as he let the flag drop from his hand and rode on.

Yaroslav looked back to see a heavy shot plow into the ranks where they had been only a moment before. The round cut a bloody swath through the line, a loud scream cutting the air, but Napoleon did not look back.

Yaroslav felt his senses reeling. What was real anymore? His sense of logic, of reality, told him that somehow this was not real. The real Waterloo had been fought on a world long since dead, a legendary home where legends had lived.

Yet now he was riding with a legend, the cheers echoing across the fields. And what was the reality of all this? How was it to be interpreted? Was this a game? What was happening to the men around him, was that an illusion? Could he be killed in this madness? He felt another shot flutter past. He didn't want to test that question out, suddenly wondering if the machine was tapping into his thoughts. If I wish my own death, would that now happen? he wondered with an almost superstitious fear.

And yet why was this happening? Was the machine insane, was this entire world insane and this was now a manifestation of it?

"You're wondering just what in hell is going on," Napoleon said, looking over at Yaroslav.

"You could say that," Yaroslav replied, shouting to be heard above the thunder of the Grand Battery.

Napoleon paused for a moment and breathed in deeply. The field stank with a rotten-egg smell, but Napoleon seemed to breathe it in as if it were a fine perfume.

"This was my world," he shouted, gesturing with his hand to all that was around them. "I don't know why he did this for me, but by God, I'll give him a fight he won't forget."

Napoleon looked over at Yaroslav, smiling.

"And you get to try it one more time."

A flash of a pained look crossed the emperor's features, and he drew closer.

"I know it is not real," he whispered, and then he paused.

"But then again," he finally said, a smile crossing his features once more, "who is to say what is real, and what is illusion. I'll leave that one to the philosophers like you."

Yaroslav looked past Napoleon to where an entire division stood in formation, flags floating on the breeze, shells bursting overhead. The sight was magnificent. It was becoming increasingly difficult to keep a sense of abandon from taking hold.

"It's a machine you're fighting against," Yaroslav said, as if trying to reassert some type of inner detachment from the incredible display around him. "It can calculate every aspect of this battle down to the final probability. It will know every odd, everything to the twentieth decimal point. It will be nearly impossible to defeat."

Napoleon looked over at Yaroslav and smiled.

"But this—" He pointed to the serried ranks of D'Erlon's corps. "—this is a different reality from pieces moving on a chessboard. This is the ultimate game, a game of timing, of knowing the precise moment to strike. In that he faces a grand master, and I shall beat him at it."

A thunderclap showered them with mud and a hot gust of wind.

"I do think our Wellington is aiming directly at me," Napoleon said. "Most unsporting of him."

Napoleon urged his horse forward, and Yaroslav followed.

"For that matter," Yaroslav said, "it can read our thoughts, we know that. It could thus already know everything you plan and act accordingly."

"A gentleman wouldn't do that," Napoleon replied, "and Wellington, damn him, is above all else one of those damn haughty English gentlemen.

"And besides, if it could, then what purpose would there be? There would be no challenge, no spirit, no game. He has made illusion into reality and must live by the spirit of that reality."

He looked over at Yaroslav.

"I think that is the key to all of this. It quite simply is bored. It has the power to make a universe." He swept his arm out with a dramatic flair. Yaroslav looked about as if almost to remind himself that he was inside the Sphere.

"It wanted something different, a challenge, and I shall give it to him."

He paused, looking over at Yaroslav.

"And then you shall write the peace as you need it to be written, that is what I shall give to you and your friends for returning this to me."

A shot hummed past in front of them, striking into a column

of men, several of them going down in a bloody heap. Napoleon barely looked.

He paused for a second and then turned back to Yaroslav.

"You thought me heartless," he said, his voice sharp with a sudden anger. "A general who loves his men too much will not win battles.

"And," he continued, his voice dropping, "he will also go mad. At least this time I will not have that thought to bother me when I watch them die."

Even though he believed it not to be real, it nevertheless did look all too real as he gazed at an infantryman, holding the body of a comrade, and though its face was that hazy indistinctness, it nevertheless had a look of anguish to it as it gazed upon the stilled body cradled in its arms.

Reaching the top of a low rise, Napoleon called for a telescope, and uncapping it he quickly scanned the enemy lines.

"They're moving some of their units to the reverse slope. Just as he did last time. Good, very good, it means they're getting hit hard. Another half hour should do it. By then the ground will have dried out a bit more."

Yaroslav suddenly realized that he was starting to feel warm, and he looked up to see that the sun was shining brightly straight overhead. He noticed as well that their ship was hovering more than a kilometer above them.

It must be quite a show from up there, he thought, remembering how so many years ago he would have been in the ship, having a drink with Aldin while monitoring some primitive conflict on a backworld for the pleasure of the Kohs. Well now he was in the middle of it.

He looked up, and unable to contain himself, he waved a crude but unmistakable gesture, at the sight of which Basak, who had been trailing behind them on foot, gave out a barking shout of approval.

Aldin sat back in his chair and roared with delight.

"Well, the old devil is certainly having the time of his life," Hobbs announced, waving a salute at the screen as if Yaroslav could somehow see him.

"I'd give anything to be down there with him," Zergh said, shaking his head with envy.

"It looks like real cannon shot flying around down there," Aldin said.

"The hell with it. I'm old, it'd almost be worth it to be able to say I rode with Napoleon at Waterloo."

"A deadly simulation of Waterloo," Oishi interjected.

The samurai got up from his chair and went to the forward viewport to look straight down at the action a kilometer below.

"Impressive though, damn impressive," the samurai said almost wistfully. "We hadn't seen armies like that in Japan since Tokugawa. My grandfather, my mother's father, was with him during the Civil Wars. I always dreamed of leading a division of mounted samurai in a charge."

"Well, it's Yaroslav that got lucky," Zergh sniffed, "and we're stuck up here."

"The Prussians are definitely on the move," Aldin said, motioning to a side monitor that was tracking events on the right flank.

"He'll be outnumbered two-to-one by the end of the day. I don't see how he can do it," Hobbs said.

"He's Napoleon," Zergh replied defensively, as if a personal insult had been leveled.

Aldin ordered up a light lunch, and the servobot returned from the galley loaded down with a tray of sandwiches and cold drinks. The shifting of several Alliance regiments down to Hougoumont, and the withdrawal to the reverse slope of most of the infantry, elicited a flurry of comments and a number of small side bets as to intentions and results. Zergh, with a brief play on the computer, brought up an old holo sim of the actual battle and projected it into the center of the room, with an overlay of the situation below so that comparisons could be made.

"I think something is stirring," Oishi said, and motioned to a monitor.

Aldin looked up, catching a worried tone in Oishi's voice. "What is it?"

"There's something moving on the far side of the sun. It's been tracking straight toward us for half an hour, weaving through the junk out there."

Aldin went over to look at the screen. It was still more than two million kilometers away, but looking at the tracking it was obvious that whatever it was, the object was coming straight toward them.

"A ship?"

"I think so," Oishi said.

"Who then?"

"It wouldn't be Bukha, he'd have contacted us. That only leaves the Overseers."

"Or Corbin."

"Damn it," Aldin hissed, turning away from the screen. "How long before they get here?"

"Hard to say," Oishi replied. "They keep changing their speed. Maybe eight hours, perhaps nine. If they go much beyond two hundred thousand k an hour they're bound to run into something, it's such a mess out here."

"Can we go down and get those fools out of there?"

"I wouldn't try it," Zergh said. "You saw the energy field that blocked it off. It might fry our systems, and stupid as it sounds, a twelve-pound shot could actually do us a lot of damage."

"There they go!" Hobbs shouted excitedly, pointing to the forward viewport, barely noticing the other crisis that was looming.

Aldin stepped away from the scanning monitor and went up to join Hobbs and the others who were pushing around the port to get a better view. Even from a kilometer straight up the sound was almost deafening. The batteries on both sides were in full play. An entire corps from Napoleon's line was advancing forward, the deep rumble of the drums, the bugles, and cheers counterpointing the deeper bass of the artillery. The large block formations moved forward with a stately grace, like an inexorable wave, the men moving in a steady cadence, a cloud of skirmishers sweeping ahead of the line, swarming out in an arc several hundred meters forward of the advance.

"Starting his move out the same way as last time," Zergh announced. "That's D'Erlon's corps hitting the left center of the British line."

A flurry of activity started on the Alliance side. Two block formations of cavalry mounted up and started to move to the opposite flanks of the French advance. On the reverse side of the low hill, other block formations of infantry started to deploy out into lines, while from the center a brigade of infantry started to move at a right angle to the advance, to position itself where the main blow would fall.

The main column continued its advance, reaching the bottom of the valley and starting up the opposite slope. The skirmishers were by now heavily engaged, driving back a thin red

line of British skirmishers who suddenly broke and ran straight
up the slope. Hobbs, who by now was betting a significant
portion of his remaining fortune on the battle, let out a groan
until he realized that they were clearing the field for the artillery to open up.

The charge now moved to a quick step, and at almost the
same moment half a dozen batteries opened up, the front of the
advance crumpling. From the right flank of the advancing column several regiments of French cavalry deployed out and
started in at a trot. On the far left of the British line their cavalry started to deploy out to counter the advance of the French
horses.

"He's still tracking in on us," Oishi announced.

"Well, we've still got plenty of time left," Aldin said, unable
to turn away from the viewport.

"I bet Yaroslav's having the time of his life," Zergh said
jealously.

"Damn it!" Yaroslav screamed, ducking low as a lazy shot,
which had skipped into the ground fifty meters ahead, bounded
up over his head with an ugly hiss and then continued on.

The battle ahead looked like complete chaos. The head of
the column continued up the slope, the front ranks going down
from the artillery blasts.

"Another hundred paces, that's all," Napoleon snapped, nervously slapping his hand against his thigh.

He looked over at Yaroslav.

"A bit too soon; another half hour of artillery from the
Grand Battery would have shaken them up enough; just a bit
too soon. It's timing, it's always a question of timing."

The left flank of the advancing column started to crumple
in, while the right flank battalions appeared to gain momentum. The distant roll of the *pas de charge* echoed even as the
column broke into a double-quick time, fifteen thousand voices
shouting. The charge swept up over the crest of the hill,
swarming two of the batteries under.

"Now comes the counterstrike," Napoleon said, and he
pointed to the devastated left flank of D'Erlon's column.

From over the crest of the opposite ridge an advancing column of British cavalry appeared, coming in hard.

"Scots Greys?" Yaroslav asked.

"The same," Napoleon replied, scanning their advance with

his telescope. "They're the best troops, and the worst led in all of Europe."

The charge came on over the slope, and the Grand Battery, firing over D'Erlon's column, started to place its shot in among them. The charge swept around La Haie Sainte and pressed in.

"Tell Roussel to move his cavalry up to support!" Napoleon shouted and another courier galloped off.

The fighting on the right flank of the advance continued to press in, but the left continued to waver; a scattering of men, turning into a steadily increasing torrent, were breaking away and streaming toward the rear.

"It's not looking good," he said quietly.

A high clarion call sounded, and to his left Yaroslav saw Roussel's cavalry division move out. Beyond the division and to the left flank, however, there was another sight that caught him by surprise: several British regiments were moving out on the far side of Hougoumont and actually advancing toward the main French line.

Napoleon noticed it at the same time and studied the advance intently for a moment.

"A smart one, that Wellington. He knows Jérôme is on my left; he's trying to draw him into a fight, to weaken my center. Courier!"

Another staff officer moved up.

"Tell my brother not to be drawn in—to hold position."

The officer saluted and galloped off.

Roussel's cavalry moved past, heading down into the valley where the entire left of D'Erlon's corps had given way, the center of the corps starting to waver as well, some units continuing to advance into the assault while others attempted to pivot. Two of the regiments were already going into square formation, thus halting the advance of regiments further back in the line of assault.

"He's got to hold," Napoleon snapped, and turned to look back at the main part of the assault. It was impossible to distinguish anything now. A steady stream of messengers started coming back from the front, calling for reinforcements to bolster the left of D'Erlon.

Napoleon waved them off impatiently, watching as an entire division broke and was routed, the enemy cavalry wading in among them.

"Tell Kellermann to get ready and for Lobau's corps to move out now!" Napoleon shouted.

Excited couriers galloped back over the ridge, and a moment later Yaroslav found that he could almost feel the rumble of fifteen thousand men of the sixth corps starting out, masked by the ridge and moving to the right.

Napoleon continued to wait, and the first refugees of the defeat of D'Erlon's left started to stream past his headquarters, rushing to get past staff officers who attempted to re-form the broken units. Yaroslav suddenly started to feel as if the battle was getting out of control. Napoleon seemed to be caught in a paralysis of inaction, unable to respond to what looked like a disaster.

From the opposite crest there were occasional flashes of French standards, the division of Durutte having taken the chateau of Papelotte, thus anchoring the advance of the extreme right; beyond the chateau a swirling cavalry action was still in progress, Jacquinot's cavalry engaged in a freewheeling brawl with that of the Alliance.

And then from the right, spilling over the crest, came the advancing wave of Lobau's corps, moving fast to the right; a solid block of men, in columns of battalions on a division-wide front, started down the slope, trumpets and the *pas de charge* rumbling. Yaroslav felt his heart going into his throat at the sight of it, a cold sweat of excitement giving him a strange chill sense.

Directly ahead, Roussel's cavalry finally brought some relief to D'Erlon's battered left, but the center of the valley was still a mass of confusion.

On the far left, the secondary battery was moving forward to bring Hougoumont into close range; however, the British regiments deployed forward were putting up a spirited fight, and it was apparent that Jérôme was gradually being sucked in.

"They're shifting," Napoleon said, offering his telescope over, and Yaroslav brought the instrument up to look. It was hard to see the opposite ridge until the smoke parted for a moment. There seemed to be a cloud of dust rising up and occasional flashes of musket barrels and blocks of men moving just beyond the ridge, barely visible. They were moving hard to their own left. He was right. Wellington, seeing Lobau, was moving to counter the blow, while demonstrating on his own right. The Alliance army was on the move, and he knew enough of Napoleonic warfare to know that it would take long minutes to change deployments once orders had been given. Even a computer enemy could not alter that.

"Now for the guard, move it all now!" Napoleon suddenly shouted.

The group broke, riding off to their respective commands.

Roussel's division of cavalry continued its move against the British cavalry that had harried D'Erlon's retreating troops, but D'Erlon's right was still holding the ridge, Lobau's corps moving rapidly to push alongside of him.

He thought a rattle of drums was sounding from behind; it grew in volume, a thunder that set his teeth on edge. Up the road from the rear came the guard cavalry with several batteries of guns, their drivers lashing the mounts. The heavy cavalry plunged up over the ridge, past where Napoleon was.

"Vive l'empereur!"

The charge swept down the hill. A flourish of bugle calls sounded in the valley, and Roussel's command, having completed its task of screening, pulled aside. The British cavalry, seeing the fresh onslaught, turned and started into a retreat.

Behind them Yaroslav saw all the Imperial Guard start to move out, moving straight up either side of the Brussels road, deployed out into columns of battalions, their front a quarter mile across, fifteen thousand men moving as one. Forward, the Grand Battery redoubled its effort, plunging a concentrated bombardment into La Haie Sainte, covering for the guard batteries that galloped up to within seventy-five meters of the chateau before turning to unlimber. Smoke cloaked the field.

Yaroslav looked to where Napoleon was pointing off to the right. Lobau's corps was moving up the slope, the men advancing at the double-quick, the forward battalions shaking out into a linear front to enhance firepower. A sheet of smoke snapped out from the British side, and long seconds later the first volley rolled across the valley and everything was lost to view.

"He's putting everything there!" Napoleon shouted. "Everything!"

The advancing column of the guard was now several hundred meters past the inn of La Belle Alliance, the column coming up over the top of the ridge.

"See, see!" Napoleon shouted, pointing to the center. "He went for it. D'Erlon breaks, and he thought he was drawing me in to support the right. He must have sent Uxbridge in with

Lambert, perhaps even Picton, to block Lobau! Now he must rebalance or in fifteen minutes the guard will cut right through the middle!"

The center of the French army was shifting to the right flank behind the chaos of D'Erlon's assault, while the guard reserve advanced straight up through for the killing blow.

A courier came riding up from the east and reined in.

"Sire, the Prussians, they are moving into the woods."

Napoleon nodded and waved the man off.

"They'll be on your flank soon," Yaroslav said.

"And if I wait for them, I'll be caught like last time. I must finish off Wellington now, then turn on Blücher. I must do it now!"

He looked over at another courier.

"Tell D'Erlon he's done all he can. Have him pull back and re-form on the Grand Battery, then prepare to shift front to the east to face the Prussians."

The valley was chaos, but Yaroslav let himself be swept away with the grandeur of it all. Behind him the guard was continuing to move at a quick pace, a mounted band playing "The Victory March of Marengo."

Napoleon looked over at them as the front of the column moved past and, unable to contain himself, tears streaked down his mud-splattered face.

"It is as it was," he said.

As if on impulse he turned his horse about and did a slow gallop across the field, moving to the front of the advancing guard. Yaroslav turned to follow him, grabbing hold of his own reins and clumsily kicking the horse to move. Basak, pulling out his great battle-ax, let out a triumphant roar and started to run alongside.

"Soldiers of the guard, your emperor fights alongside you today!" Napoleon shouted, riding up alongside the column, taking his hat off and waving it.

A bone-chilling growl went up from the ranks, the men waving their muskets, some calling for him to go to the rear, others chanting his name. With a dramatic flourish he came up to the head of the great column, and taking up the battle-scarred standard of the guard, he held it aloft, and a triumphal shout of joy went up.

"It's worth dying right now!" Napoleon shouted. "He gave it back to me for a moment, and it's worth dying now!"

"We just might do that after all," Yaroslav said. "Don't you think your job's at the rear, in command?"

"This is the moment. If we do not break him now, before two o'clock, we stand no chance of turning in time to face the Prussians. It must be now!"

He stood up in his stirrups and raised his voice to a shout. "I go in with the guard!"

Yaroslav found that there was no face-saving way in which he could turn aside. And besides, he realized, there was a fair part of him that did not want to turn away.

It'd be a hell of a story if I make it, he realized, and a hell of a story even if I don't.

The advance moved forward at a steady hundred and fifty meters a minute. From what he could see down in the valley, D'Erlon's corps was smashed except for a handful of regiments that still held the right of the line atop the crest. The ground finally started to flatten out and then gradually started to rise back up again, and directly ahead Yaroslav could now see the farmhouse of La Haie Sainte, ringed in fire, showers of rock and building timbers going up from the pounding delivered by the guard artillery that had drawn up before it.

To his left, the secondary battery was heavily engaged against Hougoumont, but several guns in the enclosed area were firing into the flank of the guard, tearing bloody furrows through the ranks. The ground ahead was chaos: dead and dying men and horses covered the field, the wheat trampled into mud. The guard cavalry, which was now forward, was nearly up to the crest of the hill, driving the British gunners back, the artillery fire slacking off at last.

Napoleon handed the standard to a waiting captain and motioned for the column to start forward at the quickstep. It was still several hundred meters out, but Yaroslav knew that timing was everything; they were now being unmasked from the smoke and confusion as they advanced straight up the slope, the *pas de charge* keeping a steady beat.

An advance line of skirmishers, moving in front of the main column, started to run, advancing toward the chateau less than two hundred meters ahead to join the guns. A musket volley snapped out, and the men charged. Moments later, from the far side of the chateau, a stream of men came pouring out, Kellermann's cavalry sweeping in to cut off their retreat.

Yaroslav realized that this was the classic combination, all three armies advancing together, each in support of the other. On the ridge beyond, there was still heavy skirmishing between the few units of D'Erlon's that were still hanging on to their position and the British and Dutch units deployed to meet them. The guns that had been pounding the chateau started to limber up again to continue the advance.

The front of the guard columns swept past the battery position, the guns moving out only seconds before their arrival. The timing of it all awed Yaroslav, who turned and nodded to Napoleon with admiration.

"Shouldn't we pull out of the charge now?" he shouted. "It's going to get awful hot once we crest that hill!"

Napoleon ignored him.

Damn, he was going all the way in, and Yaroslav found that there was nothing he could do but to follow, while Basak, waving his ax, chanted a death song.

All were crowded about the viewport or the close-up monitors. Whatever it was that was approaching them was still a good five hours out, and Aldin could only hope that things below would be finished by then.

The formations below moved with a slow, majestic grandeur. The guard units were heading straight into the English lines, forward elements shaking out from column into line formation for increased firepower. On the far right the battle was at a crescendo. Lobau's sixth corps was over the crest of the ridge, smashing straight into nearly twenty thousand of Wellington's troops. Several more British columns were moving that way, though one in the middle seemed to be breaking down, part of it turning rapidly to face the advancing guard. The front of the British division still rushed to meet Lobau, the men in the middle stopping and milling about in confusion. Several of the units in the center were in square formation, engaged against French cavalry; others were attempting to shake back out into line formation in anticipation of the infantry assault.

The cavalry sweep to the far right was swinging into what looked like open air, the few Alliance elements there breaking and running. The trouble spot Aldin could see was the center. D'Erlon was having difficulty rallying his men, and a close-up camera revealed that the corps commander was in fact already dead in the confusion.

Several English brigades were firmly wedged into the battered corps, one of them nearly up to the French Grand Battery, which could not fire, so great was the confusion in front of them. Aldin caught a brief glimpse of "Wellington," who was at that moment moving to his own center, staff galloping alongside, several infantry regiments being pulled in to join him in a mad dash to face the main attack coming straight in. The sight looked bizarre in the extreme, a First Traveler machine surrounded by men on horseback, decked out in their resplendent finery. He wished that somehow the machine were wearing a cocked hat to make the absurdity of it complete.

The real trouble though was obvious. Several miles to the right of Kellermann's flanking attack, the Prussians were advancing through the Paris Woods. Already there was light cavalry skirmishing. Within a couple of hours the Prussians would be arriving.

"They're moving somewhat faster than the historical scenario," Zergh said.

"Well, maybe he's cheating," Aldin countered. He kept trying to remind himself that, after all, this was some sort of elaborate game, but he couldn't quite get it out of his mind that this whole thing was far more important than any of them quite realized.

Then there was the mysterious other ship closing in. Just who the hell were they? he wondered.

He had to stay, at least for the moment, but if the battle was still going on, and the interloper was Corbin, he'd have to leave Yaroslav, Basak, and Napoleon behind and hope for the best.

"There they go!" Oishi shouted, caught up in the excitement of the battle below.

The advance regiments of the old guard, screaming with a near maniacal fury, went into the charge, bayonets leveled, sweeping up the slope past La Haie Sainte, which was now wreathed in smoke and flames. Napoleon moved directly alongside the lead battalions, shouting, pointing for the advance to press in.

Basak leaped forward, battle-ax raised high, running with a long-legged stride, pushing his way through to be at the front.

They crested the hill, and for a brief instant Yaroslav felt as if they had charged straight into an empty field. And then, without warning, a solid, long rank of red stood up out of the high grass. For a brief instant he thought he saw Wellington on the far side of the field, and then everything disappeared in smoke.

Several things seemed to happen to him at once. He saw Basak stagger and go down, while beside him Napoleon's mount reared and turned, the emperor leaning forward, his features gone ashen. Yaroslav felt something pluck at his left arm, and then a numbness.

A whisper of an inner voice told him he had just been shot, but strangely there was no feeling.

The charge was staggered by the blow.

"The emperor, the emperor's been shot!"

Yaroslav looked over at Napoleon. He could see the streak of blood on the tan trousers, the ragged hole. Yaroslav edged up to him.

"You're hurt!"

Napoleon looked around wide-eyed and saw that he was now on center stage, the guardsman about them standing as if riveted, while another volley ripped out from the British side.

Yaroslav, balancing unsteadily on his stirrups, stood up.

"Soldiers of France, your emperor lives. Now charge!"

Napoleon, as if recovering his senses with Yaroslav's cry, looked about and held his hand up for all to see.

It was as if an explosion were unleashed. Up forward came a wild cry, the death song of a Gaf berserker, and it made Yaroslav feel like someone was driving a corkscrew down his spine.

The army surged forward, pulling Yaroslav and Napoleon along with it. They crested up over the top of the ridge, smashing into the enemy line, bowling it underfoot, and continued on forward. The next line held for a moment, another volley slashing out, and then it, too, disappeared, and within seconds Yaroslav felt as if he were caught in a mad race.

A staff officer came up to him, grabbing hold of his reins to pull him out of the advance, and Yaroslav swore at him, wanting to continue on in, madly envious of Basak, whom he could still hear, the death song replaced with one of joy, the battle-ax rising and falling.

The old guard pushed forward, the middle guard turning to the left oblique, the division of the young guard moving to fill the gap where D'Erlon's divisions had been torn apart, cutting in behind the British units that had been impetuous enough to advance down into the valley.

Yaroslav suddenly saw Napoleon again, off his horse amid a knot of men, and following the staff officer, he came up and slid down from his own mount, grimacing with the first shock of pain from his dangling useless arm.

"How bad is it?" Yaroslav cried, feeling a genuine concern.

"Bleeding a bit."

Yaroslav knelt down to take a look. There was no arterial bleeding, that would have been trouble. The musket ball had gone clean through his upper thigh, leaving a ragged hole that was slowly but steadily oozing blood.

An orderly had already removed his own sash, and tearing up a towel, he packed the wound under Yaroslav's directions and bound it tightly.

"That should take care of it for right now; we'll get you back aboard ship and patch it up once this is over."

"There's still a battle to be won," Napoleon said almost cheerfully. "You're hurt yourself," he said, and Yaroslav was touched that the emperor had noticed.

"A bit of a scratch."

"It's broken," Napoleon said. "You'll lose your arm."

"Not likely," Yaroslav growled. "Just splint it for me."

He stifled a groan while a rough splint was fashioned from a broken board and his arm was bound to his chest.

Napoleon, favoring his injured leg, stood back up and looked over at Yaroslav.

"You are hereby appointed major general with the Legion of Honor for what you did here."

Yaroslav could not help but beam with pride.

From the low rise he looked back out over the field. The entire left of the British line was giving way, streaming to the rear, Lobau's reserve division moving out in pursuit. Straight ahead, the old guard was pushing up toward the village of Waterloo. The guard cavalry that had pulled aside to let the main assault go in was now charging, hell-for-leather, against the English right, artillery in support. Infectious panic raced ahead of it, and the formations started to break up, streaming toward the rear. Red-coated infantry came pouring out of Hougoumont, which was now threatened with envelopment from all four sides. The Alliance army was in a rout, catching the infectious panic spreading from their own left.

Hobbling, Napoleon looked around the field, breathing deeply, his eyes damp.

"This is how it should have been!" he shouted, arms extended.

The staff around him was exuberant, shouting its congratulations as the spectacle of Wellington's army collapsing and streaming to the rear was played out before them.

Basak came hobbling back, his face streaming blood, more pouring from a bullet crease to his leg, and his ax dripping red.

"By the gods, these men know how to fight!" he roared, and Napoleon went up to him, slapping the Gaf on the shoulder and looking around proudly.

A courier, pressing his way through the crush of the young guard, which was streaming past and advancing to the oblique behind the middle, maneuvered his way up to Napoleon.

"Sire, Prussian infantry are clearing the woods on the right!"

Stunned, Napoleon turned about, calling for a telescope. An aide brought the battered instrument up and stood before Napoleon so that he could balance it on the man's shoulder.

He scanned the field to the east, and as the smoke from the battle to take the ridge drifted away, Yaroslav felt his stomach knot up. Coming out of the woods two miles away was a solid black column of men.

"What is the time?" Napoleon shouted.

"A quarter after two, sire," an aide replied, holding up a glittering pocket watch.

"Too fast, far too fast," he grumbled. "Did that Wellington cheat somehow?"

"He changed things as you did," Yaroslav said. "He somehow put the spur on Blücher to move faster."

"It can't be all of his men, it can't be," Napoleon snapped, as if trying to reassure himself. "A division, two at most. They must be strung out on the road from a forced march. We should have at least had another hour."

"We don't," Yaroslav replied, and pointed down to the southeast where more and more units were emerging from the forest, extending the Prussian line southward.

"They'll be across my line of communication; if Plancenoit falls, they'll cut in from behind."

He turned away and looked back to the north, and Yaroslav sensed that the general was running a rapid calculation, weighing the odds, sensing out what needed to be done.

He looked back at his staff.

"Order the guard to halt their advance and to retire back to Plancenoit; they will be the reserve. Lobau is to press the British, drive them, don't stop. Push them back to Brussels and the sea. Kellermann's divisions of cavalry are to press in, but they're not to close the sack. Let them run, they're out of the war anyhow after this. Those damned Dutchmen and Hanoverians will be on our side anyhow within the month. D'Erlon is to rally at La Belle Alliance. Jérôme, Foy, and Bachelu are to turn to the east and form the center. Piré and L'Heretier's divisions of cavalry will screen our left and push the English back. Now all of you, ride!"

Napoleon hobbled back to his horse and grimaced with pain while a hussar gently eased him up into the saddle.

"Half a day's work done, my friends," he said. "Now let us finish the business."

"By the gods, I've never seen forty thousand men run a footrace like this before," Zergh announced, holding up his glass as if in salute to the emperor.

"All right, they've won, now let's get them out of there," Aldin said nervously, looking over to the tracking monitor, which was showing that their company was coming in at an ever-increasing speed.

"How?" Oishi asked.

"Try and get us down there," Aldin said.

Nodding in agreement, the samurai edged the controls forward and started to drop the ship down. The first hundred meters of descent the ship seemed to handle normally, and then it shuddered to a stop. Oishi eased the thrust up, they dropped a bit more, and then he was finally up to full power, but they remained stationary.

"You better shut it down," Hobbs said nervously. "If that mechanical monster should decide to suddenly shut his end off, we'll dig one hell of a crater down there and blow half the battlefield apart."

Oishi snapped the throttle off.

"Jump-down beam?"

"Through that shielding?" Zergh said. "They'll come up here looking like beef stew."

"How much time before company arrives?"

"Four hours, maybe less."

"Damn it," Aldin hissed.

"Should we leave them?" Vush asked nervously.

Aldin looked over at him coldly.

"He saved my life down on the Hole, I'll be damned if I leave him, let alone Napoleon and Basak."

"That berserker's having the time of his life down there anyhow," Hobbs interjected. "I think he'd kill you with his bare hands if you interfered in things right now. Besides, the battle isn't over yet."

Aldin looked back up at the side-mounted projection system. A full corps of Prussian troops was coming out of the woods, a second corps deploying out behind them. Further to the south, swirling columns of dust and the distortion created by the force field laid out over the battle zone obscured the view, but it looked like at least another corps was moving in.

"So what do we do?"

"I still haven't lost my bet," Hobbs said. "Let's see it out, perhaps Napoleon will get finished up by Blücher and we can get out of here before our visitors come in."

"They're hurt down there, all three of them," Tia said angrily, annoyed that the others had not even considered that fact.

"Part of the game," Vush said absently, to the surprise of everyone.

"They're going in," Hobbs suddenly cried, pointing to the monitor that was focused on a regiment of Prussian cavalry that was moving out toward Plancenoit, advancing down the road from Wavre.

"Just what the hell is he doing?" Zergh growled, and Aldin looked up to where his friend was pointing. It was evident that the new crisis was on the right. The guard divisions were already moving back in good order, having disentangled themselves from the fracas. They were in column, with flags held high, deploying back toward Plancenoit, moving through the carnage of where D'Erlon's corps had been so badly chewed up. The guns of the Grand Battery were being repositioned to face eastward as well, and the battered remnants of the dead Count D'Erlon's corps were forming. But Napoleon's left flank, which should have been moving in to cover the center and act as a fresh reserve, was advancing off in the opposite direction, the entire formation moving forward in pursuit of the retreating British.

"One corps can handle the pursuit. He's sending in two. Is he crazy?" Hobbs asked.

"That's his brother on the left; I think the other one was Foy—both under Reille. He's most likely run off on his own just like the last time."

"Well, he's going to have a hell of a hole and no reserve," Hobbs announced with a satisfied air. "I still might win this bet after all."

Yaroslav, his throat burning with a thirst he had not imagined possible, gratefully took the canteen from a guardsman. Tilting his head back, he let the water run down his throat. He tried to still his guilt with the thought that these men were not truly real. But from the corner of his eye he could see the man watching him intently, as if measuring out each precious drop that was disappearing. He stopped drinking, recapped the wooden flask, and handed it back down.

"Merci."

"An honor, sir," the guardsman said, and turning away he continued to limp toward the rear.

"What time is it?" Napoleon shouted, trying to be heard above the steady roar of musketry that was volleying out barely a hundred meters away.

"Five o'clock," an aide replied.

Yaroslav looked over at the boy, who swayed unsteadily in the saddle, a trickle of blood coursing down his face from a saber cut to the forehead.

A regiment of Prussian cavalry had cleaved right through the line only minutes before, and they had all sought safety in a square of guards. The square had actually been cracked open at one point, until a charge of guard cavalry had driven them off. It seemed as if the Prussians had realized that Napoleon was sheltered within the unit, and they nearly all died trying to cut a way in. The hole in the line had been cobbled back together with a makeshift unit patched together from half a dozen different battalions.

From La Haie Sainte down to Plancenoit, the Prussians were exerting a steady and ever-increasing pressure. Yaroslav could easily imagine that as more units came in from Wavre they were immediately deployed and thrown in. The last of Napoleon's reserves had been used long ago. He was grimly holding with what was left, riding up and down the line, urging the men on, shouting encouragement until his voice was barely a whisper, his features drawn and ashen, the wound in his leg still trickling blood.

A report had come back from the north that elements of the British had rallied several miles beyond Waterloo and that the sixth corps was battering them, coming to a near standstill, the only good news being that Kellermann's cavalry was pushing around the flank and driving what was left. As for Reille, he had simply disappeared to the north, pursuing the Alliance troops up the road toward Braine-L'Alleud.

The mere mention of Reille or Jérôme would cause Napoleon to explode in a towering rage that would take minutes for him to recover from.

His army, outnumbered two-to-one, had smashed half of the enemy, but now an equal number, all of them fresh, were closing in, and he now had but barely thirty thousand exhausted men to face their sixty to seventy thousand.

Yaroslav found that with the increasing exhaustion he had become almost oblivious to the danger that was humming all about him. The steady thunder of battle had deadened his senses, except for the throbbing ache of the bullet-shattered arm, which was now jolting him every time the horse took even a single step.

"Bring me night or bring me Ney," Napoleon gasped, pulling up beside Yaroslav.

"I don't think we can count on nightfall around here," he said, looking up at the sun, which still glowed brightly directly overhead. The ship was still there, and he cursed them. Damn it all, couldn't they see he was hurt? But at the same time he felt a strange sort of pride for still hanging on, and not simply falling down, faking a convulsion of some sort to prompt them into using a jump beam. But then again, he wondered, if they could jump, Zergh would not have missed this for anything. Wellington must have put some sort of block on that.

"Sire!"

Napoleon looked up as a blood-smeared orderly, his horse limping, came up and saluted.

"They're forming up again. It looks like a fresh division at Plancenoit."

Napoleon nodded.

"Artillery is almost depleted. If they hit again we'll break."

He nudged his horse around and started southward, Yaroslav

cursing, falling in beside him. To his amazement, Basak was still following them about, patting his ax, talking to it, chanting songs, exulting over the Legion of Merit that Napoleon had borrowed from one of his generals and pinned to the berserker's padded jacket.

A distant call of trumpets echoed, and a thundering volley of guns rolled out across the field. Napoleon reined up at the rear ranks of his guard divisions. The thin ranks waited while across the field the heavy block formations of the enemy came relentlessly forward, flanked to the north with regiments of cuirassiers and several batteries of mounted artillery. The guns pushed forward, deploying out a bare two hundred meters away.

Napoleon cursed angrily, turning to an orderly, screaming to him to find some guns, and the man galloped off.

The cuirassiers moved in closer.

"Should we form square?" Yaroslav asked.

Napoleon shook his head.

"Either way we're lost. Form square and the guns will pound us apart and their infantry will close in. Don't form square and the cavalry will crash through us.

"We stand here and if need be die. I allowed myself to leave my guard last time. I will not do so again."

The guns opened up, ranks of men going down from the sprays of canister. To the right flank of the guns the cuirassiers started forward, slowly gaining speed.

A brigade commander came up to Napoleon, looking for orders.

"Hold the line, hold the line!" Napoleon shouted, his voice coming out a hoarse whisper.

The thunder of the hooves grew louder, the ranks of the enemy spreading out, sweeping forward. The trumpets rang out, sounding the charge, and with flashing swords, an inexorable wave a quarter mile across came in, the artillery to their flank cutting holes in the French line.

The disciplined ranks of the guard waited, first rank going down on one knee, bracing musket butts into the ground, bayonet points poised upward. The second rank stood behind them, muskets pointed straight forward. The third rank raised weapons up, waiting for the command, the few squadrons of cavalry still in any order forming up behind the line, ready to seal any breech.

The charge thundered in, sounding to Yaroslav like a tidal wave rolling forward to engulf them. He had an almost child-like desire to cover his ears to block out the sound of death, to close his eyes, hunch down, and look away. If this was a game, he had forgotten it long ago. It was deadly real, the carpet of bodies around him bleeding, screaming, crawling to escape, or torn and still looking up with blank eyes.

The cuirassiers were at a hundred meters, then seventy-five.

Yaroslav knew that so much of this was a deadly game of morale, of group psychology. Unless Wellington had pro-grammed the horses to be totally insentient, they would react like any rational creature and refuse to be impaled upon the wall of bayonets, swerving aside at the last possible second. The cavalry was counting however on the simple terror that their approach would create. Yaroslav could see all so clearly just how terrifying that was. The ground shook beneath him, the air was filled with their thunder, and wild hoarse screams, sabers waving and flashing. Each man looked to be ten feet tall, and as they rode in stirrup to stirrup, it seemed as if they had become a single living machine, unstoppable. He wanted to turn to start to run. He could not imagine how any man in the line would not do likewise. Yet he knew as well that all of them, if disciplined enough, and if their courage still held after the hours of horrific pounding, had to realize that as long as they stood united they might possibly live. But if they broke, they would be a mob and cut to ribbons as the cuiras-siers waded through them.

And as he thought these things, he barely heard the shouted commands for the rear rank to fire.

A plume of smoke roiled out, and all along the line horses and riders tumbled over, high animal shrieks now sounding clear above the thunder. For several seconds it looked as if the charge had been broken, and he wanted to raise a triumph-ant shout, but then through the smoke he saw them still com-ing on, sections of the enemy line moving in. Where shots had hit the line had buckled, but the weight of the second and third line pushed around and through the tangle. The charge closed in.

He could feel the line wavering, as if a collective will were coming to a decision, the decision between an inexorable mass moving forward, and a thin wall of steel deployed to stop it.

Here and there individuals turned, looking back, the entire

line seeming to be pushed rearward by several feet, but not a single man broke and ran—they were, after all, the old guard. The charge closed in and then started to slide to a halt.

There was a clatter of steel, more shrilled screams of the horses, and a rising shout of thousands driven by terror, rage, and mad exultation. Here and there a mount, either already dying and blind or driven by madness, plunged into the bayonets, kicking and shrieking, the line beneath it buckling. At several points the wall was broken clean through, and the rear ranks of the Prussian cavalry surged forward into the gaps, like water pushing against a dam and springing through wherever a hole had been breeched.

Most of the line held, and the horsemen turned, slashing out with sabers, guardsmen thrusting upward, parrying the blows and then trying to stab rider or mount. Some of the horsemen let their sabers drop, leaving them dangling by their cinch cords to their wrists, and drew out pistols that popped off with low staccato bursts, while the rear rank of the guard worked feverishly to reload, discharging their muskets at point-blank range. Even the horses fought, turning, kicking, or reaching out to bite, one of them grabbing a guardsman directly in front of Yaroslav by the throat and pulling him up, snapping the man's neck before the horse was accidentally shot in the head by its own rider and both went down in a heap.

Most of the holes in the line were quickly sealed off, but one gap, to the south, started to broaden, Prussian cuirassiers breaking clean through into the open field behind the line. Napoleon looked over at the break in the line fifty meters to their right. A squadron of his guard chaussures galloped off to try to contain them. Forward, the battle raged on, while to the flanks of the advancing Prussians the artillery fire continued to pour in, striking so close that some of the shots plowed through their own men. To the other side of the artillery, a heavy column of infantry started to angle in, to strike the break at an oblique.

"The crisis is at hand," Napoleon announced sharply. He looked around, as if hoping somehow to conjure additional troops out of the ground, but none were to be had. To the north, what was left of D'Erlon's men were grimly hanging on. As to the pursuit of Wellington's men, Reille's corps had finally acknowledged the recall command but were still far off beyond Hougoumont.

The Prussian infantry closed in at double time, not bothering to deploy from column.

"If I had a dozen guns right now, I could blow them to hell," Napoleon snapped, and Yaroslav could not help but think of Richard's lament from Shakespeare.

The Prussian infantry forged in, striking just to the south of where their mounted comrades had started the breech. The entire line staggered, the volume of noise redoubling.

"Sire, the battle is lost!" an officer shouted, coming back from the line.

Napoleon looked around at his staff.

"Why are you staring like frightened children?" he roared, somehow regaining his voice.

He turned his horse about to face the widening breech.

"I lost the battle of Marengo at five o'clock," he cried, "and I won it back again at seven!"

He started forward.

Yaroslav came up alongside him.

"You'll get killed," he shouted.

Napoleon looked over at him.

"Go to the rear!"

"It's only a game, damn it!" Yaroslav cried. "It's only a goddamn game."

"Not for me. Not this time. I'll not lose this one again. It's better to die!" he cried, his voice carrying across the field.

A knot of guardsmen, falling back from the onslaught, turned to look at him.

"My emperor, save yourself," one of them shouted.

"I die here," Napoleon cried out in reply. A staff officer came up to grab his reins, and he reached out and with an angry jerk pulled the reins back so that the horse shied away.

"Soldiers of France!" Napoleon shouted, his voice high and clear. "Who of you will today turn your back on your emperor?"

The men around him stopped as if stricken.

"Then die with me for the glory of France," he shouted, urging his mount forward.

A drummer boy standing at the edge of the group picked up the *pas de charge*. Yaroslav watched in amazement as a thin line of stragglers, of broken and wounded men, fell in around Napoleon and surged forward, mingling in with the chaussures who struggled to contain the breech. On the far side of the break the line seemed to be melting away, but as if by strength of Napoleon's will alone the line to the north of the breech held firm.

Napoleon moved up to the very front, and at the sight of him the Prussian cavalry stormed forward, cursing and screaming, eager for the kill. Unflinching, he waited, guardsmen pushed forward around him, shouting their defiance, flinging themselves bodily in front of their emperor. Yaroslav, unable to contain himself, pulled up a lance stuck in the ground and moved up beside Napoleon, weakly thrusting it out, stunned when it caught a black-clad officer in the leg, sending the man backward. Basak was up on the other side, ax rising and falling as if his knotted arms were made of coiled steel.

The mad melee continued, and in spite of the indomitable will that seemed to radiate a resolve into those around him, Yaroslav realized that they were being swarmed under.

And then, as if from far off, he heard a roll of drums, the steady, bone-shaking roll of the *pas de charge*, a distant shout welling up to the heavens. A roaring volley cracked out.

Yaroslav, confused, looked around.

A growing cheer sounded, echoing louder and louder.

"Vive l'empereur, vive l'empereur!"

It came on louder and yet louder. And then another cheer sounded, rolling up from the south. Through the swirling confusion he could see that on the far side of the break the guard units, which but moments before were breaking apart, were now coming about, some with bayonets leveled, to charge back into the fray. Others, too exhausted to move, held their shakos aloft, waving and shouting.

"Ney, Ney!"

From out of the smoke a blue wall seemed to be advancing in, catching the Prussian columns full on the flank.

The attack before them started to break apart. A final surge of Prussian cavalry, unwilling to retreat, so close were they not only to victory but to the death of their foe, surged in, with one last desperate bid to snatch victory. Basak stood in front of Napoleon's horse cutting in low, crippling a cuirassier's mount and then with an uphanded swing cutting the cavalryman's arm off as he raised a sword up to strike Napoleon.

The charge broke apart, as Ney's troops and the remaining guard pushed in from behind.

The battle melted away.

A swarm of French infantry passed in front of the battered guard line at the double, their faces indistinct and yet nevertheless marked with exhaustion after a forced march of fifteen kilometers and a running assault at the end, accomplished in less than five hours' time.

At the fore of the advance, Yaroslav saw Ney, hat gone, red hair streaming, sword pointed forward, shouting with triumph, urging the attack in.

Weakly standing in his stirrups, he watched as the first division of Ney's assault stormed past, pouring out of the south end of the Paris Woods. It was obvious that the commands were jumbled together. Yaroslav could sense that these men must have been the strongest of Grouchy's troops, driven relentlessly, the weakest falling by the wayside during the forced march to the sound of the guns, the ranks mixing together and then surging in. But the taste of victory drove them forward. Down the entire length of the Prussian line the assault started to waver, and then as if guided by a single hand the Prussian army started to break off, turned, and retreated to the northeast. The few Prussian cavalry to the front tried to slash their way out, one of them turning and leveling a pistol. The gun went off, and an instant later the man went down and disappeared.

Napoleon visibly slumped in the saddle and seemed to reel. Yaroslav came up to his side to support him.

"A near run thing, a very near run thing," Napoleon said. He was trembling with nervous exhaustion, but there was a beaming look of triumph in his eyes.

"Should I get Ney?"

"Let him have his chase, he was always best at those things. Most of those Prussians are *Landwehr*, second-rate troops. Once broken, they'll run straight back to the Rhine."

All up and down the line cheers of exaltation sounded.

"Tell Ney to push them, to push them east."

He paused and looked about.

"I've dreamed this moment for five years. Thank you," he whispered.

He leaned back with a sigh, and for the first time Yaroslav realized that Napoleon had been hit again, an ugly stain spreading out from his chest.

"The emperor's been hit," Yaroslav cried.

Guardsmen pushed around, and reaching up they helped to

lower him to the ground, the men gathering around, their looks of joy replaced in an instant with fear and anguish.

Yaroslav dismounted, groaning and nearly losing his footing. He pushed his way through to kneel by Napoleon's side.

"It's been a good day," Napoleon whispered.

Yaroslav found that he could not speak, his throat tight with emotion.

"It was an honor to serve you."

Napoleon smiled.

"I knew I'd win you over, Marshal Yaroslav."

The old man nodded.

Napoleon looked up at a guardsman.

"André, is that you?"

"I am here, my general."

"But I lost you, it was at Arcola."

The guardsman smiled.

"I am here nevertheless, my general."

He looked around wide-eyed.

"Pierre, you fell at Rivoli. Vincent, you died at Leipzig trying to save the regimental flag. And Guillaume, how I missed you."

The cluster of men knelt around the emperor. Yaroslav looked from one to the other. All of them were silent, most weeping quiet tears that streaked their powder-stained faces, dampening their drooping mustaches.

"My old grumblers. How I killed you all. Forgive me, my children."

"We died for France, for you, my emperor," one of them whispered, his voice choked, as if comforting a child who was at the edge of the darkness.

"Emperor Napoleon."

Yaroslav looked up. It was Wellington, floating at the edge of the circle.

Napoleon looked up, squinting, as if barely able to see.

"Emperor Napoleon, I offer my surrender," the machine said. "You have won the battle of Waterloo. I am your prisoner."

Napoleon raised a hand and weakly pointed to Yaroslav.

"Marshal Yaroslav will arrange the terms."

Napoleon smiled weakly and closed his eyes.

"I die happy," he whispered.

Yaroslav leaned over him, placing a hand on his chest.

"He's going into cardiac arrest," the old man shouted. "Damn it! Do something!"

The machine looked down in silence.

"We'll have target lock in a couple of minutes," Corbin announced.

"Just don't miss," Hassan said, looking at the full magnification view of Aldin's ship, the strange confusion of the battle spread out below them.

"Miss? With these First Traveler missiles?" Corbin replied haughtily, as if the six weapons were of his own design. "Hardly likely."

Across the Cloud, the wormhole had finished its meal of a class M star, the last light of it winking out. Within seconds the several small planets that had been orbiting, but now were streaking straight out into the darkness, were captured by the wormhole and devoured.

The seething mass at the other end of the hole seemed to pulse and shudder, thinly balanced between the outward pressure of the thermonuclear furnace within its core and the ever-increasing burden of its own monumental mass, which was almost ready to start the mad rush in that would lead either to the creation of a black hole or the cataclysm of a supernova explosion.

The open end of the wormhole wavered for a brief instant, tracing out the waves of gravity that flowed about it. Locking onto the strongest of them, it leaped outward at translight speed, streaking in toward the Core Cluster as if eager to feed upon the hundreds of stars within.

The few residents still on Yarmu, a Gaf vacation world, looked up at the sun above them. A thin line appeared like an arrow driving into the light. A coiling column of fire shot out from the sun and streaked off into space.

There was a mad clamor for the last ships, their masters having counted on this event and now realizing that the cancellation of all bookings and then the reselling of tickets at a 10,000 percent markup was proving to be a most profitable venture. Several of the more suicidal patrons of the planet, who belonged to one of the more unusual Gaf cults, settled back to watch the show, not even aware that their leader was already aboard the last ship out, with plans for future investments.

An errant spin of the wormhole caught the ship, however, and the cult leader made it to eternity long before his worshipful followers.

The wormhole continued on with its deadly work, oblivious to the panic setting in across the Cloud.

chapter twelve

"Jump him up, jump him up now!" Aldin screamed. "The field's just shut off!"

Zergh was out of the room, pushing to get into the small master control room for the jump down. It'd take a minute to build up the power load necessary, and he swore vehemently while he watched the slow upward curve of power on the console.

A shimmer of light filled the room, and he felt the outrush of air. There was an audible pop, and he looked up to see Yaroslav straddling Napoleon's chest, leaning in rhythmically with his one good arm to try to keep the heart going, Basak standing protectively over them, and the First Traveler machine floating alongside.

Zergh found himself actually looking back at his console, as if somehow the machine had initiated the jump without a command, while at the same time realizing that the First Traveler device had done it.

"Get us into the medical bay!" Yaroslav shouted.

Zergh felt a moment of panic, not sure what to do, wondering if he should interrupt Yaroslav. Tia was in the doorway carrying a med portapack, a servobot behind her. She knelt down, shouldering Yaroslav aside, and slapped the pack onto the emperor's chest. The portapack computer took over, jolting a charge in, injecting medication straight into the heart. A float bed was pulled in, and the emperor was lifted up onto it, the servobot punching an artificial blood unit into his arm, while with another tentacle hooking a respiration unit in.

"How long?" Zergh asked, his voice choked.

"Maybe a minute, a minute and a half," Yaroslav said.

"Didn't we put a new heart in when we did the make-over on him?" Aldin asked.

Tia nodded and looked over at the portapack screen.

"Heart's not been hit, but one lung's got a hole in it the size of a small fist. It might be too much damage. He most likely lost way too much blood from the first wound. The second hit the pulmonary vein in the lung, and that did it."

Aldin looked over as the bed floated into the medical bay. A medbot inserted a drainage tube into the entry wound, and the tube pulsed with bright red fluid.

The float bed went into the medical bay, the servobot following, clicking with a nearly Human sound of anxiety, and the door slid shut.

Yaroslav slumped against the wall, eyes hollow with exhaustion and shock, waving Tia away when she came up to look at his arm, and then motioning for Hobbs to fetch a drink instead. Basak looked around at the group, his emotions torn between exaltation from the thrill of combat and despair over the emperor.

"Incredible," Yaroslav whispered, finally looking up at the stunned group. "He was incredible. I can see why they said his presence on the field was worth forty thousand men."

"Not like him, though," Zergh replied. "He only really exposed himself once, at Arcola; he was reckless to the point of madness this time."

"He had a chance to do it one more time," Aldin replied. "He couldn't live with himself if he had lost it again. He must have wished he had died in that fight every night of his exile when he was alone. A warrior's death to cement the legend in blood, that must have been his nightly dream."

"Aldin."

The vasba looked over to see Oishi in the doorway to the forward control and recreation room.

"We've got to get out of here now. I can still pilot us through the opening, but in another two or three minutes they'll be in position to block our escape."

Aldin nodded and looked over at the First Traveler machine

and felt a cold anger. Because of this damn machine, any hope of solving their problem had been blown.

"You most likely killed him," he snapped angrily, "and for what?"

"He won. I fought it fairly, he had his inner wish."

"Well if that's the price, I'll forget my inner wishes," Hobbs interjected.

"I am Wellington. I am his prisoner for the rest of the day, that is the game."

Yaroslav looked up.

"You are the prisoner of the emperor," Yaroslav said, "and he assigned me to arrange the terms."

"I expect to be treated with the consideration worthy of my rank as a duke, as a general, and as a gentleman."

"Fine," Yaroslav replied. "I am a marshal of the empire, appointed by the emperor, and am now in command. I accept your surrender in the name of the emperor."

The machine nodded toward Yaroslav.

"I would enjoy sharing a bottle of claret with you," Yaroslav said, "but first might I ask you a question?"

"Within reason."

"But of course, my lord."

"Then ask."

"Do you know what a wormhole is?"

"A biportal material-transformation transporter, capable of creating a field distortion to fold space and to activate—"

"Yeah, that's the one," Aldin snapped, cutting it off.

"I know of it."

"Do you know him?" Yaroslav asked, and he pointed over at Vush, who floated in the far corner, his pale features even paler as he continued to stare at the trail of blood leading out of the jump-beam room and down the hall into the med unit.

"That entity has been in my presence."

"Aldin, we've got to move now!" Oishi shouted.

He held his hand up and looked over at Yaroslav.

"Do you remember the machine that Vush and his companion took, a device to create wormholes?"

The machine floated before them.

"It is recalled."

"All right," Yaroslav said, nodding a grateful thanks to Hobbs, who drifted back into the room bearing a glass of wine. Yaroslav downed half the glass in a single gulp and sighed.

"It is believed that they took only half the machine, that there is another part that was left behind."

"That is true, element 2371881773 second unit was not taken."

"Why the hell didn't you tell us, you bastard," Vush snapped angrily.

The machine turned slightly, as if to face Vush.

"You did not accept the offer to play, you did not defeat me, you did not unlock the proper security sequence in order to elicit the necessary response. And most of all you told me to leave you alone when I attempted to warn you of the danger of the machine you and your friend were playing with."

The machine paused.

"You are scum, sir. I like my officers turned out smartly, and your dress is abominable."

Aldin could not help but smile. A friendly game of chess or whatever. It was all so simple, reminding him of an old classic story where the sign to enter a door had simply said "speak friend and enter," and all puzzled over the proper word, until finally someone had simply said "friend."

"Would you fetch the other half of the element? Such an action is within acceptable protocol of surrender, the equivalent of surrendering your sword."

"If it is wished, I am Wellington, prisoner till the end of the day and the next game."

"The machine, is it functional?" Tia interjected.

"It is functional."

"Aldin, now!" Oishi shouted. "We've got to move now!"

"Find the other half and bring it back!" Yaroslav said, his voice taking on the tone of command.

A shimmer of light flooded the corridor. The machine barely dematerialized and then it was already back, a box not much bigger than a small book resting on the floor before it.

All looked down at it in astonishment. It was jet black, no instruments visible, no controls, simply a jet-black cube that held such a dark color that it almost appeared as if space itself were floating within its confines.

"He's launched some trackers," Oishi shouted.

"At that range," Zergh laughed, "it'll take ten minutes to get to us."

"Under two minutes," Oishi replied. "They're different, already up to .002 light-speed and accelerating. Whatever it is, it's coming in fast. It's got a lock on us!"

"Get us out of here!" Aldin shouted, breaking away from the group and running into the forward control room. He pulled up beside Oishi and looked at the screen.

"Oh, shit." He sighed. The incoming vessel was still a hundred thousand kilometers away and closing fast. Spreading out from the vessel, however, were half a dozen small blips. One of them suddenly winked out with a flash, undoubtedly running into some sort of debris. The signal on the others became faint, almost disappearing, then reappearing for an instant, several thousand kilometers closer, then winking out again.

Whatever Corbin had thrown at them, it was capable of masking. It was remarkable, the blips were closing straight in, able to see them in spite of all the clutter created by the mass of the Sphere below.

"Let's go!" he shouted.

Yaroslav, still looking up at the First Traveler machine, felt the ship surge beneath him.

"Can you move this ship?" he shouted, trying to be heard above the roar of the thrust systems kicking in while the outside ports were not yet fully closed.

"Too much mass in one unit," the machine replied. "Where are you taking me? Am I to be exchanged?"

"You're the prisoner of the emperor for the rest of the day. Can't you do anything about the ship approaching toward us, the weapons they've fired?"

"Another game? Most interesting, not part of our agreement. I like to watch."

The ship bucked beneath Yaroslav, nearly knocking him over. He could feel the grating of the shattered bone in his arm, and he groaned with pain. He realized he must be in shock as well. The stress of the battle had kept him focused on other things, but now that it was over, it was all getting to be a bit too much. The machine now seemed to be far away, as if floating at the end of a distant tunnel that was now hovering straight overhead. He slid down to the floor, out cold, the others not even noticing, except for Basak, who had sat down by the door into the medical bay, cradling his blood-soaked ax in his lap and talking to it gently. The berserker slid over to sit by Yaroslav.

"It was a good day, a joyful day," Basak said.

Aldin looked back out from the control room and saw Yaroslav slide down to the floor in a dead faint and shouted for Hobbs to go look after him.

"A lot of good it'll do," Hobbs cried. "We're all going to get cooked in about ten seconds!"

"Run for the opening we came through," Aldin shouted.

"We can't, one of the incomings has tracked over that way. It's turning toward us now!"

"Sit back and hang on," Oishi shouted.

The *Gamemaster II* was already up to a dozen kilometers a second, the ground below getting ripped up by the shock wave of its passage, the smoke-clad battlefield of Waterloo behind them. He pushed the throttle up to the limit and started to climb.

"What the hell are you climbing for!" Zergh shouted. "Try and hide in the clutter, get in a gully, behind a hill."

"They're coming down, a lot of good it'll do," Oishi replied.

He pulled up to a dozen kilometers, the atmosphere thinning out, the drag dropping off, and the ship accelerated rapidly. Waterloo was now a hundred kilometers astern. He pulled a sharp turn and pointed straight at the black mountain on the edge of the city, adding another kilometer of height.

"Ten seconds!" Aldin cried, watching mesmerized as one of the incomings did a spiraling turn away from the lock it must have achieved when they were over Waterloo. The missile disappeared momentarily and then appeared again, sending out an incredible burst of a radar signal and a snap of laser light as if looking to designate them. It locked on, following their track for a second, and then completely disappeared.

It was a brilliant piece of machinery, Aldin realized, unlike anything available. It would mask to avoid having anything sent back against it, appearing only long enough to get a fix, and then masking again before a counterstrike could be locked onto it and track it for a kill. There was no beating it.

It reappeared less than ten thousand kilometers away, locked, and then disappeared. One, maybe two more. Aldin tried to point the ship's one laser gun against it, but a firing solution could not be calculated quickly enough in the fraction of a second that the device revealed itself.

He looked forward again. The mountain was straight ahead, rushing up as if they were going to smash straight into it.

"Hang on," Oishi cried, even as he slammed a full re-verse on.

The inertial damping system almost made a perfect re-sponse, but Aldin felt as if his eyes were about to pop out of his head nevertheless.

"What the hell are you doing?" Zergh screamed, reaching over as if to grab the controls from Oishi.

Oishi slammed them to a complete stop directly over the top of the mountain, while rotating the ship to point straight down.

"Holy shit!" Aldin screamed, wanting to stop him. Hobbs's high-pitched screams could be heard in the doorway. The en-tire forward screen was black as they looked straight down into the hole punched clean through the Sphere. Aldin felt his last three meals coming back up.

Oishi slammed the throttle forward, and the ship shot straight down, going into the mountain, buffeting with the tur-bulence of the atmosphere that was sucked through the hole.

The universe straight ahead was darkness. An instant later a blinding snap of light washed about them.

"Impact!" Zergh screamed.

Their ship shot out of the Sphere, and Oishi rotated it yet again as they cleared the hole. They turned, skimming along the outside shell of the Sphere. Behind them a column of nu-clear fire blew outward, a tongue of radioactive exhaust from the impact of the missile atop the mountain. The tongue of fire pulsed, began to dissipate, and then renewed itself, flaring up an instant later as if redoubling.

"The other's impacting," Oishi said, leaning back in his chair and wiping his brow with the sleeve of his robe.

"Did we get cooked?" Tia asked nervously.

Aldin looked over at the monitor, which was flickering from the EMP, and then unscrambled.

"Not much, shielding cut it down to a couple of rem, but a second earlier and we would have been inside the oven."

Zergh got up without a word and went over to help a servobot right itself, ignoring Hobbs, who was floating upside down in the corner, his float chair completely scrambled by the roller coaster ride. Pulling the servobot up, he punched the sake dispenser, poured out a cup, and came back over to Oishi. He drained half the cup and then offered it over, and suddenly his hands began to shake.

"You're chief pilot now," he said, his voice shaking almost as much as his hands.

Oishi looked over and nodded his thanks.

"We kept hanging around, waiting for the battle to clear. I kept trying to think of an escape, and that was the last alternative."

"Suppose there'd been debris in there?" Zergh asked.

"We'd be history," Oishi replied dryly.

"Speaking of history," Aldin said, and he unbuckled himself from the chair and got up, his knees feeling like jelly. "Get us to the nearest jump gate and let's head for home."

He went across the room, first grabbing hold of Hobbs's chair and flipping him back upright, laughing wanly when he saw that his friend had made as much of a mess of himself as he had. The corridor was a mess as well, pictures torn off the walls, their frames shattered. Basak rested in the corner, with Yaroslav pulled in tightly to his chest. The old man's eyes were open.

"You trying to kill us?" he asked weakly, grimacing from the berserker's embrace.

"Almost."

The First Traveler machine still floated in the corridor, Vush stretched out cold beside him.

"What happened to him?" Aldin asked.

"Struck its head against the ceiling and sleeps now," the machine replied. "Where are you taking me? I am a prisoner only to the end of the day. I must return home."

Damn, he had forgotten about the machine in all the confusion.

"Part of the game is a signing of conventions, an armistice before prisoners are all exchanged," Aldin said quickly. "The emperor alone can do that—as soon as he is fully recovered. Is that acceptable?"

The machine actually seemed to hesitate.

"Acceptable," it finally replied.

He went up to the medical bay door and punched it open. He expected far worse. Several containers were on the floor, but the medbot had secured the float bed to an anchor point before the chaos had started. It was working attentively on the emperor.

Aldin went up nervously and looked over at the monitor, expecting the worst.

"A steady pulse, thank God."

He looked back and saw Yaroslav standing weakly behind him.

"First time I've ever heard you thank a deity," Aldin replied.

The bot, with needlelike fingers, was working inside the emperor's body, reattaching shattered vessels, stitching fragments of lung back together, analyzing the genetic code of individual cells, replicating them and patching in where too much tissue had been torn apart. It was slowly working its way outward, from the deepest injury back up, repairing on a microscopic level as it went. An auxiliary arm was working simultaneously on the bullet wound to the leg, spinning out a fabric of muscles, vessels, nerves, and flesh to close the injury back up.

"Leave some sort of scar on the wounds," Yaroslav said to the bot. "It'll please his vanity."

His color was already back, the grayish blue hue replaced with a near-healthy pink. A tray to one side held a misshapen piece of lead.

"Pistol shot, lucky it wasn't a musket ball or canister, or he'd really be dead," Yaroslav said quietly.

"We should get you attended to, and Basak as well."

"We can wait. He's more important at the moment."

"Sounds like you're getting sentimental about him."

"Who, me?" Yaroslav sniffed.

"Well, he did save us," Aldin replied. "Never expected it. I think on a gut level he knew the machine was playing the game out for a reason. When that hole got slammed into the Sphere, it must have scrambled some fundamental programming for the entire Sphere. That'd explain the chaos that was going on."

"He did insist on the prisoner agreement before he'd play."

Yaroslav looked down at the emperor and smiled.

"He did almost as good as I would have."

"Now that is an admission."

Yaroslav shrugged his shoulders.

"He'd better recover. He owes me a marshal's baton. And I want a painting done, in the style of David. *Marshal Yaroslav and the Emperor Leading the Guard at Waterloo*."

"The Emperor and Marshal Yaroslav Leading the Guard."

Napoleon, his eyes barely open, looked up at them and smiled.

Aldin, reaching out, patted Napoleon lightly on the shoulder.

"Go to sleep, let the machine fix you."

"You will have your baton, Marshal Yaroslav, you earned it this day," Napoleon whispered, his voice slurring as the bot, working with a mild paralytic anesthesia, continued its repairs.

Aldin, forcing a smile, turned away.

Now the only question was how the hell to get back.

"I tell you we got him," Corbin said. "The trackers the Overseers gave us couldn't miss."

He turned a monitor around to show the top of the still-glowing mountain where five of the warheads had hit. The storm boiled and rolled, spreading outward.

"He must have been mad to go in there," Corbin said. "There was no hiding from those trackers."

"Go in closer for a look," Hassan snapped.

"What for?"

"Go in closer. There must have been a reason for him to go there, rather than turn and run."

Corbin, cursing silently, swung the ship down and approached the mountain.

"I thought an explosion would burst outward," Hassan finally said, watching as the cloud of radioactive debris, which in the beginning of the explosion had pulsed outward, now appeared to be contracting in upon itself.

Corbin felt suddenly nervous.

"There's a hole there," he finally said, figuring it was best to announce the fact rather than let Hassan find out for himself.

"A hole?"

"The explosion tore the top off the mountain, punching through to the underside of the Sphere. The atmosphere is getting sucked into the vacuum of space on the other side."

He was afraid to admit the other scenario that was already forming.

"Could the hole have been there before?" Hassan finally asked.

Corbin hesitated.

"It's unlikely. Why would they have a hole that could drain out their own atmosphere?"

"Could it have been there?"

"It's possible," Corbin finally admitted.

Hassan stood in silence, looking at the screen.

"Take us through it. That is what they did."

"They might have been caught in the burst anyhow."

" 'Might have been' is not good enough."

Hassan looked down at the smoldering explosion.

"Take us through it."

"It's deadly down there," Corbin said. "We'd have to slow to a near stop as we went through. We'd be cooked by the radiation. It'll be an hour or more before it's safe, and even then there might be so much twisted wreckage that it will be impossible to get through."

He was surprised by his own self-assertiveness and looked up defiantly at Hassan. At least the barbarian didn't understand a whit about space travel.

"Then we wait," Hassan said, his voice deceptively calm. "I trust that if they did pass through you'll be able to detect them on the outside of this ball."

"There'll be some traces of an exhaust trail. If they survived, they'll either wait to come back in to finish their search or they will run for a transfer gate back into the Cloud."

"You realize what will happen if they successfully escape."

Corbin did not reply.

"What was that?"

The Arch looked up, startled and still disoriented from the transfer jump that they had completed only seconds before.

"Something going past us in the opposite direction," Mupa replied lamely, looking over at the Xsarn pilot who nodded a confirmation. They were continuing straight in toward the Sphere even while the holo camera loop was replayed. With a combined closing speed of nearly 20 percent light-speed, it was almost impossible to distinguish anything beyond a blur. But whatever it was, it had passed less than a kilometer away to port and jumped through the gate at nearly the same instant they had emerged. The near miss reminded the Arch of all the myriad reasons of why he hated to travel. To survive for so long, only to be winked out of this plane of existence by an overeager barbarian pilot, left him with a simmering rage.

"It was them," Mupa said, his voice weak and shaky with fear from the near miss.

"Who is them?"

"The ship, *Gamemaster II*. It was them."

The Arch was silent for a moment. Couldn't Gablona do

anything right? He had the information to trace them down, the weapons to destroy them—what more did the fool need?

"Turn us around," the Arch shouted.

"But I thought we were going to look for the machine," Mupa said weakly.

"Turn us around and get after them, they've already got it!" the Arch shouted. "And I want a coded message sent out at once."

Zola settled back in his chair and nodded for the others to leave the room.

This would be a tough one to call. He was tempted to pour out a quick drink to help sooth his nerves, but not this time, maybe afterward.

In the last score of days he had managed to make a huge killing, recouping a major portion of the assets lost in the lottery and futures fiasco of the Shiga game. Transport space aboard his fleet of junk cargo ships that were going into the threatened region was making 1,000 percent more than the day before the wormhole started. There was such a shortage of shipping throughout the Cloud that even in safe regions transportation had gone up 500 percent. With his own fleet of vessels, he could keep internal shipping between his own factories and worlds at the usual cost and thus make an even bigger killing against the mad upward spiral of prices.

Real estate was going beautifully as well. A third-rate pleasure world of marginal climate and a fierce indigenous population of carnivores and insects was now a hot new development site, since it was at the far end of the Cluster. Salesmen were already hawking lots at three times the old asking price, as everyone started to come to the conclusion that life in the Core Cluster was becoming decidedly unhealthy.

The question was, should he allow it to end?

He looked at the memo on his desk, hand delivered for the sake of security. There was a slight bit of sentimental attachment that welled up for a moment. A lot of good games in the past, some of them quite profitable indeed. Beyond sentiment, there was another concern. A fair part of the Core Cluster would be rather uninhabitable if the runaway star received any more mass and detonated into a supernova.

He tried to imagine that scenario. He tried to allow himself the humanitarian viewpoint, as if by so doing he could later talk down any sense of lingering guilt. Chances were that no one would really die, even though a billion beings were in the danger zone. Every ship could evacuate most all of them in that time, he'd already checked on that one. There might be a small shortfall, but that could be easily solved—he'd skip evacuating the lawyer's planet and everyone would thank him for it.

He sat back and spun out the calculations. The insurance companies would be intact; after all, every policy ever written had included the proviso that exploding stars and impacting bodies from space were not covered. They could sue the Overseers if they wanted, and that thought made him chuckle. Give them a dose of their own morality for a change.

All those people paying passage—it was boggling to contemplate. There wouldn't be any whining about service and food aboard ship, basic emergency rations and fares 1,000 percent of normal with operational costs cut in half. And the new real estate to be sold, the construction to be done.

I'll be the richest Koh inside of a year, he thought.

He looked over at the projection charts of which worlds would be hit. And only three had major assets of his on them, all the rest were either the old territory of Corbin, the acquisitions of Bukha and Aldin, or one of the banking, legal, or administrative worlds, and who the hell needed them anyhow?

He leaned back in his chair and sighed. Friendship was friendship but a good profit line was, in the end, the bottom line.

If it had been aware, it would have known that mass had already exceeded the level whereby a supernova was all but inevitable. All that was keeping it from blowing was the central core of oxygen, superheated to half a billion degrees and thus fueling a nuclear reaction that was keeping the center burning with such intense forces that the outer shell of the star was thus prevented from collapsing in.

The sun that the cultists had been watching was gone, swallowed up, the gravitational force that had kept the planet in its elliptical orbit gone as well, so that it was now heading straight out into space. There were a lot of *ooh*s and *ah*s coming from the crowd, though the event was taking six minutes to reach them visually, and thus from their perspective the star still appeared to be collapsing in and dimming out.

Most of them were thus able to actually let out a shout of surprise when it appeared as if the show was still going on and then also suddenly stopped. The wormhole, detached from where the sun had been, first hit a gas giant further out, consuming it in half a dozen minutes, and then came back in to the small planet. There was a second of confusion and disappointment; after all, their leader had said they'd see the sky go completely dark and thus gain at that instant total knowledge of nothingness and liberation. Instead, there was still some light in the sky when from the opposite direction the wormhole bored straight into the heart of the planet from behind and within the first second caused it to start to collapse in upon itself.

Several of them had just enough time to sense that somehow things were not quite going according to plan, and were considering quitting the cult and getting a refund, when suddenly they stretched out into a long thin stream of matter and disappeared.

The planet was gone, and there was a momentary searching for the next gravitational wave to chase down. Another class M star almost won, but an ever so slightly greater presence was sensed, a burned-out black dwarf, a solid sphere of compressed iron with a mass of hundreds of trillions of tons.

The wormhole transfer gate leaped across space, actually moving in somewhat closer to its point of origin, and in less than half a minute locked onto the dark star, actually encountering some resistance as it bored into its heart before starting to pump the compressed iron out and shooting it back up to the pulsing giant.

The iron hit the thermonuclear center. Anything below iron in the order of elements would have continued to drive the reaction; iron was one element that could not. Chunks of it had been fed in before, especially when a solid planet was consumed. It would cause a confused swirling reaction in the heart of the star, actually triggering a momentary collapse of the sun's outer layers until some other element finally emerged and reignited the nuclear pile.

But this was iron, nothing but supercompressed iron pouring in at tens of billions of tons per second, instantly acting like a jet of ice water shot into a cylinder of superheated steam. The nuclear heart of the sun started to shut down, and the surface began ever so gradually to fall in upon itself. The final, inevitable supernova had begun.

chapter thirteen

"I tell you, we'll be out of fuel and in the middle of nowhere," Zergh said wearily. "We've jumped all the way down to the Milky Way, back up to the Sphere, and now halfway back into the Cloud. It's simple math, either turn off at a Xsarn world at this next gate or we sputter out when we get to our destination."

Aldin, rubbing his eyes, looked at the ceiling.

"Great, one more jump, a couple of hours of running, and now you're telling me we can't make it?"

"If you stop, Corbin will be ahead of us," Oishi said sharply. "He was less than a half hour behind us at the last gate. He'll close it the rest of the way at this one."

Aldin looked around at the group. They were all looking the worse for wear. Water had to be rationed, food was almost gone, and there was a decidedly gamy smell in the air, especially from Basak and Hobbs, who seemed to revel in an excuse for not bathing.

Aldin looked over at Napoleon.

"A tough pursuit. Do not hesitate with victory in your grasp."

Aldin nodded in agreement. If they stopped at the small Xsarn world, they'd be pinned on the ground in a matter of minutes. There was only one alternative, to run till the fuel ran out and hope they reached their goal.

"All right, we push through then."

The next transition jump point was strangely quiet. Usually there was some traffic moving back and forth, exiting out of one point and maneuvering to go into the next. He expected some form of resistance by this point. A coded Overseer message had been sent from near the Sphere, but so far no reaction, most likely due in part to a couple of turns through seldom-used jump lines, thus evading any blockades that might have been laid out. But it was coming down to the end now. There was only one way in toward Beta Zul from this direction, and they had to take it and hope for the best.

Boosting power up to the maximum, Oishi moved them across the small barren system, which was composed of a red dwarf and several dead planets, noted only for the small supplies of titanium that had been found there centuries ago and thus had resulted in this back path being laid out.

Oishi, letting the computer do the navigation, watched intently as they moved at maximum speed, doing the transit in under half an hour.

"Funny, Corbin should have come through by now," Oishi said. "He's been gaining on every transit by a couple of minutes."

"Maybe he had fuel problems as well," Tia said hopefully.

"Or he took another route," Zergh said.

"We checked that, there were no others."

"At least none that we knew of," Aldin replied. "He might have free-jumped. It was the straighter line in."

"Corbin free jump?" Hobbs said, shaking with laughter. "He's like me, too much of a coward to do something that crazy."

"Well, you've been floating around with us haven't you?" Yaroslav said.

Aldin looked over at his friend sitting in the corner with Napoleon, the two of them deeply immersed in some arcane point of tactics, both of them alternating with raised voices.

The medbots had worked their usual wonder, something he was grateful for the investment in. The units had been installed to alter replicants for the old days of gaming when substitutes had to be changed to match up with the individuals they were replacing. The system had cost millions. It had restored Napoleon when first brought aboard and had, after this latest injury, put him back on his feet in two days, Yaroslav beside him, sporting a neat circular scar on his arm, which was exposed more than once to hammer home a point when arguing with the emperor.

Wellington hovered to one side and would occasionally chime in with a comment. It conceded that Lobau's assault to the right of D'Erlon had thrown it off, since it expected Napoleon to keep the guard in reserve in anticipation of Blücher's early arrival on the field and thus assumed that Lobau was the main blow. Napoleon never confessed that he had no knowledge of the early Prussian advance until already committed to the assault in the center.

"A near run thing," the machine was now fond of saying.

There had been a formal surrender signing in the medical bay, the document drawn up by Yaroslav. The interpreting of the key point had been crucial, Wellington arguing that it was against the conventions of war for gentlemen prisoners to be used for labor. Yaroslav had countered that since the wormhole transfer gate was a substitute for Wellington's sword, all it meant was that he was being asked to give a demonstration of its use, nothing more. The agreement was finally signed when Yaroslav added the provision that all prisoners were to be exchanged back home once the "demonstration" was completed.

The latest debate between the three fell silent as they stopped to watch the final run in.

"Let's jump it," Zergh announced, and Aldin settled back for the transition.

His stomach did the usual flip over as they pulled the instantaneous leap to translight speed, and at nearly the same instant the alarms went off.

"There's something in the line!" Zergh shouted.

An explosion rocked through the ship, airtight integrity disappearing for a brief instant till the access door into the forward chamber slammed shut.

"What the hell?" Aldin and Vush screamed at nearly the same instant.

"We hit something. Something was in the line ahead of us."

Oishi scanned the monitors and looked back up at his companions, his features pale.

"We should have been dead. Our shielding never could have stopped an impact. As it is, a fair section of port side, including the medical bay, is gone."

"We never should have . . ." Oishi's voice trailed off, and he looked over at the First Traveler machine.

"According to the convention agreement, I am to aid in the delivery of what you call the device. The unshielded impact of this vessel would have destroyed it, thus preventing delivery."

"Well, nice going," Yaroslav said, almost matter-of-factly,

running a hand through his hair to straighten it out after the tornado of a temporary decompression.

"Could you have done the same thing back in the Sphere?" Yaroslav asked.

"The convention of terms had yet to be signed."

"Well, what else can you do for us?" Aldin asked.

"Energy has been dissipated," the machine replied.

"In other words, not much."

"Not much."

Aldin nodded.

"Well, somebody just tried to kill us; let's just hope there isn't a reception committee waiting on the other side."

"Corbin's ship has just come through," Mupa announced, and then turned away to look nervously back at the star that filled the entire forward screen.

The cataclysmic collapse had begun, the outer edge of the star accelerating inward. A sensitive enough eye could have by this stage detected a slight Doppler shift in color, a dropping off into a deeper red. A rapidly increasing burst of radiation was pulsing outward.

The star was going into supernova.

The wormhole line was glowing hotly, the great mass of the black dwarf pumping into the heart of the developing explosion.

The Arch watched the show intently. He knew he should be feeling some moral revulsion with all that was happening. He had supplied weapons to Corbin and the mad assassins aboard his ship to track Larice down, knowing that it would kill one of his brothers if successful. He had revealed an unknown jump point to Corbin, allowing both of them to get ahead of Aldin. He had allowed information to leak to one of the Human Kohs, who had, against all custom and tradition, scattered wreckage in a jump line with the intent of stopping Aldin after his escape from the Sphere. He was participating in the destruction of a sun that would render a not unsizeable portion of the Cloud uninhabitable.

The Arch clicked off these sins and felt no remorse.

He already had his next plan firmly laid out, giving yet more weapons to Corbin to allow him to wage war and thus plunge the rest of the Cloud into chaos. By his projections, within twenty years, the civilization, if it could be called that, of the three species would have totally collapsed and they would revert, trapped on their own worlds. Then there would be peace again, and solitude, and contemplation.

Contemplation of my own sins? he wondered. Perhaps, but there could be endless millennia to work that out, to expiate the stain and to find tranquility, something now impossible with a universe full of brawling barbarians.

"Full detonation in less than ten minutes," Mupa announced.

The Arch settled back in his chair to watch the show.

"We've got the Overseer ship on track," Hassan said, smiling and looking up at the screen.

Corbin could only nod dumbly in reply.

"If he somehow evaded the debris, we'll be waiting."

"And then what?" Corbin Gablona said coldly.

"We finish him."

"And then?"

Hassan looked over at the fat old man who sat glumly before him. He was filled with a sense of loathing for his former master, the mere thought of being subservient to him filling him with yet more rage.

I'll have you spaced, destroy the Overseers, and take over, he wanted to shout at him. But no. He would still need this one as a figurehead, a puppet to dance before the multitudes while he ruled the strings from above.

Behind Hassan, the disk of the sun continued to collapse.

Zola sat quietly watching his private monitor. It had been a tough job to sabotage the one ship that was to carry the pool of newscasters out to the rogue sun. There was to be no one there. For one thing, he had already arranged a monopoly on the holo film from Mupa, worth a small fortune in itself. And secondly, if there was any last-minute unpleasantness, it'd be bad for business to see the effort to stop the explosion being prevented in turn by the Overseers and Corbin.

He poured a drink and settled back to wait it out.

"Jump-transition point in five seconds," Zergh announced nervously.

Aldin nervously clutched at the arms of his chair. The light shift hit, and an instant later the angry glow of the collapsing sun was before him.

"We've got barely enough to make a straight in pass," Oishi announced.

"Company's here!" Zergh cried, jamming the throttle up to maximum.

The ship was bracketed with a burst of light.

"Corbin," Zergh snapped, jinking the ship to avoid the initial shots.

They dove in toward the sun, Gablona's ship moving up to match the speed they were still running with as they came out of the gate.

To one side, the Overseer ship snapped past, and within seconds was a hundred thousand kilometers astern, but Corbin was still behind them and gaining.

Aldin looked forward and found himself fascinated by the sight. Though they were approaching the sun at a high rate of speed, the disk was actually getting smaller.

It was remarkable, beautiful, radiating an unimaginable power.

"Fuel's out," Oishi cried. "We're losing control!"

Aldin looked over at the samurai and smiled sadly. There was nothing more to be done. The sequence of explosions had already started, and they were falling straight into it. He felt the gravity on the ship go with the power, his stomach lifting up inside. Too bad, he thought, I wish I could have had another drink before going.

What scared him most of all, though, was the fact that he wasn't even sure if he really cared anymore. He looked over and saw Tia and Oishi, their hands clasped. For them, he wanted something, but for himself? There was really nothing anymore. No dreams, no goals to reach. He was far too tired of the struggle that no longer seemed to matter.

He strapped himself into his chair and waited for the show to end and the lights to come up.

Several hundred trillion tons of highly compressed iron had been pumped into the heart of the storm, shutting down the reaction. The inward rush was generating at the same time a pressure increase of a full magnitude, and then another magnitude in less than a second.

A giant that had been nearly a hundred million kilometers across was now down to a million, and in that final second the iron made a final instantaneous transition to every other possible element in existence, a billion tons of mass compressing into an area the size of a thimble. Gravity had held it in upon itself. If the mass had been less, it would have simply continued to compress until finally winking out of this particular universe, disappearing down the long event horizon into another realm.

But the inward rush of so much mass created temperatures in that last instant far in excess of a billion degrees. Not even gravity could withhold this final onslaught of outward pressure.

There was only one place left to go, and that was out.

The star exploded into supernova.

The vision stirred within the First Traveler. For it was indeed just that, what others called a First Traveler, the master builder of the universe, far exceeding the powers of its long-dead creators.

It could sense what was ahead, a vision that would take several minutes to reach those around him as they tumbled in toward the explosion, their ship powerless—but contracts and surrenders were indeed binding.

"The forward monitor indicates supernova detonation," Mupa shouted.

The image was replayed on the screen, showing the last second of the inward rush, the holo relayed from the edge of the star as it started its final death throes. All that could be seen was the final incandescent snap, and the monitor disappeared, the signal dead.

The Arch looked up at the main screen, which showed the view from fifty million kilometers out.

"We better get out of here. The radiation burst will hit in less than three minutes," Mupa announced, and all in the room could detect the shocking reality of exaltation on the part of Arch of the Overseers.

Bukha Taug looked away from the screen and, lowering his face, he covered his eyes.

A lousy five minutes, that would have been all the difference. Maddeningly, the Xsarn shipping guild had suddenly announced a strike, with all pilots refusing to fly. He suspected Zola's hand in it all, bribing the guild officials to shut everything down. The plan had been so well laid out. It had been an insane scramble, a full day of waste to finally dig up a crew willing to lose their guild licenses to prepare a ship for departure.

Coming in from the Yalla jump line, he had been able to see Aldin's mad plunge straight in toward the star and intercept the holo relay of the event that must have been sent up to the Overseer ship.

It was simple enough, he had thought. Bring in a news crew not controlled by the Overseers and grounded by Zola's maneuver. Let them witness Aldin defuse the sun, and in the exultation of having saved the Core Cluster the frame-up of the war would be forgotten.

The news crew was excited to be sure, gasps of astonishment greeting the intercepted signal of detonation, the long-distance filming of Aldin's plunge in forgotten.

"Shock wave approaching. I'm pulling us back out of here in ninety seconds," the Xsarn Prime said, his voice filled with disgust.

"There goes Aldin's ship," Mari said, and Bukha felt as if he could actually pick up a note of regret in her voice, even as she snaked an arm around one of the Gaf berserkers as if seeking solace.

Bukha looked back up. The *Gamemaster II*, out of fuel and now tumbling out of control, continued a death plunge straight in toward the sun, which from this distance of nearly eighty million kilometers still appeared to be in existence.

"He's millions of kilometers further in," the Xsarn replied. "Shock wave will hit him any second."

"Corbin's coming around, the bastard's getting away," one of the minor Xsarn Kohs announced.

"What's happening?" Hassan screamed.

Corbin Gablona looked up, his stomach still in knots, a distant memory telling him just how much he hated jump-down beams.

This was wrong. The room around him was all wrong. Where was his float couch, the fine teak paneling, the plush two inches of carpet?

Where was his ship?

The battered interior of the *Gamemaster II*, that's what this was. There was another instant of memory, which was about all that time was now allowing. This was the old game ship of

Aldin's, built to go to Earth to fetch Alexander—or was it Kubar Taug? Why am I here?

Hassan and the other assassins were crowded in the room with him. Gravity was gone, the ship must have lost power. He could feel the weightlessness. He was floating. Damn, how I hate weightlessness, he thought.

Hassan, holding on to a railing, was looking back at him, wide-eyed. And behind him the sun, growing impossibly small, getting dark.

Why would it get dark?

The last second before supernova, matter rushing in at nearly light-speed before the detonation, that's why it would be dark, he realized.

"We're on the wrong ship!" Hassan screamed. "We've been jumped to their ship!"

It was a joke, a wonderful, incredible joke.

A box floated before him. It was curious, beautiful, as if space itself were contained within it, and he reached out with chubby hands to grab hold of it, pulling it in to his chest.

Corbin Gablona threw back his head and laughed.

The viewport before him flashed with a billion degrees of heat, and at the same instant a micro-servo clicked within the box. Space itself opened up within the box, a doorway swinging open into another dimension, another universe, and a very different time.

Caught between fire and night, Corbin Gablona plunged through the gate, the first Human to travel to another dimension, Hassan, the assassins, the *Gamemaster II*, the supernova, all rushing to join him.

"Hell of a nice ship," Aldin said, exhaling slowly.

Forcing a wan smile, he looked around the room. They were all here, including the First Traveler machine.

"Talk about a deus ex machina intervention," Yaroslav quipped, standing up with wobbling legs to go over to the sideboard to look for a drink.

"Has the convention of surrender been fulfilled?" Wellington asked, looking over at Napoleon. "Perceiving that you were about to crash, I exchanged your existence aboard your ship with those aboard the one in pursuit and then activated the device. As a friendly gesture I brought your friends and staff along as well."

Napoleon looked over at Aldin and grinned.

"A final custom is to escort an exchanged prisoner back to his border with full military honors," Napoleon finally said. "Yes, you have done your duty well."

"That is sufficient, then."

Aldin looked up at the screen. It was hard to tell what was happening. They were pulling away from the sun, and from this distance it still appeared to be in the final seconds of presupernova. It would be a close race to get out of the way of the shock wave.

A drone shot past in the opposite direction from the ship he assumed must be Bukha's.

Aldin punched up the commlink.

"Bukha Taug?"

"Larice?"

"Who else?" Aldin replied.

He could hear whoops of delight from the other end and then shouts of disgust.

"The Xsarn must have been a little too happy," Tia said, shaking her head.

A shouted argument broke out in the background, the news crew fighting to gain the commlink for an interview, not at all understanding just what was going on.

The drone continued to plunge in and then halted and started to back outward.

But there was no shock wave.

Curious, Aldin looked up at the monitor, which was locked onto the holo camera of the drone.

Finally there was a flash, a mild burst of radiation, and the system disappeared.

"It was late," the Xsarn shouted. "The shock wave should have hit the drone some three seconds before it did. It's slowing down."

"You activated the device?" Yaroslav asked, looking over at the First Traveler.

"As intended."

"It'll be a hell of a show if we can ever record it," Yaroslav said, "but I still advise we get out of here for right now. The system went supernova, and then he opened the other half of the wormhole, an exit point. The entire damn thing is getting sucked into another universe, and if we're still loitering here we might get sucked in as well before the other half of the machine gets pulled through and disappears."

The enormity of what they had actually pulled off finally started to settle in on Aldin, and he motioned for Yaroslav to bring a drink over.

"You heard it here first," Aldin said, knowing that within seconds it would be getting broadcast throughout the Cloud. "The crisis is over. Now let's get the hell out of here."

He shut the link off, and with Oishi pushing them up to the transit jump they followed Bukha out of the system.

Yaroslav turned and looked back at Napoleon and then at Wellington, who floated in the middle of the room.

"A near run thing," Wellington said dryly. "Upon my soul, a very near run thing, indeed."

chapter fourteen

"So I guess this is good-bye, for now," Aldin said, unable to keep a slight tremble of emotion out of his voice.

Napoleon looked at him and smiled.

"What place is there for me in your worlds?" he replied.

"Your administrative talents, they're legendary. We could use you."

Napoleon laughed softly.

"In your worlds, not mine," he said with a mock-haughty tone. "Though I hate that race, their poet Milton had summed such things up well enough."

Aldin nodded sadly. The slow, leisurely cruise back to the Sphere had been fascinating. Napoleon had held forth throughout the trip, recounting his adventures, discussing his campaigns and dreams.

Aldin looked over at Yaroslav, who was decked out in the regalia of a marshal, baton in hand, Legion of Honor dangling from his chest.

"Take good care of the painting," he said, and nodded to the gilt-framed oil that dominated one wall of the cabin. The argument between Napoleon and him had gone nonstop for hours after the unveiling of the creation of one of the servobots, until Tia had finally settled it by calling it *The Heroes of Waterloo*. It was indeed done in the style of David, showing Napoleon, Yaroslav, and Basak, all looking magnified and imbued with martial valor, holding the line in the final moments of the battle against the Prussians.

"Come by in a couple of months and check on me. We might hate each other by then and I'll want to go home," Yaroslav said.

"We've still got to fight out the campaign after our victory at Waterloo," Napoleon interjected. "Wellington insisted upon it. The Russians and Austrians still need to be dealt with. It'll be more than a couple of months, and you're still chief of staff."

"As long as there's fighting, I'll stay," Basak chimed in, looking somewhat absurd in the uniform of a general of the Imperial Guard, the bearskin hat towering him to over ten feet in height.

"Just keep it a bit safer this time," Tia said.

"We've got the medical bay transferred down there," Yaroslav replied. "Wellington knows the rules about getting us into it if we're hurt."

"A decapitation from a cannonball is a bit hard to repair," Oishi said.

"Well, there's always a little risk, but that's what will make it exciting," the old philosopher replied. "Besides, if it was totally safe it wouldn't be real."

Aldin nodded and then punched the door open. The scent of fresh air wafted in, suddenly clouded with the sulfur stink of gunsmoke from a battery firing off a twenty-one-gun salute, the concussion causing Aldin to flinch.

As the last gun thundered, a band struck up "The Victory March of Marengo," and Napoleon stepped out of the ship. The vast pavilion, all the way to the pyramid, was lined with the serried ranks of the Imperial Guard, the men standing at attention.

"What glory still to be won," Napoleon said with a happy sigh, and looked back at Aldin.

"Maybe it is an illusion, my friend. But isn't that life, after all? I was dying, dreaming that I could somehow change my past. You know what I mean, you dream so hard it almost becomes real, but then there is always the tragedy of awaking at dawn. Well, it is dawn, and this looks real enough. And who is to say that those out there, my children, are not real as well? We can build an empire here in this new world. I will fight my wars, and perhaps there will be slightly less of a sin upon my soul if they die. We will build a new empire here and have it grow. Come back someday and you will see the truth of what I dreamed, but what the world was not yet ready for. I hope you will someday find such contentment as well."

Aldin looked at him closely and smiled, unable to answer.

He wanted to shake the man's hand, but knew that somehow that would be inappropriate with an emperor. All he could do was smile and fumble a clumsy salute.

"Ah, if you ever want a command, just come here and you will know the thrill of victory."

He stepped over to Tia. Taking her hand, he kissed it lightly, and then reached up and tugged her gently on the ear. He looked over at Oishi and flashed a smile.

"I hope you find peace, warrior, but never boredom. But with her I would truly doubt that."

Putting his hands behind his back, he turned and walked down the entry plank and out onto the plaza.

"Well, can you blame me? The guy is kind of hard to resist," Yaroslav said almost apologetically. "Stay out of trouble now, you won't have Yaroslav around to bail you out at the last second anymore."

He put his hand up to rest on Basak's shoulder, and the two went down the plank after the emperor and then paused to look back.

"Don't forget to check back in. I think he might drive me crazy after all."

They followed Napoleon out onto the square.

"Well, now what do we do?" Bukha said, coming up to stand by Aldin.

He looked around at his companions, Tia and Oishi. They were happy as long as they were together, wherever that might be. He could go back to the Core for a while. After all, he was something of hero there now. The quiet negotiations with the Overseers, spiced with a good deal of blackmail of the Arch, had worked wonders. He had come to realize that they still needed the Overseers, and the story had finally been settled upon that in the end it was they who had stopped the super-nova and that he and Corbin had wandered into the scene almost by accident. Of course, the entire war was blamed on Corbin.

The fact that Vush had been set up to be the Arch and that the old Arch was sitting out a long and lonely exile of contemplation had helped to settle things a bit as well, when the other Overseers had risen up in rebellion against their leader. The right documents were found in the end to exonerate Aldin and his companions and in fact set him up as something of a hero for helping Vush to find the device.

There was a status quo returning to the Cloud. Zola, as usual, had come out on the losing end. He had, of course, pleaded innocence with the little incident of the debris, but a complete bankruptcy from overinvesting in hundreds of now-worthless planets was punishment enough, Aldin realized. Zola was the laughingstock of the Cloud, owner of swamp and ice worlds purchased from Bukha at ten times their worth, while Bukha and Xsarn Prime, using the information gained from Xsarn Tertiary, had in turn made massive investments on the threatened worlds and picked up entire systems at a fraction of their worth. The richest Kohs had come out even richer.

Aldin looked back into the ship. It was pleasantly quiet. Mari had most of his assets and had taken off with one of the Gaf berserkers. It had hurt a bit, but the quiet was worth it. If it'd make her happy, which he doubted, then that was fine enough. Even Hobbs had come out ahead, since that with Corbin gone, there were some family assets floating around with which he could rebuild his amusement emporium.

The music died away, and Napoleon stopped in front of the colors of the guard. He hesitated and then stepped up, taking the silken folds and embracing them.

"Soldiers, my children. Your emperor has returned!"

A thundering shout rose up to the heavens, and the ranks broke, the men pressing in around him, and he was lost to view.

Aldin looked over at Zergh, who was wiping tears from his eyes.

"Come on, let's get out of here."

"To do what?"

"I don't know," Aldin replied glumly. "We could retire, or maybe be vasbas again."

"You're still worth billions," Bukha interjected.

Aldin laughed sadly.

"So what."

Zergh stood silent, looking out across the field of celebration, and Aldin could see the longing in his eyes to join them. He knew that his oldest friend had no intention of leaving if he could avoid it.

From around the corner of the ship, Wellington appeared.

So this was the First Traveler after all, Aldin thought, somehow guessing the truth at last. Its programming was scrambled to be sure. He looked over at the mountain, the top of which had been blown off by the missile strikes, the outrush of air now double in volume.

The entire Sphere was winding down, though it'd be thousands, maybe tens of thousands of years before things got out of hand. And only this one surviving machine, a bit of a mad machine at that, to somehow keep it together. Someone would have to do something about it sooner or later if this magnificence was to be saved.

"The game's the thing," Wellington said, "reality an illusion, and the illusion reality."

Wellington tilted over as if to gaze into Aldin's eyes—and soul.

"Tell me, Aldin Larice, what do you dream for?" Wellington asked. "What worlds are there still for you to conquer or save?"

Suddenly, Aldin Larice smiled, finally discovering at last what he had been looking for all along.

DEL REY ONLINE!

The Del Rey Internet Newsletter...

A monthly electronic publication, posted on the Internet, GEnie, CompuServe, BIX, various BBSs, and the Panix gopher (gopher.panix.com). It features hype-free descriptions of books that are new in the stores, a list of our upcoming books, special announcements, a signing/reading/convention-attendance schedule for Del Rey authors, "In Depth" essays in which professionals in the field (authors, artists, designers, sales people, etc.) talk about their jobs in science fiction, a question-and-answer section, behind-the-scenes looks at sf publishing, and more!

Online editorial presence: Many of the Del Rey editors are online, on the Internet, GEnie, CompuServe, America Online, and Delphi. There is a Del Rey topic on GEnie and a Del Rey folder on America Online.

Our official e-mail address for Del Rey Books is delrey@randomhouse.com

Internet information source!

A lot of Del Rey material is available to the Internet on a gopher server: all back issues and the current issue of the Del Rey Internet Newsletter, a description of the DRIN and summaries of all the issues' contents, sample chapters of upcoming or current books (readable or downloadable for free), submission requirements, mail-order information, and much more. We will be adding more items of all sorts (mostly new DRINs and sample chapters) regularly. The address of the gopher is gopher.panix.com

Why? We at Del Rey realize that the networks are the medium of the future. That's where you'll find us promoting our books, socializing with others in the sf field, and— most importantly—making contact and sharing information with sf readers.

For more information, e-mail
delrey@randomhouse.com

DBDQUVSQ

Vanjoy   WEUK